NOVELS BY JOYCE CAROL OATES

FOX

FOX

A NOVEL

JOYCE CAROL OATES

HOGARTH

London • New York

Published in the United States by Hogarth, an imprint of Random House, a division of Penguin Random House LLC, 1745 Broadway, New York, NY 10019.

HOGARTH is a trademark of the Random House Group Limited, and the H colophon is a trademark of Penguin Random House LLC.

LIBRARY OF CONGRESS CATALOGING-IN-PUBLICATION DATA
Names: Oates, Joyce Carol, author.
Title: Fox : a novel / by Joyce Carol Oates.
Description: London ; New York, NY : Hogarth, 2025. |
Identifiers: LCCN 2024053359 (print) | LCCN 2024053360 (ebook) |
ISBN 9780593978085 (hardcover ; acid-free paper) | ISBN 9780593978108 (ebook)
Subjects: LCGFT: Detective and mystery fiction. | Novels.
Classification: LCC PS3565.A8 F68 2025 (print) | LCC PS3565.A8 (ebook) |
DDC 813/.54—dc23/eng/20241122
LC record available at https://lccn.loc.gov/2024053359
LC ebook record available at https://lccn.loc.gov/2024053360

International edition ISBN 9780593979440

Printed in the United States of America on acid-free paper

randomhousebooks.com
penguinrandomhouse.com

2 4 6 8 9 7 5 3 1

First Edition

Book design by Debbie Glasserman

The authorized representative in the EU for product safety and compliance is Penguin Random House Ireland, Morrison Chambers, 32 Nassau Street, Dublin D02 YH68, Ireland, https://eu-contact.penguin.ie.

FOR MARK MIRSKY

Little Lamb
Here I am,
Come and lick
My white neck.
Let me pull
Your soft Wool.
Let me kiss
Your soft face.

—WILLIAM BLAKE, "SPRING"

Or, my scrofulous French novel
On grey paper with blunt type!
Simply glance at it, you grovel
Hand and foot in Belial's gripe . . .

—ROBERT BROWNING, "SOLILOQUY
OF THE SPANISH CLOISTER"

All is possible that is not impossible.

—H. ZWENDER

FOX

PROLOGUE

There was never a time when I was not in love with Mr. Fox.

There was never a time when Mr. Fox was not my life.

Because before Mr. Fox came into my life our souls knew each other in the time before *where there is no time.*

Because we are born of such knowing. Of the time before *as when waking in the morning we carry the memory of the beautiful dreams we have lost in waking.*

In the time before *there is no time as we understand it on Earth, it is a great void like the ocean in which droplets of rain fall & vanish.*

In the time before *we are children together, there is no "age" that separates.*

This, Mr. Fox explained.

Saying, My darling there will never be a time when our souls are not joined.

Saying, Our (secret) pledge will be, we will die for each other if that is asked of us.

We will never reveal our secret, we will die together & our secret will die with us.

For there is no Death in the time before. Souls are joined in love in the time before.

This, Mr. Fox explained.

To me only, Mr. Fox explained.

I

WIELAND WATERLANDS

NATURE PRESERVE

SOUTH JERSEY

2013

THE TROPHY

I t will be no ordinary morning.

Heavy rain has fallen through the night with a din of crazed castanets. The sky at dawn is clotted with dark tumors of cloud through which a sudden piercing light shines like a scalpel.

In the mud-softened service road leading to the Wieland Township landfill, shimmering puddles in long narrow snakelike ruts. A smell of brackish swamp water from the vast marshland beyond and in the near distance black-winged turkey vultures like flattened silhouettes high in the air silently circling, swooping with a look of grisly frolic.

At 7:36 A.M. in the adjacent nature preserve there comes jolting along the service road a steel-colored vehicle with four-wheel drive to park at a trailhead fifty feet from the murky still-standing water of many acres—choked at shore with rushes, cattails, barely submerged trash, a rumor of leeches in its black-muck bottom—known locally as Wieland Pond in rural Atlantic County, New Jersey.

The driver of the steel-colored vehicle cuts her engine, headlights. Glances about the clearing to see with evident satisfaction that she is alone. No reeking sanitation trucks lumbering out to the nearby landfill at this hour, deepening ruts in the roadway. No fellow dog-walkers, hikers. No one with whom P. Cady will be obliged to exchange inane greetings.

For it is the purpose of driving out to the Wieland wetlands at dawn, on the average of five times a week, to exercise her high-energy rescue animal of mixed ancestry (terrier, hound) from the Wieland Township Animal Shelter, and to exercise herself, alone.

"Here we go! *Good girl.*"

Opening the passenger door of the steel-colored vehicle out of which leaps as if catapulted by force the small wiry dun-colored dog in a paroxysm of excitement, barking, yipping, whining, pleading, tail slavishly wagging in seeming deference to the tall bossy individual gripping the leash, her human, gripping the leash on *her* neck, speaking sternly yet not without affection as if anything uttered in fatuous human speech could have the slightest interest for the eager little dog at this crucial moment.

"This morning, you will *behave.*"

Large limpid brown eyes brimming with facile promise—*Yes, I will behave.*

"You will come back when I call you. You will not *run wild.*"

Oversized hound-paws scuffing frantically in the wet leaves, shameless whining, whimper—*Yes yes I will do anything you ask.*

"And not in the water! D'you hear?—*not in the damned water.*"

Sniffing sodden leaves at her human's booted feet. Stubby tail furiously wagging, bony rear shimmying, how then could her (naïve, trusting) human not believe such slavish deference, doggie-devotion—*Yes of course, I will obey. Just let me go!*

"I'm warning you—*do not run wild.*"

At last released from the leash, a panting yelp of gratitude before turning to bound joyously away, stopping within a few yards to sniff at underbrush, squatting to urinate, but fleetingly, for there is no time to tarry, these early-morning hikes under the command of her human are rarely more than forty minutes to an hour; restraining herself to remain on the trail at least initially, trotting in the direction in which her human habitually hikes on the 2.5-mile loop around the pond that will return them to the vehicle parked at the trailhead; but soon then, within fifty or so feet, even as her human calls after her in a voice of chiding concern the eager little dog has trotted off-trail to investigate something small scuttling in the underbrush—(rodent? black-feathered bird?)—splashing through puddles, very muddy puddles, paws sinking into muck halfway up her forelegs, still she takes time to pause every few yards to sniff, squat, urinate in quick agitated dribbles against underbrush, mounds of leaves, trunks of stunted trees in a haze of great happiness seeming scarcely to hear her human now shouting after her in a voice of outrage and indignation *Come here! Come back! Princess! Now!* as inexorably as gravity she is drawn into the marshy woods off-trail where the most delicious odors waft to her sensitive nostrils.

On this morning in late October there are a half-dozen red-winged blackbirds taunting her from six feet above, razzing her, a trespasser in their territory, if they were but large enough they might attack her, stab their sharp beaks into her, failing to find at all "beautiful"— "adorable"—her somewhat coarse brindle-brown short-haired coat, greedily they would peck out those caramel-colored moist eyes her human finds so "intelligent," captivating.

Bravely and defiantly she trots on, she *is* a trespasser, a hunter. Literally, a born hunter! Ignores the noisy bullies for these are not local predator birds (hawk, owl) large enough to carry away a small dog in their talons, and devour her.

Soon then the pleading voice somewhere behind the little dog has faded, becomes inaudible amid the cries of swamp birds and the sound of her own panting, the tumult of smells assailing her nostrils, overcharging her thrumming brain, her human's cry irrelevant as artificial light on a blind-blazing-sun day.

■

WHAT IS THAT AHEAD?—a sudden movement, a splash and ripples in the still dank water, mallard? turtle? water snake?—as she approaches on her disproportionately large paws, with a clumsy sort of stealth, crouching, preparing for the pounce, the kill, whatever it is, or was, a living thing like herself, but cannier than she, more cunning, desperate to survive, seems to have disappeared.

Cautiously exploring the dank interior of the marshland amid fallen and calcified trees, weak eyes lowered in deference to her exquisitely tuned nostrils, terrier-ears pricked upright, all of her senses alert, thrilled, her small brain near to swooning with overstimulation after seven hours of confinement in the dull-darkened house of her human; it's as if whatever force fierce as a vacuum's suction catapulted her out of the steel-colored vehicle continues to draw her forward venturing—recklessly, naughtily—ever farther from her human, or rather the memory of her human, the tall stern-voiced individual whose smallest, most petty commands she is obliged to obey, and surely will obey again, except just not yet, not now, not while trotting eagerly in this dazzling place where the most thrilling-reeking smells rush at her, some familiar, some unfamiliar, it is the unfamiliar that draws her, the tantalizing-new, new odors of carrion, irresistible as food to a ravenous beast.

Many times she has dismayed her overfastidious human by reveling in carrion, rotted flesh, stained bones the most luxuriant sensation, leaping into what she has discovered in the woods, what has seemed to be lying in wait for her to discover, rolling in it, excitedly barking, yipping, growling deep in her throat in ecstasy, the most profound kinship with whatever it is that remains of a living creature like herself, yet not-herself, deer carcass, fox, raccoon, another creature like herself: dog, most wondrous: *dog:* a carrion-cloak in which to wrap herself, myriad drunken smells swarming into her brain, overcharged as an electrical socket. Many times she has incurred the disgust of her human, unmistakably the *human words* signal the most extreme disgust, no disgust other than the *human,* as there are no words other than the *human.* At such times, discovered, reviled, chided, despaired-over, and needing to be thoroughly bathed (by her human, or by the groomer with the deft kind assured hands), she has been quick to express remorse, or has seemed to express remorse, for upsetting her human, for this is expected of her, this is her responsibility to the (needy) human, her pledge. In her doggy soul, she understands. She concurs. She is not a rebel. She adores her human, she knows that her human has been her savior since the blurred chaos of puppyhood, tossed like trash onto the shoulder of the old state highway, reddened infected eyes swollen shut, skeletal ribs, rat-skinny tail, wheezing breath and puppy-intestines swirling with parasites, discovered and brought to the bright-lit antiseptic shelter, rescued, resuscitated, with oversized puppy-ears, puppy-paws, yearning moist-brown eyes adopted out of a cage at six months, of course she understands that her human is her salvation, but her human, though sharp-eyed and often capable of reading her mind *is not here to observe,* and so for the time being she has forgotten her human, when a human *is not here to observe* it is only natural to forget the human, exploring now a patch of sinister black muck that sucks at her paws, her swift-sniffing nose has led her gaily off-trail, far off-trail, it is a thrill to forget all that her human has taught her, or tried to teach her, for the marshland is teeming with yet more life, always more life and though it is some distance away she can smell the sodden smoldering trash of the landfill, a place of slovenly treasures she has explored in the past, slipping under the rusted and partly collapsed ten-foot chain-link fence, on all sides in the landfill there are rife garbagey smells that pique a mild interest, but there again is the fresh carrion-smell, unmistakable, irresistible, and not so far from her, upwind.

Dimly behind her are pleading, plaintive cries, words recognizably *human,* yet scarcely words but mere syllables, sounds— . . . *are you? Prin-cess! Please*—hardly to be distinguished from the vulgar and menacing shrieks of crows, always at dawn there are predator-crows in the marshes, scavenger birds, buzzard hawks and vultures in a slow continuous Möbius circle above the six-acre landfill on the farther side of the pond but not this morning: no.

Beginning to exult, rejoice in whatever it is, the ecstasy that awaits: her catch, her *trophy.*

For she is a fierce hunter, or would be if properly trained, not a mere *house-pet,* destined to eat too much, to become heavy and short of breath, wheezing, sleeping away what remains of her short life, but not yet, *not yet* for she is on the scent now, she is single-minded as a missile flying to its destination trotting excitedly on, panting, tongue lolling, all of her being drawn irresistibly forward, the rich rot carrion-odor calls to her, more forcibly than any merely human voice; in a haze like lust, hypnotized, rapidly sniffing nostrils yank her forward, along a brief peninsula of land amid the marsh, on all sides broken and dying, barkless trees, human litter—cans, Styrofoam—sodden articles of discarded clothing—in the trail are tire tracks, for this trail is the width of a small vehicle, she is trotting more quickly now, urgently now, her tongue is hanging from her mouth, she is panting harder, it is the new smell, the new strong smell, the carrion-smell that has hypnotized her.

As overhead, turkey vultures circle on wide flapping wings like black crepe, eyeing her, dismissing her, a creature too small to threaten them, and alive, animated—not (yet) a meal they can digest.

Now nearing the source of the smell! Her little heart is pounding in her chest, she is so thrilled. No barking, no yipping. No crude distractions. Every sense electric-alert. *For this, I was born.*

In a tangle of flattened rushes the bloodied meat-thing lies lacerated and torn, an insubstantial object in itself, the size of a small rodent, but eyeless, presumably sightless, surely there is more, somewhere nearby there is more, but she is thrilled to discover this tidbit, this token, small jaws clamping together claiming the trophy, shaking it, to break its neck, snuff the life from it, if it were a living thing and not mere meat, *human-meat* by the smell of it.

∎

"PRINCESS DI! *WHAT* DO you have in your mouth!"

"**D**addy, *look.*"

Quickly he turns, *he* is Daddy dreading what he might see. That quavering in his thirteen-year-old daughter's voice pierces his heart.

Ten feet behind Martin Pfenning on the badly eroded wood-chip trail Eunice has come to a dead stop. She has sighted something near shore in the shallow brackish water of Wieland Pond.

"What is it, honey?"

Very still Eunice is standing, staring. What looks like something tangled, speckled or mottled, clearly out of place amid a cluster of broken rushes, cattails, algae, has captured her excited attention.

She shakes her head, shuddering. Murmurs what sounds like *ugly.*

Her small pinched-plain face has gone white, her agate eyes have narrowed. Her thin-lipped mouth works convulsively.

It is like Eunice, a nervous child, a child who has had *health issues,* to become agitated in an instant; ugly things affront her, and things in some way *not-right.* Fictitious dangers loom while actual dangers pass by without her noticing for which, Pfenning thinks guiltily, he can't really blame her since the disruption in all their lives.

He pulls his daughter to the side, to protect her. Just in case.

Hoping to hell that whatever it is in the pond, it isn't alive. Nothing venomous—water moccasin, timber rattlesnake . . .

You put our daughter at risk, Martin. In that wild place. How could you!

"Just stay here. Don't look, I'll take care of it."

Pfenning is wearing waterproof hiking boots, no problem to wade out into the brackish water though he feels at once the ground begin to shift beneath his feet, heels sinking in soft black muck. Quicksand?

Sick, sinking sensation of vertigo. A thrumming in his ears, of rapidly beating blood mixed with the indignant cries of red-winged blackbirds in trees overhead.

And if it is a rattlesnake? And if Daddy dies thrashing and choking while his child is watching?

But what's caught in the rushes appears to be harmless, only human litter. Remains of a Styrofoam food container, mottled with mud. He picks it up, flattens it with gloved hands, shoves it into his backpack with other trash he has found on the trail.

Earlier on their hike he noticed what appeared to be yellowed condoms in underbrush like clotted miniature snakes, grateful that sharp-eyed Eunice hadn't seen.

"Just trash, honey."

Eunice is cringing. Lifting a shaky hand to shield her eyes from whatever it was in the water.

"It's gone now, OK?"

"What—what was it?"

"I said, just trash. Nothing."

Eunice is peering at the stand of broken rushes and cattails at the edge of the pond, suspiciously. But there is indeed nothing for her to see.

"Why are you taking it, then?"

"Because it isn't biodegradable. It would be there forever, an eye-sore. It's the least I can do, these wetlands are a public trust."

Biodegradable. Wetlands. Public trust. These words seem to register with Eunice, with the effect of calming her. Eunice has always been impressed with adult matters.

"You know, I'm on the board here, honey. Wieland Waterlands Nature Preserve."

"What does that mean—'board'?"

"Like a committee. Trustees, donors."

"But why d'you say 'board'—like, boards for a house? Lumber?"

Though he guesses that Eunice is just being difficult, pressing her father to explain curiosities of language for which he is hardly to blame, Pfenning explains: "A different kind of 'board,' obviously. Words have different meanings."

Eunice considers this. There is something of the rat terrier in her small white face, an intensity that has never seemed childish but un-naturally *adult.* Once Eunice fixes upon something curious to her, if irksome and self-evident to others, she is reluctant to let it go.

But Pfenning is grateful, the anxious moment has passed. Why his daughter exaggerates small things like this, why she becomes so quickly distressed over trifles, he doesn't want to think.

"And you are a 'donor'—because you 'donate'?"

"Yes. I am a 'donor.'"

"You give money to 'preserve' Wieland Pond?—the bird sanctu-ary?"

"Yes. A little."

It isn't boasting, he thinks. Well—maybe it is.

A man can discover that his own child scarcely knows him in any way that defines him as an adult among adults. This should be cor-rected.

"Do they ask you for a certain sum, or do you just give it? How much do you give?"—Eunice's forehead crinkles with urgency.

"How much? I don't remember." Pfenning laughs, uneasily.

Since the separation, there has been some financial uncertainty in the family. Suddenly, Pfenning is maintaining two households on his (limited) salary.

Eunice in her interrogative mode. Pretending a naïveté that isn't really genuine, for Eunice is highly intelligent, at least intellectually.

Away from his daughter, his only, cherished child, this Daddy often feels anxiety, even anguish; but with his daughter for an extended period of time, confronted with the girl's curiously lusterless, intense gaze, that seems to scour his soul, and find it wanting, he finds himself yearning to shrink away, escape.

The essential bachelor-self, before fatherhood. Before marriage.

"She says, you have plenty of money for your 'causes.' But not for us."

She means the mother, Daddy's (estranged) wife. *She* is always a presence on these father-daughter excursions though usually neither father nor daughter will speak of this *she*.

"Really, honey? Is that what you believe, too?"

Eunice shrugs. The pinched little face closes up like a fist.

Pfenning is determined not to be upset by Eunice's remark, with all that it implies of financial dishonesty on his part. A sudden, seemingly incidental revelation of how his estranged wife is characterizing him to others. So stunningly untrue, unfair, he could howl with rage.

Instead, Pfenning gives a gentle tug at Eunice's arm that feels thin even within the sleeve of her quilted fleece jacket.

"We should walk on, Eunice. The sun sets earlier every day, it's almost November."

At the moment the sun is blindingly bright, almost directly overhead. The sky is clear and glassy-blue. In the near distance, a half-mile away, dark smoke lifts slowly, vertically from what is likely the Wieland Township landfill.

"Yes! Today it will set at five-fifty-seven P.M."

How like his daughter to be ultra-precise. A girl grimly—though in a way, happily—compulsive about homework, particularly arithmetic with its singular *right answer* amid a wilderness of *wrong answers*. Whose high grades are essential to her well-being.

"And tomorrow, five-fifty-six P.M."

"Really! That precise, is it?"

"Each day earlier and earlier until December twenty-first, the shortest day of the year—the 'solstice.' Then, the sun will set at four-thirty-six P.M."

"That is early . . ."

"But then, the next day, it will set at four-thirty-seven P.M."

"Have you memorized all these times, Eunice?"—Pfenning laughs, though he isn't sure that the subject is funny.

"No. Just around the *solstice*."

Solstice. Eunice enunciates the word with a sort of glum satisfaction, as if there were something inevitable, thus fated, inescapable, in the very sky, awaiting them.

For forty arduous minutes father and daughter have been following the overgrown trail along the eastern edge of Wieland Pond, many acres of wetlands designated by the U.S. Fish & Wildlife Service as the Jorgen Bird Sanctuary. In this area dogs must be leashed. Grim signs forbid hunting "with gun or bow." Every few yards a plaque on a tree identifies species of local birds—waterbirds, songbirds, predator-birds, turkey vultures. With the help of Pfenning's binoculars they have been sighting waterbirds which Eunice photographs with the small Nikon camera Pfenning bought for her—so far today, a smattering of wood ducks, Canada geese, a solitary snowy egret.

Eunice is assembling some sort of nature portfolio for an eighth-grade project assigned by one of her teachers at the Langhorne Academy. Since Eunice is a perfectionist, the project will have to be *perfect;* but since it is an open-ended, creative work, not a specific problem to be solved, Eunice is uncertain how to proceed. She is very good at *competitive* schoolwork—an entire class striving to solve the identical problem, as in math; but not so good imagining original work of her own.

Her teacher—a man—"Mr. Fox"—has praised Eunice lavishly to her mother and has spoken enthusiastically of her "potential"—but Eunice's grades in his class hover at B and below, frustrating to Eunice (who is accustomed to receiving A's) and if frustrating to Eunice, frustrating to her parents.

(Yes, Pfenning plans to attend the next Parent-Teacher meeting at Eunice's school and to meet the exacting Mr. Fox in person; he is annoyed that the eighth-grade teacher has been grading his daughter lower than she is accustomed to being graded.)

Eunice has refused to show her parents what she has assembled in the portfolio so far. It seems to them both that, during the fall break in the last week of October, at a time when Eunice should be less anxious than usual, she has been preoccupied with homework assignments, working late into the night.

The portfolio is encased in a slightly oversized journal with a hard cover, imprinted with bas-relief figures that might be leaves, vines, and flowers, in a luridly bright green marbled pattern like putrescent algae. Eunice is naïvely proud of her *Mystery-Journal* which she keeps with her at all times and will not allow either her mother or her father to peruse.

Has Mr. Fox given Eunice this journal?—it seems to have come into her possession without having been purchased by either of her parents. Possibly, everyone in Mr. Fox's eighth-grade English class has been given a similar journal; Pfenning isn't sure, and cannot make inquiries because Eunice will become angry with him.

Since the separation, Eunice often becomes angry with him: the Daddy.

Since the separation, Eunice has become *moody*.

She is overexcited, stressed; or she is dispirited, lethargic. She eats ravenously, or picks disdainfully at her food. She prowls the house before dawn or has a difficult time waking up in the morning, has to be shaken awake by her mother. She seems to dislike and fear the outdoors: she prefers closed-in spaces with blinds drawn ("so no one can see in"); she avoids the flagstone terrace behind the Pfennings' house because, two years before, she happened upon a fledgling robin fallen from its nest there, covered in ants.

The Daddy will long remember his daughter's terrified wail as she ran from the terrace into the house. How his heart stopped, hearing that wail; and how it jolts in his chest when he recalls it.

Eunice tires easily, she has (mild) anemia. Too much "open sky" exhausts her—wind in tall trees, a ceaseless agitation; flies, bees, hornets, mosquitoes; barking dogs, neighbors' laughter—all grate at her nerves.

This recent fixation on her eighth-grade teacher Mr. Fox and the portfolio assignment, Pfenning finds particularly disturbing.

(Is the Daddy slightly jealous of Mr. Fox?—Pfenning doesn't want to think.)

"Are you OK, honey? Don't want to turn back, do you?"

"Daddy, *no.*"

Eunice rolls her eyes at *honey.* Smiles brightly as if in mockery of a dutiful-daughter-smile.

"Anyway it's too late to turn *back.* We're halfway around the pond."

"Are we!"—the Daddy nods affably, not about to disagree.

He has been hiking ahead of Eunice since they entered the narrow path of the bird sanctuary; he makes it a point to clear storm debris from the trail to make it easier for her. It's a bad sign if Eunice breathes audibly through her mouth, her heart is racing to keep up its supply of oxygen to the brain. (Eunice's pediatrician has explained.) It's like Eunice to disdain hiking shoes, insisting upon wearing her rubber-soled sneakers (which have become soaked); she declines to wear even a child's lightweight pack saying that it makes her look like a hunchback, so Pfenning is carrying two bottles of Evian water in his backpack.

Damn!—he's disappointed that the trail around Wieland Pond has become overgrown with wild rose and brambles, tree limbs fallen months ago have not been cleared away.

Planks have been laid down on the trail where the earth is particularly wet, muddy. But these have sunk into the mud and are mostly useless.

Pfenning holds back branches for Eunice to pass beneath; still, there are thinly bleeding scratches on her small triangular face. No idea how this could have happened. He dreads some sort of accident or health crisis at the pond, for which his estranged wife will blame *him.*

Pfenning was flattered, and touched, that Eunice requested a hike in the Jorgen Bird Sanctuary with him over the fall break. This is the first time, ever: usually, Pfenning makes a suggestion to Eunice of what they might do together on the weekends and Eunice agrees, or disagrees, impassively. The separation agreement allows the Daddy a fixed number of days with the daughter each month; overnights are negotiable depending upon the mother's unpredictable mood.

He, the Daddy, lately the *estranged Daddy,* was surprised by this request; for since he moved out of the house in early September Eunice hasn't much wanted to be alone with him, and is very quiet in his company. Cheerlessly she does her homework at the kitchen table in his minimally furnished apartment in what passes as a "high-rise" (eight-floor) building in Bridgeton; it seems to the Daddy that Eunice is waiting out the clock until he returns her to her actual *home*. Only infrequently can he cajole her into watching *Jeopardy!* with him, or a Discovery Channel documentary. Most often Daddy and daughter spend their rigidly allotted hours together at harmlessly banal G-rated movies at the mall, for Daddy can't take the chance of even a PG-rated movie that might embarrass his sensitive, puritanical daughter, or himself; or in family-style restaurants, in the casual company of strangers.

It is new and disorienting for them, to be together without Eunice's mother; it feels as if they are hobbling together, missing a leg. Thus, each is grateful for strangers in their presence, friendly service people who strike up conversations with them, bemused by the courtly father's deference to the fierce-eyed, you might say *brattish* thirteen-year-old with wiry rust-red hair like Brillo, freckles splashed across her pallid face like discolored raindrops, and a prim little mouth like a doll's mouth merely painted onto the face.

Eunice's pebble-colored eyes are so thinly lashed and her eyebrows so faint, her face so plain, sometimes she is mistaken for a boy, which seems to please her. In public she makes no effort to behave as girls usually do, simpering-smiling, wanting to be liked; Eunice abhors *girly* clothes and wears drab-hued shirts, pullovers, loose-fitting corduroys, and dun-colored sneakers. Her hair is cut short, chopped-looking, as if she has cut it herself—which her mother insists is not the case.

If Pfenning calls his daughter "honey" or "sweetie" in the presence of a service person Eunice will react with comic disdain lifting her upper lip and baring her teeth in a semblance of a snarl—"Oh Dad-*dy*. Desist."

This never fails to provoke startled laughter from strangers. Daddy laughs too, feeling his face heat as if he has been slapped, affectionately.

On Pfenning's custody-days Eunice declines a scenic drive in the country or to the Jersey shore; she has said she has "zero" interest in Atlantic City, especially the "ugly stupid boardwalk." The mere mention of the Pine Barrens elicits a groan: "Bor-*ing*." A visit to Avalon, one of the most affluent beach towns on the Jersey shore, where the families of some of her classmates live, is squelched by Eunice with a yawn: "Been there, done that."

Pfenning surmises that Eunice is not comfortable being alone with him in the confines of a car, which is both hurtful to him and something of a relief.

At least, Eunice has made a serious effort to take pictures of wetlands birds; she has forced herself to take interest in flowers, plants, even *fungi*. (The word makes her giggle wildly: *"Fun-gi."*) She has covered sheets of construction paper with drawings in colored pencils and crayons, clumsily but earnestly executed, where previously she'd scorned such *kindergarten-stuff*; she preferred to immerse herself in schoolwork, nightly homework, which seemed to obsess her; studying for hours in her room, door shut against unwanted intrusions, preparing for quizzes and tests whose primary purpose seemed to be to allow her to triumph over her classmates.

Eunice is jealous of other girls in her class, it seems; at the same time, she is airily dismissive of them.

This fall, for the first time, Eunice has stayed after school to participate in activities. A quaintly named book club—Looking-Glass Book Club—which meets two or even three times a week. Neither

Pfenning nor his wife Kathryn can recall such time-consuming activities in middle school, when they were young; but then, the Langhorne Academy is one of the most selective private schools in the
country, catering to parents ambitious for their children, and a record
of "activities" is considered valuable.

Much is made at Langhorne of its graduates being accepted into
Ivy League and other high-profile universities. There is said to be
something of a frenzied effort in the Fifth Form—senior class—to
prepare students for SATs and to aid them in composing their applications; fortunately, middle-school students are spared this frenzy,
which can have devastating emotional consequences. Kathryn has
said that Francis Fox, alone of Eunice's teachers, remarked to her
that in his opinion the school's "obsession" with college acceptances
seemed to him "misguided"; in his classes of seventh- and eighth-
graders he has tried to create an air of learning as fun, joyous, playful
rather than dutiful.

Still, Eunice often seems tense, apprehensive. Since the fall term
began she has fainted twice at school; two years ago she was diagnosed with a kind of anemia that can be treated (to a degree) with
medication.

Her parents are concerned that Eunice's anemia might morph
into something more deadly—leukemia? (Who knew that there are
more than two hundred types of blood cancers?)

As if mocking their concern Eunice has hand-printed a terse little
poem in colored pencils:

(AN)EMIA

(LEUK)EMIA

Dissolving into giggles seeing the looks in their faces.

Astonishing to the parents, that Eunice seemed to know about
her medical condition when they'd taken every care to hide the diagnosis from her. They'd met with her doctor alone in his office, they'd
conferred quietly with each other when (they were certain) Eunice
could not have overheard.

How on earth does she know? Did you tell her?
Of course I didn't tell her, why would I do that?
But—how does she know?
How?—she just does.

But Eunice hasn't seemed very worried about *anemia*. The most petty things vex her but she evinces no great interest in her medical condition, as if confident that her parents will take care of it, as they take care of every other problem in her life. And no doubt, the concept of *dying, death* is unreal to Eunice, merely some weakness to which other, more ordinary children might be vulnerable, but not her.

What incensed Eunice was the possibility that anyone might know about it. Especially the parents of her classmates at the Langhorne Academy, who would then tell their children.

She'd made Pfenning and Kathryn promise they would not tell anyone. Not even relatives!

They promised. They vowed, of course they would tell no one.

"If you do, I will never forgive you. I will *hate you forever*."

Of course, Eunice didn't mean it. Pfenning is sure.

The sun has shifted overhead, beginning to descend in the sky. Autumn is a beautiful season but dusk comes ever earlier. They are now more than halfway around the pond. From the Atlantic coast in the east, plum-colored clouds have emerged. There is a sudden chill breeze.

High overhead, a quarter-mile away, is an alarming sight—turkey vultures circling in the air, silently swooping down, disappearing into the marshland.

Something dead, rotting carrion, this Daddy is hoping his inquisitive daughter doesn't notice and insist upon tracking it down to take pictures for her damned journal.

Feeling a stab of anticipation: the first drink of the day will be waiting back home when he returns. A half-glass of chardonnay, a reward to himself in the lonely-bachelor solitude of his new living quarters.

■

"DADDY, LOOK!" EUNICE HAS sighted, just barely visible through under-brush at the edge of the pond, a tall long-legged bird with a large distinctive head and beak.

"Is it—an egret?"

"I think it's a great blue heron."

"Is it *blue*?"—Eunice squints, suspiciously. "That's not *blue*."

By the time Eunice aims her camera the heron is too far away. Pfenning hears her curse beneath her breath—*Damn!*

Next is the beaver dam, a fascinating sight. Such labor! Such fa-naticism! The beaver lodge is located near the center of the pond, its moundlike roof is easily visible from shore for Eunice to photograph.

Daddy feels relief, for the distraction of the beavers, these most lovable of large rodents. So *industrious, humorless,* something very *American* about them.

The beavers of Wieland Pond are its most popular attraction, the subject of a recent photo spread in *New Jersey Monthly.*

Eunice seems excited as a fattish beaver emerges from water close to shore, swimming rapidly away. Ripples in dark water as the crea-ture disappears beneath the surface of the pond.

"Is it afraid of us? Does it think we're hunters who might kill it?"

"Probably yes. All animals are afraid of predators."

"Except predators? Are predators afraid of predators?"

"Yes. I think so."

"But beavers are not 'carnivorous'—are they?"

Daddy is stumped. Daddy thinks probably beavers are not car-nivorous but isn't sure.

Daddy reads aloud from a plaque on a tree: Beavers are mammals but can swim underwater for long periods of time; beavers are the largest rodent in North America; beavers resemble rats with continu-ally growing front incisor teeth that must be used constantly; beavers mate for life, and are "fiercely loyal" to their families. Their lodges are "ingeniously" and "efficiently" constructed to repel predators, and to control temperature in the living spaces.

Beavers are herbivores who eat leaves, woody stems, and aquatic plants. They are most practical creatures as their preferred foods are also their chief building materials: poplar, aspen, willow, birch, and maple.

Eunice snickers, hearing this. (In fact Pfenning had read the plaque aloud on a previous hike on the trail.) She is only half-listening, fussing with the camera. Startlingly intelligent in some ways, Eunice is clumsy with such devices.

"D'you need help, honey?"

"Daddy, *no.*"

Eunice is annoyed, at the query, or at being called *honey.*

Pfenning has been noticing, Eunice scarcely lifts her eyes to Wieland Pond. Its beauty is of no real interest to her. Or perhaps Eunice's brain cannot register *beauty.*

The hike in the bird sanctuary is some sort of grim duty for the girl, to be recorded in photographs for her project. It is not an experience to be enjoyed. Why, the Daddy wonders, is his daughter so perpetually dissatisfied? *On edge?*

Because unease, anxiety is coded in the genes.

Because you and her mother should not have had a child together.

But he doesn't believe that! He believes in free will, an open future.

As William James has said, *My first act of free will shall be to believe in free will.*

Or possibly, there is a situation at school. One of Eunice's teachers. Her classmates.

Pointless to ask her. She won't tell him. He knows.

He is thinking how Wieland Pond is but one pond / small lake amid the vast wetlands of South Jersey stretching to the Atlantic shore. Most of the region is uncharted, uninhabited, like the Pine Barrens. If you had a fantasy of disappearing—or causing another person to "disappear"—where would be more inviting?

Venomous snakes, black bears, quicksand. A wilderness in which cell phones are useless.

Still, there *is* beauty. Pfenning has been staring at the glassy surface of the pond. He feels mildly, pleasantly entranced. Reflected in the water are high-scudding clouds, splotches of bright autumn foliage as in a Fauve landscape to lift the heart.

"Dad-*dy*! What has happened to all these trees?"

All around them are ash trees, dying from the tops down. These are tall, beautifully shaped trees whose silvery trunks have become leprous, spectral; their branches skeletal.

"They're ash trees, honey. There's something called the 'ash borer' that's killing them."

"'Ash *bore*'?" Eunice crinkles her nose as if suspecting that this is some silly Daddy-joke.

"'Ash borer.'"

The predator beetle is the *emerald ash borer,* native to Asia. Pfenning knows this because ash trees have been dying throughout New Jersey for years. On the relatively small two-acre lot he and Kathryn own, several ash trees have been slated for removal at a minimum cost of one thousand dollars each.

"A nasty insect. Parasite."

"Like a 'predator'—a 'parasite.'"

"I guess you could say that."

"*I* said it, Daddy. Not you." Eunice laughs, she is just teasing.

Daddy laughs too. He is determined to be in a good mood. He *is* in a good mood. Smiling at his daughter eager with the effort of appearing upbeat, elated and not instead tired, downhearted.

Never does a Daddy smile so much, his lower face never aches so much, as when he is in the company of his daughter, exerting his custodial rights as he deserves. In turn, Eunice measures out smiles like a little miser.

So, what went wrong today?

Honestly, I think—nothing.

Nothing?

Well—almost nothing . . .

That merits a drink!

Once he's alone in his apartment Pfenning can review the hike, the visit with Eunice. A success, or not-a-success? Or, he can try to forget it.

He is nearly in sight of the trailhead. Beyond that will be the parking lot. The reassuring sight of his car.

"Daddy—"

"Yes, honey—what is it?"

Eunice is pointing at something in the pond. This time, she seems determined to remain calm.

He can see her lips trembling, the pupils of her eyes shrunken to pinpricks.

"Don't look at it, why don't you just look away. I'll see what it is."

Pfenning is trying not to sound exasperated. God *damn*.

No choice but to wade out into the water again. Staring at whatever the thing is, bobbing about amid a cluster of cattails some six feet from shore.

Jesus!—no idea what this is . . .

In the dark shimmering mirror of the pond's surface the filmy sky is reflected in patches. A strong brackish odor here of organic rot. Near shore the pond is only a few inches deep but its shallow muck-floor falls rapidly away, farther out the pond is estimated to be more than one hundred feet deep. Pfenning hopes he won't step off the edge, sink into water over his head . . .

He takes up a broken tree limb to prod at the object in the water. The thing is round at one end, with a smooth curved surface; splotched with mud. Birds in nearby trees seem particularly incensed by the intrusion, shrieking at him. This Daddy is swaying on his feet, close to losing his balance. Water leaks over the tops of his hiking boots.

Fortunately, the thing he has dislodged isn't anything organic, living or dead, not rotting. Just more human litter: the upper half of a child's doll.

A naked torso, bald head; no arms, and nothing below the waist.

Eyeless sockets, holes in the (plastic) head.

Yes, it is grotesque to see, to fish out of the water like this. But harmless, at least. Nontoxic.

Grunting with effort, as with exasperation, Daddy manages to maneuver the remains of the doll through the water to shore as Eunice begins to giggle loudly.

There is something alarming in her reaction. Pfenning sees that she is shivering, her teeth are chattering with cold. If her face were not so pale he'd think she might be feverish.

"So silly! Just a stupid *head*."

As Pfenning is about to pick up the waterlogged doll Eunice kicks it back into the water, laughing shrilly.

"God damn, Eunice. *Stop*."

Pfenning manages to retrieve the dripping doll, stuffs it into his backpack.

Eunice is running ahead on the trail, laughing. Daddy plods after.

His feet are soaked, his vision is blurred as if some sort of toxic gas has been released from the pond, seeping into his eyes, to his brain.

Riotous colors, red maple, golden alder. Such vivid colors mock. He is feeling sick, disoriented.

Needs a drink. One hour at Wieland Pond with his daughter, nearing Daddy's limit.

Why did you marry me if you don't love me.

Why have a child if you don't want to live with a child.

Daddy wants to protest, of course he loves his wife. He loves his daughter.

Daddy wants to protest, he would die for his wife, his daughter.

That the wife is Kathryn, who has ceased to love him after fourteen years during which (he thought) they had grown close as (sexless) siblings, and the daughter is Eunice, who seems incapable of feeling anything for anyone, makes his (unconditional) Daddy-love a challenge. But this Daddy is strong enough for the challenge.

Usually Eunice becomes short of breath if she runs, her not-strong heart can't maintain a steady accelerated pumping. Still, she is running now, as if something is pursuing her.

Her sneakers are totally wet, mud-stained. Kathryn will be angry as hell at him.

You shouldn't have listened to her, taking her out to the wetlands.

You know she's just getting over bronchitis . . .

He hurries after Eunice. He dreads seeing her stumble, fall.

Recalling how when Eunice was a little girl, four or five years old, she brought her foot down hard on a monarch butterfly in the grass, they asked why would she want to hurt the pretty butterfly, and Eunice said, scoffing, "It couldn't fly. It just looked silly."

At a Dumpster in the parking lot Pfenning disposes of the ill-smelling trash in his backpack.

His backpack is wet, smelly. He will toss it away, purchase another.

"Daddy, come *on*."

Impatiently Eunice is waiting by the car. She has tried the handle of the passenger door, which is locked. As if she could unlock the door by jerking at the handle.

She is panting, breathless. She has crossed her arms tightly over her chest in the quilted jacket as if to contain her galloping heart. The agate eyes glitter with tears of fury.

Pfenning has to acknowledge, he is somewhat afraid of his daughter—this tremulous diminutive figure, not five feet tall, weighing less than ninety pounds.

Nervous, edgy. Squinting and scowling. And unpredictable.

For no evident reason Eunice runs to the Dumpster, clamors for Daddy to reopen the heavy lid but Daddy has had enough of her childish behavior, speaks sharply to her—"What the hell? No. Get in the car, I'm taking you home."

Eunice is panting, excited, on her toes straining to push open the Dumpster lid. Pfenning pulls her roughly away, yes Daddy may be cursing under his breath, not *at* Eunice, but certainly in the presence of Eunice, for yes, Daddy is exasperated, Daddy is unnerved, and Daddy is needing a drink.

All this, Pfenning will acknowledge when questioned.

What did you do! Why did you exhaust her! You know she isn't well, she's fragile, do you want to destroy our daughter the way you've destroyed our marriage?

Deprived of the Dumpster, whatever it was she'd hoped to find in the Dumpster, Eunice allows herself to be dragged to the car. Flush-faced Daddy stabbing at the remote, to unlock the damned door.

But Eunice is near to collapsing, ghastly white-faced. Short of breath as if she has been running up stairs. Is her heart failing her? Just now, on Daddy's watch? In Daddy's arms?

"I—I did a bad thing, Daddy . . ."

"What 'bad thing'? Kicking the doll? What?"

This Daddy is stymied, he is worn out by her. *His* daughter.

Eunice begins to sob convulsively. As a young child might sob without hope. Her face is streaming tears, mucus at her nose glitters. There is nothing angry or adversarial in this sobbing, all Eunice's resistance seems to have melted away.

"Honey, come *on*. Don't cry like that. It's just a silly old doll someone threw away. Is that why you're crying? Hey."

It was an ugly sight, the doll-torso, bald doll-head with no eyes in its sockets. Yes, something obscene about it. Disgusting!

He should have hidden it from her, he supposes. Too late now.

Holding Eunice tight in a warm Daddy-embrace. To steady her. To comfort her. To prevent her harming herself.

Tight, tight in Daddy's arms, to protect the unhappy child, squatting now beside her to hold her more securely, he is frightened too, he is bewildered too, his Daddy-heart is breaking as his daughter weeps in his arms, he has no idea why.

J*ust a feeling like something wasn't right.*

Saw the tire tracks in the mud, going up the hill . . . Turkey vultures in trees.

Jesus! Wish I hadn't.

The wetlands: so dense, so silent, it exudes an air of sulfurous darkness as if ordinary light were sucked back inside it as into quicksand.

Pointless to cry for help, no one to hear.

Yet, there were settlements here, in the late 1700s. Traces of old trails remain, ancient forges, glassmaking furnaces. Kilns, bricks, remnants of long-collapsed stone houses, a gristmill. Ruin of a man-made dam at the eastern edge of Wieland Pond. Remains of a stone church, a cemetery of broken and corroded gravestones tilted as in a drunken carousal.

In the soft soil of the cemetery, scattered bones freed of coffins, risen to the surface of the earth, lurid-white in the gloom.

Cries of wetlands birds—terns, herons, Canada geese. Eerie silence of turkey vultures.

In the last century there were rumors of gangland killings during

Prohibition. Illegal liquor brought down the coast from Canada to Atlantic City, loaded onto trucks, borne into the interior of the state: Trenton, Newark, New Brunswick, Jersey City, Hoboken. Fortunes were made and lost. Murder victims were dumped into the coastal marshes, bodies ravaged by animals and decay, never found and their murderers never identified.

Children growing up in Wieland would hear tales of such unsolved murders. Men missing from their families, rumored to be buried in the marshes. Money from Prohibition times wrapped in plastic and secured in waterproof containers, hidden in cellars, in attics, in cisterns, in silos. In the wilderness. Hundreds of thousands of dollars from Prohibition times lost when a man died suddenly without sharing his secret with anyone, or succumbed to dementia and forgot where he'd hidden his money, or even that he had money.

Fallen on hard times in recent generations, these old Wieland families—Dutchins, Hannahams, Odoms, Healys.

■

USUALLY, THE HEALY BROTHERS work well together. But not this afternoon.

Unloading scrap lumber from their father's flatbed truck at the Wieland landfill and the younger brother loses his balance while backing up, loses his grip, a dozen rotted twelve-foot planks slip from his fingers causing the older brother, gripping the other end of the planks, to pitch forward, almost falling on his face.

"God *damn*. What is wrong with you today!"—Marcus is furious.

Demetrius is looking stunned himself. Being so clumsy on the job isn't like him.

Mumbling an apology: *Jesus!—sorry.*

Confronted by his brother's scorn Demetrius is mortified. Shrinks like a scolded child though he is over six feet tall, taller than Marcus. Down-looking, eyes abashed.

Only twenty but Demetrius Healy's forehead is latticed with worry-creases, just visible beneath the rim of a grimy baseball cap. His teeth are corroded, his nose broken from a childhood accident.

He has these young-old eyes, moist brooding pebble-gray gaze, you see in young persons who have had to grow up too quickly.

Trying not to stagger Demetrius stoops to pick up his end of the load. Marcus glares at him in contempt.

"You had, what?—two beers?"

Belatedly Demetrius realizes he isn't wearing gloves. He has forgotten his work-gloves, or left them in the truck, or lost them. Again.

"Shitfaced on two beers? What a faggot."

A flush comes into Demetrius's face. He has learned that it's wisest not to respond to his brother at such times.

"OK, go *on*."

Marcus pushes forward with the planks, forcing Demetrius to stagger hurriedly backward. Above them, disconcertingly near, scavenger birds circle with flapping wings, shrieking in protest as they drop the planks in a pile of refuse.

Though it isn't a warm day Demetrius is sweating inside his clothes. Can't seem to focus. Something inside his skull is beating its wings. Strong smell of raw garbage from elsewhere in the landfill, a smell that evokes memories for him, makes him want to gag.

Both Healy boys have been drinking beer, in cans, sporadically through the afternoon.

Loading their father's flatbed truck at the site of a house demolition in town, unloading it now at the landfill. Dull boring work, sheerly manual labor, no skill involved, but stressful, tiring.

In a way, wounding. Humbling. Marcus badly wants to do carpentry work like his father but the damned jobs aren't there for someone with his lack of experience.

Since Demetrius dropped out of school several years ago and has been working sporadically with his brother he has discovered that Marcus drinks at worksites if he can get away with it; Marcus often drinks while driving. Stocks up on Coors six-packs in the back of his car.

Demetrius has begun to drink, too. Not every day—not so much on Sunday, when he attends church—but during the week. Can't keep up with Marcus.

Might be the several beers he has had, or something weighing on his mind, Demetrius isn't himself today. Usually reliable, strong as a heifer, stoic and uncomplaining. Taking shit from his brother—OK, he's used to it.

Today, seems like he can't concentrate. Like a winded horse breathing through his mouth. Eyes watering from the landfill, slow-burning tires emitting a putrid black smoke rising upward indolent as a woman's beckoning hand.

Smoldering stench, hits you in the face when you first arrive at the landfill then later you discover you're not smelling it anymore.

■

POSTED AT THE FRONT gate and intermittently through the landfill are faded signs warning of *ASBESTOS*. Decades ago, siding containing asbestos was torn out of walls including the walls of public schools in Wieland, deposited here haphazardly by local workmen, among them Lemuel Healy; later much of this waste was bulldozed into a pit, covered over by gravel that is continually washing away.

Ecological disaster zone? But no one has ruled on it (yet), so—the landfill remains open.

There's a more immediate danger from predator birds defending their territory—gulls, crows, vultures, hawks. Shrieking and swooping overhead.

As boys Marcus and Demetrius frequently bicycled out to the landfill with other boys, three miles from the farm on Stockton Road, bringing BB guns, .22 rifles. Wild kind of target practice, hundreds of garbage birds trying frantically to flee, flapping their wings, squawking, can't miss, sure to hit something, the boys' blood ran high, pumping hard through their veins.

Birds of Hell, shot in midair, falling heavily to the ground. Feathered wings abruptly ceased beating and squawking silenced.

Rats too were favored targets. But rats are *smart,* flee at the sound of voices, not so easy to find and shoot.

As his brother and the other boys hooted and whooped about him

Demetrius stood silent, abashed. He'd had only a BB gun, he'd taken little pleasure in shooting even tin cans as targets.

Kill something living—why?

Boyhood is long behind him. His, and Marcus's. Things they did only a few years before seem remote now as movies they only vaguely remember seeing. When they come to the landfill now it's in their father's old Chevrolet flatbed. They are laborers. They have entered adulthood, no turning back.

Open a door and step heedlessly through, the door closes behind you, locks.

Try the handle, turn it this way, that way, yank at it, pull—*locked.*

So they are employed, sporadically. When needed. Helping out their father Lemuel Healy who has to supplement his salary as a custodian at the Langhorne Academy, this salary being hardly above the minimum wage with few benefits.

"Grab hold, hey? Wake the fuck *up.*"

On a worksite someone has got to be boss. When the Healy brothers work alone together Marcus is the boss. No question.

"You got it, kid? Jesus!"

Twenty-two, thickset and muscular as a wrestler, Marcus has a neck the girth of a man's thigh. Face shaped like a brick. His eyes are close-set, wary, and alert. His mouth in repose is a sneer, his laughter is abrasive as claws scrambling on concrete.

Girls consider Marcus good-looking, however. Women observe him in the street, in stores. Taverns. He wears his coarse dark hair shaved close at the sides of his head, longer at the crown, combed back straight from his low broad forehead as in photos of the young Elvis Presley.

Demetrius, tall and ungainly as a long-legged bird, thin scruffy whiskers barely covering his jaws, straggly uncombed hair like faded November grass. Unfairly it is said of Demetrius that he is *slow-witted.*

Sweet kid. Sad.

Like his mother, some kind of true believer in Jesus Christ. Or, trying to be.

But Marcus is annoyed, his brother is *off* today. Not looking to Marcus for signals the way he usually does, unconsciously. Half-limping, what's *that* about? (Their father is always half-limping, has a bad knee.) Glancing around the landfill covertly as an animal does, that isn't sure of the safety of his surroundings.

Had to be talked into helping Marcus today. Not like Demetrius.

Picking him up at Kroger's after his shift, and Demetrius wasn't out front waiting for him as Marcus told him to be. So Marcus was pissed having to turn in to the parking lot, having to deal with customers trying to park, pushing grocery carts, all Marcus could do not to sound his horn and yell out the window, finally there comes his brother on the run looking apologetic, like a dog expecting to be kicked.

"C'mon, Christ-sake! We're running late."

Demetrius was anxious too, that Marcus was drinking from a can of Coors, driving. Fretting that he might be pulled over by a police officer but Marcus just laughed. He knew the Wieland cops, he said. Friends of his.

Next thing that pissed off Marcus: Hallowe'en decorations in houses on Delaware Avenue.

"Jesus! Look at this shit."

Marcus spoke with an air of grievance, disbelief. Driving through this neighborhood of conspicuously repainted, renovated Victorian houses in the last few years acquired by new residents to Wieland, transfers to South Jersey: executives at Squibb, Johnson & Johnson, Bell Labs.

Gentrification. South Jersey!

Marcus has heard this word but isn't sure that he understands it nor why *gentrification* has been happening in Atlantic County. New residents with money buying "historic" properties and renovating them, sometimes gutting them entirely, retaining only an eighteenth-century stone foundation. Prices of houses rising in Longport, Avalon, Beach Haven, Wieland. The children of these new residents are likely to attend, not local public schools, but the Langhorne Academy.

Property taxes are so high now in Wieland, people who've been living here for generations have had to move out of the borough. The Healys have always lived outside town where taxes are lower. You can claim a farm deduction on state property tax if you own five acres. Bungalows, trailer villages, aging farmhouses on family farms sold off acre by acre until only the house and five acres remain.

It was a subject you didn't want to bring up with Lemuel Healy. Or any of the Healys who lived in Atlantic County.

Born and raised in one fucking place, living within a few miles of where you were born or in your parents' old house, nothing changes in your life but the state keeps raising your taxes until one day you can't afford to live in your own house.

Try to fix up your house, your taxes are raised. "Property improvement"—taxes are raised. What the hell?

The place has always been *yours,* it's all you remember, where the hell else are you going to go?

Lemuel has said he plans to die right where he is. Die in his own damn bed.

Anybody tries to come evict him, he'll blow off their heads with his shotgun. As many of them as he can get before they get him.

Think I'm not serious? Hell yes, I am serious.

Marcus thinks, probably yes. Especially when he's been drinking Lemuel is serious, like his grandfather who got into trouble shooting at that Nazi dirigible over at Lakehurst, what's-the-name: *Hin-din-burg.*

Everyone they knew resented the new residents but were grateful for them too. Money pouring into South Jersey, finally. Millions of dollars spent on restoring not only old houses but old churches, one-room schoolhouses, covered bridges. Old barns made over into houses for multimillionaires, with solar panels on the roofs; old blacksmiths' shops refashioned as antique shops.

Marcus has helped his father work construction in Longport, Avalon, Beach Haven, as well as Wieland. You had to be impressed with the luxury building materials—hardwood floors, granite-tile kitchens, state-of-the-art bathrooms, Sub-Zero refrigerators and stoves built into the walls. Marble-floor two-story foyers, large as the foyers of hotels, with winding staircases and crystal chandeliers. Slate roofs, flagstone terraces. Architectural swimming pools outdoor and in, minimum one hundred thousand dollars. "Entertainment centers" with eighty-inch TV screens. Five or six bedrooms, three-car garages, five thousand square feet minimum, multimillion-dollar houses in newly created "gated communities" with names like Pheasant Hill, Pinewood Acres, Wieland Meadow.

Why this was happening, why now, was a mystery. No one in the Healy family, none of their neighbors or friends, understood, anything to do with the economy was beyond comprehension, Wall Street, *international bankers*, it was all rigged, had been rigged since the Depression.

Indeed it was hard not to deduce, from the evidence of the visible world, at least this swath of properties in Wieland, that the world was rigged in the favor of people who have money.

"I mean, for Christ's sake look at this. Who gives a shit for Hallowe'en?"

Marcus was incensed. As if the showy decorations were a particular insult to him.

Demetrius roused himself from the deep well of private brooding, glancing around, not sure what he was seeing.

Out in the country, on Stockton Road, you'd see houses with pumpkins on front porches, cut-out witches or ghosts in front windows, kid stuff, negligible. But here in Wieland were *artistically carved* pumpkins on the porches of Victorian houses displayed like works of art. Life-sized dummies stuffed with straw, corpses, zombies, propped up on porch steps, gazing affably toward the street.

Life-sized skeletons wearing cowboy hats, enormous gossamer cobwebs covering shrubs like collapsed parachutes, what the *fuck*. You had to have money, you had to have time, you had to think you were somebody special, to set up Hallowe'en decorations on this scale, to force people to look at them and admire them.

"Crap like this is fucked-up."

Skeletons particularly incensed Marcus. Had to be reminding him, as they reminded Demetrius, of their mother who'd died the previous year: losing weight, fading, light slowly dimming in her eyes and this was the light of motherly recognition, love. The sickening shock of Ida's sunken cheeks, her collarbones pushing against her sallow thin skin; shock of upper arms no larger than a normal woman's wrist.

Demetrius has nightmares about it, still. *Like an actual skeleton pushing through, more visible every day.*

She'd wanted Demetrius to help her die, she'd said. Begged.

"Who in hell thinks *skeletons* are funny!"

Marcus braked the truck to a stop. What provoked him was a plastic skeleton on the front lawn of a jonquil-yellow Victorian house of three stories with prominent lightning rods like something in a museum. You could see that the original windows in this house had been replaced with new glass, too-bright stained glass panels beside the front door. You could see that the entire shingled roof had been replaced, at enormous cost.

As Demetrius stared in disbelief his brother kicked over the skeleton propped against the veranda of the house, a figure taller than Marcus but flimsy, breakable. Marcus next kicked an ornately carved pumpkin on the lawn, an actual pumpkin and not plastic, pulverized by Marcus's booted foot.

Demetrius realized that his brother was mildly drunk, holding a Coors in one hand as with the other he swiped at a giant gossamer cobweb, freeing a black plastic spider that fell at his feet, where he trampled it.

Returning to the truck laughing at his brother cringing in the passenger seat like a scared little kid.

"Oh fuck *you*, Demmie. Nobody's going to arrest me. Not in Wieland."

Another house, next block, Marcus did the same thing: parked at the curb, kicked another fancy pumpkin to pieces in the front yard of a big old house, knocked down a row of cartoon grave markers, another stupid plastic skeleton with smirking plastic teeth.

It appeared that someone was peering out a front window, Marcus only just laughed and lifted his middle finger to them.

Very funny to see his brother cringing in the passenger seat. Like a scared kid trying to make himself small.

Next, Marcus turned onto Vineland Avenue where, behind a ten-foot wrought iron fence, the Langhorne Academy took up an entire block.

In fact, the private school was much larger than it appeared from the street; its property stretched back for a considerable distance. Demetrius occasionally drove his father to the Academy, where Lemuel was a part-time custodian. He'd never walked very far on the campus or around the perimeter of the property but knew it comprised many acres at the outskirts of Wieland; beyond it was open land, woods and marshland.

A place for rich people. Children of rich people. Not for people like Demetrius or his father Lemuel, part-time custodian.

Here were Hallowe'en decorations like those in the yards of the Victorian houses. Ornately carved pumpkins, plastic skeletons, gossamer cobwebs ugly as bagworm nests infesting fruit trees in Atlantic County, and giant black plastic spiders in these webs. Across the granite façade of Langhorne Hall, the oldest building at the school, now the administration building, was a poster in large orange and black letters: HAPPY HALLOWE'EN.

"You're not going to do anything here, OK?—Pa works here."

Demetrius tried to speak lightly. Not a good idea to plead with Marcus.

"You could get Pa in trouble, if . . ."

"Bullshit."

Marcus cracked another Coors, considering. As if pondering some mystery of life bound up with the dignified old stone buildings overlaid with the shiny-bright Hallowe'en decorations.

"Mary Ann has a scholarship here. How's she doing, y'know?"

"No."

"*No?* I thought you and her were so close."

Mary Ann was a younger cousin who'd just started attending the Langhorne Academy, in eighth grade. Demetrius wasn't so sure how close he and Mary Ann were, any longer.

Steeling himself for Marcus to say something about Mary Ann that would upset him but Marcus had already lost interest.

"Fuck it, who gives a damn."

Driving back to the main street of Wieland, and out onto the highway headed for the landfill four miles away.

Smelling the headwind, stench of the dump almost as soon as you leave Wieland.

One mile from the entrance, your nostrils begin to pinch. Soon then, your eyes begin to water. Smells envelop your vehicle like fog: Smoldering rubber, chemical spills. Every kind of garbage-rot.

An (empty) township sanitation truck lumbers toward Marcus headed for town. Headlights on, it's a county regulation.

In the blurred seconds of their passing the bewhiskered driver's eyes catch at Marcus's eyes. Young men of their generation in Atlantic County tend to know one another and in fact this looks like a guy Marcus might've gone to school with, or his brother.

Marcus lifts the Coors can in a sneering salute. Worse shit-job than his own.

■

"OK, YOU CAN FINISH up, looks like just one more load. I've got an important call to make."

Any job the brothers undertake together, Marcus is sure to cut out the last half-hour, leave it to Demetrius to finish.

"Yeh, I can do it. OK."

"You're sure—you're OK?"

"Yeh."

Still, Marcus is regarding Demetrius as if daring him to protest; what remains in the flatbed is one more load, if two men are unloading.

Fifty minutes so far at the fucking landfill, hauling heavy lumber from the flatbed, dumping it.

Fifty minutes breathing in putrid black smoke, stink of raw rotting garbage, spilled chemicals, weirdly the smells seem to have faded.

Numbness in your nasal passages spreading up into the brain like ether.

Over the landfill, a sepia-tinged haze. Dazzle of newly dumped trash, a kitchen table with chrome legs, cracked mirror reflecting light.

Marcus asks again is it OK for (he can see) his brother is looking tired, white-faced. He has seen Demetrius gagging, trying not to vomit. *Is* Demetrius sick to his stomach, from just a few beers? Maybe the poor bastard can't drink. Marcus vows, he will be easier on Demetrius next time.

He can rely upon Demetrius to finish up a job, not to protest or complain, that's just his brother's way. When their mother was sick, dying the previous year, it was Demetrius who took care of her, Demetrius and their younger sister, Eva, who fussed, fretted, wept, complained, raged, but Demetrius was mostly quiet, stoic. As if the worst had already happened, nothing remained except to deal with it.

Now Marcus isn't sure what is wrong with Demetrius. If anything is wrong.

For the past few days Demetrius has been behaving strangely. Very quiet, distracted.

First, this morning saying he couldn't come out to the landfill with Marcus, then changing his mind once, twice. Not like him.

Couldn't be a girl. So far as Marcus knows his brother has never had anything like a *girlfriend*. Twenty years old, stricken with shyness around girls. If a woman smiled at him in the 7-Eleven or the Kroger's where he worked he'd panic.

Two years ago Demetrius stopped attending classes at Wieland High without informing anyone in the family, even their mother. Where he spent his time no one knew.

Turned out he'd been suspended from school for a week for fighting in the cafeteria, evidently a girl had been involved.

A girl!—but when Marcus looked into it he discovered that the girl was a special needs student, two hundred pounds, short, rotund, and muscular, "cognitively challenged." She'd been harassed by several girls, had attacked one of them with her fists, Demetrius was an innocent bystander who tried to intervene and wound up on the floor scrambling with the screaming girls, shirt torn, clump of hair torn from his head, bleeding from his nose. A security guard took them all into custody, all were suspended from school for a week.

It was like his brother to try to do some good, Marcus thought, and get in trouble in the process. Poor asshole!

Like he'd been their mother's caretaker. *Caretaker* seeping into Demetrius's bones like a curse he'd be obliged to look after every loser, misfit like himself needing protection.

After the week's suspension Demetrius never returned to school. Shrugging, saying the hell with it. He'd always felt like a misfit in classrooms, too tall and lanky-limbed for desks. Had trouble concentrating on reading, his eyes "jumped around" a printed page. Opening a book, something in him died. He'd gotten decent grades in what was called vocational arts—"shop"—in the company of boys like himself who in earlier decades in South Jersey were allowed to quit school at the age of sixteen to work on their fathers' farms.

Eager to get away from the foul-smelling smoke Marcus leaves Demetrius to finish the job. Wanting to call a woman he has recently met, who lives in Toms River.

He's away, not sure how long, fifteen minutes possibly, distractedly walking in the direction of Wieland Pond as he talks with the woman, laughs, in a lowered voice parrying her questions to him, which verge on inquisitive, pushy, not telling her where he is—(at the stinking town dump!)—but reiterating he's *at work.*

Relenting, saying he and his brother Demetrius are doing some work for their father, carpenter-work.

Carpenter-work! This, Michelle respects.

Marcus has wandered out onto a peninsula. Glassy water, reflected sky, must be Wieland Pond. Hears the querulous mutter of Canada geese.

Hasn't been hunting in years. No interest in Canada geese.

Overhead, not far away are vultures, circling the air flat as paper cutouts. Marcus has to raise his voice, cell phone reception is weak here.

Staring at the vultures, speaking distractedly to Michelle. When will she see him? When will he call her? Marcus is only half-listening to the woman's voice, which is not (yet) a familiar voice to him, an expendable voice, he has been intimate with this person yet doesn't really know her, or feel much enthusiasm for her coming to know him, it would be as easy for Marcus to cease thinking about her as it would be to terminate this cell phone conversation with its weak wavering reception; what he is thinking of, what the circling vultures remind him of, are the Hallowe'en decorations in town, and the Langhorne Academy where his father is a custodian, resentment he feels, bitterness he feels, people with money, Healys without money. Manual labor it's called, working with your hands, needing to wear gloves on your hands, working with all of the muscles of your body, all of the strength of which your back is capable, but you are only as strong as the strength of your skeleton, the suppleness of your vertebrae, the terror is throwing out your back the way his father has done, limping, whimpering with pain yet grateful for work, there is such shame in going on unemployment, and then, unemployment ceases after a few months . . . Having to breathe in polluted air, and grateful for that.

Marcus cuts off the woman's remarks telling her he has to go now, has to get back to work.

He'd been excited, making the call. Now, not so much.

It's like a woman, to let you down. Hearing that slight subtle reproach in Michelle's voice, like the first faint scratch on a shiny new vehicle.

All this time, Marcus has more or less forgotten Demetrius. Taking quick strides now, to return to the worksite.

Five-minute walk, Marcus didn't realize he'd wandered so far away.

But at the flatbed truck, Demetrius isn't visible.

(The truck has been emptied, all the lumber removed. Backbreaking job, Demetrius seems to have done by himself.)

"Hey—Demmie? Where're you?"

At first Marcus is just mildly annoyed, his brother isn't here. Where he should be.

Then, he's pissed. Having to search for his brother at the town dump! God *damn.*

Like a kid, not where Marcus left him. Stink of burning rubber, garbage. What a God-damned place to spend your young life.

Dangerous place, Marcus has reason to think. Pits dug thirty years before are overflowing with every kind of stinking debris. Farm pesticide drums badly rusted, lying on their sides like decayed corpses. Chemicals, raw reeking garbage. A feast for birds, flies. Poorly regulated by the county, or not regulated at all.

Weird how, as kids, they explored the landfill looking for valuable items—anything usable, not-broken. Ignoring the smoke, smells.

How much you ignore, as a kid. Some kind of blindness.

Like when it was first mentioned, *palliative care* for their mother. Marcus hadn't heard, hadn't processed the word, fuck he was going to be involved. Just—*fuck*.

Once, they discovered a vase at the landfill, that seemed beautiful to them, rose-colored, with a fluted rim, about eighteen inches high; a vase for flowers, with just the smallest hairline crack. Brought it home for their mother who thanked them, called them both *my honeys*.

My honeys!—no one has called Marcus any name like that in a long time.

Their mother washed the vase, with care. Set it on a windowsill in the kitchen where it is still, in the house that is now just Pa's house.

Not that Pa owns the property, fully. Marcus knows there's a mortgage, doesn't know for how much.

Losing patience, where the hell *is* Demetrius?

It's like his brother, not to have a cell phone. Says he can't afford one. Truth is, probably Demetrius wouldn't be able to use it and would be too embarrassed to ask Marcus for help.

Marcus has been circling the landfill. Seriously pissed. Considering driving home, leaving Demetrius to walk the three miles: serve the asshole right.

You don't fuck with Marcus, *you just don't*.

Not wanting to think that something might be wrong with Demetrius. Some kind of nerve-thing, or what's it called—*respiratory*.

Demetrius is prone to bad colds, bronchitis, even pneumonia. Weakened immune system, a doctor has said.

Fuck that, the kid is strong as an ox. He *is* strong, when he wants to be.

The look on Demetrius's face!—when he sees the truck is gone . . .

Marcus has to laugh. Would serve Demetrius right.

But: the way he dropped that load of lumber, as if his fingers had just let go. Falling onto his feet, would've broken his toes except Demetrius is wearing work-boots with reinforced toes.

Kind of thing Pa has been doing lately. *Don't know what happened, just lost the strength in my hands.*

On a construction site you see your co-workers' weaknesses when they can't any longer be hidden. Like in a family, everything up too close, intimate.

Fact is, Demetrius hasn't gotten over their mother's death. Marcus would feel sick-guilt about this but *no*. Not going there.

Marcus has left the landfill, has been walking in the nature preserve, what's it called—*Jorgen Bird Sanctuary*. Circling Wieland Pond, which looks different every few feet, different perspectives, sudden vistas of glassy water with mallards, Canada geese. Suddenly you realize you've been hearing bird cries, sharp and urgent.

"Demmie? You here? It's me . . ."

Stupid to identify himself, as if Demetrius wouldn't know who was calling his name. Marcus is becoming uneasy, none of this seems right.

He is following a service road now. Not much-used, overgrown with thistles, rutted mud leading up one of those hills they learned to identify in school—*drumlin*.

What is strange here: vultures.

Circling overhead, and in trees nearby.

Marcus sees tire tracks in the road, boot-prints. Not fresh, but not old. The tracks lead up the hill to—what? Nothing there but trees.

Also, a set of boot-prints leading down the hill. The service road turns uphill but veers to the left before trailing off into underbrush; but the tire tracks continue to the top of the hill, through tall grasses.

It's a curious sight. Marcus takes it in half-consciously. He's accustomed to working outdoors, excavation sites. With earthmoving machines. Flatbed trucks, cranes.

But weird, disconcerting—so many turkey vultures here . . .

Suddenly there's Demetrius at the top of the hill, stepping into sight. As Demetrius moves forward, vultures in a nearby tree flap their wide wings to ascend, retreat.

Marcus calls Demetrius's name, waves at him, at first Demetrius doesn't seem to hear him, or see him. Just standing there irresolute, somewhat stooped.

Not looking down at Marcus at the foot of the hill. Not aware of Marcus at all.

Marcus climbs the hill, calling to his brother, waving—finally Demetrius sees him. Still he is behaving strangely as if stunned, dazed.

"What're you doing up here? What's wrong?"

Marcus will long remember, that sick stunned look on his brother's face. Stoop of his shoulders so like the stoop of their father's shoulders.

And the vultures circling around him, scattered into the air, like dust mops vigorously shaken.

Marcus assumes the vultures have found something dead, and it is this dead thing that Demetrius has seen.

"What's it? Found something?"

Demetrius nods *yes*. But doesn't explain further.

Marcus is prepared to see a deer carcass. Not uncommon, to come upon a rotted eviscerated deer carcass.

Scavenger birds usually come after other animals have torn the carcass apart—foxes, coyotes, raccoons, black bears. These are not scavengers but they will eat a fresh corpse. Often in South Jersey you see at the side of country roads the curved rib cage of an animal, skull and large bones remaining.

Beautiful curve of the rib cage. Startling beauty in the grace of a white-tailed deer even in death.

Roadkill. Older generations of Healys brought *roadkill* home to be carefully prepared, eaten.

Marcus stands beside Demetrius who points wordlessly down into a ravine about thirty feet in depth, has to squint to make out what appears to be a vehicle, a car?—a white car upended in shallow water, trunk flung open, rear wheels and mud-splattered rear bumper exposed.

Car wreck! Plunged over the edge of the ravine.

New Jersey license plate, pale yellow. Beneath splatters of dried mud, strangely unscathed, shining.

Marcus sees now, the tire tracks lead to the top of the hill. Leaving the service road as it veers left, continuing to the top of the hill, and over.

Marcus whistles thinly through his teeth. Jesus! Has to concede, he hadn't expected this. Such a sight. Nothing like this, ever.

But Demetrius continues to point into the ravine, now Marcus sees something else beside the car: An arm? *A human arm?*

With a hand loosely attached at the wrist, fingers missing, badly mangled as if something has been chewing or pecking at it.

A few feet from the arm, the remains of a (male) torso. Naked, similarly mangled, skin waxy-white as if drained of blood.

"What the hell . . . Will you look at that."

Marcus is stunned. Blinking, staring. A moment later, seeing, in brackish water near the torso, the head.

A human head.

All this while vultures are lifting themselves noisily out of trees close by the Healy brothers, to resettle in trees a short distance away. Several in the ravine fly up, flapping their wings noisily. Uncanny, their zombie eyes and stained beaks express no alarm, no apparent concern; they move like automatons, roused by the brothers' presence as if by motion sensors.

Marcus, shaken by what he has seen in the ravine, reacts to the vultures with anger, inchoate rage. Wishes he had his fucking rifle . . .

Peering more closely at the human head below. His own scalp crawls, he sees how the scalp has been gouged. No mistaking this, a male head.

Eye sockets empty, no nose. Much of the lower jaw gone.

Human head without a face. Marcus stares, feeling sick.

Half-joking to Demetrius, how the hell did he find *this*.

Stench of decomposing flesh, wafting upward to the brothers' pinched nostrils. What they've been smelling, without wanting to think what it was.

In a weak voice Demetrius tells Marcus, he saw the vultures. So many of them, in the trees.

Tire tracks leading up the hill, he noticed too. Something about it *not right*.

Car wreck, Marcus says. Some kind of accident, they will have to report.

He's had enough staring down into the ravine. Pushes Demetrius ahead of him, they're going home.

Later Marcus will realize, he should have taken pictures with his cell phone. Once-in-a-lifetime opportunity, he lost.

Crazy kind of accident, car wreck at Wieland Pond. Dead body, part-devoured by animals. Jesus!

Halfway down the hill Demetrius has to stop, stoop over, vomit into the grass. Coughing and gagging, heaving up his guts. His face as ghastly-white as what is left of the corpse's face.

Marcus curses Demetrius, this isn't a time to lose control. Just a dead body, that animals have got to.

Demetrius wipes at his mouth with the back of his hand. In an awed voice murmuring, "He—he was all—pieces . . ."

"That's what animals do. Get over it."

Marcus speaks sharply. Marcus doesn't want to think of the torn-apart body as *he*. Seems unnatural to him, his brother would call it *he*.

Feels a need to lecture Demetrius, as if Demetrius doesn't know these elementary facts: Scavengers go for the soft parts of the body first. Eyes, belly, crotch. Tear out guts through the rectum.

Fast-talking, nervous. A kind of mania has enlivened Marcus, he needs to talk to nullify his brother's dazed silence.

Back at the truck Marcus swings into the cab. Demetrius has to heave himself, grunting with effort.

Much relief, no one is at the landfill. No one has seen the Healy brothers white-faced, hurrying to their father's truck.

Weird it seems to Marcus, that nothing has changed at the landfill. No one has observed, no one knows.

Crows, grackles—squawking over garbage, like before.

Stench of burning tires—like before, except now Marcus is feeling nauseated.

He *will* call 911. Once they get out on the highway away from this hellhole.

One good thing: whoever it is in the ravine, it's no one they know. Marcus is sure.

Could see enough of the face. Definitely, no one Marcus knows.

Terrible to see the face of a friend, a relative in such condition. Nightmare you'd never get over.

And the car: Marcus is sure he didn't recognize the car, looked like a BMW, Acura, some kind of fancy car. Doesn't belong to anyone he knows.

Out on the highway, relieved to be gathering speed. Marcus informs Demetrius, *he* will notify the police. Talk to the police. Tell them he found the wreck, found the body, spare Demetrius getting involved.

Why?—because Demetrius gets too anxious, makes too much of things. Starts to stammer. All Marcus has to do, as a good citizen, is report the wreck, tell the police where it is, if they want him to show them he will, that's OK. Least he can do, some poor bastard out there at Wieland Pond and his family won't know where the hell he is, not a pretty sight.

Demetrius tries to protest, he was the one who found the wreck, but Marcus interrupts him saying for Christ's sake stay out of it, having to talk to people makes Demetrius nervous, he can't even answer the phone without stammering.

Marcus is feeling good about this. Marcus has made up his mind.

Thinking he owes his kid brother: Taking care of their mother like he did. A year, at least. And continuing to live with Pa at the house, helping out Pa, nothing that Marcus wants to do, not ready for that burden or even to think about it.

Michelle has hinted, she'd like to meet Marcus's family sometime. Father, brother. *Fuck that.*

Out on the highway, what relief! Windows lowered, cold air rushing in. Soon enough to call 911 when they get home.

Cold can of Coors, waiting for him in the refrigerator. Remedy for trembling hands.

Thinking how their mother would be touched, to know that Marcus is looking after Demetrius. Protecting him. People say Demmie is *slow, slow-talking* but Marcus knows, Demetrius is as smart as anyone, or nearly.

Dumb sweet kid. Tripping over his own feet. Kneeling, praying with their mother at church, embarrassing to see. Well, it's good—no harm. Believe that Jesus Christ is your savior, gives a special fuck for you, if you can believe that, why not? But it's Marcus Healy who will protect his brother from what's called *trauma.*

Excitement suffuses Marcus, now he's over the initial shock. Car wreck, corpse—at Wieland Pond. *He* made the discovery, word will spread through the township. Everyone who knows Marcus Healy, his friends, relatives, guys he went to school with, works with, girls from school, women like Michelle, not to mention the Wieland cops who know him—God-damned impressed.

Pa, too. Takes a lot to impress the old man.

But, Marcus thinks, this will do it.

GRISLY HALLOWE'EN DISCOVERY AT WIELAND POND
Bodily Remains Found in Ravine by Local Resident

A grisly discovery was made near Wieland Pond two days ago on Hallowe'en afternoon by a local workman.

Marcus Healy, 22, of 1118 Stockton Road, Wieland Township, called Wieland police to report human remains sighted near a wrecked car in a ravine in the wetlands.

Mr. Healy, a carpenter's assistant, told police officers that he had made a routine trip to the Wieland landfill after which he was hiking on a wetlands trail and saw "unusual tire tracks" in a service road. Following these tracks up a steep hill Mr. Healy saw the vehicle overturned in the 30-foot ravine partly submerged in water.

Then, Mr. Healy said he had the "surprise of his life" seeing what appeared to be human remains near the wreckage.

These remains have been tentatively identified as those of a Caucasian male in his late thirties, approximate height six feet, weight one hundred seventy pounds. Tracing the vehicle's New Jersey license plate number, Wieland police learned that the vehicle is a white 2011 Acura sedan registered to a local Wieland resident whose identity has not yet been made public.

Wieland police chief Leo Paradino did not release more specific details due to the "sensitive nature" of the case. Chief Paradino did not speculate whether the deceased was believed to have died in an accident, as a suicide, or as a victim of foul play. He did confirm that there had been "significant animal activity" at the scene which would "impede identification" of the deceased.

Atlantic County medical examiner Orin Matthews will be issuing a more complete report following his investigation into the identity of the deceased and the specific causes of death, he has said. The identity of the victim will be released pending notification of his next of kin.

Marcus Healy, a 2009 graduate of Wieland High School who played varsity football for three years, helping to lead his Wildcat teammates to an Atlantic County championship in 2008, told the *Wieland Gazette* in an exclusive interview that while growing up in Wieland he had hiked and camped in the wetlands often but had "never seen anything like this before."

Asked if he thought there might be some connection between the grisly scene and Hallowe'en Mr. Healy said that that did not seem likely since the body looked as if it had been in the ravine for a while as "animals had got to it" and it was beginning to decompose "pretty bad."

Asked if he thought he would return to the wetlands for further hiking and camping Mr. Healy made it clear that he had "no plans" to do so in the near future—"or maybe ever."

WIELAND GAZETTE
NOVEMBER 2, 2013

II

TONGUE

MR. TONGUE

Who is here?—why, Mr. Tongue is here!

Who is coming to visit?—why, Mr. Tongue is coming to visit!

Mr. Tongue says *Hel-lo, ma chère Little Kitten!*

Mr. Tongue says *Close your eyes, ma chère Little Kitten!*

Mr. Tongue says *Close your eyes, ma chère Little Kitten, for Mr. Tongue will not come to visit unless those Godiva-chocolate eyes are closed! Tight.*

∎

ALL SNUGGLY IN THE silly-creaky swivel chair with the puckered-to-kiss rosebud cushion just large enough for two to sit scrunched together warm & cozy as cinnamon toast if Big Teddy Bear curls his (muscled) arm around the (slender) waist of Little Kitten slow & sinuous as a snake with the most ticklish darting-red tongue; & with the door to Big Teddy Bear's office prudently locked as it is after-office-hours at school & no light showing against the frosted-glass window in the door, utter privacy guaranteed.

Since Little Kitten has informed her mother that she will be stay-

ing after school for the Looking-Glass Book Club which (so silly
Mommy thinks) meets twice weekly & not (merely) once weekly,
Little Kitten with pert pink backpack strapped in place, somewhat
flush-faced, moist-eyed, with parted lips, awash in the dreamy after-
glow of love like the glow of radium, will not be expected at the rear
of Haven Hall for Mrs. Chambers (Mommy) to pick up until four-
forty-five P.M.; by which time Mr. Fox with fresh-washed face, fresh-
combed dampened hair, tweedy-collegiate attire discreetly adjusted,
will be ready to leave the Langhorne Academy grounds in the pearly-
white Acura bound for the privacy of his apartment across town after
a full day teaching bright seventh & eighth graders of whom a flattering number (boys as well as girls, surprisingly) are in thrall to their
very popular teacher Francis Fox.

■

WHO IS HERE?—why, Mr. Tongue is here!

Who is just a wee bit impatient?—why, Mr. Tongue is just a wee
bit impatient!

Eyes shut, quivering eyelids lowered, Little Kitten snuggles very
still as Mr. Tongue comes to visit.

Oh!—Little Kitten must resist giving in to giggles!

Must resist frantic giggles, Mr. Tongue will be offended.

This is the very first time, this will be a momentous time, that Mr.
Tongue will come to visit Little Kitten *fully.*

The previous week, in this very same darkened office in the basement of Haven Hall, in this very same creaky swivel chair, on this
very same rosebud cushion snuggled together there was some gentle
cuddling, very gentle embracing; gentle fleeting kisses light as a butterfly's beating wings against Little Kitten's forehead followed by an
overture by Mr. Tongue, clumsy, sweet-tender, but not very satisfactory, from which Mr. Tongue prudently withdrew for Mr. Tongue is
no novice & Mr. Tongue is no fool.

The challenge is to *entice,* not *frighten.*

But this Thursday, after a week of basking in Mr. Fox's attention
in class, a week in which to rehearse for this moment in the privacy

of her bedroom, Little Kitten who adores Mr. Fox has allowed herself to be lifted onto Mr. Fox's lap, that's to say onto Big Teddy Bear's lap, the palms of Big Teddy Bear's hands firmly gripping her buttocks in pink cotton panties. To prepare Little Kitten for this adventure, Big Teddy Bear has given Little Kitten a lemon meringue tart as a special treat, laced with barely a milligram of the handy benzodiazepine Ativan, a very mild tranquilizer suitable for a girl-child of no more than eighty pounds; this all innocently & unknowingly Little Kitten has ingested, resulting in her feeling, not sleepy exactly, her eyelids not visibly drooping, but a thrumming-buzzing sensation of calm coursing through her veins as she holds herself very still, shivering, yet unresisting; not daring to breathe as Mr. Tongue pokes at her tight-pursed lips (for Little Kitten *is* shy, just twelve years old & has never snuggled in any man's lap except her Daddy's lap she can barely remember, for that was years ago) then by degrees more relaxed as Mr. Tongue coaxes the prim-pursed lips to part, soon then soft-yielding lips, the lips of a young girl more accustomed to meek apology than to resistance as (very gently, not wishing to alarm) Mr. Tongue pushes farther into her mouth, which is a small mouth, a child-sized mouth.

Mr. Tongue who is warm, wetly avid, but not *too* avid. Mr. Tongue who is silly-playful but essentially calm, measured & in control. Mr. Tongue who is wriggly-ticklish, tasting of something sugary & innocent—*lemon tart.*

Little Kitten's eyes fill with quick soft tears on the verge of opening suddenly but Mr. Tongue admonishes *No, ma chère Little Kitten! Nooo* for opening eyes is forbidden, a kiss from Mr. Tongue is special.

This, the special time. Of which Little Kitten will never speak to others.

When souls are joined. Pledges are made. The most delicious secrets.

This, the special snuggly time in Mr. Fox's swivel chair in his cozy cubbyhole of an office in the basement of Haven Hall. No one else around.

Not a time you will share with anyone, Little Kitten!
Not a secret you will ever reveal, Little Kitten!

Mr. Tongue pokes, pushes, *slithers* his way ever farther into Little Kitten's mouth. As strong-fingered hands (gently) hold her head in place.

Courageous Little Kitten holding very still trying not to gag as Mr. Tongue swells by quick degrees like a balloon inside her mouth.

Mr. Tongue gliding over Little Kitten's small tongue!

Mr. Tongue sucking at Little Kitten's tongue, such a sensation!— Little Kitten is breathless, dazed as if she will faint . . .

Hands firmly grip Little Kitten's head as Big Teddy Bear murmurs softly, grunts softly beginning to rock & sway in the snug swivel chair. Gently & with no (evident) haste rocking forward & back, forward & back, warm moist breath against Little Kitten's face, Little Kitten is enraptured, Little Kitten is mesmerized, Little Kitten is feeling sleepy, so strange how in this moment of rapture unlike anything in her brief life Little Kitten is indeed now feeling very sleepy as Mr. Tongue glides deeper into her mouth, resisting the urge to glide *too deeply* for Mr. Tongue is determined to be gentle with the girl, & patient with her, & kind to her, as in class Mr. Fox is kind to her, eyes fixed upon her, admiring, patient, never disappointed in her whom he calls with infinite tenderness *Genevieve* as if the name were beautiful & melodious & not silly-sounding & embarrassing as Little Kitten believes it is; as Mr. Fox is kind to her when shyly she raises her hand to answer one of his questions as he is not always kind with certain of her classmates, coarser-skinned girls, chubbier girls, girls with faces plain as Kleenex, girls lacking that irresistible luster in the eyes, & any (& all) boys: for Little Kitten knows herself singled out by Mr. Fox, loved & cherished.

For Little Kitten *is* special. She is a lonely girl whose Daddy has left her but that was years ago, Mr. Fox is Daddy now, Big Teddy Bear–Daddy gripping her head tighter in both his hands. Little Kitten would choke, gasp, gag, struggle to free herself but dares not, for she does not want to displease Big Teddy Bear.

Ever larger, swelling in Little Kitten's mouth, Mr. Tongue is so big now, there is nothing that is not Mr. Tongue.

Rocking forward & back, forward & back, quickened, frantic until in a final thrust Mr. Tongue pushes to the very back of Little Kitten's mouth & she does begin to gag, helplessly—but there comes a sob-bing sigh, & a sudden relaxing of the hands gripping Little Kitten's head.

Now caressing her hair, soft skin of her face, soft neck murmuring *Little Kitten, I adore you, this is our secret, never reveal our secret, I will love you forever.*

Yes! Yes of course Little Kitten will keep their secret forever.

Loving Big Teddy Bear, loving Mr. Fox so, she could *die.*

THE TROPHY

WIELAND POND

29 OCTOBER 2013

"Princess Di! *What* is that in your mouth?"

Staring repelled and fascinated by the mysterious trophy in her little dog's mouth, secure between the little dog's teeth, whatever it is, could be part of a dead rat, squirrel, bird, fleshy-spongy, grayish-pink, torn, mangled, chewed, a *thing* of about six inches in length which the little dog has flipped into the air with a yelp of excitement, let fall onto the ground and snatched up again, and again tossed, and caught, and chewed, flipped and flung and chased-after in a froth of excitement that has gone on for many minutes with P. Cady in panting pursuit on the wetlands trail, calling, pleading, commanding, *threatening*.

"Stop! Damn you! *Sit*."

But no, little Di will not *sit*. Not just yet.

Eluding her human's hand grasping at her collar, daring to growl deep in her throat, not loudly, indeed near-inaudibly, so that her astonished human can pretend not to have heard, leaping defiantly away another time, not yet ready to surrender the *thing*, the precious trophy in her jaws, bony hindquarters quivering, stumpy tail held high in a blur of furious wagging that results in the little dog losing her balance for a moment, foolishly, like an acrobat in a misstep, but managing to correct the disequilibrium, if barely, all the while keeping out of the reach of her flush-faced grim-jawed human for another several minutes during which time the human's life of fifty-one years seems to flash before her eyes in a blur ending in this, this abject humiliation, a cinematic close-up in which the wounded eyes are magnified damp and baffled with tears.

Hoping that whatever it is between the dog's jaws isn't (still) alive; yet hopes it isn't (terribly) dead.

"I said: *stop*."

Clapping her hands with the vehemence of a headmistress calling an unruly assembly of adolescents to order, demonstrating now that she *is* serious, no more fooling around, *she* is the pack leader, the little rescue-pup is but the pack.

"Give that to me. Now."

Startled by the steely tone in her human's voice, blinking at her human as if unaware until this moment of her human's presence, wily little Di seems to pivot in midleap, assumes the faux-submissive posture cultivated by thousands of years of canny canine habitation with two-legged Homo sapiens, combined with the dark glisten of *soulful* eyes, and the simulacrum of *grinning* with a flash of damp teeth, the little dog comes at last meekly trotting to her human to deposit at her feet the mangled *thing*.

A mutilated, badly mangled tongue? Of some kind.

But—is it a *human tongue*?

P. Cady stoops, to see more clearly. Her glasses have steamed faintly. She must remove them, to peer at the *thing*.

A thrumming in P. Cady's ears has begun. That sound-at-a-distance of panic.

Panic. As the god Pan approaches (silently) in the forest.

In the wilderness, domain of the great god Pan, fresh-wet smells of earth, leaf mold, rotting wood, rotting organic matter, sweet-sickening stench of carrion, roots sunk deep in soil like ganglia.

Still the thrumming in her ears. She knows: only the beating of blood.

For it is not possible. Not *human*.

P. Cady's eyes see, but her brain balks at acknowledging.

Definitely the thing is meat of some kind, beginning to rot, smell—*carrion*.

By the size of it, must be a deer tongue, Headmistress Cady decides. Torn from a deer carcass.

Just the sort of (disgusting) thing her little dog adores, inexorably drawn to carrion, exactly what Princess Di would present to her human with love, with pride, a precious trophy just for *her*.

"All right. Thank you. *Good* dog."

P. Cady straightens, wiping at her eyes. She is feeling giddy—with relief.

Just a deer tongue. Torn from a deer carcass.

Go home now. Do not get involved. Now.

At her feet Princess Di is rolling over now, panting affably, tongue lolling, soft brown eyes brimming with adoration, no longer a crazed hunter, exposing her speckled tummy to be rubbed by her hot-faced human, with rough affection.

"Yes. A *very good* dog."

No difficulty capturing Princess Di now, snapping the leash to the collar. For Princess Di is a wee bit exhausted by this time, ready for home, second breakfast, nap.

"If I'd kept you on the leash as I should have, all this would have been averted. Next time, I will know next time."

Lightly chiding. Not Princess Di but herself.

Involuntarily her eyes lift, now she sees them: turkey vultures circling in the air not far away. A half-dozen, at least. A vulture has a six-foot wingspan but the black-feathered wings look shabby, rusted, small ugly heads bald, dangling legs scrawny and scaly.

She's seen them before. Has been seeing them. Could not *not* have seen them.

Alarmingly close, a vulture in a tree she has to pass, very still,

wings folded up, calmly eyeing her, P. Cady, and the little dog at her
heels, trotting back to the trailhead.

■

MORNING OF A DAY not ordinary but ordinary-seeming at this early hour
on a trail at Wieland Pond approximately sixty hours before P. Cady
will learn why the ordinary-seeming morning of October 29, 2013,
was not ordinary at all.

III

DISASTER

HINDENBURG DISASTER

The discovery of the disarticulated and partly devoured remains of the (male) body in the Wieland wetlands would be of an historic magnitude to set beside the only memorable event in the Wieland area to precede it, the explosion of the *Hindenburg* airship on May 6, 1937, nearly eighty years before.

Though the "*Hindenburg* disaster" (as it would be popularly known) had occurred not in Wieland but in nearby Lakehurst, New Jersey, it was linked in local legend to the wetlands since a local resident was believed to have caused the explosion by shooting his rifle at the immense silver airship as it glided above him in its slow stately dreamlike passage at six miles an hour to the landing dock at the Lakehurst Naval Air Station; this resident was named Romulus Healy, a forty-year-old recluse who lived in a cabin somewhere in the vast wetlands wilderness, miles from the nearest town. Healy was a former employee at the naval air station who had quit or lost his job, thus his motive for shooting at the airship billed as "the Pride of Nazi Germany" was attributed to spite, or revenge; in this version of the legend, Healy had been deer hunting when he'd sighted the airship and fired at it with no intention of causing great harm, let alone "shooting it down"—only perhaps to damage it to some small degree, for the *Hindenburg* was, at over eight hundred feet in length, containing seven million cubic feet of hydrogen, the largest aircraft in history, a mammoth and seemingly impervious target for a lone rifleman more than two hundred feet below.

Unfortunately, hydrogen is flammable, and the single shot precipitated the spectacular explosion, resulting in the almost instantaneous combustion of the entire hull of the airship and the deaths of thirty-six persons, as well as catastrophic injuries to sixty-two others.

In other accounts, likely spread by Healy himself, he had deliberately fired at the *Hindenburg* because its air fins were emblazoned with Nazi swastikas, offensive to Healy's political beliefs as a self-identified communist—(not an official Communist Party member)—who despised capitalism and capitalists, rich people, landowners, and all things to do with Nazi Germany.

In still other accounts, Healy had been drinking at the time, and had merely fired impulsively at the silver zeppelin gliding overhead, in no way prepared for the spectacular explosion that followed which he'd observed with astonishment, at a distance, an object fiery and terrible as a flaming asteroid, disappearing from view some miles away.

That the *Hindenburg* might have been sabotaged was an immediate suspicion of Nazi Germany, hurriedly denied by U.S. authorities: an investigation concluded that the explosion had been caused by a "discharge of atmospheric electricity" that had ignited the airship's hydrogen. If there were rumors circulating that the explosion had been caused by an American citizen, these were immediately squelched by U.S. authorities, for in 1937 the United States and Nazi Germany were not (yet) at war, and were not enemies; indeed, sentiment in much of southern New Jersey, a bastion of the Ku Klux Klan, was likely to be pro-German.

So it was, no official account of the *Hindenburg* mentions Romulus Healy, even in a footnote; he is enshrined solely in such marginal publications as *Tales of Haunted New Jersey, A History of the Jersey Devil,* and *Old Weird New Jersey.*

In the years after he returned to live in Wieland, having inherited his father's thirty-acre farm on Stockton Road, Romulus Healy denied having had anything to do with the *Hindenburg,* and refused to speak of it to anyone, including, it was claimed, the woman whom he eventually married, with whom he had six surviving children; it is believed that no law enforcement officers ever interviewed him, nor would he have consented to be interviewed by any newspaper or magazine.

In this way an aura of notoriety, a kind of dark glamour, accrued to the Healys of Wieland, though no connection between Romulus Healy and the "*Hindenburg* disaster" was ever established, and Healy would die, in 1987, leaving many questions unanswered. Within the family there was a sharp division between those who believed that yes, Romulus had probably caused the explosion, he'd had a drinking problem as a young man, as well as a very bad temper, and he'd been a self-declared communist; and those who believed that no, certainly not, none of that ridiculous story was true even if at one time, Romulus had (drunkenly) claimed that it was.

As a boy in school Romulus's oldest son, Lemuel Healy, was subjected to teasing by his classmates and inquisitive conversations initiated by his teachers: Was his father really the person who'd reputedly shot down the *Hindenburg*? Responsible for thirty-six *deaths*? Lemuel professed to know nothing about this, as indeed he knew nothing about it; whatever had happened had happened long before he was born, and had nothing more to do with him than the Revolutionary War, in which (it was claimed) one of his Healy ancestors had been involved, in general. His manner was curt, embarrassed; as he grew older, and more likely to flare up in anger, with quick knuckle-hard fists, such questioning ceased.

Lemuel's son Marcus, questioned in turn, would reply with a smile: "'Romulus Healy.' That was my grandfather, I guess—I never knew him. He killed, like, one hundred people in a Nazi dirigible and got away with it but they were Nazis in the wartime so it was OK."

Asked about his grandfather, Demetrius Healy flushed hotly and walked away.

Healy girls were rarely questioned about the subject, as if the *Hindenburg* disaster were a masculine matter altogether, from which females were naturally exempt.

Eventually, *Hindenburg, dirigible, Nazis* began to fade from consciousness like slow-escaping gas.

■

EXCEPT: DISCOVERING THE NAME "Mary Ann Healy," on one of his eighth-grade class lists at the Langhorne Academy in September 2013, Francis Fox, who made a point of researching any new community in which, for better or worse, he found himself, inquired of the girl if she was related to Romulus Healy who'd lived in the Wieland wetlands in the 1930s: and elicited from her a startled headshake that might have meant *No* or *I don't know.*

"Your surname is famous, Mary Ann. At least locally. D'you know that?"

Shyly Mary Ann murmured *no.* Very likely, she didn't know what *surname* meant.

Finding himself in exile in a region of New Jersey one might have thought—(*he* might have thought, glancing at a map of the state)—uninhabitable, Francis Fox had avidly researched the history of the Wieland community, and South Jersey generally—Pine Barrens, wetlands, farmland, hurricane-battered Atlantic coastline, scandal-laden Atlantic City. Nothing of significance seemed ever to have happened in this part of the state except the notorious *Hindenburg* disaster, attributed, in some quarters, to a local recluse by the name of Romulus Healy, who'd taken a potshot or two at the legendary Nazi zeppelin, precipitating an explosion and conflagration.

Too good to be true, but Francis Fox, devoted to the outré and the absurd in life, and determined to be amused by it as much as he could possibly be amused by anything in remote rural South Jersey, hoped it was true, laughing aloud as he skimmed the water-stained pages of a paperback *Old Weird New Jersey* he'd found in a bin in one of the myriad "antique shops" in the area.

Between *truth* and *legend* go for the *legend.*

In his kindly probing voice insisting: "There is something special about you, Mary Ann."

Ignoring the girl's discomfort with the conversation, and her teacher's unusual nearness to her, and her clear wish to hurry after friends exiting the room.

"I am not sure what it is, Mary Ann—it is not *self-evident*. We can explore the mystery together. That must be why you were assigned to my English class."

None of this could be remotely true. Until Francis Fox connected the shy dull plumpish girl in his classroom with the name *Healy*, he hadn't given her a second glance.

Though he'd known that, of three annual Langhorne scholarships for Atlantic County residents whose families could not afford the tuition of the private school, *Mary Ann Healy* was one, it hadn't made much of an impression upon him. Or rather, *she* hadn't.

For Mary Ann Healy was not a particularly striking girl, by Francis Fox's exacting standards. True, there was something of the dreamy Balthus prepubescent in the elusiveness of Mary Ann Healy's gaze; yet, her face was too ruddy-healthy, her body (inside an ill-fitting Langhorne uniform) no more defined than a sack of soiled laundry.

"For it can't be an accident, you know."

Still, the captive girl did not lift her gaze to his. Her lower lip trembled, arousing in Francis Fox a frisson of sexual desire, unexpectedly.

Until this moment Francis Fox hadn't really noticed that the Healy girl was "mature" for her age—physically. Which was somewhat repellent to Francis Fox, who preferred his girls wraithlike, diminutive.

Prepubescent was the key: *pubescent* with all it entailed of budding mammalian female flesh, the unspeakable horror of *menstruation*, was distasteful to him, a connoisseur of the Balthus ideal which is the essence of the *forbidden*.

Mary Ann Healy's face was round and cherubic-bland as a cream pie, if a cream pie could manage anything so complicated as a frown. Where other seventh- and eighth-grade girls could transform the dour Langhorne uniform (dark maroon corduroy jumper, crisp white long-sleeved shirt with an insipid wee bow at the collar) into an attractive, even provocative costume, on Mary Ann Healy it resembled a dowdy uniform worn by a middle-aged female of the servant class.

Francis Fox had noted, as a kind of oddity, that Mary Ann Healy was a scholarship student, which had to mean high grades, but in Atlantic County public schools, what could a *high grade* mean? He could only imagine the level of teaching in such poorly funded schools, since the level of teaching at the prestigious Langhorne Academy ranged from mildly good to mediocre, so far as he could judge—(perhaps unfairly, but *unfair* was Francis Fox's mantra)— from inane conversations in the teachers' lounge, and dull-witted surprise at his interest in spending weekends in New York City seeing plays, attending concerts, gallery exhibits.

Thus, Francis Fox's fastidious eye would have glided over the Healy girl without pausing, as it glided over the faces of most of his students, male as well as female, affably enough, finding little in it to detain his interest as (yes!) he'd found in two or three others in the class whose prepubescent faces had excited him, like matches suddenly struck in a void.

Each year, there was a beguiling Little Kitten or two, or three—to be cultivated, explored.

Francis Fox hadn't disliked this awkward girl, of course; he didn't *dislike* any of his students, on principle. Teaching middle school was not unlike grazing a buffet of exquisite foods hidden among plebeian, coarse, and unappetizing ones, it is not the fault of certain foods that they fail to arouse our appetites.

If anything, Francis Fox had come to feel sorry for the Healy girl, who lacked that indefinable quality that registered with others, particularly others her own age, as *desirable*. But the Langhorne scholarship marked her as distinctive—somehow; and the local notoriety of her family was a bonus.

"There is invariably a reason for what happens to us, Mary Ann. People we meet seemingly by chance. Students assigned to a class. Students assigned to a *teacher*. It's called 'destiny.'"

To this, the embarrassed girl nodded weakly *yes*. Her suet-colored eyes drifted toward the door.

Most girls, including the very prettiest girls, were giddily flattered to be singled out by their handsome teacher Mr. Fox for such private exchanges; but not Mary Ann Healy. *Why* was she not grateful for his attention? Francis Fox wondered, more intrigued than vexed.

It was his strategy, as soon as possible in a new term, to determine which girls, if they were attractive, were *fatherless*. For a *fatherless* girl is an exquisite rose on a branch lacking thorns, there for the picking; but a girl with a father in the family was, Francis Fox had learned from experience, so fully protected, she might as well be a rose surrounded by thorns that is also surrounded by a barbed wire fence, *off-limits*.

No idea whether Mary Ann Healy was, or was not, *fatherless*. Little interest in finding out.

Plain-plump Mary Ann, obviously a "poor white" girl, with a budding-mammalian body inside the school uniform, in hideous size-eight lace-up shoes purchased at a discount store, wiry-brush hair suggestive of a dun-colored wetlands rodent—beaver, badger, rat. An anomaly, in Francis Fox's experience.

"Yes, Mary Ann. We can explore the mystery together this year. My assignments in English class probe deeply into the mystery of 'identity.' You will keep a journal faithfully to be handed in each week as 'homework.' When such an opportunity arises before us, we must ask ourselves *why*."

Too shy or tongue-tied even to murmur *yes* Mary Ann Healy attempted a nervous smile. Her teeth were small, uneven, slightly discolored, of the hue of old piano keys.

If he were to reach out to touch this girl, a playful forefinger-poke against her arm, a casual brushing of the forefinger against the palm of her hand, how would Mary Ann Healy react?

Hairs stirred at the nape of Francis Fox's neck, such risky ventures were thrilling to him as (he had to imagine) firing a rifle at the luminous-silvery *Hindenburg* might have been thrilling, in another era.

"Mr. Fox" was the first male teacher of Mary Ann Healy's life, he supposed. There were male teachers in upper-level classes at the Langhorne Academy but no other in the middle school. Presumably Mary Ann had attended public schools in Atlantic County before the private school, all her teachers had been female.

"Come to my office after school today, will you, Mary Ann? I will give you a journal to write in—a special journal, just for you."

Blushing fiercely by this time Mary Ann Healy now managed to murmur *Yes, Mr. Fox*.

"Just for you. A special gift. But tell no one in your family—if you have siblings in the public school they will be jealous."

This, Mary Ann Healy seemed to register. Smiling, nodding.

"D'you live outside town? Does your father work—where?"

Mary Ann Healy murmured what sounded like *Him and my uncle, they own a garage*.

"A garage! Is he, by any chance, a master mechanic?"

An exuberant inquiry, to muffle disappointment. But what did Francis Fox care, if this ungainly girl had a *father*? He did not.

At last released from her teacher's scrutiny, vastly relieved to be allowed to exit the room, as one whose breath has been withheld to the point of pain, allowed now to breathe freely, Mary Ann Healy hurried out of the room in a way that might have been interpreted as rude; but Francis Fox surmised that the girl knew no better. She was from a rural family, a *poor white family*, and so lacked the social skills of her more affluent classmates at the Academy. Through the awkward exchange her suety gaze had not once lifted to his.

For much of her young life, Francis Fox supposed, the girl's precociously female body had drawn the attention of observers. As if mystified by something about her they couldn't quite name.

What is it?—she must have wondered. *Why do they stare at me?* Like one given pieces of broken glass to assemble, to fashion into a mirror out of which her own bewildered face stares up at her.

Almost, he felt sorry for this one.

BREAKING NEWS

Initially, the news is that a rogue black bear has attacked a hiker in the wetlands near Wieland Pond.

It is not the first time in Atlantic County that a black bear has attacked a hiker or hikers but it is the first time, it is believed, that one of these attacks has resulted in the hiker being not only mauled to death but partly devoured.

Body parts found scattered along a trail.

No identification yet except male, Caucasian.

If not a black bear, possibly a cougar. Though cougars have not been sighted in South Jersey in many years.

Not a wolf: no wolves in South Jersey, either.

In the wetlands are coyotes, coyote-dogs, bobcats. But these creatures are not large enough to bring down a human being.

If an animal, has to be a black bear, plentiful in South Jersey.

■

NOT A HIKER. NOT a bear attack. A suicide?

A vehicle overturned. In a ravine, in deep water, the driver trapped in the vehicle and drowned . . .

Obviously not an accident. Whoever it was he'd driven his car up a steep hill, over the edge of a precipice, the car toppled into a thirty-foot ravine near Wieland Pond.

(Was the driver alone in the car? It appears that yes, he was alone.)

Breaking news, bulletins. Local radio, TV. Newscasters have frustratingly little information for Wieland police refuse to release details of the death except to say that it did not appear to be the result of a bear attack, there should be no panic about bears, no hunters should rush out looking to shoot bears, it's illegal to shoot wild game in New Jersey except during hunting season.

Much speculation about why the *bodily remains* cannot be identified readily: Was there no wallet at the scene? Did the deceased have no *face*?

It is known that *animal activity* has made identification of the remains difficult. It is not known how, in detail.

If ID is made through dental records it could take weeks, months.

But it begins to be known definitively, as the early spark of news fans into a rushing wildfire, that the bodily remains are those of a *male Caucasian, thirty to forty years old.*

And that the vehicle found overturned in the ravine is a 2011 white Acura sedan, license plates and registration traced to an instructor at the Langhorne Academy: *Francis Harlan Fox.*

DETECTIVE Z.

He has come to speak with her privately. He has come to bring her bad news. She sees in his soft-creased face. In his zinc-eyes. She hears, in the tone of his voice. She feels her heart clench, she dreads what she will hear. Even as a part of her rebukes what she will hear—*No. Not possible.*

Since Princess Di in the wetlands. Since the *thing* in the excited little dog's jaws.

Since her decision to flee. Since she'd fled.

The *thing*, whatever it is, or was. Apparently a tongue, *a deer tongue*, torn from a deer carcass in the wetlands. Nothing remarkable, surely. Mere carrion, nothing to be concerned about.

Hurriedly she'd leashed the little dog, who'd licked her hands, wildly contrite. Hurriedly she'd returned to her parked vehicle. Driven them both home.

Do not get involved, Paige. You would be a fool to get involved.

■

SOMETIMES IT IS HER own voice instructing her. Sometimes, the recalled voice of her father deceased now for many years.

Of all things you do not wish to be, Paige, a fool is one of these.

A full day, following the hike in the wetlands. A (sleepless) night. (Sleepless for Princess Di as well, who shares in her human's mysterious distress, curled up in her fleece-lined bed at the foot of her human's hard-mattress bed with alert worried eyes, pricked-up terrier ears.)

No news! No calls.

Until, late Sunday afternoon. First of the calls, the casual-concerned voice of a woman friend—*Paige, have you heard? At Wieland Pond, a body has been found . . .*

A sensation of dread as of a shadow moving swiftly across the earth, growing ever larger, darker, an airship bearing death.

He has entered her dreams. This is her fear: something so terrible has happened to Francis Fox, she will be haunted by it forever.

I might have loved him. Except—our ages.

Of course—our ages. Not possible.

No one must know. No one could possibly know. Even Princess Di must not suspect.

■

NEXT MORNING IN HER office at the Langhorne Academy, a plainclothes Wieland police detective comes to see P. Cady, Headmistress.

Do you know anything about.

Do you have any idea where.

Do you know if.

Through a thrumming of blood in her ears she hears these words rustling like birds' wings.

It's the first Monday of November, following the fall break. The rowdy nuisance of Hallowe'en is over. Autumn foliage is beginning to fade, fall to the ground. From now on days will darken with dismaying alacrity. Afternoons will shrink. Through Wieland rumors have been circulating for several days like those quick-rising winds that presage a hurricane, six-foot waves crashing against the Jersey coast, flooding basements and ground floors.

At the Langhorne Academy, it is noted that after a full week's break Francis Fox is absent for Monday morning classes.

∎

UGLY RUMORS. UNSPEAKABLE RUMORS. *She* has not (yet) heard.

So respected is the headmistress, or so feared, when she enters the faculty lounge such rumors cease—indeed, most conversation ceases.

Still, P. Cady is well aware of the situation and has arranged for her capable closed-mouthed assistant March to take over Francis Fox's homeroom if he fails to show up by eight-thirty A.M., and his classes, if he fails to show up entirely.

"Has Mr. Fox called, Ms. Cady? I mean—has he called *you*?"

"Of course Mr. Fox hasn't called me! If he calls, he will call the office. Why would Mr. Fox call *me*?"

Incensed at March's innocent/ignorant query. Wills herself to remain calm, courteous.

P. Cady, Headmistress, is in her office in Langhorne Hall frowning at columns of numbers on her console computer when *he*—the intruder from the Wieland Police Department—insists upon speaking with her. Absurdly, this person calls himself a *detective*, like someone in a TV program.

And his surname—*Zwender*. Sounds like a fictitious name P. Cady will forget almost at once.

Stiffly formal with the man. Relieved that, at least, he is not a uniformed officer swaggering through Langhorne Hall drawing attention to himself.

Yes, P. Cady is damned annoyed at being interrupted on a (very busy) Monday morning but of course she is civil. Her headmistress's glacially friendly administrative manner includes even a swift spasm of a handshake, icy-cold.

P. Cady deduces from his nasal accent, which is not mitigated by an air of apology, that this person, this *detective*, is a native of South Jersey. Something in his very stance, the male-primate stance of elbows out, arms at his sides, hands at the ready, suggests that his identity is his physical being, a man among men; a brute among brutes; hidden inside his (nondescript, off-the-rack) clothing is some sort of holstered firearm, if not a billy club. P. Cady enjoys the detective's barely concealed surprise as she rises from behind her desk to nearly his height of six feet two not so much to greet him as to confront him.

Yes? What does Detective Zwender want with her?

Noting how Zwender glances about her office covertly. Twelve-foot ceiling, wainscoted walls, floor-to-ceiling bookshelves crammed with hardcover books, arched windows overlooking a courtyard of sculpted evergreens. On the hardwood floor a Chinese carpet, muted golds and reds in an exquisite design.

Yes, you should feel out of place here.

Yes, I am very consciously not looking down at the carpet, to see if you've tramped mud on it.

Curtly but politely P. Cady replies to Detective Zwender's questions. She does not believe for a moment that the *bodily remains* discovered in the wetlands can possibly be Francis Fox though the vehicle at the scene is registered to Francis Fox, there must be some explanation for this . . . Or, there must be a mistake.

Someone has stolen Francis Fox's car and wrecked it. Someone *drunk,* or *high on drugs,* a local youth with no connection to Francis Fox or to the Langhorne Academy. That is a likely explanation which P. Cady will leave to the detective to discover for himself.

Zwender is asking when she last saw Francis Fox? P. Cady replies that that would have been before the fall break, a week ago last Friday.

And where would that have been?

Where?—she has no idea. Possibly on campus, or in the faculty dining room. Unless there was a formal meeting she would not be able to pinpoint an actual place or time.

(No need to inform this aggressive person that she'd invited Francis Fox to her home for dinner that weekend, as she has invited Francis Fox for dinner at her home from time to time, and Francis, with much regret, explaining that he would be out of town, declined the invitation.)

"As I understand it, Mr. Fox went to New York City to see plays over the break. He teaches English and drama in the middle school— seventh and eighth grades. He advises the Drama Club."

P. Cady hears her words, at once banal and pleading. *Advises the Drama Club,* thus unlikely to have died in a car wreck and been devoured by animals.

In fact, Francis Fox is but a co-advisor of the Drama Club, which has long been advised by a senior instructor.

"Miss Cady, d'you know if this teacher of yours drove to New York?"

This teacher of yours sounds accusatory, insolent. P. Cady prefers to interpret the detective as merely maladroit.

"No. I mean—I don't know if Mr. Fox drove to New York."

Amending: "I mean—I would assume *yes.* It would be difficult for anyone to take public transportation from Wieland, he'd have to drive to Lakehurst to get a train to New York."

Wondering if this is too much information. Wondering if she is beginning to sound nervous!

"If he'd driven to New York, he'd have driven his car, yes? A 2011 white Acura sedan?"

"A—'white Acura sedan'? How on earth would I know, Detective? I don't keep a record of the vehicles my faculty drive!"

P. Cady laughs, this is so absurd. But Detective Z. does not join in.

"The vehicle found in the Wieland ravine, a 2011 white Acura sedan, is registered in the name of Francis Fox. I think you know that, ma'am?"

Ma'am. The word is a subtle rebuke, P. Cady thinks. It isn't enough to be a *head of school*—if you are female, you are also *ma'am.*

"I told you, Detective—I don't keep track of vehicles. I scarcely know how to identify my own vehicle, and I never remember my own license number."

Because such details are trivial, is the inference. This, P. Cady means as a rebuke of the police officer.

It's true, P. Cady knows little about interacting with police officers. Never in her life has she been questioned by a police officer, let alone a detective. So scrupulous she has never driven above the speed limit even on the New Jersey Turnpike where other drivers fly past like banshees in the wind. She has never parked illegally. She has never made a turn on a red light even in a deserted intersection if a sign warns *No Turn on Red.* The very notion of *illegal* is distasteful to her, like telling a lie, demeaning.

P. Cady would suppose that her father, Randall Cady, no longer living, an educator like herself, at one time an academic dean at Rutgers University at New Brunswick, would counsel her not to naïvely over-cooperate with police officers in circumstances that seem uncertain.

Possibly, the situation could develop into one involving legal matters. Public relations. In which case, P. Cady should consult the Academy's attorney . . . But she doesn't want to think about that, yet.

"Your Mr. Fox isn't here this morning, is he?"

"You can ask my assistant . . ."

"I've already asked and he isn't here, and he isn't at the address we have for him on Consent Street. If he'd gone to New York he'd be back by now, right?"

Coolly P. Cady says, "I have no idea, Officer."

P. Cady is offended by Z.'s tone. She has subtly demoted him to *officer,* does he notice?

P. Cady, Headmistress, is not accustomed to being addressed in such a high-handed way, by one who seems to already know the answers to the questions he is asking.

She supposes Z. is waiting for her to express alarm, distress. To react as a woman—*ma'am.* To react as an administrator with a concern for the well-being of a faculty member who has met with an accident of some sort, in gruesome circumstances.

Fact is, P. Cady is no-nonsense, matter-of-fact, non-alarmist. Takes pride in her strong stoic nature. *Thinks, talks, makes decisions like a man. But not just any man.*

Fact is, P. Cady is unable to believe that anything so bizarre, so *inappropriate,* has happened to Francis Fox, who has become some-thing of the headmistress's protégé at Langhorne. A kind of fever has suffused her, a mild delirium, possibly at Wieland Pond she was bit-ten by an infected mosquito, what is that condition—*encephalitis?* Since Princess Di ran away from her, misbehaved, trotted back with something disgusting in her jaws. How embarrassed P. Cady would be if anyone who knew her, knew her name and her position in Wieland, had witnessed how poorly trained her little rescue dog is, how willfully Princess Di disobeyed her human.

Leaping, lunging, snatching the *thing* in her jaws, tossing it into the air, seizing it between her teeth and giving it a good shake to break its neck, letting it fall to the ground, *groveling in it . . .*

Disgusting carrion. Rotting meat. *Bad dog!*

Not possible that is all that remains of Francis Fox's so-articulate *tongue.*

Still, more sensibly, with the part of P. Cady's mind that rejected as unlikely one or another symptom of unwellness that has mani-fested itself over the years, a pimple (cyst?) in a breast, a suety vagi-nal discharge, an alarming abdominal ache, a swollen left ankle, various joint-aches, head- and eye-aches, and other maladies which turned out indeed not to be symptoms of serious conditions but, as she'd insisted, merely *nothing*—so P. Cady can't take seriously this sensational rumor involving Francis Fox.

For how Francis would himself laugh at it: the improbability of such an ignominious end, for the Langhorne Academy's most charis-matic teacher.

"—Ms. Cady?"

Detective Z. has asked her something. Staring at her in a way as to make her feel distinctly uncomfortable. Her thoughts have been rattling past like empty boxcars.

"—Is it possible?"

P. Cady has lost the thread of the conversation. Perhaps it has been an interrogation.

Was it a mistake to have failed to consult the school's legal coun-sel? The headmistress is dry-mouthed, alarmed.

It is possible—it is not impossible—that this plainclothes police officer has come to arrest *her*.

Does he know? How she behaved at Wieland Pond the other morning? Had someone been observing, and reported her?

Seeing the badly mangled tongue in Princess Di's jaws, and then on the ground, how she panicked, and fled.

Seeing what the thing was. Had to be: *human*.

Someone might have been watching. Noted her license plate, called police.

But no: this is ridiculous. No one saw, no one was anywhere near.

Still, P. Cady is feeling shame. Fever-heat, suffusing her face. Sweating inside her tailored headmistress attire.

Of course, she hadn't wanted to become *involved*. She'd behaved in the most irresponsible way. She, routinely called a *leader of the Wieland community*.

Betraying her position, the claim of moral superiority that comes with being a head of school at the Langhorne Academy with its long tradition of the *honor code*.

If the trustees knew. If her father knew . . .

Zwender seems to be repeating a question P. Cady hasn't heard. A request to look into Francis Fox's office? The assurance is that nothing will be taken from the office without her permission.

"We'd just like to see if maybe there's a note. You know—a note he may have left behind."

"What kind of 'note'?"

"Any kind of note, ma'am."

Suicide. Isn't it obvious, they are thinking *suicide*.

"It would only take a minute, ma'am. Just to see if there was anything in his office. It would be very helpful."

Curtly P. Cady is shaking her head *no*. That is *not possible*.

"They're estimating six weeks minimum for the forensic odontologist in Newark to make the ID. So this would be helpful to the investigation."

P. Cady is insisting *No. No. No.*

Assuming there is no search warrant—*No.*

Out of fairness to Francis. His privacy, his office.

Thinking *I must protect Francis. If—there is reason to protect him . . .*

"You could accompany us, Ms. Cady. When we look through the office."

"I've told you—*no.*"

P. Cady is not accustomed to being challenged. P. Cady has not been challenged in some time—in years; and never in the office of the head of school, furnished with her particular things.

It's as if, as headmistress, her center of gravity is stolidly within her as in the base of a granite figure. So self-defined, so *weighted,* if she is thrown off-balance by an adversary like this stranger, disequilibrium overwhelms her: her limbs cannot move quickly enough for her to regain her balance.

"And now I think—I think—you should leave . . ."

Her vision is dimming, narrowing. There is a sort of tunnel, at the end of which the stranger's face peers at her quizzically; it is a face she has never seen before, without clearly defined features, crude indentations where the eyes, the nose, and the mouth should be, like a poorly carved pumpkin.

Her hands grope behind her for something firm to grasp, to restore her balance.

Whoever it is, he is calling her *ma'am.* He is asking—is she *all right?* The voice is nasal, grating at her nerves. That the voice is *kindly, concerned* is maddening to her, condescending.

"Odom? Can you get that chair?"

Another police officer! P. Cady has scarcely been aware of him, a younger man, not involved in the excruciatingly awkward interview.

A younger, heavyset man. With a pasty-pale, curiously disdainful face, a mollusk-face, disengaged, not so respectful of P. Cady, Headmistress, as Detective Z. has been.

Her legs have grown weak, her knees buckle. She has taken pride in her physical fitness at the age of (only) fifty-one; she has taken a foolish sort of pride in being routinely mistaken for a much younger person even as, as a young person, she took a foolish sort of pride in being mistaken for an older person.

But in this instant, P. Cady's legs have lost their strength. All of the light in the room is reduced to a pinprick inside her brain.

Whoever she is, this sliver of consciousness, this breath-with-a-name, is abruptly shuttered, gone.

LITTLE KITTEN, WAITING

5 NOVEMBER 2013

L*ittle Kitten, I adore you, this is our secret. Never reveal our se-cret, I will love you forever.*

Everywhere, and anywhere. These soft-whispered words are her solace. Her armor. No one will ever hurt her again.

He has promised. He will protect her. She has only to shut her eyes to summon him to her, his adoring gaze, his touch.

Ma chère Little Kitten. Snuggling in his arms. On his lap. Safe, warm, held firm in his arms.

Those closest to her, those whom she has trusted who have broken her heart—Mr. Fox will protect her from *them.*

For no matter where she is, she is with *Mr. Fox* as *Mr. Fox* is with *her.*

■

EAGER FOR PROMISES FROM Mr. Fox as a kitten is eager to lap up milk!

These nine days away from school: nine days away from Mr. Fox.

Unavoidably, Mr. Fox has had to leave Wieland for the break. He has said.

Will miss you terribly, ma chère!

Instead of those giddy hours at the Langhorne Academy there are days at home of utter boredom, emptiness. Each morning waking stunned at the prospect of *nothing*.

Like licking the interior of the fruit yogurt container. Lick lick *lick* but there's nothing there, your tongue is numbed with *no-thing*.

Wanting to hide beneath the covers, pillow over her head. Clumsy fingers touching herself with none of the finesse of Mr. Fox's fingers, no intelligence to these fingers, just stupid girl-fingers that make the decision to pinch, hard!—punish.

Faint bruise like a plum, Little Kitten's little breast. Pinch, pummel. Punch.

If Mr. Fox knew!—Mr. Fox would be *so sorry.*

Clatter of morning, mornings in the kitchen, no one in Little Kitten's life except her mother, always her mother, bright-smiling, bright-blinding as a beacon, and little brother, Billy, who never fails to get on his sister's nerves, poking and prying in Little Kitten's privacy like a tick, to her horror Little Kitten once saw this adorable pest leafing through her secret journal with the rosy-marbled cover, secret journal that is a gift from Mr. Fox, snatched it from Billy crying out in a voice Billy had never heard before in his sister, a voice of such fury Mr. Fox himself would have been incredulous had he heard: *Get out of here, you little shit! I'll strangle you.*

The look in Billy's cute little ferret-face!—Little Kitten has to laugh, recalling.

Visits from (boring) Grandma, Little Kitten's mother's mother, too much time on her hands and nothing to do with it, concerned for her daughter in the aftermath of the divorce; visits to (boring) relatives in Avalon, Montclair.

Banal inquiries—*How is school, do you like your teachers? Is the Langhorne Academy really so hard?*

People for whom Little Kitten feels what Mr. Fox has identified as *faux-family-emotions.*

Faux is French for *pretend.*

Except for Mr. Fox, everything is *faux.*

Last time in Mr. Fox's office Little Kitten wept, for how would she endure nine days away from school? Nine days away from *him*?

Gently Mr. Fox laughed, firmly Mr. Fox instructed: Little Kitten must set for herself the task of writing journal entries each day. *Pour out your heart, ma chère Little Kitten.*

And so, Little Kitten is doing just that. It is an exquisite pleasure, confiding in Mr. Fox in her journal, with the knowledge that Mr. Fox will read what she has written, soon.

No pleasure more exquisite, not even drawing a razor blade across the inside of the forearm, or the inside of the thighs, the initial pain is a kind of quivering/tingling that soon turns warm, consoling.

■

SOMEDAY. NOT SOON BUT SOMEDAY.

We will be together, forever.

Never doubt me, ma chérie!

She knows. She believes. His warm tender voice reverberates in her ears.

In her bed waking in the darkness before dawn from a sweet dream of Mr. Fox to discover that it is her own arm around her own waist, snug. Tight!

So reluctant, to open her eyes! To surrender sweet dreams of Mr. Fox.

Ah, Mr. Tongue prods against her lips! Mr. Tongue teases Little Kitten, he is ticklish-warm, he is smooth-damp and squirmy, he will not take a silly NO for an answer.

So long as Little Kitten keeps her eyes closed. Mr. Tongue does not like it if Little Kitten opens her eyes startled, alarmed.

Mr. Tongue does not like it if Little Kitten squirms, twists. If Little Kitten gags.

If Little Kitten *resists*.

Explaining to her how there has never been a time when they did not know each other. When they did not love each other.

In that time before. Before Little Kitten was born, she appeared to him in his dreams.

He appeared to her, before she understood who he was.

And so, when I saw you walk into my homeroom that morning, beautiful Genevieve, your face luminous as a flower, it was not for the first time.

And in your eyes too, in your beautiful eyes I saw that you recognized me, as well!

Of course, it is a "forbidden" love. At the present time.

The world would not understand, the world is comprised of dull selfish stupid people resenting the happiness of lovers.

The world that vilified the love of Edgar Allan Poe, greatest of nineteenth-century American poets, for his beautiful doomed cousin Virginia Clemm whom he'd first glimpsed when Virginia was but seven years old and married when she was thirteen and he was twenty-seven.

Ideal ages, for a true love match. Though the ignorant vulgar world does not approve.

In Mr. Fox's office on a corner of Mr. Fox's desk there is a bronze bust of Edgar Allan Poe the size of a man's head and on his shoulder a nasty hulking bird that has been painted black—a *raven*.

Little Kitten is intimidated by this object. Each time she enters Mr. Fox's office it is already staring at her—*awaiting her*. A man's head on a pedestal but the face of the man resembles a corpse's. And the *raven*!

Sunken eyes of mourning, grim downturned mustache-mouth of the man. Beady-blind eyes and cruel sharp beak of the raven.

Little Kitten shivers. Oh, why is Edgar Allan Poe looking at *her*?

Mr. Fox speaks casually of the bronze bust but it is clear that Mr. Fox is proud of it: the commemoration of his having won first prize in an annual poetry competition sponsored by the Poe Society of America.

Adoring Little Kitten stares at her (modestly smiling) English teacher–poet. This is *awesome*. Not only is Mr. Fox the very best teacher at the Langhorne Academy, he is also a prizewinning poet!

Sitting snuggling on Mr. Fox's lap as at last he's convinced her.

No harm will come to Little Kitten with just a wee little snuggle! That's a promise.

Little Kitten is uneasily aware of Edgar Allan Poe just a few inches away. Dour dead accusing eyes fixed upon *her*.

Playfully Mr. Fox turns E. A. Poe away from Little Kitten so that the dead-staring eyes are cast in another direction.

Little Kitten giggles, as if ferociously tickled. Mr. Fox is *so funny*.

Assuring Little Kitten, Edgar Allan Poe—("Eddie")—would have adored her; would have written a poem dedicated to her.

This very poem, whispered in Little Kitten's blushing ear:

> *For the moon never beams, without bringing me dreams*
> *Of the beautiful Annabel Lee;*
> *And the stars never rise, but I feel the bright eyes*
> *Of the beautiful Annabel Lee;*
> *And so, all the night-tide, I lie down by the side*
> *Of my darling—my Kitten—my life and my bride,*
> *In her sepulchre there by the sea,*
> *In her tomb by the sounding sea.*

■

AS THE VULGAR WORLD *couldn't stop the fated lovers Poe and Virginia loving each other even beyond death so the world will not stop me from loving YOU.*

Each time Little Kitten has knocked at Mr. Fox's office door as he has bidden her, and has stepped inside, and the door is locked behind her; each time Little Kitten has cuddled on Mr. Fox's lap, and Mr. Tongue has come to visit; each time Little Kitten has held herself very still not skittish and squirming as Mr. Tongue filled her mouth to bursting, each of these times Little Kitten has been given a present out of Mr. Fox's desk drawer *just for her*.

Little sweet-treats, tarts and scones. Foil-wrapped chocolates.

The journal with the rosy-marbled cover, unlined snowy-white pages awaiting Little Kitten's entries, Mr. Fox's gift to his favorite student, the nicest present of all.

A cuddly-fuzzy kitten with leopard spots, Mr. Fox gave her just before the fall break knowing how sad she was, how brave she would have to be to endure nine days without him.

Crying, she thanked him, he kissed away her tears.

Thanking him for the little stuffed kitten she would love all of her life.

It is true, in somber solitude Little Kitten has to acknowledge, there are other girls in seventh grade, and in eighth grade, who have been invited by Mr. Fox to join the exclusive Looking-Glass Book Club. A very special club whose membership is limited to just twelve students and this membership determined by the advisor, Mr. Fox.

A few boys are included, and these are very bright boys specially favored by Mr. Fox. All of the members are exceptional students, serious readers, their grades are uniformly high but this does not mean that they are all, like Little Kitten, *special to Mr. Fox.*

This, Genevieve understands. For jealousy is just silly. Envy of less beautiful girls, girls lacking her Godiva-chocolate eyes, just silly.

When she is being silly Mr. Teddy Bear laughs at her.

No other girl is so *dazzling-beautiful* as Little Kitten. Weighing, this very morning, reported in her journal, eighty-one pounds.

(Before this September when Mr. Fox came into her life Little Kitten never weighed herself, was only weighed at the doctor's office. Never paid much attention to her weight and so she is embarrassed to discover, in photographs, that she was almost—almost!—a chubby girl, with round cheeks! Pretty long-lashed eyes, but chubby-round cheeks. It is mortifying to her, to imagine what Mr. Fox would say if he could see these photographs, for Mr. Fox is very funny expressing disdain for certain girls in the school who are shameless *chubbies, butterballs,* and *little piggies.*)

Where once Little Kitten basked in her Daddy's adoration now Little Kitten basks in Mr. Fox's adoration, which is much more reliable, valuable. Indeed, it is the only adoration that Little Kitten trusts.

Here is a surprise, which Daddy would be chagrined to know:

under the spell of Mr. Fox, Little Kitten thrills to starve herself. For in fact she is never hungry, under the spell of Mr. Fox.

Yet, Little Kitten will eat (greedily, ravenously) from Mr. Fox's fingers: delicious lemon tarts, chocolate-covered strawberries, "organic" oatmeal cookies.

When they are alone and safe together in Mr. Fox's office with the little window high in the wall behind his desk which Mr. Fox can "obscure" by positioning a book in front of it.

Otherwise, Little Kitten scarcely eats. Proof is, Mr. Fox can feel Little Kitten's ribs, collarbones, wrist bones beneath the smooth pale skin Mr. Fox calls *alabaster*.

So thin, small firm breasts the size of plums. Mr. Tongue adores these breasts. Mr. Tongue licks, sucks.

Hairless underarms, Mr. Tongue explores. Oh, this tickles!

Little Kitten knows, Little Kitten fears, that Mr. Tongue would not wish to lick, suck, tickle if the plum-sized breasts were larger, and if hairs begin to sprout in the underarms even if these are fine silky hairs softer than the hair on her head. For Mr. Fox has expressed fastidious distaste for *older girls* in ninth grade, and beyond.

Grown women, adult women, like Little Kitten's mother.

■

IT IS BEGINNING TO be clear to Little Kitten why her father left their family. It was her mother he left, not her. Not Billy.

Compared to other mothers, Little Kitten's mother is attractive. Even what you'd call glamorous.

But—*too old*. At least forty.

Sizable breasts, like melons. Hips, thighs. Faint lines at the corners of her eyes no makeup can disguise. Slack, sagging skin at her jawline.

With horror Little Kitten observes her mother. No matter the brave smile, no one is deceived.

Vowing, she *will never grow up* to look like that for Mr. Fox will not love her as he does now.

■ ■ ■

ON BRIGHT-SUNNY AUTUMN MORNINGS Mr. Fox delights in adjusting the venetian blinds on the large plate-glass window. It is Mr. Fox's decision, to calibrate the degree of morning light flooding the room like warm honey.

Slyly adjusting the blinds so that it is in latticed sunshine that Little Kitten sits, in her (special) seat near the front of the room. Where Mr. Fox's mischievous pale-blue eyes glom upon *her*.

Mr. Fox, greeting students one by one, in the friendliest way; so that, with a particular intensity in his voice, he can declare: "And good morning, Gen-e-viève!"

A beat then, a pause. Little Kitten on the verge of a swoon.

Loving it, the caress in Mr. Fox's voice. Sly slipping-down deep-baritone voice, voice of an adult male, nothing so beautiful in all of the world.

And the name—*Genevieve*. A silly old-fashioned name she'd hated until in Mr. Fox's mouth it has become exquisite, sexy.

A *natural attraction* between them, like a magnet.

These nine days of deprivation, Little Kitten has been writing in her journal as Mr. Fox has requested.

Write as if you are speaking to me, dear Genevieve.

No one else will see, ever. Bare your heart to me.

In her journal Little Kitten has written poems, which Mr. Fox has praised in the past.

Most openly, of the misery in their family, since Little Kitten's father left. Misery of Little Kitten's mother, emptiness of their lives.

Little Kitten has transcribed conversations between her mother and certain of her women friends and relatives. (Secretly) recorded on Little Kitten's cell phone.

This material, Mr. Fox has described as "profound"—"revelatory"—"courageous."

This precious journal, Mr. Fox has called a "time bomb."

As she has sent, to Mr. Fox's cell phone, (secret) pictures of herself, (secret) parts of herself, that no one else has seen.

Even Little Kitten has never before seen such parts of herself, that require some acrobatics for her to take pictures of. And even then, she has to take numerous shots for most are blurred, indecipherable.

Laughing wildly, giddily. Laughing into her clenched fist.

Gravely Mr. Fox insists that Little Kitten is beautiful *in all ways*. This means, every part of Little Kitten is beautiful in his eyes.

Bathed in the purity of beauty.

Trust in me to preserve this beauty safely.

Little Kitten never fails to follow Mr. Fox's instructions: as soon as she sends these (secret) pictures to his phone she deletes them.

Mr. Fox is adamant: she must not keep those pictures on her phone for what if her phone is confiscated by *Them*?

Them is all the others. Ignorant others.

As soon as Little Kitten deletes these pictures she forgets them—as if they have never been.

■

THROUGH THE COLD WINTER, *we will keep each other warm.*

We will meet in secret, like this! For you are very special to me, there is no one like Little Kitten in my life.

Never has been, never will be.

Do you believe me? Kiss, if you do.

We must take care, we are in danger.

We are tightrope walkers on a high wire. There is no net beneath us.

He told her not to call him, not to text. He told her *no*.

He did not tell her *why*.

Sneaking one of the sharp knives upstairs. Fancy steak knife, with a gleaming blade.

Drawing the blade across the blue artery in her forearm, experimentally. Not hard. Just for the sensation.

What are you doing! That is bad bad BAD.

Mr. Fox would pull away her hand, take the knife from her. He would chide her with kisses hot and hard as slaps.

Mr. Tongue would chastise her, filling her silly mouth so that she could not speak.

If she is very very naughty, Mr. Teddy Bear will *spank*. Lift her jumper skirt, tug down her panties, spank spank *spank* until tears spill from her eyes.

Little Kitten should not even dream of hurting herself, that is *forbidden.*

In her journal with the rosy-marbled cover Little Kitten dared to confide in Mr. Fox what she would never tell anyone else not ever.

How when she was in fifth grade her father was gone when she'd returned from school one day, he'd left a note for her explaining he loved her and he loved her little brother but it was a time in his life when he required *aloneness* in order to be *able to think;* and her mother was crying nonstop, and her little brother was wetting himself, anxious and crying; and she'd crept downstairs into the kitchen in the night for the first time pressing the blade of the sharpest knife against her forearm but the pain was so shocking to her, the sight of the first drops of blood that seemed to spring out of her arm with a wild life of their own was so shocking to her, the knife slipped from her fingers and clattered to the floor.

Mr. Fox listened gravely. Mr. Fox was not smiling. Mr. Fox shook his head slowly in wonder.

Darling Genevieve, you are very brave—to confront this. To write of this.

To write so beautifully of this. So courageously.

But—you must promise me never to do that again—hurt yourself.

And if you are feeling sad, and feel that you should "punish" yourself, tell me!—tell me at once.

Kiss, if you promise.

Kiss kiss kiss your silly old Big Teddy Bear right now.

Wiping her eyes with her fingertips, the memory of Big Teddy Bear's wet sloppy funny-on-purpose kisses ending in tickles all over her ribs!

And Little Kitten confides in Mr. Fox, in the rosy-marbled journal, how on Facebook she stares mesmerized at her father (whose name is David, a name she can speak aloud now) and his *other family* living in La Jolla, California—pictures of happily smiling people, her father in the midst of strangers, the man named David (who once was

Daddy) with a beard and little mustache and hair now lighter/blonder than she recalls, in clothes that don't seem right for him, like an actor miscast.

Especially Little Kitten is stricken with hatred, jealousy, envy of the *other daughter,* a stepdaughter, nine years old.

Not a pretty girl! Not at all.

Wishing this *stepdaughter* would die. And the new wife. And Daddy could shave off the stupid beard and come home.

There are earthquakes in California. Very easily, the house could collapse, a ceiling fall on the stepdaughter. Or childhood leukemia. And the wife with a pink-gum smile, too wide for her narrow face.

But this has not (yet) happened. With the part of her brain that wielded the knife Little Kitten knows that it is not likely to happen.

Well, Daddy does call, on birthdays, Christmas. Daddy does—sometimes!—start to blubber on the phone, as Little Kitten grips the phone in stony silence.

He does send gifts. For Little Kitten, clothes. (She doesn't want to think the *other wife* has selected them.) And she knows that he provides *child support, alimony.*

These entries in the journal, Mr. Fox reads with particular care. In the margins of the journal Mr. Fox comments in his precise hand praising her for her *courage, candor,* and her *unique writing style.*

Mr. Fox communicates in block-printing, for students now have difficulty reading "cursive"—"handwriting."

To surprise Mr. Fox during the interminable fall break she has dared to disobey him and sent pictures (of herself) to his cell phone.

Giggling to herself, lying on her bed, on her back with legs spread, the cuddly-fuzzy kitten with leopard spots placed on her (bare) tummy.

And another in the bathroom, in the shower. Peering into the cell phone through a haze of plunging steamy water.

Kiss kiss kiss I love you Big Teddy Bear.

These pictures Little Kitten has sent to Mr. Fox's phone believing that Mr. Fox would forgive her for disobeying him, because Mr. Fox would be delighted to receive the pictures, but Mr. Fox did not reply, not once did Mr. Fox reply.

No way to know if Mr. Fox received the pictures. Or, if he did, if he liked them.

Still, following Mr. Fox's instructions she deleted the pictures from her cell phone.

Never leave a trail, ma chère Little Kitten.

Delete, delete, delete.

■

MR. FOX'S HOMEROOM BUT—where is Mr. Fox?

Something is wrong this morning. Very wrong.

For always Mr. Fox is here in homeroom when students arrive, relaxed and smiling with the air of a magician awaiting his audience.

Eight-forty-six A.M., Mr. Fox is forty-six minutes late.

Ugly rumors. TV news. Her mother's grave face, Little Kitten ran away to hide.

Oh will you *shut up*. I hate you!

And now in homeroom, somber faces of classmates. Why are they waiting, what is wrong?

Whispers, muttering. Little Kitten *does not hear*.

After fall break it is November, the air has turned cold. Lights are *on* in Mr. Fox's homeroom, there is no honey-warm autumn sunshine spilling through the window today.

Spotless whiteboard at the front of the room. In preparation for Mr. Fox, who loves to cover the whiteboard with green marker, tall words with exclamation points, clever cartoon figures.

Several times, Mr. Fox has asked Little Kitten to read from her journal to the class. Only special students are invited by Mr. Fox to read their work to the class.

Little Kitten has been so nervous! The first time, she read a book report from her journal singled out by Mr. Fox as *of the quality of a college essay.*

("*To Kill a Mockingbird* is an esteemed classic of American literature which is as timeless today as in 1960 when it was first published under the authorship of the thirty-four-year-old first-time novelist Harper Lee.")

Little Kitten was so nervous! Her voice thin and quavering, her knees trembling.

But Mr. Fox had led the applause! The first time in Little Kitten's life anyone ever applauded *her*.

Soon then, Mr. Fox invited her to come to his office after school. Deserted corridor, Mr. Fox's office door open, welcoming.

There comes Mr. Tongue poking at her lips, tickling, so funny, she squirms, wild giggles arise, she has no choice but to allow Mr. Tongue to poke into her mouth, for Mr. Fox is holding her head, firmly.

With her own fingers (chilled, stiff) Mr. Fox has gently pushed her hand down inside her panties. He has urged her, guided her, to touch herself *there*.

Mr. Tongue, filling her utterly. In Mr. Fox's arms, so snug. She does struggle, he holds her firm. Because he holds her so firm it is not possible to struggle. It is a relief not to struggle.

Kiss, kiss, there are different kinds of kisses. He has promised to keep the pictures secret, just for him. On his cell phone. He will show no one of course. Between them, all is *secret*. Because it is *forbidden*.

He feeds her lemon tarts, chocolate-covered strawberries. His mouth to hers. She is so, so in love with Mr. Fox.

Her own fingers, shyly slipped into her panties, and up inside her. Drawing in her breath sharply. The sensation is strange, hurting. It makes her very nervous. Mr. Fox soothes her, kisses her. He will take pictures of her, not her face, she cannot be identified, just her slipped-down panties, the smooth skin between her legs, her fingers moist. She would like to push away his hand holding the cell phone but she does not want to offend Mr. Fox.

When there is love, there is nothing forbidden between us.

Only when there is not love, there is the forbidden, and shame.

Such terrible things she has been hearing. Her mother, on the phone. Her friends. Something has happened to Mr. Fox, something awful.

He is missing. He is not here. He is away. He did not tell her, warn her, before the fall break.

". . . cops found him in a car crash, he was killed . . ."

". . . he was drowned, and his body was dragged all apart . . ."

". . . but was it *him*? They don't know for sure."

". . . black bears . . . Jesus!"

". . . *not* black bears, asshole."

Little Kitten presses the damp palms of her hands over her ears. Little Kitten is fierce not to hear.

■

AT LAST: AT 8:56 A.M. a figure appears in the homeroom doorway.

But the figure is not Mr. Fox. Plain-faced as a large upright root vegetable, if a root vegetable had a face.

"Hello! I am your substitute homeroom teacher for today. I am taking Mr. Fox's place for today. I will also be teaching Mr. Fox's classes if he isn't back by then. My name is—"

Flat dull dread dun-colored name is "March."

Whoever this is, not clear if it's a woman or a man. Everyone in Mr. Fox's homeroom stares at the *substitute homeroom teacher,* appalled.

Even the smirking boys, appalled.

As the girls sit affrighted, hands to their mouths.

Stunned silence, then an outburst of whispers, murmurs as the substitute teacher tries to restore order, squinting out into the classroom of suddenly *unruly prepubescents.*

"Excuse me! Let's have some quiet here. Let's have some *respect.*"

Amid uplifted voices Little Kitten stares blankly at the figure at the front of the room—Mr. Fox's room. Her eyes have so filled with moisture, she can barely see this person. Her stricken little heart is pounding against her ribs.

In a quavering voice March declaims: "I have told you—I am your substitute teacher for today. You will sit quietly in your seats as I take the roll. The bell for first period will ring in just three minutes. But do not leave this room until you are dismissed. Quiet! (No, I *do not know* when Mr. Fox will be back.) *You*—sit down! And you, *you are not yet dismissed.* I insist upon order, and I insist upon respect. I will be reporting back to Headmistress Cady's office. I will now read the roll, you will raise your hand when you hear your name. 'Atkinson, Denis'—"

So quickly it is happening, Little Kitten is feeling light-headed, her pen slips from her fingers and clatters to the floor, in the next instant Little Kitten herself is *on the floor.*

Fallen sideways from her desk, falls heavily for a girl of less than ninety pounds, dark-brown Godiva eyes sightless, the cries of her classmates distant from her, unheard.

Ma chère, our (secret) pledge will be, we will die for each other if that is required of us.

ATLANTIC COUNTY EVENING NEWS

19 NOVEMBER 2013

*D*rug-related shootings in Atlantic City. Suspected arson in Vine-land. Heavy rainfall expected over the weekend turning to snow showers. Continuing joint investigation by Wieland police and New Jersey state police regarding the yet-unidentified remains of a man (Caucasian, late thirties) found in the wetlands near Wieland believed to belong to a Langhorne Academy teacher missing since late October . . .

He is entranced. Appalled. Staring at the TV screen mounted on the wall where a blond-highlighted newscaster speaks in a thrillingly low voice as a video plays—not for the first time: this footage has been rerun for days—of a tow truck straining to lift a scummy-white automobile out of a ravine as a small gathering of men, presumably police officers, stand on a steep hill grimly observing.

Made to realize that, unhappy as he is, the *estranged Daddy* is at least not reduced to human remains part-devoured by wild animals . . .

"Jesus! Poor bastard."

With a shaky hand Pfenning pours the remaining chardonnay into his glass. His first drink of the day.

Dusk of a bleak blear November day that began twelve hours before in a similar twilight before dawn. And now Martin Pfenning has returned from the bright vacuous busyness of work (Bristol Myers Squibb, Bridgeton branch) and is alone in his living room in the sparely furnished two-bedroom apartment several miles from the house in Wieland from which (unwillingly, involuntarily, through no fault of his own) he has been expelled by the *estranged wife*.

It has come to this: an obsessive defining of his circumstances, his ontological being, so reduced, so diminished, a raging incantation in the brain of an individual who once believed he knew who he was. Permanently.

For *how* has it come to this: at the age of forty-one alone in an apartment he scarcely recognizes each time he enters it, seated in front of a giant TV screen seeking some sort of (sick, sad) solace in local news of persons even more unhappy than he is.

It is hard not to feel a kinship with the "missing" Francis Fox whose affable smiling face Pfenning has been seeing for weeks on TV or in the local newspaper. Fox is, or was, an attractive youngish man, with a slight gap in his upper front teeth that gave him a look of boy-ish naïveté and earnestness; handsome in the clean-shaven way of the British actor Hugh Grant, or George Clooney; a genial, playful masculinity that didn't seem to take itself too seriously, and didn't seem to threaten. You could see why middle-school children would like Mr. Fox: especially the girls.

As a high-school teacher Francis Fox would have been too attrac-tive to his girl-students. Was that why he preferred to teach middle school? To spare temptation on both sides?

Kathryn certainly seemed to like him: "'Fran-cis Fox.'" Pfenning first heard the name, its droll alliteration suggestive of a child's lov-able storybook character, from his wife.

At the time Pfenning hadn't paid much heed. Though it might have seemed odd to him, Kathryn was speaking admiringly, rather than critically as usual, of a teacher of Eunice's: her standards for their daughter's teachers at the Langhorne Academy were high, as the tuition was high, on a par with tuition at an Ivy League university.

This would have been weeks ago, early in the term. When it had seemed that the *estrangement* might be only temporary—a matter of correcting a misunderstanding or two.

Realizing he'd been oblivious to so much. Having taken for granted that his wife, being *his wife,* would always be content with their domestic situation; assuming, naïvely, that the strife of finding a mate, marrying, fathering, was now safely behind him.

Now, his nerves are raw, alert. Watching Atlantic County TV news with a drink in his hand.

Feeling the irony, a kick in the gut, the smiling face of a local man on TV after the man's death. If Pfenning had given it much thought he might have been slightly jealous of Francis Fox, admired by Kathryn (who isn't easily impressed), but now jealousy seems beside the point. The *estranged wife* has no interest in another man, Pfenning is sure.

(And in this lies the probable explanation of the mystery: Kathryn has no interest in *men.*)

In the most frequently displayed photograph of Francis Fox the man is standing in front of a quaintly ivied beige-brick wall squinting into sunshine, shading his eyes with an uplifted hand; his smile isn't cocky but hesitant, hopeful. He is wearing a pale-blue oxford shirt with a button-down collar. His hair is wavy, wheat-colored, curling over the collar. On the third finger of his uplifted hand there's a ring, hand-tooled silver, just visible. He might have been in his early thirties at the time of the photograph, an instructor at a private prep school in Pennsylvania.

. . . one of the most popular teachers, his subjects English and drama, only just Francis Fox's first year at the Langhorne Academy . . .

Pfenning thinks: if Fox could have known, when that picture was taken, where it would wind up, and when, and why, he wouldn't have been smiling.

"None of us would be smiling. If we could know."

A new habit, talking to himself. Alone in his bachelor quarters.

Where once he'd have called out to Kathryn to comment on something on TV, now he simply thinks out loud, no pretense of speaking to another person.

He is testing his voice, rehearsing. No longer married, or rather no longer living as a married man in the casual intimacy of domesticity, when he's alone in this apartment he can go for long hours without speaking at all; at Bristol Myers Squibb his business-voice, his professional voice, continues as always, undiminished, retaining its old authority, like the recorded voice of a person no longer living.

 . . . *after our break,* Atlantic County Evening News *continues with an exclusive interview with New Jersey Lottery's latest Powerball winner, ninety-one-year-old Morris Carey of Barnegat . . .*

The bright-blond newscaster disappears in an instant. There is no blank black screen to allow the viewer's brain to adjust but rather an immediate advertisement. Slick, glossy, peppy-musical, giddily smiling interracial couple like so many in TV advertisements in recent years, thrilled with their TriState Insurance coverage.

Quickly Pfenning mutes the sound. The happiness of others, including even the faux-happiness of TV actors, is abrasive to him as fingernails scratching a blackboard.

A curious interlude, Pfenning thinks: when a man must be officially declared *missing* because it isn't (yet) demonstrably provable that he is *dead.*

Reminds him of the *Tibetan Book of the Dead,* which for some reason he read as an undergraduate at Brown. Forty days of a twilit existence in the Bardo state, neither alive nor fully dead, before the soul is reborn in its next incarnation.

You have to believe in *soul.* You have to believe in *reincarnation.*

But if the body is badly torn apart, does the soul escape *whole?* Can a soul be injured, wounded, by the suffering inflicted upon its body?

At first it was expected that the ID of the "remains" would be made by the second week of November—but that time has passed. For insurance purposes, Pfenning assumes, the ID of a badly mutilated corpse has to be definitive.

He hasn't heard anything about Francis Fox's "next of kin"—if the man has any. Nothing of Fox's background, his relatives. He is, or was, unmarried? No wife, children? No one?

Unless Pfenning has missed it, it isn't even clear how the deceased died. Driving up a steep hill and into a ravine isn't likely to have been an accident but it isn't a very efficient way to kill oneself. And if it was a murder, not a very efficient way of murdering someone.

An investigation has been "under way" for weeks. Authorities have assured local residents that there is no reason to fear "foul play" of a kind that might endanger anyone, nor is there reason to fear black bears or "rabid foxes."

An initial autopsy has been "inconclusive"—the remains too ravaged. Pfenning doesn't want to speculate what this means.

His own life, his own situation, is the mystery that dominates his thoughts. For Pfenning can only think of himself as *blameless*. The breakup of his marriage, his family—the strange behavior of his daughter . . .

Kathryn has said *Don't be ridiculous, Martin. We don't love each other. It's been over now for years.*

That isn't true!—Pfenning wanted to protest. Though obviously on Kathryn's side, it seems to be true.

Belatedly wishing that he'd accompanied Kathryn to teacher-parent sessions at the Academy. He was always too busy, she had so much more time than he . . . He might've shaken Francis Fox's hand, a painful memory which now at least he and Kathryn could share.

It's said that an anxious malaise has settled upon the Langhorne Academy. A number of Fox's students have been absent from school. One of Fox's seventh-grade students, a girl, is said to have been hospitalized after cutting her arms severely; another, an eighth-grade girl in Eunice's English class, is said to have disappeared, a suspected runaway. And there have been others.

It isn't clear how Eunice feels, Kathryn has told Pfenning. She keeps her feelings to herself.

Frustrating, indeed baffling, that Francis Fox never once gave Eunice a grade of A+—to which she was accustomed from her other teachers; her highest grade from Mr. Fox was a tantalizing B+.

Yet, Fox spoke enthusiastically of Eunice (to Kathryn) as "remarkably mature for her age, intellectually"—"potentially one of the brightest students" he'd ever taught.

(Pfenning had to smile at this. It would have given Eunice little pleasure to hear herself described as *potentially one of the brightest*—merely *one* among many.)

Kathryn said: "Francis Fox isn't an ordinary teacher. He presses 'gifted' students to work really hard. He thinks that Eunice's high grades have come too easily to her, she doesn't exert herself enough *creatively*. This portfolio she's doing for his class—he expects it to be 'brilliant.'"

"Does he! That's—impressive . . ."

"He sees it as his mission to encourage gifted students to 'surpass' themselves."

Pfenning supposed Kathryn must be right. He had no doubt their precocious daughter was capable of much more than the routine schoolwork demanded of her.

In this new disjointed phase of his life Pfenning calls the *estranged wife* several times a week. Usually in the early evening. It's rare for Kathryn to call him unless to alert the *estranged Daddy* that an upcoming visit with his daughter is being postponed.

Conversations between Pfenning and Kathryn are usually curt, courteous, pragmatic. Pfenning would linger but dares not. He takes care to maintain an even, affable, reasonable-Daddy manner; any hint of *wistful, pleading, pitiable Daddy* is muted.

Absolutely, any hint of *reproachful, smoldering-angry Daddy* is muted.

The subject of their conversations is nearly always their daughter: how is Eunice, when will Pfenning see Eunice, can Pfenning speak with Eunice on the phone? Usually, after a little delay, Eunice will come to speak with Daddy, in a subdued voice; her playful-defiant public manner with Daddy falls flat on the phone. But since their hike in the bird sanctuary Eunice has been reluctant to speak with Daddy at all.

The day following their hike, the "remains" of the unidentified body were discovered at Wieland Pond. Pfenning wonders how close to the hiking trail.

He has heard that a torso, legs, a head were found—horrible to think that he and Eunice might have stumbled upon these! Eunice would never recover from such a trauma, nor would Pfenning.

The doll's head floating in the water. How that spooked Eunice, out of all proportion to the situation.

Uneasily Pfenning recalls how Eunice was behaving that day. Trying to retrieve the doll's head from the Dumpster, laughing hysterically . . . He had to hug her, hard. To calm her.

He has heard, when emotionally fraught children become upset, it is good to hold them, to comfort them. Children diagnosed as "autistic"—"on the spectrum."

According to the separation agreement with Kathryn, Pfenning has the right to visit with Eunice more frequently than he has. But if Eunice claims to be "unwell" there is little the *estranged Daddy* can do except be a good sport.

Three weekends in a row Eunice hasn't felt "well enough" to spend time with Daddy. He has made dates, Kathryn has called to cancel, apologetically.

At such times Daddy feels a twinge of relief. But then, immediately, guilt for this relief—almost a panicky sensation that if he is prevented from seeing his daughter for very long, he will never see her again: he will cease being Daddy.

And now, this totally extraneous distraction: Eunice's English teacher Francis Fox whose disappearance has evidently stirred much speculation and emotion at the Langhorne school.

Pfenning asks Kathryn if it's this Fox business that is upsetting Eunice, that's why she isn't feeling well enough to see him; and Kathryn says she doesn't think so.

"She doesn't talk about Mr. Fox at all any longer. A substitute has taken his place, classes are being held as usual, she has plenty of homework to occupy her. The school has sent everyone emails about therapists available for students during this 'highly stressful time.' There've been candlelight vigils for Mr. Fox, even prayer meetings."

"Prayer meetings!"—Pfenning was amazed, the Langhorne Academy prided itself upon being secular.

"Eunice hasn't attended these," Kathryn said quickly, "—you know how she is: how private."

Still, Eunice's health has been poor lately. She has had a sinus infection, bouts of nausea, diarrhea; she is wakened in the night by bad dreams, drenched in sweat. She has missed school days, which is unlike her—in the past, even with a bad cold, she insisted on attending school, fearing that she would fall behind if she missed a single day.

Kathryn has restricted Eunice's TV time, to prevent her from seeing local news broadcasts, and she has restricted Eunice's computer time, though this is difficult to enforce with a thirteen-year-old.

"Everyone must be talking about it at school," Pfenning said. "There isn't much we can do about that."

"Well—you know, Eunice doesn't have many friends. She comes home immediately after school, she has quit after-school activities like the book club. I pick her up every afternoon now at three-thirty. She refuses to take the bus."

The Langhorne Academy has its own half-sized bus, a replica of a public school bus in bright yellow with black trim; this bus leaves the school once a day, and is not available at later times. But Eunice has said that she hates the bus, hates having to sit by herself or worse yet with some idiot girl who chatters at her.

Either Eunice resented not having friends—not being "liked"—or she was disdainful of classmates who tried to befriend her.

"And something strange, the other day," Kathryn said hesitantly, "—I was changing Eunice's bedclothes, and I found a ring—a large, heavy ring—a man's ring—beneath her pillow. It was nothing I'd ever seen before, an expensive ring I think it must have been. When I asked Eunice what it was she snatched it from me, she seemed angry with me. She said she'd found the ring at school and was going to turn it in to the lost-and-found but had forgotten about it, but she would turn it in, the next day. It was quite heavy, sterling silver I think, with some sort of dark stone like an onyx, much too big for any

child to wear, an adult man's ring. Next day after school I asked her
about the ring and she said she'd turned it in to the lost-and-found . . ."

"And that's it?"

"Y-yes . . ."

"Why is that so strange, Kathryn? Eunice found a ring, she turned
it in."

"But why was it under her pillow?"

"She's thirteen years old, Kathryn. Does there have to be a reason?"

"Also—her raincoat was stolen a week or two ago. At school."

"Stolen? At the Langhorne school?"

"Yes, I know—it's hard to believe. It was a new coat, I don't think
you'd seen it yet—a pretty dark rose color—just polyester and cotton,
and not one hundred percent rainproof—but Eunice liked it, and you
know how picky she is about clothes."

"And someone at the school just—stole this coat?"

"She said she'd left it on a bench and when she went back, it was
gone."

"Did you call the school?"

"Oh yes, of course. I've made several calls. And Eunice checked
at the school lost-and-found. But it was never found."

"It hasn't been lost very long, has it? Maybe it will turn up."

"She says it wasn't lost, it was stolen."

"We can get her a new coat . . ."

"I told her I'd replace it immediately, just order another online.
Not to worry about it, but Eunice said no, she didn't want that coat
again. She'd decided she didn't like that coat after all."

Pfenning laughed. "Well! That's our daughter."

Kathryn laughed, in sudden rapport with him. "Yes—well."

Meaning Of all the strange things about Eunice, this is hardly exceptional.

Even as an infant Eunice had seemed funnily willful. Kicking,
thrashing, whimpering in her crib and when one of her parents hurried to her, staring up at them with large imperturbable eyes, suddenly silent, impassive.

But then, scoring in the highest 1-percent on tests measuring cognition. Learning to read at an unusually young age.

"I really would like to see Eunice, Kathryn. You know, she's my daughter too."

"I know, Martin."

"But maybe you don't know, actually. I'm living alone and half the time I wake up not knowing where the hell I am. According to the agreement, I'm supposed to see her much more frequently than I do . . ."

A moment's silence. Never good to speak reproachfully to the *estranged wife*, Pfenning should know by now.

"But if she doesn't want to see you, Martin—that's how it is."

Doesn't want to see you. These are words that stung, even if they are true.

Pfenning felt a moment's vertigo, hating his wife. The very smugness of Kathryn's pretense of sympathy with him, the less-loved. The loser-parent.

"Does Eunice *not want* to see me, or is she really ill and doesn't want to go out? Why can't I speak with her?"

"Martin, I can't force her."

"You could encourage her . . ."

"Martin, I *can't*. You know what Eunice is like."

But do I?—Pfenning wasn't sure. As he wasn't sure what Kathryn was like, any longer.

Why wouldn't Eunice talk to him? This was puzzling, frustrating. Prior to the *estrangement* Eunice had seemed to favor her father, not her mother. The corporate-lawyer Daddy, not the stay-at-home mother with a master's degree in library science, put to only intermittent consulting use.

In fact, Pfenning had felt a petty sort of gratification, that their daughter preferred Daddy to Mommy, and that he could feel gracious, generous about it—speaking positively of Kathryn to Eunice, buoying Mommy up, complimenting her when he could.

Eunice had asked Daddy, not Mommy, to take her to Wieland Pond so that she could take pictures of waterbirds for her portfolio.

Happily he'd complied, she'd taken pictures with the camera he'd bought her, all that had gone well enough. He'd thought. But she'd behaved strangely, on the trail. Fearful, anxious. This couldn't be attributed to concern for her English teacher since at the time Fox hadn't been missing.

Three weeks ago. End of October.

Pfenning hadn't told Kathryn about Eunice's behavior on the trail—always he wanted to suggest that, in his company, their daughter was relaxed, enjoying herself. He would never have told Kathryn about the doll's head floating in the pond, how it had seemed to frighten Eunice. He didn't mention Eunice rummaging in the Dumpster to retrieve the doll's head when he'd disposed of it. He didn't mention her bursting into tears. He didn't mention hugging Eunice tight as in a straitjacket, to calm her.

The crazed beating of her heart, her scalding-hot breath, he didn't mention to Kathryn.

The strange uttered words, barely audible—*I did a bad thing, Daddy.*

For Pfenning was not *troubled Daddy,* Pfenning was *damned-good-sport Daddy.*

As if he'd just thought of it Pfenning suggested that he take Kathryn and Eunice both out to dinner that weekend, since Eunice didn't seem to want to spend time with him alone; and Kathryn said hesitantly, "Well, maybe. Or dinner here. That might be better. Eunice has gotten fussy about what she eats, she wants to see how it has been prepared."

Pfenning was surprised, touched. "Kathryn, I'd like that very much. Thank you."

"I'll call *you.* Early next week."

So it wasn't to be *this weekend.* But *next week* sounded like a plan at the time: a promise.

■

TONIGHT PFENNING IS (STILL) waiting for the call. He has calculated the risk he might be taking if he telephones Kathryn, annoying her, possibly sabotaging a call from her, nullifying the chance for a dinner together by a rash action of his own.

Or, Kathryn might say *Martin! I was just about to call you, can you come for dinner tonight?*

Pouring himself another glass of wine. Such comfort in wine, warming his throat, chest.

The TV is muted, giddy neon-bright images careen across the screen. It is nearing eight P.M. At Kathryn's, dinner is rarely later than six-thirty P.M.

Pfenning is trying to feel hopeful. Trying not to feel dismayed, disheartened. Their daughter is entering *puberty,* that problematic phase. Maybe that's all that is wrong. He recalls that Eunice was less fearful as a younger girl than she is now. She was a bright, bold, tomboy sort of girl, though she didn't play outdoors. Only in the past year has Eunice become wary, silent, sulky-sullen, sarcastic. Pfenning sympathizes with her: something is happening which she can't control, a shifting of consciousness among her classmates. Her pretty girl-classmates are drawing attention to themselves in a way that Eunice can't. Boldness, intelligence are not enough. Even teachers prefer the prettier girls, it's said to be a fact. Even Francis Fox, probably.

Except, Fox praised Eunice, to Kathryn. That must have meant something to Eunice, must have signaled hope.

In seventh grade, the change began in Eunice. She lost her confidence, certainty. She began to be anxious, worried about schoolwork for the first time. Grim. Few friends. Impatient. Came back home early from a friend's house, no explanation.

She is afraid. Afraid of what lies ahead.

Puberty, sexual maturity. Eunice will have a difficult time navigating the rough waters to come in high school.

Father of a boyish girl, a plain-faced girl, Pfenning wonders if Eunice is a form of himself. What is undefined in him, undefined in her. For resolutely Eunice is not *girlish, feminine,* nothing soft about her. Agate eyes, cool and assessing. Wiry little monkey-body, tiny breasts and narrow hips.

Kathryn has said she doesn't think that Eunice will have her first period for another year or more. She hoped so, menstruation would infuriate and humiliate Eunice, who disliked her body already. Though Kathryn was trying to prepare her, and health classes at school were preparing her.

Pfenning has been reading a disturbing article in, was it *Harper's?* The phenomenon of puberty in ever-younger American girls, some as young as nine. *Nine!* Fortunately, this did not happen to his sensitive daughter.

When the phone rings close beside his head Pfenning is startled—wakened. Has he fallen asleep? It's 8:40 P.M.—he has been asleep an hour, his mouth is dry, sour.

Fumbles for the phone. It's Kathryn, sounding urgent.

"Martin. Come over here. We have to talk."

Even then, groggy with wine-induced sleep, the *wistful estranged Daddy* is expecting the *estranged wife* to suggest dinner. He hasn't eaten since lunch. He's starving, light-headed. But Kathryn doesn't say a word about dinner. Is this ominous?—Pfenning tries not to think so.

Twenty minutes driving from Bridgeton to Wieland along country roads. Trying to remain calm, matter-of-fact. Trying not to think— *Something has happened to Eunice now. Like the other girls in Fox's classes . . .*

He hopes to God that she hasn't hurt herself, like the girl who allegedly slashed at her arms. Must be hell for the family, their twelve-year-old daughter in the hospital under a suicide watch. His heart goes out to them.

Chambers is the name, he has heard. No one he knows. For which he is grateful.

He has entered the Village of Wieland, population 2,300. Past the hulking water tower illuminated at night, Day-Glo graffiti *Wieland Wildcats* a familiar eyesore Pfenning tries in vain to avoid glancing at when he drives by. Public school kids, private school kids, two distinct castes, that rarely mingle.

Along Main Street driving past darkened storefronts, only Ricco's Pizza still open at this hour, in happier times Pfenning might've stopped here, brought pizza home for supper except Eunice isn't any longer a child who loves pizza, she's acquired finicky food preferences—no sausage, no melted cheese, no *nasty fried dough.*

In the residential neighborhood of expensively renovated Victorian houses. Theirs, on Ashland, is one of the more modest yet still impressive, on a two-acre lot amid tall elms and fir trees.

The porch light is on as if to welcome him but the door is locked when Pfenning tries to enter, he's hurt, annoyed, why would Kathryn lock the damned door if she knew he was coming? *She* invited him.

Of course, Pfenning has a key. It's his house, too. But he waits prudently for Kathryn to open the door.

Without a smile, scarcely with a greeting, Kathryn opens the door to him. Her face is strained, her hair disheveled. Pfenning feels a stab of dismay, loss, but it has become a familiar sensation in his gut: a literal loss of equilibrium, quicksand beneath his feet where once there was solid ground.

Since the *estrangement* Kathryn seems to have stopped lightening her hair, it is perceptibly darker at the roots, yet also threaded with gray. When did this begin?—Kathryn is not yet forty.

He has been gone from the household for less than two months— yet it seems much longer.

"What is it? What's wrong?"—anxious Daddy glances about for his little girl but Eunice is not in sight.

Kathryn appears to be genuinely distraught. She doesn't invite Pfenning into the living room, doesn't ask him to sit down. Pfenning wonders if he dares remove his fleece jacket, if this would be a breach of manners? In his own house? In a stammer Kathryn tells him that Eunice told her something "very upsetting" that evening.

Out of nowhere, about two hours ago. Kathryn is visibly trembling, recalling.

Eunice was doing homework as usual in her room, or so Kathryn assumed. She began to hear Eunice talking to herself. Laughing, angry, arguing. Kathryn went to the door of Eunice's room and listened, wondering if Eunice could be on the phone with someone— (not that Eunice was ever on the phone with anyone)—when Eunice began screaming suddenly.

Kathryn opened the door, and saw to her astonishment that Eunice was sitting on the floor of her room, tearing pages out of the journal with the green-marbled cover, throwing them into the air, laughing wildly. Her face was streaked with tears and her eyes were glittering.

"I managed to calm her, a little. I didn't even ask what was wrong, I just held her like a baby. And finally she told me, Martin—what you'd done to her. The last time you were with her."

Pfenning isn't sure if he has heard correctly. "What I'd done to her?—but what?"

"At the pond. That hiking trail. The day before Hallowe'en."

"I—I don't understand . . . What is she saying I'd done?"

"She said, 'Daddy hugged me *so hard*. I hate it when Daddy hugs me *so hard*.'"

Pfenning is stunned. He does remember hugging Eunice— hard . . . But only to calm her, she was weeping hysterically.

"Eunice told me that you kiss her, too. You kiss her 'in a bad way'— 'with his tongue.'"

Pfenning protests, this is not true at all. Nothing like this . . .

"She said you'd found a broken doll in the pond, the upper half of a doll. You'd fished it out of the water, and rubbed it all over yourself, including 'between the legs.'"

Pfenning is speechless. Kathryn is keeping a little distance between them, and is not looking at him. Her face is suffused with disgust.

"*What* is she saying? Kathryn? This is—this is not . . ."

"'Daddy hugged me hard, Daddy kissed me with his tongue, I hate Daddy kissing me like that, *I hate Daddy and never want to see him again.*' That's what Eunice told me."

In appalled silence Pfenning listens. It will be one of the catastrophic moments of his life: wholly unanticipated, inexplicable, as if the very earth has opened before him.

"She made a gesture as if she was rubbing something against the pit of her belly. The gesture was so obscene, I grabbed at her hand, to stop her."

"Kathryn, I did not do anything like that. Any of that. Not remotely any of that."

"Were you drinking? Eunice says you drink, a lot. 'Daddy's breath *smells*.' She has said that in the past."

Pfenning stands confused, defeated. His head swirls, he cannot think how to defend himself.

Kathryn is saying that he should leave. She will call her lawyer in the morning.

"You can't see our daughter again. She is traumatized."

Traumatized. The most banal of words, overused, cheapened, a cliché—yet, here is Kathryn uttering it almost calmly, her eyes lifted glaring to his face.

As if he hasn't heard what Kathryn has said Pfenning demands to see Eunice, of course he has to see Eunice, immediately, this has to be straightened out tonight. He doesn't want to accuse his daughter of lying but she must be, what is it called—*confabulating*.

Kathryn says no, absolutely not, Pfenning can't see Eunice, he has to leave. Now.

"How do I know that any of this is true? How do I know you're not lying?"

Pfenning pushes past Kathryn, pushes away her grasping hand, hurries upstairs panting to Eunice's room, knocks on the door, calls, "Eunice?—honey?"—not waiting for a reply but pushing at the door, stepping inside, bold brazen desperate Daddy; and there, on the floor, as if primed for this moment, is Eunice red-faced and screaming at him.

Pfenning has the impression of a child much younger than thirteen, a child in a tantrum, face contorted and unrecognizable, wet with tears and mucus.

"Go away! Go away! I don't want you here! I hate you!"

The carpet is strewn with shredded pages, which Eunice has torn from a journal her English teacher, Fox, allegedly gave her.

"Eunice, what is wrong? Why are you so—angry? Why at *me*?"

Kathryn is tugging at Pfenning's arm. She apologizes to Eunice for having let Pfenning get past her.

"You need to leave now, Martin. Just *go*."

"This is ridiculous, Kathryn. Eunice—listen to me . . ."

"No! Just *go*." Kathryn yanks at him, furious; for a moment Pfenning considers shoving Kathryn away, hard.

Instead he turns away dazedly. Descending the stairs. *His* stairs, so familiar to him after years in this house even as he has become unfamiliar to himself, panting sweating desperate Daddy.

Kathryn shuts the door to Eunice's room. Kathryn follows after Pfenning close as a dog in pursuit of an intruder, ushering him to the front door.

Still Pfenning is trying to explain to Kathryn that Eunice was "excited and emotional" at the pond, she seemed frightened of a small doll floating in the water, just a doll's head in the water, he retrieved it to throw away (as he removes debris from the trail each time he hikes there), he threw the doll's head into a Dumpster but Eunice tried to pull it back out.

It is true, he *did* hug Eunice, to calm her, she was crying, upset, near-hysterical but she seemed to grow calmer when he held her securely . . .

To this faltering explanation Kathryn scarcely listens. She tells Pfenning that he must leave, immediately. If he does not she will call 911 and have him arrested.

"Kathryn, how can you mean that? This is a tragic misunderstanding. You must know that Eunice is—she's confused, she's making things up . . . None of what she said happened, at the pond. I would never, you know that *I would never . . .*"

How like a guilty man Pfenning is sounding. Hears the weak, pleading-Daddy voice with dismay.

"It's all over, Martin. No more. Just *leave*."

Pfenning has no doubt, Kathryn will call 911 in another minute. Never in her life has Kathryn behaved like this, so in defiance of him, so *certain*.

Though she is mistaken, as his daughter is mistaken, yet fury like flames rages in them, of utter *certainty*.

Pfenning sees: signatures on a formal separation contract are but

the first cause of an action that ends with an excited call to 911, uniformed police officers rushing at the *estranged Daddy* to drag him off
handcuffed, so roughly the poor bastard loses his balance, falls to his
knees, is jerked upright with such force both his wrists are sprained . . .

Blindly out the front door, which is slammed behind him.

Stumbling on the front walk wet with leaves. Makes his way to his
car parked in the driveway, formerly *his* driveway. Half-falls into the
car, sick with shame.

Is he drunk? He believes that he is stone-cold sober, tragically
sober, but his head is swimming, his balance is askew.

Not sure if he can trust himself to drive. Disequilibrium settles
upon him like a noxious gas, he fumbles for his car keys.

So much has happened!—in so brief a period of time. He'd just
muted the TV. An hour, two hours. Yet Martin Pfenning's life, so precious to him, so richly complicated, has become a mere page torn out
of a notebook, crumpled in a fist, tossed away like litter.

Retracing the drive to Bridgeton. Resisting the impulse to press
the gas pedal to the floor. Determined not to swerve off the highway,
crash into an abutment, make an end of it, the *estranged Daddy's* miserable life, but no, he will not, won't give Kathryn the satisfaction, his
hatred for her is a raging flame, the woman has turned his daughter
against him.

She has been hoping for something like this. Now, she has triumphed.

THE WRAITH

This journey she will make through the remainder of her life.

Behind her eyelids the apparition beckons: Mr. Fox's (kindly) face in which Mr. Fox's (adoring) pale-blue eyes are fixed upon *her*.

You see, I am not dead! I am exactly the way you remember me.

Making her way gliding enchanted along the basement corridor of Haven Hall blurred as in shimmering water at last at Mr. Fox's office door with its frosted-glass window and a neat little white card listing Mr. Fox's office hours and inside the office (for the door has opened soundlessly, a mild breeze has blown it open for it seems not to have been locked allowing the sleepwalker to step inside) the single window set high in the wall emitting a gauzy sort of late-afternoon light, a desk and a swivel chair behind the desk and facing the desk a smaller cane-backed chair with a cushioned seat.

On a corner of the desk, to your left as you enter, the foot-high bronze bust *Edgar Allan Poe 1809–1849*.

Against one wall, bookshelves. Half-filled, for Mr. Fox is still "new" at the Academy, he has not quite moved in.

Still, the bookshelves contain multiple copies of paperback books which Mr. Fox gives to students. He is impulsive, generous with such gifts not just to his favorites but to all students who *take an interest.*

On the opposite wall are several large gaily colored posters: flowers with widespread petals, sinuous big cats (leopards, cheetahs, tigers) with tawny eyes, Alice in Wonderland with crimped hair flaring about her head, long-necked, startled-looking, wearing what Mr. Fox has identified as a *pinafore.*

The drawing of Alice on the poster is by *John Tenniel.* More famous in his time than *Lewis Carroll* himself.

One hundred years ago, or more. When girls of *good families* wore proper dresses even for everyday, with thick cotton stockings and prim little shoes.

But it is foot-high bronze *Edgar Allan Poe 1809–1849* with a raven hunched on his shoulder that draws the eye. Its base is engraved with letters so small you have to squint to read *Francis H. Fox first-prize winner Nevermore Competition, Poe Society of America 2011.*

Mr. Fox laughs, indeed the bust is *aggressively ugly kitsch.* Heavier than it looks, not a very good likeness of Poe, and the dead eyes of man and bird *stare.*

Those special students whom Mr. Fox invites to his office will never forget the foot-high bronze bust of Edgar Allan Poe with the raven on his shoulder.

She is not really a favorite of Mr. Fox's—is she?

Dares not think so, dares not hope.

After so many weeks, months of abject yearning, self-loathing for that yearning, she dares not think *Yes. I am.*

■

IT SEEMS THAT SHE has entered Mr. Fox's office but it is *so strange*—for Mr. Fox is not there!

Never has she entered Mr. Fox's office except if Mr. Fox is there!

Impossible to be inside Mr. Fox's office if Mr. Fox is not there and so, if she is there, Mr. Fox must have opened the door for her, to allow her inside.

Silly timid knocking at the door half-hoping that Mr. Fox will not hear, she will be released, she will vanish into airy thinness like a wisp of smoke.

But he has heard the knock on the door. Of course he has heard the knock on the door, he has been awaiting the knock on the door for Mr. Fox's ears are *sharp,* his eyes are *sharp,* all of his senses are alert for he is *Mr. Fox.*

He has been awaiting her. He has been expecting her. He has summoned her. He would like to discuss her most recent journal entry, which he finds *teasingly intriguing.*

Or, he would like to discuss her most recent grade. Not a high grade, not nearly so high as she should be earning, why is that? *Why is she failing to recognize her deepest self? Why is she sabotaging her destiny?*

The heart in her skinny flat chest is beating so quickly she has become light-headed. She is in danger of fainting for she is weak, anemic, would Mr. Fox catch her in his arms if she began to faint?— silly heart fluttering, failing.

Suddenly she realizes, she can't breathe.

Cries and cries, tries to scream, she is choking, gagging, something nasty has been shoved into her mouth, a giant tongue shoved deep into her mouth as her head is gripped tight as in a vise, she is writhing, kicking, struggling to save her life, a violent convulsion shudders through her body as if a giant sinewy snake is thrusting into her, into her mouth, into her throat, deep into her throat, in desperation to save herself she is tearing pages from the journal with the marbled cover of which she has been so proud, the *Mystery-Journal* (she has called it) (for it will explain her life to her), in a fury trying to wrench off the cover but the journal is too sturdy, too well-made, a very special object not easily destroyed by weak-faltering hands.

IV

"NEVERMORE"

BAR HARBOR, MAINE: EXILE

APRIL 2005

For the moon never beams, without bringing me dreams
Of the beautiful Annabel Lee.

Anywhere he flees they track him. Harpies swooping out of the mist-shrouded Maine sky in pursuit of a man's softest parts: eyes, buttocks, groin.

And once the Harpies have flayed him, eviscerated and emasculated him, prized open his rib cage: his palpitating heart.

■

THIRTY-THREE YEARS OLD. His first full-time job since leaving graduate school: English instructor for seventh- and eighth-grade English at the Newell Johnson School in Quakerbridge, Pennsylvania. Frank Farrell is young, naïvely optimistic, over-trusting in his own good nature and in the good nature of others.

God damn I am (only) guilty of loving too much.

Loving not wisely but too well.

The Harpies have run him aground. He's been unshaven for five days. Unbathed. His breath is sour. Hair stiff and matted, crawling up the back of his head like something alive digging its tiny claws into his scalp.

Exiled to Bar Harbor, Maine. "Suspended" from his teaching duties at Newell Johnson for the remainder of the term.

Drove nearly six hundred miles in nine hours, of which at least seven hours were through pelting rain on hazardous interstates from Quakerbridge, Pennsylvania, north into desolate coastal Maine as a desperate man might keep himself afloat in a rushing river by the agitation of his arms incapable of thinking of what has come before, what lies ahead.

Only now: stay alive *now*.

No one knows he's here except his lawyer and the kindly owner of the beach house who has lent it to him *until all this blows over*.

Wind-lashed Maine coast isn't a terrain he knows or would wish to know. Thirty degrees colder in April than you'd expect. Below the bluff, down a treacherous flight of wooden steps white-splotched with the droppings of gulls like leprosy or the acne of a brain beset by spurious notions of guilt not his own but foisted upon him by dwarf-souled others.

Not what you'd call "beach," just unyielding hard-packed sand, ugly boulders contorted and twisted like giants' shoulders.

Crazed Atlantic surf of the hue of pewter, foam, froth, curdled seaweed, rotting and skeletal things underfoot, screaming glaring-eyed gulls overhead. Fortune has flung him here like something you'd shake off your shoe.

He's become a solitary guy running on the beach. Early morning, dusk. Compulsive running, joyless. Running for his life.

Frank? Hey, it's Simon Grice, give me a call.

Soon as you can, OK?

Playing and replaying the message, trying to decipher what the guileless words imply, what's the tone of the lawyer-voice, decides it's neutral, or maybe (just slightly) optimistic, unless *fucking grim. Cut your wrists.*

Only the first (exhausted) night in Bar Harbor he'd been able to sleep and he'd slept thirteen hours like sodden laundry.

Waking to his cell phone ringing. Vibrating-ringing. *No. Not yet.*

Running now below the bluff along the beach where the sand is hard-packed as concrete. Frantic to save his life leaking from him like the dribble-urine of sheer panic.

Love you, love you so much I could die.

The girl's voice, almost too soft to be heard. Blown away by bone-chilling gusts of wind.

In pursuit, the Harpies. Shrieking beaks, razor-sharp talons, small beady-glaring eyes of raw jealousy.

For (let's be frank) (*he* is Frank!): These are older females sick with envy of the young. These are older females who have aged out of love. Older females avid to punish the young.

That they would punish *him* is the irony. He, who'd only wished to respect the (pure, virginal) love of the girl for him, that had stirred a kindred feeling in him as a lighted match brought perilously close to flammable material explodes into a conflagration.

How is it the fault of the flammable material that the match ignites it? *It is not.*

How is it the fault of first-year instructor Frank Farrell that older females on the Newell Johnson faculty became jealous of his popularity? That a mother no longer young, formerly beautiful but no longer beautiful, became deranged with envy of her own daughter?

Had I ever met the mother, yes I think I did—but only just spoke politely to her, at a Parent-Teacher reception, exchanged insipid cheery remarks, did not respond to her (subtle, but obvious) attempt at a flirtation, for which (little did I guess at the time!) the Harpy would never forgive me.

As the older females on the faculty would never forgive him with his master's degree in an authentic subject (English) from an Ivy League university (Columbia) shining like a gem amid the dross of their undistinguished degrees in secondary education from Penn, Drexel, Rutgers.

Older females on the board of trustees. Older females jealous of his darling Miranda.

That she was *his*. That she would wish to die for him, in defiance of their demand that she betray him.

It is not (entirely) accurate to claim that all of the Harpies in pursuit of Frank Farrell are female but those who are not *female* are not altogether *male,* either.

Headmaster Higg. Closeted middle-aged gay except *gay* isn't in Higg's dour vocabulary.

(And Higg was once *his* champion!—impressed with the degree from Columbia University's revered English Department.)

(Impressed that Frank Farrell is rumored to be related, through his mother's family, to the legendary Biddle family of Philadelphia.)

Also in pursuit are Miranda's vindictive mother and a friend of the Myles family reputed to be a brilliant "feminist-activist" lawyer in Philadelphia.

A bloodthirsty pack! And all of them jealous of the love of twelve-year-old Miranda Myles for her seventh-grade English teacher, Frank Farrell. That Miranda was *his* and not *theirs,* they could not bear.

Infuriated, that a man like Frank Farrell could never feel the slightest attraction for any of them, nor even gaze upon them without a shudder of disdain, distaste.

That no man could feel for them what he'd felt for Miranda. That no man had (probably) ever felt for them what he'd felt for Miranda.

That their (not-young female) bodies could stir only disgust in any man.

How dare they judge *him*! Sheer sexual jealousy.

Such thoughts fill Frank Farrell with the strength of loathing, that he will, he *must* overcome his enemies who are bent on destroying him.

Running on the beach in this desolate place. Breathing in quick gasps through his mouth as a runner should never do. As a long-distance runner on the varsity track team in high school in East Orange, New Jersey, he'd never done.

Weird to think, when he'd been twenty-three, Miranda Myles was but two years old.

Mr. Farrell, how could you! The girl is just a child . . .

How could you betray our trust in you . . .

Sinkholes in the hard-crusted sand, suddenly. He stumbles, nearly falls. If he sprains an ankle in this deserted place shrieking Harpies will swoop down to tear the living flesh from his bones, pluck at his eyes and swallow them whole.

So vivid is this hellish vision, he could swear he has seen it.

◾

LOVE YOU, LOVE YOU *so much, Mr. Farrell, don't make me live without you.*

He'd interpreted Miranda Myles's declarations to him as metaphorical. He had not interpreted them as literal.

◾

TWO AND A HALF HOURS on the interstate beyond Bar Harbor, Maine, is New Brunswick, Canada.

There, he might begin his life again. In a foreign country where no one knows him.

Back in Quakerbridge, Pennsylvania, his enemies want nothing more than to hunt Frank Farrell down, humiliate him and castrate him. He will never surrender!

If he confesses, they may not pursue criminal charges. If he resigns his position, voiding his three-year contract with the Newell Johnson School, they may simply let him go. Of course, his teaching career will be ruined.

Simon Grice is negotiating, he has said. It is just as well that Farrell is out of town.

Trying not to be angry at Miranda for this catastrophe. The poor girl could not have known how her reckless behavior would endanger the very person she loved . . .

The Harpies had driven her to it, persecuting her with their prurient questions. The mother had been the worst, and the litigious feminist-activist.

I will never tell them our secret, Mr. Farrell. I promise, I will die before I tell anyone.

Farrell has learned that the northern U.S. border is very different from the southern U.S. border. Here are no armed guards, no barbed wire fences. No drug cartels smuggling cocaine.

At any remote spot along the five-thousand-five-hundred-mile border you can cross into Canada on foot undetected. No need for a passport.

Except: in his haste to leave Quakerbridge he hasn't brought any legal documents with him to Bar Harbor. No birth certificate, social security card. He has no relatives in Canada. No one he knows who might help him.

He will ask his lawyer: Is there extradition from Canada to the United States? On (bogus) charges of *statutory rape, sexual assault of a minor*?

In the 1960s and 1970s American conscientious objectors to the Vietnam War were not only allowed into Canada but welcomed, seeking asylum from the bellicose U.S. Many eventually became Canadian citizens.

Farrell's lawyer Simon Grice hasn't been very helpful or confiding. He scarcely listened when Farrell spoke wildly of "seeking asylum" in Canada. He insisted upon an initial payment, a retainer fee of five thousand dollars—"Nonrefundable."

(*Nonrefundable*. Meaning that if Grice decides not to take on Farrell's case after he examines the charges and evidence and interviews a few people, he gets to keep the retainer. Outrageous!)

Still, in Canada, no one would know the name "Frank Farrell" unless he told them. And why would he tell them?

He would need a new name, new papers. But he would have no identity in Canada, he couldn't be a teacher, couldn't be employed at all.

How to create a new identity out of—nothingness?

There is no avoiding it, Farrell must return to Quakerbridge. He must defend himself. Clear his name, demand his reinstatement at the school in good standing.

For he is *innocent of all charges*. For there is no *proof*.

He will explain to the investigating committee: "Interpretation" is the issue. Where Miranda spoke literally, he heard metaphorically. One could argue from a neuropsychological perspective that "misinterpretation" is not an aberration of human experience, but is indeed inevitable in human experience.

Love you so much I could die.

Such a misinterpretation could not possibly be criminal because it was unintentional, indeed it was innocence itself, inexperience, on the part of Frank Farrell, for which no just court would punish him.

My punishment is, I have lost my darling.

My heart is in tatters, my life is in ruins, that is my punishment and there is no punishment more profound.

This, he will explain to them.

Except, he feels such contempt for them.

None of you has any right to judge me. To judge us. We reject you!

He has been running for more than an hour. He has lost track of time. His breath is ragged, he is beginning to stagger. Sweaty inside his clothes, yet shivering. Not sure where the hell he is. Still in Bar Harbor? In the distance is a pier, near-invisible in mist.

Higher on the shore, bizarrely shaped sand dunes suggesting the coiled contours of the brain.

Everywhere underfoot are broken things. Seashells, turtle shells, fish corpses, desiccated jellyfish. Fossil-scribbles in the sand. Trilobites? Nothing seems accidental, all a kind of calligraphy.

Sick with regret, they'd never been truly alone. He had promised her—*Someday, darling. Soon.*

Oh but when, Mr. Farrell? Where will we go?

Not even eight months he'd known his seventh-grade student Miranda Myles altogether. But only the last three months in a way that might be called *intimate.*

Three months! Difficult to believe, a lifetime crammed into so small a space of time.

First day she walked into his homeroom, just after Labor Day, September of the previous year. *His* first day too.

Beautiful flaxen-haired Miranda Myles, he made a little check by her name on his class list.

Though pretending not to know her name, at first. As if confusing her with other girls in the class seated near her.

Balthus!—he thought. One of the painter's prepubescent girls, a wan sort of beauty, dreamy, like a sleepwalker. Large slow-blinking eyes, slightly parted lips. *Thérèse Dreaming, Katia Reading. The Golden Years.*

Her lifetime crammed into that space. The remainder of Frank Farrell's life in tatters.

For he will never recover from this catastrophe. He is a changed man, entirely.

Recalling how they'd first touched hands, shyly. His touch—his forefinger and thumb closing about Miranda's (impossibly small) wrist.

His first time touching any student in any way.

His first time touching anyone so young, in this particular way.

Farrell has young nieces, nephews, who were never of any interest to him. He doubts that he'd ever touched them at all. Stooped to kiss? No.

Children are, by definition, deeply boring. They are more interested in themselves than in you.

Indeed if there is the opposite of a *pedophile,* that is Frank Farrell! Though he is not a *pedophobe,* certainly.

Farrell has always been contemptuous of Nabokov's *Lolita,* for instance. He knows that the notorious novel is a handbook of sorts for pedophiles but he found it boring, pretentious, and offensive when it wasn't plain ridiculous.

Only a sick pervert would behave like Humbert Humbert. Asinine name, asinine literary style. Forcing sexual relations on an eleven-year-old girl—loathsome. (Anatomically impossible? The engorged penis of a mature male, forced into the tiny vagina of a child? This would cause rupture, hemorrhaging, possibly death.) Farrell skimmed through *Lolita* with mounting repugnance, finally tossing it aside in disgust.

Farrell's romantic relationship with Miranda Myles had been totally different from (fictitious) Humbert's with (fictitious) Lolita. Farrell had not the slightest interest in forcing sexual intercourse upon the girl, or involving her sexually in any way; that was disgusting to him. Their romance might have been *erotic,* to a degree, but it was certainly not *sexual.*

Very gently he'd kissed the inside of her wrist, where faint blue veins were visible through her translucent skin.

He'd touched her throat, an artery pulsing there. Alabaster skin like Poe's Virginia, that left him breathless, light-headed.

Framing her perfect oval face in his hands, kissing her small mouth—lightly, as a butterfly's touch.

Tears welled in her beautiful hazel eyes. A flush rose into her face.

Oh, Mr. Farrell, I love you so, so much . . .

Numerous times she'd come to his office late in the afternoon when no one was around. When he'd "signaled" with his eyes in class, their special/secret communication.

Including Miranda Myles among the students selected each Friday to read from their journals to the class. Praising Miranda to encourage her, but not so effusively that she was embarrassed; making sure that he praised all the students who read.

Good work. Brave work!

"Dig deeper."

Innocently it began and only some time later after Farrell had touched the girl in the cozy privacy of his office, kissed her, held her on his lap and whispered to her a favorite poem or two—(*She walks in beauty, like the night . . .*)—did he realize that he could not so easily draw back.

Understanding (naïvely, belatedly) that possibly, just possibly in the ebullience of a mood he'd behaved incautiously.

For lovesick Miranda began to come to Farrell's office when he hadn't "signaled" her—when he was busy with other students, or colleagues; when he hadn't time for her, however he might regret it.

That little Myles girl is waiting for you again—so Farrell's colleagues began to say to him, pointedly.

Miranda Myles lingering puppylike in the corridor outside Mr. Farrell's office stricken and staring toward his door. Worse, seated on the floor with knees drawn to her chest, patiently waiting to see him.

Farrell was embarrassed by her presence. Yet gratified, that such a pretty girl should appear to be—well, *infatuated* with him.

Didn't want anyone to notice. Yet, wanted them to notice.

Wanted them to envy him. Yet, not to blame him.

In retrospect he supposes that he should have been more cautious. He'd felt something of the drunken inflation of ego of the popular teacher—very like a balloon expanding with helium gas.

They adore me, I can do no wrong. Hey!—I'm enjoying this.

Not anticipating how the giddy romance with Miranda might end, for none of it was *calculated.*

Though (Farrell is thinking now) he should have known, perusing her journal. Such raw emotions, so openly revealed! Many passages about the death of Miranda's father when she was nine years old. Fragments of poems, childish little drawings. Cascades of hearts filled in with red ballpoint ink.

These passages Farrell marked with asterisks in red ink of his own. Writing in the margins of the journal—*Exquisitely written, Miranda!*

And—(*Expand here? Deeper?*)

Soon Miranda began addressing Farrell directly in the journal, as if she were writing a long, meandering, heartfelt letter to him. Telling him what no one else at school knew—her father had *taken his own life.*

Farrell had thought how poignant this was. The quaint euphemism—*taken his own life.*

Pages in Miranda's journal were devoted to the lost father: how he'd been living away from home when he'd died; how, for days, Miranda and her sister were not informed that he'd died; for months, that he'd died *by his own hand.*

Writing to Farrell that she could *never trust them again my mother especially.*

Farrell was sympathetic—of course.

How could you not be sympathetic with a girl whose father has killed himself? *A very pretty tremulous-lipped twelve-year-old girl whose father has killed himself?*

He'd extracted from her a promise that she would never ever tell anyone about her visits to Mr. Farrell's office. She would never ever reveal their secret friendship.

But then, Miranda wanted to be with "Mr. Farrell" more frequently. Whatever semblance of self-confidence she'd seemed to have when he had first glimpsed her, she'd lost entirely. Forlorn and needy as a puppy. Waiting in the corridor to see him, no matter if Farrell was attending a faculty meeting that dragged on past five P.M. Trailing after him to his car. Worse, surprising him at his car, where he hadn't seen her. Asking if she might come to his apartment—*For just a little while. Please!*

Did Miranda have any idea what she wanted from Farrell, really? At twelve she was not so naïve that she didn't know what male-female relations were yet—in the way of a dreamy Balthus prepubescent— she surely imagined that such crude physicality could never be a reality for her.

Farrell was becoming alarmed. He *was* attracted to her, and he *was* excited by her even as he began to wish that she would simply stop coming to school, just—disappear.

No other teacher of Miranda Myles could hope to compete with Frank Farrell—unfortunately! Except for the girls' gym instructor, who was a feisty androgynous figure with hair buzzed up the sides and face piercings, they were a dull-dreary lot.

Gently laughing at Miranda. Urging her to laugh at herself. Stroking her arm, kissing her forehead, the tip of her nose, her mouth. *Miranda, you don't know what it is. "Making love"—you have no idea.*

All I know is, Mr. Farrell—I love you.

Taking care not to force her in any way. Never to initiate anything with her, only just to respond to her (apparent) wishes.

Kissing the delicate blue veins on the inside of her wrist. Kissing her forehead, her eyelids.

Asking, *Should I kiss you in a special way? Would you like that? If you say no, I will stop, darling.*

Faint with yearning. That buzzing sensation in his brain. What you might feel lifted suddenly from sea level to a great height, an altitude of many thousands of feet. Dazed from a lack of oxygen in the brain.

Farrell is sure, he has no doubt, Miranda never named him in the journal. He saw the journal frequently, two or three times a week, it was a way they communicated together in the guise of homework assignments; he never saw his name or any reference to himself except now and then the initials *ML* ("My Love"). Miranda knew, of course, why their special friendship had to be kept secret, she was an intelligent girl, she understood that he would lose his job if they were discovered; she would have to transfer to another school.

Never never never tell anyone, darling! Do you promise?

Cross my heart, Mr. Farrell, and hope to die.

Now the Harpies are claiming that Miranda left behind a diary after all. Simon Grice has informed him.

Not the journal but a diary of which Farrell hadn't known, they refused to allow him or his lawyer to examine this diary or even to see the passages they considered "incriminating."

But he knows, Miranda would never betray him.

Love you, love you to death. I promise.

Since arriving at the beach house he has been fantasizing how it would be, if Miranda Myles were with him in this place. They'd never been alone together, really. Never in any truly private place. In any bed.

Waking to the sound of the crashing surf, wind from the Atlantic. Forlorn cries of gulls.

He could weep, missing her. How she'd lingered in the corridor by his office for lengthy periods of time until he was free to see her. If just for a few minutes. *So faithful.*

Never was he with Miranda for more than two hours at a time. Usually much less.

Of course, these were intense hours. Breathless hours. Such a pitch of excitement, such a thrill of the forbidden, he could not have borne the strain much longer.

For there is nothing like the *forbidden,* to heighten passion.

Bursting a grape against the roof of the mouth. Was that Keats? The most exquisite pleasure, perfect because fleeting.

But if the girl were here with him in Bar Harbor, if they were obliged to have meals together, to share living quarters together, what on earth would they talk about over such a period of time? Days, weeks? Farrell cannot imagine.

With no need to hide from prying eyes, no need to conspire together, no need to steal kisses, quick embraces . . .

The delight of teaching middle school is that Farrell talks *at* his students, not *with* them. He asks questions, they answer. It's like Ping-Pong—fast, but he sets the pace. He wins the games. He wins *all* the games. He's a naturally gregarious teacher, quick-witted, funny, he has no wish (like certain of his colleagues, he has gathered) to bully students, or give them low grades; the atmosphere in Mr. Farrell's classes is relaxed, genial. He is amazingly patient, kind. Sometimes he seems to be laughing at them—but not cruelly. He wants his students to like him, he doesn't want them to cower in fear before him. He recalls from his undergraduate psychology class how the behaviorist B. F. Skinner conditioned his laboratory rats by rewarding them when they did something right but never punishing them when they did something wrong. *That* is the secret of a happy classroom.

But Frank Farrell doesn't want to have conversations with his students. What could be more boring!

He has no interest in even upper-level girl students at the school, some of whom are bold enough to seek "Mr. Farrell" out in his office with one or another transparent question. ("Mr. Farrell? Who is your favorite writer? Is it true that you write poetry?") Politely, but very firmly, Frank Farrell discourages these girls. He finds it a strain to maintain a conversation with most adults, who babble away about nonsense and expect you to chime in; the patter of adolescents is especially wearying, except in short doses interrupted with kisses by Mr. Tongue.

Yes, he misses Miranda! His heart is broken, he has lost her love.

How it began, why Mrs. Myles became suspicious sometime in March, Farrell isn't sure. He thinks it might have been Miranda bursting into tears for no evident reason, which she'd begun to do, most annoyingly. No appetite, losing weight. Said to be "listless."

Cutting herself on the insides of her forearms, not deeply. But unmistakably.

He'd scolded Miranda, he had not liked such behavior, either. He did not find it titillating, as sickos online, in certain Internet chatrooms, which Frank Farrell tries to avoid, seemingly do.

Disgusting, graphic pictures of young girls crying, black-eyed, bruised, whipping welts on their smooth young naked backs. Frank Farrell deletes these shocking photos, and worse, as quickly as they flash onto the screen.

He'd kissed the wounds Miranda hid beneath her sleeves. He'd extracted from her a promise not to cut herself again but she disobeyed him, cutting herself in a shocking place—the insides of her white thighs.

Darling, why are you doing this? Why are you hurting yourself?

Because you don't love me enough.

Of course I love you—enough for right now . . .

If you loved me I could come live with you right now.

That's impossible. You know that's impossible. I've explained, and you understand.

No. I don't understand.

Those many hours kissing, pleading, begging, cajoling, and again kissing, her hair, her warm forehead, her cheeks, her feverish lips.

Once begun, no way to end. Farrell realized belatedly.

For each school day became crucial. A (melo)drama.

Would he look at her, smile at her, in English class? Or would he not?

Would Miranda stare at him in open unabashed adoration eager to laugh at his silliest jokes or would she slump in her desk staring at her wan little clasped hands?

Would he detect shadows beneath her eyes, her downcast hazel gaze? If he were to investigate would he discover fresh cuts in her arms, beneath her sweater sleeves?

In class he was too conscious of her. Wanting to be free to be funny, silly, make everyone laugh; use the whiteboard for cartoons. *She* wanted only to know *Am I loved?*

How was he to blame?—loving not wisely but too well.

He would learn afterward that Miranda had given up all her after-school activities. She'd ceased seeing her friends. She'd lost weight, she had become dangerously thin . . .

Still, all that mattered now was that Miranda hadn't betrayed him. She had told no one. Though the Harpy-mother had interrogated her. Though the investigating committee had questioned her relentlessly, reduced her to tears.

As Grice said wryly, *Don't worry. If they had the evidence to arrest you they would have arrested you by now.*

And so, Farrell would be very foolish if he incriminated himself voluntarily.

Eventually he will meet with the investigating committee. But with his lawyer present. In a formal, not an emotional, atmosphere.

He is certain that he can explain, even to coarse-minded vulgarians, the uniqueness of his relationship with Miranda Myles. How he will stress, for this seems to be their obsessive preoccupation, that their relationship was *not sexual.*

An unusual friendship, perhaps in a way a *romance*—but definitely *not sexual.*

Of course Frank Farrell has had what are called "sexual relations" in the past. But these were with girls or women his own age. Not at all complicated, fairly ordinary, even banal relations primarily sexual, sensual, not emotionally engaging.

His love for Miranda Myles was very different. A pure love *like gold to airy thinness beat.*

What he felt for Miranda was what Poe felt for his cousin Virginia who was but seven years old when Poe first met her.

Seven! At such an age a girl-child is purely a creature of beauty, innocence. Scarcely is a child so young a physical being. Rather more like a doll, with soft flawless skin.

Pure love. Ideal love. Fated love.

Out of respect for Miranda he made himself receptive to her love. He could not reject it—he could not reject *her.*

Frank Farrell's fault was, he is not a cruel person. He is not a selfish person. Not cruel enough to reject Miranda Myles, break her heart.

He will never share this information with his adversaries because he is a gentleman, and because he loved Miranda Myles, but the fact is: Miranda pursued *him*.

You could say, Miranda seduced *him*.

From the first day she stepped into his classroom.

Her eyes which were such beautiful eyes lifting to his, the adoration in her perfect face.

How she smiled, how she laughed at her teacher's silliest jokes! He had to make an effort not to look at her too often.

No idea (of course!) that she would behave as she had. Do such harm to herself . . .

At their first meeting Farrell tried to explain this to Simon Grice but Grice lifted a warning hand—*No. Enough. Don't tell me.*

If I am defending you, I am defending you. You don't need to be "innocent"—what you claim to be "innocence" is irrelevant. I am looking at the evidence being brought against you. I am looking at the charges. A lawyer earns his fee by defending his client against a specific set of charges.

As an officer of the court a lawyer cannot support his client in perjury.

If you tell me too much, and later lie under oath, I will be forced to recuse myself.

Farrell insisted, he wasn't going to *lie*! Not under oath, or otherwise.

He will not perjure himself, Grice needn't worry. He will not behave in any way other than ethically, for that is his upbringing.

(Though beginning to wonder if the lawyer he has hired, recommended to him by the kindly woman who lent him her beach house in Bar Harbor, one of the few persons in Quakerbridge who is *on his side,* is the right man for the task.)

He's an eloquent person, Frank Farrell. He hopes to impress Grice by quoting Kierkegaard—*The crowd is a lie.*

And—*The individual is the highest truth.*

Trying to explain to the porcine-faced lawyer that only the individual is authentic, for only subjectivity is the life within: the most intense life, pure sensation before it rises to the level of consciousness.

In a sense (he argued) *objectivity* does not exist. The "objectivity" of penal codes is but a *pseudo-objectivity* since it exists, if at all, purely within the subjectivities of human beings, each biased, a partial vision.

In love, we form a bond with the beloved. All the rest of the world is shut out—irrelevant.

Lovers speak their own private language. No one else can interpret this language.

That this love would be so crudely, vulgarly (re)defined as "pedophilia" is outrageous.

Outrageous, as it is wildly inaccurate.

(It is very hard for Farrell to utter the obscene word *pedophilia*.)

(That he has been accused of being a "criminal pedophile" is particularly painful to him.)

His argument is that all laws—all "law"—are local; therefore a single law can have no universal application. If individuals like Miranda Myles and Frank Farrell refuse to identify themselves as *citizens*, it's within their rights to nullify "law . . ."

Grice was listening to Farrell with a creased forehead as one might listen to someone speaking in a foreign language in which from time to time a random syllable surfaces that is familiar.

Rudely Grice laughed aloud.

"'Nullify law'!—how d'you propose to do that, Frank?"

■

SODDEN WITH DRINK. Tavern is closing. Farrell has an impression of a tent folding, darkening, or is it a Harpy's giant wings closing, he will be trapped inside.

How'd he come here. Where *is* here. Climbing a jittery set of wooden stairs up from the beach. Gusts of wind, swaths of rain, red neon lights beckoning—*Molson*.

Christ!—he's soaked through. Teeth chattering.

Noisy place but he's grateful to hide within the noise. Doesn't want to recall his abject plea to Simon Grice, laying his heart bare, the coldhearted bastard's refusal to smile, to nod, to confirm.

Like playing a musical instrument and your audience is a warthog. Not that a hog isn't intelligent but a hog is insensitive, indifferent.

Nullify law: why's that so ridiculous? You hear of *jury nullification*, often.

In the end Farrell had no choice but to sign the contract Simon had prepared. Pay the five-thousand-dollar retainer with a check that decimated his account newly established in a Quakerbridge bank.

Smoke-haze. Laughter. Men at the bar who know one another. His age and older. Year-round residents of Bar Harbor, which is a swanky resort town in the summer. Farrell feels no kinship with these men. Doesn't know if he's lonely for male companionship or con-temptuous of such weakness. (Where are *his* friends when he needs them? Scattered all to hell since college.)

These men have all gone to school together—probably. Tattoos, beards. Beer bellies. Booming voices. Though Farrell too is unshaven there's no mistaking Frank Farrell for one of these *locals*.

Fills him with maudlin melancholy, he's a *local* nowhere.

One of the bartenders is a woman, that's unexpected. Good!

Her eyes glide over the solitary drinker at the end of the bar, rim of a baseball cap pulled low over his forehead. Hunched shoulders, nylon jacket. Asking, when she swipes the bar near him, is he visiting here?—obviously Farrell isn't a local.

Yes, Farrell says. Visiting.

There's hurt in his face. Woundedness. In a kindly voice the bar-tender inquires where he's staying and he tells her the name of a lane which he mispronounces—*Petit Manon*. This is impressive to her, it seems. Prime real estate near the marina.

For two hours he's been drinking beer(s). Maybe he's had enough?

Touched that the bartender is friendly to him, a woman in her late thirties he guesses. Women *are* friendly to Farrell. Not knowing of his notoriety back in Quakerbridge, Pennsylvania. Slanderous rumors of *unprofessional behavior, relations with a twelve-year-old, criminal pe-dophila*.

None of it true. Grounds for a defamation suit.

He suggested this to Grice, *countersuit*. Grice murmured something affable as if to humor him.

But the bartender isn't judging Farrell. She smiles at him, she is welcoming to him. One of those good-sport females, not glamorous but attractive, a buddy-girl, a girl with older brothers. Farrell responds to such women passively, as they are likely to take the initiative with him. He doesn't lead them on as there is nowhere to which they might be led.

Orders another beer. Succession of beer(s) to stupefy his senses, which have been abraded raw over the past week. Well, yes—*his* heart has been lacerated. No one has given much thought to *him*.

Wanting badly to lay his head down on his arms, on the bar. As loud voices, laughter wash over him.

The woman's name is Gladys, she tells him. He sees in her ruddy-friendly face a possibility of tenderness, forgiveness.

Comfort of the female body yet (also) a kind of threat. Too much flesh, often they have massive thighs, you can't really judge when they are clothed. Soft-flaccid large breasts, suffocating.

Farrell tells her, after a moment's hesitation, his name is Francis.

(He's never felt that "Frank Farrell" is a name worthy of him. His full name, "Frank Harrison Farrell," is even clunkier.)

Gladys is too old for Farrell by, what?—twenty years. Instantaneously that's established: faint lines in the woman's forehead, dyed-looking frizz-hair, something worn and battered in her bemused eyes yet when she offers to drive Farrell back to where he's staying in town, he is close to tears, eager with gratitude. *Yes! Yes thank you.*

No idea how he'd get back to the beach house otherwise. No idea from which direction he's come on foot.

There's a second bartender, male. Closing up the tavern. Suddenly everyone has left. At last the damned TV is *off*. Gladys is laughing, not in a cruel way but as an older sister might laugh, a mother helping Farrell zip up his jacket, where the zipper has become snarled, walking him outside to her car.

The generosity of women! Farrell is continually astonished. He is *blessed*. A man can be a pure unabashed bastard yet there's a woman who will forgive him.

Hell, women will forgive you before they even know what they're forgiving.

Impulsively Farrell tells this woman, his name is *Francis*. She laughs saying, yes you told me, Francis: I'm Gladys.

In the car Gladys asks Farrell where he's from and he tells her Nowhere Special, USA.

Christ!—his legs are cramped in this car. What's it, a compact? Economy? Some kind of Nissan.

He's living now near Philadelphia, he says. Teaches at a fancy prep school.

He's in mourning. A lost love, who died. Beautiful young girl.

At once Gladys is sympathetic. Saying, she hoped the girl wasn't Francis's daughter?—and Farrell says *Yes. She was a daughter.*

Bumpy road, ascending. Fortunately Farrell remembers which beach house he is staying in on Petit Manon Lane.

Quite a large house, dark-shingled. Chimneys, wraparound porch. At least an acre of land above the ocean. Gladys is impressed.

Belongs to his family?

No, a friend.

A very nice friend.

Yes. She is.

Farrell has temporarily forgotten this woman-friend's name, back in Quakerbridge. She is the mother of one of his eighth-grade students who has *staunchly* defended him. Will not believe the nasty rumors about him. Has written to Headmaster Higg *vouching* for him. A well-to-do divorcée with a plain sweet chubby daughter who is also one of Mr. Farrell's *staunch* student admirers . . .

Oh, Mr. Farrell's students adore him! Most of them, anyway. That's why it's *so unfair.*

Hears himself tell Gladys again, he's in mourning. Anguished voice. Genuinely anguished. Tears run down his stubbled cheeks. Gladys is tenderly solicitous, touching his icy fingers. She is so, so sorry.

Farrell repeats that a beautiful little girl has died, she has died by her own hand, the adults around her who could have saved her failed her, and he is one of them.

Gladys asks if Farrell can get out of the car? Can he walk by himself? He is light-headed, his legs feel weirdly numb.

Gladys slips an arm around his waist, helping him walk to the house. She is a sturdy woman, with muscled legs. Always there are sturdy buddy-women who come forward when they are needed like a chorus in a Greek tragedy.

Farrell leans on Gladys's arm. He is shivering. His hands are icy-cold. He has lost all shame, he is sobbing. *A beautiful little girl has died because adults failed her.*

In Farrell's jacket pocket Gladys locates the key to the house. Sudden intimacy as in a hospital—Gladys might be a nurse. Forgiving, no reproach. No judgment. Farrell allows the woman to maneuver him into the house. He is passive, he will follow her lead. She switches on lights, gives a faint whistle.

Living room with vaulted ceiling, fieldstone fireplace. Polished plank floors. A multimillion-dollar property though not smelling too fresh at the moment, Farrell was drinking beer here too, earlier that day.

Loses his balance, sits down heavily on a rattan sofa. His head feels as if it's loose on his shoulders.

Gladys asks if she should help him into bed? Or onto a bed? Will he be all right by himself?

No, Farrell says. His face is damp with tears. His voice is hoarse with anguish. Holding out his hands for the woman to grasp, to warm.

"No! I am not *all right* by myself."

■

IN THE MORNING WHEN the phone rings Farrell fumbles to answer it.

"Frank? I've been trying to reach you. They're ready to negotiate."

QUAKERBRIDGE, PENNSYLVANIA: THE HANDSHAKE

APRIL 2005

B y the time he returns to Quakerbridge, Pennsylvania, he's ready to confess.

Doesn't believe that he is *guilty* of anything essentially but there's a black-bile taste in his mouth, might as well be *guilt*.

For the fact is, the girl is dead.

That is a fact. That is an unassailable fact.

Frank Farrell is stone-cold sober. Hasn't had a drink since the tavern in Bar Harbor. Feels like hell. He *is* contrite. Sick. Sick with shame.

It is three weeks to the day since Miranda Myles was found dead in her bedroom, wrists and forearms slashed.

It is fifteen days since Frank Farrell was *suspended from teaching duties* at the Newell Johnson School.

Porcine-faced Grice regards Farrell's misery-face with, what?— Sympathy? Pity? Barely disguised contempt?

Tells his bloodshot-eyed client, of course he feels bad. Anyone would. Any teacher of any student who'd died would feel *damned bad*.

He's seen pictures of Miranda Myles, Grice says. She was a very pretty girl. Obviously a sensitive intelligent girl. But her eyes . . .

"Her eyes?"—Farrell asks. "What about her eyes?"

"Her eyes were unusually large, verging on *protuberant*," Grice says. "Sign of a high-strung, emotional person. As the mother is, excitable."

"Wait. I don't think . . ."

"They've admitted, the Myles family, that Miranda had therapy as a child. After her father died. Very possibly, she was *on the spectrum*."

On the spectrum—Farrell frowns. This isn't true, he is sure.

Grice persists: "It's an anecdotal impression, not a clinical diagnosis. One of your colleagues suggested it in those very words—*on the spectrum*."

"Who was that?—one of my colleagues?"

"They're not all your enemies at the school, Frank. They don't want to jeopardize their standing with Higg but they will go on record, they believe *you* and not the charges against you. Two or three of them—women."

Farrell feels dazed, relieved. *Not everyone at Newell Johnson abhors him as a pedophile monster!*

"It's generally acknowledged that the poor girl must have been unbalanced, considering what she did. Mutilating her arms like that. And she'd been starving herself for weeks—you have to wonder what her mother was thinking, indifferent to the girl's condition. *There's* parental neglect, obviously."

Farrell is sad, this talk of Miranda Myles in the past tense. He hasn't really grasped her death yet. Absorbed it. If he returns to his classes, Miranda Myles's desk in his fourth-period English class will be vacant . . .

But it doesn't look as if he will be returning to his classes, Higg has banished him. In a fury of disgust Higg has banished him. The board of trustees has banished him. The committee of Harpies has banished him.

Sick with self-disgust and shame Farrell has come to the law office of Grice, Murke, Mudge & Pettigraw in suburban Quakerbridge. He is shaky, his head pounds with pain. His head pounds with ontological malaise. He has lost entirely his resolve to defy the Newell Johnson School. Only dimly can he recall climbing the rickety steps to the tavern at Bar Harbor, how drunk-sick he was before collapsing on a bed that night with just his running shoes tugged off by now-forgotten Gladys.

But Simon Grice does not appear impressed with Farrell's contrition. As he wasn't impressed with Farrell's original arrogance.

Explaining to him as one might explain to a slow-witted child that the situation he's in is not at all uncommon: an employer is attempting to violate the terms of an employee's contract *for cause.* As Farrell's attorney he is questioning that *cause;* he is prepared to refute that *cause;* indeed, he is negotiating for a settlement.

"This isn't a nineteenth-century Russian novel. You are not going to bare your soul and confess before a public tribunal. You are not going to confess out of misplaced altruism or worse yet, martyrdom. You are not going to throw yourself down to kiss the earth which you have defiled, like Raskolnikov."

It will be Farrell's word against the claims of the Newell Johnson School, represented by the headmaster Higg. For there is *no evidence of irrefutable wrongdoing* brought forward by Higg.

No evidence in the girl's diary.

(Turns out, there *is* a diary. Not the journal that Farrell gave to Miranda Myles but a smaller diary in which Miranda wrote profusely of her love for her English teacher who had, among other things, she claimed, *saved her life.*)

Grice has demanded to see this diary but has not, yet. Passages have been read aloud to him by the school's counsel and will be read aloud to Farrell if he requests it but Grice advises Farrell not to request it.

"You will only be upset. You will feel an irresistible desire to answer, to refute, to explain, to defend—so, no."

Seeing the expression in Farrell's face Grice assures him, it's just the girl's word against his. She had quite an imagination, it seems. But no one can prove that anything remotely resembling what she wrote actually happened or that there was ever a *Mr. Tongue* or a *Mr. Teddy Bear.* Ridiculous!

At this, Farrell is stricken silent. Grice hurriedly continues assuring him it's perfectly plausible that an emotionally unstable girl of that age, who has lost her father, would imagine a torrid romance with her seventh-grade English teacher, a good-looking youngish man, who was kind to her.

The fantasies of pubescent girls are notorious, Grice says. Recall Salem, Massachusetts: Hysterical girls accusing older women of witchcraft. Causing innocent parties to be executed. Not just women but men as well. Historical fact.

Proof that the girl was unstable is self-evident: she took her own life.

No normal, well-adjusted twelve-year-old would commit such a desperate act. *By definition* Miranda Myles was psychologically un-stable.

Farrell listens, pained. All that Simon Grice is saying is true, and yet . . . And yet, *it is not the total truth.*

"I think—I am to blame. I mean—encouraging her. Writing in her journal. She never talked about her father to anyone—she said—but she was able to write about him. Once she began, she wrote and wrote. She wrote poems, little stories. Her words were so sad, so beautiful, so much more profound than her classmates' writing. I asked her to speak with me after class, she came to my office, she started crying and—and so—I comforted her. One thing led to another."

One thing led to another! The most banal of clichés and he, Frank Farrell, is uttering it.

"It was natural to comfort her," Farrell says defensively. "It was—it was *not*—calculated."

"Of course not. None of this was 'calculated'—and you are prob-ably not remembering entirely correctly, Frank. It's my understanding that the girl came to *you*. She lingered after class, many times. She came to your office. The assignments you gave her were identical to the assignments you gave to the other students—she was the one who obsessed over them. You asked her to read her work to the class but you asked others as well. She *was not* a favorite of yours, you have *no favorites*. She came voluntarily to your office, and she came too often to your office. She followed you to your car. You asked her to stop but she did not stop. You were concerned—of course."

Adding, as in a practical aside: "But here you should have sent the headmaster a note for his file, about her, to prepare for possible trouble. An unnaturally needy, obsessive student. In the future you'll know better."

"'Future!'"—Farrell laughs bitterly. "All my future is *past*. The tragedy was Miranda's father committing suicide when she was nine years old. Long before I came into her life."

"Yes, a tragedy," Grice says, patiently, "—but not *your* tragedy."

There is nothing that Farrell's accusers can do if he holds firm to his story, Grice says. If he doesn't weaken. There isn't a shred of actual evidence. Miranda never accused him, never complained of him to anyone. On the contrary, she said what a wonderful teacher "Mr. Farrell" was. His colleagues have said they often saw the girl in his office, and in the corridor outside his office, that's exactly what he said. She was never a passenger in his car. She was never at his house. He has sworn that.

"If they try to terminate you without a considerable severance package we will sue."

Severance? Sue? Farrell isn't sure if he is hearing clearly.

"We will also demand a strong letter of recommendation from Higg, with the proviso that you and I both read it. If you follow my counsel you will wind up with a sabbatical year and a better job."

Farrell's head is spinning. *Sabbatical? Better job?*

In an expansive voice Grice tells Farrell he has informed Higg that he's prepared to file a countersuit against both Higg and the school, accusing "defamation of character." He has hinted he will disclose to the public that, contrary to Higg's fraudulent assertion that nothing like the suicide of Miranda Myles had ever happened before in the hundred-year history of the Newell Johnson School, there has been a considerable number of nervous breakdowns, drug overdoses, fatal "accidents," and suspected suicides at the school in the past decade, in the upper grades especially.

Not to mention sexual assaults, rapes. Male students assaulting female students, never reported to legal authorities, never disciplined by the school with its fear of bad publicity.

"I told Higg: if they take us to court on this, I will drag out the sorry, sordid history of the Newell Johnson School. Local media will go into a frenzy. The school will hemorrhage students. Within a year they will be shut down. They will go bankrupt."

Farrell listens, humbled. He has a vision of the limestone façade of the school's oldest building collapsing into ruins. Has *he* precipitated this, closing his thumb and forefinger around a twelve-year-old girl's delicate wrist one day in his office, with the blind bravado of one diving from a high board for the first time in his life?

He had something to say but Grice's voice has expanded to fill the room, like hissing gas.

"Frank? You've been listening?"

"Y-Yes. Of course . . ."

"Well, that's it for now. I'll be meeting with Higg this afternoon. Any questions?"

Farrell rises to his feet, unsteadily. His head is abuzz with questions. He feels like a condemned prisoner who has been spared through a technicality, he cannot begin to fathom the technicality, it is best for him to remain silent.

"No questions? Just as well. Go see a movie, relax. I'll call you tonight or tomorrow. I may have some good news."

Grice's handshake is brisk. Farrell's hand feels crushed even as it's quickly released.

In a haze Farrell turns to leave the lawyer's office. How bizarre it is, like a dream that has come to no clear conclusion, he is free to simply walk out of this claustrophobic space.

Where?

■

HE *IS* A CONDEMNED prisoner, spared by a technicality.

So grateful to have been spared, he could throw himself down and kiss the earth which he has defiled—almost.

Vowing, he will make amends for the tragedy of Miranda Myles. He will change his life. He will do good in the future—he will *be* good.

In his life never another Miranda Myles!

V

THE HIRE

THE LANGHORNE ACADEMY

WIELAND, NEW JERSEY

APRIL 2013

*H*iring will be on the strict basis of merit.
    But not a white male. Probably, no.
This is the (tacit) mandate. No one has actually uttered these words aloud.

■

ONE OF THE LANGHORNE Academy's middle-school teachers is retiring, a new position is opening, the school is flooded with applications.

P. Cady, chair of the hiring committee, is determined, with the (tacit) approval of the Academy's board of trustees, that she will hire a woman for the position, preferably a young woman of color or of an ethnic minority underrepresented in the Langhorne faculty, which is 90 percent "white."

(It is P. Cady's predilection to designate "white" in this way, with quotation marks, as if it were a linguistic or biological curiosity.)

The position will involve teaching three sections of seventh-grade English and three sections of eighth-grade English, as well as supervising after-school activities as required, and serving on school committees as required; with a salary in the top one percent of comparable teaching positions in the United States, befitting a private school of the prestige of the Langhorne Academy.

(How can the Langhorne Academy afford to pay such high salaries, in an era in which both public and private school teachers' salaries have generally stagnated?—there have been rumors.)

Since its founding in the late nineteenth century the Langhorne Academy has been staffed primarily by (white) men, a situation that began to change, with evident reluctance, in the late decades of the twentieth century; in the twenty-first century the ratio of male to female teachers is at last nearing equity though the most senior, highest-paid faculty positions are still held by (white) men.

A succession of (white) men have been headmasters of the Academy since its founding: P. Cady is the first headmistress, having come to Langhorne from the Lawrenceville School, where she was dean of students.

(Even now wincing to recall the opposition of a small but influential cadre of male Langhorne alums to her appointment, a campaign of cruel and protracted misogyny that, P. Cady suspects, continues to the present day, smoldering like an underground fire without her knowledge.)

Publicly P. Cady has stated that hiring at the Langhorne Academy is strictly on the basis of merit, and this is the essence of the announcement in professional journals, seeking applicants for the new opening; but of the leading candidates for the position, winnowed down from more than one hundred applicants, the hiring committee, led by P. Cady, favors a young Black woman with an advanced degree in African American and gender studies from Wellesley College, a young Korean American woman with equally impressive credentials currently on the faculty at the Phillips Exeter Academy, and a young Latina woman with degrees in education and psychology from Northeastern, currently teaching at the Brearley School. An outlier in their midst is a single (white) male candidate with an impressive résumé and a strong personal recommendation from a niece of P. Cady, an administrator at the Guggenheim Memorial Foundation.

(Is P. Cady unreasonably influenced by her niece's recommendation?—in fact, P. Cady *is not*. She has no intention of hiring a *white male* no matter how warmly her niece Katy recommends him.)

Interviews with the candidates are scheduled for the final two weeks in April. In addition, each candidate is required to teach a class of eighth graders while the committee observes from the rear of the room. P. Cady is sympathetic with the young women, performing under duress; recalling how when she first began to teach she was stricken with self-doubt; her first interviews did not go well.

As a young woman imagining herself in the eyes of her (male) interviewers—*too tall, ungainly.*

Forcing herself to speak slowly, calmly. Trying not to suggest that she was *overprepared, ambitious*. Not *shrill*.

Not *feminine*. Yet clearly, though not troublingly, *feminist*.

So very prudently P. Cady has made her way through the dense thicket of her professional life, with such concern for fair-mindedness, integrity, and unremitting self-discipline, she feels a tinge of envy for a generation of women younger than she, who seem scarcely to comprehend how difficult it was in the earlier era just to be taken seriously by the dominant sex when, at the age of twenty-two, Paige Cady (as she was known at the time) had no recourse other than to blush and stammer *thank you* when the chair of the committee examining her master's thesis ("Heroic Narrative in Classic American Literature") had pronounced it so good, *it might have been written by a man.*

Wanting badly to say to the genially smiling professor *Really? Which man? Any man? You?*

But to have spoken her mind at such a crucial moment would have been to sabotage her career at its start. Like bringing down your heel on a caterpillar before it has metamorphosed into a butterfly . . .

Twenty-nine years later. P. Cady is still not (quite) in a place where she can *speak her mind* without risking consequences.

■

IN ALL, SIX CANDIDATES are invited to the Langhorne Academy to be considered for the position. Five of these, young women, acquit themselves reasonably well in their interviews and in the classroom; but it happens, unexpectedly, ironically, that the least-favored candidate, the lone (white) male, whose visit is at the very end of the interview process, is the most impressive.

His name is "Francis Harlan Fox"—a name ideally suited for a man in his mid-thirties who exudes an air of zestful energy, enthusiasm. Pale-blue-eyed, with a charming gap-toothed smile, Fox is both boyish and avuncular, an ideal type for middle-school teaching. You do not want a stern, old-style *patriarch,* not in the twenty-first century; but you do want an individual for whom authority comes effortlessly.

Obviously, Fox is sharp-witted; but he is also modest, even self-deprecatory; he is winningly funny as one of the less aggressive TV stand-up comics is funny, inviting laughter but not forcing it. He is tall and "fit"-looking, but not too tall, and not too "fit"-looking; he dresses casually, yet with an unmistakable preppy élan. He is carrying a bookbag, or is it a backpack? He doesn't sit at the teacher's desk at the front of the room, he prefers to move about. Yet, he does not nervously *pace.*

Within minutes, with the ease of a professional magician, Fox has won the rapt attention of the classroom of eighth graders.

Poetry is Fox's subject for the class: in particular, Edgar Allan Poe's "The Raven."

This most robust-rhyming poem Francis Fox recites in a spirited voice, making of the hackneyed rhymes something new and disturbing; he leads a discussion of the poem in which more than half the class participates; with the patience of one steering a small boat so inconspicuously it would appear that the boat is steering itself, he draws out of the class of thirteen-year-olds the poem's *deeper, secret* meaning.

Fox declares that all great poems have double meanings: "What the poem tells us, and what the poem doesn't tell us." Unexpectedly, he passes out sheets of colored paper and asks the students to "quick-scribble" poems of their own employing "strong rhymes" and "secret meanings."

At the rear of the classroom P. Cady and the other members of the hiring committee are astonished. Students known to be shy, reticent, indifferent, or bored in their regular English classes are eager to read their poems aloud for Mr. Fox, and some of the poems are indeed original, clever; there are hilarious rhymes; waves of applause. Francis Fox is certainly *inspirational*.

At the bell, students seem reluctant to leave. Usually, they hurriedly exit a classroom but here are a half-dozen lingering to speak with Francis Fox, who appears to be taking their questions seriously, replying to them most genially. A few give Fox their poems, which he folds up carefully, like treasure, and puts in his bookbag.

Quite a performance!—P. Cady thinks. But *she* is not deceived.

"Very well done, Mr. Fox!"—P. Cady has no choice but to shake the man's hand, with a grimace of a smile.

She has not called him Francis, as her committee colleagues have. She has allowed him to register that her admiration for his teaching, as for his candidacy in general, is more restrained than the admiration of her colleagues.

Seeing the disappointment in Fox's face as politely she explains, she will have to miss the luncheon with him following the class— "Something urgent has come up, unavoidably."

As she discreetly absents herself from the committee meeting on Monday, anticipating how the vote will go, and not wanting to display vexation, disapproval, dismay, or worst of all anger to her colleagues when they vote to make the offer to Francis Fox which they do, unanimously.

Unanimously! P. Cady is chagrined.

"How could they! Betraying me."

Was there not a (tacit) understanding among the committee members that a minority candidate, a woman, would be offered the position?—*not another (white) male.*

Any one of the young women candidates would have been agreeable to P. Cady. But—of all of the candidates—*Fox!*

Though P. Cady is the most liberal, the most reasonable, the most generous and fair-minded of administrators she is resolved that this appointment *will not go to Fox.*

It's clear to P. Cady that the committee has been taken in by Fox's undeniable *charisma,* which seems to her showy, superficial. They have been beguiled by Fox's (seemingly) guileless blue eyes and quick smile. They may have been stirred to envy just a bit by Fox's ease at teaching their students. It would be pointless to argue with them, they have voted sincerely—if ignorantly.

True, Fox's résumé is impressive. His curriculum vitae is impressive. He has taught longer than any of the young women candidates, and has stronger recommendations; he has taken courses in secondary-school education to supplement his graduate work in English; he is even, evidently, a published poet. Undeniably, he is an excellent middle-school teacher. Yet—P. Cady's heart is hardened against the man.

She is reluctant to veto the decision of the hiring committee but as headmistress of the Langhorne Academy she is obliged to reject any decision of her faculty that is mistaken or misguided.

Pointless to honor the democratic tradition at the Academy if poor decisions are made in a democratic process, defeating the very purpose of democracy.

"I should have gone to the meeting! I should not have recused myself."

(It's to Princess Di that P. Cady makes such declarations in the solitude of the household they share. But Princess Di only gazes upward silently at her eccentric and unpredictable human, brown eyes brimming with compassion, empathy, incomprehension.)

"*Why* did I recuse myself! I have only myself to blame."

Here is the dilemma: P. Cady handpicked the hiring committee herself, choosing exactly those individuals, three women and two men, whose judgment she most respects; she cannot reasonably reject their decision now.

(Seeing that her human is troubled Princess Di gazes upward at her more intensely, as if trying very hard to speak. In the effort her little bottom wriggles, and her stubby tail wags, as if in an uncertain wind. The brimming-brown eyes urge *Compromise!*)

P. Cady will compromise by bringing Francis Fox back to Wieland, for a second interview in the privacy of her office.

"This time, I will ask Fox rigorous questions. No one will interrupt. He will not slide by on *charm*."

■

"HELLO, MR. FOX! Come in, please."

Briskly P. Cady greets Francis Fox as he is escorted into her office by her assistant March, briskly P. Cady shakes the candidate's hand without looking him fully in the face. She has reserved forty minutes for this interview. She has not scheduled lunch to follow.

P. Cady thanks Fox for returning so soon to Wieland, which is after all an *out-of-the-way place* . . .

It's the sort of remark that P. Cady has cultivated in her years as an administrator, one that makes a reply difficult since its expression of gratitude is couched in an attitude of reproach.

If Fox is looking startled, like one who finds himself on a tilting floor where he expected something solid, P. Cady does not notice. Fox manages an affable reply: Wieland is not *out-of-the-way* to him, he says; he is very interested in the "ecology" of the Pine Barrens, he loves to hike, he is a bird-watcher . . . He is not a city-dweller.

City-dweller. This term seems self-conscious, quaint. Does anyone really think of himself as a *city-dweller?*

Nothing the man says is remotely authentic, genuine. Everything about "Francis Fox" is a performance—P. Cady *knows.*

Though Francis Fox seems prepared to discuss the "ecology" of the region—(a subject in which, in fact, P. Cady is interested)—the topic of Wieland being an *out-of-the-way* place is abruptly dropped.

If Fox is waiting for P. Cady to allude to his interview of the previous week, and to his exemplary classroom performance, he must wait in vain.

With a smile that might be measured in single-digit millimeters P. Cady invites her visitor to take a seat facing her as she regards him from behind a massive mahogany desk, clearly an inheritance from a more genteel time, the desk of an old-time *headmaster,* if not a nineteenth-century ship's captain. Her office is spacious, high-ceilinged, with walls of built-in cherrywood bookcases, and floor-to-ceiling windows overlooking the fountain at the center of the school grounds. The room, the furnishings, the very orderliness of the neatly shelved books suggest a settled world into which an outsider, like the *white male job-candidate Fox,* is not welcome yet out of civility cannot (yet) be expelled.

For this private interview Francis Fox has dressed with more formality than previously. Where P. Cady remembers him as tieless, now he is wearing a dark blue bow tie; where he wore a green-striped shirt, now he is wearing a long-sleeved white cotton shirt. He is not so boyish, or so avuncular; he is *gentlemanly.* Tweed jacket, sharp-creased trousers. Polished black leather shoes. Glimpse of silver cuff links.

Still, he is carrying the ridiculous dark-green bookbag, or backpack. A youthful touch, and Fox is how old?—late thirties.

And he's wearing a ring on his right hand P. Cady hasn't noticed previously. Chunky octagon-onyx ring, also ridiculous. Why do men wear *rings?*

"Why do you think, Mr. Fox—'Francis'—that you would be happy at the Langhorne Academy? Is there any particular reason you are interested in us?"

How abruptly the interview has begun. P. Cady lifts her steely gaze like a rapier to Fox's face: sees that indeed, Francis Fox is a bit crestfallen, not smiling so affably now, his forehead has lost its boyish smoothness. The pale-blue eyes are clouded with a kind of male hurt, bafflement. Almost, P. Cady can feel the effort of the male brain *calculating* how to reply to such a question.

If the interview is a kind of chess game, P. Cady has begun aggressively; she is not one for subterfuge or circumlocution.

Canny Fox manages a plausible reply: speaks of the Academy's reputation among private schools, its rigorous academic tradition, its emphasis upon creative arts; if he came to Langhorne he would be interested, he says, in establishing a book club for middle-school students, as well as a drama club—casting school plays with middle-school students, junior versions of Broadway shows like *Annie, Into the Woods,* even *Sweeney Todd . . .*

Not very graciously P. Cady is leafing through Fox's application folder, only half-listening.

Something in Francis Fox has triggered memories of her father, Randall Cady. No idea why, it has been years since her father's death, which she recalls as slow-approaching as a train in the distance and then abrupt, rushing as a train passing within a few feet.

No idea why, Paige Cady loved her father very much, more than she loved her softer, more pliable mother; yet she'd never felt comfortable with him. Like P. Cady he was an educator but on a grander scale, not a prep school headmaster but a financial officer at a large state university, overseeing an immense faculty, dealing with a budget many hundreds of times greater than the Langhorne budget. Publicly he professed pride in his daughter's accomplishments yet she felt his (secret) disappointment, that she had earned only master's degrees (two: in English and in education) and not a PhD; that she hadn't become a university professor but had settled for a career in private school education.

Settled for is unfair, perhaps. Secondary-school teaching is not to be slighted, one could argue that it is more crucial than university teaching, for young students.

But why she'd done this, P. Cady could not have explained.

Except: as a university professor she'd have been too explicitly following the path her father had expected, with its many opportunities for missteps, stumbles; she'd have been expected to compete with other young academics to publish research, scholarship, a continuous stream of papers and reviews in her field. It is P. Cady's way to write with fastidious slowness for she *overthinks.* Too much pressure!—she might have failed, conspicuously; her father would have known.

If she'd failed as a secondary-school teacher, or if she'd flourished, as (in fact) she has, her father took little notice.

How she regrets that Randall Cady is *gone . . .* He will never know of her stature within the prestige-private-school community.

Her skills as an administrator, a fundraiser. *That* might have impressed him.

A greater regret, she'd failed to tell him that she'd loved him.

Even when he was dying, in a hospice attached to Robert Wood Johnson University Hospital, New Brunswick. Nor did her father tell her, if indeed he loved her.

She'd planned to tell him, she'd rehearsed the words. *Daddy, you know—I love you . . .*

Time passed too swiftly. At the end. And suddenly, it was too late.

". . . until last spring, when I realized . . ."

P. Cady rouses herself, as if from a bad dream. What has this obviously insincere male candidate been saying?

A bias against males, especially straight white males of the kind that, when P. Cady was younger, might glance at her startled, stare at her strong-boned handsome face, note her poise, appreciate her wit, but were reluctant to approach her.

Here a question for the (eager, fawning) candidate: He has taught at four schools in nine years, isn't that most unusual? Why has he moved around so much?

(Obviously a *red flag* on the man's résumé.)

(Why haven't the committee members noticed this?—P. Cady is vexed at them.)

Fox explains that he was "very happy" at each of the schools and had no particular wish to leave but he also—somehow—acquired "some sort of reputation" as a teacher that led to his receiving offers from rival schools . . .

"So, you were made offers you 'couldn't refuse'—is that it?"

P. Cady speaks as if bemused. Not overtly suspicious.

There have been offers he did refuse, Fox says quietly. The résumé in his file is just a "small portion" of his teaching career.

"And there's a year when apparently you didn't teach, between the Newell Johnson School and the Winnetka Academy, what did you do during that interim?"

Smilingly Fox explains, as if he has been hoping he might be asked that question, that that was a "sabbatical" year. A "token of apprecia-tion" from the Newell Johnson School since, in addition to his teach-ing and advising, he'd done several "highly successful" fundraising events for the school.

"A 'sabbatical year'—for a middle-school teacher? That must have been a considerable 'token of appreciation.'"

P. Cady speaks ironically even as a part of her brain registers *fund-raising*.

Yes, Francis Fox would be an attractive asset for a private school, in the matter of fundraising; for, in a private school, fundraising is essential, and nonstop. (Male) Langhorne alums would feel comfort-able with Francis Fox, who far more resembles one of them than any female minority candidate could.

"And what did you do, Mr. Fox, on your 'token-of-appreciation' sabbatical year?"

". . . during that year, I took courses . . . That summer, I enrolled at . . ."

P. Cady has assumed an interrogative manner while Fox continues to speak forthrightly, with a kind of wounded male dignity, that touches P. Cady in spite of her distrust of him.

Either the man is unwilling to acknowledge P. Cady's animosity, or he is unaware of it.

". . . hoping to gain a deeper understanding of . . ."

P. Cady observes the candidate's mouth. A wily mouth, a prac-ticed mouth. Clean-shaven jaws, a just-perceptible cleft on his chin. Without an enthusiastic and flattering audience the middle-school teacher is looking years older, luster has faded from his face. In that instant P. Cady feels an unexpected empathy for Fox.

Recalling how as a younger instructor she was somewhat the same. "Paige Cady"—shy, reticent, self-doubting, not at all combative or assertive; yet, in the classroom, after an initial, tentative year, she'd learned to be forceful, even dynamic.

It was some sort of trick, lighting up a room: smiling, wit, keep things moving, ask sharp questions.

P. Cady had never learned to be quite as *entertaining* as Francis Fox but she acquired a particular sort of droll humor specific to a classroom of adolescents, and rarely displayed outside it.

For teaching is site-specific: not *identity* but *performance*.

More favorably disposed now, P. Cady peruses Fox's letters of recommendation. The letter from Otto Higg, headmaster of the Newell Johnson School, is profuse with praise: *superlative classroom teacher, magical rapport with students, warmly collegial, enthusiastic participant in school activities (including Parent-Teacher meetings), middle-school book club advisor, drama club co-advisor, alumni fundraising drive . . .*

Each of Fox's recommendations resembles this one. Kent School, Brookdale School, Winnetka Academy. *Most popular teacher, outstanding academic record, advisor to the student literary magazine, advisor to the middle-school book club . . .* Not in Fox's file but in a drawer in P. Cady's desk there is even a personal, unofficial letter from her niece Katy testifying to Francis Fox's qualifications for a teaching position at the Langhorne Academy: *Personal integrity, commitment to teaching. Respect for his subject.*

Yet, P. Cady is not convinced.

Bluntly she asks Fox if he doesn't think it's unusual for a teacher to move around so frequently? Would he remain at the Langhorne Academy if he received a better offer, after just a year or two?

Quickly Fox assures P. Cady that there could not be a *better offer*.

"It would be a great honor to teach at the Langhorne Academy— I'm sure I would never want to leave."

P. Cady smiles at this extravagant claim. But Francis Fox appears sincere, in his chastened way.

Adding, "It isn't a matter of money, Ms. Cady. No one goes into private school teaching for the money. And anyway—I have very few expenses."

Not a very prudent remark to make to a prospective employer! P. Cady's impression is that, judging by his tasteful clothes, and the quiet understatement of his manner, Francis Fox does not lack for funds.

Traditionally, so many who gravitate toward private school teaching and administration, as to literary publishing, have come from genteel-moneyed backgrounds: Francis Fox would appear to be one of these scions.

"I know, Ms. Cady, it does look as if I've been restless. 'Four schools in nine years.' But I am prepared to settle down now . . ."

Settle down. As if the likelihood of tenure at Langhorne is not unreasonable for this candidate to expect.

Sheer ego, P. Cady thinks, amused. Yet, she can understand why her colleagues on the hiring committee were so persuaded by him.

Fox flatters you, by seeming to be "equal" to you. What a gentleman!

"Excuse me, Mr. Fox, but—do you have a family?"

"Of course. My parents are retired, living now in Sarasota, Florida."

"You are not married, I see. Do you have plans to marry? A companion or, what's the term—'significant other'?"

P. Cady is embarrassed to ask such a question since she would not wish the question to be asked of her.

With a pained smile Fox assures P. Cady: "No. I do not."

"You haven't been married, I assume. You don't have children . . ."

"I have not been married, and I have not had children. I've been so focused on my work during the school year, and in the summer I've taken courses, or traveled, or worked on my poetry—I seem not to have given a thought to marriage."

There is something grandiose in this statement, P. Cady is reminded of the swagger of Oscar Wilde. That subtle ironic emphasis of the word *marriage.*

P. Cady nods, Fox's reply is reasonable to her. *She* has scarcely given thought to marriage in a quarter century.

"I've never really given much thought to cultivating a 'personal, domestic' life—you know, the American ideal. My experience of actual families, married life, the lives of couples with whom I have been close over the years, hasn't much appealed to me."

As if detecting something receptive in P. Cady's face, Fox speaks with sudden candor.

Nor does he care to have children of his own, he says, preferring to invest time and energy in other people's children, whose lives he believes he can benefit all the more, because he *does not* have children of his own.

P. Cady nods *yes*. This is so.

Still, Fox continues wryly, he *is* a godfather, he has a "godson"—strange as it sounds. A favor—an honor—he did for a college friend in Philadelphia years ago.

P. Cady doesn't mention that she, too, is a godparent, a "godmother"—though her friendship with the girl's parents has somewhat atrophied, she has not seen the girl or her parents in several years. (But why has she allowed the friendship to fade? She feels a twinge of loss, melancholy.)

It's a strange custom, Fox says, as if P. Cady has agreed with him. Acting as a *godparent*. Dating back to an earlier era when human lives were much more precarious than they are now, and a child might require more than one father or mother for survival.

His godson is in his teens now, Fox says. The grandson of Fred Biddle, whom he, Fox, has met only a few times, though he still keeps in contact with his godson, once or twice a year.

Biddle. The name resonates like the ringing of a gong—(Philadelphia, Quaker, abolitionist history, family wealth, philanthropy).

P. Cady has discovered Fox's personal letter in his file, which she hasn't read carefully until now. She notes that Fox has listed among his special interests nineteenth-century American art, in particular Luminism; P. Cady too much admires the Luminist painters, indeed the Romantic painters of the Hudson River School, about whom she wrote in her master's thesis on the "heroic" in American literary culture.

Luminist painters occupy a special place in P. Cady's heart since her grandfather owned several large landscapes by Albert Bierstadt and Thomas Cole, and a small, shimmering-sunrise painting by James Whistler. She cannot resist boasting to Francis Fox that she grew up seeing these paintings in her grandfather's house in Highland Park, New Jersey, most of which were eventually donated to the Williams College museum.

Amazement in Fox's face. A glimmer of hope in the pale-blue eyes.

He's sure that he has seen these, Fox says excitedly, in the Williams museum, which he visited researching a paper he was writing on the Luminist movement . . .

He has never seen a reproduction of the Whistler painting, Francis tells P. Cady. He has never met anyone who even knows about that exquisite painting.

Maybe you will see one at my house—P. Cady resists the impulse to say.

In the headmistress's house, P. Cady has hung several paintings and watercolors remaining from her grandfather's collection; it would be more generous to give them to a museum, but P. Cady is reluctant to part with this connection to her past, just yet.

By this time P. Cady is warming to the candidate: noting too that Francis Fox has listed bird-watching as a particular interest. She feels a frisson of guilt, she'd cut him off abruptly when he spoke of wanting to visit the Pine Barrens.

Her favorite local place to hike and look for birds is the Jorgen Bird Sanctuary at Wieland Pond, she tells Fox. The most beautiful birds you will see there are snowy egrets, great blue herons, (mute) swans, and bluebirds.

Fox nods enthusiastically. *His* favorite birds have been mostly the more common perching birds—cardinals, robins, nuthatches, chickadees. But he is looking forward to seeing more egrets, herons, waterbirds, hawks . . . Never in his life has he seen a bluebird!

"Oh, there are bluebirds here in South Jersey, Mr. Fox. Not as many as there once were, but they are surviving, in bluebird houses specially constructed for them adjacent to open fields. Also, bitterns—including even 'least bitterns,' that are very shy, in the marshes at Wieland Pond."

"We could go together sometime to this—'Wieland Pond' . . . "

An outburst of boyish enthusiasm, which startles P. Cady into silence.

Imagining herself with Francis Fox as a companion! An entirely new idea. Preposterous, of course. Not likely.

(P. Cady rarely hikes with a companion. Though there are women colleagues at the Academy who are also hikers, who often invite her to join them. Her reluctance is, if she hikes with a companion she will have to keep rambunctious Princess Di on a leash, or not bring her at all.)

(Also, it is awkward to hike with subordinates. Teachers whose salaries she helps to determine, whose careers she oversees.)

The subject shifts to music. Fox had piano and cello lessons as a child—never very talented but at least he learned to appreciate "genuinely talented" musicians.

P. Cady laughs in agreement, this was her experience too. Though her mother was quite a talented pianist, for an amateur.

Fox remarks, his favorite piano composer is John Field.

P. Cady laughs again, for what an eccentric thing this is to say! Why John Field, and not Chopin? Liszt? Mozart?

Of course, Francis Fox isn't altogether serious about Field, a little-known Irish precursor of Chopin. Fox is probably the only person P. Cady has met, she says, apart from musical people, who has even heard of Field.

"Well," says Fox ruefully, "—I could play Field. I couldn't play Chopin."

"*I* could play Chopin. But only the slow preludes."

Encouraged by the shift of tone in their conversation Fox removes from his bookbag a half-dozen student portfolios he has brought to show the headmistress of the Langhorne Academy, which his English students at the Newell Johnson School have created. These are oversized journals with striking marbled covers; inside are drawings, watercolors, poems, prose poems. Some of the inserts are printed pages, others are handwritten. P. Cady is impressed that Fox's students have worked so hard to please him. This looks like work more appropriate for upper-level students than middle-school. Fox tells her that he has done some printmaking, bookbinding, he has helped his more talented and motivated students to bind their poetry into chapbooks, which he shows her also.

As if a prep school headmistress isn't inundated with *exceptional student creative projects*! Still, Fox's samples are impressive.

Even more, P. Cady is impressed by a poem of Francis Fox's published in *Nevermore: A Journal of the Poe Society of America* (December 2011), on the occasion of Fox having been named first-prize winner in the Poe Society's annual competition.

"I hope you don't mind, Ms. Cady, I've brought this for you . . . It's a good example of my more recent poetry."

P. Cady sees that there is a personal inscription inside—

FOR P. CADY, WITH WARMEST REGARDS,
FRANCIS HARLAN FOX, APRIL 28, 2013

P. Cady thanks Fox, glancing at the poem of six stanzas, which she sees is a *rhyming poem*, in emulation of Poe. She will read it later, she tells Fox.

"Oh, no need to read it, Ms. Cady! I just wanted you to have it. Not everyone appreciates abstruse verse in emulation of Edgar Allan Poe."

On this jubilant note it seems that the interview has concluded. Forty minutes have passed swiftly. P. Cady rises from her chair, thanking Francis Fox for having returned to Wieland even as Fox murmurs an apology for having not been at his *strongest, emotionally*: it has been a difficult time for him.

He didn't share with the committee but will share with her, he'd lost his beloved dog just two weeks ago, his closest companion for the past eleven years.

P. Cady tells Fox, she is very sorry to hear this. For a moment she has no idea what to say.

She wonders if Fox is such an effective teacher because the effort and ebullience of classroom teaching helps to deflect sorrow . . .

Indeed, Fox's face has lapsed into melancholy. P. Cady sees that he is a sensitive person whose persona belies his truer self. Bravely he came for an interview the previous week, with remarkable energy he taught an eighth-grade class to be observed by strangers, despite his grief after losing his closest companion.

It is one of the terrors of P. Cady's life at the present time, that something will happen to Princess Di. That she will lose *her* closest companion and be obliged to maintain a brave persona as if her heart hasn't been broken . . .

P. Cady asks Francis Fox what breed his dog was, he tells her that the dog wasn't a pedigree but a "mutt" from a rescue shelter in Connecticut: part golden retriever, part boxer, hint of terrier blood.

Francis Fox happily shares with P. Cady pictures on his iPhone of a dog with moist-brimming brown eyes, sand-colored fur, a red-plaid scarf tied about its neck.

P. Cady is moved. What was the dog's name?

"Christabel."

"Ah! Coleridge?"

Of course, Coleridge. Fox is an English teacher. "Christabel" is a poem by Coleridge about purity assailed by sin, sexuality. As P. Cady recalls, it is a sort of vampire poem, not unlike more lurid sensational poems by Edgar Allan Poe.

"Here is Princess Di. I'm afraid she is also a 'mutt'—but an entitled one. Shamelessly spoiled."

Cannot resist showing Fox pictures on her iPhone of the little terrier-hound mix gazing at the viewer with limpid brown eyes.

"Adorable!"—Francis Fox exclaims.

The first dog of his life, Fox tells P. Cady, resembled Princess Di to an "uncanny" degree—"Her name was Bibi."

It is revealed that Francis Fox has been a donor to animal rescue shelters in Quakerbridge, Pennsylvania; Kent, Connecticut; and elsewhere; and that he particularly sponsors elderly "special needs" dogs. It is revealed that P. Cady is a donor to the Wieland Animal Rescue; and that *she* sponsors several "special needs" animals there.

With disappointment P. Cady sees that indeed the interview is ended, unfortunately she has another appointment now. Impulsively she invites Francis Fox to have lunch with her that day if he doesn't mind waiting until one-thirty P.M. She was very sorry to have missed lunch with him the previous week.

There's a private room in the faculty dining room, P. Cady tells Fox, where they could speak at greater length about his ideas of teaching middle-school English and drama.

"Thank you, Ms. Cady! That would be—frankly, that would be wonderful . . ."

Francis Fox smiles a bit dazedly, like one who is taken aback by an unexpected stroke of luck. P. Cady suggests that he stroll about campus, chat with students, visit the library, visit the chapel, return at 1:20 P.M. to this office and she will take him to the dining room.

As soon as Fox has departed P. Cady hurriedly asks her assistant March to call several parties for her: the chair of the Langhorne board of trustees, a personal friend of hers; the director of alumni and development; the director of student life; the assistant head of school; the reunion and class campaign coordinator; the chair and head of theater.

P. Cady apologizes to all for inviting them to lunch at such late notice but it is something of an emergency situation. Truly she is sorry but if they are free she would like them to meet an outstanding candidate for their middle-school vacancy.

"We need to make this candidate—Francis Fox—an offer he can't refuse."

THE NEW LIFE

MAY 2005

W*here Farrell is, Fox shall be*—a witty variant of Freud's boastful *Where id was, there ego shall be.*

No more giddy-felicitous day than May 9, 2005, when "Frank Harrison Farrell" became "Francis Harlan Fox" by order of a petition filed in the Court of Common Pleas of Lower Merion County, Pennsylvania.

Appealing to a family court hearing officer—(who would then take his petition to a judge)—Simon Grice argued that his client had little choice except to change his name: Frank Farrell had been the "blameless victim" of a "savage campaign of defamation" initiated by a vengeful employer seeking to void his faculty contract at the Newell Johnson School in Quakerbridge, Pennsylvania.

"For months, my client was subjected to vilification in the suburban Philadelphia area as his name was leaked to the media by the Newell Johnson School as a 'pedophile molester of middle-school students'—slander that was subsequently rescinded after the school issued a public apology and made a significant settlement. But damage to the reputation of Frank Farrell is irrevocable and so on his behalf I am petitioning the court to allow him to change his name: 'Frank Harrison Farrell' to 'Francis Harlan Fox.'"

Acting on behalf of Frank Farrell, Grice presented copies of documents to the court: Farrell's birth certificate, social security card, and state-issued driver's license; notarized confirmations of Farrell's fingerprint ID and a document confirming that Farrell had no criminal history in any state; a certification that there were no legal judgments, decrees, or other matters against Farrell; and a certified check for three hundred thirty dollars payable to the Lower Merion court.

For this service, Frank paid Simon Grice a fee of twenty-five hundred dollars in addition to the considerably higher fee he'd paid the lawyer for negotiating a settlement with the Newell Johnson School awarding him a full year's salary; a nondisclosure contract forbidding the school to speak of Frank Farrell in any way detrimental to his reputation; and, most wonderfully, the right to oversee letters of recommendation drawn up by the school.

Soon then, it became known that Otto Higg was to retire as headmaster of the school at the conclusion of the term.

The hearing officer returned from the judge's office to inform Simon Grice that his client Frank Farrell had been granted the right to change his name; a revised birth certificate had been issued for him, stapled together with the original birth certificate.

"Congratulations, Francis!"—Grice's manner was typically droll.

Out on the street, Frank Farrell, now Francis Fox, felt a swoon of elation, like one inhaling ether. He'd folded the birth certificate to put in his pocket but removed it to reread another time.

"'Francis Harlan Fox'—my new life . . ."

Grice grunted a vague reply. The men had come to the courthouse in separate cars and were about to part.

"This will never happen again, Simon! I—I am determined."

"The name change, d'you mean?"

"No. The trouble at the school. The misunderstanding."

"The girl cutting her wrists?"

"Well—the misunderstanding."

"Yes. Right."

"Shall we have a drink together? We can celebrate my 'new life.'"

Grice thanked him but explained that he had an appointment in Philadelphia.

"Just a half-hour! To celebrate all that you've done for me . . ."

It was true, Frank Farrell, now Francis Fox, felt much gratitude for Simon Grice though he didn't feel altogether comfortable in Grice's presence; it seemed to him that Grice regarded him with disdainful eyes, when he looked at him at all.

The lawyer was one of those annoying individuals who resist the charms of others, as if out of spite. No matter what he'd said Grice seemed amused by him as an anatomist might coolly appraise a living body, undeceived by its outward appearance.

There have not been many in this category, Frank/Francis thought. Those individuals immune to *him.*

Another time he invited Grice for a drink—"On me, Simon!"—and Grice repeated that he had an appointment in downtown Philadelphia, unfortunately.

"But it's my 'new life,' Simon! Only you and I know."

Wanting badly to review with Simon Grice the terms of the settlement with the Newell Johnson School. A year's salary! A promise of a "highly positive" recommendation! Wanting badly to gloat over the defeat of Otto Higg. Is there anything sweeter than the humiliating defeat of an enemy?

But no, Grice didn't appear to be interested. A final handshake crushing Fox's hand but releasing it almost simultaneously.

"Simon! I'll keep your card . . ." Calling after Grice as he walked away.

But without a backward glance Grice has walked out of earshot.

ONE DOZEN ROSES

APRIL 2013

One dozen blood-red roses are delivered to Katy Cady at 8 West Seventy-ninth Street, New York City, with the triumphant note:

THANK YOU MY DEAR, DEAR FRIEND

THANK YOU FOR YOUR FAITH IN ME

LOVE, FRANCIS

At once Katy Cady calls Francis Fox on his cell phone. Her voice is tremulous as a girl's.

"Do these beautiful roses mean that Aunt Paige has offered you the teaching position?—so quickly? Oh—I am so happy for you, Frank! I mean—'Francis'!"

Aunt Paige. Francis Fox has to laugh, that stone-cold-eyed cunt is someone's *aunt*.

Yes, it is good news, he assures Katy Cady. Yes, the good news has come more quickly than he could have hoped.

Yes, he is very grateful to Katy Cady—*My closest dearest friend.*

Yes, he *is* very happy. Yes, he loves her.

(Yes, he knows she loves him.)

Yes! He is hoping to see Katy Cady soon, he will take her to dinner so that they can celebrate his new position at the Langhorne Academy which (he is sure) he owes entirely to her.

Apologizing, can't talk now, he's in his car, driving, will talk to Katy again soon, hoping to see her soon, *Yes!*—he will call *her*.

■

IN FACT, FRANCIS FOX is on his way to Atlantic City for the first time. One of his *rewards* to himself.

Richly deserved after he was made to grovel at the feet of P. Cady. Glaring-eyed Pallas Athena, size-ten boot on the nape of Francis Fox's neck.

Though in the end he triumphed over the stone-cold-eyed cunt. Yes!

■

KATY CADY. FRANCIS FOX'S oldest friend though (in fact) he has known her for only thirteen years.

If he could love an adult woman, would it be Katy Cady?—possibly.

No way of knowing with certainty if Katy's appeals to her aunt Paige were influential or not but he'd guess *yes*—to a degree.

Katy assured him, she'd written several emails to her aunt in addition to a formal letter on Guggenheim Memorial Foundation stationery praising Francis Fox as a teacher, idealistic educator, lover of literature, loyal friend, person of *unusual integrity.*

To these appeals, Aunt Paige replied tersely, which is characteristic of "P. Cady," but thanked her.

Katy assured him, P. Cady is not the cold dominatrix-type person she appears to be in public but *warm, fair-minded. Generous.*

In any case, Francis Fox will behave as if Katy has really helped him, and he is grateful. It is his principle to flatter people who have been generous to him whether they've actually helped him much at all. One dozen red roses to Katy Cady is damned expensive, but—look on it as an investment.

Conditioning others to think well of us, not to wish to harm us, but to conflate in some way *helping us* with *helping themselves*—this stratagem, Francis Fox has cultivated over the years, following the great B. F. Skinner's tenets of behaviorism. One is always conditioning others in order to make use of them at some future date; one must never condition others in a way to wish one ill. A warm smile, a squeeze of the hand, the communication of tenderness, *listening attentively, or giving that impression*—all these are valuable.

Sweet naïve girl, Katy Cady, practically in tears over the roses! Francis Fox *does* love her, in his way.

Yes, Katy Cady is a *girl*, you'd hardly call Katy a woman except in years which must be about forty by now.

Too old for *him*. By decades. Francis Fox laughs, amused.

It's always amusing to Francis Fox, formerly Frank Farrell, how mature females glance at him with *that coquettish sort of interest* as if imagining that a man who looks like Francis Fox might return their interest, as if in some way it is their right, if they are attractive, still more if they are very attractive, as the world has conditioned them to believe of themselves and expect of others.

Totally unaware that (some) men are immune to them. Indifferent to them. And these men are the ones to exert the most power over them, if it's worth the effort.

Fortunately, Katy Cady has no inflated vision of herself. She understands, she *sympathizes,* that men are not likely to stare after her in the street or devote their lives to her.

Plain-faced girl with eyebrows so pale as to be virtually invisible, scanty eyelashes, eyes of the hue of ditch water, ruddy-cheeked, with limp hemp-colored hair. Already in graduate school Katy seemed middle-aged, a soft comforting presence as of a cushioned easy chair, molded to the contours of a fleshy body. Never was Katy Cady a prepubescent *kitten,* never one of Balthus's slender dreaming vacant-eyed girls.

Never a female of the slightest interest to amorous Mr. Tongue.

Worse, Katy Cady has the most ridiculous name: *Kat-y Cad-y.*

Grating to Francis's sensitive ears, a clumsy-clunky succession of syllables with the charm of a fingernail scraping a blackboard.

He has wanted to ask Katy outright, how can she stand being called such an unmelodic name?—why not ask people to call her Kathy, or Katherine?—but he has hesitated, for perhaps Katy would have no idea what he meant. Her eyes would well with tears of hurt, she would bite at her cuticles, an annoying habit of hers.

They first met in the fall of 2000 in a graduate seminar at Columbia University, in Renaissance drama. Twenty-eight-year-old Frank Farrell had befriended the slightly older Katy Cady sensing how devoted a friend this earnest plain-faced girl might be to him, how grateful for male attention, let alone affection; that Katy turned out to be a brilliant literature student, as well as the daughter of a well-to-do Upper East Side family, were bonuses he felt he'd earned.

"There is a special rapport between us. What the Romantics meant by 'soul-mates.'"

He'd squeezed her hand to suggest the Platonic assurance of a soul-mate rather than the romantic urgency of a lover. They would spend hours together in coffee shops discussing French literary theory and "deconstruction," so abstruse, and so wearying, Frank had to rely upon Katy to decode it for him; it was bullshit, he guessed, but *très chic bullshit*. She helped him write crucial papers, which invariably earned him A's, even as Katy, disadvantaged by her sex as by her unprepossessing appearance, struggled to earn A–'s from their male professors. She was a *staunch supporter* when an (unsubstantiated) charge of plagiarism made by his advisor abruptly terminated Francis's graduate career in English literature.

Katy had gone on to earn a PhD in Renaissance studies while Frank had been allowed to transfer to the Columbia School of Education, to earn a master's degree; a far better fit for his particular talents for, as a (male) middle-school teacher, with his warmly dazzling manner, he would have little serious competition.

It has become one of the curiosities of their friendship, that Katy Cady imagines she knows Francis Fox intimately, while in fact Katy knows nothing of his personal, private life. She knows nothing of his (fatal, delicious) predilection for prepubescent girls; she knows nothing of the real reasons he has had to seek new employment, abruptly and "unjustly" dismissed from teaching positions at several schools.

When Francis informed Katy that he'd changed his name from "Frank Farrell" to "Francis Fox"—that he'd had no choice, his former name / reputation had been defamed by the headmaster of the Newell Johnson School, "inexplicably, and cruelly"—she believed him unquestioningly.

A more skeptical person would have been suspicious of Frank Farrell / Francis Fox by then but dear Katy, for all her intelligence, and the breadth of her learning, is totally devoid of suspicion where Francis Fox is concerned. She will hear no criticism of him.

Indeed, Francis is not unlike Harry Houdini. Finding himself entrapped, *seemingly insisting upon getting himself entrapped,* then wriggling free. A charmed life!

Occasionally in the throes of an infatuation Francis has been tempted to share his secret with Katy: an infatuation with one of his kittens. How he longs to talk about—*Miranda, Cecilia, Taylor, Chloe* . . . He can share his obsessions only with strangers, anonymously on the Internet. Though Katy seems warmly understanding of Francis, and *forgiving* by nature, she may be repelled if he speaks too frankly, and their friendship will abruptly end.

Once, visiting Katy Cady in New York, he took his friend to the Metropolitan Museum, so that, as if by chance, they might stroll past several Balthus paintings. When he asked Katy what she thought of the paintings her reply was vague, disappointing—she'd heard of Balthus, of course, but knew nothing about his work. She could see that there was a sort of "classical" look to the portraits of young girls, and the curiously flat interiors; but that was all Katy saw. What to Francis Fox were highly charged, erotic images that captured his attention utterly were, to Katy Cady, no more emotionally charged than the most banal Cubist still lifes.

As he lingered staring at the luminous paintings Katy grew restless beside him. At last, hesitantly, she tugged at his arm—"Frank?"

Roused from his trance he was startled, annoyed; wishing that
ruddy-cheeked Katy Cady were somewhere far away to leave him
here with Balthus's dreaming girls, alone. But he managed to smile at
her of course.

Shyly Katy said, "I always think when I'm with you, Frank, that
people will see us, and think we are a couple."

"Well. We are a couple. Who says that we are not?"

A startled light glistened in Katy's eyes, Francis Fox would long
recall.

Was he misleading his dear friend? Or was it beyond Francis's responsibility, that Katy Cady was so eager to believe him?

That evening at dinner Katy surprised Francis with a gift: a man's
sterling silver ring inset with an octagonal stone, that had once belonged to her father.

In fact, the ring had originally belonged to her father's father. A
family heirloom, who knew how old.

Francis was embarrassed by the gift, and by Katy's pleasure in giving it to him. He protested, he couldn't accept such a special ring, an
heirloom; Katy should keep it, to give to someone within her family.

"Oh but you are closer to me than almost anyone else in my family, Frank. It's a 'friendship ring'—I want you to have it." A blush rose
into Katy's face.

It would be cruel to deny Katy, he'd thought. And the ring fit, or
nearly.

On his right hand, third finger. *Friendship ring.* Not to be confused with a wedding band. The ring was indeed sterling silver and
the smooth dark octagonal stone an onyx. Francis would have it ap-
praised, the work of a well-known Manhattan silversmith of the early
1900s, now worth approximately two thousand dollars, considerably
less than he'd anticipated.

Francis saw that Katy's eyes were welling with tears. Clearly
she'd been planning this intimate dinner (at the Carlyle, elegantly

dim-lit and quiet) that meant so much to her and so little to him. Thinking, with a stab of guilt—*The poor girl is in love with me. God help her.*

No choice but to accept the ring. A gentleman does not disappoint. It was of obviously high quality, exquisite silverwork, blunt black onyx stone, giving to Francis's ordinary-sized hand a certain macho brio.

"You're very kind to me, Katy."

"You're very kind to *me*, Frank."

Over the years Katy Cady has remained the most loyal of friends: she writes to Francis frequently, and doesn't take offense if he is slow to reply, or fails to reply at all; she sends him cards, and gifts; sometimes, if she is feeling brash, she signs a card *Your soul-mate Katy.* Like weather, she is always *there.* In her sweetly naïve way Katy seems to be awaiting the occasion when Francis Fox will declare his feelings for her.

Not vanity so much as the desperation of the faithful, Francis thinks. If they persevere their devotion will be rewarded one day by their God.

But how boring it is, to be *adored* by a person for whom one feels nothing but the most *sibling* sort of friendship.

Circuitously, Francis has hinted that, if he could secure a decent-paying teaching position in New York, he might move there; he and Katy might rent apartments in the same building. (*Rent?* Francis assumes that Katy would purchase a condominium, and another for him—she would call it an "investment.") When he visits New York he stays with Katy in her three-bedroom brownstone on West Seventy-ninth Street at Central Park; a guest room is always available for him, *his room.* Together they visit museums, attend plays, concerts, gallery openings. Katy is always eager to introduce Francis to her friends.

Yes, he has several times relied upon Katy, to loan him "emergency funds"—the (tacit) understanding between them being that Francis need not repay the loan, will indeed forget the loan, nor will Katy remind him—ever!

Eventually, when he is older, and the spell of his kittens has abated somewhat, as he guesses (hopes) may happen in middle age, Francis thinks he might travel to Europe with Katy Cady. She has spoken longingly of Rome, Florence, Venice—how Francis would love these cities! Katy is a rich girl: she has an inheritance: like many good-hearted persons she is embarrassed about having money, and so it is a kindness to allow her to pay for their excursions together, to allevi-ate her sense of guilt.

But might Francis marry Katy Cady? One day? There is that pos-sibility, as appealing to him as hospice care to a person not yet hospi-talized.

When Francis has had to seek new employment Katy Cady's first suggestion has always been the Langhorne Academy. Despite its prestige, Langhorne has been one of the last places at which Francis has wanted to teach; the very name is dull as a dirge; so far from New York City, in a remote, mosquito-infested region of New Jersey!—but this time, he had few other options, for every other school to which he applied had turned him down.

Despite the nondisclosure contracts forbidding former employers to speak ill of Francis Fox, and despite the surpassingly enthusiastic letters of recommendation they have written for him, his reputation as a *difficult person, problematic hire for middle school* has begun to be known in the small world of prestige private schools, as over time a deathly radioactive element might leak from its solid lead container.

"But you will love the Langhorne Academy, Francis!"—Katy de-clared. "It has a remarkable library for a prep school, first editions of your favorite writers."

(*Favorite writers?* Francis can't recall what these might be.)

With girlish pleasure, like one plotting with a best friend, Katy prepared Francis for his interview(s) at Langhorne. In several lengthy phone conversations she told him about "Paige Cady"—the headmis-tress's area of specialization in nineteenth-century American literature and art, her predilection for hiking, bird-watching, the piano music of Chopin and Liszt, dogs—"Any talk of dogs will win over Aunt Paige, I promise! She has an adorable little terrier-hound mix with a sweet, silly name, I forget what it is." Cunning Francis Fox would wear a bow tie and a tweed sport coat for his private interview with the headmis-tress; in his personal research into the Cady family of New Jersey he'd discovered photographs of P. Cady's father, Randall, a prominent New Jersey educator, who wore bow ties and tweed sport coats. He made sure he could discuss the Luminist artists—Frederic Church, Albert Bierstadt—since P. Cady's grandfather was a collector of their art. (Enormous *très kitsch* landscapes blandly picturesque as calendar art, ideal for jigsaw puzzles. On Francis Fox's walls are reproductions of Balthus's dreamy girls gazing at themselves in mirrors, or, as if teas-ingly, at Francis Fox gazing mesmerized at them.)

With a kind of girlish boastfulness Katy had said, "Aunt Paige! People are so afraid of her, who don't know her. 'P. Cady' wields good-ness the way Amazons wielded swords."

And: "Aunt Paige appears cold, heartless, 'disinterested.' But she's fiercely loyal if she decides that you're worthy. She gives away most of her money, she doesn't take a salary from her school at all. She went to Bryn Mawr. She is the very embodiment of the honor code. She feels that women should be 'leaders.' She has told me that I'm her 'favorite' niece. So I think you will like each other."

Katy Cady clapped her hands together like a schoolgirl delighted with herself.

But Francis Fox's private interview with P. Cady did not begin promisingly at all. The headmistress barely glanced at him when he entered her office, rudely she riffled through his application folder as if she'd never seen it before. Only half-listening to him—and he was speaking so winningly!

P. Cady was an intimidating figure, his height or taller. Broad slop-ing shoulders, an androgyne face, impassive, composed. Nothing *womanly* about her. Of an age beyond forty—fifty? Handsome sculpted face, the face of Pallas Athena, deep-set eyes that gave the impression of not blinking, as a reptile's eyes might, lidless. And her voice too, deep-modulated, composed.

Why do you think, Mr. Fox—"Francis"—that you would be happy at the Langhorne Academy? Is there any particular reason you are inter-ested in us?

Enunciating "Fox"—"Francis"—as if she knew very well that these were fictitious names which she found laughable.

Only barely did Francis Fox manage to control his mounting rage at the woman. The condescending manner, the reptilian gaze. High-ceilinged office, massive mahogany desk. Chinese carpet on the floor, frayed with time yet still vividly colored. A clutter of framed diplomas, photographs of P. Cady with (presumed) persons of significance in academic gowns, brass plaques, citations.

The merest caprice of chance had established "Paige Cady" as his superior, and "Francis Fox" as her inferior, groveling for her approval: if there were justice in life, in this *feminist-saturated* culture, their situations would be reversed, and *she* would be begging *him*.

Gritting his teeth, grinding his back molars like a dog eager to bite but restraining itself. Perspiring with the need to say something rude to the Langhorne Academy headmistress that would resonate through decades, stride out of her office slamming the door.

But no. Francis Fox knew better. *Do not ever make an enemy needlessly. Of an enemy, make a friend.*

How foolish it would be, how myopically counterproductive, to have come so far, not once but twice, to the Langhorne Academy in South Jersey, and sabotage his prospects with a futile insult!

With effort steering the interview in a direction favorable to him. As in a rudderless boat, steering with a pole, resisting the powerful current, surreptitiously.

In the end Francis Fox triumphed. Just barely. P. Cady smiled at him, baring her teeth in a smile like Medusa's, rose from behind her desk, and shook his hand.

Invited to lunch, dazed with the turn of fortune. And, not surprisingly, the offer that followed: the highest salary Francis Fox had ever received, with a three-year renewable contract.

Still, he hates "P. Cady." For making him grovel, pressing her boot on the nape of his neck.

Though he does respect the woman—true. Has to admire her.

No ordinary woman, as Francis Fox is no ordinary man: *alpha female, alpha male.*

An unmistakable rapport between them, she had to acknowledge finally.

Still—P. Cady is on Francis Fox's *revenge list*. For the time being.

Recalling with a smile how elated he felt, departing after lunch at the Langhorne Academy. In his car in the visitors' parking lot where no one could observe him ripping off the bow tie, tossing it onto the floor by the passenger seat, where, he sees, the damned thing still is.

■

CELL PHONE RINGS, CHRIST!—it's Katy Cady again. Wanting (he guesses) to thank him another time for the roses, congratulate him another time on the new teaching job but he doesn't answer, lets the phone ring and go to voice-mail.

Entering now the (dismal) outskirts of Atlantic City. To his left the Atlantic Ocean—suet-colored, just barely visible behind garish billboards, run-down motels, fast-food restaurants. In the near distance are sleek glittering high-rises—*Borgata Hotel Casino, Harrah's Atlantic City, Golden Nugget*.

Early dusk, lights are coming on. He's looking for *Econo Lodge,* 1829 Ocean Highway, near the boardwalk. Stuck in a stream of slow-moving traffic.

Atlantic City is less than an hour's drive from the quaintly "historic" Village of Wieland. Distant as another planet.

He will be moving to Wieland by the end of the summer. Beginning his new life.

He has vowed: no more *kittens*. At least, not his girl-students.

In the meantime, checking out Atlantic City. First time, (surely) last time. Too squalid for his refined taste.

Text message from *E*. This is the third text message, each time *E* has told him the name of a different motel, not *Econo Lodge* after all but *Flamingo Inn* a half-mile up the strip.

At such times he is strongly tempted to keep driving. But, he never does.

Meets *E* in the parking lot, has to be her, skinny stork legs, high-heeled boots to her knees, faux-leather miniskirt, dyed-maroon hair unless it's a wig, probably a wig, synthetic as nylon. Small squinched-in face, heavily made up, not bad-looking but pasty-white skin, he wonders if she's a crack addict like most hookers.

Hiya, mister!

Hi.

In the motel room, a strong smell of disinfectant, insecticide. Lightbulb has burnt out in one of the squat pear-shaped bedside lamps. Cigarette scorch-burns on the chenille bedspread. On a bureau, a vase of grimy artificial roses.

He's a teacher-type, librarian? Probably married with kids. Shy, eyes evasive. Doesn't know what to do with his hands. Not accustomed to this sort of thing, E takes the initiative. He's awkward, an amateur, *she's* the pro.

C'mere! I won't hurt you.

Mister? Hey.

Feels a moment's intrigue, the erotic possibilities of pity, but no, the hooker is too old, in the glaring overhead light she's at least twenty. Skinny-scrawny body but not prepubescent as he was promised.

Stunned by disappointment. A mean little whiplash of a taunt—*What'd you expect, sucker?*

He's looking as if he'd like to be anywhere else but here, hesitating as if he's about to leave, toss some bills onto the bed and flee, muttering some sort of apology or excuse, but no, before the mascara-inked eyes he's filling slowly with contempt as with a virulent gas. Not a shy fumbling guy after all is he? Not a sucker is he? Beneath the cosmetic mask E's composure fades rapidly as he orders her—*Strip.*

Hookers are cows, contemptible. Pimps are bulls. In this sleazy room he has rented, thirty-nine dollars plus tax, *he* has the authority of the pimp.

There follows then a confused scene as of a handheld camera jostled. The mascara-eyes blink rapidly, moistly. Pupils like caraway seeds. *I said, strip.*

The sequined tank top is loosened on the skinny torso, a scattering of pale bruises revealed on the pasty-pale chest. (He feels a sharp sensation of desire, seeing these bruises.) Wriggling out of the faux-leather ridiculous skirt. The glistening-red mouth is agape like a fish's. She is frightened. She has misjudged him. In a shaky brash voice she demands cash up front, he says *No.*

He has changed his mind, he says. Now that he's had a look at her. *Get dressed. Get out. You're ugly. You're too old. You're diseased. You're a crackhead. You disgust me. Go the hell away.*

With a cavalier gesture he tosses bills onto the bed, tens, twenties, not many, he's suffused with scorn, triumphant with scorn, turns and leaves the acrid-smelling room without a backward glance.

VI

A NEW LIFE

A FOX AT THE LANGHORNE ACADEMY

FALL TERM

2013

And so, he has learned caution.

In this new setting, in this *new life*. Wieland, New Jersey, which is no-man's-land, a place of exile he will learn to call home.

He *will* call home, and be happy here. He has vowed.

Maybe he will marry? Maybe—it's time!

∎

MARRIAGE, THINKS FRANCIS FOX wryly, is usually preceded by *falling in love*.

The greatest of all challenges for a man: *falling in love*.

(That is, with someone beyond the age of consent.)

(For Francis Fox *is determined not* to court disaster ever again. After nearly being arrested at the Newell Johnson School, and that misunderstanding at the Kent School, he has *learned his lesson* for the final time.)

He has moved to Wieland, New Jersey, at the end of the summer. With the assistance of his dear friend Katy Cady he has acquired a position on the middle-school faculty at an excellent prep school—

though seemingly remote, the Langhorne Academy is about equidistant from Atlantic City and Philadelphia. (Not that Francis Fox has any desire to explore decaying Atlantic City again. *He does not.*)

On (wittily) named Consent Street he has acquired an apartment at a reasonable rate within walking/bicycling distance of the Langhorne Academy. He has acquired a secondhand English racing bike from a shop in town. He has located a Kroger's, a Walgreens, a wine-liquor store where (so soon!) the proprietor recognizes him when he enters. He has introduced himself to both librarians at the Wieland Public Library, taking pleasure in their startled-woman-eyes lifting to his face like candles lit.

In the doldrums of late August stoically awaiting the start of the fall term and his first paycheck. In the doldrums of late August determined to remain calm. Calm before storm.

One drink a day!—maximum. Or at the most, two.

Through long solitary days on Consent Street sequestered in the air-chilled apartment with shades drawn against the tropical South Jersey heat scrolling his way through myriad websites on the Internet as a snail makes its way through clotted filth.

He has vowed *No.* Yet, *No* is not so easy to maintain.

Chat rooms, websites, "subscription only"—*Nymphets, Girls at Play, Little Heidi, Princess Lo, Little Jills & Big Jacks.* Contemptible, most of these. Not worth his attention. Crude, dopey, lacking *élan.*

Mr. Tongue has a (private) collection of select kitten photos taken surreptitiously on his cell phone over the years but *never would a gentleman post such precious mementos* on the common coarse Internet for sick-fuck morons to drool over.

"*Nyet.* Not ever."

Relief when at dusk the torpor-heat begins to lift. In khaki shorts, T-shirt, running shoes walking/running/walking on the near-deserted school campus which turns out to be larger than he expected—seven hundred twenty acres.

A good deal of the Langhorne property is playing fields, stretches of close-mowed grass kept alive and brightly green by underground sprinkler systems.

Affluence!—Francis Fox's heart becomes a fist, bitterly he resents the rich.

Rich people's children, *his* students. He is their *Mr. Fox*.

Hire Fox to fuck your children. Fuck you all, thank you very much.

Pausing to stare, smiling: in the near distance, foxes run gliding like flame across the playing field into a grove of trees.

These appear to be mature foxes. Beautiful wild creatures surviving at the periphery of the suburban and the rural.

The most feline of canine mammals. Lush tails, russet-red coats, shiny black muzzles, and shining eyes. Elusive at dusk, stopping the observer dead in his tracks.

Lifting a hand to wave. A fox freezes, stares. Fellow carnivore.

But no, the fox has vanished. Both foxes have vanished. *He* trudges on.

A loop of the Langhorne property eventually takes Francis Fox into a no-man's-land belonging to Atlantic County, not so well-maintained, bike paths, coarser grass, burnt-out grass, litter. High-pitched laughter of local kids, high-school louts, smoking something acrid-dry—is it weed? Here in Wieland?

Staring at him in silence. Is he a cop? Is he a *fag*?

Hair shaved close to their skulls. Lips twitching with the need to sneer.

He's a stranger in Wieland. No one they've seen before. Interloper in their space wearing dark-tinted aviator glasses, hair grown long and wavy onto the nape of his neck. A silver ring on his right hand glitters.

Not sure, maybe he *is* a cop? Or—*fag*?

Still, Francis Fox is in charge. Teacher-authority. In no haste turns with a casual lift of his hand, might be signaling *Hi, goodbye, guys* or might be signaling *Fuck you, losers.*

Returns to the Langhorne property without a glance behind him.

(With a part of his mind envisioning one of the skinheads taking aim at his back with a .22 rifle. Skinhead-buddies high on weed urging him *Pull the trigger, whack the fag!*—but with imperturbable sang-froid Francis Fox refuses to glance back, still less to break into an undignified run.)

(Here in South Jersey in what circle of Hell to which he has been exiled, how appropriate to be murdered by local anonymous louts, die shuddering face in the dirt, dragged into the brush, rot and dissolve to skull, rib cage, scattered bones no one will ever identify. Francis Fox reverts to Frank Farrell reverts to no one, nothing.)

Just slightly abashed he returns to the campus. Fortunately no one is here to observe him sweating, short of breath.

Indeed the Langhorne Academy is an impressive place. Stolid-stone buildings facing a grassy square. Twelve-foot ebony obelisk commemorating the founding of the school in 1811 by abolitionist Quakers.

On a plaque in front of the library it is noted that in the 1880s, the renowned architect Frederick Law Olmsted, Sr., was hired to design the main campus in emulation of British public (that is, private) schools Eton and Harrow except that, from the start, the Academy was coeducational.

So accustomed to "historic" private school campuses, Francis Fox scarcely sees them any longer. *His* habitat, where a fox is as camou-flaged as a lion amid tall sere grasses in the African plain.

Predator, prey. The most desired prey is the prey that has no idea it is being *preyed upon.*

The most desired prey is grateful to be *preyed upon.*

Still, Fox has promised himself *Nevermore!* Not here.

■

SCHOOL SPIRIT. IF YOU don't feel it, you can easily give the impression of feeling it.

To that end Francis Fox takes care to attend school sporting events. Mr. Fox will be seen at two or three football games a semester, boys' basketball is always watchable, girls' volleyball, basketball. Mr. Fox sits in the bleachers with other lone faculty members. He cheers, applauds. He congratulates winning teams. He commiserates with losing teams. He tries not to stare too avidly at the younger cheerleaders. It has never (yet) been the case that one of Mr. Fox's girl-kittens has been on a school team nor would he wish to see one of them panting and sweating on a basketball court, wings of perspiration dampening her uniform, or galloping along a hockey field wielding a stick like a Fury. *His girls are not athletic.*

Their ankles are nearly as slender as their wrists. Gently he can circle both with his thumb and forefinger. Nor do they—ever—(usually)—*sweat.*

Never does Francis Fox socialize with students. Not a good idea even if they beg you.

For it is not in gatherings that Francis Fox comes *most alive.* That is strictly *in private.*

■ ■ ■

SURPRISING TO LEARN THAT the Langhorne Academy has a large staff for a relatively small school: one hundred and five teachers, eight hundred and sixteen students.

Of these eight hundred and sixteen students nearly seven hundred are residential students living in four houses on campus: the Lower Division, the Quad, the Crescent, and the Upper-Fifth (seniors). The remaining are day students who live in the area and commute from their homes to the school.

Not that Francis Fox is calculating, but: in the past he has learned that residential students are off-limits since their close proximity in the residences and their extreme curiosity about one another greatly increases the likelihood that, if one of them enters into an intimate relationship with anyone, but particularly a teacher, very soon everyone in the residence will know about it.

No nightmare quite like such exposure. That morning you are summoned to the headmaster's office before your first class . . .

Nothing like that will happen here in Wieland. Or ever again!

Succession of days leading to the start of the fall term. Faculty meetings, staff meetings. Already Francis Fox's face aches with smiling. But he *is* smiling.

Welcome Back! reception at which a cursory assessment of colleagues does not yield much promise: most of the plausibly marriageable women appear to be already married, and of these, few would be

of interest to Francis Fox in any case even as most of the apparently
unmarried women are of absolutely no interest to him; possibly it's
the grave atmosphere of the Rotunda (as the Olmsted-designed
building is called) but with its poor acoustics and shadow-casting
lighting even young persons look middle-aged as the middle-aged appear on the cusp of *elderly.*

Yet undiscouraged Francis Fox makes his smiling way through the
gathering like a sea lamprey through a school of oblivious lake trout.
Gripping a plastic cup containing cloyingly sweet sherry. Pausing to
be greeted repeatedly, hand shaken, plastic name tag squinted at—
Francis Fox. Amid a blur of faces after twenty fatiguing minutes by
desperate chance meeting the greenish-gray gaze of *Imogene Hood,*
like Francis Fox a "new hire" at Langhorne, an assistant librarian.

Soon then, these two are speaking animatedly together. As in a
romantic film of the most trite sentiment yet vast relief, drowning
persons grateful for a proffered hand in rescue, giddy with relief—
Are you the one? The one who will save me?

A sudden couple, Francis Fox and—(what is the woman's
name?—he hasn't heard clearly)—beneath the leaded-glass dome of
the Rotunda at the edge of the gathering where the din isn't so loud.
Scarcely does it matter what is said, most of it will be quickly forgotten, where are you from, where have you taught before, have you
found a place in Wieland?—where?

Titles of books suitable for twelve- and thirteen-year-olds, reading
lists, required, recommended, on reserve in the library—a subject of
(presumed) mutual interest.

Animal rights?—somehow, the subject has shifted, Imogene
Hood (for that is the newly hired librarian's name) is speaking passionately, Francis Fox inclines his head to listen, national animal
rights legislation is badly needed, campaigns against meat-eating,
vegetarianism, veganism, each year more idealistic young people forswear meat, many forswear dairy products, salvation of the planet,
meat-eating is retrograde, cattle grazing on huge swaths of land a
doomed and futile practice, cruelty of factory farms, agribusiness,
climate change, *it is not too late.* Francis Fox is touched that his

librarian-colleague feels so intensely about this subject, of course Francis Fox feels intensely as well, snubbing a platter of that particularly delicious salty-greasy appetizer *pig-in-a-blanket* for indeed such crude meat is repellent, disgusting. *He* has not had a steak in years, doubts that his stomach could digest beef now.

None of this is remotely true. Much else will be uttered by Francis Fox that is not remotely true, he is intrigued to discover what it will be in this young woman's company.

For he is feeling how fortunate he is, exiled in Wieland, New Jersey, as in one of the more remote circles of Hell, to have found an unattached female so soon, of his approximate age, reasonably attractive, obviously intelligent yet warmly friendly, overeager yet not embarrassingly overeager, in flat shoes of the kind called *ballerina* which schoolgirls used to wear (but no longer), so that she stands an inch or two shorter than Francis Fox.

Never will Francis Fox stand beside a woman who is taller than he, nor even his own height, if he can help it! An instinct of which he is only part aware.

At his most winning, in such circumstances. That gap-toothed smile, manly yet not *too* manly.

To condition others to like you—that is the challenge of any human encounter.

To condition others to like you so that you have blocked their inclination to dislike—distrust—you: that is the challenge.

Imogene Hood: like any girl who has grown too tall too quickly in school she carries herself with an air of awkward apology, inclined to stoop, to ingratiate herself with others. Her forehead is creased with earnestness. Her smile is aggressively friendly. Her prematurely silver hair flutters about her narrow face. Even as she laughs like a schoolgirl at a droll witticism of Francis Fox's her gray-green eyes regard him warily—*I have been hurt badly in the past, I am not sure if I am willing to be hurt again.*

He will not hurt this woman, Francis Fox thinks gallantly. No more than he would squash a flailing butterfly beneath his heel.

Their meeting at the reception, the warmth and vigor of their conversation, has not gone unnoticed among their new colleagues, Francis Fox senses with a little stab of pride. For of all attributes, it is *normal* that Francis most craves: *normal male.*

Altogether natural then that Francis invites Imogene to have dinner with him after the reception at the historic Wieland Inn, if she is "free"—rapid-blinking surprise and slow-stunned delight suffusing the librarian's face flushed from sherry to which she is not accustomed, murmuring *Yes thank you, Francis. What a, a lovely idea . . .*

And so it will happen, Francis Fox will escort Imogene Hood to a succession of Langhorne Academy events. Student concerts, student plays, student exhibits. Sports events: where, in the bleachers, Francis and Imogene will be invited to sit with their (married) colleagues.

In Wieland, Francis Fox and Imogene Hood will be acknowledged as a couple. They will be acknowledged as an ideal couple—*so suited for each other.* English teacher, librarian—*bookish.* Of the same approximate age, and so it is commendable of Francis Fox not to prefer a younger woman, or a more beautiful woman, as another man of his type might: a handsome bachelor, with a most delightful sense of humor and impeccable good manners. It will be noted how courteous Francis is with Imogene, how intently he listens to her, rarely, indeed never, disagrees with her, no matter how eccentric some of her opinions are; how gracious Francis is helping Imogene with her coat, which seems perversely to have too many sleeves, or too few; opening doors for Imogene, pulling out chairs for her at a dinner table, deferring to her with an incline of his handsome head.

But then it will come to be noted that *Francis Fox behaves in a most gentlemanly way with all women, with—everyone!*

Nor will it go unnoted in Wieland that, in Francis Fox's company, Imogene Hood seems to bloom. She too becomes quick-witted, clever like her companion. She dresses more stylishly—long flowing bright-colored scarves, woven shawls, carved-looking necklaces, shell earrings—(gifts from Francis Fox?). For special occasions Imogene even wears makeup, lipstick, eyeliner, eyebrow pencil which gives to her usually pixilated face an air of startling definition, like those faces in Matisse paintings in which a solid black line will define the profile of a nose, the curve of a jaw.

True, like many naturally shy people Imogene tends to chatter nervously but Francis seems not to mind, nor even to notice. (Though privately regarding his companion as one might regard a runaway baby buggy careening down a flight of steps, you feel a twinge of concern, alarm, yet mostly you feel exasperation, impatience, a wish to see the damned buggy crash and the wailing baby silenced.)

Yes but you could, you know. Marry her.

. . . why in hell?

You know why, asshole.

Establishes himself as *friend* verging onto *companion:* insists upon driving Imogene to the medical center at Bridgeton for a colonoscopy, waits in the hospital lounge contentedly making his way through a swath of seventh- and eighth-grade homework assignments which he reads rapidly as always, his practiced eye skimming through paragraphs of earnest stammering prose pausing only to mark, with a red pen, minor or major infelicities of grammar; then driving drowsy part-sedated Imogene back to her home, declining to come inside, insisting it was no trouble for him, none at all even as Imogene teary-eyed in her weakened state thanks him, thanks him, *thanks him as her dearest friend.*

If at times Francis Fox's attention detaches itself from the social setting in which he finds himself smiling and affable to shift to another dimension entirely, where dwell recollections of the amorous adventures of Mr. Tongue, unfortunately soon resumed in the early weeks of September, despite the very best intentions on the part of Mr. Fox, or if dreamily Francis is recalling exquisite passages in Kawabata's *House of the Sleeping Beauties,* or summoning to his ardent inner eye the coolly erotic *jeunes filles* of Balthus, his pantomime of rapt attention to the bright-dazzling repartee around him is so skillful that no one notices.

P. Cady will invite Francis Fox and Imogene Hood to a dinner in the headmistress's residence, a sign that their status as a *couple* is formally acknowledged, and seemingly approved; at this dinner of twelve guests, most of whom are senior faculty and administrators, P. Cady will say to Francis Fox (who seems forever flummoxed in her presence, uncertain how to address her): "Francis, please! Call me Paige—haven't I asked you?"

Abashed, Francis says hesitantly, "Paige . . ."

P. Cady laughs heartily at Francis Fox, but (he wants to think) with affection.

Francis's first invitation to Headmistress Cady's residence! Amid such exalted company he understands that P. Cady, for whom he feels much ambivalence, if not actual hostility, has decided that she "likes" him—as other heads of school over the years decided that they liked Francis Fox, and before him Frank Farrell, seduced by his intelligence, sense of humor, flair for conversation and for flattery skillfully maintained in their presence as a juggler keeps in the air a half-dozen balls at once.

Typical of such authoritarian personalities, Francis Fox thinks, to single out a subordinate to favor, elevating him above others who might be more deserving; typical of such personalities not to see how naïve their trust might be. Francis smiles thinking that *he* wouldn't be such a sucker as to fall for Francis Fox; but then, he isn't the much-lauded headmistress of the Langhorne Academy blinded by her own vanity, as by her magnanimity, a fifty-one-year-old virgin Pallas Athena led to assume that anything she does, or says, or believes is beyond doubt or reproach.

At the end of the evening P. Cady will draw Francis Fox aside to remark to him that, if he is interested in hiking at Wieland Pond with her and Princess Di, they are usually there most mornings at seven A.M.

Francis will stare blankly at his hostess for a moment, remembering then the picture of the silly little dog she'd shown him on her iPhone, quickly saying, with a delighted smile, "Yes, I would like that very much, thank you—'Paige.'"

∎

". . . SOMETIMES, I think you are just not *here*."

Staring blankly at Imogene Hood, who is accusing him of—what? Not listening to her?

Of course, Francis *has been listening*. While at the same time brooding on a recent interlude in his office in Haven Hall, the bold way in which Mr. Tongue introduced himself to little Genevieve Chambers, whose quivering fawn-body and lovely dark eyes are more vivid to Francis in recollection than the reproachful face of the adult woman before him to whom he says wittily, with his disarming-fox smile, scarcely missing a beat, "But where d'you think I am, Imogene? If I am not *here*?"

Francis Fox is a master of the playful, the *lite*. Never any point in acknowledging a wounded female's reproach.

In the weeks following the *Welcome Back!* reception, Imogene Hood will begin to feel unease with the very affability, geniality, *equipoise* of her friend who is quite unlike any (male) friend in Imogene's experience. Francis is unfailingly agreeable, slick and glossy as a poster. His gap-toothed smile is infectious—Imogene has begun to notice creases bracketing her mouth from the contagion of nonstop smiling. Already in their still-fledgling relationship Francis has given Imogene tasteful gifts of the sort found in museum gift shops—a silk scarf imprinted with images from Van Gogh's *Self-Portrait*, an umbrella with an ebony black cat's head handle. He will have lightly kissed her cheek in greeting and in parting. He is warmly if glibly affectionate with Imogene as with Katy Cady (of whom he has virtually ceased thinking, having failed to answer poor Katy's emails and phone messages most shamefully) and other women who comprise Francis Fox's small but loyal harem of adult-women friends. Francis is good to them when he thinks of them. He is not cruel, or unkind, not usually.

Still, Francis does misjudge women, sometimes. He believes himself a puppet-master of their moods and whims but he may be wrong to assume that essentially they feel for him the sort of superficial emotions he feels for them.

Francis's sense of social interaction is *repartee*, not conversation.

Francis avoids the strain of *conversing* as Francis avoids the tedium of *emotional rapport*.

A paradox which Imogene Hood admits: even as she has become increasingly wistful in Francis Fox's company, she has become increasingly fixed upon Francis Fox, in his absence. As if a part of Imogene's brain understands that this man will never seize her hand, kiss her hard on the mouth, push his tongue into her mouth, make love to her even as, knowing this, she is resolved to *not know*.

Certainly never guessing that her affably smiling male friend in his late thirties is most deliriously deliciously *shamefully* in love with one of his seventh-grade girl-students.

For at school, Francis Fox takes care never to betray his intense interest in any individual students, passing in the corridor, for instance, or dropping by the library. He is as likely to exchange warm greetings with a boy as with a girl—he is *more likely* to pause to chat with a boy than with a girl, in a public setting.

But what has happened to Francis Fox's fantasies of *marriage*? He has not abandoned them utterly.

Until the very eve of his death he will continue to contemplate, as one prods an aching tooth, Imogene Hood as a theoretical wife; more suitable to him temperamentally than Katy Cady?—except that Katy has a trust fund and Imogene has only her Langhorne librarian's salary. In moments of sober repose observing Imogene Hood with the grim-smiling resolve of a hungry carnivore contemplating a head of cabbage.

And so he assures Imogene: "I am *here*. I am always *here*."

Pretending not to know what Imogene is saying, or what the hurt in her pebbly-gray eyes means.

I am falling in love with you, Francis—why do you not care for me?

As if reading her mind, the flurried thoughts passing through her mind, Francis takes Imogene's hand and squeezes it gently, reassuringly.

Imogene swipes at her eyes. "Well. Please ignore me, Francis. I'm just silly."

Silly: a diminished word. Francis is grateful to this woman, she is ideal for him.

In an insipid romantic comedy of the sort in which the swoony British actor Hugh Grant might be a principal performer this would be an emotionally intense/sincere scene in which all that has been suppressed is given a voice, and the would-be lovers are jolted into a new, deepened sense of their feelings for each other; in actual life, in *this* life, such sentimental revelations are rarely realized, let alone voiced.

Soon then, the fraught moment passes, the subject shifts to the timely concern of book-banning in American public schools, reading lists at Langhorne, required and recommended titles appropriate for middle- and upper-level students. Prestigious American private schools are nearly all liberal, and proudly hostile to anything so populist as *book-banning*. Imogene mentions that one of the upper-level instructors has put Nabokov's *Lolita* on a recommended list for advanced placement English students, to which revelation Francis flares up at once, indignant.

"What! *Lolita*! That's ridiculous. *Lolita* isn't fit for high-school students. That novel is *pornography*!"

At first Imogene wonders if Francis is joking. In their previous conversations he has been entirely open-minded, liberal to the point of indifference about such subjects; he has never expressed any view to Imogene remotely puritanical or censorious.

"I'm sure that I read *Lolita* when I was in high school," Imogene says, uncertainly. "Or maybe it was college. Some of us passed a copy around . . ."

"Really!" Francis stares at her, coldly.

Imogene tries to explain: "It's a work of literature, a 'classic'— don't you think? Notable for Nabokov's style. The story is titillating but the prose is actually somewhat dense, for most readers, especially teenagers. It's the wit that makes it palatable."

Francis Fox is frowning, scowling. Imogene is astonished that he seems personally affronted.

"Humbert Humbert is a pervert, and the novel is indefensible. A man of, is it forty, forcing sex on a girl of eleven, disgusting! Also, anatomically impossible."

Imogene has no idea what to think. *Is it anatomically impossible?* She has never given the matter any thought.

For several heated minutes Francis continues to fulminate. He is incensed, he says, that *Lolita* is so admired a novel. He has read it just once—skimmingly. He felt little interest in Lolita, an annoying brat who didn't seem at all "authentic" to him.

Real girls that age are shy, Francis insists, frightened of male adults. The last thing they are is smart-aleck seductresses.

Lolita was obviously based on a young boy, Francis says, and Humbert Humbert was a homosexual in the mode of Aschenbach of *Death in Venice*. Nabokov himself may well have been a homosexual, which would account for the homophobia in his fiction. But Nabokov hadn't the honesty to confront his homosexuality, in the tradition of Marcel Proust, who created his fictional Albertine, a gay man's notion of a girl, in *Remembrance of Things Past*.

There is a reason, a very good reason, Francis says, why Poe's marriage to his thirteen-year-old cousin was a *mariage blanc*. Sexual relations with a girl so young, for a fully mature male, are just *not possible*.

Imogene Hood is confused, why is Francis now talking about Edgar Allan Poe? Why so *urgently*?

"There are just some things only a sick fuck will do! A swine."

(Imogene is shocked—she has never heard Francis utter an obscenity before. She has rarely heard him utter a profanity.)

It will begin to dawn on Imogene, something is very disturbing here. Francis Fox may have been a victim as a child of sexual abuse himself. She has never seen him so agitated.

Wishing she might comfort him—but dares not touch him in such an incensed mood.

Between the two, *touching* has not (yet) developed; though Imogene imagines a time when she might casually reach over and stroke her friend's arm, to calm him . . .

Francis Fox declares that *Lolita* is all the more disgusting because it's a *classic* as well as *pornographic*.

"It's outrageous that students at a school of this caliber are being encouraged to read filth! If it were up to me, I would ban the novel entirely—I wouldn't allow it to be published. I certainly wouldn't allow copies to be in public libraries at taxpayers' expense, let alone in school libraries. I hope it isn't in our library here, Imogene!"

Francis glares at Imogene as if she is personally to blame. Imogene shakes her head vaguely *no*.

Reluctant to confess to Francis that, yes, *Lolita* is on the school library shelf, along with Nabokov's *Speak, Memory* and another title, possibly *Pnin*. But she, a mere junior librarian, newly hired, had nothing to do with this!

Imogene Hood is moved by Francis Fox's certitude on the subject of *Lolita*. He is not being frivolous now, he is not smiling. She admires this—certainty. She will defer to Francis, he has earned her respect; she will fall more deeply in love with him, having seen this side of him—an individual not merely charming, not merely insouciant, but possessed of a strong moral core.

Moral core. A kind of old-style, intrepid manliness rarely seen today.

■

WHICH IS WHY WEEKS later when the Wieland detective Zwender interviews Imogene Hood on the subject of Francis Fox, Imogene will flare up in indignation at the suggestion that Francis might have been "involved" with any of his students.

For cruel, crude rumors have been rampant, since Francis Fox has gone missing.

Since a police investigation has begun, following the discovery of Francis Fox's car in the ravine at Wieland Pond, and the discovery of the (not-yet-identified) human remains at the scene—a firestorm of rumors.

Imogene's reddened and swollen eyes well with fresh tears. The thin, papery-white skin of her face looks strained; her colorless lips tremble; she clutches at a wadded tissue, as a small child might clutch at a rattle. Confronted with a barrage of questions from this steely-impassive stranger who regards her with a flat zinc gaze, Imogene Hood can only stammer in reply.

For she is one of those at Langhorne who still believe fiercely that Francis Fox is alive, somewhere; there has been a misunderstanding, confusion involving his wrecked car and the (dismembered) body in its vicinity, which will be explained when Francis returns.

Imogene insists to the detective that Francis Fox is the *most moral* person she has ever met. Francis Fox would *not ever* behave in any way unprofessional or hurtful to anyone, let alone students. Francis Fox is kind, generous—thoughtful . . .

"Francis doesn't care to 'socialize' with students at all. We were invited as a couple to chaperone the homecoming dance but Francis declined. He said it was 'awkward to mingle socially' with students. He firmly believes that professional educators need to 'establish boundaries' with their students. Which doesn't mean that Francis doesn't like his students, of course he does. And so, I—I resent your line of questioning, Officer—about these ridiculous rumors . . ."

"'Ridiculous,' are they? 'Rumors'?"

"Yes—*ridiculous*. Suggesting that Francis had favorites among his students . . ."

"'Students'?—boys as well as girls? Both?"

"I—I don't know. I don't listen to them. No one would dare say such things to *me*."

Even as another, younger police officer records the interview on an electronic device Zwender takes notes on a small notepad. His manner is unperturbed, impassive; Imogene has the vague impression of a gentlemanly person, in his fifties, with a kindly creased face. There is something awkward, eccentric about the man: he is left-handed, requiring him to hold his hand upside-down as he writes, gripping an old-fashioned fountain pen. With an air of mild curiosity Zwender asks: "And so *you* didn't notice, Ms. Hood, that girls were often in Fox's office? Young girls?"

"Girls are often in teachers' offices! And Francis is a middle-school teacher—of course his students are *young*. This is a school, Officer."

Adding, "Francis is also a faculty advisor. He's in charge of a book club, and a drama club . . . But it isn't that unusual, students sometimes have 'crushes' on any of us."

"On you as well, Ms. Hood?"

"Well, yes. In a way. Is that so hard to believe?" Imogene's voice shakes with exasperation.

Zwender lifts his flat zinc-eyes to Imogene Hood's face. His expression is blank as a sheet of paper.

"It was reported, Ms. Hood, that the door to Fox's office was sometimes shut later in the afternoon when he was in it, having office hours."

"Reported by whom? One of Francis's jealous colleagues? *That* is a rumor."

On this morning, Francis Fox has been missing for twelve days. An absolute identification of the remains in the ravine has not yet been made. It is an interregnum in which it is still possible, though increasingly implausible, to hold fast to the belief that Francis Fox is alive; Imogene Hood has reported to work in the library each morning as if nothing were wrong.

(Well aware that yes, people are observing her. The senior librarian, teachers, students including Mr. Fox's students, some of whom have red-swollen eyes as well.)

(Are they whispering among themselves *Poor Ms. Hood! She and Mr. Fox were secretly engaged . . .*)

"Did you have a close relationship with Francis Fox, Ms. Hood?"

"Y-yes. I am Francis's closest friend in Wieland."

"An intimate relationship?"

"Y-yes . . ."

"How long have you known the man?"

"Just since—the start of school . . . But it seemed that we'd known each other all our lives."

"But he didn't inform you that he was going away last week?"

"I think he'd said—he had tickets for plays in New York. But I don't know that he actually went."

"Why do you say that?"

"Because he—we—he'd made the suggestion that we might go together, or meet in New York, at the start of the fall break. But—something must have happened, Francis seems to have gone alone. I was waiting to hear from him."

Imogene speaks vaguely. Her eyes fill with tears.

"He didn't call you? He didn't explain?"

"He may have, in some elliptical way, which I didn't understand at the time."

"What do you mean—'elliptical'?"

"Sometimes Francis will say something like a riddle. He likes to tease, he has a sense of humor . . . Only afterward you might understand."

"Did you contact him during the week?"

"I—I did. I called, and left a message. I sent emails."

"And he never replied?"

Imogene Hood wipes at her reddened eyes, abashed. "I—I guess not."

"But you are Fox's closest friend in Wieland, you've said?"

"Yes! You've asked me that already."

Imogene Hood is stricken with embarrassment. It is possible— she dreads to think so, but certainly it is possible—that Wieland police officers will discover emails of hers sent to Francis, if they take possession of his cell phone or computer. Possibly, they will discover through interviewing fellow tenants in Francis's apartment building on Consent Street that a woman resembling Imogene Hood came to his apartment not once but several times during the fall break.

Possibly, they will learn that Imogene knocked shyly, daringly at Francis's door. Possibly, they will learn that Imogene shaded her eyes peering through windows in his first-floor apartment seeing nothing, no movement inside.

(Were these actions recorded on surveillance cameras? Imogene feels a rush of something like panic.)

Steeling herself for further questions from Zwender. Humiliating questions, rude questions Imogene Hood isn't sure she can answer truthfully.

"You say that you had an 'intimate' relationship with Fox, Ms. Hood? What exactly does that mean?"

"That—that means that it's a private matter. My privacy, and Francis's."

"Did you cohabit with him? Will we discover items of yours in his apartment, if we search it?"

"I—I don't know. I don't like this line of questioning."

"For instance, in the kitchen in his apartment? In the bathroom? Are we likely to discover things of yours in the medicine cabinet, prints of yours on the faucets? In his bed, traces of—what we call DNA?"

Hot-faced, Imogene refuses to answer. Tactfully Zwender changes the subject, like one backing a vehicle around in a tight space, in no evident haste.

"Well! Is there any likelihood, Ms. Hood, that the remains found in the ravine do not belong to Francis Fox? That is, do you have reason to think that the remains belong to someone else, who might resemble Francis Fox, and the man is elsewhere?"

The tone of this question is unassuming, neutral. Yet, Imogene registers that it is an outrageous accusation made against Francis, as if, in some mad devious plot, he arranged for another body to be discovered in the ravine, unidentifiable.

"No. I don't know. This is very upsetting . . ."

"Francis Fox is who he says he is, you are sure? Not someone else?"

"What do you mean, 'someone else'? I don't understand."

Imogene has the impression that Zwender and the young police officer are sharing a thought, some sort of silent communication, though neither glances toward the other. It is curious that the younger officer seems scarcely involved in the interview, except to record it.

"Are you suggesting that Francis staged the accident? With his car? Is that what you are suggesting?"

Blood rushes to Imogene's face, it is not typical of her to speak so boldly; but the mild-mannered detective doesn't take offense.

"Not at all. I am just asking *you,* Ms. Hood."

"Well—I am just telling *you,* I think the idea is totally absurd, and insulting."

"Just a few more questions, Ms. Hood. We appreciate your cooperation, we know that this is very difficult for you. Can you say—did your friend ever mention 'enemies'? Anyone who might want to hurt him?"

"Of course not! Everyone liked—likes—Francis . . ."

"Enemies elsewhere? At previous schools he'd taught at, before coming here?"

"No!"

"You didn't meet his family? Though you were on 'intimate' terms with him?"

"Not—yet. No."

"You didn't meet other friends of his, from before he'd come to Wieland?"

"No, and *no.*"

"And Fox wasn't suicidal, in your opinion?"

"He *was not* suicidal."

Imogene has become shaky with exhaustion. She hears her voice pleading with the detective that she is very, very tired and can't speak with him any longer. She has a full day at school before her. She does not intend to go home but to fulfill her duties. She has told him everything she knows, please will he *leave.*

"Understood, ma'am. Thank you for your time."

He will leave his card with her, Zwender says. He will get in contact with her again, if necessary.

But then, unexpectedly, though Imogene should be relieved that Zwender and his companion are preparing to leave her office, she finds herself following them to the door as if reluctant to let them go.

"This—is confidential, Officer! You must tell no one. Can you promise?"

"Of course, Ms. Hood. 'Off the record.'"

"Is that device off?"—nervously Imogene indicates the recorder, which the young police officer appears to be shutting off.

"Absolutely, Ms. Hood. You can speak in confidence."

"We—Francis and I—are not formally engaged but there is an 'understanding' between us. Very soon after we met he spoke of me as his 'soul-mate.' He escorted me to school events, and to Philadelphia to the art museum. We had a tentative plan to meet in Manhattan over the break and see an August Wilson play . . . You see, Francis is a very private person. He has shared confidences with me. He has hinted of—abuses—'wounds'—in his childhood. He didn't go into details but it was clearly very traumatic. This is why Francis is so adamant about adults not taking advantage of children. Not being 'involved' with students. Something terrible seems to have happened to him when he was a boy. It might have been a man, or an older boy who victimized him . . . He spoke of being in therapy, and making progress. He is a *wounded being*. But all of this is confidential, Officer. *You must not tell anyone.*" Imogene pauses, breathing quickly.

"Certainly, ma'am."

"Do you—can you tell me—do you have any idea where Francis might be?"

Zwender murmurs something evasive, apologetic.

"He *is*—alive? Isn't he?"

This question, Zwender seems not to hear. He moves away accompanied by the younger officer, a heavyset young man who nods briskly at Imogene without speaking.

Together, the two descend the stairs of Haven Hall and emerge in chill November sunshine, Zwender in the lead, as his younger companion trails behind him, short of breath; neither speaks until, approaching the Wieland police cruiser in the parking lot, Zwender calls back over his shoulder, bemused: "What d'you think, Odom? Poor girl's in love with Fox, eh?"

With difficulty Officer Odom fits himself into the driver's seat of the cruiser. His thick thighs jam against the steering wheel, his barrel-torso only just fits behind it. Even his voice is reluctant, issued with a sullen sort of effort:

"Fox! That sick fuck."

VII

IN BELIAL'S GRIP

THE RETURN

Eight A.M. bell rings.

She enters his homeroom in Haven Hall, second floor. Passes through latticed sunshine reflected in the hardwood floor, less than eighteen inches from him as he feels a kick low in the gut, quickly looks away, groping for the support of something, anything behind him: edge of the desk.

Is it—? Cannot be: Miranda Myles, returned to him.

■

BUT NO! RIDICULOUS.

Slantwise he looks again, of course this twelve-year-old sylph isn't Miranda Myles returned to him from the dead like Poe's Annabel Lee embalmed, perfect and unyielding to mortality, crude decomposition.

This girl, Francis Fox has never seen before. Not so tall as Miranda was but definitely one of those prepubescent females Balthus adored.

In fact, she bears an eerie resemblance to Balthus's *Thérèse Dreaming* except that her legs are not luridly bared but chastely obscured by the pleated skirt of her school jumper.

Through lowered eyes Francis studies the girl whose name he does not (yet) know. Through tremulous lashes, stares. It is a feat he has perfected, staring avidly, hungrily at one of his students—(but few: Francis Fox has highly cultivated tastes)—while giving the impression of scarcely observing anyone at all, in fact standing quite casually, class list in hand, leaning against the teacher's desk at the front of the room, ankles crossed, the very epitome of prep-teacherly poise.

Scanning the class list. Which one is *she*?

Shaken by the sight of the girl. So close, she passed before him on her way to a desk by the window, almost he can imagine a faint fragrance of shampoo . . . After his resolve to be decent, to be wary, to be cautious, to be *celibate*.

Lines of Browning rush through his brain like electric jolts.

> . . . *my scrofulous French novel*
> *On grey paper with blunt type!*
> *Simply glance at it, you grovel*
> *Hand and foot in Belial's gripe.*

Seeing the girl so suddenly, unexpectedly, he feels Belial's grip at his throat. And at his groin.

Belial: along with Lucifer and Beelzebub, one of the all-time great demons. Celebrated in ancient Hebrew texts, in Milton's *Paradise Lost,* and in these lines of Robert Browning's "Soliloquy of the Spanish Cloister"—one of Francis Fox's favorite poems, parts of which he has memorized.

Simply glance, you grovel. Hand, foot, and swollen cock in Belial's sweaty fist.

Sadly true, desire enters through the eyes. At least male desire. Leaping like flame.

He has become uncomfortable in his newly purchased Banana Republic chinos. Feels his face flush with heat. But Mr. Fox is an old pro, he will persevere.

Friendly-smiling Mr. Fox! Seventh graders filing into room 207 of

Haven Hall are pleasantly surprised to see that their English instructor is male. Youngish-avuncular, not at all the stern-Dad type. His smile is gap-toothed but not *too* gap-toothed. His clothes are preppy but not *too* preppy. His russet-brown hair is just slightly long at the sides and back but not *too* long. By the end of the first class period the boys will have detected something conspiratorial, (mildly) rebellious in his manner even as the girls will have detected something so thrilling, so roughly tender, they have not (yet) a vocabulary to express it.

Recalling how, when first he stepped in front of a middle-school class, almost a decade ago at the Newell Johnson School, he felt a surge of elation, a visceral thrill almost sexual in its intensity, realizing how his very *maleness* assured authority. *Maleness* like a scepter in the eyes of prepubescents accustomed to female teachers, all smiles and eagerness to please. *He* smiled with the magnanimity of the sun shining upon all who were fortunate enough to gaze upon him but he did not ever appear eager to please, that was not Mr. Fox's way. Instead, Mr. Fox would encourage students to compete with one another to please *him*.

For weeks Francis Fox has been preparing for this morning. Like an athlete of old who has taken a vow of celibacy to more effectively channel his (manly) strength. For the monastic-looking Langhorne Academy is Fox's *last chance,* he understands. He has been very lucky, before this. He has been astoundingly lucky. And so if here in South Jersey he falls prey to Belial's grip another time, it will be the *last time.*

The last students enter the room. Ludicrous school uniforms: boys in jackets and ties, girls in jumpers, long-sleeved white blouses. It might be the 1950s, that safe time before the rise of feminism.

A final bell rings. In the periphery of his vision the girl who resembles Balthus's Thérèse is seated to his right, by a window, second desk.

Class list! Snakily his gaze slithers down columns of printed names. Have to love the girls' names: *Ashley, Genevieve, Amanda, Olivia, Michelle, Adrienne.* Boys' names interest him less.

Gravely Mr. Fox reads the class list. It is his first encounter with their names, the first time they hear their names pronounced in his voice, there is something ritualistic in this for Francis Fox knows that children this age, regardless of their (relative) insignificance in the world, take their names very seriously, and are easily embarrassed by them.

Politely he tells them: if he has mispronounced a name, will they please correct him; and if they have another name, a nickname, which they prefer, will they please tell him?

Always a kind of hush as he reads names on the first day of class. In this case Mr. Fox too feels a frisson of suspense.

"'Chambers, Genevieve'"—the third name he reads, which is *her* name.

Shyly she lifts her hand. A girl who, for all her beauty, is uneasy in her body, uncertain of her attractiveness, her worth. On the class list Mr. Fox places a small star beside her name.

Other students merit mere checks. Mr. Fox's special girls, *kittens-to-be,* small stars.

"'Genevieve' is French, elegant—most unusual." In a kindly voice he speaks so that the girl will know that he isn't teasing but serious.

"People call me, like, 'Gen' . . . "

"*I* prefer 'Genevieve.'"

By this time the girl is blushing. Lifting beautiful widened dark eyes to his face as in that instant Francis Fox's vows of celibacy melt away, of no more substance than cotton candy in the rain.

Sharp intake of helium, filling lungs, heart. Shot in the heart.

■ ■ ■

My body of a sudden blazed;
And twenty minutes more or less
It seemed, so great my happiness,
That I was blessèd and could bless.

This rhapsodic stanza from William Butler Yeats's poem "Vacillation" Mr. Fox recites to the class. By custom it is his "first day" poem with which he dazzles seventh graders.

(Secretly, it is Francis Fox's ode to himself: his sense of himself in a classroom where, in the eyes of twelve-year-olds, unobserved by skeptical adults, he is suffused with certitude that he is indeed *blessèd,* and can *bless.*)

First days, first impressions. Francis Fox believes in strong *first impressions.*

It is inspiring even to Francis, hearing himself speak in exalted terms of the "challenging path" that lies before them over the course of the fall semester.

He tells them—*assures* them—that they will learn to write in his class. They will learn to think with clarity and force. They will learn to observe. They will learn to doubt and question. They will learn to expand their vocabularies even as they will acquire the skill to write sentences using the fewest, most effective words possible.

Selections from an anthology of classic American literature they will be reading, critiquing. Papers they will be writing, projects they will choose, a personal journal due at the end of the term—"All of it your original work. Unique to *you.*"

Looking about the room as he speaks, *his* room. Already as he read the class list with the aplomb of a magician Mr. Fox memorized the students' names, when one of them raises a hand to answer a question he will call the student by name, impressing them all. There is no need for him to look pointedly at Genevieve Chambers in the second-row seat beside the window, of course he is well aware of her, the little Balthus beauty, he is performing for *her* as the others look on.

For a *kitten* in any class of Mr. Fox's more than justifies the effort he expends upon the class lavishly, extravagantly, their Houdini.

Fact is: the girl is *there,* she will be *there* and in his homeroom tomorrow, and the day after tomorrow, week following week until the end of the term in mid-December. Seated in an ideal position to gaze up at him like any adoring *kitten.*

For in his innermost heart Francis Fox isn't an adult male but a prepubescent like these twelve-year-olds. All of his life shimmers before him, an untrodden path, unexplored; not a much-trodden path, littered and defaced, along which he is staggering no longer young, losing his looks by inexorable degrees and filling up with self-loathing as a septic tank fills up with excrement . . .

Time for a joke! He has been purposefully intimidating them, scaring them. Now time to make them laugh. Give them permission to laugh. Keep their eyes riveted on you. Move about the room but do not appear nervous. Do not *pace*. Lace your remarks with mild expletives—*hell, damn, God damn*—that make them giggle. Encourage them to think that you are one of them. Almost.

Their first homework assignment, due the next day, is a "carefully considered and original" critique of a Robert Frost poem from the anthology. The Langhorne Academy is famous for its high standards, its heavy workload. Where public schools have lowered standards and cater to infantile "contemporary content" the most select private schools adhere to classics, high-quality authors like Frost.

"Keep in mind: you are not in elementary school any longer. The transition from sixth to seventh grade can be a little rocky."

With relief they see: Mr. Fox will not humor them, but Mr. Fox will guide them. Here is an adult who is *on their side*.

By the end of the hour he has won them over entirely. He will be their puppet-master, they will adore Mr. Fox all the days of their lives.

WOMANSPEAK

SEPTEMBER 2013

He is listening. *Is* listening.

As the world is suspicious of a man *alone* so the world is not-suspicious of a man who is one-half of a *couple.*

Walking together, where?—somewhere.

Hasn't heard a word the woman has been saying for the last ten, fifteen minutes in her warmly animated earnest voice though Francis Fox is listening, certainly he *appears to be listening,* as Imogene Hood speaks with (girlish) (grating) enthusiasm of the excitement of returning to school in the fall, that feeling of exhilaration, how contagious their students' enthusiasm is, almost you feel that you are *their age* again . . . Hears himself agreeing affably if vaguely even as his thoughts swerve in another direction, how like a racing car driver he is, wrenching the wheel to one side, what pleasure in veering off the roadway and into the forbidden, in Belial's sweaty grip recalling with an inward swoon the Balthus–look-alike–girl in his homeroom and his eleven A.M. class drawing his attention to her like a magnet, glowering radioactive magnet at which he must not / must look.

That breathy-giggly voice he'd had to stoop to hear—*People call me, like, "Gen"* . . .

But not Mr. Fox. *He* prefers "Genevieve."

(He prefers "Genevieve" for its poetic proximity to "Guinevere," fated queen of Sir Arthur, of whom, he's sure, twelve-year-old Genevieve Chambers has never heard.)

(*He* will be Lancelot, in this intense and forbidden relationship, which must remain secret.)

Saturday, after the first week of classes at the Langhorne Academy. A single week! A single downward swoop as in downhill skiing leaving the skier dazed, breathless, but exhilarated as Francis Fox in the bracing climate of his new life is indeed exhilarated promising himself a reward when finally he's alone later that night.

Privacy of his bedroom in the apartment on Consent Street.

Single glass of Italian red wine. No yammering female voice in his ear. No need to feign *enthusiastic attentiveness*.

Just his laptop, treasure trove of (most exquisitely forbidden) loves.

■

BUT YES, FRANCIS *IS* listening. Has been listening.

Together approaching the headmistress's residence on the Langhorne campus as a bell in the chapel bell tower solemnly tolls six P.M., for dinner on the Saturday evening following the first week of classes at the Academy; or has the dinner ended, abruptly at eight-thirty P.M., on schedule, and so they are walking to Francis Fox's car parked nearby.

Or has time pleated mysteriously (as frequently happens when you are mesmerized by the most fantastic thoughts playing in your head in a continuous and inexhaustible loop) and the couple are headed up the fine-cracked walkway to Imogene Hood's rented duplex on Hurley Street a mere half-mile from Francis Fox's rented apartment on Consent Street . . .

Soon!—the evening will be over.

Soon!—Francis will be alone in his bedroom.

Yet still, he is politely attentive to his companion Imogene Hood wine-warmed and loquacious reminiscing of autumn in New England: what *spiritual renewal* in autumn, the change of light, the shortening of days, how powerful a sensation it is—*nostalgia* . . .

Bittersweet memories of growing up in Northampton, Massachusetts, where her father was head librarian at Smith College . . .

Nostalgia! Francis Fox has no choice but to feign interest. Faux sympathy, of which he has an inexhaustible reserve.

Thinking: what a purely bogus (bourgeois) sensation. *He* has never felt a moment's nostalgia in his entire life.

Nostalgia: yearning for something that never was recalled with much maudlin emotion as if it had ever been.

Francis Fox feels not the merest wisp of nostalgia for the childhood of "Frank Farrell," which he can barely remember and which he may have conflated with films and TV of the era of an equal banality and tedium. Long estranged from his thoroughly undistinguished parents, siblings. Descended from thoroughly undistinguished ancestors. Not even a modest fortune in the Farrell family, no estate to inherit even if (a sizable *if*) he'd have been a probable heir.

Nor does he feel nostalgia for the America of his childhood, post–Vietnam War burnt-out decades (1970s, 1980s) of no more interest to him than used toilet paper flushed into an abyss.

His generation means nothing to Francis Fox. As far as Francis Fox is concerned he is *unique* and shares no values, memories, sentiments with anyone else of any age.

Only Francis Fox's *kittens* possess meaning for him. For only *kittens* arouse Francis Fox's (erotic, forbidden) desire.

Though it must be admitted, within a very finite period of time—(a school year, a single semester, sometimes a mere month)—Francis Fox's obsession with a *kitten* gradually wanes, sometimes abruptly ceases, never to be revived; as a fiery blaze subsides to a mere fire, a mere flame, eventually mere smoldering embers, then—nothing.

Twelve years is the prime age, Fox has found. Thirteen can be exquisite.

By the age of fourteen often the fatal mammalian coarseness has set in, inexorably: tiny breast-buds begin to thicken; hips, thighs, legs of even the most lithesome prepubescent girls begin to fill out. The exquisite child-face is lost, the fuller adolescent face emerges with its self-indulgent pouts and blemishes. Sprouting hairs at underarms and crotch, bristling on legs like tiny wires—repulsive to one with Francis Fox's fastidious tastes.

And other symptoms of *maturation*, too crude to consider.

Not a single *kitten* of the past could Francis Fox bear to see again. Not even Miranda Myles, who would have been, by this time, too old for him.

(Unfortunately there have always been *kittens* who have tried to keep in contact with their beloved Mr. Fox, before him Mr. Farrell, mailing notes, cards, valentines from high school and college and even beyond college, clippings of weddings, births . . . Such mementos, flattering to Francis Fox's pride, he sometimes keeps, but more often tosses away as soon as he receives, with a shudder of distaste.)

(Especially, Francis Fox is revolted by the thought of a former *kitten* who has become a *mother.* That tiny hairless girl-vagina unspeakably swollen, thickened, stretched, despoiled—an obscenity.)

(For what value is it to be told *I will love you forever, Mr. Fox, you came into my life & changed my life forever* when the feeling cannot be reciprocated? When the feeling is so tritely sad, or so sadly trite, it evokes no response more animated than pity?)

For there's no time for dwelling in the past. As Mr. Fox has often quoted Henry David Thoreau to his middle-school students: *God himself culminates in the present moment, and will never be more divine in the lapse of all the ages.*

Seeing again vivid in his mind's eye as a scene glimpsed through a telescope the classroom in Haven Hall, *his* classroom. Dreamy latticed light from leaded windows in an aura around the (slightly bowed) head of Genevieve Chambers, the most prized beauty is the beauty unaware of itself, dark eyes melting in submission to her teacher as the eyes of a speckled fawn small enough to fit into the (gentle) jaws of a fox . . .

I will not hurt you I promise, dear Genevieve.

The last thing I would want to do is—hurt you.

Already, in the wake of carefully prescribed homework assignments, that encourage students to write in an *autobiographical vein,* Francis Fox knows that Genevieve is a day student at the school, not a boarder; she lives in the Village of Wieland on a street quaintly called Church Street with a mother and a younger brother but her father seems to be "away"—intrigued, Francis will soon learn what that means. Genevieve's first homework grade from Mr. Fox has been B– with the kindly admonition in red ink *Lacks depth & development but highly promising*—which will inspire the *kitten-to-be* to try harder.

Of course, Francis Fox always has alternative *kittens-to-be.* At the start of a new year he peruses his (girl-)students closely, marking names on his class lists with stars. If Genevieve Chambers is too risky, or unapproachable, or reveals herself to be less desirable, he has three other girls in reserve, among his seventh- and eighth-grade classes.

The first week of any school year is rushed, vertiginous, giddy as a toboggan run. It is thrilling, exhilarating. All predators know that their initial prey may elude them, the experienced predator knows when to retreat, and recalculate.

The fox trotting as if casually, casting a net with sharp eyes, sniffing the wind.

Literally sniffing as certain girls drift by Mr. Fox's desk, or in the corridor of Haven Hall, in their wake a faint fragrance of vanilla soap, floral shampoo, that indefinable scent of soft fair poreless ivory-pale skin that causes the salivary glands to secrete—*prey* . . .

Francis's heart trips. A smile spreads through his groin. Yes, he is happy!

In this phase of his life which Francis has every reason to believe may be the start of *a new life, an ascendant life,* and not rather, as Francis cannot know, *a rapidly depleting life* as of a spinning/ diminishing spool of thread on a bobbin.

All this while in his ear is the voice of the woman to which he half-listens, inclining his head in her direction as they walk companionably side by side, Francis Fox politely attentive, gentlemanly though he has begun to suspect that something has gone amiss—he has lost the thread of Imogene Hood's words, he hears now a tone of sobriety, solemnity. For Imogene is speaking of family memories, childhood griefs, the loss of Imogene's mother when Imogene was nine years old, more recently the loss of her father, an unexpected death, for Imogene an uncertain future . . .

They are standing in front of Imogene's rented duplex on Hurley Street. A wave of dismay sweeps over Francis. He murmurs something sympathetic, meant to comfort, even as he tries to retrieve key words of Imogene's.

Nostalgia. Loss, grief. Future.

He has been made to feel uneasy, Imogene Hood has been speaking to him as one might speak to an intimate friend, not to a man whom she scarcely knows, whom she has met just recently; she seems to have alluded wistfully to planning a *future,* of—*children?*

Family life, having children—vaguely, Francis thinks he has heard this.

Why is Imogene telling him these things? Why Francis Fox? In a circuitous way expressing the wish that—exactly what?

Blood rushes into Francis's face, he is stricken with embarrassment for Imogene.

No one so quick with speech as Mr. Fox in a classroom but now, Francis Fox has been rendered speechless. Racking his brains for how to placate the distraught woman whose eyes are brimming with tears, her mouth trembling. How, without insulting her? Not too obviously misleading her.

An incurable blood disease? In remission, but incurable.

(But no: Imogene is a *good woman.* A *good woman* would leap at the prospect of caring for a man. Any wreck of a man.)

A secret wound? Psychic wound? "Trauma."

Too secret, too painful for him to give a name to.

In the awkward silence Imogene invites Francis inside her house for a drink.

A drink? But—Imogene Hood doesn't drink! And so far as the Langhorne community knows Francis Fox limits himself to a single glass of wine at a meal, which glass (it has been observed) he rarely finishes.

In the near distance the bell in the bell tower is tolling nine P.M. Saturday night!

Absurdly early but Francis tells Imogene in an apologetic murmur that it is late for *him*. He gets up early in the morning, weekends as well as weekdays, he has a swath of homework papers to grade over the weekend . . .

This is true: Francis Fox has several dozen seventh- and eighth-grade English assignments to grade. The Langhorne Academy has a reputation as a school with a heavy workload and Francis Fox will be no slouch in upholding this reputation though in fact Francis has mastered the skill of "correcting" middle-school papers as his eye skims them so rapidly that an entire page can be assimilated in the blink of an eye. Often, he is also watching a video on his laptop.

Imogene is wiping at her eyes with a tissue. She has seemed about to speak, perhaps to reiterate her invitation to Francis, to come inside for a drink, but falls silent instead. She is a tall slope-shouldered woman, thicker at the thighs and hips than in the torso, with a plain-radiant face exuding sincerity, honesty, integrity. Her eyes are beautiful bovine eyes, Francis Fox feels a stab of unease seeing these eyes awash with tears, and hopes that he is not the cause.

Is Francis expected to embrace Imogene, to comfort her in her distress? The poor woman is shivering as if with cold on this balmy evening in early September, a convulsive shiver passes over her.

What to say to Imogene, to allow her some measure of dignity! And to allow Francis to escape, at least for the time being.

Yearning for the seclusion of his apartment though it is sparely furnished, not very attractive. Eager to be alone.

A secret wound of which I dare not speak. "Trauma."

He will suggest that he has been wounded in love. He has been betrayed in love. He has lost faith in love.

He has been *deeply wounded* in the past. Can't risk . . .

But does he want Imogene to think that he may—might—be *gay*? Would that be a good idea, or a not-so-good idea?

"Yes. I have paperwork too. For the weekend."

Imogene speaks with the most subtle sarcasm. A mere eyelash of sarcasm.

Francis sees that she isn't crying but—laughing? Silent laughter racks her body. A glisten of merriment in her eyes.

"Goodnight, Francis. Thank you for escorting me to the dinner."

"Hey, thank *you*, Imogene. Are you—all right?"

"Yes, Francis. I am 'all right.'" Imogene laughs again, silently.

Francis tries to think of something appropriate to say, something warm, witty, consoling, conciliatory, but Imogene has turned casually away, preparing to enter her house. It is certainly unlike Imogene to leave Francis so abruptly, without their having made a plan to meet again soon.

"Well—goodnight . . ." He smiles weakly, inanely.

He is hurt that Imogene doesn't invite him for a drink again even as he is vastly relieved that she does not. Calling after her to ask if she is *all right* but Imogene seems not to hear, shutting the door firmly behind her.

Francis remains on the walkway, stunned. He is turning the ring which Katy Cady gave him around his finger, it has grown loose. He has not expected this. He has been so gallant all evening—he has *exhausted* himself in gallantry. He watches as lights are switched on in the duplex, behind drawn drapes he can see a wraithlike shape. He is stricken with regret, guilt.

Of course, you have disappointed her. You could have had a drink with her . . . You could even have held her for a few minutes, comforted her. What a shit you are!

But could Francis have held Imogene in his arms, even to comfort her?—he isn't sure. Hairs stir on the nape of his neck at the prospect.

It's an unfortunate fact, which Imogene Hood certainly must know: though she and Francis are a *couple* in the eyes of the Langhorne community they are not a *couple* in any intimate sense.

They have shaken hands in greeting, but they have not held hands; they have brushed lips against cheeks, but they have not kissed. A neutral observer would be more likely to identify them as longtime husband and wife than lovers.

Frequently it has happened in Francis Fox's life, that adult women whom he befriends become disappointed with him. But he does not mislead them, he is sure. It is they who are eager to do favors for him, prepare meals for him, give him gifts, loan him money sometimes without being asked—it is not *his fault* . . .

Most often, the women forgive him, eventually. In the life of a lonely solitary woman, a Francis Fox is yet a prize.

But Imogene Hood is new in his life. It worries him that she has become unreasonably impatient, so soon.

It isn't too late. He could move boldly, rap on the door.

He will tell Imogene that yes, he would like a drink after all. (Steeling himself for inexpensive white wine from a New Jersey winery like the piss-poor "chardonnay" served at P. Cady's dinners.) He will tell her . . .

A light is switched on upstairs in the duplex. Here too a wraithlike figure glides behind drawn drapes.

Is it some sort of romantic-erotic relationship the woman wants? Or just emotional solace, support? Francis can supply this, he thinks, if required. Emotions are easy.

Irresolute on the walkway Francis is trying not to envision his friend upstairs in her bedroom. Imogene Hood, partially undressed. Bereft of clothing, her body exposed and vulnerable. Francis knows from unfortunate experience that a mature woman is always much larger, more mammalian, unclothed than clothed; her breasts seem to spill from her with a lurid life of their own.

He shudders, repelled.

Imogene Hood lifting her face to be kissed, eyes half-shut in ardor—the vision fills Francis with dismay, disgust.

No no no no no. Just not possible.

Sad fact: even as a young girl Imogene Hood wouldn't have been Francis Fox's type.

■ ■ ■

"THANK GOD."

What relief to be alone! At last.

The past forty minutes have been particularly draining, exhausting; he fears that dear wounded Imogene might be drifting from him, as even a not-fully-inflated balloon might yet be blown into the upper branches of a tree, out of reach.

He will think of Imogene later. Tomorrow is soon enough.

Now, he pours himself a glass of red wine. Very good, not cheap, Italian red wine.

Retreats to his bedroom, and his laptop. His cell phone, purposefully left behind to prevent his glancing at it surreptitiously and compulsively through the tedium of the evening, has been charging for hours on the bedside table.

This past week, cautiously, and discreetly, Francis has been taking cell phone pictures of certain of his girl-students, while they were absorbed in impromptu writing sessions at their desks; these images, the majority of which are of Genevieve Chambers, he will send to his email account, to store in his computer under *K Files.* On this computer Francis has accumulated an archive of images dating back to the late 1990s, hundreds of pictures of prepubescent girls of whom most were *kittens* in their time. Some of the photographs show the subjects at a little distance, like these, others are intimately close-up, and blurred. In some, the girls appear to be asleep, heads resting on their arms, eyes shut and mouths slack and hair spilling about their heads.

Francis Fox's favorites—*Sleeping Beauties,* as he calls them. (In homage to Yasunari Kawabata's *House of the Sleeping Beauties,* a tenderly erotic novel Francis has read so many times that pages in his paperback edition have fallen out.)

But it is enormously risky, to cause a prepubescent girl weighing less than one hundred pounds to fall asleep in a teacher's office, even into a very light sleep. Scarcely a milligram of Ambien will do it, secreted in a sweet treat—two milligrams would be a catastrophe. At the Kent School, besotted Francis Fox took foolish chances which *he will never take again.*

It's a measure of Francis Fox's gentlemanly discretion that he has not recorded the names of these girls, nor their locations, only just dates. Nor has he any written records on the premises. Absolutely nothing in his office at school—of course! Each *kitten,* in each phase of Francis's life, has been unique, much-cherished; but each *kitten* has driven out memories of previous *kittens,* for Francis Fox is a serial romantic, not by nature a polygamist. So it is, he has forgotten most of his *kittens'* names. So many times in the trance of an erotic reverie he has gazed at these flawless child-faces, they have become abstract to him, like Cubist deconstructions of faces; only the most recent are of interest, as they represent the yet-unknown, the unconquered.

At the present time, the predominant interest is Genevieve Chambers. After only one week, Francis has become (mildly) obsessed with the girl; he has taken several striking pictures of her on his cell phone, for Genevieve is, not surprisingly, extremely photogenic, in poses of extreme absorption as she leans over a notebook, writing with her arm bent at the elbow, as if she were shielding what she is writing. In this fetching pose her hair spills over her shoulders, not straight but subtly wavy, a beautiful wheat-color, glittering as if with mica. Downcast eyes, thick lashes and clearly defined brows, a short, snub nose . . . He imagines himself lifting her fragrant-smelling hair, gently kissing the nape of her neck. Surely, *this will happen.*

Francis congratulates himself on his good luck: because it happened to be vacant this beautiful *kitten-to-be* took the ideal seat in his classroom. During classes, five days a week from eleven A.M. to eleven-fifty A.M., her diminutive figure will be within the periphery of her teacher's gaze whether he actually looks at her or not. And always, unfailingly, he, Mr. Fox, will be at the center of *her* attention.

Francis had required of all of his students that they write autobiographical journal entries at home, quickly and without revision, inspired by a sequence of Robert Frost poems; in class, they were to transcribe these entries into more formal, measured English using subordinate clauses and punctuation including commas, semicolons, and colons. Not a difficult exercise, for most students, so Mr. Fox will glance through the papers over the weekend and ask selected students to read aloud "exemplary" work to the class, on Monday.

Whatever Genevieve Chambers has written, no matter how vacuous, how trite, Mr. Fox will be sure to ask her to read to the class and to praise her for it, though not excessively. He has already indicated to her that her work is *promising*—he will hint that it *falls short.* For Mr. Fox is a master of praising, he knows how to modulate praise, how to withhold it, if necessary; how to relieve a student's anxiety by subtle praise, without exactly removing the possibility of criticism to come. If there is inflation, there must be, to a degree, deflation. Then again, if it suits his purposes, inflation.

In this, as in other classroom interactions, Francis Fox follows the lessons of behavioral psychology: all of life is a matter of *conditioning,* and he is the puppet-master of *conditioning* in the strictly controlled classroom setting, not unlike a Skinner box.

Francis has noticed that one of his eighth-grade boys, in his two P.M. class, a high-browed, fair-haired brat absurdly named Jeffrey Swanson III, is inclined to be just slightly smirky, and so Mr. Fox will quash this smirkiness in the bud by subjecting Jeffrey Swanson III to a bout of (mild) criticism in front of the class, followed by qualified praise; from experience Mr. Fox knows that if he allows Jeffrey Swanson III to disrespect him, or even to appear to almost disrespect him, at the start of the term, he will regret it later. Francis Fox is highly sensitive to prepubescent-boy rebelliousness, as predators have developed sharp olfactory senses to detect the presence of other predators, and knows how not to merely quash them, but enlist them as allies.

And there is a singularly homely, ferret-faced eighth-grade girl in an afternoon class, one Eunice Pfenning, who has stared at him all week, without once smiling; this little bitch too he will quash, or squash, like a roach beneath his heel, if she continues to prove resistant to Mr. Fox's charisma.

He has done it in the past, if provoked. He has *always* routed his student-adversaries, sometimes before they realize that they are adversaries. In middle-school teaching as in warfare, a *preemptive strike* is often the wisest strategy.

Francis has never driven any student to self-harm, he is sure. Not deliberately. A number of potential troublemakers were so outfoxed by Fox, over the years, neither they nor their parents knew what happened exactly to derail their promising academic careers and shunt them into the bin of the miscellaneous *average,* squirming like lobsters awaiting execution. Instilling a fatal *self-doubt* in the prepubescent soul is pathetically easy to do, like the kind of brain surgery once executed with an ice pick.

On his laptop Francis enlarges several pictures of Genevieve Chambers. In all but one, Genevieve is totally absorbed in writing; but in one, her head appears to be slightly raised, her lowered eyes appear to be about to lift, as if to meet Mr. Fox's ardent gaze, or as if aware of Mr. Fox's ardent gaze, through the magnifying lens of the cell phone camera.

Such innocence! Francis Fox doesn't doubt, it is genuine. *Exquisite.*

Never has Francis posted pictures of *kittens* online—of course. And if he did, he would obscure their faces so that they would be unidentifiable. Admittedly, he has been tempted. Admittedly, he could use the money, if he established a website, for subscribers. His harem of *kittens* is far more beautiful than more blunt, banal images one is likely to find elsewhere on the Internet but Francis is not likely to take such a risky step.

In this phase of his life in Wieland, South Jersey, which has seemed to Francis Fox a kind of sanctuary to which he has come as an asylum-seeker from enemies elsewhere, passionately he vows, "I will *never.*"

SOUL-MATE

D oorbell rings! Though it's Sunday a special delivery arrives for IMOGENE HOOD.

One dozen resplendent crimson roses with a handwritten note attached, composed in stanzas like a poem:

> Dearest Imogene,
> I am so sorry, a misunderstanding may have arisen between us innocently as toadstools in the night for which no one is to blame.
>
> In my life there is an old wound—a "toxic trauma"—of which I find it difficult to speak even to those cherished by me to whom I should not find it difficult to speak at all.
>
> Someday perhaps I hope to share with you the nature of this wound. But I shrink from burdening another with my private grief incurred at so young an age, it predates full comprehension.
>
> It is a confidential revelation, I hope you will protect as a secret, for the past several years I have been undergoing therapy, and I am indeed making progress (I think).

I will hope to share some of this with you someday, dear Imogene. In the meantime I hope you will be patient with me. You see, I am fearful of intimate emotions—of "touch"— for I have been badly injured.

I feel the highest regard for you and would not hurt you for any reason. It is hurtful to me, to think that I may have hurt my closest friend inadvertently.

Precious friendships are gifts, like grace. Coming to us undeserved. But I will try to deserve you for you are a most remarkable woman—unique in my life—indeed, a soul-mate.

Please have patience with me. I am making my way slowly to a fuller being—to "health." I shrink from asking another for help until I am "on my feet."

I would not burden another with my grief, who has a profound grief of her own to bear. Yet the promise has been made to me, someday soon I may be whole, and may hold out a hand to another.

In the words of W. B. Yeats, one day I may be blessèd, and can bless.

With love & hope, with remorse & tenderness,
Your friend & soul-mate Francis

Reading this handwritten message, and rereading, Imogene is suffused with emotion. Tears spill out of her eyes, in rivulets down her cheeks. She has spent a sleepless night. She has berated herself, for behaving so *pettishly* the night before. She sees now, understands now, something, not clearly but dimly, as through a smudged glass, *something* shimmering just beyond her grasp, for which she feels grateful, yet a kind of dread, as in one who is affiancing herself to a hooded figure, a face without features, a dybbuk of some sort, a fate.

Yet: better *a fate*, than *no fate* at all.

Imogene's first impulse is to call Francis Fox to thank him for the roses and for the cri de coeur which she will never share with another—but she resists.

She will see her friend the next day. She will grip his hand in silence. In recognition, commiseration. In forgiveness—of each other.

My soul-mate.

DIRTY GIRL

SEPTEMBER/OCTOBER 2013

lready at birth she was a chubby baby: eight pounds, three ounces.

Already a label was affixed to her: *macrosomic.*

Soon then, a chubby toddler. A chubby child. Just four years, two months old when the tiny twin flesh-buds in her chest began to emerge and to *feel funny.*

Her head was unusually large for a child of her age, covered in curls of the hue of pale apricot which would gradually fade to sparrow-brown. Her eyes of no discernible hue were close-set, small in her moon-shaped face. Her cheeks were chubby, looking as if they'd been pinched, reddened by rough/affectionate fingers. A round little pot-belly, chubby legs, chubby ankles and feet. By the age of five she stood four feet six in stocking feet and weighed ninety pounds.

It did not seem right, a child of such a size still had *potty problems.* It did not seem right, a child of such a size sometimes *wet the bed,* for which she was scolded as an older child might more reasonably be scolded with the consequence that, scolded, made to feel shame, and anxiety, she was more likely to *wet the bed,* incurring disapproval, disgust, and further scolding. She had been known to have *potty acci-*

dents even in church, to her mother's dismay. And even in her first-grade class, to her teacher's disgust. The pediatrician to whom she was brought at the suggestion of the Healys' family doctor speculated that she might have an endocrine problem, or a pituitary-gland problem, or a genetic problem, for she was abnormally tall and chubby for her age. Her genitals were "abnormally" developed and hypersensitive. Her "cognitive skills" lagged behind her "physical development"—by several years. The circumference of her head was measured. Her (baby) teeth were examined. X-rays revealed that while her chronological age was six, her "bone age" was nine.

At age six years, nine months, the first soft fine hairs began to appear on her body. Silky hairs in her underarms, small wiry hairs in the area of the soft white chubby groin. The tiny twin buds in her chest grew jiggly, the tiny roseate nipples *felt funny, hurt.* When she touched them in the bath her mother slapped her hands away. *What is wrong with you! Stop that.* Dared not scratch between her legs where sometimes it itched because her mother would slap her even harder if she saw and even if her mother didn't see she somehow knew. *Dirty girl! That's not nice.*

Always she was judged harshly because she looked older than her age by several years. It seemed wrong, willful, spiteful on her part that she failed to understand the simplest commands even if uttered in a loud voice. And she could not speak as other children spoke who were her size, without stammering and stuttering and blushing furiously. She was made to feel stupid. She was made to feel clumsy. She was made to feel ashamed. Her own doll given to her by her grandmother was a reproach to her, an insipidly pretty girl-baby-doll with flawless smooth skin, no fleshy knobs on her flat chest and hairless everywhere except on her head where blond ringlets spilled to her shoulders. A girl-baby-doll with a serene smiling face and shiny-marble eyes that never filled with tears.

She will remember: In the doorway Daddy stood staring in his garage mechanic's coveralls dark-stained with grease. Steam filled the bathroom, where she lay naked in hot soapy water as her mother bathed her for she could not be trusted to bathe herself. For there were parts of her, crevices, cracks, and fissures, in which filth accumulated and had to be scrubbed clean. *Go away, close the damned door!* her mother cried as with a swerve of her arm she caused the door to shut, hard in her father's stricken face.

Stricken face of the father who suspects some sort of joke is being played on him which he does not understand.

Soon then Daddy ceased hugging her, touching her. Ceased coming into her room to say goodnight where she lay in bed in chubby baby-fat inside her flannel nightgown waiting without daring to breathe. If she lay very still. If she lay with her hands outside the cover on either side of her body without touching. But it was not enough, it was never enough, Daddy ceased coming to kiss her goodnight, all that was finished when she was seven years, nine months old.

Forever after this she knew herself stared-at, but not *why.*

Her brothers were older than her, by years. They too stared at her in curiosity, then in discomfort, then in dislike. When others were present they did not acknowledge her at all for she was embarrassing to them, she had no clear idea why.

If no one observed Pete might tickle her roughly beneath her arms and up inside her shirt until she squealed with laughter like sobbing. Calling her *Little Piggy,* his lips drawn back from his teeth as a dog will do.

Her brother Kyle ignored her, mostly. Already Kyle was in high school, working after school at the gas station with their father.

At school, she was seated at the rear of the classroom because she was as tall as the tallest boys and these boys teased and tormented her mercilessly. Her teacher was suspicious of her since in homework assignments she made few mistakes while in class taking quizzes or answering when called upon she did poorly.

At school, she was called *Mary-YANN* by teachers in a tone of exasperation and reproach.

She was learning to perceive her soft chubby shameful body from above. She was learning to inhabit her body like a bird in a slovenly tree. She was learning not to glance into mirrors unless she narrowed her eyes to slits and even then, she never dared to look into a full-length mirror, only into a small mirror framing her face abashed and abject as a plate of mashed potatoes left to harden.

The fleshy knobs in her chest continued to grow!—even if she pushed them flat with the palms of her hands or punched or pinched them. Ever more silky hairs flourished in her underarms, and hairs not so silky but wiry-itchy flourished between her legs.

Eyes moved upon her and fixed upon her, particularly her chest. Chest and hips. In bafflement. In disapproval. She overheard relatives marveling *Jesus, what've they been feeding her!* She was often very hungry and fearful of starting to eat at mealtimes because she would not be able to stop. Still they would marvel *She eats like a horse, look at her!* But truly she was not *fat,* she was only just *chubby.* Again she was taken to be seen by the pediatrician, who weighed her, measured her, examined her except this time she put up such a panicked resistance which not even her mother could subdue, flush-faced and furious he decided not to examine her between the legs. She was declared to be "healthy"—yet, she was declared to be "abnormal" for a female of her age. There was talk of additives and hormones in food, estrogens in chickens, antibiotics, "trans fats" and "dyes." Pesticides in soil, water, air. Household toxins—detergent, bleach, soaps, especially the harsh lye soap her father used to wash up after work.

Her father was not living with them now but she was assured *It isn't your fault. None of you kids' fault, he's a son of a bitch.*

Still, she seemed to know that of course *it was her fault.*

She was not allowed to see her mother cry but she could hear her mother cry. The bedroom door closed against her.

When she was eight years, seven months old something terrible happened to her.

Yet in happening to her this terrible thing happened to her *because of her.* For it did not happen to any other girl in third grade.

In the girls' lavatory in the toilet stall discovering clots of blood, blood-clumps in her underwear and between her legs leaking like pee. In the toilet bowl in slow curls like worms unfurling. She had never seen anything so terrifying. Mesmerizing. Could not look away nor even shut her eyes. That this thick clotted smelly rust-colored blood was leaking out of her was unfathomable. A sight so obscene, so unspeakable she could not cry out, a hand clutched at her throat choking her.

Trying not to cry because once she started she could not stop crying like a baby wailing brokenhearted for no one will hear. Trying not to make any noise of alarm or distress as often she did at home where her brothers might hear. Jamming her fists against her mouth. Gnawing at her knuckles. Shameful for this blood had come from the place where pee comes from and there was the shame of *wetting her bed.* Chickens in the backyard she'd seen with their heads chopped off, spouting blood in small gushers. Bleeding to death piteously as their scaly legs kicked. Something shameful in such sights. A living thing suddenly in the dirt fallen. Blank-staring eyes in the decapitated head. With badly trembling hands she wadded tissues to soak up the blood that kept trickling from somewhere deep and high inside her. Anything and everything she did was wrong but there were degrees of wrongness. Clumps of toilet paper pushed into her already soaked underpants, clumsily secured with a safety pin found on the lavatory floor but not really secured, the toilet paper would soon work its way loose and slip down her leg. She was light-headed, faint. Pain throbbed in the pit of her belly like an animal clawing from inside.

When finally she returned from the lavatory her teacher saw her in time. Spared her the disgrace of entering the classroom. Rivulets of blood down the girl's chubby legs soaking into silly white cotton socks. Ghastly-white-chubby face like flour. Panting through the slack dazed mouth. Hurriedly her teacher blocked her entrance, led her to the office of the school nurse, who could barely disguise her surprise, dismay at the sight of her. *Third grade? Starting her period? Why's a girl so big in third grade? How old is she?*

Her mother was called on her cell phone, to bring her home midday. Smelling of rank blood, sobbing in shame. Her mother tried to comfort her but scolded her too—*What am I going to do with you now? You will be in danger every day of your life.*

And on the phone with her sisters—*Yes! She is! Today! I had to bring her home from school, she's started her period! She is not—even— nine years old and she's started her period and we were all—what?— twelve?—thirteen when we started?—and that was bad enough . . . Oh God, what am I going to do with her?*

She was taken to another pediatrician recommended by relatives, in Bridgeton. This doctor did not seem so surprised or alarmed by her condition though he looked upon her with a pitying sort of sympathy, reluctant to touch her so his nurse examined her instead, including even between her legs gently, gingerly where the child-vagina, the child-vulva appeared swollen, reddened. *Early menarche. Precocious puberty.*

Possibly, she'd been fed too much milk. All sorts of growth-inducing hormones in milk. Or it could be a brain disorder, tumor pressing upon the pituitary gland. Wouldn't know unless she had a CAT scan and those are expensive and there was no medical insurance for such expenses, in fact her mother would have trouble paying the pediatrician's bill but reluctant to leave his office for nothing had been decided, no solution offered, pleading with the doctor *Can't you help us somehow, is there some kind of vaccination you could give her, boys will take advantage of her, they already tease her, pick on her, she isn't able to take care of herself, she isn't mature enough, she's too trusting . . .*

No wonder that men and older boys stared at her. She *was* just a little girl, you could see in her face. But in her body, you saw something else. A miniature woman, near-adult. Except no, obviously not an adult, her movements childlike, childish, her high-pitched voice, her frightened smile.

Always that *certain look* in male faces as if they were seeing not her, but something inside her of which she was herself unaware, and could not disguise.

Sunday at the lake with her family, relatives. How the bathing suit made of a rough nubby pink fabric clung wetly to her pear-shaped breasts, rotund buttocks, and belly. One of her aunts hurriedly wrapped a beach towel around her. There were awkward jokes, not-funny jokes that, inside the beach towel, Mary Ann was naked. Her brother Pete told her to put on clothes, she was embarrassing them. Her cousin Demetrius told Pete to let her alone, there was nothing wrong with her, she had as much right to be there as Pete did. Demetrius was a tall lanky spindly-limbed boy of sixteen with purple blemished skin and a tendency to stutter when he was excited. Pete was not so tall as Demetrius but hard-muscled and cunning with a mean streak like an actual fissure through his low forehead and thick-ribbed hair. He came at Demetrius at an angle striking him in the solar plexus hard-fisted as a boxer causing Demetrius to stagger gasping for air as if his heart had stopped. When Pete lifted his fists dancing about in comic jubilation Demetrius managed to throw himself at his cousin in a sudden embrace bringing him down and falling upon him. The boys wrestled grunting as others looked on in astonishment. Pete cursed Demetrius and tried to knee him savagely between the legs, Demetrius seized Pete's head in both his hands and pounded it against the sandy ground until Pete screamed that he was being killed. By this time adults were pulling Demetrius from Pete shouting for him to stop. Pete made an effort to stand, blood streaming from his broken nose. Seeing Mary Ann shivering in the beach towel he screamed at her—*What're you looking at, fucking dirty pig you caused this!*

Demetrius ran off, was not seen again that day at the lake.

Not ever again will Demetrius and his cousin Pete be what you'd call *friends*.

■

FREAK! FREAKY!—DIRTY GIRL in dreams as in actual life she heard these words which were sometimes taunts, sometimes accusations, sometimes uttered in vehement disgust but sometimes, which frightened most, in a kind of reluctant and resentful awe.

Coming up close behind her at school. Big boys in the elementary school corridor nudging against her. *Hey! Dirty little girl, lookit those titties!*

Such eager, *ardent* disgust in male faces, she could not comprehend.

Pushing and crowding against her laughing like monkeys. She learned to murmur *Let me alone* in the most abject way.

Learned to murmur *Sorry* in the most abject way.

Like a dog cringing before it is kicked as a way of (possibly) deflecting the kick.

Learn young: all kicks are deserved.

For if you are kicked it was you who provoked the kick.

Girls she admired, wished she could *be,* avoided her. Even her girl-cousins who should have been her friends. Boys her own age, in her own class, avoided her.

As soon as the boys turned fourteen or so, they began to notice her. Intensely.

At her father's Sunoco garage, one warm summer day in shorts, T-shirt. Loose-fitting clothing her mother had checked out yet still Billy Odum, Hank Dunchin stared at her with the intensity of piranha fish, her father was furious with her and with her mother, saying to her mother *Christ's sake look what she looks like. Can't you use some judgment, what is wrong with you!*

Never looked in the mirror especially if she was unclothed. Never looked down at her body if she was unclothed.

She avoided the outdoors, safer to remain inside. No one staring at you when you turn around, you didn't know had crept up on you.

She didn't mind helping her mother in the kitchen and with housework. As long as she was meek and yielding in her mother's company her mother was kind to her, and seemed to love her, or anyway not dislike her. She took refuge in books, schoolwork. She was grateful for school was a way to earn merit. Despite the fact that she was a Healy, and alarmingly mature for her age, her teachers had to concede that Mary Ann was surprisingly intelligent. Her homework papers were neat, her handwriting was legible. She stammered if addressed too bluntly. But by sixth grade she had acquired a reputation for taking home library books each week and turning in book reports to her teacher, for extra credit, on Monday morning without fail.

In rural Atlantic County there were many Healys, and relatives of Healys by marriage. They were an old South Jersey family believed to have been prosperous bootleggers many decades ago. There were Healys who were prison guards at the South Jersey Men's Facility at Argyle, and there were Healys who were in law enforcement, but there were also Healys who'd been incarcerated for a variety of crimes—drug dealing, burglary, assault, writing bad checks, involuntary manslaughter. One of Mary Ann Healy's uncles had been charged with unauthorized dealing in firearms but had been sentenced just to probation and there was a rumor that her father, Blake Healy, had *gotten on the wrong side of the law* when he'd been a hotheaded kid but had never been incarcerated a day in his life.

Half a mile away on Stockton Road lived Blake's older brother Lemuel, who did part-time carpentry for a local contractor and worked as a custodian at the private school in Wieland. It was said of Lemuel that he had a *drinking problem,* he'd *let the property go to hell.* Lemuel's sons, Marcus and Demetrius, were friendly with Mary Ann's brothers when they were growing up, the boys were often together at one another's houses. When Lemuel's wife, Ida, was terminally ill, wasting away with cancer, Mary Ann's mother often came over to make meals for the family. She volunteered Mary Ann to help out as well—Mary Ann loved to *feel needed,* like a nurse.

By this time Marcus had moved out of the house and lived somewhere in town. The younger brother, Demetrius, remained to take care of his mother and to work part-time in town; he helped out his father and his brother, when they required him. Demetrius seemed to have no core identity, no *being* of his own. His face was often impassive, as if he were waiting to know what to think, how to react. He was the only boy among the relatives who didn't seem to be embarrassed of Mary Ann, or resentful of her, or obscurely angry with her: he did not seem to "see" her at all.

It was said of Demetrius that he'd had to grow up too soon, taking care of his mother for more than a year. There was no one else, none of Ida's family could come to live with her, having families, and medical problems, of their own. Ida had had three surgeries for breast cancer and one final, devastating surgery for colorectal cancer. A warm and vivacious woman, already by forty-six she'd begun her long decline. Whatever medical insurance Lemuel had as a custodian at the Langhorne Academy, it did not cover home care. After Ida's death Demetrius became yet more reticent, reserved. He was known to slip from the house if relatives came to visit, to disappear out in the woods behind the house. If forced into conversation he spoke with maddening slowness like one for whom speech was not natural but had to be forced, at some risk; as if speaking were a kind of tightrope, you could easily fall off.

"That boy has 'old eyes'—an 'old soul.' Children like that tend to die young."

"That's just made-up, Grandma. That isn't real."

Mary Ann spoke hotly, in resentment. She would not hear such things said about Demetrius.

"Well. We can pray it isn't."

"That's just something you said, Grandma. It's silly."

It was not like Mary Ann Healy to speak sharply to adults. She was most tolerated when adults felt sorry for her, and speaking sharply jeopardized their sympathy. She had not realized until this exchange that she loved her cousin Demetrius more than she loved her brothers—much more. Or anyone in her family including her mother.

Like a thunderclap out of a cloudless sky the news came that: Mary Ann Healy was awarded a scholarship to the private school in Wieland, where, her mother said excitedly, she would consort with "a higher class of people" and be treated differently than she was used to.

Also, she would be wearing a school uniform—"That will make a difference, too! About time." Her mother spoke with a grim sort of hope.

An Atlantic County scholarship, as it was called, was considered an honor but it was an intimidating honor which Mary Ann would have rejected if she'd had any choice, which (of course) she did not.

Relatives were split over the news, which was reported in the local newspaper: some thought it was thrilling, impressive; others were not so sure. For Mary Ann *was* something of a liability, no one knew what to make of her.

One thing was certain: if the girl remained in Atlantic County public schools she would have to drop out by ninth grade, she'd be such a magnet for the most aggressive boys.

Such a risk for *getting knocked up*. A girl so young, and so naïve.

Mary Ann's mother had become pregnant at the age of seventeen, too God-damned young. She'd hoped to live in Atlantic City after high school, learn how to deal blackjack and work in one of the glamorous casinos—*Tropicana, Caesars, Harrah's*.

At least she'd been seventeen before it had happened to her. Getting involved with older guys. Winding up with Blake Healy.

Poor Mary Ann with her mature figure, childish doll-face, would never make it to fourteen without guys all over her.

When he was told about the scholarship her father whistled through his teeth: Tuition at the Langhorne Academy was sixty thousand dollars a year? Just going to school, which was free, could be worth *sixty thousand dollars a year* to some people?

Some things, you had to shake your head in bewilderment. It was as if people with money needed ways to spend it.

"Fucking 'tuition'—too bad we can't cash it in," Blake Healy said, quickly adding:

"Just joking."

It was a curiosity, another way people with money spent it, that most students at the Langhorne Academy were *boarders*. They lived at the school, on the campus, in what were called *residences*. They had meals in dining halls, they spent much time at athletics, they were in one another's company constantly, in a way Mary Ann could not imagine. How like a nightmare you could never escape, living with young people her own age and older, vulnerable to their rapidly shifting moods, at their mercy; steeling yourself against their alliances with one another, which excluded you; having to be grateful for any small crumb of kindness or friendliness, if you could trust it.

More than once she'd seen, or imagined she'd seen, girls glancing at one another even as one of them was talking with her, being "nice" to her, an instant's rapport among them that excluded Mary Ann Healy.

Why?—because you are a cow. Because you are a PIGGY.

Because you are sexy but stupid.

Because you are a "poor white" and don't belong here.

Mary Ann did take pride in the girls' uniform: a maroon corduroy jumper with a pleated skirt past the knee, worn over a long-sleeved white blouse. It was a distinctive *look*, it communicated dignity, class. In the Wieland schools girls wore torn and much-laundered jeans, already by seventh grade some of the girls wore jeans so tight their crotches were outlined, the cracks of their asses; as young as thirteen they wore goth makeup, mascara, starved themselves on Diet Coke, smoked cigarettes, pot. Her mother had insisted that Mary Ann's uniform should fit her "loosely"—Mary Ann was allowed to wear a jumper two sizes too large, and in addition, if she wished, an unbuttoned cardigan sweater over the jumper, to further disguise her figure.

Still, Mary Ann would hear sniggering remarks in hallways, on stairs, walking on the Langhorne school grounds—*Lookit her! Oh man—lookit those boobs!* Muffled whistles, lewd moaning sounds of boys in passing who made a point of ignoring her otherwise.

Overall it seemed to be true, as Mary Ann's mother had said, that there was a *higher class* of person at the Academy. Langhorne students were much better behaved than students in Atlantic County schools. In their school uniforms—boys in jackets and ties, girls in white blouses, jumpers—they more resembled poised young actors on TV and in movies: they seemed to have flawless hair, teeth, complexions. They made their way without particular haste through school corridors as if they had no idea that you could run, shove, scream in the halls, you could knock one another down stairs, you could scrawl obscene graffiti on lockers—in fact there were no lockers at the Langhorne Academy, students carried books in backpacks, and these backpacks were not covered in lurid Day-Glo stickers of skulls, swastikas, swollen red lips. Classes were one-third the size of classes in the public school, or even smaller; many classrooms did not have seats in rows but arranged in circles. Teachers, too, were better-looking, much better-dressed, than their colleagues in public schools. They spoke quietly, rarely needing to raise their voices. If they asked questions, most of the class would raise their hands immediately, eagerly. It is true that now and then a student, usually a boy, might nod off in class, having stayed up too late the night before; but it would never be the case that everyone in class would drift into a light doze. No student would utter an obscenity in a Langhorne class, make a rude gesture at a teacher, stalk out of the classroom. Cell phones were not allowed in classrooms, therefore cell phones *were not* brought into classrooms. Every night there was homework, on weekends there was twice as much homework. Mary Ann felt as if she were being made to run a race with weights on her ankles, panting, stumbling, desperate to keep up with the others, no chance of excelling as she had in her old school. No matter how hard she worked her grades were rarely above B–.

Here too, books were her refuge. At Mary Ann's former middle school there had been a very small library, and a single librarian (who was also an English teacher); here at the Academy there was a much larger library, and several librarians. One afternoon when Mary Ann came harried and panting into the library in the hope of avoiding several older boys who'd been tormenting her, a young librarian approached her, not to scold, as Mary Ann anticipated, but to strike up a conversation with her, asking her name, what sort of books she liked, which grade was she in, where was she from?—seeming to know that Mary Ann wasn't a typical Langhorne student but a local resident. The librarian introduced herself as Ms. Hood.

So nice to her, so friendly, Mary Ann wanted to cry. Here was an adult who did not stare at her body, looked her in the eye, spoke to her in a normal way as if she were a normal girl and not a freak.

Fifth period was Mary Ann's study hour, she could spend it in the library. Ms. Hood drew books from shelves to recommend to her— *Anne of Green Gables; The Secret Garden; Emily of New Moon; The Blue Castle; Are You There God? It's Me, Margaret.*

So absorbed in reading, Mary Ann lost track of time. A bell ringing woke her from her trance, study hour was over.

Mary Ann was allowed to withdraw four books at a time from the library, sometimes returning a book the next day.

"Didn't you like this, Mary Ann?" Ms. Hood would ask; and Mary Ann would say, "Oh I *loved* it. I read it all last night."

Mr. Fox, Mary Ann's eighth-grade English teacher, was impressed too, that Mary Ann Healy was such an avid reader, and wrote book reports that were, as he said, not merely descriptive but, to a degree, analytical, though he never gave her a grade above B−; like other (male) adults he seemed somewhat discomforted by her.

Though he did not stare rudely at her as if undressing her in his mind nonetheless he was stiff with Mary Ann as if she were distracting to him. Alone of her teachers Mr. Fox expressed an interest in Mary Ann's background. He seemed to know about a "Healy ancestor" of hers who was "famous"—"infamous"—for something weird like shooting an airplane out of the sky, many years ago before even her parents were born. Had she ever heard of Romulus Healy? *No?*

Mr. Fox was curious about where exactly she lived, and whether her family were "landowners"—a term new to her. Mr. Fox was even curious about her father's employment, asking about the gas station—"Does your father own it, or lease it?" He asked her if her family was proud of her for having won a scholarship to the Academy.

Proud of her! Such an idea had never entered Mary Ann's mind.

No one was ever *proud of her,* not ever. She was sure!

Embarrassed of her, or ashamed of her—more likely.

Mary Ann did her best to answer Mr. Fox's questions in some way that was polite and plausible though often she had no idea how to answer. (Did her father own or lease the gas station? No idea.) She was eager to escape her teacher who was like a bright blinding beacon in her face—she could not look away from him yet she could not shut her eyes against him. She could not press her hands over her ears, to keep from hearing his voice. Others in the class, especially girls, crowded about Mr. Fox, whom they found *cool, sexy,* but she was not one of these. The only adult with whom Mary Ann felt comfortable at school was the librarian Ms. Hood.

She'd discovered that Ms. Hood's first name was *Imogene.* She had never heard a name so magical.

One day Mary Ann brought a little present for Ms. Hood: a sachet she'd made from lavender that grew wild behind her house.

Making such sachets was something everyone in the family did. Women, girls. Yet Ms. Hood seemed surprised and pleased, as if she'd never heard of such a thing.

"Mary Ann, thank you! What is this for?—to put in a drawer, with clothes?"

"To keep away moths. So moths don't eat your wool clothes."

"That's so thoughtful of you, Mary Ann. It's exactly what I need."

No one had ever told her such a thing—*exactly what I need.* No one had ever expressed gratitude for anything Mary Ann had ever done, in her memory.

Wanting to hug Ms. Hood but standing very still. As if tears might spill from her eyes if she moved. The brightly lit library was her refuge, she hated to leave it and return to the rest of her life, in the classroom and in her home, unpredictable to her as a rowboat lurching and swerving along a swollen creek.

■

DIR-TY GIRL! WHERE'RE YOU going so fast?

Hey—Mary-YANN, show us your titties.

Walking quickly away. Not daring to break into a run for then they will run after her whooping and yipping like a pack of dogs.

More aggressive than usual, these must be older boys from the high school. Boys in her class rarely bother her for she towers over most of them.

A cloudy-gusty day in early October. After school, hurrying to catch the school bus which will bring her to within a quarter-mile of her home on Stockton Road.

Mary-YANN! Hey, babe! Lookit here . . .

Biting her lips, trying to keep from crying. The boys are close behind her, trying to make her trip. One dares to pinch her upper arm. Another pinches her hips, thighs. One or two lunge at her as if to pinch her breasts, jiggling inside a half-buttoned cardigan sweater.

She gives a little cry, begging them to leave her alone.

At a distance, several high-school girls are observing. They dislike the Healy girl, one of the redneck local girls, they feel sorry for her and they are disapproving of her for bringing out the worst in boys, even "nice" boys—boys they want to like.

"Hey!—stop that. What are you guys doing?"

An adult male is scolding them, one of the instructors—Mary Ann's English teacher, Mr. Fox. Out of nowhere Mr. Fox has appeared speaking with authority, and loudly.

The boys are not Mr. Fox's students but they know who Mr. Fox is and are intimidated, abashed. Francis Fox takes pleasure in asserting such gallantry, it is both genuine and exhibitionist, he knows that there are observers, he will be admired. Word may even make its way to Headmistress P. Cady.

Canny Langhorne students revert to good behavior if an instructor is in sight. They understand that their lives are being prepared for them by adults wielding authority. Unlike public school boys they understand that they are meant to be special, privileged. It is their default, as failure is the default of their less affluent contemporaries. A network of adults will nourish them, cultivate them, pass them on to other adults. It is a world of *recommendations*. It is a world of *reputations*. But in this world their lives can be derailed, overturned. If they cross a certain line. If they make a serious blunder, and are caught. By instinct they know to placate some adults more than others. Adults who wield power, and are willing to use it. Instructors like Francis Fox, who, within a few weeks, is beginning to acquire a reputation at the Academy.

A popular teacher, a demanding teacher, a *man*. They can see in Fox's affable gap-toothed smile a certain vigilance that has earned their respect. The pale-blue eyes are friendly but can turn hostile. Fox can be funny in class but Fox can be witheringly sarcastic. Word has spread quickly through the school, Fox is *cool*. Fox will not tolerate *bullshit*.

As the boys stand meekly before him Francis Fox scolds them as "embarrassments" to the Langhorne Academy. He demands their names, and makes a show of memorizing their names. He warns them that if they ever—*ever again*—harass this girl, or any other girl, he will file a report on them with the dean of students, there will be a mark on their transcripts that will turn up on their college applications.

Sexual harassment it's called. Not just *harassment* but *sexual*. Fox wields these words like cudgels.

He has filed such reports in the past, Fox warns them. At his previous school he made sure that sexist behavior was not tolerated, and was "swiftly punished."

Like a drill sergeant in a movie Fox insists that each of the boys mutter an apology to Mary Ann Healy, who cowers behind him, mortified. When they fail to speak audibly Fox forces them to repeat their words.

Dismissing them then with a snap of his fingers. *"Go."*

It's a performance Francis Fox thoroughly enjoys, his first here at the Langhorne Academy, a role for which he was born. Nothing so pleasurable as bullying bullies. And he is taller than they are, an *adult*. Adrenaline pumps hotly through his veins.

The poor Healy girl stands stunned before him like a creature who has been struck over the head, speechless. He feels sorry for her but exasperated by her. Vacant moon-face like one of those insipid rotund females in a painting by Francis Fox's least-favorite artist, Botero.

"Mary Ann. That *is* your name, yes? Come on, I will escort you to the bus."

Mary Ann has no choice, her glowering English teacher escorts her to the rear of the school, where the yellow bus awaits, motor running and exhaust spewing as if with impatience. There is swagger in Fox's stride, it has not escaped his notice that the driver as well as students at the bus have been observing the scene, and are sure to be impressed and relate the tale to others.

In this way, unexpectedly, and to the misfortune of both, Mary Ann Healy falls desperately in love with her teacher Mr. Fox.

CUSTODIAN, HAVEN HALL

SEPTEMBER–OCTOBER 2013

Problem is, Pa is afraid to acknowledge that he's becoming what's called *crippled*.

Problem is, Pa is limping, his right knee hurts like hell. Sometimes, his lower back is so painful he can hardly get out of bed.

Everyone urges him to see a doctor. Pa's face shuts up like a fist. He refuses to discuss it.

Marcus tells Demetrius: "Christ's sake, go with Pa to the fucking school. Help him. It's the least you can do."

Demetrius is stung, why's this *the least* he can do? No matter what he does, if Demetrius does it, and not Marcus, it's *the least*.

Marcus has always been embarrassed that their father is a *janitor*. Not enough work for Lemuel as a carpenter in Wieland, he's had to be a *janitor* at the rich kids' school, scrubbing rich kids' filthy toilets, trying to pass himself off as a *custodian*.

He, Marcus, isn't going to settle for some shit job like that: *janitor*, *custodian*.

Demetrius says stiffly OK. That's enough about Pa.

Hotly Marcus says, fuck *he'd* get himself into such a situation, married, kids, stuck in one place, he's thinking of joining the navy like friends of his, see the world.

See the world. Demetrius laughs, OK. You can *see the world* for me.

■

DO WHAT HAS TO *be done. That is all.*

Somehow it happens like so much in Demetrius's life, he falls into a pattern of behavior at the behest of another, as a consequence of the need of another: first, his mother; now, his father.

He loved his mother, that was OK. That was hard, but OK.

How he feels about the old man isn't so clear. But it's going to be OK.

Demetrius never says *no* to his father. If he'd dared say *no* once, he would never not say *no* again.

Accompanying his father to work in Wieland at the Langhorne Academy on those days when his father needs him. Not much to say to each other in the flatbed truck which sometimes Lemuel drives, sometimes Demetrius. Lemuel Healy has a late-afternoon shift at the school, five P.M. to eleven P.M. weekdays. (Rarely does Lemuel stay until eleven P.M. if there is no one around to observe him leaving; with Demetrius lending a hand, father and son can leave the grounds as early as nine P.M.) There are several custodians at the school, each with his own buildings to maintain; Lemuel is one of the senior custodians, after twelve years of part-time employment, at a wage well above the minimum wage paid to public school custodians. It is Lemuel's belief that he has a reasonably good reputation with his supervisor based upon friendly remarks over the years; he is particularly proud that the headmistress of the school once encountered him in Haven Hall and took time to compliment him on a "beautifully maintained" building, making it a point to ask his name. ("A real lady," Lemuel Healy has said of P. Cady, "—you can tell, she isn't from around here.") But lately Lemuel has been obsessed with worry that he won't be able to continue much longer doing work that requires lifting, bending, protracted exertion, remaining on his feet for hours;

gauging with his eyes whether what he has cleaned is thoroughly *clean*. (Of course, nothing is thoroughly *clean*; that would require virtual sandblasting.) Especially, he is anxious that he will be seen limping, wincing with pain, dropping something because his strength suddenly fails him; he will be reported to the supervisor, who will either coerce him into retiring or, possibly worse, insist that he see a doctor, undergo tests, have surgery.

Especially, Lemuel dreads *spinal surgery*.

Since Ida's death, terrified of any kind of doctor, any kind of test, hospitals. It's in hospitals that people die.

Or, if they don't die in the hospital something inside them dies, that never returns.

That light going out in the eyes.

So many times the old man has fretted about these matters, to Demetrius, to Marcus, to whoever will listen, Demetrius has a strong impulse to clamp his hands over his ears.

If you will just stop, Pa. I can do it if you will stop.

"If I can lean on you, I wouldn't need the fucking cane."

Muttering in Demetrius's ear. Gripping Demetrius's upper arm so hard it hurts, leaning on him as the two make their unsteady way to the rear of the building.

"Take it slow, Pa. I got you."

"Fucking 'slow'—how else am I going to take it!"

Pa can't resist sneering even as he's hanging on to Demetrius to keep from falling.

Demetrius is stoic, silent. Fuck Marcus, and fuck Pa. Half the time Pa's breath smells of whiskey.

Isn't it a worse risk, Lemuel Healy's breath stinking of whiskey on the job, than being noticed limping?—Demetrius wants to ask.

Futile to reason with the old man. Futile to reason with anyone, Demetrius has learned. The closer you are to anyone, the less sense they make to you. Given up expecting anything in his life to make sense: keep your mouth shut, say as few words as possible, do what they ask of you, what's required. At his mother's bedside he learned. At the medical clinic he learned. At the graveside he learned. Exert yourself to the fullest so that you can respect yourself. Keep in mind the example of Jesus Christ on the Cross.

So that you fall into bed exhausted, sink like a stone into the depths of sleep awakened only by cramps in your legs and feet, smelling your body as if, in the night, you've been laboring too, as by day.

Each night thinking with a swell of elation *Thank you, Jesus! I got through it.*

Not that the old man doesn't work hard, once he gets to the school. Pa is crazy to work as quickly as possible before his back seizes, which (of course) can precipitate a seizure.

But needing help, clearly. It's an effort for Demetrius just to drag the cleaning equipment out of the storage closet. Heavy-duty vacuum cleaner, wet/dry vacuum, Kaivac bathroom cleaner. Floor scrubber, carpet extractor, sweeper, mop. The old man takes pride in knowing how these devices work, showing Demetrius how to operate them. Like Lemuel is a young father again, with a young kid. Most nights Lemuel starts out strong enough but soon slows down while Demetrius pushes ahead with vacuum cleaner, cleaning cart, scrubbers, mops, bleaches.

Not such hard work, not like construction, or working a cement truck, but tedious, and demeaning, *smelly.*

Fortunately there's rarely anyone around to notice them. Fortunately the supervisor is gone by five P.M., the few security guards—known here as proctors—have little interest in custodial staff.

If anyone asks who he is, Lemuel tells Demetrius, say he's just *helping out* his old man this one time only.

Avoid looking at anyone. Keep to yourself. *Keep your mouth shut.*

Trash, garbage, dirt, grime, scum, filth accumulate daily, hourly in any space inhabited by children, adolescents. In any space inhabited by people. Long corridors with hardwood floors requiring daily vacuuming, mopping, and polishing. Scrubbing sinks, lavatory floors, toilets. Emptying trash containers including those in girls' lavatories containing smelly sanitary napkins, tampons, dried-blood-reeking, wrapped haphazardly yet with a touching hope of decency in yards of toilet paper. Polishing mirrors, windows. Smooth reflective surfaces in which, wraithlike, with a lean, high-cheekboned face and gaunt eyes, the face of Jesus hovers startling Demetrius out of his trance seeing it's just *his*—his face.

Floors shining like idiocy, why must floors *shine?*

Disinfectant, ammonia fumes making him light-headed. Reminding him of the sharp sad smell of isopropyl alcohol he'd soaked tissues in to clean the plastic port surgically implanted in his mother's upper right chest.

Crazy thoughts drifting through his brain like chub through seaweed seeking—what?

Jesus help me to do what has to be done. Amen.

By the time Demetrius starts working at the Langhorne Academy at five P.M. he has already put in a full shift at Kroger's. Six A.M. unloading trucks at the rear of the store, stocking shelves, bagging groceries. Custodial work as needed: he's the guy to summon to clean up spillage in a store aisle when a customer causes something breakable to fall from a shelf. He's the guy to bring shopping carts back to the store, left by customers in the farthest corners of the parking lot. Mostly he works in silence, efficiently and reliably. Never has much to say but his co-workers seem to like him, one of the (female) cashiers calls him Demmie in a way to make his face redden with a pleasurable sort of embarrassment. He enjoys the others joking and laughing together but always it's a relief to leave the store, be away from people, their eyes on you, sympathetic or pitying or curious, some of them (like the cashier) possibly expecting something from you which you have no way of providing nor even of knowing with certainty what that something might be.

After five P.M. the building Demetrius's father is responsible for keeping clean is mostly empty. Classrooms, teachers' offices, corridors. After-school activities are ended, or ending. Athletic events draw the most excitement at the school, in the gymnasium or on playing fields which Demetrius has no opportunity to see though he frequently hears shouts, cries, whistles, and applause wafting through an opened window as if from a distant planet.

Not envy he feels. Not jealousy. More like loneliness.

■

HIGH-PITCHED NERVOUS GIGGLING?—dim-lighted basement of Haven Hall.

Switching off the floor-polisher he hears it. All of the offices in this corridor appear to be empty, locked; yet, the giggling is coming from one of these.

Maybe Demetrius has heard this before, other afternoons. In this same corridor. Not really noticing. None of his business.

The frosted glass window in the door is opaque but there's a dim light inside. Demetrius notes the name beside the door—*015 Francis Fox. Office hours 4–5 P.M. & by appointment.*

It isn't unusual that students meet teachers in their offices after classes end. But it is unusual, this late. For this *is* late, in Haven Hall. And it is unusual, an office door *shut*.

Earlier in the day, the teachers' office doors are open. All of them, open. Students trail in for individual conferences, conversations. Why the Langhorne Academy costs so much, why public schools cost nothing.

Demetrius pauses to listen: more giggling, a man's deep voice, an inaudible exchange.

Maybe it isn't a student in the office with the (male) instructor. Maybe the giggling is an adult woman, another teacher.

Anyway: none of Demetrius's business. As the old man would say with a shrug—*Fuck all.*

Pushes on, he has work to do. Hours of work. Already his shoulder and arm muscles are aching. His face throbs with heat.

But following this, beginning to notice a girl, a very young-looking girl, a very pretty girl, lingering near Fox's office. On the stairs, in the corridor. Shy, frightened. Excited. Shiny-eyed. Gripping a journal with a fancy cover against her chest.

Sometimes the girl is there when Demetrius arrives, sometimes he sees her later. No other instructor with an office in the basement of Haven Hall remains as late in the day, well after dusk, as Francis Fox.

Once, Demetrius sights this girl—(certain it's her: doesn't want to stare)—as he and Lemuel are approaching the school from the parking lot: she is standing on the walkway in front of the rear entrance, a lone solitary figure as other girls in maroon jumpers pass by her talking and laughing.

Silky darkish-blond hair to her shoulders. Very young: twelve? Must be seventh grade. Looking years younger, far less mature than Demetrius's cousin Mary Ann Healy, who is in eighth grade at the school.

Soon then, a day or two later, happening to see this girl slipping into Fox's office as the door is opened to her, and shut quickly behind her.

Not that Demetrius can be absolutely certain it's the same girl. No.
Of course it's her! You know it is.

None of his business. Makes him feel sick. Gut-sick. A girl so young!

Soon, Demetrius begins to notice, without wishing to notice, other girls waiting to see Francis Fox. Most of them are attractive but one is strikingly unattractive—a rust-red-haired girl with a small triangular face whom Demetrius has seen sitting on the floor across from Fox's office, pleated skirt falling carelessly between her legs. This girl never glances up at him, a custodian would be invisible to her. She is scowling, brooding, leafing through a textbook, scribbling fiercely in a journal.

A journal with a fancy cover, like something carved.

Boys too wait to see Fox, occasionally. It seems that the man is a very popular instructor. Once, Demetrius sees three girls waiting outside 015 Haven Hall: two of them sharing a bench, the other, the rust-red-haired girl, on the floor, back to the wall. Each of these girls is stiffly oblivious of the other two though each is bent over scribbling into a journal with a fancy cover.

Fuck all, it's nothing to you. Bullshit!

One late afternoon pushing the floor-polisher along the corridor Demetrius passes by Fox's office surprised to see the door open, several students cozily crowded together around the instructor's desk, there is laughter, rowdy high spirits. Is there music? Someone's cell phone? Hip-hop? Or is Demetrius imagining this? He has a glimpse of Fox, the teacher, the adult, leaning back in a swivel chair behind his desk, laughing, fully at ease, basking in the moment; feeling a sharp stab of loss, no teacher at any school has ever behaved in such a way to him, not ever. Can't imagine what these kids might be saying to their teacher, or he to them; in all his years in school Demetrius had never more than an awkward exchange with a teacher, usually about a test he'd done poorly on, or homework he hadn't completed.

Not just he found school hard. He'd been too tall for them, probably. Already by eighth grade. He was Marcus's height, by thirteen. They felt threatened by him. They confused him with Marcus, who'd been a surly student. Other Healy boys, who hadn't liked being in school, and allowed teachers to know.

Mrs. Ryan the social studies teacher who seemed to be *trying*. But holding her breath speaking with Demetrius as if some smell wafted from him, from his clothing, about which Demetrius had no clue . . .

How many times, his feelings had been hurt. He was a big baby!— Jesus.

Wanting to be liked, just had no idea how you went about it.

Maybe it's his teeth, Demetrius thinks. Discolored, crooked. Langhorne students have perfect teeth like actors on TV.

Eventually Demetrius learns that Francis Fox is the faculty advisor for the Looking-Glass Book Club, which meets on Thursdays after classes, in the Haven Hall library on the third floor.

Passing by the library window which opens onto the corridor Demetrius has glimpsed a gathering of boys as well as girls—though mostly girls—seeing that the silky-haired girl is among them. Twenty or more, seated in a circle, some in chairs and some on the floor, gazing up raptly at Francis Fox, who is speaking to them.

Demetrius is relieved not to see Mary Ann there.

Relieved that no one notices him: if they glance up, their eyes simply fail to connect with his.

Stoop-shouldered young man in work-clothes, not so much older than they are but *work-staff, invisible.*

■ ■ ■

THEN, THIS HAPPENS.

Six-twenty P.M. damp-mopping the floor in the basement of Haven Hall and out of nowhere the silky-haired girl appears at the farther end of the corridor slowly approaching the (shut) door of 015 Haven Hall. Inclines her head meekly as if listening for a voice inside.

(No voice? By the girl's posture tense as an arrow pulled back from its bow it would seem that there is none.)

Shyly rapping on the frosted-glass window. Waits for a response but there is no response.

Not daring to breathe—(as Demetrius is not daring to breathe)—as if half-hoping there is no one inside awaiting her, she will be spared the ignominy of rejection . . .

Demetrius is able to see the girl clearly: She is thin-armed, thin-legged, the corduroy jumper fits her loosely. She seems to have lost weight recently. Ivory-pale face like a face in an old picture book.

So beautiful! Demetrius's heart lurches.

After some hesitation the girl again raps her knuckles against the frosted-glass window and this time she is admitted, a shadowy figure looms in the doorway, with a nervous giggle the girl ducks beneath the figure's arm disappearing inside the office as the door is shut firmly behind her.

Forgotten mop gripped in his hands Demetrius has been staring, enthralled.

It is late for a student to be meeting with a teacher in Haven Hall. The basement corridor is deserted, everyone else has departed.

Knock on the door! Whatever is about to happen, stop it from happening.

Aiding and abetting a crime against a child. You must intervene.

An adult male, a twelve-year-old girl. There is no "consent" at the age of twelve.

Disgusting stories Demetrius has heard from his brother, guys taking advantage of young girls. Some of them Healy relatives.

He could open Fox's door, he has his father's key to offices in Haven Hall. Pretend he didn't realize that anyone is inside.

Except: Pa would be furious with him. Bringing trouble onto both of them.

He's acted impulsively in the past. It has never gone well. Intruding in others' business, asking for trouble.

That fracas he got into in high school defending the special-needs girl who'd been bullied by other girls, knocked to the cafeteria floor as a crowd gathered around them hooting with laughter. A school security guard took them all into custody and Demetrius was suspended from the school with the others as if he hadn't been trying to help.

Abrupt end of Demetrius's education, he never went back.

Only his mother consoled him—*Demetrius, you are blessed by God to do what you are called to do.*

His brother laughed at him—*Asshole!*

It wasn't true as people said that Demetrius was expelled from school. After ten days' suspension he was readmitted but didn't want to return. Several of his teachers pleaded on his behalf but he'd turned his heart against the school. *Fuck all it was no place for him, he wasn't wanted there.*

And what the hell difference would it make, if he had a high-school diploma. He'd be working at Kroger's anyway. Taking on part-time construction work, carpentry. If he was lucky, getting hired at the Langhorne Academy taking his father's place on the custodial staff.

Damned if he's going to knock on Fox's door. Best to mind his own business. The school should be protecting the girl, not Demetrius.

Soft laughter inside the dim-lighted office. Lowered male voice like a rough caress.

Demetrius finishes mopping the corridor. His face is burning, bleach fumes make his eyes water.

Meets up with the old man in the teachers' lounge on the first floor, where Pa is sitting slouched, half-dozing waiting for Demetrius to drive him home.

On Pa's breath, fresh smell of whiskey. Must be bringing a pint bottle with him in his pocket, Demetrius is pissed as hell.

"OK, Pa. Let's go."

■ ■ ■

AT THE AGE OF twenty Demetrius has had little experience with girls. Thoughts of *sex* are distressing to him.

Girls and women are intimidating to Demetrius. If they approach him aggressively. If they seem to be flirting with him. As they might flirt with a large harmless-seeming dog.

Anyone who shows interest in him, Demetrius distrusts. What he admires in the Langhorne students is how invisible he is in their eyes.

The silky-haired girl. She has never seen him, he is sure. Girls in the Langhorne uniform look through him, he is safest this way.

What he knows of life: it is hazardous, capricious. Things happen, and then other things happen. In a rowboat in a fast-running river without an oar.

Cautious at the Langhorne school where he has no business being. Pa has told him always knock on a door even if you're sure the room is empty.

Excuse me? Custodian.

Another evening, he's back in Haven Hall. This time all the offices are dark.

015. Francis Fox. The office has a low ceiling, a single window high on the rear wall which has been left open two or three inches.

Like a bloodhound sniffing the air seeking *her* scent.

Smelling something else: pastries?

In Fox's wastebasket are remnants of fruit tarts—lemon, strawberry. What looks like a chocolate-covered strawberry. Dirtied paper napkins, candy wrappers, tissues.

Wads of tissues, stiff-crusted. Demetrius stares in disgust but isn't going to examine closely.

Isn't going to sniff at these. No.

Empties the wastebasket into the wheeled trash receptacle in the hall.

He will spend a minimum amount of time in 015, hurriedly cleaning the floor, the teacher's desktop. Takes care to close the door so that, if anyone passes in the corridor, they won't see him inside.

On Fox's desk is some kind of sculpture, what Demetrius might call a "statue"—a man's head and shoulders, and a crow-like bird on his shoulder, facing the door.

A plaque identifies the man as *Edgar Allan Poe 1809–1849*. Heavy, ugly thing. The eyes are blind but protuberant. The lips are drawn back tight from the teeth. The crow-like bird's claws appear to be sinking into the man's shoulder gripping him in place.

Fascinating to Demetrius, how the sinewy feathers in the bird's wings are mimicked in the sinewy waves of hair carved into the head. Sightless eyes of the bird mimicked in the sightless eyes of the head.

No idea how you make a statue like this. Not carved like stone but some kind of metal, possibly molten, in a mold.

The sculpture commemorates a poetry prize. *Francis H. Fox first-prize winner Nevermore Competition, Poe Society of America 2011.*

Demetrius runs a damp cloth lightly over the sculpture. Tempted to knock it over, onto the floor. But if it broke? The bird might snap off, Pa would be blamed.

Posters on the wall: dreamlike flowers close-up, in soft pale hues. Cats of Africa: lions, leopards, panthers, cheetahs. Poster for the Looking-Glass Book Club with an illustration of a girl of a bygone era in old-fashioned clothes, with an unnaturally long neck and a surprised expression.

On Fox's bookshelves, paperback books for young readers. None of the titles are familiar to Demetrius. He can't remember the title of a single book he has ever read. (Printed words quiver in his brain, he can't force himself to sit still and *read*. Mary Ann once told him she thought he had something called *dyslexic? Dyslexia?*)

Demetrius opens Fox's desk drawers one at a time. Hairs at the nape of his neck stir for what if he is caught? Going through a teacher's desk?

In the first drawer, a box of Godiva chocolates, fancy-looking candies wrapped in foil. Tempted to slip one into his pocket but better not, Pa might smell chocolate on his breath and ask about it. The old man is unpredictable that way, noticing things you wouldn't expect and not noticing things you would.

In other drawers, a bag of chocolate chip cookies, white plastic plates and forks, napkins. In the center drawer, lesson plans, class lists. Grade book.

Demetrius runs his eye down the class lists. The girl with the silky hair must be one of these names.

Here is something curious: Fox has marked just a few names, girls' names, with small red stars. *Her* name is one of these, Demetrius is sure.

He discovers his cousin Mary Ann Healy's name in an eighth-grade list. No star beside her name, he's relieved to see.

In a lower desk drawer Demetrius discovers a card with an old-fashioned kitten illustration.

MR. FOX I LOVE YOU!!!

YOUR KITTEN

Is this the girl? The girl he saw slip into Fox's office?

Also in the drawer are more cards, childish drawings of hearts, roses, kittens. Poems by *YOUR KITTEN*.

"That fucker! Son of a bitch."

So soon in the fall term, already these girls have fallen under the spell of Francis Fox.

Of course, they're just children. Naïve, ignorant.

But what is the man's secret? He's so much older than they are, why aren't they suspicious of him? Disgusted by him?

Fox is evil. He should be stopped. Someone should stop him.

In another drawer, a small hand mirror. A mirror to allow Francis Fox to peer at himself, in secret?

Demetrius's eyes narrow, seeing his face. How raw, exposed he looks. His blemished skin is glaring.

Each morning early Demetrius shaves hurriedly. Trying to minimize time spent looking into a bathroom mirror. By early evening his angular jaws are stubbled.

But your eyes are beautiful, Demetrius. You are a custodian of souls. In your heart, you are beautiful.

He owes it to his mother, to try to remember. The world wears away our memories like wind. He must make a conscious effort to remember.

Clutching at his hands with her cold hands. He'd spread his fingers over hers to warm them.

"Hey? What the hell—?"

The office door has been pushed open, a man stands in the doorway staring at Demetrius.

Fox! In corduroy coat, tie, chino trousers. A look on his face of incredulity, alarm.

At once Demetrius has dropped the mirror, shuts the drawer with his knee. Stammers something explanatory about *just finishing up.*

"Going through my desk? That's what you're doing?"

Demetrius draws himself up to his full height, not knowing how to respond. He has been taken entirely by surprise. He sees that the teacher is agitated, angry. Yet, Fox can't be sure what Demetrius has seen, which drawers he's opened.

Fox saw the cleaning equipment outside the door, he knew that someone was working inside. But wasn't prepared to see Demetrius peering into a desk drawer.

Because the son of a bitch has something to hide.

Demetrius backs off from a confrontation. He will not meet Fox's glaring eyes. Stammers a weak apology setting the emptied wastebasket beside the desk as if to establish that this is his major purpose—emptying trash.

For a moment it looks as if Fox is going to stand in the doorway and block Demetrius's exit but he steps to the side. Demetrius is telling himself that Fox has not seen exactly what Demetrius discovered. The chocolates, the poem, the mawkish cards—Fox can't be certain for those drawers are shut.

The teacher's face is unevenly flushed. His breath comes quick, audible. He must have returned to his office for something he forgot, he is carrying a briefcase.

At least, Demetrius thinks, he hasn't been caught stealing anything. Not even a Godiva chocolate.

As if he intends to berate him further Fox follows Demetrius into the corridor. Then, he seems to change his mind, asking in a voice affable, conciliatory: "Are you on the custodial staff here? You seem kind of young to be a janitor."

Putting his hands on the heavy floor-polisher Demetrius avoids meeting Fox's gaze, no interest in engaging with the excited man.

"D'you belong to a union? Do janitors here belong to a union?"

Demetrius shakes his head in silence—*No*. Or, *Don't know*.

No idea how to reply to Francis Fox. Demetrius has never exchanged a word with anyone at Langhorne. Like a cornered rat Demetrius could defend himself with his fists but until then, his instinct is to retreat.

Fortunately, Francis Fox lets him go. Wanting no more trouble than Demetrius does.

■

THAT NIGHT DRIVING HIS father back home, pitch-black countryside beyond Wieland in a trance of consternation, shame. Replaying this scene like a video.

Lemuel senses Demetrius's agitation. "Something wrong? What's wrong?"—Pa is acutely sensitive to things going wrong.

Demetrius shrugs his shoulders. Nothing wrong, he's just tired. Fucking tired.

He's fucking tired, his father says.

"Nobody saw you tonight, did they?"—working himself up to being anxious. Worse than a woman, sometimes. Demetrius has to placate him.

All of his life since the age of eleven: placating others. Why Demetrius Healy was born.

"Nothing's wrong, Pa. Everything is OK."

Lemuel sighs, shifts in his seat. He doesn't entirely trust Demetrius but he isn't going to accuse him of lying.

Telling Demetrius that he got a lot done tonight. More than usual. Cleaning and polishing lighting fixtures in the foyer, aluminum surfaces, tiles. For each, special chemicals are required.

Slowly, carefully, taking his time Lemuel cleans filthy chalkboards, erasers, and eraser trays. Fussy work in cramped areas for which Lemuel with his arthritic joints and watery eyes is best suited now that Demetrius has taken on most of the heavy cleaning.

Sometimes Demetrius wonders if Pa's supervisor knows that one of his custodians brings his son to work with him to do the heavy work.

Two for the price of one. Fuck!—Demetrius grinds his back teeth.

How the scene in Fox's office played out. He sees it like a scene in a movie. Demetrius going through the teacher's desk, taking a chance. And the door is pushed open, he and Fox stare at each other.

Might've ended with Fox yelling for one of the proctors. Demanding to see Demetrius's ID.

Instead: it was instantaneous between them like an electric current leaping from one to the other, the acknowledgment on the part of Fox that Demetrius with his ropey-muscled arms and lean face was the taller and (very possibly) the stronger of the two, as he was the younger, an instinctive sizing-up between two males.

Demetrius trusts to instinct. Fight like hell if your life is threatened.

But if not, get the hell out.

Smiling to think that he frightened Fox. He thinks he did.

In a movie the scene wouldn't have ended as it did. In a movie there would be no point to such a scene unless something dramatic happened between the custodian-intruder and the teacher.

One of the men kills the other, in such a scene. Has to be.

Yet, not in this case. Not enough motivation for either man to commit a violent act.

And no weapon: neither had a weapon.

Except: the ugly sculpture on the teacher's desk. Demetrius recalls how heavy the thing is, how unwieldy it would be to seize it, bring it down hard on Fox's head, hard enough to crack the man's skull.

You'd get just one chance. First blow, would have to be final.

But why would he do something like that?—Demetrius shudders.

He would not do anything like that. Not Demetrius Healy, whom his mother loved so deeply. Jesus has loved so deeply.

He will be cooler-headed in the future, Demetrius thinks. The girl, the silly silky-haired girl who'd been nibbling at fruit tarts and chocolates, all the silly girls leaving poems and cards for Francis Fox, let them take care of themselves.

■ ■ ■

HISSING STINGING RAINDROPS OUT of a thunderous sky strike the pavement like bullets.

This autumnal afternoon in October. Sudden chill, smell of cold damp stone.

He has pulled the car around to the rear entrance of Haven Hall so that his father doesn't have to walk far, now on his long legs Demetrius is running from the parking lot back to the building head bowed against pelting rain when he sees her—the shock of it, *her*—sheltering from the rain in an archway.

Tears streaking her face, that might have been raindrops.

Raindrops streaking her face, that might have been tears.

It's the girl with the silky dark-blond hair: *Your Kitten.* Demetrius has not seen her in a while, he has begun to think he will not see her again.

Not that he has been looking for her. He has *hoped not* to see her.

Observing the small forlorn figure now from a little distance. She seems subdued, listless. In a raincoat, a hood pulled partway over her head. Must be waiting for someone to pick her up. Which would mean that she isn't a boarder at the school but a local resident.

Demetrius could speak with whoever it is who arrives. A parent, a mother.

Has he broken your heart? Fucking son of a bitch.

His own heart is beating quickly. Running from the parking lot through the rain has been invigorating to him. He is feeling excited, hopeful—not sure why.

Could kill him, for you. No one would know.

This thought has come to Demetrius out of nowhere like an arrow plunging into his breast.

Of course, she isn't a silly girl. She is just a girl, a blameless child.

Inside Haven Hall Demetrius's father is waiting for him. By now he will have unlocked the custodian's closet. Wondering where the hell Demetrius has got to but Demetrius is reluctant to leave the girl.

What he should do: Approach her in a way not to alarm her. Speak quietly to her. Allow her to know that—he knows.

What your teacher is doing to you. I know . . .

Or, he could wait to see who arrives to pick the girl up. A parent, a mother, someone who loves her, will protect her.

All he would need to do would be to approach the vehicle on the driver's side, tap on the window, stammer a few words—"Excuse me? I think you should know—one of the teachers is taking advantage of your daughter . . ."

Taking advantage of your daughter. Not a way that Demetrius speaks, such words are not in his vocabulary.

And is this true, does Demetrius really *know*? Making such an accusation could be the biggest mistake of his life.

He doesn't even know if this girl is Your Kitten. Maybe there is no Your Kitten. What proof does he have, why should he get involved, the private school is an alien and hostile environment, no one here wishes him or any Healy well. Students here are rich spoiled brats, the last thing you want is to confront a parent, best thing for Demetrius is get to work, get the work done, get the hell home.

■

IT'S ALSO IN EARLY OCTOBER that Demetrius begins to see the rust-red-haired girl with the peevish hatchet-face and pellet eyes more frequently.

At first he's scarcely aware of her. For it's the other girl—*Your Kitten*—that Demetrius broods over.

On the steps to the basement of Haven Hall the rust-red-haired girl walking with trancelike slowness like one whose coordination is slightly impaired. Outside Fox's office waiting with the grim forbearance of a

midget pit bull while another student confers with him inside. Upstairs
in the corridor outside the library where the Looking-Glass Book Club
meets on Thursday afternoons.

The rust-red-haired girl is older than Your Kitten. An eighth grader,
probably. The pellet eyes raking across Demetrius's face exude not
only prepubescent misery but something like incredulity, fury.

A spoiled girl accustomed to getting her way, Demetrius perceives.
A spoiled girl baffled and thwarted when not getting her way.

Standing irresolute in the hall outside the library where the
Looking-Glass Book Club is meeting as if she wants to join the others
inside but can't or won't. Purely yearning yet stubborn, resistant. Is
she waiting for someone to come out into the hall and notice her, and
invite her to join them in the library? Waiting for Francis Fox himself
to invite her? Or is she, despite her peevish expression, stricken with
prepubescent shyness?

"Stop looking at me! I'll report you."

Demetrius is taken by surprise. He has not been looking directly
at the rust-red-haired girl but he has been aware of her as he pushes
the floor-polisher along the corridor.

Averting his eyes Demetrius stumbles an apology. *Sorry!*

Usually, Langhorne students see through Demetrius as if he
doesn't exist. This one is staring at him incensed, her small close-set
eyes filled with tears.

Demetrius moves quickly past the girl as his father has instructed
him he must do in such circumstances if he finds himself in confrontation with one of *them*.

He is shaken, frankly scared. *I'll report you.*

He resolves, he will avoid this girl if he can. She is not one of the
meek hopeful girls who hang about Fox's office and she is nothing
like the silky-haired Your Kitten.

Yet, the following week Demetrius can't avoid seeing the rust-red-
haired girl again, outside Fox's office. It is just past five P.M., Fox's
door is open and another student is inside. Haven Hall has not begun
to empty out; other teachers are in their offices conferring with stu-

dents. Demetrius is trying to recall if teachers at the Wieland school even had offices like these, he's sure that they did not.

With grim forbearance the girl is seated on the floor with her knees drawn up tightly against her chest, pleated skirt spilling carelessly about her legs. She seems to have been there a long time, unmoving. Fortunately, this time she is totally oblivious of Demetrius passing by.

"Eu-nice? Are you still there? You can come in now, dear."

Dear. Has to be a joke. No one, least of all Francis Fox, could think of this homely girl as *dear.*

But Eunice scrambles eagerly to her feet at the invitation of the bemused voice as a dog might leap up summoned by its master. Eunice enters the office as another student exits.

Demetrius, at the farther end of the hall by now, pushes on without a backward glance.

■ ■ ■

THANK YOU, JESUS.

Thank you, God.

Demetrius has never understood what relationship there is between these two—*Jesus the Savior, God the Father.*

No one has explained it to him. If it was explained at Sunday school, to which, years before, for a vague while, Demetrius was sent as a little boy, he has long forgotten.

There is another figure too—the *Holy Spirit.*

Truly, no idea what the hell the *Holy Spirit* is!

Out of embarrassment no one in the Healy family would speak of such things. Marcus would choke with laughter, Lemuel would scowl. The only person who's ever spoken of *Jesus* and *God* to Demetrius was his mother, Ida, who prayed with him, and for him, on her knees beside her bed, until she became too ill and too weak.

But it was only when she'd become sick that she spoke of such things. Demetrius thinks of *Jesus,* and of *God,* in association with the nauseating odor of isopropyl alcohol, the odor of stained sheets, a breath smelling like damp pennies in the palm of a hand.

Still, Demetrius is determined to give thanks that things are what they are and not worse. His father's arthritis is bad but not (yet) *crippling-bad*.

His own life isn't so bad, he has a decent-paying job where (he wants to think) he's respected. A son helping his father is a good thing.

Always wisest to be grateful for what you have, which might be taken from you at any time.

∎

MID-OCTOBER, CHILLY DAY. Already by five P.M. the sun is sinking in the sky, there's a smell of sodden leaves. Demetrius has dropped Lemuel off at the rear of Haven Hall, he's parking their car in the staff lot. By chance crossing the lot he happens to see two figures ahead that look familiar: the taller, the man, is Francis Fox; the other, his cousin Mary Ann Healy.

His cousin! Demetrius stares in disbelief. Fox is walking in long strides to his car, Mary Ann is following after him half-running.

His cousin!—one of Francis Fox's girls?

Fox's hair stirs in the wind as if with impatience, irritation. He is dressed casually but stylishly. Mary Ann is wearing a loose-fitting jacket over her school uniform. Her hair is disheveled, her cheeks flushed. She seems to be pleading with Fox who speaks sharply to her without looking at her and without breaking his stride.

Demetrius shrinks back hoping not to be seen. He has not encountered the middle-school teacher since Fox pushed open the door to his office and accosted him. He has not seen his cousin since Mary Ann began school at the Langhorne Academy.

Fox walks swiftly to his car, a white Acura; Mary Ann stands staring after him forlorn as an abandoned puppy. As Fox backs up the car, to swing around and exit the lot, Mary Ann decides impulsively to run after the car, and as the Acura moves forward somehow it happens that she is struck by the left front fender—glancingly—but enough to be knocked to the ground.

Demetrius shouts at her, running forward. Mary Ann sits stunned on the pavement as the Acura gains momentum moving away.

"Jesus! Are you all right, Mary Ann?"

Demetrius helps Mary Ann to her feet. She isn't hurt, she insists hotly. Her cheeks are very flushed, damp with tears. She doesn't look happy to see Demetrius.

"He almost ran you down! He just drove away!"

"I said—I'm all right. Please don't shout . . ."

"You were knocked down by a car for Christ's sake. I should take you to the ER for X-rays."

"I told you, Demmie—I'm all right. Why are you here?"

"Never mind why I'm here. I saw what happened. Is that son of a bitch one of your teachers? He should be reported to the police, he left the scene of an accident."

"It wasn't his fault! He didn't see me. It was my fault, I—I can't talk to you right now, Demetrius, I have to take the bus home . . ."

"I can drive you home. I can drive you to the ER."

"No, please. I told you—I'm all right. Nothing hurts. Please don't shout, Demetrius, people will hear us."

Mary Ann is looking frightened, clutching at Demetrius's sleeve.

"What were you and that man talking about, Mary Ann? It looked like you were having an argument."

"We were not having an argument! Why are you spying on me?"

"I'm not spying on you. I just want to know what the hell is going on with you and this—Fox."

Mary Ann stares at Demetrius astonished that he knows Fox's name. She pushes away from him, she is indignant, abashed. As Demetrius calls after her Mary Ann walks resolutely away from him, limping slightly. He is hesitant to follow her. He doesn't want to attract attention, there are Langhorne students at a distance, queueing for a bus.

It will be a matter of deep perplexity to Demetrius, that the girl-cousin for whom he has always had tender feelings, whom he wishes only to protect, is annoyed with *him*.

Calling after her pleadingly, he will drive her to the ER . . .

Mary Ann doesn't seem to hear. She breaks into a run, limping. The school bus awaits in a courtyard nearby. Demetrius looks after her clenching his fists.

God damn motherfucker Fox, he will kill the bastard with his bare hands.

∎

FURIOUS! SICK WITH RAGE, wouldn't be able to sleep, has to see his cousin that night, demand to know what the hell is going on, but arriving at his aunt's house at ten P.M. Demetrius is conscious of annoying his aunt Pauline sprawled on a sofa barefoot and in sweatpants in the dim-lit living room drinking from a can of beer and watching *Forensic Files* on a wall-screen TV. An aroma of something cheesy, scorched-baked-dough comes to his nostrils.

Demetrius has always been a favorite of his aunt's but Pauline is scowling at him now saying Jesus! it's late, Mary Ann is in her room doing homework, every night there's a shitload of homework from the new school, ten times more demanding than the Wieland school so Mary Ann doesn't have time to help me out like she used to, no wonder the place is looking like a pigsty. Every night there's a crisis doing the damned homework, every night Mary Ann cries herself to sleep, doesn't have any friends at the new school, says they laugh at her behind her back, it's a shame they let themselves be talked into sending Mary Ann to the private school on that scholarship, first time her and Blake have agreed on something in a long time so they might change their mind and take her out of the Langhorne school except everybody made such a fuss when Mary Ann got the scholarship, they'd be saying she flunked out if she quits now.

Pauline asks Demetrius if he'd like a beer, Demetrius thanks her saying he'd like to but can't stay long, has to get up early in the morning, he's got to be at Kroger's at six A.M.; he really just wants to talk to Mary Ann for a few minutes. Pauline peers at him suspiciously asking why, what's going on, is Mary Ann in some kind of trouble she doesn't know about?—but before Demetrius can think of an answer Pauline's attention is drawn back to the TV, a rapist-murderer is being arrested.

Demetrius uses the opportunity to slip away, at the rear of the house rapping on the door of Mary Ann's room saying *Hey? It's me,* pushing open the door before Mary Ann can respond telling him not to come in.

So many times Demetrius has been in this house, him and Marcus, hanging out with their cousins, Mary Ann's older brothers now living elsewhere, as Marcus is living elsewhere. Demetrius has to think he's kind of stuck in his life, even Mary Ann is getting older, growing up, he's still the kid he was at fourteen, fifteen, long-limbed and gawky and his skin blemished, has to make himself realize that he's out of school, twenty going on twenty-one, his mother has died and is not going to return, no one will ever love him as his mother loved him, not even Jesus.

Though in recent years he's been thinking there's a special feeling between him and Mary Ann, she loves him, or anyway likes him in a special way, a feeling for Demetrius she doesn't have for Marcus, or any other boy, but now it's like a needle in the heart, he sees the look in Mary Ann's face at the sight of him like she's embarrassed, guilty, but exasperated too—*Last person she wants to see right now, asshole: you.*

Mary Ann stares at Demetrius not knowing what to say. Sprawled on her rumpled bed amid a clutter of books and papers and part-eaten pizza crusts, not in the school uniform as Demetrius somehow envisioned but in jeans torn at the knees, soiled pullover Orlon sweater stretched at the neck and snug-fitting at the bust. She's barefoot, her hair is disheveled and her face slightly swollen. Her eyelids are puffy as if she's just been roused from a deep sleep and slow-blinking now trying to factor Demetrius in, what his appearance in her room might mean.

About Mary Ann on the bed are scattered papers, textbooks, a journal with an ornate cover into which she has been writing in purple ballpoint ink. She's twisting a homemade beaded bracelet around her wrist nervously.

Seeing the look in Demetrius's eyes Mary Ann shuts her eyes tight assuring him she is *all right,* she is *not hurt,* it's *none of his business* what happened today at school.

"Bullshit, it *is* my business! I saw you running after that mother-fucker tonight."

Demetrius sees a mark on the inside of Mary Ann's forearm, tugs up her sweater sleeve to reveal an ugly purplish-yellow bruise. Mary Ann shrinks from him, pulls the sleeve back down to her wrist.

"I had this before today. Anyway, it's nothing."

Demetrius is hurt, his cousin isn't at all welcoming. That special feeling between them, that unspoken alliance, is broken now; Mary Ann is sullen, unsmiling.

"I told you, Demmie, it was an accident. I slipped, I fell but I didn't hurt myself. Mr. Fox didn't even see me."

"But what were you doing there? Following him in the parking lot?"

"I had a question about a homework assignment . . ."

"'Homework'! Like hell."

"Yes! Homework! Every night we have journal entries . . . I had a question, that's all."

"Is that it?—the journal you write in?"

"Yes. But you can't see it."

In a childish gesture Mary Ann hides the journal beneath a pillow.

"Our journals are 'confidential'—'private.' No one gets to read them except Mr. Fox and we don't even have to show Mr. Fox every-thing unless we want to. There is always a 'margin of secrecy.'"

"Let me see."

"I *will not.* This is none of your business, Demmie. Why are you even here?"

"Because Fox is what d'you call it—a *pedo-file.* An adult who likes children. Young girls."

"He is *not.*"

Mary Ann laughs contemptuously. Demetrius looms over her as she lies on the bed.

"Just tell me what's going on with you and Fox. Then I'll go home."

"Nothing is going on!"

"He tried to run you over. I saw it."

"He did not! I fell."

"He tried to kill you . . ."

"He *did not.* I slipped and fell. It was my fault—I'm clumsy."

"What were you doing running after him?"

"Why were you there? Why are you *here*? I think you should go home."

"I was at the school because I drove Pa there. I'm here because I need to do something about Fox."

"He's my English teacher! He's the only teacher who ever liked me. I just wanted to ask him a question. What happened was an accident. Now go away."

Demetrius's brain feels tangled like pondweed at Wieland Pond. He has come to be certain he saw Francis Fox deliberately try to run over Mary Ann in the parking lot. If called upon to testify as a witness he will raise his right hand, solemnly swear, *Yes. I saw.*

"Oh, Demmie. I wish you knew."

"Knew what?"

"Mr. Fox. How special he is. How kind and generous he is. Not like people in our family. Not like people who live out here. He gave me this journal, it's special for *me.*"

Mary Ann rolls over, retrieves the journal from beneath the pillow. She opens the journal so that Demetrius can see it from a few feet away, but doesn't let him take it from her.

"These little stars, see these little red stars?—they mean 'very promising.' There's one on almost every page. Mr. Fox has been letting me do my homework over again if it isn't right the first time. That's special to *me,* he says that I've been disadvantaged by my education and background. 'You can transcend your genetic history by an act of will.'"

"'Genetic history'—what the fuck's that? Like, our grandparents? Great-grandparents?"

"In the beginning Mr. Fox didn't grade my homework at all, he said it 'wasn't ready' to be graded. Then, he gave me C's. But then, he gave me a B–. Now see here," Mary Ann says excitedly, turning pages, "—he gave me a B+."

Demetrius is feeling deflated, disappointed. There's a feverish glow to Mary Ann's face that is hurtful to him.

Last Christmas she gave Demetrius one of the beaded bracelets her grandmother had taught her to make. Wild birds' feathers, bright-colored yarn, glass beads woven together on an elastic band which, she insisted, a boy or a man could wear, but Demetrius was reluctant to wear, and had put the bracelet away for safekeeping in his room. Had to wonder if Mary Ann had forgotten about the bracelet since she hadn't asked him about it afterward.

"Mr. Fox assigns us poems and stories from the anthology and then we're supposed to write about our own lives, using them for 'inspiration.' He says, write about something that happened to you but make yourself into your favorite animal and change other details too. It's our exercise in *spiritual transformation*. 'What is it you plan to do with your one wild and precious life?'"

Demetrius has been staring at his girl-cousin in a way he has never stared at her before. Is she quoting poetry? Whose poetry? Mary Ann has never confided in him so intimately, in so deep-thrilled a voice; she is lying on her back on the bed, flexing her toes sensuously, reading from the journal in a hoarse, husky voice.

She's in love with him—Fox! In love with that motherfucker.

A flame seems to rush over Demetrius. He snatches the journal from Mary Ann's hands.

"This is bullshit, Mary Ann. Fox is just some bastard who wants to fuck you, get it?"

Mary Ann winces at the crude word *fuck*. Never has her cousin uttered this word in her presence.

Scornfully Demetrius leafs through the journal. Poems written in purple ink, inside shakily drawn hearts, by "Mary Ann"—love poems! In a mocking voice Demetrius reads:

"*Dear Mister Fox!*
Since you have come into my life

My life is like a flame.
My life is a fire, a sun, a moon,
All the stars glimmering together
And no one is to blame."

"This is such bullshit, Mary Ann. Jesus!"

Mary Ann tries to seize the journal, Demetrius pushes her back onto the bed.

"Go away! Go home! I hate you!"

Demetrius tears the page out of the journal, crumples it in his fist, and tosses it onto the bed, tosses the journal after it. Mary Ann screams at him:

"I love Mr. Fox more than anybody in the world and *I hate you.*"

Without a word Demetrius exits Mary Ann's bedroom, exits the house by the kitchen door to avoid his drunken aunt Pauline in the living room watching *Forensic Files.*

■

IT WAS LIKE A gamble, and he lost.

(Possibly) he expected a different reaction. (Possibly) he half-expected his cousin to agree with him, even thank him.

Not the way it turns out.

Hate you. Love Mr. Fox.

HAPPY BIRTHDAY!

18 OCTOBER 2013

"Happy birthday, Francis!"

Jubilant ringing of the doorbell in the rented apartment on Consent Street, Fox opens the door warily and is stunned to see Katy Cady in a wide-brimmed hat beaming at him.

Like a maiden in a nineteenth-century bucolic painting Katy is all but staggering beneath an armload of bounty: a pot of yellow chrysanthemums so festive-bright they hurt Francis's eyes, gaily colored food containers, an unwieldy but surely very expensive designer handbag. She has brought a *birthday dinner* for them both, she declares.

Birthday? Francis Fox tries to think: *is* it his birthday?

Has he made plans with Katy Cady, to celebrate his birthday? But—when did he make these plans?

"Aren't you going to let me in, Francis? You seem *surprised*."

"Of course, Katy—come in . . ."

Staring at this radiant ebullient woman whom, in the exigency of the moment, Francis might almost have difficulty identifying: for the ringing of the doorbell in this generic-neutral zone Francis has established for himself in Wieland is so rare, its sound fills him with apprehension, dread—(who in Wieland is daring to ring Francis Fox's doorbell at six-fifteen P.M. of a weekday?)—if not exasperation—(not Mary Ann Healy, the infatuated girl wouldn't dare seek out her English teacher in his home—would she?); but rallies with a grimace of a smile which might be mistaken, by a hopeful woman friend, as warmly welcoming.

Francis relieves Katy of her armload of parcels. There is a comical near-mishap, the chrysanthemums almost tumble to the floor but Francis seizes the pot in time, and sets it on a table. He is a bit dazzled by his friend's sudden appearance: Katy's skin glows with ruddy health, her amber eyes shine inside the lenses of the transparent pink frames Katy has worn, in one minor variant or another, since Francis first met her.

A hurried hug, brushing of Francis's numbed lips against Katy's cheek, squeezing of fingers as Francis tries not to inhale too deeply the woman's odor of heated urgency, yearning, determination intensified as in a bell jar by several hours of nonstop driving from New York City for even at this juncture, Francis is reminded of the thrillingly scentless perspiration of his *kittens*.

"Did you forget that today is your birthday, Francis? You *did*! You most certainly *did*! You should look guilty, Francis, you are so, so neglectful of yourself!"—Katy chides Francis Fox affectionately. "And you forgot that I was coming tonight, didn't you! And bringing dinner for us all the way from Le Bernardin."

Francis leads Katy into his apartment, which is as sparely furnished as a minimalist stage set. He has delayed unpacking his belongings, he has been too distracted. The living room walls are bare. The carpeted floor feels bare, a dull sand-color. In his bedroom at the rear he has begun to hang reproductions of his favorite Balthus paintings, which he has no intention of hanging in his living room.

"So very nice to see you, Francis!"—Katy cries; even as Francis murmurs, "So very nice to see *you*, Katy."

Now vaguely, guiltily Francis recalls receiving emails, text messages, calls from Katy Cady in recent weeks which he hasn't gotten around to answering, nor even in most cases reading; he has been so busy with teaching, and faculty meetings, and the intricacies of cultivating *rapport* with potential *kittens,* he has not had time. It's likely that Katy proposed a birthday celebration for this very night and Francis skimmed through the message, failing to absorb it.

"You work too hard, Francis! You're becoming a workaholic! You need someone to look after you, to prevent you from exhausting your-self. When I didn't hear back from you about tonight—(when you didn't answer your phone)—I spoke with Aunt Paige and she assured me that you are well but working very hard and everyone is impressed with you—*she* is certainly impressed. You've organized a book club? Already? Aunt Paige said, 'Katy, I'm so grateful to you for helping to bring Francis to us, thank you *again.*'"

These breathless cadences of speech don't sound at all like P. Cady to Francis's ear but he isn't about to question Katy in her extravagant mood.

"Our dinner is a surprise. I think you will like it. I hope you're hungry, Francis!"

It has always seemed distasteful to Francis Fox, to remark upon another's appetite: surely nothing is more private? Food, drink, sex. Sensuous experiences are not really to be shared, essentially.

Imogene Hood has invited Francis to her house several times for dinner, a strain for Francis unless someone else is included, not usu-ally the case. Headmistress Cady has invited Francis to dinner sev-eral times, less of a strain since others are present, and Francis has more of an audience for his dazzling conversation, largely wasted on just a single admiring friend.

"You do recall that we planned this, Francis, don't you? At the end of August when you'd just arrived here and were feeling lonely. You said."

So wistfully Katy speaks, Francis hears himself agree. It is his weakness—he yearns to placate, to please. To say what an ardent listener hopes to hear.

"Le Bernardin is your favorite, yes?"

"Y-yes. But—*oui.*"

Over the years when Francis has visited Katy in New York City they have often had dinner at the elegant French restaurant in Midtown, with Katy paying the bill; it should be touching to Francis that Katy has gone to the trouble of bringing food prepared by the Bernardin chef all the way to South Jersey but it weighs upon him instead as an eccentric whim for which he is obliged to be grateful, and Francis resents feeling *obliged*. In Katy's presence he is inclined to feel as if he's wearing one of those lead-lined vests dental patients are made to wear when enduring X-rays.

The prestigious restaurant wouldn't provide anything so plebeian as take-out food; Katy must have made some private/costly arrangement.

All this fuss over you by Katy Cady. Why, do you think?

Francis would have been happy to have dinner at the Wieland Inn in kitsch-romantic-historic surroundings where he could at least order a ten-ounce plank steak and fried onion rings and the most expensive wine on the menu. (Not that the Wieland Inn has an impressive wine list but Katy hasn't thought to bring wine from New York City; the only wine Francis has on the premises is the kind he calls *maintenance*—wine with no distinction beyond its properties for self-medication.)

"Has anyone else remembered your birthday, Francis? Your parents? Your mother?"

Your parents. Your mother. Francis tries to think, how would one plausibly reply to this query? Katy too often inquires into Francis's family, as if hoping to bore into his life. He doesn't want to sound as if he's estranged from his parents (too melodramatic!) but he doesn't want to sound as if he's on folksy parent-son terms with individuals he hasn't glimpsed in so long, their faces have faded from his memory like old Polaroids.

"You know old WASP culture, Katy: we don't fuss over trifles."

"Oh, I know!" Katy Cady, a genuine daughter of old WASP ancestors, is quick to agree.

But *is* this Francis Fox's birthday? (Was October eighteenth Frank Farrell's birthday?) Francis has a vague memory of having invented an October eighteenth birthday at some point in his relations with Katy Cady, no idea why; it is like Katy to have made a note of the date.

"This apartment of yours is so—impersonal," Katy says. "I guess you haven't entirely moved in yet? Where are your books?"

"Most of my books are in boxes," Francis says, "—my boxes are mostly in storage."

"Your kitchen is small but everything looks new—the stove looks *untouched*. Is this dust?"

Francis laughs, uneasily. His friend's hyper-scrutiny is making him nervous.

"Well, as a bachelor you probably don't prepare your own meals. You're probably invited out to dinner all the time. Aunt Paige told me that you've come to her house for dinner, with a 'woman friend.'"

Woman friend lies lightly on Katy's tongue, not at all a reproach.

"Not too often. Certainly not 'all the time.'"

"Is she a colleague? The woman friend? A teacher?"

"A librarian."

"A librarian on the Langhorne staff—?"

"Everyone I know in Wieland is on the Langhorne staff," Francis says, "—I'm a stranger here, essentially."

Francis has been turning the ring Katy gave him around his finger, for it fits him loosely; he must have lost a pound or two without realizing it. He has seen Katy glancing at his hand as if to reassure herself that he is still wearing the ring.

Wanting to assure her—*But only you are my soul-mate, Katy.*

Katy asks Francis how his experience has been teaching at Langhorne, and is he happy here? Has it been a good decision, to come here? Katy assures him, her aunt Paige has told her that he is already a popular teacher; but then, Francis Fox has been a popular teacher wherever he has taught.

Francis says modestly that he isn't sure of that but he does treat his middle-schoolers like adults—"I never talk down to them. I don't speak platitudes to them. I allow them to know, I am *on their side*."

None of this is true exactly but all of this is plausible. Though Katy has never witnessed Francis Fox in the classroom, nor spoken with any of his students, she is an adamant admirer of his teaching.

Francis is flattered that P. Cady has been speaking of him. Only just arrived at the prestigious Langhorne Academy, already Francis Fox is on his way to becoming one of those *legendary* teachers celebrated in the memoirs of famous graduates!

"Aunt Paige is just a little hurt, I think, that I didn't invite her to host this dinner for you. She would have been eager to have us both. She has an excellent cook. She does want me to stay the night at her house, of course. And we're invited there tonight for dessert—as late as nine P.M., she says. I told her I would ask you, Francis. I didn't want to presume anything."

In her wistful mode Katy Cady is most appealing to Francis and in this mode, most difficult to resist. Francis has to guard himself against giving in to a request he may subsequently regret.

"I don't think so, Katy. Maybe another time."

How earnest Francis is! P. Cady, Headmistress, cannot fail to be impressed that one of her most recent hires has passed up an opportunity to visit the headmistress's house, which would fill many another teacher at Langhorne with envy if they knew; how certain it is, Francis Fox is not an ambitious careerist but a dedicated teacher.

Francis reminds Katy that private school teaching is arduous. It is nothing like university teaching—of course. Nothing like working for a genteel foundation (like the Guggenheim Memorial Foundation). Four classes, each day. Five days a week. And every night homework, which a serious teacher will grade conscientiously.

"Oh, I know, Francis! I understand," Katy says quickly. "It would be too late after dinner, to visit Aunt Paige. But we will hope for another time, when I visit you again. I will tell her."

(In fact Francis is jealous of his private time each night from eleven P.M. to midnight set aside for scrolling the Internet on his laptop, perusing a galaxy of *kittens* as an explorer might peruse a map of undiscovered territory.)

"I've come to the conclusion, Katy, that it may have been a good thing that I was excluded from the higher academic life. Middle-school teaching is much more challenging, and can be rewarding . . ."

Francis speaks thoughtfully, as if he has spent much time pondering this nuanced issue.

In Francis's small kitchen Katy has been busying herself preparing their dinners. Francis detects a dispiriting aroma of fish, no doubt (pricey, tasteless) Chilean sea bass with cloying lemon-butter sauce or worse yet, an "Asian" glaze: heating in the oven for just a few minutes at 375 degrees Fahrenheit. To deflect the subject of Francis's thwarted academic career she searches for plates and cutlery in the kitchen, to set on a table in the living room.

Francis is thinking of the squalid interlude of his being accused of plagiarism by a vindictive professor at Columbia, as one might prod an infected tooth, to arouse pain, the luxury of an old grievance. Always useful to stir guilt in Katy Cady as in anyone better off financially than we are. No matter what they do for us it is never quite enough, and they know it.

Katy murmurs, "I know, Francis. That was so unfair . . ."

"It *was* unfair, but I've moved on. There are rewards in middle-school teaching I could not have anticipated."

"Well, you don't have to teach forever, you know, Francis. You could take time off—a year, two years. If you were interested in travel . . ."

Francis is searching for napkins in the kitchen. He will store these promising words away for safekeeping.

Thinking how much more promising Katy Cady is, as a potential wife, than Imogene Hood! With Imogene, the two of them would be teaching forever at the Langhorne Academy; they could never afford to retire, still less time off for *travel.*

By retirement time, Francis wants to think that his weakness for *kittens* will have subsided. It is not likely that such a consuming and dangerous obsession will prevail for decades as it is depicted in Kawabata's *House of the Sleeping Beauties:* a world in which elderly Japanese men pay exorbitant sums for the privilege of merely lying beside young girls while the girls sleep—a pitiful fetish.

Francis is scornful of such weakness. A kind of senile voyeurism.

His *kittens* are likely to doze off in his lap, snug in his arms; but his *kittens* are not fastidiously untouched, as in *House of the Sleeping Beauties.* Mr. Tongue, Big Teddy Bear are the most discreet lovers.

If Katy Cady were not taking up so much space in the kitchen Francis could lose himself in a shuddering recollection of how little Genevieve Chambers slipped into his office that afternoon; consuming an entire apricot tart, unknowingly ingesting a comma-sized particle of Ambien to soothe her nerves, cause her eyelids to droop, all resistance fading from her slender limbs so that, to Francis's delight, she would have fallen to the floor except in a dreamy panic she'd twined her arms around his neck, to stop her fall. The most adorable Little Kitten in thrall to Mr. Tongue.

This is our secret, ma chérie! Till death undoes us.

"Francis? What are you looking for?"

"Napkins . . ."

"I've already put them on the table!"

Francis gives himself a playful shake as a dog might, to wake up more fully.

Now it happens: just six minutes before the oven timer is set to ring Katy Cady asks Francis if she might use the bathroom in Francis's apartment, of course Francis says *Yes*, just down the hall, past the small room that is his study; only belatedly does Francis realize that he should have hurried ahead to tidy up the bathroom, for no doubt the mirror isn't clean, nor the sink and toilet; fortunately not *filthy* as in some bachelor quarters, for Francis cannot abide filth (of the kind that is visible); then, in a wave of sheer sick cold horror realizing that his laptop is open and prominent on the little table he uses for a desk, facing the window overlooking the parking lot; a single stroke of any key will bring the screen alive, suffused with soft-focus close-up pictures of the most delectable little kittens in various states of undress and distress . . .

"Jesus!"—Francis steadies himself against a kitchen counter. He is light-headed, faint. So taken by surprise at Katy's arrival he'd totally forgotten the Dark Web (as philistines call it) he'd been surfing in the interstices of grading eighth-grade critiques of a story by Zora Neale Hurston assigned by an edict of the English department to all middle-school students this week.

"God help me . . ."

So abruptly the unthinkable has happened, a visitor of Francis
Fox's simply slipping away, out of his sight, having made a most reasonable request to use the bathroom in his apartment, already Katy
has been away for what seems like a suspiciously long time as Francis
oozes sweat like hot little beads of acid thinking *She has seen, it's all
over* in despair that his new life in Wieland, New Jersey, will end, has
been sabotaged by his own complacency. Stunned, sickened, righ-
teously repelled Katy Cady will depart the premises as if fleeing a fire
or a plague; she will drive immediately to P. Cady's residence and
denounce him, and expose him; and condemn him; and destroy
Francis Fox who might protest in vain to both incensed women that
it was by sheer chance he'd stumbled naïvely into the Dark Web of
pullulating filth, as despicable to his eyes as to theirs.

They will never believe you. Who would?

As if the minimally furnished stage set were illuminated by a flash
of lightning it is revealed to Francis Fox that he has no choice except
to murder Katy Cady.

He cannot let her escape the apartment with this shocking knowledge of his private life; it would mean the collapse of his assiduously
constructed career at Langhorne, in which Genevieve Chambers is
enshrined, intricately woven as in a sacred mosaic. It is Katy Cady or
Little Kitten—no hesitation between the two.

But this is absurd, Francis Fox isn't capable of murder. He is not
handy; he has no weapons except kitchen utensils, and these are not
his own but rented; in a haze of panic he pulls open drawers, rum-
mages through cutlery, knives, an ice pick—all dull. He discovers
what appears to be a steak knife but its blade too is dull.

Not nearly sharp enough to slash through skin, cut through bones,
tendons, trachea. And his hands are too weak, if he could bring himself to strangle anyone, *he would fail*. He has no experience with
anything approaching manual labor. He once walked away in defeat
abandoning a vehicle by the roadside because he could not change a
tire. And he'd hoped to marry Katy Cady one day! A rich girl who
adores him, who has never been critical of him as others have, who
has already given him so much more than he deserves, a true *soul-*

mate. He is an ingrate bastard but how is it Francis Fox's fault that prepubescent girls are attracted to him, and linger by his desk after class; and linger outside his office; and slip notes beneath his office door. *It is hardly his fault* that one of the most beautiful twelve-year-old girls he has ever seen seems to have fallen under his spell, and pleads with him with her eyes—*Mr. Fox, I love you . . .*

But Katy Cady for all her sweetness and docility is as puritanical as most females, and fatally judgmental. With her conventional upbringing and lack of imagination she can't fail to be revulsed by images of scantily clad young girls on a computer screen unless—possibly—she could forgive Francis, if he explains the circumstances: if he acknowledges his weakness, which is fundamentally a yearning for beauty, and innocence, and purity of heart, of a kind so powerfully expressed by Edgar Allan Poe in his adoration of his young cousin. Yes, it is Eros, but it is not mere frank crude *sex.* Francis will explain that he has sought professional care; he is coming to terms with a long-buried trauma of his childhood, when he was seduced and violated by a trusted family friend, or by a Catholic priest; indeed a priest who was a trusted family friend. In therapy for several years he is "making progress"; before today he had not glanced at the Dark Web for months.

Forgiveness is a charitable act, an act of generosity, like tossing pennies to beggars. Forgiveness appeals to most mature females, like Katy Cady and Imogene Hood and (possibly) P. Cady.

Yes but even if Katy forgives Francis she will know too much about him. At any time she could tell her aunt Paige; if the mere possession of (so-called) child pornography is some sort of ridiculous felony in New Jersey, Katy could blackmail Francis for the rest of their lives emotionally, morally. He could not bear to be in thrall to another person, especially Katy Cady before whom he would also be deeply, excruciatingly embarrassed.

"Francis? That's a—a nice view from your 'study' window—are those beech trees?" Katy asks with shining eyes, and genuine enthusiasm; though the view from Francis's window is of no more distinction than a Dumpster still Katy is smiling so happily, Francis understands that of course she didn't peer at his computer screen.

Katy Cady isn't the kind of person (like Francis Fox himself) who would violate another's privacy, *he is perfectly safe for nothing has changed*.

"But why are you looking so anxious, Francis? You really have a good deal of work to do this evening—I guess—I am so sorry to be disturbing you. I only wanted to bring you a nice birthday surprise. Because you do work so hard. Do you forgive me?"

Francis is feeling so light-headed, he has had to sit down. Relief sweeps over him as paralyzing horror had a few minutes before, leaving him weak, dazed. As if he'd stumbled off a cliff but fell only a few feet, and has not broken a single bone, landing upright.

"Forgive you? Of course I forgive you, Katy. You are the kindest person I know. I've been missing you. I've been so lonely here . . ."

Reaching out to squeeze Katy's fingers as the oven timer rings for the first and final time in Francis Fox's occupancy of the apartment on Consent Street, Wieland, New Jersey.

THE RAPTOR'S EYE

SEPTEMBER–OCTOBER 2013

The raptor's eye is not exclusively for prey. The raptor's eye is as keenly alert to adversaries in the field.

Already by the end of the first week of classes at the Langhorne Academy Francis Fox had identified several potential troublemakers among his students; by the end of the second week of classes Francis has disarmed, or made alliances with, all but one of these, by happenstance the sole girl among them.

This, the ferret-faced agate-eyed rust-red-haired thirteen-year-old Eunice Pfenning in his two P.M. eighth-grade class whose seat was at the approximate center of the small classroom giving her grim-scowling presence the prominence of an irritant in an eye, impossible to ignore as it is difficult to dislodge.

What is wrong with her, why doesn't she like me? How can she not like—"Mr. Fox"?

It was a puzzle to Francis Fox, a riddle. His pride was abraded as with a Brillo pad. His vanity was flummoxed as in a distorting mirror that made him appear not handsome and charismatic but clownish.

Students *always* smiled, laughed at Mr. Fox's jokes. Students *always* raised their hands eagerly in response to a provocative question posed by Mr. Fox. Yet, there sat the ferret-faced girl unimpressed and unmoved with arms folded tightly across her narrow chest suggestive of the flat segmented body of a scorpion poised to sting if one draws too near.

Initially, Francis tried to ignore the girl—the irritant in his eye. There is little pleasure in engaging with unattractive individuals, you are obliged to look at them. Francis Fox's ideal of female prepubescent beauty is such that he feels a genuine jolt, pain in the region of his heart, when he sees a girl as homely as *Eunice Pfenning*. Even the name is unattractive, sexless as a turnip.

Francis made discreet inquiries and learned that Eunice Pfenning was a local Wieland resident, a day student at the school since fifth grade. Consistently high grades, always on the honor roll, praise from her teachers.

Praise from her teachers? How was this possible?

It was a mystery to Francis Fox, that he could not seem to win over this student. He tried not to look at her peevish little face but the effort of trying not to look at her was distracting to him, who was usually so at ease before his classes.

Is she unhappy? Is she depressed?

(Does she see through Mr. Fox's subterfuge?)

Francis Fox encouraged discussions in his classes and the two P.M. eighth-grade class was particularly lively. Yet, disdainful Eunice Pfenning rarely participated. Her prissy expression suggested that the remarks of her classmates were boring to her and the revelations provided by her teacher did not impress her, like magic tricks performed by an inept magician.

Where ordinarily Francis would never have given a plain drab creature like Eunice Pfenning a second thought now he found himself thinking of her obsessively.

Waking with a jolt in the night in the throes of a deliriously pleasurable dream of Genevieve Chambers cuddling on his lap, as Mr. Tongue dared to poke into the pursed lips that are a weak defense against him, to stark grim thoughts of the ferret-faced rust-red-haired Eunice Pfenning *who refuses to be seduced by Francis Fox.*

"Jesus! I hate her."

In a calmer mood reasoning: not all his students are required to adore Francis Fox. He is not a vain person, he is sure. He does not *expect* adulation.

But he does expect respect, and it is most unusual, unnatural, *pathological* when a student is rebellious for no reason.

Since he first began teaching middle school years ago Francis Fox's nightmare has been: One by one students refuse to be charmed by him. One by one they stare coldly at him, not smiling at his jokes.

Until finally "Mr. Fox" is exposed—a charlatan, a failure. In his most lurid fantasies his students rise from their seats, swarm at him like ravenous rodents, tear him with their teeth, devour him . . .

Which is why Francis must identify potential troublemakers as soon as possible. Isolate potential mutineers, divide them and conquer them through intimidation, flattery, praise, a subtle threat of aggression while always leaving open the option for them of *becoming Fox's friend.*

Almost always, the potential troublemakers are boys. Fox is particularly attuned to bullies, smart alecks, show-offs—immature replicas of himself, readily disarmed.

A hostile girl is a surprise. A mystery. It seemed likely to Francis Fox that the ferret-faced girl was cognitively impaired in some way, though (evidently) intelligent.

Possibly *on the spectrum.*

Fortunately, Eunice Pfenning seemed to have no allies. Such a plain sour-faced girl wouldn't attract friends. Though seated at the center of the classroom Eunice was nonetheless isolated as in a bell jar, a singular specimen: a girl with lashless staring frog-eyes, peevish-pale face, and joyless heart.

"And—Eunice? What do *you* think?"

Francis Fox never failed to query Eunice Pfenning in a friendly voice, respectfully; it was his protocol to involve everyone in a discussion, including those who held back, did not raise their hands out of shyness, or insecurity; ironically, Eunice could often provide exactly the answer Francis Fox was hoping for from the others.

Yet, no matter how friendly-seeming Mr. Fox was, Eunice would reply in a near-inaudible voice, tersely, flatly, without a smile, as if she were reluctant to participate in a discussion so banal.

Either Eunice locked eyes with Francis Fox's eyes, in a cold reptilian glare, or refused to lift her eyes to his, as if he did not exist.

Of course, in his classroom role as adult, in his performance as genial Mr. Fox, Francis gave no sign of being insulted; like a seasoned musician who has struck a wrong note he simply moved on, as if there were no wrong note at all.

Though there came a rush of adrenaline sharp as a jab in the groin—*Squash the smug little cunt like a scorpion.*

■

THIS, MR. FOX WOULD surely do: not openly, but by degrees.

Handing back the first graded paper of the term, a critique of Jack London's *Call of the Wild,* and seeing with satisfaction how the ferret-faced girl stared at the red-inked C– at the top of her paper, quickly folded the paper and laid it flat on her desk and her hands over it numbly, with an air of dissociation, disbelief.

Take that, you homely little bitch.

See what Fox can do if you defy Fox.

When after class Eunice Pfenning crept away in shame and humiliation to examine the paper more closely she would discover that it was riddled with corrections and queries from her sharp-eyed teacher in red ink like blood-splatter. At the very end, a remark meant to burrow under her skin like an infected tick: *Banal ideas & unimaginative writing lacking focus, insight. Might have been written by a computer & seems hastily written even for a computer. Try again?*

No doubt, the sour little bitch had never received a grade so low. The blow to her self-esteem would be considerable. Already the look of insufferable smugness had drained from her face.

It was true, Eunice Pfenning's critique of *The Call of the Wild* was the most impersonal writing of its kind Francis Fox had ever encountered in one so young. Clearly the girl was highly intelligent but not imaginative, and didn't seem to comprehend the nature of fiction and storytelling; yet Francis could as easily have given her an A for the highly detailed critique, as another teacher might have.

It is Mr. Fox's general strategy to grade low at the start of the term, and gradually raise grades as the students' writing "improves." Which usually it does, since students will learn to provide what their teacher requires.

Even brilliant students require challenge, and Mr. Fox is one to challenge brilliance.

(To his credit, Eunice Pfenning did not seem to him a truly *brilliant student*. Certainly an A-level student, highly intelligent, methodical rather than inspired.)

But Mr. Fox would soften the blow, as Mr. Fox often did, by allowing students the option to revise, rewrite—"Try again. Try better."

In the adult world beyond school, Mr. Fox tells his students, it is routine to try again, to try many times. It is not realistic to be judged on a single effort.

"Always keep in mind these stirring words of Henry David Thoreau: 'God himself culminates in the present moment, and will never be more divine in the lapse of all the ages.' Your future lies ahead of you to make of it what you will."

Eunice Pfenning was one of those students eager to rewrite the assignment, and for this new and improved version, which would have merited an A from another teacher, Mr. Fox grudgingly raised her grade to C.

Though with a smile returning it to her. *See? Mr. Fox is on your side, you homely brat.*

In the corner of his eye seeing how disappointed Eunice was with this new grade. Her pinched little face seemed to shrink, and her skinny shoulders slumped.

Eunice Pfenning was absent from class for two days, with an excuse of "respiratory ailment."

How idyllic the classroom, without the smirking little face at its center! Francis Fox felt as if he were on a holiday, every student adored him.

But when Eunice returned to class, far from being chastened, she appeared unchanged. As if the ferret-face stoniness were a mask she couldn't remove, a permanent smirk about her thin little mouth. But now she looked embittered, as well. Her fingernails were shockingly short, bitten. For much of the class she sat quietly staring down at her clasped hands on her desk oblivious of her classmates' laughter at their teacher's clever jokes as if she were deaf; when at last she lifted her head the narrowed eyes moved past Francis Fox's head as in a trance of detachment beyond hurt.

Francis was reminded of Botticelli's Saint Sebastian, the white-skinned Christian martyr dreamily indifferent to arrows piercing his body.

So it was Francis Fox's will, pitted against hers. Damned if he would give this homely little bitch the grades she deserved, so long as she resisted him.

■

CASUALLY FRANCIS FOX BRINGS up the subject to Imogene Hood.

"Have you ever had a student who is hostile to all your efforts? Not actively hostile, not outwardly arrogant, just *passively aggressive,* staring coldly at you, refuses to smile, to laugh at your jokes, to engage normally?"

Imogene seems bemused by Francis's question: she doesn't ordinarily tell jokes to her students, she says.

But yes of course, as a librarian she has occasionally confronted hostile students, more often withdrawn or sulking students, though not (yet) at the Langhorne Academy. She has never felt that the student was hostile to her *personally.* And in Francis's class, whoever it is is surely not hostile to *him.*

Imogene speaks so reasonably, Francis concurs. Even as he seethes with indignation, certain that Eunice Pfenning's hostility is *personal,* and for no reason he can comprehend it is directed at *him.*

"This girl is also singularly unattractive. She has a pinched little face like a ferret. She exudes bitterness, spite. No matter how nice I am to her, she refuses to even look at me."

It's unusual for Francis Fox to speak so vehemently, Imogene tries to console him. The girl is obviously unhappy, she says, she came into his class unhappy, it has nothing to do with him.

"All you can do is continue to be nice to her, Francis. She's just a child, you are an adult. Eventually she will probably behave more reasonably. How is her work?"

"She's accustomed to A's. But she isn't getting A's from me, yet."

"Maybe that's why she's hostile to you?"

"She's hostile to me because she's a spoiled brat. The kind of smart-ass girl who kills herself in college."

Imogene stiffens even as she seems not to hear this chilling remark from her friend.

"But yes, I will be nice to her—of course, Imogene. Mr. Fox is nice to all his students."

In the faculty dining room Francis Fox brings up the subject of the *mysteriously hostile spiteful student* to his fellow teachers. Nothing evokes such ardent conversations among teachers as problematic students—how to deal with them? Confront them, ignore them? Droll classroom anecdotes, accounts of bratty students and interfering parents, tales of disaster barely skirted—sharing these is a primary solace of teachers.

Francis Fox presents himself as a thwarted idealist, flummoxed by one student in just one class like an abscessed tooth he can't help prodding.

"She stares at me like a basilisk! It began on the very first day of classes. I believe she must be 'on the spectrum'—though it isn't noted in her file."

His companions ask what is the girl's name?—but Francis demurs, of course he can't reveal the name. He is protective of his students, he says, even those who test his patience.

Francis is assured by the others that they all have problematic students from time to time. The Langhorne Academy is difficult to get into, students tend to be competitive, under pressure from their parents who are grooming them for the Ivy League.

"They're fixated on grades. Even in middle school. It's unfortunate but there's nothing we can do about it. Teaching high school is worse, you have to worry about students becoming suicidal."

Suicidal! If only the ferret-faced girl were suicidal, that would be a consolation. But Eunice Pfenning is too spiteful to harm herself, Fox thinks.

Sitting at a lunch table with fellow teachers, listening to them, or half-listening, is comforting to Francis, calming. To learn that others encounter maddening students like Eunice Pfenning whom, however hard they try, they can't seduce.

Seduce is not the word. No.

Can't reach is the preferable term.

Francis knows also that speaking with (apparent) frankness to his colleagues, asking their advice, presenting himself as disadvantaged, will diffuse whatever dislike they might be feeling for him as a new faculty member who seems to have a favored relationship with the headmistress, having been invited to her house for dinner. *For of course they know all about P. Cady's dinners,* to which they have not been invited.

They have surely heard that Mr. Fox is already very popular with his students—his classes are said to be *cool, awesome.* They have begun to notice, or will shortly begin to notice, that girls linger in the vicinity of his office, among them very pretty girls.

So it's a practical measure, that Francis Fox befriends his colleagues. The women are inclined to like him in any case, the men may need a little more persuasion; but if he invites them to lunch, if he invites them to have a beer with him in town, if he chats with them about sports, drops by their offices and continues to ask their advice, and to show gratitude for their advice, they are not likely to resist the Fox charisma.

■

SQUASH HER LIKE A *scorpion beneath your foot.*

Such a mean-spirited little brat would squash a butterfly beneath her foot. Francis could imagine her gleefully shaking a bird's nest, squashing robin's eggs. Wouldn't be surprised if Eunice Pfenning tormented animals, as she has tormented him since the first day of classes.

Each Friday students in Mr. Fox's classes are invited by their teacher to read their work aloud to one another; in Eunice Pfenning's class only Eunice has not yet been invited to read her work. Francis wonders if the others have noticed. (They seem so little aware of her they would probably not notice if she disappeared from the class.) He is sure that Eunice is well aware of not being included but her pinched little face is so stubbornly impassive, he can't guess if she is wounded, or furious, or indifferent.

A few select students in Mr. Fox's classes are invited to join the Looking-Glass Book Club. With grades hovering in the range of C, Eunice Pfenning is not (yet) qualified for the book club.

(Of course, Fox's favorites belong to the club. These include but are not limited to the very prettiest girls, like Genevieve Chambers; less attractive girls are included if they are deserving, and have winning personalities, as well as a few boys who have impressed Francis Fox with their intelligence, personalities, and admiration for Mr. Fox.)

Where originally Francis had come to dread his two P.M. eighth-grade class, with the cold-staring Eunice Pfenning at its core, more recently he has come to anticipate the class with a stirring of adrenaline, like one preparing for a fight which, he has no doubt, he will win.

Following the Skinnerian principle of intermittent reinforcement, in which an experimental subject is rewarded for their effort not continuously, or predictably, but intermittently, or unpredictably, Fox will grade Eunice Pfenning in a way designed to shatter her defenses: it will be impossible for her not to feel relief, gratitude, some measure of happiness when her grade improves, thus she will be *conditioned* to seek a higher grade; she will therefore experience disappointment, hurt, helplessness, and despair when her grade is lower than it was previously since, so far as she will be able to determine, the quality of her work is more or less consistent. A sort of *learned helplessness* will be absorbed by the girl even as she is compelled to work ever harder, by the encouragement of her (seemingly) sympathetic teacher.

The great B. F. Skinner's experiments usually involved rats or pigeons but applied as well to human beings, especially young, impressionable persons.

Handing back papers to the class, pronouncing names one by one, all but Eunice Pfenning to whom he says, gravely, in his kindest teacherly voice: "Eunice?—I will need to speak with you during my office hour."

Awaiting the return of graded papers is always stressful for students. By the time Mr. Fox turns his attention upon her the ferret-faced girl is cringing at her desk, agate eyes narrowed to slits. Conspicuously, Mr. Fox does not hand back Eunice's paper.

The class passes in what must be a haze for the girl, stiff-sitting in her desk in the midst of warmly animated discussions by her classmates, eyes downcast, small mouth made smaller as if she were sucking her lips inward. Out of kindness, Mr. Fox does not call on Eunice today.

After school Eunice is obliged to wait in the corridor outside Mr. Fox's basement office while a giggly seventh-grade girl confers with him for long minutes, then lingers in his doorway before reluctantly departing.

In his office at last and seated in a chair facing Mr. Fox across his desk Eunice Pfenning is given her paper which has been marked at the top in glaring red ink NO GRADE.

Eunice's paper is an elaborate, three-page critique of several poems by Edwin Arlington Robinson which everyone in the class critiqued but no one so methodically, in such dogged detail, as Eunice Pfenning.

"D'you know why there is no grade for this paper, Eunice?"

Eunice is staring at the paper held in trembling hands as if she has never seen it before. Francis sees with gratification that her grubby little nails are close-bitten, and that, in such intimate quarters, Eunice Pfenning is even less attractive than she is in their class.

"N-no . . ."

"Sorry? I didn't hear you, Eunice."

"No . . . I don't know."

"It's a promising paper, Eunice. There is at least one good idea here. But I have to ask you, frankly: Is this your work? Or is it copied from the Internet?"

For a moment Eunice seems not to hear. Then she says, almost inaudibly, not meeting Francis's eye, "Y-yes . . . I wrote this myself."

"Really!"

Francis looks at her searchingly, sympathetically. As if waiting for her to realize that she is misremembering.

"I've shown this to some of my colleagues. They seriously doubt that this sort of poetic exegesis could be written by an eighth grader."

Eunice Pfenning sits stiff, unmoving. Nothing to say in her defense.

"If I show this to your English teacher from last year, what do you think she will say?"

"I—I write differently now—for you . . . I—spend more time."

"Did anyone help you with the critique? At home?"

Eunice shakes her head *no*.

"Did anyone read it? Make suggestions?"

Eunice sits mute, staring at the paper, which is bleeding from dozens of razor-cuts from Mr. Fox's scalpel-pen.

It is amusing to Francis Fox that Eunice Pfenning cannot help but think of him, not as an adversary who wants to crush her, as one might crush a beetle beneath his heel, but as a kindly teacher who seems to be generally perplexed by her failure to turn in good work. That she is *highly intelligent* but for some reason has yet to live up to her potential in his class. That she has at last written a passably good paper does not, as she might reasonably expect, merit a higher grade than usual, but suspicion.

"You are sure, Eunice? This is your own work? You didn't memorize something you'd read without realizing it?"

"I—I don't think so . . ."

"It might be entirely unconscious, Eunice. 'Memorizing'—'regurgitating.' Can you absolutely swear, this isn't what happened?"

Eunice opens her mouth to speak but cannot. A sick, sinking expression in her face.

"And you said, you have sworn, no one has looked at this paper?"

At this, Eunice looks at her hands. Cannot meet her inquisitor's gaze. Francis thinks—*Aha!*—*one of her parents has read it.*

"Eunice? No one has looked at this paper?"

Hesitantly, Eunice shakes her head *no*. But it is not an emphatic *no*.

"Are either of your parents educators, Eunice?"

Educators. The word seems to confound Eunice.

"Let me rephrase: is either of your parents in the teaching profession?"

Eunice shakes her head *no*.

"Neither of them has looked at this paper?"

At last, in a plaintive voice, Eunice confesses that her mother read the paper: "I didn't want her to—she snuck into my room and found it. But—only after it was finished. And I didn't change anything, no matter what she said." Eunice swipes at her nose, deeply mortified.

All this, Francis Fox seems to be pondering. As if it were wildly uncommon that a student might show work to parents for advice. As if a well-intentioned parent might not offer unsolicited advice. Indeed, Francis would be surprised if this were not common: he'd shown his graduate papers to dear Katy Cady, and to a few other ultra-smart young women students, and usually followed their suggestions without question.

In a grave voice Francis reminds Eunice of the Langhorne Academy honor code. Which all Langhorne students have pledged to follow. "That no one helps you with your schoolwork, your work is entirely your own. And this critique is entirely your own?"

"Yes. It *is*."

"Your mother didn't offer suggestions?"

"Yes, but—I don't pay attention to her . . ."

"Do you *ever* pay attention to your mother?"

This is a note of whimsy, unexpected as a tickle in a prepubescent underarm: but Eunice is too tense, too anxious, to feel it.

A remarkably stubborn, willful girl, Francis Fox thinks. Hardly a *girl* in his lexicon.

Francis feels a stir of satisfaction. He has managed to pierce the cocoon of the spoiled brat, Eunice no longer smirks at him in class, and is far from smirking now.

During office hours Francis Fox sits facing the (open) door. Students sit in a straight-backed chair, backs to the door. So positioned, in a swivel chair that gives him the advantage of further height, Francis seems to loom over most students; often, a student will shrink back from him. But Eunice Pfenning is making a pitiful effort to sit taller, as if to confront him.

Such a scrawny girl! No dreamy Balthus like Genevieve Chambers, no fleshy little rosy-cheeked Renoir like the Healy girl, rather a scribble-sketch of an androgynous female by Giacometti.

Eunice has been glancing at the oversized bronze bust of Edgar Allan Poe positioned on the corner of Francis's desk a few inches away. The large head, blind-staring eyes, grotesque-comic raven crouched on his shoulder.

Francis explains: "It's a commemorative sculpture—a poem of mine won first prize in a national poetry competition a few years ago."

Poem. Mine. Won. Competition. Francis sees that this has impressed Eunice Pfenning.

"You can see the plaque, I think—'Edgar Allan Poe.' 'Nevermore.' D'you recognize the poem the sculpture is illustrating?"

"'The Raven.'"

"Very good, Eunice! Yes."

Eunice smiles quickly, a twitch of a smile. (Is her teacher praising her? Is this real?)

"Do you like Poe's poetry, Eunice?"

Eunice hesitates as if suspecting that this is a trick question. She murmurs something inaudible that might have been *I guess* or *I don't know.*

"Later in the course we will be studying Poe. I will ask students to memorize and recite some of his poems. And if you want to read his most famous short story, which we will also be taking up in November, it's in our anthology—'The Tell-Tale Heart.'"

At this point, Eunice astonishes Francis Fox by mumbling that she has already read the story. She has been "reading ahead" in the anthology.

"Well! Good for you, Eunice. But it might be more prudent, you know, to concentrate on your present work. To improve your weaknesses."

Returning now to the subject of the NO GRADE paper on Edwin Arlington Robinson, explaining to Eunice that her critique, though well-written in a dogged, methodical way, has fallen into a category of "questionable" schoolwork, for which a grade of NO GRADE is recommended.

Strictly speaking, Francis Fox is supposed to report such suspicious papers to a faculty committee, which will review the paper, and interrogate Eunice about its originality; but he has thought of a way around the conundrum, if Eunice is willing to rewrite the critique, every sentence revised, he will consider it an entirely new work, and grade it accordingly.

Eunice is rapidly blinking, breathing shallowly through her opened mouth. She appears on the brink of fainting. Blithely Francis Fox continues:

"Now, Eunice, this is the grade that I would have assigned if I were totally convinced that this work is your own, but following the directives of my conscience I cannot assign"—Francis writes "B" on a notepad, and shows it to Eunice, who stares at it as a ravenous creature might stare at a morsel of food, in silence; then, he tears out the note, crumples it, and drops it into his wastebasket.

"So? Will you rewrite the paper? Due tomorrow, in class. *But keep this conference confidential,* do not tell a soul."

Eunice tries to speak but is barely audible. "Y-yes, Mr. Fox . . ."

"Andre! Hel-lo! I'll see you in a minute, this young lady is just leaving."

Another student has arrived, hulking in Mr. Fox's doorway. Francis dismisses Eunice Pfenning, who departs his office as a sleepwalker might make her way in unfamiliar terrain, stumbling a little, but persevering.

Next day, somewhat to Francis's surprise, Eunice hands in the (revised) paper, which he skims to see that it does appear to be totally rewritten; this *is* impressive.

On the following day, which is a Friday, Mr. Fox asks Eunice to read her critique to the class, which she does in a breathless faltering voice; at the very end of the paper Francis has graded it B.

It is touching, Eunice Pfenning is terrified of reading aloud to the class of students whom (it seems evident) she disdains; she is totally unprepared for Francis Fox to declare, when she has finished, "Brilliant, Eunice!"—leading the applause from Eunice's classmates.

A blinding light has been shone in Eunice's stunned face, she is too dazed even to smile.

■

HOW DISAPPOINTING IT IS, then, for both teacher and student, that Eunice's next critique, an analysis of several poems by e. e. cummings, merits only a C−, with a terse commentary in red ink—*Promising argument but very average prose. At least it's clear that this is your own work.*

In the corner of his eye Francis sees tears glistening on Eunice's cheeks. It's the end of class, a very pretty girl-student is lingering at his desk, it's to this student that Francis Fox gives his fullest attention and when he turns back he sees that Eunice Pfenning has crept away.

Maybe have mercy on the miserable brat now? Maybe.

■ ■ ■

"HELLO, MR. FOX? I'M Kathryn Pfenning—Eunice's mother."

An attractive dark-haired woman of approximately his age. Her eyes are fixed intensely on his face, she is smiling uneasily. Francis has no choice but to shake her hand which is a brisk chill hand. Hearing her name he feels a twinge of guilt faint as an earthquake measuring 2.5 on the Richter scale.

It's a convivial Parent-Teacher evening at school. They are meet-

ing in the third-floor library of Haven Hall. Mrs. Pfenning has crossed
the room to speak with him.

Five weeks since the start of the fall term. Like a creature trapped
in a bog desperate to save itself poor Eunice Pfenning has been struggling all these weeks to improve her grade.

Francis would steel himself against a confrontation with an angry
parent except to his relief Eunice's mother is not at all angry but
rather abashed, apologetic. She has questions to ask of him of the
kind Francis might reasonably expect.

Francis explains to Kathryn Pfenning that her daughter is "exceptionally bright"—"highly motivated"—but her work in his class has
fallen short of her "potential."

Potential: one of those vague terms which teachers wield like ma-
gicians, which arouses hope and despair simultaneously.

". . . is there anything more that Eunice can do? Extra work . . ."

Francis is reluctant to say that Eunice has already done "extra"
work for him—twice the work her classmates have done.

"I hope you don't mind—I've brought one of Eunice's 'critiques'
which I'd like to discuss with you. Eunice doesn't know that I have it,
of course. I took it from her room. She would be mortified to know
that I'm speaking with you."

Francis stares at the paper, which he'd "corrected" mercilessly
with a barrage of red marks and a grade of C–.

"She would be furious, too. Eunice would never, ever agree to my
making some sort of special plea with you . . . She would never forgive me!"

How surreal this is, Francis thinks. Two adults involved in a conversation about the spoiled little ferret-faced girl whom he finds so
repellent.

However, in his role as kindly conscientious Mr. Fox he spends
ten minutes leading the concerned mother through a line-by-line critique of several short poems by Carl Sandburg which earned for Eunice the disappointing grade. Francis is prepared to be defensive but
Mrs. Pfenning has few questions for him, concentrating on trying
to comprehend his teacherly points about grammar, poetic form,

"focus"—though there is essentially no logic behind them, as another teacher of middle-school English might have noted.

In fact, Francis gives A's to students whose work is less focused than Eunice's, if he feels more warmly disposed toward them.

Francis offers to go downstairs to his office and bring back an A paper by one of Eunice's classmates which they might go over, to provide some context with Eunice's work, but Kathryn Pfenning demurs: "I will defer to your judgment, Mr. Fox."

Her daughter has always received high grades in all of her classes, in the past, Kathryn tells Francis; but obviously eighth-grade English is more difficult.

"I did wonder whether Eunice's teachers were reading her work carefully or just giving her A's because she's obviously smart. Eunice can seem mature for her age but in fact she's immature—physically, emotionally. In your class she seems to have had a kind of wake-up call. She has never worked so hard. My heart breaks for her—she would be furious if she knew I was telling you this. I see her light beneath the door of her room hours after she's supposed to be in bed. She is so, so determined to improve in your class!"

"I know she is, Mrs. Pfenning. I'm impressed with Eunice's optimistic attitude."

"She's grateful that you allow her to revise and rewrite, Mr. Fox. That always gives her hope . . ."

"Please call me Francis."

"Please call me Kathryn."

Francis is touched if a bit mystified that Kathryn Pfenning seems to be genuinely concerned for her daughter. The peevish, self-centered little brat—how could any reasonable person care for *her*? He could see that a parent might forgive a beautiful child (like Genevieve Chambers) if she behaves badly—(*he* would forgive his Little Kitten almost anything)—but Eunice in no way resembles Genevieve Chambers.

DNA, the blood-connection. Explains so much without really explaining anything.

"Is Eunice your only child, Kathryn?"

"Yes. How did you guess?"

"Randomly. Blindly."

It's meant to be a joke. Kathryn laughs, uneasily.

"I suppose that we've spoiled her, just a bit—my husband and me. It's so much easier to get along with Eunice if she gets her own way— she can be headstrong. You would understand, if you had children."

To this remark Francis makes no reply.

No one's business but his own if *Mr. Fox* has children or not.

"Oh, I'm sorry, Mr. Fox—I mean, Francis. That was presumptuous of me."

Francis never waves away an apology, however unmerited. To wave away an apology is like tossing away dollar bills, one can always find use for them.

He would never have guessed that a mother of the ferret-faced girl would be such an attractive woman. Not Francis's type certainly, her face too solid, square-jawed, much too old for him yet gracious, warmly engaging. Her dark hair is threaded with silver, elegantly; even the fine lines on her face exude dignity, class. Impressive that Kathryn doesn't seem bitter that fate has played a cruel trick on her, burdening her with Eunice.

What a charade life is! Individuals obsequiously accepting roles they feel obliged to play, unable to see what a neutral observer can see at a glance.

Francis wonders if Eunice's father feels the same way. Doting upon a spoiled child, helpless to resist because the child is "his."

Though it is significant, Eunice's father hasn't come to the Parent-Teacher session.

While suggesting to Kathryn Pfenning that he is totally sympathetic with Eunice's hope of improving her grade Francis confides that, in his opinion as a new faculty member, there is far too much emphasis on grades at the Langhorne Academy. The school takes pride in the high number of graduating seniors who go on to Ivy League universities but there are those who fall by the wayside, no less talented but not so competitive as their classmates, less skilled at test-taking.

"Grades are not everything, you know. Learning should be enjoyable, fun. Writing should be playful. I try to emphasize the imaginative side of English—grammar is but the foundation."

Kathryn listens, subtly rebuked. It is difficult to reply to Mr. Fox when he is making such a reasonable point. He says:

"Eunice is a superior student who belongs in the highest percentile but she is working below her capacity. I think you are correct, Kathryn—her teachers in the past didn't challenge her. It would be helpful to her if she listened to her classmates when they read their work aloud but my impression is that Eunice is too disdainful to listen."

Gravely Kathryn listens. It is clear to Francis that any criticism of her daughter, however mild, is absorbed as a criticism of *her*. A parent who so identifies with her child that there is no boundary between them.

Francis has found that in his role as "Mr. Fox" if he speaks with conviction and exudes an air of concern, and sympathy, even the most unhappy parent will nod anxiously in agreement.

The (naïve) assumption is that teacher and parent are united in a common goal: the well-being of the student. There is not the slightest hint in Mr. Fox's affable demeanor as in his smile that he takes revenge seriously.

Once Francis makes a decision about a student it is difficult for him to rescind it. It would be a sign of weakness, vacillation. If he has resolved to exercise the Skinnerian procedure of intermittent reinforcement he feels obliged to carry the experiment through to some sort of satisfactory conclusion, for him.

"Is there anything in your daughter's personal life that might be affecting her schoolwork, Kathryn? Something that distracts her?"

"I—I'm not sure . . ." Kathryn speaks evasively. "I suppose so."

"Your husband isn't quite as concerned as you are with your daughter, I take it?"

"Oh, no! Martin is as concerned as I am. But he's always working late, over in Bridgeton. Most nights he doesn't get home until after seven P.M."

After a pause adding: "I think you should know, we've been separated since the end of the summer."

Separated! Another father, out of the picture. This is good news. The ferret-faced girl falls into place, a girl whose father has abandoned her, no wonder she thinks that she dislikes Francis Fox.

Eunice's behavior makes perfect sense. He could never quite believe that the girl disliked *him*. Rather, she resists laughing with the others. They are all rival siblings, Eunice must hold herself apart from them, to impress Mr. Fox.

Kathryn says, in a faltering voice: "Eunice isn't happy that Martin and I are separated. Anything that upsets her routine is frightening to her. And now her classmates are 'maturing'—especially the girls. She was confident in grade school, but no longer. I think now she's jealous of the girls, and she's afraid of the boys. Teenagers are so *judgmental*. There's so little we can do to protect her. She isn't allowed to use the Internet unless I'm in the room with her but that can't last much longer. I dread some kind of 'cyberbullying'—that goes on even at this school. Sexual abuse of young girls . . ."

Francis Fox frowns, he isn't so sure of this. Eighth grade? He has heard rumors from his fellow teachers, amusing to him, if disgusting, like the antics of monkeys. "Blow jobs"—middle school? Ridiculous.

His Little Kitten is not of that sordid world, certainly. Her shyness as Mr. Tongue approaches is certain proof.

Kathryn has been saying that Eunice was always somewhat slow to develop. She talked early on but didn't walk well. She has always been high-strung—"skittish." They discovered that she has a medical problem, a minor congenital condition, though it is not serious—not progressive . . .

Kathryn hesitates to say more, and Francis does not inquire. For a moment at the table in a corner of the library they sit silently, as others' voices rise and fall around them.

"It must be a challenge to have a gifted child."

"Oh yes, it is."

Never has Mr. Fox met parents who don't believe that their child is *gifted*.

Indeed, what child, at the Langhorne Academy, is not *gifted*?

Francis Fox is vastly relieved, never to have had children. Several aborted fetuses dispersed among several young women, so far as Francis knows. The oldest child would be sixteen by now. Ghastly!

If a boy, they'd be at each other's throat. As a father he wouldn't put up with insubordination. Fuck little Oedipus.

But if a girl . . . For a delirious moment Francis feels light-headed. Imagine a baby girl, a girl-toddler, the most incredibly soft-smooth-pale-porcelain skin, enormous beautiful eyes and eyelashes like a doll's, then a young child, an older child, a prepubescent girl-child climbing onto Daddy's lap . . .

Oh, Daddy! I wuv you, Daddy!

But beyond that, any age beyond that—no interest. Disgusting, to think of one's own daughter in the throes of puberty: leaking blood, burgeoning breasts, cosmetics. No!

Francis recalls: how he and P. Cady bonded over a decided lack of interest in progeny. Exquisite moment when he understood he'd won the stone-cold heart of Pallas Athena, that had been eluding Francis Fox's charisma.

"Mrs. Pfenning—Kathryn! I'm so sorry."

Kathryn Pfenning is brushing at her eyes with her fingertips. Thinly from the corners of her eyes tears leak, she has been moved by Francis's remarks.

Francis reaches out to touch the woman's hand. No resistance, he folds the chilled hand in his, to comfort.

(An animated discussion is taking place elsewhere in the library, no one is aware of them.)

In a rush of words Kathryn confides in Francis that her life has reached an "impasse." Her marriage is ending—"evaporating." Her husband has become a stranger "lost inside his own head." He spends time at his work—obsessively at his computer—late at night; she has sent him away, he frightens her. She is most worried about their daughter. She would die if something happened to Eunice!

Yet she isn't at all close with Eunice. She has tried—but she has failed. She is terrified that she is losing her capacity to love. Beginning with her husband . . .

"It's like water draining away. I can almost see it—'love' can drain away."

Francis is stunned by this revelation. All such sudden revelations, from women, to *him*—not pleasant surprises, though flattering.

Managing to stammer a reply: "You will feel better in time—probably. This is just a phase. You're upset about your daughter, and your husband . . ."

Ruefully Kathryn laughs. "'Just a phase'—my mother used to say that. Totally undermining anything I was feeling. All of life—'just phases'—one by one."

Such intimacy makes Francis Fox uneasy. In poems and short stories sudden, abrupt, life-altering intimacies are the "climactic" moments of revelation, but in life such moments are not really wanted, at least not by Francis Fox.

Unlike most of his Langhorne Academy colleagues Francis Fox doesn't much mind the Parent-Teacher sessions scheduled for once a month in Haven Hall. "Mr. Fox" in J. Press blazers (navy blue chambray, russet-brown linen), fitted shirts, and designer denim takes pride in charming whoever speaks with him, as a skilled tennis player might take pride in playing with amateurs in such a way that, though he defeats them effortlessly, they imagine that they are near-equals: this requires a very special tact, which few have.

But here, this evening, with Mrs. Pfenning, a startling *rapport*. The distraught mother of his least-favorite student, whom he has never glimpsed before in his life, seated close beside him at the library table with tear-brimming eyes; in a curious state of passivity, helplessness, as if her torrent of words has exhausted her.

Francis has an impulse to shield his eyes from her, as if the woman were but partly clothed, her naked, vulnerable body exposed to him.

"I am so sorry to hear that, Kathryn . . ."

"Oh, I'm sorry, to be burdening you . . ."

"No, no! It isn't a burden . . ."

"It's just that—I have no one else to talk to . . ."

"I know! I mean, I can understand . . ."

". . . marriage is, can be . . ."

". . . from the outside, can seem . . ."

". . . not what it is! Not what you think it is."

There must be something in "Mr. Fox" that he cannot see himself, that elicits such responses, primarily in women, as well as in girls. (Not all girls. But most.) As if, being hollow at his core, empty, "Mr. Fox" somehow attracts the *fullness* of others.

That must be it: sincere and ardent emotion flowing into an empty vessel, under the (mistaken) assumption that the vessel will nurture and not poison it.

Still, Francis is shaken by the sudden *rapport* with this stranger.

Of all strangers, the mother of Eunice Pfenning.

"Well, Mrs. Pfenning—Kathryn—it has been a pleasure to meet you . . ."

"Mr. Fox, a pleasure to meet *you* . . ."

Each is relieved, the consultation has ended. Francis Fox is on his feet. Kathryn rises slowly wiping at her heated face with a tissue.

Vehemently Francis promises: he will reach out to Eunice—"the very next day."

He will challenge Eunice to write in a more "natural, imaginative" voice and not in her usual "machine-like" way.

"Thank you, Francis. *Thank you.*"

Awkward moment when it seems that Kathryn Pfenning might throw herself into Francis Fox's startled arms but somehow instead the two adults merely shake hands in the most conventional of ways, the moment passes, and is lost.

■ ■ ■

"EUNICE? COME IN, PLEASE."

Eunice Pfenning creeps hesitantly into Mr. Fox's office as if doubting that she is welcome though Mr. Fox is waving her gaily inside.

His manner is cheerful, ebullient. He has good news for her, it seems.

At least, it *seems*. Thirteen-year-old Eunice cannot be sure for her English teacher Mr. Fox is the most unpredictable adult she has ever encountered, he has become mesmerizing to her, as a cobra would be mesmerizing, rising up before us in sinewy unspeakable beauty.

It's the very day following the Parent-Teacher meeting. Francis Fox is fulfilling his promise to Eunice's mother for Francis Fox *never fails to fulfill promises*. As in a genial parody of a prep school teacher Mr. Fox is wearing a corduroy blazer of the subtle hue of ripened wheat, blue-striped Brooks Brothers shirt, and a blue polka-dot bow tie that mirrors the icy-blue merriment of his eyes.

"Have a seat, Eunice. You've been in my office before, yes?"

Meekly Eunice concedes *Yes*.

Eunice sits tentatively on the edge of the straight-backed chair. Her small narrowed eyes dart about the room furtive as mice. She is a squirrely little creature, breathing through her mouth, as if asthmatic. Astigmatic?

On the spectrum most likely. *Minor medical condition, congenital.*

An unwanted intimacy, such knowledge. The mother (unwittingly?) betraying the privacy of the daughter. Francis's campaign to squash his nemesis like an insect is undermined if he learns too much about her. He has no wish to feel sorry for her!

Wan afternoon sunshine slants through the single window in the basement office illuminating one of the O'Keeffe posters on a wall. Giving an eerie life to the lusterless blind eyes of the bust of Edgar Allan Poe prominent on the edge of the desk.

"You've met my doppelgänger-friend and fellow-poet Edgar Allan Poe, I think, Eunice?"

Eunice nods *yes*. She has been glancing nervously at the bust.

Glancing nervously too at her English teacher who seems to have taken on the air of a subtly different person than Mr. Fox of the classroom: looming surprisingly tall in his swivel chair as if the floor on his side of the desk were higher than the floor on her side.

Though Mr. Fox is smiling his encouraging Fox-smile as he did that afternoon at the end of their class, summoning her to his office after school, at four P.M. on a "crucial" matter.

Eunice surprises Francis by asking, awkwardly, if she could read the poem of his that won the poetry prize? She makes this request in a way that suggests that she has rehearsed the words beforehand.

"*My* poem? You want to read?"

Francis is astonished at the request. At once, greatly flattered.

That Eunice Pfenning of all his students would remember this detail. Such an inscrutable little creature, partly stricken with shyness, partly pushy. Few eighth graders would dare to make such a request of their teachers. Has he misjudged her?

Possibly the pinched little face, the perpetual scowl, haven't meant disdain for him, but simple shyness.

Or, distrust of an adult male since her father has separated from her family.

Whether voluntarily or not, the father has *abandoned* the daughter. No doubt, Mr. Pfenning is approximately Francis Fox's age.

And she is an only child, as he would have guessed. Not really her fault that with her "congenital" medical condition she has been spoiled by protective parents.

Francis is flattered, yes. Not one of his Little Kittens has ever requested a poem of his but of course Francis has recited many poems to them leaving the girls weakly swooning, faint with love of their blue-eyed English teacher.

However, Francis doesn't want prickly Eunice Pfenning perusing his award-winning poem—an ingenious bricolage of images, phrases, and mordant cadences purloined from a miscellany of poetic forebears from Poe to Frost, Eliot, Roethke, Lowell, Plath, so finely enmeshed no unsuspecting reader could identify them; nor does he want the homely girl lingering in his office, where, in forty-seven minutes, Genevieve Chambers is expected to knock the "secret knock" at his door, which will be discreetly closed at that time.

In Mr. Fox's desk drawer are fresh-baked blueberry tarts and chocolate-covered Godiva strawberries dusted with a mere pinch of Ambien innocent-looking as powdered sugar, awaiting the deliciously tender, sweetly naïve kitten-mouth.

"Another time, Eunice! I promise. But today our subject is *you.*

We are going to reexamine your most recent critique and see how it can be improved."

With a gravely creased forehead Mr. Fox reads through Eunice's homework assignment as if it were a document of great literary merit. When he comes to one of the red-inked queries he pauses to ask if Eunice can rephrase the sentence, which she manages to do, with his guidance.

"You see? Already, your paper is *improved*."

Finally, as if it were a bonus, Francis asks Eunice which of the several poems is her favorite.

It's a friendly question, not a trick question, but fright seizes Eunice as if she fears there must be a correct answer she will fail to provide.

"A—a 'favorite'?"

"Yes. A 'favorite' poem among these."

Eunice pauses, quickly scanning the paper, as if she has forgotten its contents entirely.

Gently Mr. Fox says that *his* favorite Sandburg poem is "Fog"— "A perfect little poem for middle-school readers. It's mercifully short, it does not *fatigue*. A single, singular metaphor: 'little cat feet.' What if the poet had said 'little kitten feet,' Eunice?"

It's a radical new idea to Eunice, that anything printed, anything important enough to be in the class anthology, might have been other than it is.

"'Kitten' would be silly!"

"Why would 'kitten' be silly?"

"You wouldn't say 'little kitten'—a kitten is already *little*."

Eunice dares to laugh, scoffing.

"And what *is* a metaphor, Eunice?"

Unhesitating, with the confidence of a robot, Eunice recites:

"'A metaphor is a figure of speech in which a word or phrase is applied to an object or action to which it is not literally applicable.'" This definition, word for word Mr. Fox wrote on the whiteboard earlier in the term.

"And what is another example of a metaphor, Eunice?"

Eunice's eyelids flutter. She is eager to reply but seems flummoxed.

Francis smiles encouragingly at her as one might at a much younger child.

"'The fog comes trudging in on ponderous elephant feet.' That is another metaphor."

Eunice giggles as if tickled.

"'The miasma comes staggering in on drunken camel feet.'"

Eunice giggles delighted, slightly scandalized. That poetry can be *funny* is a surprise to her.

Francis is gratified, he has made the little bitch laugh at last. Giggling as if tickled with rough fingers as only Mr. Fox knows how.

But no, not this girl. Not the slightest wish to tickle Eunice Pfenning!

"Reconsidering your paper, Eunice, I believe I can plausibly raise your grade. Though it is unfair to your classmates who have not been given this unique opportunity to revise the assignment, thus must remain confidential between us. And I have hope for your next assignment, and assignments to come, which will surely earn A's. You are an *exceptional student,* Eunice. *Potentially.*"

Meekly Eunice murmurs *Thank you.*

Francis returns the paper to her now marked, in red, C+. This, Eunice stares at with a most piteous sort of gratitude.

The sneering girl who was disdainful of Mr. Fox at the start of the semester is now grateful for a mediocre grade which could as readily be A.

Still, C+ is an improvement over C−. As C− was a stunning setback after B, so the next grade may be a whimsical leap forward, if Mr. Fox is feeling generous.

Again Eunice murmurs, her face reddening, *Th-thank you, Mr. Fox.*

She will certainly show her mother this paper with its new grade. And Kathryn Pfenning too will feel encouraged, uplifted.

Kathryn will assume that her conversation with Francis had an immediate effect upon her daughter's grade. *That* will be flattering to her.

It's a human weakness, Francis knows, that perfectly intelligent, reasonable people will nonetheless succumb to flattery if it is adroitly administered.

Never a bad idea to cultivate friends among the parents of one's students. Never a bad idea, if you live a risky life as Francis Fox does, a most *risky risqué* life, to establish ardent supporters among the very individuals who, if they only knew more, might be your mortal enemies; far from being angry with Francis Fox for tormenting her daughter, Kathryn Pfenning will be delighted with him for treating her daughter so kindly.

Because I am making a special case of you. Because you are special, you are deserving of being treated specially.

Francis recalls those few, but ardent, mothers of students at the Newell Johnson School, who fiercely supported Frank Farrell when vicious charges were brought against him by Headmaster Higg. One of the mothers, very likely in love with Frank, though irremediably married, had even lent him her beautiful house in Maine to which he could flee, to save his life that had been unraveling like an old sweater.

Francis smiles, recalling. Hoping to hell such desperation doesn't envelop him again but if it does, Kathryn Pfenning will be on his side.

"Before you leave, Eunice . . ."

In a gesture of impulsive generosity, unplanned, Francis reaches into a desk drawer and pulls out a journal to give to Eunice. The journal has a strikingly elaborate marbled cover, intricate leaves and tendrils, of the bright hue of fermented algae; it is the least attractive of a dozen such journals he purchased at a fire sale in a secondhand shop in Wieland, all with marbled Pre-Raphaelite covers looking as if they cost much more than fifty cents apiece.

"A special gift to you, Eunice. For your class portfolio, due at the end of the term."

Eunice fumbles to take the journal from Mr. Fox's fingers. Her face is stunned with disbelief.

"This is a 'magic journal,'" Francis says solemnly. "You must tell the truth when you write in it, otherwise there will be a curse on you."

Eunice laughs again, uncertainly. A slow smile transforms the pinched little face, Eunice looks almost *girlish*.

"A curse? What kind of curse?"

"It's forbidden to say."

"Are you joking, Mr. Fox?" Another time Eunice has dared to utter the magical words *Mr. Fox*.

"Mr. Fox never jokes! You know that. Haven't I told our class— 'There are no jokes.'"

Eunice nods uncertainly. *Yes, there are no jokes.*

In a lowered voice, with a glance at the opened doorway behind the girl, Francis says: "You must keep the contents of your journal secret from everyone, Eunice. Your parents. Relatives. Friends."

Thinking cruelly—*Friends! As if she has any.*

Hearing his voice riffing like a jazz musician with his instrument. No idea what Mr. Fox will say next but it is always inspired, memorable. This particular student is likely to remember every word uttered to her in Francis Fox's office on this and subsequent days for the remainder of her life.

"I require of a certain caliber of students that they turn in journals to me once a week. These are the élite who then qualify for the Looking-Glass Book Club. In the journal you can write about anything, Eunice—personal, private, domestic, thoughts about the world, books you've been reading, secrets of your household, 'censored' material, anything and everything. For you, I would recommend exploring the outside world: trees, waterways, birds. You give the impression of being imprisoned, trapped inside your hard little skull. You must *get outdoors*. If you designate some pages as PRIVATE, I will not read these. I respect the wishes of my élite students."

In fact, Francis usually doesn't read PRIVATE pages in students' journals for he has little interest in them, except (of course) in the journals of his special girls. He would be very upset if his special girls tried to keep secrets from him.

(Genevieve Chambers has been astonishingly frank, even reckless in her *intimate passages* for Mr. Fox in the rose-marbled journal he gave her, as she has been reckless in sending him certain "selfies" in her nightie. Like sediment at the base of a bottle Francis's senses are stirred by the mere recollection.)

"I would suggest, Genevieve—I mean, *Eunice*—that you push yourself out of your comfort zone. You might experiment with writing with your nondominant hand. You might experiment with illustrating your journal entries with colored pencils. You can include photos. You should wander in the woods and get lost, for once. Have you ever been *lost*?"

"N-no . . ."

"'One cannot be found who has not been lost.' D'you know who said that, Eunice?"

Eunice shakes her head meekly. Francis Fox does not identify the quotation.

"You see, Eunice," Francis enunciates the name with exaggerated care, so that it sounds like *You nice,* "—you are certainly an élite student but your destiny is sheerly hypothetical at this point. It is not yet realized."

Eunice has been staring intently at Francis Fox's face as if hoping to discern, beyond the kindly smile, a deeper truth; but the icy-blue merriment in Francis's eyes is an impediment.

She has been dismissed. Like one dazed, entranced, Eunice gathers her things together, slips the gift-journal into the bookbag, murmurs near-inaudibly *Thank you, Mr. Fox,* and turns to leave as if blindly.

Your destiny is sheerly hypothetical. A blessing, or a curse? A knife with a double-edged blade, any way you grasp it your fingers will bleed.

∎

NOW WHY DID YOU do that, asshole?

For the hell of it, that's why.

Because I could, that's why.

Like training a dog, just as easy.

But: now the homely little brat will adore you.

Now you will never be rid of her.

Francis Fox swallows the last of the wine. It's a rich dark-fruity Barolo, he has treated himself tonight after an interlude of stress.

He isn't worried. He will be rid of the ferret-faced girl whenever he wishes, rid of any of them, all of them, Little Kitten included, whenever he wishes. *He* is Mr. Fox.

Snap of his fingers, easy as pricking a bubble, press *delete,* he's the puppet-master.

■

AT FIRST IT'S AMUSING to Francis Fox, that the ferret-faced girl is now smitten with him.

Where once the squinty stone-colored eyes fastened upon him in dislike, disdain, disapproval now the eyes fasten upon him in adoration.

Francis takes a kind of petty pride in the fact that Eunice Pfenning has joined the ranks of her classmates in smiling at Mr. Fox's witty remarks and laughing at his jokes; her laughter is distinct from the laughter of her classmates for it is shrill and startled-sounding, grating to the ear. When Mr. Fox poses a question to the class Eunice is no longer shy about raising her hand; if no one else supplies the desired answer Mr. Fox will call upon her with a neutral smile: "Eunice? What do you think?"

Though Francis rarely listens to her answer—as he rarely *listens* to any student—he certainly gives that impression, which cannot fail to be gratifying to Eunice Pfenning.

By mid-October the other students no longer ignore Eunice—in fact, they often glance at her in startled admiration of her intelligence, or with growing irritation; her voice can sound shrill, *brattish.* But Eunice seems scarcely aware of them. Her focus is solely upon her English teacher at the front of the room who is often on his feet, skillfully wielding a marker on the whiteboard, provoking laughter, steering the class like the captain at the prow of an old-time sailing ship.

(No one could guess that there is just one person in this class for whom Mr. Fox performs, not the homely Pfenning girl but a lithe little beauty named Olivia, sleek-black-haired, enormous dark eyes, pouty lips—seated in the third row, far right. Thirteen years old but looking a wee bit younger. Mr. Fox is suffused with energy in Olivia's presence though he takes care never to stare at her; though he is thrillingly aware that little Olivia stares at *him*. If something goes tragically amiss with Genevieve Chambers, Olivia Trask will be a delightful surrogate to cultivate.)

Francis takes pride too in the fact that Eunice's writing has actually improved. She has learned to vary sentences and to employ more "colorful" language. She has begun to be "witty"—in obvious emulation of Mr. Fox in the classroom. In her journal, which she entrusts with Mr. Fox each Friday, she never fails to include several reviews of YA books from the school library. ("A classic of American young-adult literature, *A Girl of the Limberlost* by Gene Stratton-Porter is in danger of being 'lost' to readers of today who do not appreciate blatant sentimentality.") To Francis's disappointment she never writes about herself or her family, no mention of her mother. No mention of the "separated" father. She is making an earnest if awkward effort to write about nature and she has begun to include colored-pencil drawings of trees, flowers, butterflies that aren't bad, to Francis's casual eye, but aren't particularly good, either. No talent for art but at least, at his behest she is *trying*.

Francis enjoys the ritual of handing back graded papers, seeing apprehension, even anxiety in student faces, a kind of choked anguish in Eunice's pinched little face. He has to smile, these privileged private school kids *suffer*, they are so competitive and insecure. Like garroting: you choke the victim for a while, then allow her to breathe and revive, then you choke her again, then allow her to breathe and revive, for as long as possible. Somehow it happens that Eunice Pfenning's name is the last called, her paper handed back last.

The look of stunned surprise when Eunice receives from Mr. Fox her first paper graded B+ with the grandiloquent scrawl *Very good, Eunice!*

The puppet-master smiles benignly. A puppet is *always grateful* to merely exist.

Gratified too, to think that Kathryn Pfenning must be overjoyed. Francis likes exerting power no matter how petty. In fact, the more petty, the more pleasure in its exertion; and how good it is for the mother of a Langhorne student to feel gratitude to Francis Fox for his efforts on behalf of her daughter.

Mr. Fox is the only teacher to care enough for Eunice to challenge her! The only one to see her potential.

(It has crossed Francis's mind that he might contact Kathryn Pfenning. The *rapport* between them was immediate, powerful. A still-young woman separated from her husband would be eager for male company of an unthreatening nature. Francis might suggest meeting for coffee at Wieland's lone coffee shop or [more boldly] for a drink at the Wieland Inn. It is tantalizing to him, to recall how Kathryn spilled out her heart to him, how he touched, then held, her hand, to comfort her; how she confided in him, that she was losing her capacity to love—*I can almost see it—"love" can drain away.*)

(The more obsessively Francis has been pursuing the twelve-year-old Chambers girl, the more unobtrusively he has been establishing playful connections with backup kittens Olivia, Taylor, and Brooke, the more prudent it would be to establish a relationship with an adult woman, the mother of one of his students, in case Mr. Fox needs a friend in the Langhorne community.)

Of course, Eunice Pfenning *is* a very good student. It requires no special acumen to recognize this. Nor to surmise that the girl has been spoiled by teachers as well as doting parents, and needs to be made to work harder. Francis Fox has made a career out of discovering the obvious and cultivating it for his own purposes.

Yet—God *damn*. Annoying as mosquitoes buzzing about his head, after each class, or nearly, Eunice Pfenning has taken to lingering in the vicinity of his desk with questions to ask. Francis is coming to realize he was better off when the homely little brat hated him.

Fortunately, other students hang about Mr. Fox's desk as well.

Girls, boys. Each has a question. After a polite interval Mr. Fox can shake them all off and escape.

"Sorry, kids! Have to leave."

Genuine regret, you can see that Mr. Fox *would much rather* hang out with them than hurry off to wherever he is going.

Yet: at the end of the (long) day there is Eunice Pfenning loitering in the basement corridor of teachers' offices, looking as if she has been there for a long time, like a homeless person encamped.

Often, ignoring a bench, she sits on the floor directly opposite Mr. Fox's office, knees drawn up to her chest, pleated skirt tucked carelessly about her legs.

Seeing Eunice in this posture outside his door Francis looks quickly away. Is the girl lifting her knees, in some way displaying herself, for *him*? (As in a cruel parody of *Thérèse Dreaming*?) The thought makes him feel ill. He assumes that Eunice has no idea what she's doing, how she presents herself, typical behavior of a child *on the spectrum*.

Best to nod at her, unsmiling. Stern.

Questions which Eunice has for him are invariably trivial, involving her portfolio. How many pages for this subject, how many for that. She seems resolved to create *the very best eighth-grade portfolio* for Mr. Fox beating out all competitors.

Since Francis gave her the journal, she has been clinging to it like a baby clinging to a spittle-soaked blanket.

This afternoon, Eunice has no appointment with Mr. Fox. To keep her, and a few other avid students, at bay, Mr. Fox has had to limit student conferences to no more than once a week for each student, no longer than fifteen minutes.

Of course, Mr. Fox doesn't mind intense private conferences with favored girl-students but unfortunately, there are few of these.

This afternoon students appear promptly at his door, and leave promptly. He has blocked out fifteen-minute interludes to fill his schedule until five P.M.

Through these appointments Eunice Pfenning persists in waiting, in her awkward ungainly position on the floor, trying to read, and to scribble into her journal with the too-vivid green-marbled cover.

How faithful she is! How *dogged*.

At last, after more than an hour, Francis calls out in just barely disguised exasperation: "Why don't you go home, Eunice? I've told you, my office hour is booked solid."

At once the nasal voice replies: "But one of them might cancel, Mr. Fox! We might have time."

We. What on earth does that mean?

Francis gnashes his teeth. God *damn*. If Eunice is out there when Genevieve arrives Genevieve will stop dead in her tracks and tiptoe away. This has already happened once, to Francis's severe disappointment.

Should wring her neck! God damn.

All too frequently Mary Ann Healy also shows up outside Mr. Fox's office with no appointment. Mary Ann is another besotted eighth-grade girl-student for whom Francis feels little more than exasperation.

Mary Ann Healy and Eunice Pfenning are acutely aware of each other without exchanging a single word: each seeing in the other a pitiful mirror of yearning.

"Fuck it!"

Too restless to grade papers. Haunted by the last time Little Kitten was in his office, in his arms, with the sweet-trusting naïveté of Alice in Wonderland nibbling at a delicious apricot tart, so sweet, so trusting, recall that Lewis Carroll's Alice was only seven years old and Little Kitten is twelve years old, yet childlike, unresisting . . .

He has closed the door, not quite shutting it. Pacing inside his office as a caged fox might pace. Lightly panting.

As five P.M. approaches—footsteps in the corridor but they pass by the door.

Five-ten P.M. Five-fifteen P.M. Little Kitten isn't coming to Mr. Fox this afternoon? She promised, just the day before. And in class this morning, gazing at him with her liquidy eyes, that stirred his senses, left him feeling vertiginous. Even as he had a class hour ahead!

He has prepared his special tarts. Just a trace of powdery Ambien on them.

But where *is* Little Kitten?

In a way, Francis thinks stoically, it's a relief if Genevieve fails to come to his office. No need to contend with prepubescent emotions, worries, fretting, giggles, kiss away tears, make an effort to be patient, *nice.*

Mr. Fox, Mr. Teddy Bear, Mr. Tongue—all very *nice.*

Never do they do anything that Little Kitten doesn't invite. Or seem to invite.

But sometimes, Christ!—just want to grab with both hands, shove into your mouth, and tear with your teeth.

In fact, Francis is (almost) coming to prefer Little Kitten reduced to a video on his cell phone at which he can glance during the day at a whim, daringly in a classroom while teaching, or in the company of garrulous fellow teachers in the lunchroom who would fall in a dead faint could they see what "Mr. Fox" is perusing surreptitiously while grinning affably at their jokes.

In the faculty men's room, in the rushed interim between classes. In the privacy of a toilet stall.

For here is Little Kitten luxuriant in a moment of exquisite tenderness. Not fretting, not anxious but just enough sedated, she is *pure kittenhood.* No willful personality to intrude. Eyes shut, lips partly open, not asleep yet not awake, no resistance as gently—very gently!—Mr. Teddy Bear slips his big-bear hand (warmed!) between her knees, stroking the smooth skin of her thighs, she stirs, she whimpers, her eyelids flutter but do not open, Mr. Teddy Bear grips her tight whispering *Don't be afraid, ma chère, this will not harm you in the slightest but make you very happy and make Mr. Teddy Bear very happy too.*

Francis feels light-headed, recalling.

Online, perused by "paid subscribers"—("paid" is something of an exaggeration since roughly one-half of the six thousand subscribers to *Sleeping Beauties* have opted for a two-week free trial)—Little Kitten is not recognizable, Francis has skillfully altered the picture so that her features are blurred.

Yet, Little Kitten is immediately recognizable, to Francis. *My Kitten*.

Francis prefers the computer, he thinks. To life.

So close, gazing wide-eyed at you but without seeing *you*.

Like the beautiful drugged virgins in Kawabata's *House of the Sleeping Beauties*. Never waking, never conscious of the enthralled elderly visitor lying beside their naked bodies.

Just take sleeping girls as sleeping girls. Is this the wisest wisdom of life?

Twenty past five. Fuck, Little Kitten *isn't* coming! Francis Fox grinds his back teeth. About to slam out of the office cursing but pauses prudently to look out into the corridor, and there is Eunice Pfenning in the identical pretzel-position hunched over her journal, lost in whatever impassioned gibberish she is writing which she will be showing to her English teacher all too soon.

Obviously, Genevieve sighted the ferret-faced eighth grader as she was descending the stairs, and shrank away. "Mr. Fox" will receive a repentant text message shortly framed by insipid heart and kitten emojis.

Sighing, like one stuck with the task of hoisting up a ragged flapping flag.

"Eunice. You can come in now, dear."

Dear. Francis is reckless, uttering *dear* in this way. Of course he is being playful, joking—a bitter joke, but on himself.

"Thank you, Mr. Fox!" Eunice Pfenning scrambles up wide-agate-eyed, eager as a puppy.

THE REQUEST

OCTOBER 2013

Scrolling through recent emails he'd neglected to open Francis Fox is surprised to discover one from Kathryn Pfenning, sent at 11:28 P.M. the very night of the Parent-Teacher meeting, asking if they might meet again. *Preferably off-campus? In the Broad Street coffee shop?*

Despite their singular rapport at the time Francis has more or less forgotten Kathryn Pfenning in intervening days. Interludes with Little Kitten in the privacy of his office, yet more mesmerizing interludes with the video recording of Little Kitten in the privacy of his bedroom, at midnight, have blurred the memory of the woman.

Francis feels now a wave of something like guilt, trepidation.

What did he say, to encourage Kathryn Pfenning to write to him? Mother of one of his students, separated from her husband?

Francis is moved, flattered. But troubled. As in a romantic comedy in rapid forward motion he sees the two of them in the coffee shop enacting a scene made careworn and trite by multiple showings, stumbling through banal dialogue toward a "foregone" conclusion; some sort of falling-in-love interregnum involving drives into the South Jersey countryside and walks along the beach with a lyric-musical soundtrack; more comedy, less romance: pratfalls avoiding detection by Kathryn's precocious-brat daughter Eunice, complications with the estranged husband whom Francis would be obliged to meet, unless Francis simply refuses to meet; sudden swerve to somber drama when Francis disappoints Kathryn as (of course) he must, and will; for the naïve woman has totally misread affable charming Francis Fox and it will be entirely Francis's fault, if he allows her this folly.

His responsibility, Francis thinks, to not-proceed. Though he feels kindly toward Kathryn, and wishes that they might be *soul-mates,* as he is with Katy Cady and Imogene Hood; but Kathryn is a married woman, and Francis has no interest in tangling with an estranged husband, and there's ferret-faced Eunice like an unwieldy bitter pill no man could force himself to swallow—of all Francis Fox's students, *her!*

If Kathryn were the mother of sweet-kitten Genevieve, a different story. But that story is not this story.

Francis pours himself a glass of red wine, and ponders how to reply; how to evoke both *genuine regret* and *genuine moral integrity* within a single brief document.

> *Dear Mrs. Pfenning—"Kathryn"—*
> *Thank you for your email!*
> *I would like very much to continue our conversation which has lingered in my memory—but I don't think it's a good idea at the present time.*
> *Mostly, I am thinking of you, and of your daughter. If your husband is estranged from you at the present time there is the hope that he will return and your differences will be reconciled for the sake of Eunice particularly.*
> *It was a true pleasure to meet you and to speak with you as (I guess I should confess) I have not spoken so warmly and openly with anyone in a very long time and especially not in Wieland! But as you must know—it is made clear to us—it is not "professional ethics" for a Langhorne teacher to meet pri-*

vately with the parent of a student, as it is not ethical for us to accept gifts, dinners, etc. Our code of ethics forbids any relationship however innocent that might compromise a teacher's objectivity in teaching the student.

At Langhorne, it is drilled into us—and I guess I agree—that the well-being of students takes all precedence. Entering into a special friendship with you would inevitably give Eunice an advantage over my other students which would be unfair to them and make Eunice uncomfortable, I am sure.

She is such a special student!—a quite remarkable intelligence, just beginning to blossom. "A terrible beauty is born."

However, dear Kathryn, I will hope that I might make your acquaintance some time in the future if both our circumstances alter.

Sincerely, and warmly—
Francis Fox

Francis peruses this, and wonders: Is *I guess* too hammy, used twice? And what of the ridiculous line from Yeats, applied to a frog-eyed little thirteen-year-old brat struggling to get a grade beyond B?

He could spend more time but—"Fuck." It's getting late, time to snuggle in bed with his laptop kittens, and another glass of wine.

Clicks *send.*

NOCTURNAL

M*is-ter Foxxx . . .*
A high keening cry like that of a nocturnal creature.

His eyes leap up from the laptop screen. He listens. His heart is pierced. What is it?

. . . autumnal wind rattling something loose at one of his windows.

■

MIS-TER FOXXX . . .

Three times distracted from the laptop, three times making his way cautiously through sparely furnished darkened rooms to a window, a door—at last to the rear door of his apartment overlooking a dim-lit parking area where, leaning out into the chill October air in shorts, cotton T-shirt, barefoot, he sees what appears to be a small figure at the edge of the parking lot crouched beside a Dumpster.

He rubs at his eyes, the figure is gauzy as a waning dream image. He hears a startling sound like breaking glass, a tinkling, giggling . . .

"Who the hell is it? *You?*"

Francis steps outside to see more clearly. The figure—stunted-seeming, of a height below five feet—a fleshy-mammalian female body inside disheveled clothes—runs suddenly toward him, at him like a propelled missile. Her face appears swollen, flushed. Her eyes are unnaturally glittering as a doll's eyes. She veers near him, her fingers would clutch at him but he shrinks back alarmed as she passes close by him giggling frantically, reeking of alcohol.

Is this Mary Ann Healy, is she *drunk?* Francis has never seen his girl-student in such a state, the sight is shocking to him, astonishing.

Mary Ann Healy, always so meek, so abashed, so *self-abnegating* in Mr. Fox's eighth-grade English class, sitting quietly at her desk in the posture of one who wishes only to escape scrutiny, rarely participating in class discussions but gazing in mute bovine adoration of Mr. Fox who ignores her, fails to see her at all, for she has proved to be of little interest to him.

How does Mary Ann Healy know where Francis Fox lives? *Why* is she here?

He is stunned at her audacity. Mortified to be made to know that his private life (which is to him indeed *private*) can be so easily invaded by one of his students!—for Francis Fox is complacent in his sense of being so superior to his students, no one would dare to behave insolently toward him.

The nerve of this girl, crouching behind his apartment building in the middle of the night, calling out *Mis-ter Foxxx* in a mock-mournful cry like the call of a loon.

Francis is incensed: What if other tenants in the building have heard her? What if they are looking out their windows even now? *Calling 911?*

He's sure that his fellow tenants, whom he scarcely knows, know of *him.* Instructor at the Langhorne Academy, always well-dressed, well-groomed; exceedingly polite if he encounters them but never lingers to chat, he's so busy.

Already this has been a day of mortifications for Francis Fox: when Genevieve Chambers disappointed him by failing to come to his office as they'd planned. *Mr. Teddy Bear has been missing his Little Kitten!*

She'd texted him a hasty, not-entirely-grammatical apology with the excuse that another girl was waiting for him outside his office door, she hadn't dared come forward and be seen—*Will Mr. Fox forgive Little Kitten?*

Yes, he would forgive her, Francis supposed. Cursing himself, what folly!

Lovesick, heartsick, gutsick Francis Fox. He has gone too far, yet he hasn't gone far enough. He has missed the very best of life. He has wanted to suck the marrow out of the little girls' delicious white bones, nothing less. Yet—they elude him: they die, or they get old. Or they run from his office like squirrely little cowards before Mr. Teddy Bear can work his special magic on them.

Yes but Mr. Fox has sunk his sharp fox-canines into them. Scars they will wear secret inside their clothes for all the days of their maimed and stunted lives.

Never anyone who loved me like Mr. Fox! Never anyone I loved like Mr. Fox.

Yes, I would die for Mr. Fox.

(*Did I die for Mr. Fox?*)

Next day he would write to Genevieve of course. One of his teacherly-formal messages which, if discovered by a suspicious third party, would prove to be undecodable. He has invested too much ridiculous emotion in his current Little Kitten to repudiate her in the name of sanity, his own well-being.

In the meantime Little Kitten can spend a sleepless night wetting her pillow with sentimental tears, first of a succession of sleepless nights, wondering if Mr. Fox has ceased to love her.

No. Mr. Fox has not ceased to love Little Kitten. If only!

But this one, Mary Ann Healy. No possibility of Francis feeling anything like desire for *her.*

"Mary Ann! Listen to me! What are you doing here? How did you get here? You need to go home *now.*"

His voice is lowered, cautious. She doesn't seem to hear. Running flat on her heels, clumsy, yet coquettish, hair in her face, eyes glassy and mouth twisted into a clownish grin. Something has altered Mary Ann Healy, her manner is brazen, reckless. Where in the past Mary Ann has seemed to be shrinking inside her fleshy body now she seems to be flaunting her body, in snug-fitting jeans torn at the knee, a flimsy jersey top that slides off one naked shoulder even as Francis Fox stares in dismay.

His eighth-grade student! Disobeying him so openly, as she'd never have dared to do in their class.

"It's one o'clock in the morning, Mary Ann! Do your parents know where you are? Do they know someone has gotten you drunk? *What do you want with me?*"

Tempted to seize hold of her arm as she runs past him, brushing outspread fingers against him, a rough touch to his arm that is shocking to Francis, deeply alarming. How has Mary Ann Healy dared to touch *him*?

Tempted to drag her indoors, out of the sight of strangers who might be watching from darkened windows, serve the little bitch right if he yanks her arm out of its socket, he is *very angry*.

Though Francis has been drinking also, since early evening. Rapid-fire correcting of student papers is best accompanied by calibrated rewards, a half-glass of red wine for each five papers graded, a reasonable bargain. Francis is certainly not drunk, as Mary Ann Healy is drunk, he is clear-headed as usual, perhaps clearer-headed than usual, all his senses alerted at the possibility of being discovered with a thirteen-year-old girl-student whose (slovenly, soiled) clothes look as if they've been pawed-at and whose breath smells lewdly of alcohol, laughing-sobbing *Mis-ter Foxxx, Mis-ter Foxxx* like a vixen in heat.

Francis wants to protest: He is thirty-seven years old. He is this girl's teacher. He will not only be fired from his position and publicly humiliated, he will be arrested.

If she accuses him. If it occurs to her. If she realizes, how Mr. Fox for all his authority is at her mercy.

Here is irony: Francis is innocent, he has never once touched Mary Ann Healy.

One of his girl-students whom he has not only never touched but for whom he feels not the slightest desire to touch.

On the contrary, since Francis protected Mary Ann from the boys who were tormenting her, he has had to avoid her. In recent weeks she seems to be everywhere he is, in Haven Hall corridors, on stairs, on walkways, in the faculty parking lot where presumably Mary Ann has no purpose being.

It was amusing at first, until it wasn't. That a girl so precociously sexual in appearance, a girl whom other (male) teachers might find attractive, should have so little appeal to him; amusing, that a thirteen-year-old should be pursuing *him*.

Barefoot on concrete, too aroused to feel the cold, Francis is standing just outside his rear door, in shorts, T-shirt. He is but half-clothed. He *has* been drinking. His brain clatters like an old-style computer that will require hours to come to a solution.

Thinking—*Kawabata knew what Nabokov was too stupid to grasp: you want them comatose, mute, their eyes shut and their mouths stopped, their hot hive-brains shut down. Wild creatures, needing to be tamed.*

Shrill laughter like a creature being killed. Brashly she runs at him with blind-seeming eyes, dares to paw at him, clutch at his arm, her eyes are dilated, sweat gleams on her forehead and the loose-fitting jersey slips farther off her shoulder, of course she is naked beneath, a loose heavy chalk-white breast exposed, with a flushed-purple nipple, Francis shoves her away in panic.

Mis-ter Foxxx I love you

∎

INNOCENTLY IT BEGAN ON the very first day of the fall term when he'd noticed her name on his class list—*Healy, Mary Ann.*

A scholarship student, one of very few locals. And an "historic" name, in South Jersey at least.

But Mary Ann Healy seemed scarcely to know about the notoriety

of her family name, and scarcely to care. In this, Francis Fox surmised, the girl was emulating the indifference to history characteristic
of her social class: rural, poorly educated, anti-intellectual, resistance
to "ideas."

He would make a difference in her life, he'd thought (initially).
Mold her like shapeless dough into an intelligent, inquisitive individual in defiance of the Langhorne élite who looked down upon
such scholarship students.

He'd given Mary Ann Healy one of the fancy journals with a cover
marbled like autumn leaves believing that it might inspire her to write
a personal account of her life as a Healy, familiar with family tales of
the recluse who'd (allegedly) shot down the *Hindenburg,* "the Pride of
Nazi Germany," in 1937, causing the deaths of thirty-six people yet—
(how was this possible?)—never been charged with any crime; but
Mary Ann seemed embarrassed by the subject, acutely self-conscious
and uninspired. Writing book reviews of puerile YA novels with schoolgirl enthusiasm seemed to be Mary Ann's métier, dullest of subjects.

Couldn't she interview older relatives?—Francis asked patiently.
A grandparent, someone who might have known Romulus Healy?

(But when had Romulus Healy died? Nineteen eighty-seven?
That wasn't so very long ago, certainly.)

(Romulus was said to have sired six children. How many grandchildren, and great-grandchildren?)

Out of ignorance or sheer female-flesh obstinacy Mary Ann Healy
murmured that they would think it was *weird,* people in her family
would laugh at her, nobody ever talked of anything like that, that happened so long ago.

Seventy-six years wasn't that long ago, Francis objected. Was she
one of Romulus's grandchildren?

Mary Ann murmured what sounded like *No* or *Don't know.*

"Don't *know*? Mary Ann, how can you *not know*?"—Francis tried
to disguise his impatience.

The girl's blank moon face was mottled with embarrassment, her
gaze mutely downcast. Indeed it was like trying to communicate with
uncooked bread dough.

"Well, Romulus was a relative of yours," Francis persisted. "I'd think you would want to know more about him. It may be just local history but at least it's *history.*"

History! At this a faint shudder passed through Mary Ann like an electric current.

Pressed by her English teacher to write about Romulus Healy, Mary Ann resorted to copying passages from kitsch-histories like *Tales of Haunted New Jersey* from the school library; at least, these were footnoted and properly credited, which seemed to him impressive in an eighth grader, though still he was disappointed in her.

"Mary Ann, anything that can make you *special,* you should cultivate. Even if you have to exaggerate a bit. Otherwise, you will be like everyone else."

Mary Ann smiled wistfully. As if to be *like everyone else* were possible for her, in her alarmingly voluptuous young body.

She didn't care so much for "history," Mary Ann told Mr. Fox in a pleading voice. As her father said, things that happened once weren't going to happen again. *She* wanted to be like Miss Hood: a librarian.

Librarian. Mary Ann pronounced the word with such reverence, Francis had to laugh. Absurd! A girl as physically developed by thirteen as Mary Ann Healy need not set her sights on so ordinary a life, routine and circumscribed as the life of spinster Imogene Hood.

But Mary Ann persisted: "I guess—I love books. I can trust books . . ."

Shrinking just slightly, hurt that her English teacher seemed to be sneering at her, as so many others did.

She'd asked Miss Hood and Miss Hood said you can go to "library school" in college and learn to be a librarian. She hoped to do that, and work in a library like the Wieland Public Library where she could read all the books on the shelves and order new books and when students came in the library she could help them pick out books to *expand their horizons* as Miss Hood said.

Francis listened in disbelief, eyes glazed with boredom. This ridiculously sexy little girl, a plump Renoir with a pretty-vapid doll's face, prattling about books and libraries!

Next, Francis urged the girl to write about her own life, if she couldn't manage to write about her family history, thinking that, looking the way she did, a young female in rural Jersey among mostly uneducated people, she'd have experienced sexual harassment if not sexual abuse of some sort, which would make for interesting journal entries; but to his frustration, these passages too were utterly pedestrian.

> Grandma's canary lost his mate and stopped singing and so another female canary was put in his cage but still he wouldn't sing but the female had eggs and when the little birds hatched the father-canary taught the little canaries to sing and so there were three canaries singing at one time which made everybody happy to hear especially in the morning.
>
> Kyle's Jeep he'd bought second-hand broke down in the Pine Barrens and he had to hike out eleven miles he said and then the tow truck couldn't find the Jeep so it is still there somewhere . . .

Francis's lower jaw felt unhinged from yawning. Leafing through the journal in search of he didn't know exactly what but certainly not this recitation of domestic banality lacking subtext and significance.

One day asking Mary Ann Healy if anything made her angry?— and she said, with surprising vehemence, "When people look at me without looking at *me*."

"Well, can you write about that? Boys, men?"

Inspiring Mary Ann to write just a single paragraph in her neat schoolgirl hand, in purple ink:

> I hate him! I would run away from him to hide but you would find me, in a corner where I was hiding he unzipped his pants and took out his ugly thing I hid my eyes not to see, he was jerking at himself and grunting and I hid my face, I felt sick, I would not look at him he said, look! what

are you afraid of, look, but I would not, I hate him so much. They are all like that, that is why I love books because you can trust books, books are your friends.

This entry in Mary Ann's journal Mr. Fox marked with an enthusiastic red star and a B+ saying the subject had promise but did Mary Ann realize that she'd made a small mistake, she'd written the word *you* when she'd meant *he*?

Also, the entry was too short. Could she say more? Could she identify this boy or man who behaved in such a disgusting way, when did this happen, how old was she, did she tell anyone else about it, did she tell her mother?—but Mary Ann balked saying she didn't want to write more about *that*.

"That's why I like school, Mr. Fox. I like to read books and think about them. I don't even like TV so much like my mother does. I guess—I guess I am sorry—I just don't want to write about *that*."

"Has anyone in your family touched you like that, Mary Ann? You have older brothers, don't you?"

"Why is that all you want to know about, Mr. Fox! That is what I *hate*."

Mary Ann spoke in dismay, tears shining in her eyes. Behind her, the opened door of Francis Fox's office, very likely a student or two waiting to see Mr. Fox, late afternoon after classes, quickly now Francis wanted the girl gone, her voice had lifted dangerously, this was no ethereal Little Kitten but a fleshy flush-faced girl who looked more like eighteen than thirteen.

Dismissed, Mary Ann rose to leave, in her agitation forgetting the journal with the marbled cover, which Francis pushed at her across his desk: "Don't forget this, Mary Ann. It might be, for all you know, your *lifeline*."

Francis had to concede defeat, he'd failed to inspire the girl to write about anything interesting. Her revulsion at sex was reasonable: since childhood she'd probably been a target of sexual interest of older boys, men; it would make sense, she'd have little sexual desire of her own. Hoping to be a librarian was in fact a practical solution for one in retreat from the physical life but it certainly did not make her very interesting, as, he had to admit, Imogene Hood, Francis's closest friend in Wieland, was not very *interesting*.

Still, out of a kind of sociological-scientific curiosity, for Francis considered himself something of a polymath, he retained a peripheral interest in Mary Ann Healy, as a sort of South Jersey specimen. Was she a product of inbreeding? Scrolling the Internet Francis discovered a condition called *precocious puberty*, of which he'd never heard before.

Twelve percent of white American girls are now beginning puberty before the age of eight. The average age of menarche is dropping yearly.

Eight! Francis was dismayed, disgusted. How was this possible? A child of eight—puberty? Could this mean—pregnancy?

It was revolting to him, deeply upsetting, to think that a slender ethereal girl like Genevieve Chambers might, at twelve, already have begun her so-called menarche . . .

"Not possible. Not Little Kitten."

According to the online article, normal girls usually began menstruating at much older ages in the past: fourteen, even fifteen. Twelve would have been distinctly young. But for some reason in the twenty-first century an eerie phenomenon was being noticed by medical researchers to which the name *precocious puberty* had been given.

Twenty-three percent of Black girls, fifteen percent of Hispanic girls, twelve percent of white girls are beginning to menstruate at ever earlier ages.

Francis read on, in horror. The very words were repugnant to him: *menstruate, menarche, puberty.* As if an exquisite Balthus painting were defaced by crude graffiti.

There were numerous theories attempting to explain *precocious puberty*: the "obesity epidemic" in the United States, unparalleled among industrialized Western nations; "endocrine disruptors"— chemicals that interfere with the body's hormonal processes (found in pesticides, shampoos, deodorants, perfumes). Non-environmental factors like early childhood stress, absent or abusive fathers, adoption.

Though growing up in the identical milieu boys experience *precocious puberty* far less often than girls.

Pheromones, olfactory and auditory cues. Poverty, mistreatment, sexual activity at an early age, trauma. Neural pathology.

Mary Ann Healy was a victim of her body's hormones, essentially. A reasonably intelligent girl trapped in a body that didn't represent her, it was unlikely that she would ever be taken seriously by either men or women. A pure product of biology, primed to reproduce. In fact, Mary Ann looked pregnant, with a round little tummy, heavy breasts and hips, no matter how loose-fitting her school uniform.

Francis, who considered himself a feminist, an enlightened male, had to concede that he tended to underestimate the girl, when he thought of her at all; nothing further should have developed between them.

■ ■ ■

"MR. FOX? I HAVE a present for you."

Seeing Francis's look of exasperation, quickly amending: "I can leave it on your desk. I'll just—I'll just leave it . . ."

Shy-stubborn, meek-willful, the Healy girl is at his heels again. Following him in the corridor after their class, knocking at his office door without an appointment.

Weeks following his interceding with the boys who'd been taunting Mary Ann. He feels sorry for Mary Ann Healy but wishes to hell he'd never seen her.

Francis has explained to Mary Ann that Langhorne teachers are not supposed to accept gifts from students but Mary Ann seems not to hear. Her eyes shine with the puppy-pleasure of being in Mr. Fox's company.

Earnestly Mary Ann explains that her presents are all handmade, *her* hands. She did not buy them in a store.

"Mary Ann, I don't think that makes any difference. 'Handmade,' 'store-bought' . . . It's unethical for us to accept gifts from students."

Unethical. Is this Francis Fox speaking so piously?

Francis stares at the thing Mary Ann is holding: some sort of sewn or woven pouch, of the size of a grapefruit, which she calls *sa-shay.*

Sachet? It smells strongly of lavender, Francis's nostrils pinch at the odor.

A *sa-shay,* Mary Ann explains, is something you put in a closet with your clothes, or in a drawer with sweaters, to keep moths away, and to "smell nice." Her grandmother taught her to make *sachets* using lavender from her own herbal garden.

"My grandma also taught me to make bracelets like this," Mary Ann says proudly, showing Francis an awkwardly woven bracelet of colorful yarn, fluffy bird feathers, and glass beads on an elastic band on her wrist. "I could make you one too—men can wear them, too."

Francis declines with thanks. Telling Mary Ann again that accepting gifts from students is unethical at the Langhorne Academy but Mary Ann is looking so wistful, he doesn't have the heart to decline the lavender sachet as well.

"But no more, Mary Ann. Just this. And it has to be a secret between us."

"Yes, Mr. Fox! *A secret between us.*"

Frequently it has happened that girl-students develop a crush on Francis Fox when he has absolutely no interest in them. Such pre-pubescent attachments are flattering to him, if embarrassing, and sometimes annoying; usually, the attachment wanes when Francis doesn't encourage it, or at the end of a school term. It is rare that even a highly desirable kitten will endure beyond the summer break and into another term.

Francis resents time spent thinking about the Healy girl, as he resents time spent thinking about the Pfenning girl, when he could be basking in dreamy thoughts of Little Kitten.

Francis would like to ask Imogene Hood if the girl is a nuisance to her too but is reluctant to bring up the subject; when he's with Imogene it is usually Imogene who does most of the talking while Francis's thoughts drift elsewhere like whitish vapor in an opium den. But he does notice a scent of lavender in Imogene's company, and elicits from Imogene the information that yes, Mary Ann Healy gave her a little gift of a homemade lavender sachet.

"She's an earnest student, isn't she," Francis says in a neutral voice, and Imogene says, more enthusiastically, "She's such an avid *reader*. She's a scholarship student here, her family background is very 'working-class.' Mary Ann is literally the only student I've ever encountered who has expressed an interest in being a librarian."

"Is she!"—Francis expresses genuine surprise.

Waiting in vain for Imogene to mention, at least in passing, that Mary Ann Healy is very *mature* for her age, at least physically; but Imogene speaks only of the girl's interest in books, and in the library.

(In recent weeks, steeped in his infatuation with Genevieve Chambers, Francis has had less time to spend with Imogene Hood; he is conscious of Imogene feeling slighted, hurt. Vaguely he has suggested to Imogene, or allowed Imogene to think, that over the fall break she might meet him in New York City to see a museum or a play; as, vaguely too, he has allowed Katy Cady to think that he might be coming to New York City to see her over the break, to stay in her apartment for a few days while they go to plays, museums . . . Francis isn't serious about any of these plans, which he has more or less forgotten; he has been fantasizing a way to meet with Genevieve over the break, not at the school, which will be closed, and not in his apartment where she might be seen but—where?)

"Yes, she's very serious. It's touching . . ."

Francis inclines his head, not sure what Imogene is talking about so earnestly. As he listens, he realizes that the topic is still Mary Ann Healy.

"She admires you so much too, Francis. Her second choice for a career is English teacher, she told me."

"Did she!"—Francis manages a weak smile.

Soon then excusing himself, to escape from Imogene before she brings up the subject of their "mutual plans" for the fall break.

Next day, this happens: returning to his office in the company of a colleague whose office is beside his Francis is appalled when the colleague (a fellow English teacher named Quilty) stoops to pick up a folded sheet of paper pushed partway beneath Francis's office door, saying with a toothy smile, "A billet-doux from one of your girl-students, Francis?"—as if it were quite well-known among his fellow teachers, that girl-students are pursuing Francis Fox.

Forcing his usual smile Francis tugs the paper from Quilty's fingers before Quilty can see what it is. It's a brazen gesture, possibly even a rude gesture, but Francis isn't going to take a chance allowing this pushy son of a bitch to peruse a private message from one of Francis's besotted girl-students.

No apology for his behavior, not even an embarrassed murmur, all Francis can think to say to Quilty is *Fuck you* which he isn't going to say aloud.

Once Francis is in his office with the door safely shut he unfolds the paper (which emits a telltale fragrance of lavender) to read, in chagrin, these words in purple ballpoint:

> *Dear Mr. Fox!*
> > *Since you have come into my life*
> > *My life is like a flame.*
> > *My life is a fire, a sun, a moon,*
> > *All the stars glimmering together*
> > *And no one is to blame.*
>
> ***I Love You***
> *Your Student Mary Ann*

Arteries in Francis's head swell to the point of bursting.

Not only does Francis feel revulsion at such frank forthright emotion aimed like a missile at him, Francis is revolted by the maudlin bad taste of the "poetry"—mitigated only just slightly by the fact that the girl is an eighth grader and what can one reasonably expect of an eighth grader?

"God *damn.*"

Francis rips up the paper, shoves the pieces into his pocket so that they won't be discovered in his wastebasket and fitted together by that God-damned nosy young custodian.

His face smarts with heat, for what if Quilty saw the poem? Quickly scanned the poem, committed it to memory? Saw the signature—*Your Student Mary Ann?*

Following this incident Francis Fox is visibly cool to Mary Ann Healy. He does not smile when the anxious girl greets him with her wide hopeful smile in class. He does not look at her, not once during the class period. The next grade he gives her for a homework assignment is C− with the brusque comment *Commonplace, banal, unoriginal, trite.*

So stricken is Mary Ann by Mr. Fox's sudden hostility she redoubles her efforts to see him, speak with him. She leaves another purple-ink message smelling of lavender pushed beneath his office door.

> *Mr. Fox forgive me, I am so sorry.*
> *Please tell me what to make things right?*
>
> *Your Student*
> *Mary Ann Healy*

No comma where a comma is required, an entire word missing!—this is a scholarship student at the Langhorne Academy?

Francis tosses out the sachet smelling of lavender. Last thing a man wants, his clothes smelling like God-damned lavender.

Soon then he discovers Mary Ann Healy following him at a little distance like a kicked dog. Heedless who might be noticing her, and him. He is sure that all of his colleagues are aware of Mary Ann Healy and whispering together about her and him, God knows what slander. All he can hope is that Imogene Hood doesn't hear this vile gossip, still more Headmistress Cady.

At least, no one has a clue about Genevieve Chambers, he is sure. So far, Francis has been discreet about meeting the girl, he believes that he is fully in control of the situation.

But Mary Ann Healy is another matter. She has become reckless, even defiant. One wet dank October afternoon daring to follow Francis from Haven Hall to the parking lot beneath dripping trees determined to get his attention, pleading with him to look at her at least, reiterating how sorry she is, how she needs to speak with him, despite the stiffness of Francis Fox's posture, rigidity of his head as he stares straight ahead resolved to ignore her, it's clear that she is of no more significance to him than a small yapping dog, each plea is a new blunder, all of these blunders irrevocable yet (still) Mary Ann Healy is determined to pursue Francis Fox even as he hurries away from her, climbs into his car slamming the door behind him, guns the motor leaping forward knocking her to the pavement with a little cry—*Ohhh!* As if something very small, bat-sized, has had its neck wrung.

"God *damn*."

Ignoring the girl sprawled on the ground with books strewn about her Francis Fox speeds out of the parking lot in the dazzling-white Acura without a backward glance.

■

IT WAS NOT HIS fault, how was it his fault.

She—the girl—stepped in front of his car. Deliberately.

No blame of his but he will be blamed. He fears.

■

LOVESICK FOR THE ONE girl who eludes him. Little Kitten who has been making excuses not to see her besotted Mr. Fox. Even as other girls lie in wait for him like wild creatures infected by rabies and by rabies empowered to behave most brashly, halfway he expects to stumble over one of them in the corridor outside his office.

Suffused with chagrin, frustration, rage that Genevieve Chambers is lately resisting meeting him in his office though clearly—(he can see in her eyes, she gazes at him reverently in the classroom)—she adores him, despite her shyness she adores Mr. Tongue's vigorous kisses, Mr. Teddy Bear's warm caressing paw, gripping at her lover's arm to steady her trembling as he holds her tight, fixed in place, her luminous skin heated, beautiful dark eyes liquidy and clouded about to spill over in tears.

Just to recall leaves Francis light-headed, faint.

In class this very morning scarcely daring to glance at Genevieve Chambers fearful of raw desire glaring in his eyes.

In class performing solely for Genevieve (yet) oblivious of her. As once he performed for Miranda Myles.

That is the teacher's trick: to perform for the single, singular, privileged student in such a way that she worships him anew even as she doubts her standing with him.

And so this evening following the frustrations of the day—(Mary Ann Healy following him into the parking lot! stepping in front of his car!)—allowing himself the illicit luxury of driving past the Chambers house. For in her intimate journal entries Genevieve Chambers has revealed her home address as in heedless headlong infatuated-schoolgirl prose she has provided many details of her personal life and the life of her family—(including excruciatingly detailed conversations with her mother, one of that ever-growing army of left-behind/outgrown first wives)—a delight to Mr. Fox no matter if the entries are often ungrammatical, poorly punctuated, with misspellings that would ordinarily offend an English teacher's fastidious eye but in this case the English teacher finds quaint, charming.

Ah, the Chambers house!—impressive large white Colonial at the corner of Church Street and Richmond Avenue, five or six bedrooms at least, three-acre landscaped lot. A single vehicle (classy BMW, looks like) in the driveway, parked slightly askew, which sends a (hopeful) signal that only one adult is living in the house and that adult the left-behind/embittered first wife who is Little Kitten's sole remaining parent in Wieland.

(And not a very vigilant parent since wily Mr. Fox has practically seduced her twelve-year-old daughter just slightly beyond the mother's purview.)

Yes, it is risky. Driving past a student's house. Even after dark!

Yet Francis is sure he is safe: he *is* Francis Fox, blessed with good luck. No one is likely to take note of a clean-shaven white man in a reasonably new-model upscale car (Acura) driving through this sequestered residential neighborhood. Even if Francis dares to park at the curb cutting the headlights to stealthily observe the Chambers house with a pair of binoculars (kept in the Acura glove compartment for just such felicitous occasions), squinting to see through the thumb-smudged lenses, a not-quite-focused vision of second-floor curtains delicate as lingerie though (of course, being practical-minded) Francis Fox doesn't really expect to see anything, not a glimpse of lithe Little Kitten gliding past the window half-dressed, in just teeny girl-panties and (possibly) no top at all, this is but a whimsical gesture, harmless, even innocent; in homage to the purity of his love; besotted by the visionary—

> Let me pull
> Your soft Wool.
> Let me kiss
> Your soft face

—though Francis isn't drunk, though the first drink of the day eagerly awaits him in the privacy of his apartment, hardly a crime to park his car, peer through binoculars (he has not used them in a very long time, he swears) for doesn't Francis owe himself this small reward after the clownish indignity of the Healy girl pursuing him in the faculty parking lot, blushing-moon face and voluptuous female body jiggling in full view of anyone who'd chanced to be watching the spectacle.

(Recalling now that in the corner of his eye he was conscious of a tall lanky figure, not a student but [possibly] a staff worker, also in the parking lot, an accidental encounter yet this young man seemed to

know Mary Ann Healy; in the confusion of the moment Francis didn't
have time to actually see this person, didn't recognize him, all his effort was concentrated in trying to avoid Mary Ann Healy, escape
Mary Ann Healy, oblivious of the fact [if it was a fact] that as he'd
gunned the motor of the Acura he'd struck the damned girl with the
left front fender, knocked her down, but no scream, no outcry, hadn't
felt much of a jolt, determined not to notice, not to obsess, desperate
to escape the scene, not a glance in the rearview mirror and next he
knows he is exiting the Langhorne Academy campus, he is *gone*.)

Tonight he will contrive to send a text to Little Kitten. Though
this is risky indeed. He has instructed Genevieve always to delete his
texts immediately and to delete all record of her texts to him but can
he trust her? A twelve-year-old kitten is moody and capricious as a
flame in a draft. And this kitten skittish, easily frightened.

Still it is hard to resist driving past the Chambers house. Knowing
that beautiful Genevieve is inside. Slow-circling the block of large
houses on large landscaped lots, passing the house a second time,
curious to see if anything has changed in the few minutes he has
been away, for instance in the upstairs room Francis has come to
believe must be *her* bedroom. Does a citizen of Wieland, New Jersey,
not have the right to be driving on any public street on his way to the
7-Eleven, in fact the liquor store next door, Francis is no more than a
mile out of his way here on Richmond Avenue. And sometimes he
shops for groceries (did lovesick Poe shop for *groceries?*—hard to
imagine) at grungy Kroger's where once (he'd swear) he glimpsed the
lanky-limbed young Langhorne custodian he'd caught rummaging
through his desk in Haven Hall unless he was imagining *that*. (For
Francis Fox has become somewhat paranoid here in South Jersey
where his cultivated tastes, educational background, and hauteur
make of him an *outlier*: a puppet-master in search of a worthy puppet.)

Sudden vision: Genevieve Chambers in T-shirt snugly fitting her
petite torso, snug-fitting shorts, slender white legs, walking alone on
a tree-lined road and Francis happens to be driving on that road, recognizes his seventh-grade student, pure chance he has sighted her

and pulls up beside her in the dazzling-white Acura calling out *Hello!*
My goodness! Is that—Genevieve?

Natural to ask if Genevieve would like a ride home? Or—a ride
out into the countryside?

How far to the Pine Barrens? Half-hour, forty minutes?

Mr. Tongue is avid to kiss in his special Mr. Tongue way. Mr.
Teddy Bear, avid to caress in his special Teddy Bear way.

But: Forbidden. High alert. Simon Grice would be appalled.

Stay on campus. Haven Hall. Privacy of Mr. Fox's office, door
shut. No car. No plausible reason for a Langhorne teacher to be in a
car with a student. Mere glimpse of the guilty couple through the
Acura windshield would end Francis Fox's promising new career.

Priggish Simon Grice would disapprove of Francis Fox né Frank
Farrell behaving recklessly (again). No emails, no text messages, no
cell phone photos! Your attorney advises you: no electronic trail, no
paper trail.

One bit of helpful advice Simon Grice had given: if a girl-student
appears to be becoming inappropriately attracted to him, lingers after
class, comes to his office, leaves notes for him, billets-doux and love
poems, it would be a very good idea to file a report with the school
administration, just in case.

In case you are accused. In case they try to blame you, *and not* her.

Francis has been considering filing some sort of report to the
school administration about Mary Ann Healy. An eighth grader who
has developed an unhealthy fixation on her English teacher, sends
him personal notes (including a mawkish love poem), followed him
into the faculty parking lot, stepped in front of his car as he was
driving away . . . But if Francis reports his student he will have to
insist that he has given her no reason, he does not return her feelings, *she is not his type.* Even in his zeal to do the right thing the
feckless teacher may find himself in trouble with the administration.

Also, Francis feels sorry for Mary Ann Healy. First in her family to
attend a private school, first in her family to win a scholarship. Over
her head at the swanky school, she will never be accepted by her

spoiled-brat classmates as one of them. Francis is but exasperated with her, pities her, has no wish to do her harm.

The Pfenning girl is almost as much of a nuisance as Mary Ann but apart from waylaying him after class and stationing herself outside his office with the tenacity of a pit bull she is not really a threat. (He is sure.)

Ridiculous that girls/women are attracted to Francis Fox when he is not attracted to them. Unnatural, somehow. Disagreeable.

He is the puppet-master, *he* is the one who chooses. The girls Francis falls in love with are solely his choice for it is one of their attractions that they are *prepubescent*: that is, *presexual*.

Not children, for Francis Fox *is not* interested in children. Of all perversions, pedophilia is most offensive to him as to any decent human being. Plus, children are *boring*.

Zero interest in girls younger than twelve. As fourteen is the outer limit, fifteen impossible.

Nor does he approve of makeup on girls' faces. For Francis Fox, luminous beauty is the beauty requiring no cosmetics.

Headlights flash onto him in the front seat of the car, quickly Francis lets the binoculars fall from his hands.

Heart clenches: Is it a police car? Wieland cruiser? (The raptor's eye has taken note of local law enforcement vehicles: stark-white, with blue letters *Wieland Police*. To be avoided.)

Yes? No?—no . . .

The ordinary-civilian vehicle passes, another time Francis Fox has been spared. Though trembling badly, he is grateful.

This is a sign, friend: *Go home.*

■

MIS-TER FOXXX . . .

High keening cry like that of a nocturnal creature.

No choice (he thinks) but to let Mary Ann Healy into his apartment. Can't shut the door against her, it's past one A.M., the October air is cold and he feels sorry for the damned girl though he is (also) furious with her.

Can't call 911. No police on the premises!

Can't call her parents, Francis dreads being associated with a drunken disheveled thirteen-year-old who happens to be *his student*.

"All right, come in. Come on!"

Disgusted-daddy. Not a role to which Francis Fox has aspired.

Like a feral animal Mary Ann Healy approaches the sliding glass door which Francis has opened partway, steps cautiously into the sparely furnished living room. Her bloodshot eyes dart rapidly about. Francis could laugh, is she suspicious of *him*?

The drunken girl smells strongly of her body, and of alcohol. Francis's impression has been that she is barefoot, in fact she's wearing soiled sneakers without socks. Her torn jeans are soiled too, a size too small for her shapely hips and buttocks. She's sniffling as if chagrined.

In a near-inaudible voice with lowered eyes Mary Ann asks to use Francis's bathroom. No choice but to say yes even as Francis feels a jolt of panic for what if this distraught girl locks herself in his bathroom? Slashes at herself with a razor blade from the medicine cabinet? *How could Francis Fox possibly have not foreseen this?*

His mouth has gone dry, he swallows compulsively. Recalling how Katy Cady used his bathroom, how his brain clattered frantically trying to imagine ways to murder the woman who was (Francis would insist) his truest *soul-mate*.

The mistake is, letting them inside. Females, uncontrollable.

Fortunately, Mary Ann doesn't lock herself in the bathroom. There is rushing water, a toilet flushing. When the girl reappears her face is less flushed, her disheveled hair has been wetted, tamped down. He sees that she is wearing the homemade woven bracelet on her right wrist, the bird's feathers are not so fluffy or clean now.

Muttering what sounds like *Thank you, Mis-ter Fox* . . .

Francis steps into khakis, no time for a belt. Searches for his car keys, he will drive the girl home. He is grim, determined. By two A.M., he thinks, the problem should be solved.

Anything to be rid of her! A predator-fox cannot think clearly if backed into a corner like a rat.

Mary Ann protests she doesn't want to go home.

She could sleep on the floor, she says. *Please, Mis-ter Fox . . .*

Francis all but shouts *No. Ridiculous.*

"You're not sleeping here and if you did, it would be on a sofa, not the floor. For Christ's sake."

Stubbornly Mary Ann explains that she told a friend of her brother Kyle's that she needed a ride into Wieland, she was spending the night with a girl cousin, so this guy drove her into town, her mother isn't expecting her home so it's OK for her to stay away overnight . . .

"No, it is not 'OK.' I'll drive you home."

Francis is reluctant to touch Mary Ann Healy even to nudge her toward the door. She stands flat-footed, inert; eyes teary and downcast, loose-fitting jersey top slipping from her shoulder. Slovenly, yet (Francis supposes) seductive.

Not a candidate for *Sleeping Beauties*. But yes, there are websites on the Dark Web that would welcome pictures of a girl like Mary Ann Healy.

"I said: I'm driving you home."

Francis has opened the front door of his apartment. Has to hope to God that no one is watching from the walkway or the street, if so he is finished, *fucked*.

Pushing Mary Ann outside. Reluctantly she moves, as an unwieldy bundle of soiled laundry might move if it had animation.

Trying to remain calm, matter-of-fact as a middle-school teacher confronting a soluble problem he asks Mary Ann where she lives, in her chastened voice she tells him. She has begun to cry.

"Jesus!—just stop. No one is hurting you."

Driving into the night out of darkened Wieland and along Stockton Road which soon becomes a two-lane country highway. By his calculation Mary Ann lives less than three miles away, not far; he recalls from her journal entries that she lives alone with her mother in a farmhouse once belonging to her grandparents. No father.

Thank God! No redneck father with a shotgun.

Still there is the matter of a drunken juvenile girl in his vehicle.

Looking as if someone has been pummeling her, tugging at her clothes. Francis is trying not to think what this might entail if a police cruiser glides up beside him.

Asking Mary Ann who bought her alcohol? (Not beer. Her breath doesn't smell of beer.) Has she been drinking—whiskey?

"Was this some guy you're mixed up with? Your brother's friend? Did he do something to you?"

Mary Ann hides her face, crying harder.

"Hey. Who is it? How old is he?"

Trying not to lose patience. Trying not to glance at Mary Ann huddled in the passenger seat uncomfortably close.

He hears her murmuring something that sounds like *I only love YOU*.

Not sure if he can ignore this. Pretend not to hear.

Trying to remain calm. Not panic. Tempering his voice so that he sounds casual, even teasing, like somebody's daddy:

"Hey. You do not love ME. You're being silly, and you know it."

"No. I am not, Mr. Fox. *I am not silly, this is the rest of my life.*"

"What do you mean—'the rest of your life'?"

This sounds alarming, Francis has no idea what Mary Ann means. He knows that teenage girls are wildly unpredictable, emotional. His own dear Kitten Genevieve has confessed to "cutting" herself, God knows why. And there was the tragedy of Miranda Myles of which Francis rarely allows himself to think.

Melodrama! So female-humid, suffocating.

Asking, half-pleading what does she want with him?—and Mary Ann says, "I want to love you, Mr. Fox," and Francis is shocked as if Mary Ann has uttered an obscenity instead of the word *love*, hears himself stammering, "But—you have your father, Mary Ann—your parents, your family—they love you . . . ," his voice trailing off weakly as Mary Ann protests, "Not the way I love you, Mr. Fox," and Francis says, "But—I'm too old for you, old enough to be your father—and I'm your teacher," banal words unworthy of one for whom words have been so important, one whose very personality has been shaped by the capacity of carefully selected words for seduction and deceit, to which Mary Ann responds with the clumsy ease of a child whipping a Ping-Pong ball back into the face of a startled adult, "Oh, Mr. Fox!—we could love each other now but not, like, live together or anything—that people would know about . . . Until I'm older, graduated from high school . . ."

Snuggling close to him, peering up at him, pleading, desperate, inanely smiling, bloodshot eyes glittering with tears, swiping with her fingers at her runny nose.

"I just want to, like, *die* if you don't let me love you, Mr. Fox. I mean—I don't want to *live*."

"But you don't mean this, Mary Ann!—really. You're thirteen—I'm three times your age. You have no idea what an adult man is like. You're a smart girl!—you know better. You want to be a librarian—didn't you say? Tomorrow everything will be different . . ."

In a trance driving along the highway. Desolate countryside, out of which mailboxes emerge from time to time atilt in tall grasses, like totems of another era, passing too swiftly for Francis to register the numerals scrawled on them but he assumes—*he has to assume*—that the Healy farmhouse is somewhere ahead.

If he can just get her home. Let her out of his car in the driveway. Out of his life, his responsibility.

Obviously Mary Ann Healy is a deluded girl, a pathetic girl. Possibly, a sexually abused girl. But *not his responsibility.*

Recalling with a pang of loss the cozy perimeters of his bedroom from which he'd been rudely, abruptly torn by the forlorn cry in the night which he had not understood initially was a cry for help. In his memory warmly nostalgic as an illustration by Norman Rockwell: the laptop with its thrumming life, the unmade bed in which rumpled sheets which seem to show the contours of the user's body, the glass of tart red wine on the bedside table awaiting him if he can only get back to it safely . . .

"It's tomorrow now, Mr. Fox. It's that late. I *said*—I don't want to live if you won't let me love you."

Now Mary Ann is speaking sharply, with an air of reproach. In an instant, the blame is on Francis Fox.

Mary Ann makes a gesture as if to seize the steering wheel, Francis blocks her with his elbow. He's taken by surprise, confused—have they arrived at her house? Does she want him to turn in to a driveway? Mary Ann is flailing at Francis, slapping him. She is sobbing angrily. Her hot little hand drops to his thighs, his crotch in the khaki trousers, dear God what is she doing?—Francis shoves her away astonished.

"Stop that! You're drunk."

"*You're drunk.* I hate you."

In sudden fury Mary Ann fumbles for the handle of the passenger door. Manages to open the door even as Francis frantically brakes the car, grabs at her arm but can't prevent her from throwing herself out of the moving vehicle—"Jesus! Again! Are you trying to drive me crazy!"—as in hellish mimicry of the scene in the faculty parking lot Mary Ann Healy has again fallen beside Francis Fox's car, rolling along the ground with the momentum of the fall.

Francis brakes the car to a halt on the shoulder of the highway. His heart has almost stopped, he is terrified that he has killed the girl this time, what will he do with her broken little body? He can't report this, he can't acknowledge any of this. Though he is blameless he knows *he will be blamed.*

(No shovel in the trunk of the Acura! And even if there were a shovel in his distraught state Francis hasn't the stamina to dig a grave, his nerves are shot, he would have to drag the girl's body by the ankles deep into the marshy field beside the highway and hope that the body might sink out of sight in the brackish black water . . .)

To his infinite relief seeing that Mary Ann has scrambled to her feet, limping like a wounded animal away from the car and into the marshy field where he sees, or thinks he sees, a faint path through underbrush.

Is this a shortcut? To the Healy house? Lights are glimmering in the near distance, on the farther side of the field.

His face is covered in sweat, in rivulets sweat runs down his body thrumming with adrenaline, his heart is hard-thudding. He waits, he knows better than to try to drive too soon.

Then, executing a careful U-turn on the road to bring him back to Wieland.

Fortunately there are no other vehicles in sight, no one to observe. No one to note the license plate on the white Acura mysteriously parked on the shoulder of the road by a marshy field into which a young girl has fled limping and sobbing.

■

ANOTHER TIME, HE THINKS, he has escaped reckoning. Like Houdini!

ABSENCE

25 OCTOBER 2013

Inhaling shakily as he enters the classroom at 12:52 P.M.: only a few students have arrived, Mary Ann Healy is not among them.

Bell rings. One o'clock. The last of the students streams into the room, all but one seat is occupied.

Second row, third seat from the front. Empty.

Friday afternoon before fall break. Students chatter together excitedly, there is a current of restiveness, energy.

"Qui-et, please! It is not break *just yet.*"

Mr. Fox takes attendance. Mr. Fox is scrupulous about taking attendance.

Healy, Mary Ann. Absent Oct. 25.

Noting in his attendance book, this is Mary Ann Healy's first absence of the fall term; until today, Mary Ann has had perfect attendance.

Through the duration of the hour-long class, the empty seat in the second row, third seat from the front remains empty.

Possibly, Mary Ann Healy's seat will remain empty through the remainder of the term.

Possibly, Mary Ann Healy will never again return to the Langhorne Academy.

Late October, pellucid-blue sky through the leaded-glass windows, hurting his brain.

How is it his fault, it is not. Not his.

■

WADING IN NOT-DEEP BUOYANT water, still you can lose your footing, lose
your balance and fall and inhale water sputtering and choking but
that will never happen to Francis Fox who has boasted that he can
teach middle-school English in his sleep.

Do I sleep or wake?—whichever.

Glancing repeatedly at the empty seat amid the occupied seats as
if he half-expects to see someone there. Ugly emptiness like a socket
from which an (infected) tooth has been yanked.

Staring at a gaping hole, a socket in a gum, you could never imagine a *tooth.*

As (Francis is thinking) the other students scarcely notice that
Mary Ann Healy is absent.

For an absence is not equivalent to a presence, it is but an absence: a nullity.

Don't want to live if you won't let me love you.

It will be noted: Mr. Fox is in a somber mood today. Mr. Fox is not
in a joking mood today. Mr. Fox is easily distracted today. Shadows
like bruises beneath his eyes, faint creases in his forehead like strands
of cobweb.

Particularly, the girls in the class take note.

Something on his mind, you can tell. Mr. Fox is so sensitive!

Staring at the empty desk. Missing a beat. Are they waiting for
him to say—what? Trying to remember what the discussion has been
about. Passages of the long poem by Walt Whitman?—about which
these smart kids have much to say to which he should be listening
attentively as if he gives a God damn what they think, any of them,
but of course he does care, *Mr. Fox cares.*

Mr. Fox is the only one who cares, Mr. Fox cares like hell.

I love Mr. Fox he is the only adult in my life no bullshit.

He is somewhere far away, he is not here. Oxygen isn't reaching his brain. Fighting a yawn that feels like a sinewy snake twisting his lower face out of shape.

The empty seat in the second row. What's it got to do with him?

"O-kay"—(drawling out the word, making it loud, jovial-percussive)—"who's going to read from their journal for us today? Volunteers?"

Mr. Fox's first smile of the class period and it's a dazzling smile tossed out into the classroom like a net.

DESTINY: A KNOCK ON A DOOR

25 OCTOBER 2013

What was your dream last night, dear? Did someone come to you?

Don't be embarrassed, dear. Look at me!

Mr. Tongue came to visit you last night, didn't he? Because you were a very naughty Little Kitten and disappointed him not once but twice?

Where did Mr. Tongue visit you, dear?

In your bed? In the night? Beneath the covers cuddling with you? Inside your nightie?

■

FEEDS HER WITH HIS fingers, lemon tart dusted with powdered sugar.

Delicious lemon tart, and delicious kisses. Sticky fingers and sticky tongue!

In the seashell-ear promising never a time when he will not love her.

Never a time when they will not be together.

For in the time before she was born, already Mr. Fox knew her: had dreamt of her.

For the poets tell us it is an illusion—time, years, "age." When you are in love you are the same "age"—it is your souls that love, that never age.

So he knew, as soon as she walked into the classroom on the first day of class. Saw her face, and she saw his.

In that instant, like a struck match.

■

IF YOU WANT TO *make Mr. Teddy Bear very very happy, know what he'd like for his birthday?—a selfie on your phone. Little Kitten in her nightie in her bed!*

On the stroke of midnight tonight. Six selfies is the request.

Send to Mr. Teddy Bear, then delete from your phone!

Very important, dear—send the pictures, then delete.

No evidence, ma chérie! Not a shred.

■

GENTLY KISSING THE WARM nape of the white neck, beneath the silky wheat-colored hair.

Gently kissing scars small as commas on the inside of her forearm where the (sad, naughty) girl cut herself when Daddy first went away before Mr. Fox came into her life to save her.

Gently lifting the pleated skirt, to kiss the warm inside of thighs lightly scarred too from slashes with a razor blade gripped in shaky fingers.

Kisses to heal, to make well. Sticky kisses, sticky-sweet tickly-tongue!

Little Kitten you must promise: you will never "cut" yourself again.

Never never never "cut" yourself again!

Mr. Teddy Bear will be upset if you do!

Mr. Teddy Bear will cry if you do!

But if you do, if the terrible urge comes over you as you have de-scribed so courageously in the journal, take pictures of the little wounds with your cell phone, and send to Mr. Teddy Bear immediately because Mr. Teddy Bear loves his Little Kitten so, he wants to know what hap-

pens to his Little Kitten at all times and he will want to kiss kiss kiss the little wounds and make them well when you are together again.

And always remember to delete these pictures from your phone.

No evidence. Not a trace, chérie!

Promise?

■

YES, IT IS VERY very sad, this Little Kitten's daddy has been *cruel.*

This Little Kitten's daddy is *away, gone* from his family.

In her journal this Little Kitten has poured out her heart as her teacher has encouraged her, swiftly writing late at night in her bed not pausing for punctuation, scarcely pausing to breathe in passages of startling frankness detailing secrets of her parents' *sad, sick* marriage and the divorce that followed in poems cascading down the page festooned with black butterflies and hearts describing how the cruel daddy first *abandoned* his family and then *remarried! Now has a new baby.*

But Mr. Fox has intervened. Mr. Tongue, and Mr. Teddy Bear. All devoted to *her.*

Such praise for her in Mr. Fox's English class, she has wept with happiness. Mr. Fox is so enthusiastic, he leads the applause and all the students join in. Genevieve is not the only student so favored but Genevieve has been given to know that *she is unique among middle-school poets* whom Mr. Fox has taught in his entire career.

It has been such fun, rehearsing with Mr. Fox the poems she will be reading, in fact reciting to the Looking-Glass Book Club.

These are love poems in iambic pentameter, with a rhyme scheme of A B B A that Mr. Fox has praised as *most ingenious.*

Mr. Fox has impressed upon the class the importance of rehearsing, revising. In the privacy of his office Mr. Fox tutors his "select" students.

Amid these "select" Little Kitten is *most select.*

As Edgar Allan Poe's hauntingly beautiful young cousin was to the poet, so Genevieve is to Mr. Fox the love of his life as she is also a *fatherless girl* whom it is his destiny to protect.

Hearing this, Little Kitten wipes at her eyes. Beautiful dark eyes filling with moisture.

Oh but Little Kitten is becoming *so sleepy.* A Little Kitten is most delectable when she can barely stay awake, her head on Mr. Fox's sturdy shoulder.

A special poem for Little Sleepy-Head Kitten whispered in her ear as she drifts into that warm-cozy state neither awake nor asleep.

> *Little Lamb*
> *Here I am,*
> *Come and lick*
> *My white neck.*
> *Let me pull*
> *Your soft Wool.*
> *Let me kiss*
> *Your soft face.*

■ ■ ■

HE LAUGHS ALOUD, HE is suffused with happiness.

"Thank God!"—he has avoided disaster (again).

For: the troublesome Healy girl seems to have disappeared from his life. At least for now.

Absent from school, not only Mr. Fox's English class but (he has learned) from all of her Langhorne classes that day.

He will not think of her. He has had enough of thinking of her. He will lose himself in thrall to Little Kitten who alone is worthy of Mr. Fox's adoration.

But not as in the days of hapless Frank Farrell. No more falling-in-love at risk to himself.

He is the hypnotist now, *he* is the puppet-master, never again will he relinquish control.

For in the quiet time after his final class Little Kitten has come to him in his office. Tremulous, breathless, meekly begging forgiveness.

She *has* been naughty but it was not her fault entirely. She *has* been frightened of him but that is silly, she knows.

Asking with her eyes *Do you still love me, Mr. Fox?*

Yes yes yes Mr. Fox still loves his Little Kitten. Come here!

A final meeting of the Looking-Glass Book Club before the break: that is the excuse.

Genevieve has explained to her mother, this meeting is expected to last longer than usual, possibly as late as six P.M. Genevieve will text her mother, to pick her up at the front of Haven Hall when the book club is over.

It is the Friday before fall break. All day the campus has been emptying out. Boarding students are going to their homes for the nine-day break, parents have driven to campus to bring them home. There is an atmosphere of muted festivity, a kind of melancholy. Local students go nowhere except to their usual homes. Haven Hall has become near-deserted. The library has closed earlier than usual. Faculty offices in the basement are darkened—except for one.

Tap-tap-tap on Mr. Fox's door, a secret code known to just Little Kitten.

Opening the door to Little Kitten, pulling her inside. Mr. Tongue has been ravenous all day!

Little Kitten is skittish, excitable. It is always a surprise—a shock—that Little Kitten is *real.*

Feel her heart beat!—Mr. Fox presses the palm of his hand against her chest that is both soft (small breasts) and bony (ribs close beneath the skin).

Half-carrying her giggling to his swivel chair behind the desk. Snug in his arms.

It has been so, so long. He *is* ravenous.

Open your mouth, dear!—feeding Little Kitten pieces of lemon tart lightly dusted with powdered sugar.

Lemon tart, sweet kisses. Sweet kisses, lemon tart. Sticky! Giggly.

Kissing her drooping eyelids. Left, right.

Kissing the white neck, the soft skin at the nape of the neck. The silliest most skittish kittens are easily tamed if one knows how.

(Mr. Fox is recording on his cell phone, these precious minutes. This puppet-master is no fool.)

(To be enshrined forever in *Sleeping Beauties*.)

Kissing away tears. Tonguing the warm cheeks where tears have streaked in thin rivulets. A kitten is always on the verge of tears as a kitten is always on the verge of wild shrieking laughter.

What a sweet little mouth, dear! Mr. Tongue adores it.

Gently easing his hand beneath the pleated skirt, gently firmly at the soft fork of her thighs, sharply she draws in her breath, he pauses, waits until she relaxes drowsy and without volition then resumes the slow rhythmic caress even as Mr. Tongue gently pokes into the soft hot lemony little mouth just slightly resistant to him . . .

Just a few feet away: a knock at the door.

Rude, sudden, unwelcome: not a surreptitious *tap-tap-tap* but a solid knock, then a second knock, with a fist.

At once Genevieve's eyes fly open. In an instant the mood soft as a gossamer cobweb is destroyed.

Shhh!—Mr. Fox presses a forefinger against the girl's lips.

In his swivel chair frozen in place, not daring to move.

Whispering to assure her that the door is locked and that whoever is there will go away if no one answers.

But Genevieve scarcely hears, she has panicked.

In an instant no longer languid, loving. No longer sweetly-limp as a rag doll sprawled in Mr. Fox's arms. Not his delightful Little Kitten but a twelve-year-old graceless and strong as a young heifer detaching herself from him roughly.

On her feet, but dizzy. Swaying.

"I—I have to leave, Mr. Fox. I told my mother I would call her . . ."

"Call her—*when*? It's still early."

Reduced to begging! Jesus.

God damn he is disappointed in this Little Kitten!—so skittish, childish. In a similar situation at the Newell Johnson School (office, door shut, knocking, trapped! panic!) Miranda Myles was gaily reckless, tugging her shirt out of her school jumper, lifting it, shocking her teacher exposing bare girl-breasts scarcely the size of Seckel pears and whispering in his ear words truly shocking to him, an inexperienced middle-school teacher, words he had never imagined hearing from the lips of an innocent twelve-year-old girl . . .

"Mr. Fox, I—I really need to leave . . . Please."

Genevieve rests a shaky hand on the bronze head of Edgar Allan Poe to keep her balance, almost causes the bust to topple off the desk but Francis quickly intervenes holding her upright, and repositioning the bust.

Jesus!—if the girl faints in his office, and he can't revive her . . .

Little Kitten has ingested no more than a milligram of Ambien, he is sure. Harmless. But he was planning for her to remain with him until six P.M., more than an hour from now when the effect of the sedative would have begun to wear off.

This is serious: if she is going to walk out that door, she'd better be *awake.*

Gripping her shoulders, giving her a little shake. Head rattles like a doll.

Francis loves to touch the girl, shake her around a little. Nothing like taking hold of a full-grown woman—*that* is gross. Genevieve is a sweet-rag-doll kind of puppet, soft-bodied, unresisting, there's a stark-sexual excitement in measuring his strength and size against her strength and size for when upright seated together they seem (almost) equals but that is very deceiving.

(Jesus: Are her eyes dilated? Will the mother notice?)

(Trust a prepubescent girl to deceive her mother!)

Assuring the wary girl in a calm-adult voice that whoever is outside the door will go away if no one answers the knock. (Maybe whoever it is has already gone away since there has been no further knocking.)

Francis is more indignant than alarmed at this intrusion. Francis is sure that no student of his would dare to knock on his office door without an appointment.

Nor is it likely to be a custodian: since he discovered the young man snooping through his desk a few weeks ago Francis has insisted that his office be cleaned only once a week at a time when he isn't likely to be using it, late Monday afternoon. *And today is not Monday.*

Still Genevieve is desperate to leave. All but struggling to get free of him as if Mr. Fox has become one of those embarrassing old-guy relatives, uncle, grandpa, hugging too long and not letting go.

Hard fact is: Once they are out of your arms they are *out of your arms*. Once the spell is broken.

No choice but to sigh heavily, acquiesce with a smile as one does humoring a willful child.

"Of course you can leave, dear. But let me look out first . . ."

Francis is trembling, himself. Hoping to hell that the girl doesn't see the tremor in his hand.

Steels himself, opens the door: not guiltily but matter-of-factly, peers out into the corridor. No one?

No one in sight. Along the corridor office doors are primly darkened.

Unless—at the end of the hall? A shadowy figure in the stairwell, easing out of sight?

Francis tries to think who this might be: not a custodian, whose cleaning cart would be in sight; not another teacher, they've all gone home; possibly a student but not one of Mr. Fox's students.

Not annoying ferret-faced Eunice—wouldn't dare knock at Francis's door. Not after he chided her. And not Mary Ann Healy, he is certain that Mary Ann Healy will never dare approach him again.

Tempted to try to cajole Little Kitten into staying for just a little longer since there is (evidently) no one outside in the corridor and Mr. Fox is very, very hungry for more loving but he sees that the white-faced girl is desperate to escape, the mood of Eros so carefully orchestrated by Mr. Fox with assistance from Ambien and sugary-crumbly baked goods has been shattered entirely.

Of all moods the *erotic* is most fragile. The most *fickle*.

"Mr. Fox? I—I'm going now . . ."

Unsteady on her feet Genevieve shoves her arms into the sleeves of her jacket, pulls up the hood to hide her flushed face. Her eyes are blinking rapidly as if she is trying to bring them into focus. So nerved-up, she seems to be *panting*.

"All right, then. *Go*."

Deeply wounded and deeply resentful for in her haste to escape Genevieve is scarcely aware of him.

Not even a kiss on the cheek let alone a deep tongue-probing kiss with Little Kitten's arms tight around his neck as he has trained her to do.

Abashed Mr. Teddy Bear, rudely dismissed. Tender Mr. Tongue, dismissed.

Not even a final whisper in his ear—*Mr. Fox, I love love love you!*

Not even a final fluttery kiss in the air between them—*Mr. Fox, goodbye!*

VIII

THE INVESTIGATION

HUMAN REMAINS FOUND AT WIELAND POND
IN OCTOBER IDENTIFIED
Francis Fox, 41, Langhorne Faculty Member
Missing Since Late October

A body discovered near a capsized vehicle in a ravine near Wieland Pond on October 31 has been positively identified by Atlantic County medical examiner Orin Matthews as that of a recently hired Langhorne Academy faculty member, Francis Harlan Fox, 41.

Police had initially ascertained that the wrecked car in the ravine, a 2011 Acura, belonged to Mr. Fox. However, due to "significant animal activity" it was not possible to identify human remains at the scene with "one hundred percent certainty" except through dental records which were not immediately available for New Jersey State forensic odontologists to examine.

Mr. Fox, formerly of the Newell Johnson School (Pennsylvania), joined the faculty at the Langhorne Academy in the fall of 2013 as an instructor in English. According to Headmistress Paige Cady, Mr. Fox was a "very popular" teacher and "much-loved" colleague who had taken a "strong personal interest" in the Langhorne Academy, acting as a faculty advisor for the *Langhorne Literary Magazine* and establishing after-school activities for middle-school pupils including the Looking-Glass Book Club. Mr. Fox was also a prizewinning poet with a national reputation, according to Ms. Cady, and a "generous donor" to wildlife preservation.

Police Chief Leo Paradino told the *Wieland Gazette* that the investigation into the cause of Mr. Fox's death is "ongoing." Chief Paradino declined to say whether authorities are leaning toward accident, suicide, or homicide.

Detective Horace Zwender of the Wieland Police Department confirmed to the *Gazette* that the investigation is "ongoing" and that a number of "persons of interest" in Atlantic County are being interviewed. "If anyone has information that they believe might help our investigation, please do not hesitate to call the Wieland Police Department at 856-020-0147."

WIELAND GAZETTE
NOVEMBER 27, 2013

WET-WHISKERED KISS

NOVEMBER 2013

How many autumn nights since *it* happened, long arcs of night like wheels straining to carry a vehicle steeply uphill with enormous effort even as the ground beneath is soft black muck in which wheels spin and she is trapped within the effort of the straining wheels, eyes struggling to focus through pupils the size of caraway seeds, mouth an anguished O struggling to breathe as her limbs weakly flail and flounder and her brain is fainting for lack of oxygen even as another mouth boldly seeks hers—to force breath into her lungs to revive her, or to suck what breath remains from her lungs to extinguish her?—wakened with a jolt for something wet and cold has kissed her in her sleep, in the anguish of sleep a mouth daring to brush against her mouth, in terror that *he* has kissed her, as she wanted so badly for him to kiss her in life, as in confused dream logic recalling that the beards of the dead continue to grow, hairs sprout from their heads and stubble from their jaws and so (she reasons) the kiss is *his kiss,* his the wet-whiskered muzzle-mouthed kiss against her mouth, wet slap of tongue, with a sharp cry of surprise and revulsion she is fully awake sitting up, heart pounding waking from sleep as in an astonishing defiance of bedroom protocol the panting little terrier-hound has clambered up onto her bed sniffing, licking, wetly nuzzling her mouth as she sleeps.

"Princess Di! Bad dog! What are you doing!—get *away*."

Trying not to panic but desperate to slap, shove the hot little body away from her, seeing something in the glassy-brown eyes she has not seen before; and when Princess Di falls to the floor with a graceless thud, yellowish teeth bared and wet tongue lolling, a near-inaudible growling deep in the throat, which she has not heard before.

SLEEPING BEAUTIES 2013

27 NOVEMBER 2013

"Jesus!"—staring at the screen in disgust.

What his eyes are seeing, which his brain refutes.

He, who has gazed upon glistening brains oozing from the crushed skull of a bludgeoned victim, and glistening intestines spilling from an eviscerated rape victim hauled out of a marsh in the Pine Barrens, as well as numerous battered, beaten, bloodied bodies during the course of a thirty-year career as a police officer in Atlantic County, New Jersey, finds himself struck dumb by the lurid images in Francis Fox's MacBook Air, inside the innocuous-sounding *K-Files*. It seems that Fox has created a website called *Sleeping Beauties 2013*.

Hairs stir at the nape of Zwender's neck. Feels like he's about to stumble into one of those sinkholes at the Wieland landfill, reeking with rotting garbage and chemicals.

■

THIS IS UNEXPECTED, ZWENDER has gained access to Francis Fox's computer so easily. No password needed, just strike a key.

Obviously, the pedophile Fox hadn't expected to die when he did.

Or how he did. Assumed he'd be back within a few hours, didn't trouble to shut down his computer radioactive with felonious filth.

Never anticipating any need to protect *K-Files, Sleeping Beauties* from the eyes of a stranger.

In the eight-man Wieland PD Zwender is the senior officer, most experienced in investigative law enforcement even as he is the least skilled in computers. When computers are seized as evidence in purported crimes it's forensic computer experts at the New Jersey Crime Investigation Bureau in Newark who deal with them, crack passwords and encryptions, retrieve deleted material from the bowels of a computer in procedures as arcane to an officer of Zwender's generation as advanced calculus or astrophysics.

A weird world now, Zwender thinks. So much criminal activity has become online. Vast empires of crime invisible to the eye but readily accessible to those who can navigate the "Dark Web."

Though people still die in actual life. What begins online can shift to actual life.

Zwender has no doubt that Francis Fox's child-porn website precipitated his death. Possibly even the curious circumstances of his death.

The incriminating MacBook computer is innocuous-looking, child-sized. Discovered in Fox's airless bedroom in the first-floor bachelor-apartment on Consent Street, on a small bedside table beside a bed hastily made-up, comforter and pillows askew. In the bedroom, a melancholy odor as of spilled, stale liquids—wine, semen; through a part-opened closet door, a glimpse of shoes on the floor, and stylish-looking clothing crammed together on cheap wire hangers. The plank floor is uncarpeted, there's a single window obscured by a grime-encrusted venetian blind.

He cut something of a glamorous-bachelor figure, in life: Francis Harlan Fox. Zwender has studied photos, and has interviewed witnesses to the life, or to that fraction of the life that Fox revealed to others. But in a man's private quarters it's the condition of a venetian blind, or the stale-sour smell of his bedding, or the contents of his personal computer that most reveal his soul.

On a wall facing the bed is a glossy reproduction of a painting, European-looking to Zwender's inexpert eye, subdued colors, nothing blatant or sensational, a slender girl of about thirteen reclining on a chaise longue, one leg bent at the knee and lifted provocatively as she gazes dreamily at her face in a hand mirror oblivious of the presence of another (a male figure hunched over at a fireplace) in the room.

The girl is fully clothed, no one is touching her, this is not pornography. Disturbing to some eyes, or arousing—but not obscene. Not the kind of underage pornography that would get a consumer or a purveyor like Fox arrested in New Jersey.

Sleeping Beauties 2013 qualifies as child pornography, however. Intimate pictures, videos of girls who appear to be as young as twelve in various states of undress, and undergoing some sort of (blurred) sexual fondling by an individual identified as male only by his hands.

(The hands, too, are purposefully blurred but Zwender can discern a ring on the third finger of the right hand. Small dark oblong blur, possibly a black onyx in a silver or platinum setting. Typically stupid amateur, neglecting to remove the ring even as he's committing a felony to post on a global site!)

Fox's little MacBook is a treasure trove of child pornography under other files as well. A pedophile will have downloaded a ton of pornography because never do you discover a modest cache of pornography in a computer like this. Child, adult, "soft," hard-core. Most disgusting sexual sadism including even videos of rapes, murders, necrophilia, there's always an abundance, a sinkhole of evil smut that can never be filled.

Zwender became a police officer in his mid-twenties, soon then acquired a wife, children, a normal-seeming life among civilians. He has long separated his private life, the normal-seeming civilian life, from his life as a police officer. Still, scrolling through *Sleeping Beauties 2013* he finds himself thinking of his own daughters, when they were the age of Fox's girl-victims.

Years ago, now. And fully grown into adults, in no need of their father's protection.

But still, Zwender can remember. His heart is beating hard, in rage.

Whoever killed Fox, this is why.

So far as the public has been given to know the Langhorne middle-school teacher died in some sort of car wreck attributable to his being relatively new to the Wieland area, and apparently lost on a wetlands service road. His car had veered off into a ravine filled with rain . . . The Atlantic County coroner has tentatively ruled *accidental death* subject to a police investigation. (Among the more sensation-minded, suicide has been rumored but is a distinctly minority notion.)

To Detective Zwender's seasoned/skeptical eye neither accident nor suicide but a clumsily executed *homicide*.

The degree of blunt-force trauma to the back of Fox's head—not merely a fractured but a *shattered* skull—isn't compatible with the circumstances of the wreck, in which the front of the head would have been injured by striking against the windshield of the car; but the condition of the head itself, its ravaged and battered state, has made precise determinations difficult for the medical examiner.

Other details, not released to the media, would seem to rule out both accident and suicide. It's clear to Zwender that Fox was killed elsewhere and his body transported to the ravine, in his own car.

So hateful an individual, having abused any number of girls in Wieland and elsewhere, it is quite natural that someone would hate him enough to murder him; unfortunately for law enforcement, those with motive are likely to be numerous, scattered, anonymous.

Except: Someone with a knowledge of service roads at Wieland Pond. Someone *local*.

"Jesus!"—now Zwender *is* disgusted.

Seven thousand three hundred and twenty-two persons have sub-scribed to *Sleeping Beauties 2013* as of this morning.

Zwender has discovered dozens of pictures and videos of a slight girl of about twelve with glossy wheat-colored hair, heart-shaped face, blurred/pixelated features. The girl is often seated on a man's lap, she is squirmy and giggly as a nervous child, frightened, yet flirta-tious; in some photos clearly drugged, hardly able to keep her eyes open. Her mouth droops, lips damp with saliva.

In all the photos Zwender has seen the girl is wearing what appears to be a dark maroon jumper over a white blouse: the Langhorne girls' uniform.

Is this girl Genevieve Chambers, the seventh grader who slashed her wrists soon after her teacher Francis Fox was found dead at Wieland Pond? Though Fox tried in an amateurish way to disguise her features Zwender is sure he can recognize her.

Zwender has spoken with Mrs. Chambers. He has not (yet) been able to speak with the hospitalized girl.

There are many other unsuspecting girl-students entrapped in Fox's website. Like beautiful iridescent-winged moths entrapped in a spider's web. Similarly unresisting, limp. In similar states of erotic dishevelment. And the same male hands fondling them, with sinister gentleness. The same dark-stoned ring. In the background a book-case that is just partially filled, paperbacks with titles on their spines that will be readily discernible when the image is magnified by a computer expert: another stupid-amateur mistake of Francis Fox's.

Occasionally there's a glimpse of a small window high on a wall, poster-sized reproductions of photographs, artwork, a picture of a startled-looking girl in a pinafore with crimped hair and an unnaturally long neck—is this Alice, of *Alice in Wonderland*?

A piss-poor job Fox did of it, disguising his tracks. A man who'd gotten away with doing whatever he'd wanted to do for most of his life, doing it sloppily, negligently, not giving a fuck what harm he brought to others but brazening his way with what's called *charisma*.

Zwender thinks: *charisma* is just another word for *bullshit*.

Fortunately no one in Wieland seems to know about the website maintained by a Langhorne middle-school teacher. No one at the school. Such scandalous news would spread quickly. It will spread quickly if *Sleeping Beauties* is discovered by the media, linked to a pedophile teacher at the prestigious Langhorne Academy who has been found dead in mysterious circumstances.

Loathsome pictures of middle-school girls posted online, available to a global market of pornographic consumers yet locally unknown. So far as Zwender knows.

You would have to examine the blurred/pixelated faces closely to identify them. You would have to know precisely whom you were looking for, as Zwender does. You would have to have a sharp eye, a suspicious mind, a grim determination to seek out the predator and destroy him utterly.

You would have to deliberately seek out *Sleeping Beauties 2013* on what's called the "Dark Web." You would have to pay for a three-hundred-dollar annual subscription to be allowed to scroll through the website as Zwender is doing now, for free.

■

"ODOM? COME LOOK."

Casually Zwender calls to the junior officer elsewhere in the apartment.

Officer Odom, a heavyset young man in his late twenties with a soft sulky mouth, a habit of deep scowling silences. Latex gloves strain Odom's large fleshy hands cruelly, his forehead oozes sweat like the tears of a mollusk. Odom has been entrusted with, among other ignominious tasks, bagging the contents of trash containers in the Fox apartment.

Gratifying to Zwender, that Odom will see he's gotten into Fox's computer. That will impress Odom, who's taken a course or two in computer science at Cumberland County College and thinks he knows computers.

"Yah, what is it?"

Peering at the laptop screen over Zwender's shoulder. Zwender can register by Odom's sharp intake of breath when Odom realizes what it is he is seeing.

"Jesus *fuck*."

As Zwender scrolls down the screen, teasing titillating images of the (blurred/pixelated) young girl snuggling, squirmy and giggly, on the (faceless) man's lap move up jerkily.

"Is this—*his*? Fox?"

Zwender tells Odom yes.

"It's a—website? That perverts subscribe to? We need to take down this shit!"

"We can't take it down, Odom. It's evidence."

"'Evidence' for what? Fox is dead. Nobody knows about this but you."

"There's a division to deal with this—online kiddie porn. We aren't going to touch it."

"Are these girls in his classes? At the school? He's been taking pictures and posting them on a porn site?"

Odom is speaking excitedly, rare for Officer Odom. Zwender doesn't think that he has ever seen the heavyset young man's eyes entirely open as they are now.

Not generally known in the Wieland PD is the fact that Daryl Odom is obscurely related to his supervising officer Zwender— (Odom is Zwender's eldest cousin's eldest son's son)—but between the two there is no blood-bond, not a hint of favoritism on Zwender's part; Odom understands that Zwender is a coldhearted son of a bitch who could (probably) shoot you between the eyes without flinching if he had a good reason to do so though Odom grudgingly admires Zwender, and respects him; Zwender would not consider that Daryl Odom, not yet thirty, only a year or two on the job, merits any serious opinion at all.

Both Zwender and Odom are from South Jersey families in which police officers, prison guards, and individuals with criminal records are frequent but the families live in separate counties—Atlantic, Cumberland—and have little to do with one another.

Zwender moves to close the laptop and Odom dares to reach out, to stop his hand.

"This is fucked-up, Horace. Let me fix it."

"It will be shut down. But not by us."

"Just let me fix it, OK? Once this is entered into evidence it's out of our hands . . ."

"Absolutely not, Odom. Get the hell away."

"Who the fuck would know? It's just you, right? Who else knows?"

"I'm giving you an order, Odom. Stand back."

"These are girls in Fox's classes? Right here in Wieland? People could recognize? The motherfucker did a shitty job disguising them . . ."

Odom is incensed, he's from a Christian-family background. See-ing lewd pictures of girls so young, who look as if they're being abused, who *are* being abused, is shocking to him, even his breathing is af-fected, labored as if asthmatic. Zwender is impressed, Odom clearly *cares*.

But also, Zwender is annoyed, offended. His junior officer is try-ing to tell him, a senior officer, a detective of the highest rank, how to proceed, when Odom knows better. Any kind of tampering with evi-dence, let alone destroying evidence, could get them both fired.

Odom is arguing if no one knows about the website except Zwender and himself he could just delete it—all of it. In an instant, gone.

Zwender is arguing that they can't know who might know about the website and its link to Francis Fox, there could be a pedophile-watch team monitoring *Sleeping Beauties,* some state or even federal department the Wieland PD doesn't know about.

Odom insists, just let him take the laptop, no need for Zwender to observe what he does with it, and Zwender tells him to back off, that isn't going to happen; and Odom says in an aggrieved voice, "If it was your daughter? This girl here—'Little Kitten'—looks like she's high on something, that sick fuck must've been drugging them right in the school. Let me delete it, OK? Websites disappear all the time like into a black hole. Like flushing a toilet."

"How can you be so sure that no one has linked the website to Fox? We'd be destroying evidence."

"Look, the motherfucker is *dead.* There's no case to build against him. *Dead* means you can't be made *deader.*"

"We take down the website, we don't delete it. It's evidence."

Zwender checks again: now there are seven thousand three hun-dred and twenty-seven subscribers to *Sleeping Beauties 2013.*

Enough of Odom panting like a sheepdog against the nape of Zwender's neck. He isn't about to abrogate his authority to a junior officer.

"Just back off, Odom. Drop it. *No más.*"

Odom steps away. The pallor of his face gives to his skin a translucent quality. He is quivering with indignation, he is *fierce* in the defense of girls unknown to him, other men's daughters.

Yes, impressive. But not professional.

Odom exits the room, walking heavily. Cursing under his breath which Zwender can't quite hear.

Zwender pulls the power cord from the wall, carefully shuts up the laptop, and secures it in a plastic bag. He too is wearing latex gloves, encasing his fingers tight as sausages.

Forensic specialists will peruse the site, Zwender is taking the crucial evidence with him back to Wieland police headquarters. Marveling at how easily he opened the laptop, located Francis Fox's (secret) (perverted) (damned) soul. Even if he doesn't get credit for it, *he* knows, and so does Odom.

But too damned bad: Francis Fox is dead. Zwender won't have the pleasure of arresting the pedophile. At the fancy private school, everyone staring. What's her name—P. Cady, Headmistress—staring in astonishment.

Yanking Fox's hands behind his back, handcuffing the pervert in a way to make him cry out in pain like a pig at the slaughter.

■

ON THEIR WAY OUT of the Fox residence (sealed off with yellow crime scene tape by order of the Wieland PD) the men are silent and avoid looking at each other. Zwender is furious with Odom for disrespecting him, Odom is sullen with dislike of the elder police officer.

The elder Zwender charges ahead while the younger, heavyset Odom lags behind though it is Odom who will drive the Wieland PD cruiser.

Each man is thinking that he has had enough of the other. (Though junior-officer Odom has no way of avoiding senior-officer Zwender, who is his supervisory partner; and Zwender has to acknowledge, there's no one else in the eight-man department with whom he could bear to work in such close quarters.)

Daryl Odom is a smart-ass but he *is* smart. For all his faults.

Murmuring now, as he shoves the key into the ignition of the cruiser: "See, my girl is just nine. Junie. If anybody like Fox touched her I'd blow his fucking head off."

Not an apology exactly but Zwender interprets it that way and by his silence tacitly acknowledges that he doesn't object to Odom blowing off the head of a pervert-pedophile in such circumstances.

THE DETECTIVE. THE GUILTY PARTY.

29 NOVEMBER 2013

She has been waiting for him. Like a creature with its leg caught in a trap, awaiting the trapper to return to deliver the coup de grâce.

Still, when Headmistress Cady's assistant March informs her that the Wieland police officer Zwender has come to speak with her, and is waiting in her outer office, P. Cady feels a thrill of something like terror.

"Tell him—I can't see him now. Not this morning."

March goes away, is gone very briefly before returning to inform P. Cady in a grave voice that Detective Zwender insists upon seeing her immediately.

"Tell this person that 'immediately' is not possible. My morning is fully scheduled."

March goes away, is gone very briefly before returning to inform P. Cady in a grave-quivering voice that Detective Zwender insists upon seeing her. *Now.*

"Tell him—well, yes. All right."

Haughtily P. Cady begins, then her voice falters, seems to break. *Yes. All right.*

But for a long minute she remains seated at her desk as within a fortress that will protect her. Inertia weighing upon her like a leaden vest. She has not slept fully through any night in weeks. She has not slept fully, fearing dreams of *remains*.

"Ms. Cady?"—March's voice has never sounded so thin, hesitant.

A roaring in P. Cady's ears as of a distant cataract. Incapable of motion or even of drawing breath in a paralysis of being like a soul at the precipice of Hell lacking strength to move either forward or back.

"Ms. Cady?"—March stands uncertainly in the doorway.

Shakily rising to her feet. Must hide from her assistant the terror she feels.

The tight-fitting mask *Headmistress P. Cady* settles over her face.

■

POLITELY HE INFORMS HER, he would like to speak in private with her.

Politely P. Cady tells the police officer, her office *is* private.

"Ma'am, maybe just come with me. Outside."

Headmistress Cady hates being called *ma'am*. Reduced to a sort of uncooked dough, shapeless and boneless *female*.

"I would prefer that we talk in my—"

"Just, it would be more comfortable, for you. Ma'am."

P. Cady has the idea, the way Zwender is looking at her, that it is for her own good, to come with him. *More comfortable*: what can that mean?

Succession of sleepless nights. Since the remains in the ravine at Wieland Pond have been positively, irrefutably identified. Dental records, but under another name; a birth certificate, revealing that the deceased man had not only had another name but was older than he'd claimed to be. *Her* young friend, protégé. P. Cady's very equilibrium has become impaired, when she walks she has found herself needing to touch a wall or a chair to maintain her balance.

Remains. No more chilling word in the English language, in reference to what was once a living human being.

". . . sorry to further disturb you, Ms. Cady. I know that it has been a shock, and a personal loss . . ."

"Am I under arrest, Officer? Is that what this is?"—attempting an awkward sort of joke for which her lauded administrative skills have not prepared her even as Detective Zwender regards her with cold zinc-eyes, and does not smile at her joke.

"You'll see, ma'am, it's more of a private matter."

Feeling the teeth clamp more tightly about her leg, digging into the flesh, the trapper approaching to make his claim.

At least Zwender doesn't seem to be accompanied by his heavyset sulky-eyed junior officer this morning who'd fixed P. Cady (she recalls, with a shiver of dread) with a look of sheer misogynist contempt.

Outside, the November air is startlingly cold, wet. The opaque sky is eerily radiant.

Descending the stone steps of Langhorne Hall P. Cady nearly stumbles. Zwender at her elbow steadies her, to her chagrin.

She has always been a very fit person. She *is* a very fit person.

Crossing the green in front of Langhorne Hall. Walking beneath dripping trees in the direction of the playing fields determined to keep her balance, not to betray unsteadiness on her feet.

Passing the twelve-foot ebony obelisk but to P. Cady's disappointment the Wieland detective seems scarcely to notice.

How beautiful the sculpture seems to P. Cady, in this muted light. In commemoration of the founding of the school by Quaker abolitionists in 1811. Everyone who visits the Langhorne Academy admires the ebony obelisk and asks about it except Detective Zwender who is clearly not interested.

He is a barbarian, they all are. Hoping to bring you down as they brought Francis down so that they can gloat.

The sky *is* unnaturally bright though occluded with clouds. P. Cady's eyes narrow reflexively as if in anticipation of pain.

"Is this more disturbing news, Officer? Is it about—*him*?"

Hard for P. Cady to utter the name *Francis Fox* in any way associated with past tense.

Hard for P. Cady to recall the circumstances of her first encounter with Detective Zwender which did not end well.

Impossible to believe that Francis has died. Is dead. Bodily remains in the ravine subjected to "significant animal activity."

Did she faint?—such weakness, such deep unmitigated shame.

Did she faint, fall?—in this man's presence?

Vague memory that Zwender actually caught her, to prevent her falling. They brought a chair for her—the sulky-faced younger police officer dragged it over.

Or did P. Cady fall to the carpeted floor of her office, the chair brought to her too late.

At that time Zwender requested permission to search Francis Fox's office and P. Cady refused. Zwender had wanted P. Cady to acknowledge that *of course Francis Fox was dead* but she refused.

Out of loyalty to her friend, refused.

Out of sheer patrician stubbornness, refused.

Has the head of the Langhorne Academy deliberately impeded the Wieland police investigation into the death of Francis Fox, has she behaved less than admirably as well as less than reasonably, P. Cady does not want to consider.

Like all persons of authority P. Cady fears those whose authority is greater than hers.

If he wished Zwender could gloat now. For Fox *is* dead, and *was* dead.

If he wished Zwender could gloat, the attention focused lately upon the prestigious Langhorne Academy has not been flattering.

But in fact (P. Cady has to concede) Zwender seems concerned for her. He has been walking at a pace matched to hers. Solemnly he suggests that she sit on a nearby bench, he has something to tell her that might be upsetting to her.

Ridiculous! P. Cady is not an infirm/elderly person needing to *sit*.

Nonetheless weak-kneed suddenly, agreeing to *sit*.

Anticipating an unpleasant surprise but in no way prepared for what follows.

■

BENEATH THE WHITE-GLARING NOVEMBER sky at an hour of the morning when (certainly!) P. Cady would be normally at work in her office in Langhorne Hall she finds herself seated shivering on a bench at the edge of a playing field where adolescents in bulky clothing run with hockey sticks shouting at one another like gleeful young beasts intoxicated by the cold air, smell of wet leaves, the thrill of playful combat even as in a low-baritone male voice as matter-of-fact as if he were reading a weather forecast Zwender is telling her that a "considerable quantity" of pornographic photographs and videos has been discovered on Francis Fox's personal computer in his apartment on Consent Street and these include not only links to websites containing child pornography but a website recently established by Fox himself called *Sleeping Beauties 2013,* a mixture of new and older photographs and videos he evidently took of middle-school-aged girls over a period of years at the Langhorne Academy and other schools.

Worse, the photographs and videos record sexual abuse of these girls, clearly by Fox himself.

And though Fox tried to disguise the girls' features it wasn't difficult for Zwender to recognize at least one of them, a seventh-grade student at the Langhorne Academy currently hospitalized in Bridgeton after an apparent suicide attempt; nor was it difficult to recognize the setting for the most recent postings, Fox's office at the Langhorne school.

"The girl is Genevieve Chambers. You know about her, Ms. Cady, right? The girl who tried to kill herself a few weeks ago."

"Genevieve Chambers! Y-yes, I know about Genevieve, but I—I—didn't know why she—tried to hurt herself . . ."

P. Cady's voice trails off, she is stunned, bewildered. The astonishing revelations Zwender has made have left her speechless.

"You didn't know about any of this, Ms. Cady? Right? The person you knew as 'Francis Fox' was a serial predator, a pedophile, he's been posting pictures and videos of some of his Langhorne students on a website? This is all a surprise to you?"

"I—I can't believe . . ."

"Ma'am," Zwender says coldly, and now indeed he seems to be

gloating "—it's of no significance whether you 'believe' or not. These are facts, we have evidence. And Genevieve Chambers didn't 'try to hurt herself'—she did hurt herself, she almost died."

"I—I see. I'm so sorry . . ."

P. Cady stammers, stunned. Her head feels as if it might explode, she is overwhelmed by what Zwender has told her.

"But it's all news to you? That 'Francis Fox' was a pedophile, abusing twelve-year-olds? In your school? *In* the school literally, in his office?"

"If—if what you say is true . . ."

" 'If'? You really think this is 'if'—like, something I am making up, out of thin air?"

"I—don't know what to say, Officer. This is—such a shock. I thought that you were going to tell me details about Francis's death but this—is so much worse . . ."

Zwender allows P. Cady to speak, in her stunned faltering voice. No idea what she is saying. Like the survivor of a wreck, crawling out of the wreckage, managing to breathe, utter words that establish her survival but evaporate like vapor.

No idea what she is saying except *Sorry.* Repeats *Sorry.* Dares not say *I can't believe this, this cannot be true, not Francis Fox who was my friend.*

"Yes, you should be 'sorry,' Ms. Cady. Of all people, *you* should be sorry."

P. Cady would protest but she is too bewildered, confused. No one ever speaks to P. Cady like this!

On the playing field an argument has erupted, there are shouts and laughter.

Braying of raw adolescent voices. P. Cady would like to clamp her hands over her ears.

But here is some small relief: No one has noticed her here at the edge of the playing field. No one has so much as glanced at her and Zwender—two adults, middle-aged, of a category in which adolescents take very little interest.

Even in this moment of catastrophe, her life fallen in rubble about her feet, and this terrible man gloating over it, P. Cady has enough presence of mind, or vanity, to register relief, she has not been identified; nor did anyone particularly note her walk across campus in the company of the plainclothes detective.

Zwender's hostility is another shock to P. Cady. In some naïvely wistful way P. Cady hoped to believe that the detective was her *friend, protector.*

Even as the trapped animal wishes to console itself that the trapper is coming to free it, not slaughter it.

"What I want to ask you, Ms. Cady, is why you hired this man, and brought him to Wieland? You weren't aware that Fox had been fired from every school he'd taught at? You didn't look into his record, you didn't find it suspicious?"

"We—we did look at his record. Of course. But . . ."

Trying to recall: the hiring committee wanted Fox, after his visit to the school; after his dazzling classroom performance; after he charmed everyone at lunch. While she, the ex officio member of the committee, had been dead set against another him. And yet—somehow—Fox had been hired.

How could she explain? Wanting to hide her face in her hands, and cry.

Cry and cry, for her heart is broken. Francis Fox deceived *her.*

If what Zwender says is true, if there is evidence. What did he say?—*child pornography, website, sexual abuse.*

In disgust Zwender is saying that Fox's website *Sleeping Beauties 2013* had more than seven thousand subscribers when it was taken down—"Sicko pedophile-perverts like Francis Fox himself."

P. Cady is stunned to hear such obscene words uttered aloud.

Stunned to find herself in (male) company in which such obscene words are uttered aloud with impunity.

Sicko pedophile-pervert. Is that what Francis was?

Her friend, Francis! Who seemed so sincerely to like, admire *her.*

With a part of her mind P. Cady will never believe this. Never accept.

At the same time wanting to protest to Zwender, to placate the detective's disgust (which is at least partly a disgust aimed at her) that—in fact—she was suspicious of Francis Fox herself, at first.

For this is true! This is true: She questioned Francis Fox closely in their private conversation in her office. She was determined not to hire the man, nothing about him appealed to her, not just that he was a *white man* but that even in his effort to be deferential to her he exuded an air of what was called white privilege, specifically *white male privilege*; he could not help himself. He was too dazzling with the students, too *charismatic*. It would be no surprise, some of these impressionable young adolescents might adore a man like this fatally.

No, she didn't trust the grandiloquent letters of recommendation. She didn't trust *him*.

An attractive man and he knew it, and knew that P. Cady knew it: a contest of wills in which, by seeming to concede to her, the man had in fact actually won, though P. Cady in her naïveté assumed that she had won.

True, she *had* won, by insisting that the board of trustees hire Francis Fox, the very candidate she'd vowed she would never hire.

How did that happen? How did he deceive her?

Like one who has narrowly survived a catastrophic accident that has left her traumatized P. Cady recalls only the outlines of the event—the interview in her office—but not the event itself.

The sleight of hand of the master magician. He distracts your attention away from the hand that plies the "magic"—the deception.

Francis lied about so much, it has been revealed since his (official) death. He even lied about his age: he wasn't thirty-seven but forty-one, born in 1972.

The forensic odontologist's ID was delayed because "Francis Harlan Fox" wasn't his original name, his dental records were for "Frank Harrison Farrell" whose most recent dental records were with a dentist in Quakerbridge, Pennsylvania.

All this has come to light in the past week, the result of the Wieland police investigation headed by Detective Zwender.

P. Cady tries to explain to Zwender: There *was* suspicion of Francis Fox, at first. But his letters of recommendation were uniformly excellent, no one so much as hinted that he'd been fired from his previous schools. The hiring committee voted unanimously to hire him, the board of trustees was easily convinced that he was the best candidate for the job, he'd even won a poetry contest! He'd been published in a national poetry magazine.

At this, Zwender laughs aloud. *Poetry!*

"All I can say, Officer," P. Cady tries to speak with care, not wanting to challenge Zwender, let alone seem to be defending Francis Fox, "—is that we had no idea. I had no idea. No one came to us complaining of him. No student, no parent. This poor girl Genevieve . . . Did she tell anyone?"

"It's common that abused children don't know they are abused. The girl thinks she loves him—loved him. She thinks he loved her."

"Is this—Genevieve? She has said this?"

"It's been reported to us. Her mother won't allow anyone to interview her."

"It's been reported to you—*what,* exactly? That the girl has said she loves Francis Fox, or that Francis Fox has abused her?"

Zwender concedes, the word *abuse* is his word, not Genevieve Chambers's. Nor has the girl's mother reported "abuse"—yet.

They have only the online evidence so far, Fox's photographs and videos. Which are incriminating, or would be incriminating, if Fox were alive.

"He'd posted selfies the girls took in their beds, and must have sent to him on their cell phones. Some of the photos are close-ups of 'cutting'—bleeding wounds in the girls' arms, thighs. It was discovered that Genevieve Chambers had older, healed cuts on parts of her body."

Zwender speaks with such disgust, P. Cady winces. It is difficult for her to fathom what the detective is saying.

Close-ups of "cutting"—"bleeding wounds"? Sent to Francis, who posted them on the Internet?

"You know, Ms. Cady—'Francis Fox' wasn't even his name. He'd changed his name. You didn't find that suspicious?"

"But we didn't know that at the time! How would we have known . . ."

This is unfair, how could P. Cady and her staff have known! Francis's former schools cooperated in using his new legal name in place of his former name for their recommendations; even P. Cady's niece Katy had never thought to mention that "Francis Fox" had been "Frank Farrell" when she'd known him at Columbia.

(Blithely Katy explained to P. Cady: "Oh yes—Francis used to be 'Frank Farrell.' He had a very good reason for changing his name! He explained it all to me. I don't remember the details but Francis was treated very badly, slanderously, at the school in Quakerbridge. The headmaster there took an irrational dislike to him and tried to fire him for no reason except that there was jealousy of his popularity with the students . . .")

Zwender tells P. Cady that in their investigation they've learned from several sources that young girls were often seen in Fox's office, or waiting outside his office, late in the afternoon or early evening. Two or three girls were often there. And sometimes a girl would be looking agitated, upset. Sitting on the floor outside his office, and his office door closed but Fox was inside apparently with another student. They'd reported these incidents to their department chair and also to the headmistress's office but never had any response.

"I never knew that! I didn't see any reports . . ."

Is this true? P. Cady tries to think. If there were vague accusations made against Francis Fox she possibly/probably dismissed them. Francis was *enthusiastic* about students, everyone knew. He seemed to thrive on teaching. He'd told P. Cady more than once that his Langhorne students were "the very best students" of his life. As he'd told P. Cady, in his interview with her, he had no children of his own, his students were all the children he wanted or needed, like P. Cady herself. And one of her confidantes, a supporter of Francis Fox, had mentioned to her that several of the older teachers were jealous of Francis because he was young, popular.

"You know how it is, Officer, there are always rumors . . . Teachers can become jealous of one another."

"Did you investigate these rumors?"

"Did I investigate? No. I did not. I didn't even know about them."

"Really? At such a small private school you never heard rumors—?"

"That—that is not the role of a headmistress, to poke into petty disputes among the faculty . . ."

"So, you didn't investigate. Just as you didn't investigate Fox's background."

You see, this is all your fault. The abused girls, the pornographic website. The dead man in the ravine.

P. Cady feels a sharp pain in her brain as if Zwender, her torturer, were driving a spike through her skull.

Never has P. Cady felt so defeated, so annihilated by anyone, even her father; but her father, even as he criticized her severely, had never ceased loving her, while Detective Zwender feels no love for P. Cady at all.

Has it caught up with her now, her life of privilege and piety, her rectitude, her very sense of *duty,* how like a sewer backing up, acid-bile in her mouth, all that through her life she denied knowing, refused to know, her blindness, stupidity.

Believing yourself so special, because you are "good."

Incapable of making a mistake. Incapable of acknowledging a mistake.

That has been the root of it, P. Cady thinks. Believing that she is special in some way. Because she has lived so fiercely for others, given so generously and aggressively of herself, having no inner being of her own.

Overhead the November sky is glaring with light. Banks of clouds, yet a diffused light, a kind of elliptical glare, hurtful to the eyes.

"I—I will resign. If this is my fault. If—what you say is true . . ."

Zwender laughs, even now P. Cady is pleading *if.*

■

"MA'AM, HERE."

Zwender gives P. Cady a fresh tissue from a little packet of Kleenex, to wipe her eyes.

Large widened eyes warmly brown, like those of a terrified cow. And her face no longer stony-composed but crumpled like wet tissue.

Takes pity on P. Cady knowing that the headmistress of the Langhorne Academy has been humbled, broken before his eyes. He has
kicked the arrogant female over into the mud, where she lies exhausted; she has aged a dozen years, as he has looked on impassively;
he has vanquished her utterly; he has despoiled her pride. Never will
the woman entirely recover from the pounding revelations of the last
half-hour because never will she entirely forget.

A pleasure that is almost sexual. Possibly it *is* sexual.

"No need for you to resign, ma'am. Not just yet. They will need
you especially now, they will be looking to you for guidance."

"But I—I've failed the school . . . The students . . ."

Even now, P. Cady is speaking hesitantly, peering up at Zwender
in appeal. So badly she wants him to comfort her, to tell her that none
of this is her fault.

Desperation of the trapped creature, peering up at the trapper.
Begging for life however reduced, humbled.

With a twinge of resentment Zwender recalls when he first met
P. Cady in her office in Langhorne Hall: how the headmistress of the
fancy school stared coldly at him, treated him like a tradesman or a
deliveryman, didn't seem to know who he was, or to care. She refused
to acknowledge that Francis Fox was likely to be dead and she refused to allow Zwender to search Fox's office, impeding the investigation into Fox's death at a crucial period in time.

As if she didn't want to know that he was dead. Or why.

Zwender has had access to the office in Haven Hall only recently,
after the positive ID of Fox's remains. Because of the headmistress
valuable time has been lost, crucial evidence has (probably) been
destroyed.

Furious with "P. Cady" but doesn't want to crush the woman utterly. "P. Cady" is an innocent fool, well-intentioned like so many
deluded females suckered into falling for a "charismatic" psychopath;
it would be a blunder to alienate her, frighten her, and send her to the
Langhorne attorney with whom Zwender would then have to deal.

Zwender loathes lawyers. Worse than their clients, because purely
mercenary.

No doubt, the Langhorne Academy retains fancy lawyers. Hopes to hell he doesn't have to tangle with them.

"Ms. Cady, I'm sorry to have distressed you further. I understand, this has been a terrible shock to you."

In a kindly voice now, no longer judgmental or jeering. As P. Cady gazes up fearfully at Zwender like a kicked dog steeling itself to be kicked again.

Zwender assures P. Cady that she is hardly alone in being victimized by Francis Fox. Pedophiles like Fox depend upon the naïveté of people around them. They are like parasites boring into living things, hiding in their guts while they devour them from the inside. By the time the victim realizes it's too late.

The serial pedophile is like a serial killer: hiding in plain sight.

He's usually a nice guy, everyone likes him. It's rare that a young girl isn't *in love with* her abuser, that's how the abuse is possible.

"You probably don't know, Ms. Cady, that one of Fox's seventh-grade students at the Newell Johnson School in Pennsylvania actually did kill herself by slashing her wrists. Fox—his name was 'Farrell' then—managed to escape being arrested because the girl never accused him or acknowledged that they were involved. He didn't post pictures of her online, and no witnesses could testify that they'd actually seen him abusing the girl. He hired a lawyer to defend him and wound up with a settlement from the school that included nondisclosure contracts and a guarantee of 'highly positive' recommendations. And so, you hired him and brought him here."

In a state of numbness P. Cady listens to this new revelation. A girl—twelve years old—has *died*? Because of—Francis Fox?

Not possible. Not Francis. There must be some mistake . . .

But no, there is no mistake. *She* has committed the mistake.

You hired him, and brought him here.

Never has P. Cady felt so vanquished, so forlorn. So beaten down, exposed. As if this terrible man, a stranger to her, has stripped her bare in a public place for all to stare at her in horror and repugnance.

Zwender tells P. Cady not to worry, the Wieland PD is not going to release most of this information to the public. There will be no mention of Fox's website, which has vanished from the Internet.

"We're keeping all information regarding the alleged sexual abuse at the school and the pornographic website confidential, Ms. Cady. You'll be relieved to know, yes? We're doing this not to protect the reputation of the Langhorne Academy, and not to protect your reputation as headmistress, but to protect the girls whose pictures were on the website, and their families, whose lives would be destroyed if news got out."

Zwender is speaking in a voice heavy with irony. Still, P. Cady is so relieved by these words she could faint.

Could murmur *Thank you!*—but the words stick in her throat.

Could seize Zwender's hand and kiss it kneeling before the man groveling in abject gratitude murmuring *Thank you!*—except that Zwender would fling her away from him in disgust.

Zwender tells P. Cady that they will be continuing with the investigation into Francis Fox's death—of course.

He and Officer Odom will be interviewing people on the Langhorne staff and they will be expecting cooperation.

Yes, P. Cady concedes weakly. She will cooperate. Her staff will cooperate.

They will want to talk to the custodial staff as well. They will begin by talking to the school officer in charge of the custodial staff.

Custodial staff? P. Cady has no objection, she thinks.

"When we were finally able to look into Fox's office, we discovered that it had been thoroughly cleaned with disinfectant and bleach. Floor spotless, walls wiped down. Did you give instructions to someone on the custodial staff, to clean the office like that?"

"I—I did not 'give instructions' . . . No, Officer, I did not."

"You didn't? Then who did?"

P. Cady shakes her head helplessly.

So very tired. She has never been interrogated like this: the terrible man has been abusing her for what seems like hours. Her head feels as if he has been beating it with a bat. When will it end!

She *will* resign as headmistress, she cannot bear such scrutiny. A police investigation focused upon the Langhorne Academy will draw the worst sort of publicity, P. Cady will never outlive it.

She will retire from the Langhorne Academy entirely. No more teaching, though her happiest moments have been in the classroom. No more public life, no more well-intentioned educator interfering in the lives of others. P. Cady's pretensions have been stripped from her, indeed she has been kicked into muck akin to the dense black muck of the marshes at Wieland Pond, that sucks alarmingly at your feet if you step into it by mistake.

"Are you all right, Ms. Cady?"

"Y-yes. I am all right."

But how eerily bright, the opaque sky! Glowering, opalescent. Near-blinding.

The interview is over, it seems. The playing field is empty. Without her noticing the contentious athletes have vanished.

P. Cady finds herself on her feet, she will shrug off the detective's arm if he makes a gesture to steady her.

She would walk alone back to her office but Zwender insists upon accompanying her.

Strange, she is out of breath almost at once. She is light-headed, the white sky makes her eyes hurt.

Envisioning with an almost sensual yearning the familiar screen of the console computer on her desk. The solidity of her straight-backed chair, as she faces the screen like one facing an unsparing mirror.

As soon as she is back in the headmistress's office safe and alone she will begin to compose her resignation letter to the Langhorne board of trustees.

Except: Much of what Zwender has been telling her is confidential. It may never be released to the public . . . How should she proceed?

Again passing by the twelve-foot ebony obelisk, so striking to P. Cady's eye but of so little interest to Zwender. P. Cady feels a twinge of loss, sorrow.

"Officer? How—how do you think Francis Fox died?"

P. Cady's question is naïve, wistful. She steels herself to hear something very ugly but Zwender says only that that is the purpose of the investigation, to look into the death; his reply is stiff, formal.

"Do you think it could have been an accident?"—this query too is naïve, childlike.

Zwender frowns, as if determined not to smile. But his manner seems bemused.

"Ms. Cady, we don't know. The investigation is ongoing."

"Some people are thinking . . . Francis may have taken his own life."

"Well. That's another possibility, isn't it."

"Do you think so?"

"That it's a 'possibility'?—maybe."

"But—is it a probability?"

"A 'probability'?—impossible to say."

Zwender is guarded, wary. P. Cady hesitates to ask the detective anything further, he has retreated into his authority; he is the one to ask questions, not answer them.

P. Cady has avoided discussing the grim facts of the death of Francis Fox; P. Cady has avoided thinking about the death of Francis Fox. When the local news station reports on the Wieland police investigation P. Cady often switches channels, in an effort to forestall panic.

She does know, she has not been able to avoid knowing, that speculation into the cause of the middle-school teacher's death at Wieland Pond flourishes unchecked, in Wieland as in Atlantic County generally. If it becomes known that Francis was a *serial pedophile* as Zwender has called him, speculation will flourish like wildfire, there will be even more focus upon the Langhorne Academy, the most ignominious and damaging sort of publicity.

In the hesitant voice of one who does not wish to seem to be intruding in another's profession P. Cady says, "In the newspaper it was stated that Francis hadn't been wearing a seat belt at the time of the accident. I mean—at the time the car fell into the ravine . . ."

But is it an *accident*? Is the more accurate word *wreck*?

Pointedly, Zwender says nothing. As if allowing P. Cady to continue, to make an utter fool of herself.

"And also, I—I think I'd read—no one could find Francis's wallet in the car or in the ravine, or a wristwatch, or—personal items that were missing, he must have removed. If it was deliberate—I mean, driving his car up the hill and into the ravine . . ."

If it was deliberate. What is P. Cady saying?

"Is that what you're thinking, ma'am, that your 'Francis Fox' drove his car up the hill and into the ravine, all deliberately, and this was for what reason?"

"I—I would think that, if it was deliberate, it was because Francis had become depressed, suicidal . . ."

"Because of his behavior, as a pedophile? Abusing his students? That's the motive for 'suicide'?"

"Well, what do you think, Officer? It may have been all too much for him, he decided to end his life . . ."

"Did 'Francis Fox' impress you as the kind of person to kill himself out of conscience? Remorse?"

"Well—I don't know, Officer. I think—I didn't know Francis at all. I don't know what he might have been capable of."

"That I can believe, ma'am. That's why there are investigations into suspicious deaths."

"In the newspaper it was stated—the medical examiner said—'inconclusive' . . ."

"It *is* 'inconclusive.'"

"So, Francis might have taken his own life. Out of disgust with himself, or despair. It might be one of those 'deliberate accidents'—like a depressed person taking an overdose of drugs. Do you think that's a possibility, Officer?"

P. Cady hears the desperation in her voice. She sees a flicker of irritation, exasperation in the cool zinc-eyes.

"Why don't you assume that, Ms. Cady? If it makes sense to you and gives some sort of comfort. Suicides don't always have obvious reasons for killing themselves but in this case, Francis Fox certainly did."

Comfort! But this is kindly meant, P. Cady wants to think. Not mocking, jeering. Not pitying.

"Yes. Trying to make things right, in a desperate way. Remorseful. But not thinking clearly, depressed . . ."

"'Clearly depressed'!—right, ma'am."

They have been standing at the foot of the limestone steps of Langhorne Hall. Zwender gives P. Cady his card, tells her to call him or text him if she remembers something essential; turns then to walk away leaving her staring after him with smarting eyes.

Suddenly, he is gone! Her tormentor.

Though P. Cady has wanted to be gone from the man, though she has wanted to clamp her hands over her ears and scream at him to leave her alone, she hates and despises him, his smug self-righteousness, now the detective's departure seems abrupt to her, even rude.

Also, the opalescent glare of the sky has given her a mild headache of the kind that is called a "cluster headache"—if P. Cady doesn't take care, within an hour or two the headache will burst open inside her skull like an umbrella sharp with quills.

Yet: feeling a sick sort of relief, at least her father is no longer living and can know nothing of the guilt staining his daughter's soul like black muck.

■

IN THIS WAY THE *detective entered my life. Not a bearer of life but a bearer of death and the illumination of death which will be my redemption.*

WRECKAGE

29 NOVEMBER 2013

In the stillness of the headmistress's residence at 6:40 P.M. as P. Cady enters through a side door, in the scant seconds before Princess Di, hearing her human return, rushes panting and whimpering with joy to greet her, P. Cady is startled to hear a voice somewhere close by.

Her niece Katy? *Here?*

Her heart clutches. She loves her only niece but does not want Katy in Wieland.

Then, she realizes that Katy is not in the house but merely leaving a message on the answering machine. A most poignant message, which brings tears to P. Cady's eyes.

Hello? Aunt Paige? Are you there? [Pause]

If you are there please please can you pick up, Aunt Paige? [Pause]

I need to speak with you, Aunt Paige. I—I need . . . [Long pause]

When you get this message, Aunt Paige, PLEASE call me back tonight, it doesn't matter how late you call me, Aunt Paige, THANK YOU. [Pause]

Aunt Paige, I am so—I am so lonely without . . . [Pause]

The click of a receiver, Katy Cady has hung up.

P. Cady suspects she knows what Katy was saying before the message cut off—*I am so lonely without him.*

Or, as Katy has said so frequently on the phone to P. Cady—*I am so lonely without Francis.*

Since Francis Fox's disappearance from their lives Katy has been calling daily. Sometimes, twice daily. For Aunt Paige has always been closer to Katy than Katy's own mother from whom she is somewhat estranged.

Should P. Cady call Katy back at once, since clearly Katy is upset; call Katy later in the evening, when Katy may be less upset; wait for Katy to call her again.

Delete the message. Don't call.

Standing irresolute in the hallway by the phone stand even as the small wiry brindle-coated terrier-hound mix comes bounding at her mistress in a paroxysm of excitement, panting, whimpering, small body wriggling with the deranged-pendulum wagging of the stubby tail, nudging her hard little head against P. Cady's shins, on oversized hound-feet teetering, pawing P. Cady's thighs, pleading to be lifted into P. Cady's arms, allowed to lick P. Cady's face, reassured that she is loved, she is adored, she will be taken for a walk immediately, it is past time for her evening walk, she is so excited! anxious! impatient!—not at all happy with having to wait for her human to return home, wait wait wait for her human to change from headmistress attire into worn corduroy trousers, shapeless pullover sweater, water-stained running shoes, wait with mounting frustration as her human procrastinates lingering in the kitchen for a moment to herself, for a moment in which to pour for herself no more than two inches of wine into a sparkling clean glass, to savor the aroma of the wine before swallowing, in the hope of steadying her nerves, restoring some of the strength sucked from her by the vampire-detective six hours before.

Laughing startled, scolding—"Oh, Princess Di! That hurts, your teeth are sharp and you are *nipping*! Will you please *get down*."

∎

THE WRECKAGE OF THIS DAY, P. Cady will not soon forget.

Will not soon forget the playing field, the harsh white sky, adolescent children whose shouts hurt her ears.

Thoughts in such a churn she cannot be said to be *thinking*. Chaos in her brain like a dam that has been breached.

And now, this strange behavior of Princess Di. Where usually returning to the headmistress's residence at the end of a long day is comforting to P. Cady, lately she has felt uneasy not knowing how Princess Di will greet her.

When she has to work late on campus, P. Cady instructs her housekeeper to leave dinner for her in a warm oven; if Princess Di is particularly restless and fretful, to walk the dog for at least twenty minutes.

Today, Princess Di hasn't been walked since early that morning. She is nerved-up, anxious. Her elation at being reunited with her human is tinged with something like resentment, covert-doggie-hostility.

P. Cady has to concede, Princess Di has been behaving strangely since that terrible morning at Wieland Pond: October 29.

When the little terrier-hound mix misbehaved shockingly, running off-leash disappearing into the woods, into underbrush, trotting through fetid marshland dirtying her paws and splattering her underside with black muck in search of carrion in reversion to *terrier-hound* behavior of the most bestial sort.

Disobeying her human. Refusing to listen to her human calling plaintively after her. Behaving as though her human had ceased to exist, of no more significance than squawking crows, grackles in the marshes.

Suddenly then reappearing, taunting her human with further disobeying in plain sight, cavorting, whimpering with sensual pleasure, defiantly displaying a *trophy*.

In a rapturous trance tossing the soft-rotted meat-thing into the air, catching it between sharp teeth, refusing to surrender it when her human commanded her to open her jaws . . .

What appeared to be the tongue of a large animal, presumably a deer, badly mangled, rotted.

"Oh God. Please *stop*."

It's to herself P. Cady speaks. She has *got to stop* thinking about it.

She has told no one of the horror for there is no one to tell. Her failure to recognize what *it* was, and to report *it* as a responsible citizen would do.

Zwender knows. Must know. Suspects. Does not trust me.

Too often in her wretched dreams P. Cady is back at Wieland Pond running panting after the headstrong little dog she cannot catch, always Princess Di is trotting before her with *the soft-rotted thing* in her jaws but there is no one to tell of her misery for she is certainly not going to confide in her excitable niece Katy, any more than she would confide in the Wieland detective who has treated her with such condescension and contempt.

You must stop thinking about it. You will make yourself ill.

And now in recent weeks P. Cady has been rudely awakened from sleep by the squirmy little dog clambering onto her bed, cold damp nose sniffing at her neck, licking her face with a damp sinewy tongue, shoving her muzzle at P. Cady's mouth in a clumsy semblance of a kiss propelling P. Cady into heart-pounding wakefulness.

At first, no idea what is happening. What has lunged wetly bristling against her mouth slack in sleep.

Then realizing: Princess Di.

"Bad dog! Stop! Get down! Get *away!*"

In a panic pushing the misbehaving little dog off her bed, hard onto the floor. Shocked to hear a deep, near-inaudible growling in the little dog's throat and to see in the glaring glassy-dilated eyes no glimmer of recognition.

"Princess Di! What is wrong with you!"—rush of adrenaline as if her life is threatened.

Never before has P. Cady slapped or struck at her beloved Princess Di. Never has she screamed, shouted at the dog in such panic.

"*Bad! Bad! Bad!* Don't you ever do that again!"

Shaken, trembling, shuts herself in the bathroom to escape the hot-panting little dog staring at her with glassy eyes from a distance of about six feet, belly close to the floor and hind legs curiously elevated as if she is about to spring.

P. Cady washes her feverish face in cold water, washes her mouth (her lips tingle as if tickled by something obscene, an unpleasant sensation slow to fade), rinses her mouth with Listerine, spits into the salmon-colored fluted-marble sink.

In the mirror above the sink, the face of a woman of youthful middle age looking strained, haunted.

Eyes in urgent appeal—*Oh God what is happening to me? My life has become wreckage.*

Against the bathroom door, a sound of claws. Panting.

Beneath the bathroom door, curved-spiky claws scrambling to gain entry.

"Bad dog! How dare you! I told you—*stop.*"

P. Cady pushes the door open, knocking the little dog away. Prepared to kick the little dog away.

Thinking—*Thank God, this animal weighs less than twelve pounds.*

Wanting to think—*This is a cartoon interlude. This is not real and will not last.*

Soon then, the fraught moment does pass. If it were a scene in a film, the musical score would have changed from screeching violins to calm raindrop notes, subdued.

Visibly, Princess Di comes to her senses. P. Cady's voice triggers something in the little dog-brain. Recognition floods back into the liquidy-brown eyes. The little dog is immediately repentant, remorseful. Wagging her stumpy tail in abject surrender, begging to be forgiven by her tall indignant human.

You see?—I am not bad. I am not a bad bad bad dog, it is all a misunderstanding.

Long ago, I was bred to hunt vermin. Burrow into their snug little tunnels, drag them out and break their necks between my jaws and shake shake shake them but you have taken that happiness from me, in exchange I promise to obey you, adore and worship you.

P. Cady strides out of the room ignoring Princess Di who trots behind her at a discreet distance in the very posture of abject canine remorse, tail between her haunches.

Downstairs P. Cady pours herself a glass of white wine to settle her nerves. It is anguish enough that Francis Fox is gone from her life, and what scandal threatens to rush over the Langhorne community like filthy water, now this worrisome behavior of Princess Di.

Tries to laugh, it *is* absurd.

It is well-known, seemingly well-adjusted rescue animals may suffer from anxiety recalling cruel treatment in the past. They may lash out in panic if mistreated, frightened. A rescue animal may growl deep in its throat. A rescue animal must not be unfairly blamed, in such circumstances.

It is well-known, there are no bad dogs, only dogs poorly trained by bad masters.

"Princess Di, you know better. You *do not* growl at me. Ever."

Princess Di peers up at her human squinting and blinking with hope. Her stubby little tail thumps once, twice.

"You do not climb onto my bed unless you are invited."

Admittedly, P. Cady does allow Princess Di to sleep on her bed sometimes, though never *in* the bed.

From the first night Princess Di spent in the house she'd slept in P. Cady's bedroom, at the foot of her bed, in a donut-shaped faux-fur doggie bed designed to assuage canine anxiety.

"Are you calmed down now? Will you be a good dog now?"

Princess Di does appear calmer. Subdued.

Her reward: a brisk walk in the neighborhood.

Not an unfamiliar walk which is good for tonight, after such agitation, after such a baring of canine teeth, and the growl deep in the throat, *familiar* is comforting.

No doubt, the little terrier-hound mix yearns for the abundant wildness of Wieland Pond and its unspeakably wonderful treasures but P. Cady has not taken her to Wieland Pond since October 29.

Since October 29 P. Cady has not returned to Wieland Pond or the bird sanctuary, her favorite places in Wieland. Never again.

Since the discovery in the ravine. Since the *remains*.

Walking Princess Di until the little dog's short legs tire. Until P. Cady's legs tire.

For it is good to be exhausted, an antidote to insomnia.

P. Cady cuts short her walk with Princess Di, returns home. Anxious not to miss a call from Katy precisely because she dreads a call from her niece.

Feeds Princess Di so distractedly, she empties an entire can of dog food into the little dog's bowl, where one-half usually suffices; picks through the tasteless meal her housekeeper has left for her in the oven.

Slouched on a leather sofa in her study. Too exhausted to return to work.

Seeing again the Wieland detective staring at her with flat zinc-eyes, suffused with contempt.

What a fool you are. Headmistress!

But—I only meant well . . .

She should apologize to the Langhorne community, P. Cady thinks guiltily. To poor Imogene Hood, who has been so devastated by the loss of Francis Fox; to her maddeningly naïve niece, Katy.

It will be impossible to tell these women of the (alleged) evidence that Francis was involved with girl-students; (alleged) evidence that he posted pictures and videos online, on what the Wieland detective has described as a child-pornography website subscribed to by *sicko pedophile-perverts.*

Zwender!—he only pretended to be sympathetic with her. In fact, Zwender is satisfied that Francis Fox is dead. You could see, the look in his face. He and his henchmen—local law enforcement—will thoroughly enjoy the investigation into Francis's death as it will be a humiliation of the deceased Langhorne teacher, a public evisceration of his character.

P. Cady was warned, when she became headmistress of the school. Local residents resent the Academy and its staff though the school is one of the largest employers in Atlantic County and brings in a large amount of revenue; Zwender is a local resident, and not above personal bias.

But several Langhorne trustees are influential residents of Wieland. The mayor of Wieland (with whom P. Cady is also acquainted)
and other county officials including the township tax board who will
certainly not want the reputation of the prestigious school damaged.

Still, P. Cady will resign. The only ethical decision!

Even if Wieland police never reveal their evidence, as Zwender
has promised. Even if the community never knows the (alleged)
monster Headmistress Cady hired to live and fester in their midst.

A genuine relief, to reenter private life.

But: she dreads the inevitable meeting with the Langhorne attorney, who has become a personal friend of hers. For one must tell at-
torneys the unvarnished truth. All P. Cady can hope for is not to burst
into tears. Imagining the look of horror/disgust on the man's face
when she informs him *I am afraid I have some bad news about Francis
Fox* . . .

How warmly Francis admired the Luminist paintings which
P. Cady inherited from her grandfather, including a large Hudson
River landscape by Thomas Cole; he astonished her with his seem-
ingly casual knowledge of lesser-known Luminist artists like Susie M.
Barstow.

By sheer coincidence P. Cady happens to own a single watercolor
by Barstow, ornately framed, hanging in a rarely used parlor in the
headmistress's house, which she was eager to show him—*Sunset in
Keene Valley, 1887.*

Francis agreed with P. Cady, there was no essential difference
between the work of Susie M. Barstow and her famous male
contemporaries—yet, Barstow was virtually unknown, forgotten soon
after her death in 1923.

How unjustly women are treated!—Francis Fox exclaimed. It is
up to men, men in power, men with influence, responsible men
aware of their own privilege, to repair that harm.

Soon then P. Cady moved the Barstow watercolor from the parlor
to the front hall of the headmistress's residence where it is hanging
now—so positioned, the first artwork a visitor sees.

P. Cady wipes at her eyes, it is so *unfair*. She felt such rare *rapport* with Francis Fox.

Past ten P.M. If Katy doesn't call soon, she should call Katy.

But—so tired! Slouched on the leather sofa with her eyes closed. Feeling as if she is submerged in a wrecked vehicle, in foul dark water.

If in a wreck, lacking the strength to struggle for her life.

At P. Cady's feet Princess Di is drowsy after her late walk and late dinner. Leaning her warm weight against P. Cady's ankles. In her remorseful state the wiry little dog knows better than to beg to be lifted into her human's lap, or to dare crawl onto the lap to be cuddled; she is not usually allowed on certain pieces of furniture for her sharp little claws can damage vulnerable fabrics like leather.

Sensitive animals can gauge our feelings for them, beneath even the gestures we make to them, to assure them that all is well.

Princess Di knows that she is not fully forgiven for her bad behavior, only just part-forgiven.

Though she is certain that she is fully awake P. Cady sees again the playing field, the shouting adolescents running with hockey sticks, the cold zinc-eyes of the Wieland detective blaming *her* . . .

Suddenly then, the Wieland detective lunges at her: pushing his bristly jaw and mouth roughly against her mouth.

P. Cady gives a cry, in an instant her eyes fly open. Princess Di has clambered onto her lap again, bringing her wet muzzle close against P. Cady's mouth, sniffing urgently, panting, nudging.

"No! Stop! God damn you."

P. Cady pushes the little dog away, knocking the hot little body onto the hardwood floor. Hearing the near-inaudible growl deep in the dog's throat. Seeing the glassy eyes empty of recognition as the eyes of a hyena would be.

She has leapt to her feet, to defend herself. As if a wild animal has attacked.

My tongue. It's my tongue she wants.

■ ■ ■

PHONE RINGS, AT LAST! P. Cady sees her tremulous hand reach out to answer.

It is 10:55 P.M. Late for Katy to call. This call that is dreaded. Several glasses of wine have been required to fortify P. Cady's nerves.

"Aunt Paige! Hel-*lo*. I've been waiting for you to call me . . ."

That tone of reproach. P. Cady feels her heart harden.

Explaining, she was out at dinner with trustees. Only just returned home.

"It *is* late, Katy. I'm afraid I can't talk long tonight."

But that sounds harsh, P. Cady doesn't mean to sound harsh. Her nerves are tight-strung after the skirmish with Princess Di.

"Oh, I know, Aunt Paige! I know. It's late for me, too."

Aunt Paige. P. Cady has never felt comfortable being called *Aunt*.

Quick step from *Aunt* to *Auntie*. No one wants to be called *Auntie*.

"Is there any—news, Aunt Paige? I mean—"

"No. Nothing."

P. Cady tries to reply casually. Yet, Katy seems to detect something amiss.

"But there must be—something? You said there wasn't any news yesterday too. Did any detective ever come to talk to you?"

"No. Not to *me*, particularly."

"Have detectives talked to anyone? That you know about?"

"Well, probably yes. I would think—yes. Quite a few people by now."

"Do they know anything more about what happened to Francis? If it was an accident, or . . ."

"If they knew, I think they would tell us. All they say officially is that the investigation is 'inconclusive.'"

Katy has become convinced that Francis died in a "tragic accident." Driving alone at night in an unfamiliar place, became lost, followed a trail thinking it was a road, drove over a precipice and into a ravine . . . When Katy speaks of this sequence of events her voice begins to quaver. P. Cady listens to her niece with sympathy, it is all so preposterous and yet *not impossible*.

P. Cady hasn't driven out to Wieland Pond to examine the terrain, she could not bear to see the site of Francis Fox's death, but she has seen photographs and videos on TV. No one could possibly have driven up the hill and over the ravine except deliberately, P. Cady is certain.

It has not (yet) occurred to Katy that Francis may have taken his own life. Still less, that he may have taken his life out of remorse for his predatory behavior, his shame at having harmed young girls like Genevieve Chambers.

". . . it just seems so obvious. The medical examiner must be an idiot."

Some days, Katy has called her aunt Paige twice. She has broken down on the phone, weeping.

P. Cady's niece, clinging to her like an orphan.

Clinging to theories, narratives. Explanations.

However calmly Katy begins one of these late-night conversations soon her voice will begin to falter, break. Soon, an adult woman will begin to cry like a child.

But tears are useless!—P. Cady wants to tell her.

She never wastes time crying. What point, if there is no one to hear?

(Princess Di would become distraught if P. Cady broke into tears. So far as Princess Di knows, P. Cady is her pack leader. A pack leader *must not* betray weakness.)

". . . the girl in the hospital? Is she . . ."

Unfortunately, Katy knows about Genevieve Chambers. Katy follows the online news more obsessively than P. Cady and has established contacts in Wieland whom she calls frequently; but Katy has no idea of what Zwender has told P. Cady, nor is P. Cady likely to tell her.

The *dark side* of Francis Harlan Fox. P. Cady has an image of a luminous moon one-half of which is obscured by a shadowy smudge.

"Have you seen the girl yet, Aunt Paige? Is she going to be all right?"

"I haven't seen Genevieve—she's been in intensive care. But my assistant calls the hospital regularly, to get reports. I've spoken with Mrs. Chambers—understandably, the poor woman is very distracted. I've indicated that whatever help we can provide . . ."

"This is one of Francis's seventh-grade students? Upset at his death? That is so touching!"

P. Cady has told Katy that a number of Francis's students are upset over his death—Genevieve is one of them.

P. Cady has spoken with Mrs. Chambers on the phone just once—feelingly, but guardedly. Though she is genuinely concerned about the twelve-year-old girl she has been warned by the Langhorne attorney not to imply that the school is responsible in any way for Genevieve's behavior; she has directed March to send flowers to Genevieve's hospital room, a dozen white roses, a dozen white carnations, nothing showy or extravagant.

It is true, a kind of hysteria has afflicted the Langhorne Academy since Francis Fox's disappearance. Students have been absent from classes, or attend classes haphazardly; they are visibly emotional in class; the infirmary is said to be full. Several boarding students have left school to return home. There have been nighttime candlelight vigils behind Haven Hall, poetry readings in honor of Francis Fox, flowers (both fresh-cut and artificial) placed daily in front of his office door, which have to be cleared away by custodians. Reports have come to P. Cady that students who never glimpsed Francis Fox are claiming that he has appeared in their dreams, girls high on drugs ("ecstasy") pray and weep together in the chapel; there are instances of contagious fainting in the residences, dining halls, classes. One of Francis's eighth-grade students, Mary Ann Healy, recipient of a county scholarship, is said to have run away from home, reputedly staying with relatives in Atlantic City but nowhere to be found when her parents drove to Atlantic City to bring her back home; another eighth grader, Eunice Pfenning, recently collapsed at school with dangerously low blood pressure, and had to be taken to the nearest ER; several of Francis's girl-students are said to have become anorexic. But boys are behaving strangely as well: there are reports of "pilgrimages" to Wieland Pond (seven miles away), hikers lost in the marshlands overnight.

A nightmare! How astonished Francis Fox would be, if he could know!

P. Cady dreads more students injuring themselves. If these isolated incidents coalesce into something like "breaking news"—picked up by the media. What a catastrophe it would be, a Langhorne student taking her life as rumors of a pedophile teacher at the school begin to circulate . . .

P. Cady has directed the dean of students to plan a memorial for Francis Fox as soon as possible, in the largest auditorium at the school, hoping to stave off unsupervised student gatherings and further self-destructive behavior. A beautiful ceremony in Francis's honor with music performed by the school orchestra, the choral society, poetry recitations, eulogies by Mr. Fox's students . . .

All of this, or most of this, P. Cady has told Katy, who is eager to hear anything and everything involving Francis Fox, however remotely it is related to her. Especially as the hour grows late, Katy seems anxious to keep P. Cady on the phone.

Circling the same subjects. Sifting through the same finite set of facts. Expressing disbelief, incredulity. Raw grief.

P. Cady has told Katy—until today, truthfully!—that she knows very little about the private life of Francis Fox, surely no more than Katy knows. Francis died without a will, apparently—not surprisingly, considering his age and health; he'd named no heirs, no next of kin; there were few personal documents in his apartment but he did have the notarized certificate issued by the State of Pennsylvania in 2011 recording his change of name from "Frank Harrison Farrell" to "Francis Harlan Fox." Less than fifteen thousand dollars in his combined savings and checking accounts in the Bank of New Jersey; no substantial possessions since the wreckage of the Acura. An older stepsister living in Sarasota, Florida, has no interest in flying to New Jersey to deal with her deceased stepbrother's estate, and was content with arranging for his cremation over the phone, choosing the least-expensive option and insisting upon a "private ceremony" with no one outside the family involved.

P. Cady had tried to appeal with the stepsister over the phone, practically begging her to allow a small circle of Francis's friends and colleagues to attend his cremation at a mortuary in Bridgeton, but to no avail—the stepsister spoke curtly, saying to P. Cady that she was a very busy person who had no more time for "empty sentimentality" than her stepbrother would have had for her, if their situations were reversed.

P. Cady tried to ask if Francis's ashes might be given to her but the stepsister interrupted rudely saying *No*.

"What a terrible, coldhearted sister," Katy said vehemently. "A monster."

She would have paid for the cremation, and a proper burial. If only she'd been the one to speak with the stepsister . . .

P. Cady lets this pass. No point in not humoring her niece on this subject.

"It seems so very lonely for Francis," Katy says. "All that he meant to so many people, lost. Even his ashes . . ."

"Well. It's lonely for us all, Katy. We have no choice but to carry on."

Carry on. Francis would wince at the cliché, P. Cady can almost see his droll expression.

"Maybe we could arrange to be given his ashes, Aunt Paige. I mean—purchase them. If the sister isn't interested . . ."

This is a wistful notion Katy has aired in the past. P. Cady knows better than to disagree.

Another wistful subject is Francis's ring: the ring that Katy gave him.

A black octagonal onyx in a sterling silver setting. An heirloom ring with a special meaning to her, as to Francis.

No ring seems to have been found in the wrecked auto or in the ravine. No wristwatch, no wallet or personal items were found by searchers at the scene.

Why is that?—P. Cady has wondered.

It would seem to suggest that the wreck wasn't an accident, that Francis had prepared for it by removing personal items. Some sort of care, deliberation. But why?

Not to obscure his identification, for the Acura's license plates would easily be traced.

Maybe tossed into Wieland Pond close by. But lost forever in the depth of the pond, in all that black muck.

Vaguely and bravely Katy has several times said she plans to visit the scene of Francis's accident. She too will make a pilgrimage. When she is feeling stronger. She will look for the ring, *her ring*. She has a *distinctive feeling* about the ring.

"Except, it's such a beautiful ring, it's possible that someone has kept it. One of the police officers . . . Who would know?"

Katy has raised this possibility in the past. P. Cady usually murmurs in vague assent, hoping that Katy will shift to another subject, as she does now inquiring when there will be a memorial for Francis—"I mean, for adults? For people who knew him, and loved him?"

"We're hoping later in the term, maybe December. There is so much unresolved right now, Katy."

"December! That will be complicated by Christmas."

"Well, January is complicated by the New Year, the spring term . . ."

"I want to speak at that memorial, Aunt Paige. I was Francis's closest friend, you know."

"Yes. I know, dear."

"Though we lived apart, and didn't see each other often, we spoke on the phone at least once a week, and we emailed and texted. Francis spoke of us as *soul-mates*—a beautiful Romantic tradition. Like Percy Shelley and Mary Godwin. Heathcliff and Catherine. Edgar Allan Poe and—what was her name?—Violet?—Virginia. Francis was particularly admiring of Poe and Virginia."

P. Cady thinks grimly—*Virginia, the thirteen-year-old girl-bride. Poe's cousin.*

"We celebrated his thirty-seventh birthday together, I brought him an exquisite dinner from his favorite restaurant in New York City . . ."

"Yes, Katy. I know. You stayed here at the house that night."

"We were *so happy* that evening. Oh, God."

Katy is eager to discuss a memorial service for Francis but P. Cady reminds her that the situation at the school is precarious right now, the well-being of her students has to come first. A tsunami of grief has swept over the school affecting even students who didn't know Francis personally. P. Cady has asked parents of the most distraught students to keep them at home until they are feeling more stable, it isn't good for students to infect one another. Hysteria is a contagion. Adolescence itself is a kind of contagion. The school has hired two new therapists, "grief counselors."

P. Cady *is* responsible. She hired a predator, she is the guilty party.

Though it is crucial not to suggest that the Langhorne Academy is in any way responsible.

"Aunt Paige? You're quiet tonight. Is anything wrong?"

Is anything wrong! P. Cady laughs, this query is so naïve.

Telling Katy yes, many things are wrong, all of Wieland is under a sort of accursed cloud, this *unresolved* issue of Francis Fox's death, its unanticipated consequences.

Wanting to tell Katy that she will be resigning her position, possibly at the end of the fall term.

But Katy will only react in astonishment, and disappointment. And disapproval.

But, Aunt Paige, the school will be lost without you! You have been such a leader, and a fundraiser! Why on earth would you want to RE-SIGN?

This, P. Cady can't face. Easier to resign in secrecy, clear out her things from her office and disappear.

Easier to take her own life, as Francis seems to have done.

But—with such consequences! P. Cady would not wish such consequences on her innocent colleagues.

". . . come visit? Stay with you a while? I'm feeling a little stronger now."

She can take a leave from the Guggenheim Foundation, Katy says. She has told the executive director, who is a friend of hers, that there has been a *death in the family,* she might be needed to stay with a grieving older relative for a while.

P. Cady shudders at the prospect.

Grieving older relative. Not *her.*

"It's just that I'm so lonely, Aunt Paige. Could you use a lecturer? Does the school teach art history? I could show slides, I have an entire syllabus on nineteenth-century American women writers and artists."

"Katy, I don't think so. There are no openings . . ."

"If there's no salary, that's all right! I don't need a salary, any more than you do."

P. Cady feels her face burn. She doesn't want it generally known that she turns back her salary at the Langhorne Academy, it is a violation of protocol for Katy to speak so carelessly. Even some of the trustees don't know this.

"I—I do have a salary here, Katy. I don't know where you got that information from."

"Oh, sorry!" Katy's apology is marred by muffled laughter.

Feeling as if the walls are closing in. P. Cady and her niece are too much alike.

High-achievers, addicted to work, restless when not at work. Inclined to fret, like birds pecking feathers out of their own breasts.

Unspoken between them would be the loss of Francis Fox. And if Katy were to spend time in Wieland she would certainly learn more about Francis Fox than she would wish to know.

"I don't think it's quite the right time, Katy. So much is in turmoil here . . ."

"But I could help you, Aunt Paige! I could set up a scholarship fund in Francis's name. I could endow literary prizes in Francis's name."

". . . right now, it's an awkward time. There are problems I can't discuss . . ."

"And that beautiful old house is so big, Aunt Paige! It's crazy to live alone there, just you and Princess Di."

P. Cady feels her heart clutch. That old reproach, she's heard or imagined she's heard in others' voices. *A woman alone, without a family. A woman. Alone.*

Acquiring a PhD in English literature from Columbia would be a coup for a prep school, and Katy Cady is a published scholar, and everyone would like her—Katy is so friendly, guileless, unthreatening.

"How *is* Princess Di?"

P. Cady has been hearing a scratching sound at the study door, which she has secured against the damned little dog. She plans to drag Princess Di's faux-fur bed out of her bedroom and into a guest room. She will barricade her bedroom tonight and sleep alone undisturbed.

For it is true, she is sure. Princess Di has been morbidly intrigued by her mouth, by her tongue inside her mouth. A moving tongue. *An alive tongue.*

P. Cady isn't in a mood to discuss Princess Di. She has wondered if solitary women chattering about their animals are not somewhat ridiculous.

"She's alone too much. When I stayed overnight at your house, I could see how lonely Princess Di was. She followed me around, she practically begged me to take her for a walk."

"Yes. I should hire a dog-walker."

"*I* could walk her, Aunt Paige. I love that little dog."

Is this true? P. Cady has a vague memory of Katy frowning at Princess Di leaping and pawing at her legs, giving the little dog a surreptitious swat when she thought P. Cady wasn't watching.

"Katy, I've tried to explain that it isn't a good time right now. Maybe in December, if there's a memorial. I can understand that you're missing Francis terribly but I'm at school through the day, I wouldn't have much time to spend with you . . ."

"Oh for God's sake, Aunt Paige! You wouldn't have to babysit me. I've told you, I could give lectures. I have wonderful slides. I could take a sabbatical from the foundation. I think I need a change of scene. I need to make a 'pilgrimage' to—that place you call—is it Wieland Lake?"

P. Cady listens in silence. She loves Katy Cady, but finds her exhausting. The prospect of her niece visiting her in this house, still less staying for an extended period of time, makes P. Cady feel faint.

"It's just—I—I loved him so much, Aunt Paige. I can't believe that I will never see him again."

"I know, Katy. I'm so sorry."

"We could have had a beautiful life together, Francis and I! He loved teaching but he was sympathetic to my suggestion that we travel in Europe, we'd talked of renting a villa in Venice. Francis could concentrate on his poetry, and I could concentrate on my book on nineteenth-century women photographers . . ."

It is past midnight when P. Cady persuades her tearful niece to hang up the phone, go to bed.

■

PAST MIDNIGHT WHEN SHE goes upstairs, Princess Di behind her at a discreet distance in the abject-canine posture, tail between haunches.

In Princess Di's shimmering brown eyes, the most intense ardor. Pleading for forgiveness from her human. Her bizarre behavior of earlier in the evening has been forgotten, or nearly. P. Cady wonders if in her weakened state, after the brutal beating by Detective Zwender, she has exaggerated it.

Hasn't the heart to lock the little terrier-hound out of her bedroom as she planned. Too cruel, Princess Di will whine and whimper through the night as if her little heart is broken; she has never spent a single night alone since being brought home from the Wieland rescue shelter.

"Oh, all right. But—*be a good dog.*"

Hurriedly, P. Cady undresses. Cannot face what awaits her in the morning.

Continuing the investigation. Expecting cooperation.

What was he asking her—about Francis's office? That it had been cleaned *too thoroughly?* How was that her fault, too? *Was* that her fault?

She pleaded that she knew nothing about the office. She, headmistress of the school, has virtually nothing to do with directing the custodial staff. But her protestations sounded weak, unconvincing.

But when should she resign? Such an important decision can't be made unilaterally, she will have to confer with one of the trustees. But then, she would be asked *why*.

Impossible to speak of Francis Fox as Zwender spoke of him. Such ugly words as *sexual abuse, child pornography*. No one at the Academy must ever know!

Sitting on the bed, hugging Princess Di who quivers with love, relief that her human has not cruelly rejected her but seems to have forgiven her. Tears are streaking P. Cady's cheeks, Princess Di licks the tears away.

"Princess Di, you are my only solace. My heart is broken, I will never have faith in any human being again."

Of course, Princess Di's bad behavior is forgiven: their household is too small for one abject creature to refuse forgiveness to the other.

FEATHER BRACELET (1)

30 NOVEMBER 2013

Turning in his fingers, in brooding wonder, the badly water-stained handmade bracelet found on the floor of the passenger seat of Francis Fox's wrecked Acura. A bracelet of feathers and glass beads attached to a stretch wristband.

The work of an earnest child, a young girl who was (surely) one of Fox's victims.

No one in H. Zwender's life has ever made H. Zwender such a bracelet and yet in a way this bracelet is *for him*.

Turning it in his (gloved) fingers, staring.

In the Wieland police department after the others have gone home. After the jocular noises of the others have ceased. Seeking out the feather bracelet in the evidence room.

Slips on latex gloves, to examine the bracelet reverently, tenderly in his hands.

Whoever made the feather bracelet, unknowingly making it *for him*.

FEATHER BRACELET (2)

With latex-gloved fingers H. Zwender positions the stained little feather bracelet on the Formica-topped table for the father of Mary Ann Healy to identify.

The homemade bracelet of miniature feathers and colored glass beads, retrieved from Fox's wrecked car.

The bracelet which has been positively identified by Mary Ann Healy's mother as belonging to Mary Ann Healy.

But Blake Healy seems not to recognize the feather bracelet and stares perplexed, as if this is a riddle to decode and he doesn't like it.

"What the hell's that thing? Something I'm supposed to know?"

"Does it look familiar, Blake?"

"Something, like, to do with Mary Ann?—is that it?"

"You don't recognize it?"

"Something kids made? Fuck I'm supposed to know—why?"

Healy speaks in explosive grunts, barely coherently. Black hairs in his nostrils bristle with indignation.

Thirteen-year-old Mary Ann Healy has been missing from home since October 25, and has ceased attending classes at the Langhorne Academy; she has called several times to assure her mother that she is all right but she does not want to come home; she refuses to give any reason for leaving home without informing anyone, and she refuses to say exactly where she is. (Though it seems to be understood that Mary Ann is in Atlantic City, where she has female relatives.) If her mother presses her Mary Ann begins to cry and breaks the connection.

Fingerprints belonging to Mary Ann Healy have been found in the bathroom of Francis Fox's apartment on Consent Street. Colleagues of Fox's at the school have reported seeing the eighth-grade girl frequently in Fox's office and in the corridor outside his office; one colleague reported seeing a "shocking scene" in the school parking lot when, it appeared, the eighth grader was in a distraught state and Fox "almost ran her down with his car." (Yes, this was reported to the headmistress's office but nothing came of the complaint.) Though neither Zwender nor Officer Odom has (yet) identified Mary Ann Healy on Fox's website *Sleeping Beauties* Zwender is confident that Fox posted pictures of her which they will discover sooner or later among the hundreds of erotically posed *kittens*.

It is H. Zwender's hypothesis that Blake Healy is very likely—very *probably*—the individual responsible for Francis Fox's death, in a rage at the English teacher for abusing his daughter—for who else would have a motive to fracture Francis Fox's skull and contrive an auto wreck to conceal the murder? Who else, in the Wieland vicinity, has a criminal record for aggravated assault? Only an adult male could commit such a crime, Zwender reasons—it's impossible to imagine that Mary Ann Healy herself could have managed such a violent act, still less the aftermath. (So far, however, there is no forensic evidence linking Healy with the probable crime scene and there are no witnesses to claim even seeing the two men in close proximity.) Yet more frustrating to the detective, neither Blake Healy nor his wife, Pauline, seems even to realize that their eighth-grade daughter was involved with her English teacher.

All Blake Healy seems to be incensed about is that his daughter is a *God-damn runaway.* He has driven twice to Atlantic City to bring her back, in vain. He has been harassing relatives who live in Atlantic

City, demanding that they tell him where Mary Ann is, because he knows that they know, but they claim that they don't know. He has threatened these relatives, and they have threatened to report him to the Atlantic City police. In Wieland he has been demanding that police arrest Mary Ann and bring her home as a *runaway juvenile*— she is only thirteen! In an aggrieved voice Healy tells Zwender that an older daughter of his (from his first marriage) behaved in a similar way years ago and when Aimée did return home, she was eight months pregnant, at the age of fifteen; he and his wife (at the time) had to deal with the pregnancy, the birth, and all that the baby cost; even now, he's still handing out money to Aimée who's a single mother with another kid, a "mixed-race" kid, living in Toms River.

Healy's roughly handsome Irish face is flushed with chagrin, re-sentment. Clearly he expects Zwender to sympathize with him: They are of the same age, or nearly. They both attended Wieland High School years ago, overlapping by a year or two. Healy is unshaven, slovenly dressed in grease-stained T-shirt, coveralls, smelling of his body. His hair lifts in tufts from his deep-furrowed forehead. The backs of his hands are covered in dark hairs; his fingernails are edged with dirt. Healy is part-owner (with a brother) of a Sunoco service station on the outskirts of Wieland; of several stations in the area it's the most run-down. From a report typed up by Officer Odom at Zwender's request Zwender learns that Healy has a police record dat-ing back to 1969, when he was sixteen years old; he has citations, arrests, probation for assault and battery, public disturbance, DUI; in 1989 he was sentenced to eighteen months in the state prison for men at Trenton, on a charge of aggravated assault, of which he'd served seven months. Exactly the profile of a hot-tempered man, fa-ther of an abused young girl, who might smash in the skull of the girl's abuser in a fit of rage, and improvise a way to cover up the crime that involves heavy machinery, wreckage.

Not premeditated murder, Zwender is thinking. Not a homicide charge at all.

It is Zwender's plan to suggest manslaughter to Healy—"voluntary manslaughter"—an act "committed in the heat of passion resulting from a reasonable provocation." Persuade Healy to confess, it's in his best interest to confess, to cooperate with law enforcement, the county prosecutor will take such cooperation into account; and he, H. Zwender, will argue for the minimum sentence of five years, considering the nature of the *provocation*.

Or maybe, Zwender could convince Healy to confess to the killing of Fox in self-defense, in a (wholly probable) situation in which the aggrieved father of the abused girl confronted the girl's abuser in his office at the Langhorne Academy, and was threatened by the abuser, and had no choice but to defend himself by smashing in Fox's skull— "involuntary manslaughter."

Minimum sentence two to four years, parole for good behavior after merely one year. A bargain!

In prison, Blake Healy would be a hero. Killing a pedophile-predator who'd abused his daughter. The parole board would be eager to parole him at the earliest time.

No one in law enforcement in Atlantic County would object. No local resident would object. Even without knowing that Fox was making money from online child pornography, which would have to remain strictly confidential, the consensus of sympathy would be for the local resident Healy, and not the outsider Fox.

Zwender is filled with such revulsion for the pedophile-predator Fox, he has been insomniac for weeks in sympathy with Fox's killer, whoever the man is. Residents of Atlantic County are sick of seeing dimpled-smiling Francis Fox on local TV news, swoony "Mr. Fox" of the Langhorne Academy in preppy Brooks Brothers clothes, invariably described as "popular"—"much-loved." Enough!

Any longtime law enforcement officer understands that there are individuals so loathsome, they deserve being murdered, as there are those hapless others who, in the exigency of the moment, as if fulfilling an unvoiced wish of the community to expunge evil in its midst, rise up as angels of wrath, self-sacrificing as Jesus Christ on the cross: if not the father of the abused and denigrated Mary Ann Healy, then who?

It has seemed so *probable*. It has seemed, to H. Zwender lying awake each night for weeks in a blizzard of thoughts like neutrinos piercing his skull, so *inevitable*.

Daryl Odom too, usually resistant, pulling in opposition to H. Zwender's best hunches, has come to believe that the father of Mary Ann Healy, incarcerated for assault, a known local brawler and drinker, is likely to be the killer, if there *is* a killer.

But as the interview progresses by fits and starts like a bulldozer making its way through a toxic landfill Zwender is beginning to realize that Blake Healy is possibly—probably—not his man.

"Your official residence is 388 Stockton Road, Wieland. You said you weren't at that address right now? How long have you lived apart from your family?"

"I don't *live apart*," Healy says irritably. "I just moved out for a while. She wanted me to go, she says she didn't but she did. Pretending like she was afraid of me—that somebody might hit her. Now she won't tell me where Mary Ann is, she knows because Mary Ann told her but if I look for her there, she won't be there."

"Has your daughter ever left home before like this?"

"No! At least, I don't know about it if she did."

"Do you have any idea why your daughter left home?"

"Ask my wife. If Mary Ann ran away it's that bitch's fault."

"Why would that be, Blake?"

"*Why?* Ask my wife. She's the parent responsible."

"Was your daughter upset about something? At school?"

"How the hell would I know? You cops, arrest her and bring her back. Bring her back in handcuffs."

"Did Mary Ann ever talk to you about her school? Any of her teachers?"

"No. Not that I remember."

"Her English teacher Mr. Fox?"

"Who?"

"Her English teacher—Mr. Fox."

"What about him? Is Mary Ann flunking at the new school already?—she just started."

"Blake, when did you see your daughter last?"

"When did I see her last?"—Healy's face is contorted with the effort of trying to remember. "Maybe—around Labor Day . . ."

"Mary Ann is a new student at the Langhorne Academy? A scholarship student?"

"Yes. Everybody's proud of her for that."

"Are you proud of her?"

"Yes! I guess so. Just the tuition, it's more than I make in a year. They wear uniforms, it's like a military school, there's *discipline*. I don't even know where the fucking school is, it's in Wieland somewhere. Never get in that part of town. But Pauline says Mary Ann isn't happy there, she'd be better off back in her old school."

"Why is that, Blake? Do you know?"

"Pauline says she cries a lot in her room. She wouldn't tell me, she doesn't tell me things like that."

"Why does she cry, did Pauline say?"

"I don't know, Jesus! What is this shit you're asking me? Why don't you ask Pauline? The two of them talk together, like they don't talk to me. Not that I give a damn, I'm through with them. She's in Atlantic City, she won't come home and *she*—her mother—is protecting her. Could wring their necks, both of them."

"Your daughter doesn't talk to you?"

"Does your daughter talk to *you*? Nobody's daughter talks to them if they can help it. If I come to the house, Mary Ann stays in her room half the time, doesn't even come out for supper if I stay for supper. Pauline says she's writing things like poems, she has a special notebook she writes in, and she does get good grades for that, Pauline said."

"That's for her English course? A special notebook?"

Healy shrugs, how'd he know? Stifling a convulsive yawn.

Zwender has been speaking sympathetically to Healy, not wanting to upset the man, who is easily excitable; now, Zwender shifts to the subject of Francis Fox, expecting that Healy will stiffen and look away from him, or become defensive; but when Zwender asks if he has ever met his daughter's English teacher Mr. Fox, Healy looks blank. Not a feigned, guilty blank but a purely blank blankness like a concrete wall.

"'English teacher'? Why'd I meet an English teacher?"

"Did Mary Ann ever talk to you about Mr. Fox?"

"Mr. Fox—no. We don't actually talk so much, since I moved out. She blames me but it was her mother, not me. It's hard to talk to them, you wind up pissed at them. My other daughter's the same. My boys, it's hard to talk to them but in a different way, it's like there isn't that much to say but, if there was, the boys would talk to me. They ask advice, sometimes. They see me somewhere, they come right over and say hello. My daughter, though, like if I saw her somewhere like the mall, she'd pretend she didn't see me." Unexpectedly, Healy laughs, the deep gut-laughter of disgust.

"Has that happened?"

"What happened?"

"Your daughter has avoided you in public?"

"Well—she *would*. If she saw me, like in Atlantic City. Her bitch-cousins are hiding her, I know. They are going to regret it if I find out."

"Have you been threatening them? Relatives of yours?"

"No, I have not! Who says so?"

Zwender ventures to ask Healy another time if he met Francis Fox, and Healy looks blank, as if he has never heard the name until now; Zwender asks if he has ever been in Francis Fox's apartment, and now Healy looks utterly baffled.

"Who?—Fox? When was this?"

"Blake, we've been talking about Francis Fox, the Langhorne English teacher who was found in the ravine back in October, dead; the man who was your daughter's teacher."

"He's *dead*? What happened?"

"Haven't you been following the news, Blake?"

"What news?"

"A teacher at the Langhorne Academy was found dead, we are trying to determine how he died . . ."

"That's the one in the wreck? The car went off the road? Was it a bridge, that the railing broke and he drowned?"

Zwender is feeling thwarted, balked. Trying to question Blake Healy is like tugging at a locked door that will not budge. Zwender is accustomed to cagey, cunning, childishly deceitful interviewees; he is accustomed to blatant liars who quiver with excitement when they lie, as if lying to a police officer were a sensuous experience, deeply daring, thrilling. But Blake Healy is not one of these, he seems to be genuinely confused, like a man with a hearing impairment trying to decipher a foreign language.

Zwender is aware of Daryl Odom smirking at the back of the room. Zwender feels a thrill of rage—*Fuck you, Odom.*

Trying another tack asking Healy if he ever hikes at Wieland Pond?—even as he knows it's an asinine question to put to the auto mechanic.

"'Hike'?"—Healy cups his hand to his ear as if doubting he has heard correctly. "You mean, like, walking around? Like in the woods? Who the fuck has time for *that,* I'm at the fucking garage from eight A.M. to six P.M."

Healy laughs, this is so ridiculous. His breath smells like sour malt.

The interview seems to be ending. Far from leading Healy to a confession as he'd anticipated Zwender has lost his man, as one might lose a tattered kite drifting idly away, caught and broken in a tree, transformed to litter. More questions Zwender has prepared for Healy seem pointless. His instinct tells him that Healy isn't involved in any way with whatever happened to Francis Fox; the man hasn't even a clue that Fox has been murdered and that he, father of an (abused) girl, has been a person of interest in the homicide.

"You going to tell me what this is?"—Healy indicates the feather bracelet on the Formica-topped table.

"It's a bracelet belonging to your daughter," Zwender says bluntly, "—and made by your daughter. Your wife recognized it at once."

"So? Why's it here?"

"Because it was found on the floor of the passenger seat of a car owned by your daughter's English teacher, that was involved in a wreck. Because it suggests a connection between your daughter and this English teacher."

At once Healy flares up: "You mean, a grown man? Mary Ann is riding around in a car with a grown man? Her English teacher? Where is this son of a bitch, what's he think he's doing with my daughter? She's thirteen years old, that's against the law, isn't it? A grown man, a teacher, giving my daughter a ride? In his car? Where the hell? What's his name? Is this the new school she got the scholarship to? I told Pauline, I didn't want her going there, she won't fit in there, I don't want people looking at her and feeling sorry for her, I could wring their fucking necks and I'll wring his neck, what'd you say the name is?"

"No, you don't understand, Blake—the English teacher is *dead*. Mr. Fox is *dead*."

"How's Mary Ann riding around with him, then? When was all this?"

Zwender has had enough for the day. His nostrils pinch with the acrid unwashed odor of Blake Healy. He shuts his folder, puts away his notepad. Politely thanks Healy for coming to police headquarters, helping with their investigation. Tells Healy that they might be contacting him again.

Zwender is about to give Healy his card and is taken wholly by surprise as with no warning Healy lurches to his feet like a bull that has been stunned, but has recovered, summoning back his strength, in an instant revived, with a clumsy yet powerful swing of his thick-muscled arm, fist like a rock striking the side of Zwender's head with a volley of curses—*God damn son-of-a-bitch motherfuckin fucker*— propelling the detective against a wall, an adult male of approximately one hundred ninety pounds standing six feet two inches no more resistant to this blow than a mannequin would have been and with legs tangled in a chair so that, as Zwender falls, falls heavily, the chair overturns upon him even as Daryl Odom has ceased being amused and moves with unexpected alacrity across the room, pushing aside the table, kicking away a chair, strong enough to overpower the infuriated Healy, bringing him to his knees, forcing him down onto his stomach on the floor, jamming his knee hard enough in the small of Healy's back to crack a vertebra or two, all the while shouting at him as he was taught at the police academy, fierce, exuberant, triumphant as other police officers run into the room, to assist in subduing the man, forcing his arms up behind his back so that he screams in pain, cuffing his wrists behind his back.

Through this, only H. Zwender is oblivious. Only H. Zwender is *out of time: concussed.*

THE PRAYER

5 DECEMBER 2013

J ust *a feeling like something wasn't right.*

Saw the tire tracks in the mud going up the hill . . . Turkey vultures in trees.

Jesus! Wish I hadn't gone up to look.

■

ON HIS KNEES AT his bedside in a trance of terror.

Rehearsing *his story. His account* that will explain.

Praying to God, and to Jesus who is Demetrius's special friend. Praying that he will be believed.

■

HE'S SORRY, MARCUS IS SAYING.

He is so damned sorry, Marcus is saying. His face is clotted with guilt. Something like shame. *Letting you down, Dem. I didn't want to . . .*

He's been summoned to the Wieland PD. Not once but twice. Couldn't figure out why, *he* was the one who'd called 911.

Last time he'd call 911. First time and last time he tried to do the right thing, what you are supposed to do. But in the future fuck that!

Asking him about what he'd seen in the ravine which he'd already told them more than once. Why he'd climbed the hill to look into the ravine which he'd already told them more than once. Whether his brother was with him initially or had only come when he'd called him which he'd told them more than once.

No idea why. Like they were suspicious of him—why?

Because he'd been on the hill, and Demetrius had been on the hill, they'd left footprints, boot-prints, and these would have to be identified. So the detective informed him. It was just routine, a process of "elimination."

The detective was polite enough. The detective smiled at him once, twice. The detective assured him it was routine seeing that Marcus was looking worried or maybe Marcus was looking puzzled or maybe Marcus was looking pissed he'd have to bring his work-boots to the station and leave them for a few days.

And Demetrius too, he'd be called to the station. Same thing.

Exactly what it meant, and why, Marcus didn't understand. The detective didn't explain. If you ask them a question they don't seem to hear. They ask questions, not answer questions. Though Marcus was the one who'd called 911 like a fool.

Bring their boots to the station, that was all. Just routine.

There were two of them but only the older one was asking questions. At some point asking about Demetrius and he'd had to say that Demetrius was with him, when he'd found the wreck.

Why did you tell us that your brother wasn't with you, the detective asked.

Marcus didn't know. Said he didn't know at first.

Then, tried to explain: He didn't want his brother to get involved. Didn't see any point to it. All he'd done—all Marcus had done—was call 911, right? Demetrius hadn't had anything to do with it.

But, so—he'd told the detective that Demetrius was with him.

That they'd both climbed the hill. Because there were footprints, that they were trying to identify.

So, he was sorry: It's like once their names got in the police computer they were on the record. Once on the police record, you couldn't get off.

Yes, he could kick himself in the ass, that he'd ever called 911.

First time, last time. Trying to be a good citizen.

Same thing if you register to vote, they get your name in the computer.

He asked them why they wanted to know about the boot-prints, all they said was "elimination" and "routine."

Saying he's sorry, he might've fucked up. Trying to explain to them that he didn't tell them about his brother at first, didn't want him to be involved, you're my kid brother and you had a tough time at school and didn't answer questions so well, I just wanted to spare you. That was all.

That was what Mom would want, right? Just to keep you out of it.

Because you might have to miss work, if they keep you a while. They say it won't take time but they make you wait.

Marcus says he will go to the police station with him, maybe he can help. If Demetrius needs help. Like, just talking to them. I can say you don't talk too well sometimes, it's just your personality.

Marcus speaking in a grave voice. Three days' stubble on his jaws. Sucking a can of Coors. Guilty-eyed, not meeting Demetrius's eye.

Then saying, well—maybe he told them that he, Demetrius, was the one to find the wreck. Because of the vultures.

And they asked me why I'd been lying. Well, I said—I wasn't *lying*. I didn't think of it that way, *lying*.

As Demetrius listens appalled. Seeing his brother has worked himself up into a state of maudlin sentiment as if he has discovered a vein of emotion in himself he'd no idea was there, like digging into clayey soil and discovering rich dark fertile soil a few inches beneath.

"So, OK: if you want me to come with you I'll take time off from work. They won't let me in the room with you probably but I can wait just outside. OK?"

Demetrius listens without comment. Jesus listens without comment.

What it will be, it will be.

■

FROM SODDEN MIDAFTERNOON SLEEP Pa staggers into the kitchen wild-white-haired in stocking feet, smelling of his underarms. Lemuel's face is mottled from where he's been sleeping on a creased pillow-case, his breath is sour as fermented fruit. Complaining bitterly to Demetrius he was all morning at the God-damned police station mostly just waiting in a room like they'd forgotten him, finally this detective comes in, face looks familiar and name is familiar—"Zwender"—(is this the cop who killed another cop in Wieland, years ago?—but the claim was self-defense or some bullshit)—but the detective doesn't seem to know him, calls him "Mr. Healy" and is polite at first, just a few questions he wants to ask about Lemuel's "custodial work" at the Langhorne school, his shift, late-afternoon to nine P.M., right?—asking does he clean offices in the basement of Haven Hall?—did he clean offices in the basement of Haven Hall on certain dates in late October which might be October 24, October 25, October 26, or any date following, into early November?—Lemuel is taken by surprise by such a question, no way he can remember these dates, or any date, months are just blurs to him of no more significance than swirls of dust or leaves blown by the wind, in fact years are blurs, he'd have a hard time saying exactly what year it is if you woke him from one of his deep sodden sleeps; but has to tell the detective *Yes* since Haven Hall is his assignment, cleaning teachers' offices is part of his work but whether he'd cleaned offices on these dates, or whether Demetrius did, he couldn't remember, probably it was Demetrius but he isn't about to tell the detective this so he says *Yes*; then he's asked about a certain office, 015 Haven Hall formerly occupied by a teacher named—is it *Frank? Fox?*—not a name Lemuel recognizes but nods vaguely, not that he knows the names of any teachers in fact, no more than a blur to him, basement floor of Haven Hall is a warren of small offices, junior staff, cubbyhole offices not like the larger offices on higher floors with windows of fancy leaded glass, he doesn't know anyone's name why the fuck should he?—015 Haven Hall means nothing to him so he's stunned by the next question, *Why did you clean Mr. Fox's office with disinfectant, Mr. Healy, and wipe down the walls?—Why did you clean that particular office so thoroughly?*—in a panic by now sweating inside his clothes, shaking his head, no idea, no idea what the hell the detective is talking about—*Who instructed you to clean the office so thoroughly, Mr. Healy? Was it your supervisor?—Was it the headmistress?*—in a weak voice protesting no one ever told him to clean any teacher's office in any special way, sometimes there's boys' lavatories have to be cleaned like you'd clean a pigsty, with extra-strength cleanser and bleach so strong you have to wear a mask but not a teacher's office, not ever that he could remember; but the detective keeps asking him, not so politely now, and Pa is getting desperate trying to think of an answer so that he will be released from this place and allowed to return home, he's in pain, arthritis in his knee, back hurting like hell he needs to *self-medicate* as it's called, dying for a beer, one of his Oxycontins, can't think of any answer because who would clean any office at the school with special cleaning equipment except a custodian on the staff who is supposed to be Lemuel Healy—"So finally I said maybe it wasn't me after all that was supposed to clean the office, and he asked who it was then, and at first I said I didn't know, but he kept asking me, like he knew that I was lying, just staring into my eyes like boring into my brain so finally I—I told him it was you."

Astonishing to Demetrius, his usually reticent father has spoken at such length. More than Pa has said to him in years put together. Like a rising wind, rattling windows, causing tree branches to thump against the roof, these words to which Demetrius listens with a slow-pounding heart seeming to know how they will end.

It was you.

■

ON HIS KNEES, AT his bedside. Hiding his eyes.

Though his mother is dead, yet his mother is close beside him at such times as Jesus comes into his heart to help him shape these crucial words.

Just a feeling like something wasn't right.

Saw the tire tracks in the mud going up the hill . . . Turkey vultures in trees.

Jesus! Wish I hadn't gone up to look . . .

And then I called my brother, to come look with me.

"BAD DADDY"

7 DECEMBER 2013

D*addy, I did a bad thing.*

So softly Eunice speaks on the phone, the Daddy can hardly hear her. In fact, the Daddy isn't sure if Eunice has said what (he thinks) he has heard or, muffled in the hoarse-muttering way in which his daughter speaks when she is abashed, like fluid sucked down a drain, the more alarming/accusatory *Daddy did a bad thing.*

■

THE *BAD THING* THE Daddy has been doing, he has to acknowledge, is learning to live alone.

Learning to live alone, again.

Like learning to walk again, after a collapse, paralysis.

Learning to breathe again. Learning *it can be done.*

Learning to live (alone) without giving a damn about the Daddy—the person he's been for the past thirteen years, the role he's been playing with more animation than enthusiasm.

Since November 19, the single worst day of his life. So far.

The day, the evening, when his daughter screamed at him out of a face contorted and unrecognizable—*Go away! Go away! I don't want you here! I hate you!*

And his wife, looking at him with undisguised disgust, loathing—*It's all over, Martin. No more. Just leave.*

Single worst day of his life yet it is weeks later, Martin Pfenning is still *here*. Has to smile at the improbability that he is *still here*.

Learning to live again as he once lived—alone, not unhappily—in that gravityless interregnum between leaving the shelter of his parents' home at the age of eighteen (just in time!) and becoming a married man at the age of twenty-seven (too soon!).

A kind of free-fall, a liminal space, characterized by interchangeable places, dorm rooms, shared apartments, a co-op in University City, Philadelphia—living amicably, affably, with friends, housemates, a shifting cast of persons no single one of whom had the power to pierce Pfenning's heart with a mere word, or words; no single one of whom he cared for deeply, beyond the perimeters of easygoing affection, camaraderie, practicality.

Quarrel with a friend, you can both walk away. Maybe you'll walk back, or maybe not, that's your prerogative.

Quarrel with a wife, it's carved into your very body. Bleeding wounds, even the scabs hurt.

Quarrel with a child, there's no quarrel. In a quarrel *a child is always right.*

And Kathryn is right, he has come to realize. Pfenning didn't love being the Daddy.

He *performed* the Daddy. He did a damned good job (he thinks) of *performing* the Daddy for thirteen years.

Some of the times, he detached himself from the performer and stood to the side admiring, impressed. Thinking—*Hey, is that really me? Is that how I really feel?*

And—*Guess I must love them. If I am the Daddy.*

Circle of admirers, applauding. Kathryn's parents, his parents. Relatives. Impressed that Martin Pfenning, always somewhat immature, over-smart, over-ambitious, has been able to love not only a woman, but a *daughter.*

No wonder fatherhood is so applauded, Pfenning thinks. It is an utterly unnatural state of being.

Surely Homo sapiens is polygamous. Absurd to think that we are meant to be *monogamous*. At least the male of the species.

Absurd to think that we are meant to *care so very much* for offspring. In the course of the average male life, how many offspring is he meant to sire?

In Pfenning's case, just one. Fatally, one.

If he'd sired dozens of offspring, which isn't far-fetched to consider hypothetically, he would certainly not be grieved, wounded, traumatized by his single child hating him, loathing him as a child-molester, lying about him to her mother.

Not just the lie, but *why*. Cannot comprehend *why* Eunice would say such vicious things about the Daddy, who's been so very kind, so very patient, so very *loving* toward her even when she's been a heedless brat.

Did she, does she, blame the Daddy for the Pfennings' separation? Is that the motive?

But then, Eunice should blame the Mommy, too. For Kathryn is obviously the prime mover in the separation.

Of course, gentlemanly Daddy was the parent to *move out*. Not realizing that as soon as he'd *moved out* it might seem to his emotionally fraught young daughter that he was abandoning her.

Yet, pointless to blame Kathryn. He'd left her alone to care for Eunice, too often. Too many years. Hadn't told her about the transfer to Bridgeton, a promotion with a gratifying raise in salary, until he'd all but accepted.

Pointless to try to fix blame, the only recourse is to move forward. Find a way into a future since, in any case, the future rushes at us, heedless of our wishes.

Surprisingly, Kathryn hasn't told anyone about Eunice's charges. Not yet.

For weeks he's been expecting a knock at the door. Possibly, in the most lurid of scenarios, Atlantic County sheriff's deputies showing up at the high-rise executive suite in Bridgeton with a warrant for the arrest of Martin K. Pfenning.

Child sexual abuse, child negligence. Bad Daddy.

But no one contacted him. No authorities.

Causing Pfenning to wonder: has Kathryn questioned Eunice more thoroughly, has she begun to doubt their daughter's accusations? Even as Kathryn has consistently refused to allow Pfenning to return to the house, or even to speak with Eunice on the phone.

Daddy hugged me so hard. I hate it when Daddy hugs me so hard.

Hate Daddy kissing me in a bad way. Daddy kissing me with his tongue.

These words have haunted Pfenning, he has (literally) heard them in his sleep.

In fact, Pfenning has rarely hugged Eunice hard—she isn't the sort of child who is amenable to hugs, or kisses. He hugged his daughter in a simulacrum of a (normal) Daddy hugging a (normal) daughter whom he loves. Quick squeezes, bantering and joking, flurry of Daddy-kisses, then a release.

Never has he kissed Eunice with his *tongue.* The thought is repulsive to Pfenning. He is filled with rage at the accusation, that his thirteen-year-old daughter, whom he has tried to love, whom he has tried to endure, would fantasize something so disgusting, let alone utter it aloud.

Must be some ugliness she'd seen on the Internet. Maybe a graphic comic someone at school had shown her.

(But Eunice has no friends, Pfenning has been told. Hard to believe, a thirteen-year-old girl boastful of having no friends.)

All this turmoil began in September, Pfenning recalls. Possibly, in that English class taught by the late Mr. Fox.

The poor grades Fox had given her, that seemed to have driven Eunice to distraction, obsession. The journal with the toxic-algae cover, into which neither the Daddy nor the Mommy was allowed to look.

Yet, Kathryn defended Fox, insisting that he was only challenging Eunice because she was potentially brilliant, a truly gifted child.

In fact, Eunice had been improving; her last grade from Fox was B+.

How petty this is!—Pfenning thinks in disgust.

Petty, ridiculous. Humiliating.

As if the child's soul is being "graded"—found wanting.

Yet it seems possible, Pfenning's little family has been torn apart because of it.

That Martin Pfenning is Eunice's father, he is obliged to love her. Since November 19 trying to calibrate what that must mean.

That Martin Pfenning has been banished as Eunice's father, he is not obliged to love her, nor even to endure her. Trying to calibrate what *that* might mean.

Trying to calibrate—*Does he want to return, if they want him back?*

Or—*is it too late?*

■ ■ ■

"MARTIN? I AM SO SORRY. I think that Eunice might have—must have—'confabulated . . .'"

On the phone Kathryn is—almost—repentant. Yet still there is an air of reproach in her voice when Pfenning remains silent, taken by surprise by the unexpected call, and uncertain how to reply.

It is what he hoped he might hear from Kathryn, weeks ago. When he was too stunned to know how to react.

". . . it's a kind of misremembering. Or, something like a dream, a nightmare. Eunice has been agitated for weeks. As you know. She has never worked so hard in school in her life. She hadn't been sleeping, at the time she said those things to you. Since the disappearance of her English teacher, and then—his death . . ."

But how was that his fault?—Pfenning is thinking. Why would both Eunice and Kathryn blame *him*?

"We need to talk, Martin. Eunice wants to see you. Can you come for dinner? Tonight?"

Tonight? It is 7:40 P.M., Pfenning has been drinking for the past forty minutes. Slouched in front of TV news with the sound muted.

Pfenning asks Kathryn if she is sure that Eunice really wants to see him?

"Yes! I think so. I am sure. She says she misses you."

"Maybe I should speak with her, first?"—Pfenning dreads driving to the house, being turned away.

He has lost trust in his daughter. Screaming at him she never wanted to see him again, that look of hatred in her face.

He has lost trust in himself, as the Daddy. For commingled with the sense of loss, shame, loneliness has been a slow-mounting sense of relief. *No more Daddy.*

Nonetheless he has made it a point to call Kathryn every day. Sometimes twice a day. When Kathryn hasn't answered the phone, which has been most of the time, Pfenning has left polite messages. Always speaking calmly, not at all defensively.

She didn't notify authorities, didn't report him. At least, he thinks so.

In his messages he never challenged Eunice. He was not going to blame her for the false accusations: Eunice is a child, immature for her age, much in need of therapy. But he will not be the one to suggest this, Kathryn would fly into a rage.

He only allowed Kathryn to know how he felt: How surprised, stunned, alone, lost in his new living quarters in Bridgeton. How he misses his family. Has missed his family for months.

He feels no guilt for there is no reason for guilt; he feels sorrow, for there is reason for sorrow.

My heart is broken. Is that ridiculous, maudlin?

Or is he playing a role even now? Half-wishing that Kathryn would hang up the phone and release him.

Carefully he sets his half-filled wineglass on a table, waiting. He hears Kathryn's voice uplifted, calling upstairs to Eunice. He does not hear a reply.

After a full minute, or more: "Martin, hello? Are you still there?"

"Yes. Of course."

"Eunice says yes, she will come downstairs if you come here. We can have dinner together—she says. (She's been boycotting meals here, at least with me!) There was something at the school for Mr. Fox, Eunice had to miss. She hasn't been out of her room for two days. She's still coughing."

"Is she!"—Pfenning feels benumbed, he has heard these words or their equivalent before.

"Martin, we need to be patient with her, not angry. I know, you must be angry with us both, but—please don't blame Eunice, she's just a child."

Rebuked even slightly, Pfenning feels his face burn. And this too, familiar.

"Yes. Of course, you are right."

As a boy Pfenning recalls being told that the three most gratifying words in the English language are *You are right*.

"So, you're coming over? Now?"

"If you're sure . . ."

"Yes, I am sure! That's why I called you, Martin."

Even now, determined to appeal to Pfenning, Kathryn can't help being impatient with him. Summoned to the very house from which for the past eighteen days he has been cruelly evicted, the Daddy is now expected to be grateful, eager as a banished dog.

"I'll be there by eight o'clock."

Crazy kick in the heart of elation, hope. Decides not to finish the half-glass of wine.

In the bathroom, hurriedly rinsing his mouth, hoping that Kathryn won't detect the smell of wine on his breath.

Should he shave again, lightly? It has been more than twelve hours.

Confabulated. How much kinder a word than *lied*.

But of course it is the more accurate term. An utterance by someone not fully rational, guided/misguided by emotion; particularly, an utterance by a troubled child.

■

DRIVING TO WIELAND, TAKING care not to speed. Risky driving when he has been drinking.

Though Pfenning has never been picked up for speeding, nor has he ever been picked up for impaired driving.

It's a windy night in early December, moonless sky like cracked concrete. A smell in the air of the ocean not far away.

Thinking how ironic it is, this summons of Kathryn's has come too late.

For he has ceased loving them, he is sure. Ceased caring if they love him, or hate him.

That is freedom: the cessation, not of love, but of caring if there is love.

It was the morning after the catastrophic incident when Pfenning desperately needed Kathryn to call him, or to come to him. But she did not. In such circumstances even a rational man may think—*If I kill myself, she will be sorry.*

But he hadn't, so she wasn't. And so, he has ceased caring.

He survived by immersing himself in work at Bristol Myers Squibb. A project director is most productive when he has nowhere else to *be*, ten hours a day minimum.

For this, Pfenning drew praise from his division supervisor. Pfenning has even hinted that he is interested in being transferred to a larger corporate branch in White Plains, New York, provided there is a significant raise in salary along with a promotion.

For one who has lost his family, a consolation prize. But, still— a *prize*.

So long Pfenning has been the Daddy, he's defined himself by *wife, daughter* like a cloak in which to wrap himself. A signal sent to other men, especially older men—*You see, I am one of you. A man among men.*

Too young he stepped into the role like an inexperienced actor brashly stepping onto a stage, no idea where the script will take him.

And now, the script is being taken from him—forcibly.

Yet Pfenning is deeply grateful that Kathryn didn't have him arrested. She has not publicly humiliated him. (Yet.) A call to police, or a call to her attorney. A truly vindictive wife would have called Atlantic County Family Services, to report an abusive father. A wife bent upon destroying her husband utterly would call her family, his family. His employer.

Pfenning *is* trembling, his thoughts career so crazily. But there is no need for fear—is there? The estranged wife has invited the husband to dinner.

Feeling a glimmer of hope. Yet, Pfenning is ashamed of that hope.

Like a man so ravenous for food he will crawl on his hands and knees, eat from a bowl on the floor like a dog.

Recalling how Kathryn spoke of Eunice's teacher Francis Fox whom she'd met at one of the Parent-Teacher evenings. The admiration in her voice, her idealization of the man, amusing to Pfenning at first, later annoying. He'd resented this "Fox"—the intrusion into his life.

The disruption of his life. Somehow, Fox is to blame.

What particularly stung Pfenning was that Kathryn had been speaking of Francis Fox the way, years ago, when they'd first met, he'd overheard her speaking of him to mutual friends. *So kind, so thoughtful. So smart.*

He'd been thrilled that Kathryn had so admired him even as he'd felt that her estimation of him was exaggerated. A very attractive young woman, whom he'd known at a distance, who'd seemed aloof to him, wary of intimacy.

"Everyone I knew, my friends from high school—no one was a 'virgin' except me. And in college, of course. Like diving into water when you don't know how cold it is or how deep, I wasn't ready. I'm not sure if I'm ready now," Kathryn said, laughing breathlessly, "—but I'm going to *dive.*"

Pfenning had been immensely flattered. He hadn't been much more experienced than Kathryn, though she didn't know that.

Falling in love as in a mutual hypnosis. Delirium!

For what was love but a kind of rope you gripped. The promise was that you could tug this rope and it would haul you forward, it would not fall loose in your hands.

Planning to marry before they'd taken time to determine if they wanted children for each was reluctant to impose upon the other. Pfenning was one of a new generation of young men, exceedingly aware of women—women's rights. Determined not to make the mistakes of older male generations.

Yet, once Kathryn became pregnant, roles of *female, male* emerged irreversibly. Kathryn gave up her part-time work, Pfenning took on the patriarchal role of *provider*.

An older friend told Pfenning that once you have children you have your reason to live—"No more need for philosophizing."

At the time, he was grateful for this insight. A promise of a life to come suffused with meaning.

Now in the Village of Wieland which seems darker, less lighted, than Pfenning recalls. Approaching the house on Ashland Avenue from which he'd been exiled he feels a vertiginous sensation. If this were a late-night TV program, one of the true-crime programs he sometimes watches if he can't sleep, a solemn voice-over would identify this as *the house of the crime.*

■

"MARTIN, HELLO! COME *IN*."

Awkward moment as Kathryn hesitates before stepping forward to embrace Pfenning and Pfenning instinctively stiffens, not sure what to do with his hands.

Pfenning has been steeling himself for the sight of his daughter's pale freckled face which he has imagined obsessively and so he is both disappointed and relieved that Eunice isn't waiting for him with her mother, but is upstairs in her room. In a lowered voice Kathryn says: "She's worried that you might be angry with her, Martin. But she will come downstairs for dinner, she has promised."

"Well—good!"

Kathryn leads Pfenning into the living room as if he were a guest. She asks him if he would like a drink and Pfenning says quickly *No thank you.*

Possibly a test. Pfenning is determined to pass the test.

Together they sit on a sofa in the living room speaking quietly like conspirators. Pfenning glances about the familiar room thinking how unreal it seems to have become, like a poorly designed stage set.

And here he is, the Daddy back in his role, and his daughter's mother speaking to him in tones of regret without exactly apologizing.

". . . had to believe her, Martin. I mean—I could not *not* believe her, she was so upset."

"Of course. I understand." Pfenning feels an impulse to take his wife's hands, comfort her for having treated him so cruelly. Even if a child is uttering the most outrageous accusations a loving mother can't not believe the child.

Gratifying enough to Pfenning, that Kathryn seems to have decided to believe him instead of Eunice. Or to realize that Eunice was "confabulating."

But can he assume this? Matters in his family life have become so precarious now, Pfenning feels as if he is inching out onto thin ice that might shatter at any moment.

Kathryn reports to Pfenning that Francis Fox's classes are being taught by a substitute teacher named March who lacks his authority and charisma; this substitute can't hold the students' attention as he did. Students in Eunice's class claim to see Mr. Fox's "shadow" in the room. Girls have screamed and fainted, even boys have been upset. "'It was like the invisible man in the movie,' Eunice told me, 'you couldn't see anyone exactly but you could feel the air around him. And a kind of shadow moving on the wall.'"

Pfenning feels hairs stir at the nape of his neck. What on earth is Kathryn telling him—Fox has returned from the dead to *haunt* his classroom?

Pfenning asks if Eunice is frightened and Kathryn says not at all—"She just laughs. Our daughter doesn't believe in ghosts."

However, Eunice has been unwell. She has been missing classes. She has had stomach upsets, a sinus infection, headaches. Last Thursday she fainted in her English class, had to be taken to the ER in an ambulance, spent two nights in the Bridgeton hospital—the identical hospital in which another student of Francis Fox's, a seventh-grade girl, was hospitalized after a (rumored) attempt to commit suicide.

It turned out that Eunice was seriously dehydrated, her blood pressure was dangerously low. Unknown to Kathryn she'd been making herself vomit after meals and had lost eight pounds.

Pfenning tries not to react with indignation. Kathryn didn't tell him this though he's been calling her faithfully each day, leaving messages which she never answered.

Presumably she didn't want Pfenning at the hospital. No time for the Daddy.

"Did Eunice wonder why I wasn't there?"

"Martin, I don't know! It was a stressful time, I don't think she was much aware of her surroundings."

"I should have been at least notified, don't you think?"

"If her condition had been critical, yes of course. But it was mostly dehydration, the doctor said. And anemia. She'd been forcing herself to vomit, which can lacerate the esophagus. It was—as I said—a stressful time . . ."

Pfenning has been listening for footsteps overhead. Sounds of Eunice preparing to come downstairs. The palms of his hands are slick with sweat.

If his daughter accuses him again? If she looks at him with loathing—again?

Pfenning is tormented by the possibility that Eunice has deliberately prepared a scene in which he, the Daddy, will be rejected/humiliated again.

Mental illness, in that case. Not meanness, or malice, or punishing Daddy-who-has-abandoned-her.

Kathryn excuses herself, calls to Eunice upstairs. Pfenning waits in silence glancing uneasily about the room.

It *is* a familiar room. Yet, Pfenning could readily be convinced that he has never seen it before. On a table beside a taffy-colored leather chair, a color that strikes Pfenning as singularly unattractive, *his* books he'd been reading when with rude abruptness his wife informed him that it might be advisable for him to move out for a while . . .

Pfenning regards these books with curiosity. He has not given them a thought in months. Why did he think that closely reading, even annotating, *The Sixth Extinction, Why Nations Fail,* and *Thinking, Fast and Slow* could possibly have any significance in his life? Back issues of *The New Yorker, Harper's* as well.

What a luxury, to feel that there is some purpose to expanding your knowledge, consciousness. To feel a small thrill of adventure, settling back in your quiet household for an evening of *reading.*

For what is *reading* but the dissolution of the merely personal into the impersonal, a triumph of mental concentration.

Lately, Pfenning has scarcely been able to concentrate on TV news, let alone print. Let alone lengthy, fastidiously researched books. He has become morbidly fascinated by the investigation into the (mysterious) death of Francis Fox which seems in some gruesome way to run parallel to his own private unraveling.

Miserable as Pfenning is, Fox seems to have come to a worse end.

Kathryn returns, smiling uneasily. "Let me put dinner on the table, Martin. I'm sure that Eunice will join us. Vegetarian pasta—almost the only thing she will eat these days."

Vegetarian pasta! Pfenning is grateful that he had a late lunch.

". . . though she might be feeling that you don't want to see her."

"But why would I be here, Kathryn, if I don't want to see her? The fact that I am here, that I've come when you've summoned me, should suggest that I do want to see her—of course." Pfenning speaks patiently, without a glimmer of irony.

"Well—you know, Eunice is a *child.*"

"Not a *child,* a *young adolescent.* Thirteen is not three!"

"Martin, please. She might be listening. We both know that there are ways in which Eunice is mature for her age—and there are ways in which Eunice is immature."

Pfenning feels a stab of pain behind his eyes. A familiar pain for which the (partial) solution is a full glass of wine, in the privacy of his bachelor's quarters.

Pfenning tells Kathryn it was kind of her to invite him to dinner tonight but he thinks it is too stressful for them all. He doesn't think he can manage vegetarian pasta, his stomach is easily upset these days. He doesn't think he can manage an actual meal. He has adjusted to a quiet life, without drama. A life alone, concentrating on his work.

"'A life alone'—what do you mean?"

"'A life alone'—concentrating on my work."

As Kathryn stares at him in astonishment Pfenning tells her he is thinking of accepting an offer of a promotion and transfer to White Plains. Since it has been looking to him as if she wants a divorce . . .

"I've never suggested a divorce!"

"You said 'It's over, Martin. We never really loved each other.' You never explained exactly why, why at this time."

"But—I didn't mean that . . ."

"You certainly sounded sincere, Kathryn! Then you banished me from the house, you believed those outrageous things Eunice said about me. I've felt like a tightrope walker, I need to be nearer the ground. Returning here I will be on the high wire again, the slightest breeze could knock me off."

"But—we want you back. Eunice does!"

Pfenning laughs, weakly. Where *is* Eunice?

"You know it's been a terrible strain for her, these past few weeks. All of Fox's students have been affected. They are obsessed with him. They have prayer vigils at night in the residences. Some students don't even believe that he is actually dead, they think that someone else's body was in the ravine. Or, they are haunted by him—they 'see' his ghost. Some have tried to harm themselves like that poor girl Genevieve Chambers, they've had to drop out of school. Eunice has said she is sorry, she wants to tell *you*."

Pfenning hears the appeal in Kathryn's voice, the genuine hurt, surprise. His wife banished him as a pedophile, a child-molester and incestuous monster, he saw the loathing in her eyes, that seems to have supplanted in his memory the love he'd once seen, or imagined he saw; and now, Pfenning is supposed to forget that, as if it never happened.

He does love Kathryn but her vanity takes his breath away. She assumes that if she has changed her mind and feels differently now, Pfenning must feel differently, too.

If the (empowered) female beckons him, summons him, the (emasculated) male must come at her bidding.

"Kathryn, Eunice isn't ready to see me tonight. We'd better wait for another time."

Pfenning is on his feet, anxious to leave. He feels as if his head will split with pain.

"Oh no, Martin! Wait."

Kathryn tugs at his arm, leaning close. Pfenning hasn't been touched in such a way in a very long time and feels a sudden pang of sexual yearning.

Kathryn is looking strained, even haggard. Her eyes are rimmed with shadow as if, like Pfenning, she has endured sleepless nights. Yet, her lips have been darkened with lipstick. She has been regarding Pfenning with something like hope, expectation.

"Let me go speak with her, Martin! Please wait."

Kathryn hurries upstairs to confer with Eunice, returns to tell Pfenning that Eunice does want to speak with him on the phone. She can lift the receiver upstairs, he can lift the receiver downstairs.

Pfenning laughs sadly. A game! All right.

"It's a way for her to communicate, Martin. She won't have to risk leaving her room."

"I understand, Kathryn. It's an excellent compromise."

Pfenning is determined to be genial, good-natured. Soon, he will be free to retreat to his bachelor's quarters in Bridgeton.

Pfenning picks up the phone saying brightly, "Hello? Hi, there." As if he were speaking to a much younger child. "It's Daddy."

Even his voice is altered. The Daddy-voice reasserting itself.

At last, Eunice speaks in a near-inaudible voice, somewhat hoarsely.

"Daddy? I—I did a bad thing . . ."

"Well, honey. That's all right." Pfenning speaks encouragingly, but Eunice doesn't explain. "What did you do, Eunice?"

". . . told a bad lie about you."

Eunice's voice is so soft, Pfenning isn't sure that he has heard her.

"Did you! And why, Eunice?"

A lengthy pause. Pfenning can hear Eunice breathing against the phone receiver. A soft murmur that might have been *Don't know.*

Pfenning waits but Eunice seems to have nothing more to say. He has been gripping the cordless phone tightly.

"Maybe we can try to forget it, then? Should we try?" Pfenning says in the bright-Daddy voice. "Why don't you come downstairs? Mommy has made dinner for us."

At this, Eunice erupts unexpectedly saying, "Mommy *has not* made dinner. Mommy *bought dinner.*"

Eunice laughs shrilly, and hangs up the receiver.

Pfenning, feeling foolish, replaces the phone. A thin film of perspiration covers his body.

Kathryn asks if Eunice admitted that she'd made things up about him and Pfenning says *Yes.* She admitted she had lied.

"Did she say why?"

"No. She did not say why."

"Did she say she was sorry?"

Pfenning tries to recall. No, Eunice did not say she was sorry.

"I think so. Yes."

But now, the ordeal is over. Pfenning is impatient to leave. He has no wish to go upstairs as another father might have done under the circumstances and speak with his daughter, hug her, kiss her goodnight.

Never kiss Eunice again. Never that risk.

Never touch her.

Explaining to Kathryn, he really has an upset stomach; he is having tests next week; his internist thinks he might have gastric ulcers or colitis. (This is true.)

Kathryn looks genuinely disappointed, hurt. Pfenning hurriedly hugs her goodnight, doesn't kiss her; he is wondering if, if he'd tried to kiss her, Kathryn might push him stiffly away.

And what if they'd shared dinner, spent the evening and then the night together, Pfenning welcomed again in his old bed, and in the morning Kathryn accused him of harassment or worse.

Was it possible? Yes. If not probable.

In human relations, who can predict. How *wearisome,* to be obliged always to try to predict the behavior of others.

Kathryn follows Pfenning outside, telling him again how sorry she is. Pfenning assures her he understands, he will call her in the morning.

"Eunice *is* sorry, Martin. She has agreed to see a therapist, she has promised. I do wish you would stay a little longer, and have dinner with me . . ."

I have had dinner with you in the past. Many times. And see what came of that.

Pfenning climbs into his car, tremendously relieved. He will be back in his safe place in Bridgeton by eleven P.M. which is his favorite time for watching local TV news.

Tonight we have an update on the Wieland Police Department investigation into the allegedly accidental death of a Langhorne Academy middle-school teacher in October.

In his car, key in the ignition. At Eunice's second-floor window a small shadow-figure stands as if frozen in place as the Daddy pulls away from the curb.

Like Houdini, he is thinking. You're here, then you're gone.

"GOOD DADDY"

8–11 DECEMBER 2013

Except: in fact, the Daddy is not *gone*.

Next morning Kathryn calls Pfenning at his office to tell him in an agitated voice that a Wieland police detective wants her to bring Eunice to the police station for a short interview regarding Francis Fox, in Kathryn's presence; initially Kathryn refused, saying that Eunice's fragile physical condition made an interview impossible; but the detective assured her that it would be more like a conversation, not at all stressful, conducted by a female officer and guaranteed not to last more than ten minutes.

"I asked Eunice, certain that she would say no, but—she said yes, she would! But she wants 'Daddy' to come with us."

"Really! Eunice said yes?"

Pfenning is forever mystified by his daughter. He would have expected her to say no.

"So, will you come with us, Martin?"

"Of course. I wouldn't let you go alone."

Pfenning recalls, he has had a call from a Wieland police officer himself which he hasn't gotten around to answering.

He assumed the request has to do with Francis Fox. It is generally

known that Wieland police officers have been casting a wide net in
their investigation of the alleged accident, with an emphasis upon
certain of Fox's students and their parents; these are not interroga-
tions but casual interviews. No one is under suspicion of any crime,
no one is a "person of interest." But it's a ridiculous waste of time,
Pfenning thinks, for him to be interviewed about a man whom he
never met. Ridiculous too, for Eunice to be questioned.

Still, Pfenning will accompany his wife and daughter to the police
station. Wouldn't think of allowing them to go alone.

■

THE WIELAND POLICE DEPARTMENT shares a single-story brick building
with the Wieland Public Library; Pfenning has visited the library
often, the police department never.

There, in a small windowless room, as Pfenning and Kathryn look
on, a woman police officer of approximately Kathryn's age encourages
Eunice to speak of her English teacher Mr. Fox. For instance, the officer asks, in a friendly voice, did Mr. Fox ever ask her to come to his
office after class?—to which, eyes shyly downcast, Eunice shakes her
head *no*.

Did Mr. Fox ever ask anyone else to come to his office after class?

Eunice shakes her head *no*.

Did Eunice ever hear that Mr. Fox asked anyone to come to his
office after class?

Eunice shakes her head *no*.

Still smiling, though obviously disappointed, the officer asks if
any friends of hers told her that Mr. Fox had asked anyone to come to
his office, and again Eunice shakes her head *no*.

"Are you sure? Take your time, Eunice. There's no hurry about
answering."

"I don't have any friends. I told you—*no*."

Now Eunice is speaking more sharply, irritably.

Pfenning is wondering if what Eunice is saying can be true. He is
sure he heard from Kathryn that Eunice had several conferences
with Mr. Fox which were immensely helpful to her.

It's a feature of the Langhorne Academy, in fact, that teachers spend time with students individually. Yet, Eunice insists upon not acknowledging this.

Pfenning wonders what Kathryn is thinking, beside him. She too has been listening intently to the interview. Is Eunice lying, or is Eunice "confabulating"?

More likely, Pfenning thinks, Eunice is simply frightened. The police department setting is intimidating to her, the fact that a woman police officer is speaking to her. The fact that there is something problematic about her former English teacher, his life or his death, that requires investigation.

While at home Eunice exudes an air of willfulness and self-assertion that belies her age, size, status in the household, here at police headquarters she appears diminished and withdrawn. At home, her emotions determine the very atmosphere of the household; here, she is of no significance, a child among adults, a nonentity. Her small triangular face is waxy-pale, her mouth appears shrunken, eyelashes and brows nonexistent; she has lost weight recently and now more resembles a child of ten than a girl of thirteen.

"Is there anything about Mr. Fox that was special, Eunice? Just take your time, no hurry about answering."

To this question Eunice says, with surprising clarity, "Yes. Mr. Fox *is* special."

"'Mr. Fox is special'—how, Eunice?"

A subtle distinction, which Pfenning hears: Eunice has corrected *was* to *is*.

Still Eunice speaks softly, in her passively aggressive way, forcing the police officer to hunch forward to hear her, saying that Mr. Fox is the "most original" teacher she has ever had, who gives assignments that are "inspiring"—"He makes you work so hard you want to *die*. And you *do*."

"Really! That's very interesting, Eunice." The woman officer smiles perplexedly.

"He lets you 'revise' an assignment—to 'improve.'"

"Yes?"

"Special students, he gives special assignments to, to 'challenge' us."

It is strange, Eunice speaks with a kind of childish enthusiasm that seems, to Pfenning, uncharacteristic of her; as if she were emulating such enthusiasm, as another child might express it.

"He says for me to write with my 'nondominant' hand—that's my left hand. He says to use pastel crayons, charcoal sticks to draw the 'wordless.'"

Mr. Fox is just *the very most wonderful teacher.*

Mr. Fox *isn't really gone away like people think but is still— somewhere.*

Eunice's parents are surprised that she has brought with her, in a bookbag, her journal with the bright algae-green cover which she has refused to show them, and which she identifies as her *Mystery-Journal.* Proudly she opens the journal to show selected passages to the woman officer without allowing the woman to see the passages clearly.

"These poems I wrote, Mr. Fox marked with little red stars— meaning 'potentially excellent.'"

The woman squints dutifully at the journal, nodding as if impressed.

"Here—a quote from Henry David Thoreau—'God himself culminates in the present moment, and will never be more divine in the lapse of all the ages.' This means, Mr. Fox says, that you can always 'reinvent' yourself, there is always the time that is ahead."

Again, the woman nods, with a forced smile.

"Mr. Fox told me to 'lose yourself in nature'—you can't be found unless you are *lost.*"

Now that Eunice is speaking more volubly, and enthusiastically, the woman officer has clearly lost interest in the interview. Whatever she hoped to draw out of this eighth-grade student of the late Francis Fox, Eunice has failed to provide.

The woman thanks Eunice, and Eunice's parents, for taking time to come to the police station; she says something complimentary about Eunice's *Mystery-Journal,* and expresses admiration that Eunice is a poet; she gives the parents a number to call if Eunice remembers anything else that is "special" about Mr. Fox.

Also: both Kathryn and Martin Pfenning are advised to make arrangements at the front desk to return to the police department within the next several days, for brief interviews.

"But why?—I never even met Fox," Pfenning says irritably. "I don't know anything about him."

"I did meet Francis Fox," Kathryn says, guiltily, "—but I don't really know anything about him either. The poor man!"

On the drive home Pfenning regards his daughter through the rearview mirror above the dashboard. Eunice appears wan, shrunken. The enthusiasm she expressed for Francis Fox has seeped away like air out of a balloon. Sprawled in the back seat of the car, clutching her journal against her chest as if she is too weak even to peer into it.

Pfenning can't resist asking Eunice, in a casual way, not at all accusingly, if in fact she had conferences with Mr. Fox in his office? "Tutorial sessions"? Didn't she tell her mother about these at the time?

Kathryn reaches out to touch Pfenning's wrist, in rebuke. *Don't upset our daughter, she has been through so much.*

Kathryn's gesture is annoying to Pfenning, frankly. He is going to repeat the question which Eunice seems not to have heard, or is ignoring, but sees through the rearview mirror that Eunice's eyelids have shut, her mouth is slack, damp; she seems to have fallen into an exhausted sleep.

Kathryn whispers in Pfenning's ear: "Martin, for God's sake! Don't torment her."

■ ■ ■

FEELING ALMOST GIDDY. ADULT, responsible, hopeful, *good.*

Returning to Wieland police headquarters several days later, to be interviewed by a senior detective who introduces himself as H. Zwender. Pfenning checks himself thinking that H. Zwender is wearing the kind of clothes you'd expect to be on sale at JCPenney—the store's "upscale" clothing line for professional men which means a suit coat with boxy shoulders, loose-fitting in the torso, oddly shiny dark-brown plastic buttons like plastic eyes on a child's toy. Necktie dull-brown with a small pimply check. Nondescript white wash-and-wear shirt with too-short sleeves, cuffs out of sight.

Despite his prole attire the detective's manner is civil, congenial, even gentlemanly; his handshake is brisk, forthright. His face is curiously swollen, however, his left eye badly bruised. His hair is silvery-gray, close-cropped; on the left side of his part-shaved scalp is a luridly reddened patch, ugly black stitches at which Pfenning does not want to stare and which Zwender makes no effort to explain.

Their conversation will be brief, Zwender says. He knows that Pfenning is a busy man—"an executive at Squibb"—and does not want to inconvenience him.

(In retrospect, Pfenning will perceive that this innocuous remark is laced with malice. At the time, Pfenning takes the remark at face value.)

It will not be an interrogation, H. Zwender assures him, just an interview. Yes, it will be recorded. That is "routine." H. Zwender and his task force are investigating the death of Langhorne faculty member Francis Fox on or about October 25 in the vicinity of Wieland Pond, and the detective has a few questions to ask Pfenning, as the father of one of Fox's eighth-grade students.

At this Pfenning feels a frisson of excitement. He has been fascinated by accounts of the (mysterious) death of Francis Fox for weeks and here is a person—Detective H. Zwender—who is in possession of facts not available to the public.

He wonders if Zwender has been wounded *in the line of duty*. If the injury to his head was caused by a bullet grazing his skull. And his face pulpy; the left eyelid swollen almost shut.

Yet, the detective's manner is matter-of-fact, calm. Pfenning supposes this is deceptive, to put a civilian at his ease, to his disadvantage.

"Should I 'lawyer up,' Detective?"—Pfenning hears himself joking, inexplicably; as awkwardly as if he'd clapped Zwender on the back.

To Pfenning's relief H. Zwender chooses to ignore the feeble joke. He invites Pfenning to take a seat at a Formica-topped table, facing him; not in the small room in which Eunice was interviewed but in a larger and grimmer room, lacking windows, at the rear of which a heavyset young man with an impassive moon-face is sitting. Zwender introduces Officer Odom who will be participating in the interview and recording it.

Zwender begins the interview by asking Pfenning if he'd had the opportunity to meet Francis Fox, his daughter's English teacher, and Pfenning says, "No. I have not."

Zwender asks Pfenning if he'd had any contact or correspondence with Francis Fox, for instance email or phone calls, and Pfenning says, "No. I have not."

"No Parent-Teacher meetings, where Fox was present?"

"No. None."

"D'you mean, no Parent-Teacher meetings at all, or no Parent-Teacher meetings when Fox was present?"

"Both. That is—none."

"You haven't gone to a Parent-Teacher meeting at your daughter's school?"

"Not this year."

"But—last year?"

Pfenning tries to think. *Did* Kathryn talk him into attending last year, when Eunice was in seventh grade? He thinks not, has no memory of such a meeting.

(Kathryn called him that morning to tell him that her interview at police headquarters was very brief, lasting less than fifteen minutes. Pfenning wonders now if she told Zwender that Pfenning hadn't attended Parent-Teacher meetings with her—a trivial point, but one he doesn't want to get wrong.)

"I don't know what this has to do with Francis Fox, Detective. He wasn't on the faculty last year."

"But, you are in the habit of attending these meetings, Mr. Pfenning? Usually?"

"N-no. Not usually."

"So missing meetings where Francis Fox was attending was nothing unusual, you would say."

"Is that a question, Detective? I don't understand what it has to do with—Francis Fox."

Pfenning speaks forcefully. Zwender appears to back down, doesn't pursue the subject.

Pfenning has been studying the detective: a man of youthful middle age with flat-metallic eyes, thinning silvery-gray hair in a crew cut, a cordial manner; obviously, in clichéd speech, a seasoned veteran; a small-town police officer who has risen through small-town ranks to the highest post of senior detective, a puny sort of authority, Pfenning guesses, bringing with it a yearly salary that is a fraction of the salary Pfenning makes as a project director at Bristol Myers Squibb.

Judging from Zwender's nasal New Jersey accent, he's a local. Has to be demoralizing, a local from *here*.

Has to be demeaning to Zwender, encountering new residents in this part of New Jersey who have moved here as part of an executive class.

"Mr. Pfenning, did you ever meet with Francis Fox in his office at the school?"

"I told you—no. I've never met Francis Fox anywhere."

"You were never in his office at the school?"

"His office at the school? No. I have no idea where that is."

"But you've never been in it?"

"No. I told you—*I have not*."

Pfenning is becoming annoyed. Is this police strategy, to ask a simple question repeatedly, in the naïve hope that the interviewee will blunder and give a wrong answer?

Zwender asks if Pfenning has ever been inside Francis Fox's apartment on Consent Street, and Pfenning says, irritably, "No. I just told you, Detective. I've never met Francis Fox."

"And also, you've never been in his apartment? No?"

"No. I have never been in his apartment."

"Or in his car."

"In his car! Of course not."

"It isn't likely that prints of yours would be in Fox's apartment, or in his car, Mr. Pfenning?"—Zwender asks imperturbably, like a boy goading a snake with a stick, to see it react. "Or in his office at the school?"

"'Prints'? *Fingerprints*? What are you talking about?"

"You won't mind if we take your prints, then?"

"But—why? I've told you . . ."

"It's a routine procedure, Mr. Pfenning. Where there are many unidentified prints, we try to identify as many as we can."

"'Unidentified prints'—where? I've never been anywhere near Francis Fox."

"There won't be any prints of yours in Fox's office, or in his apartment, or in his car, then. So, there is nothing to be concerned about, Mr. Pfenning."

"But Francis Fox died in some kind of freak car accident, didn't he? Why are you asking all these questions?" He is feeling less assured now.

Zwender continues to scribble notes, with an imperturbable expression, as if he were unaware of Pfenning staring at him. In his eyes a metallic glint, and in the quills of his silvery hair as he leans forward, turning his left hand as he writes, in that curious posture in which left-handed persons write, as if in a mirror-parody of the writing of the right-handed.

Pfenning feels a sensation of cold. *This is a homicide investigation, not an accident investigation. It is a murder, and they are going to make you the murderer.*

Seeing that Pfenning is looking shaken Zwender assures him that the interview is "just routine"—he and his team are interviewing many people. They are looking into the circumstances of the death of Francis Fox but it is not a homicide investigation at the present time, and he, Martin Pfenning, is not a "person of interest."

Pfenning is so weak with relief, he could weep. Yet, he is utterly innocent of—anything! Ridiculous, to feel so grateful. So guilty.

Even if he wished Fox dead many times, he did nothing to make Fox dead. Dares not explain this to Zwender.

"Are you all right, Mr. Pfenning? Would you like to stop, for some water? Odom?"

Officer Odom, at the rear of the room, lurches to his feet with a grunt, goes next door to fetch a paper cup of lukewarm water, handing it carelessly to Pfenning.

Pfenning sips at the water, which is undrinkable. Sets it aside. Regarding Zwender warily as one might regard a coiled snake.

"Tell us what you've heard of Francis Fox? From your daughter, for instance."

Pfenning's mind is blank. A harsh wind has broken windowpanes, wind is howling through a house. What has happened? He has nothing to explain.

"What I've heard of Fox? He's a popular teacher, or was—it's said. Eunice didn't think so much of him initially, but lately, he'd given her good grades, he told my wife that Eunice had 'great potential.'"

"Did your daughter ever speak of Mr. Fox to you?"

"To tell the truth, I don't always listen. Kathryn listens. Eunice talks mostly to Kathryn, they have time for each other. I—I don't have that kind of time. My life is concentrated on my work."

"So your daughter didn't often speak of Mr. Fox to you?"

"No. Not much."

"Not much?"

Pfenning hesitates. How much does this terrible person know? Zwender has burrowed into an innocent man's life like an infected tick.

But Zwender can't possibly know how much Eunice has been speaking about Mr. Fox. Complaining bitterly about him, more recently praising him, obsessing over him. *In love with him.*

But that is ridiculous! Eunice is an immature child, incapable of anything like *love.*

Wondering if he should call a lawyer. (But why? There is no suspicion of murder and even if there were, Pfenning is not the murderer.)

Pfenning tells Zwender that, from what he has heard from his wife, Eunice had a more challenging time than usual this term; usually Eunice earns high grades and the praise of her teachers, but this was not the case with Francis Fox.

"But you didn't meet with Francis Fox, to discuss your daughter's grades?"

"N-no, I did not."

"Your wife did, but you did not?"

"I planned to. I had it on my calendar. The upcoming Parent-Teacher evening . . ."

"But you've said, you heard about your daughter's grades from your wife, not from your daughter. Why is that?"

"That—that is because—my wife and I have been separated . . . Since September, I don't live in Wieland any longer, in the house jointly owned by my wife and me, on Ashland Avenue, but by myself in a high-rise apartment in Bridgeton. We talk mostly on the phone— I call her. And mostly we talk about Eunice. My wife tells me about Eunice. I see Eunice mostly on weekends but we don't talk, exactly. We are together but—we don't talk. Not much. That—that is why, Detective."

At last, Pfenning has confessed. He and his wife, separated. A matter of shame, ignominy. But now relief: he can breathe more freely. He has not told anyone at his office. He's avoided this acknowledgment until now. For what relevance does it have? What connection with Francis Fox? None.

Hears himself saying bitterly, "Fox poisoned my marriage, and my family—my daughter. My life. He's like a parasite, he has burrowed into her brain . . ."

"'Burrowed into her brain'—? How?"

"My daughter is a changed person. He has got his claws into her somehow."

"How has she 'changed'? What was she like before?"

"'Before'—?"

"Before Fox."

Pfenning shakes his head, not sure how to respond. Eunice's behavior with him began to change when he left home, when Kathryn asked him to leave home, but when was that?

"Mr. Pfenning, the other day when one of our officers interviewed your daughter, with you and Mrs. Pfenning observing, your daughter said of Francis Fox that he is 'not really gone away like people think but is still—somewhere.' Is this something that Eunice has said to you personally?"

Pfenning laughs, annoyed. "Eunice says all sorts of things she doesn't mean, Detective. You can't take children seriously. I think she likes to confound people—adults."

"Though your daughter said this very clearly to our officer, she didn't mean it? She was—*lying*? Is that what you are claiming?"

Pfenning wipes his face with a tissue. His heart is beating rapidly, he is in the presence of an enemy.

"Detective, my daughter *does not lie*. She—sometimes—'confabulates.' She is thirteen years old, and very bright. She doesn't believe in ghosts!"

"Mr. Pfenning, we've been interviewing students from Fox's classes who have told us near-identical things. 'Mr. Fox is not really gone but in his classroom'—'In bright sunshine you can almost see him.' Mostly these are girls but there are a few boys, too. 'He's listening to us and laughing at us'—one boy said."

"They're just kids. They say all sorts of things they don't believe. They *want* to believe in ghosts . . ."

"Eunice says more or less the same thing but she *does not* believe?"

"Certainly not, Detective! If she were here right now, and I questioned her, she wouldn't say anything so silly."

"I was observing the interview through a monitor, Mr. Pfenning. It was my impression that your daughter was serious in what she said. Our officer reported that she was shivering—trembling."

"Eunice was probably laughing at the officer. She'd be laughing now, adults taking her so seriously. My daughter is the only student of Fox's *not* seeing his ghost, I'm sure."

"Just to reiterate, Mr. Pfenning: You never sought out Francis Fox to discuss your daughter's work in his class, you've said? Or—you *did* meet him?"

"I said *I did not* meet him."

"If we check your prints, Mr. Pfenning, they won't match any prints in Fox's office, or in Fox's apartment, or in Fox's car?"

"No!"

As Pfenning's exasperation mounts Zwender becomes calmer. No doubt, a strategy of police interrogation.

"Anything further you'd like to say about Francis Fox? Any rumors you'd heard?"

"No. I don't hear 'rumors' about my daughter's teachers."

"Anything passed on to you by other parents of Fox's students?"

"I don't know other parents of Fox's students. And I don't spread rumors. Sorry."

"And your wife? Did your wife mention anything unusual about Francis Fox?"

"You spoke with Kathryn yesterday, didn't you, Detective? She would have told you."

"But I'm asking you what your wife told *you*."

"Nothing. That I remember."

"Is it 'nothing'? Or—'nothing that you remember'?"

Pfenning shakes his head vehemently. God damn if he's going to repeat his wife's inane praise of Francis Fox, it's enough to make a man vomit. No more!

"How many times did Mrs. Pfenning meet with Francis Fox, d'you know?"

"Just once."

"That you know."

"*Just once*. I would know if—if it was more than once . . ."

Pfenning hears himself stammer. The way in which Detective Zwender contemplates him, flat zinc-eyes bemused, Pfenning has all he can do to keep from shouting in the man's face *Leave us alone, we had nothing to do with Francis Fox dying and dead.*

"And you don't remember anything that your wife said about meeting with Francis Fox. Not a thing?"

"Not a thing."

Pfenning guesses that, in her interview with Zwender, Kathryn reiterated the same ridiculous things she has always said of Francis Fox sounding like a woman besotted. And so, no. *He* is not going to repeat it.

Zwender switches to a new subject: is Pfenning familiar with Wieland Pond and the hiking trails there?

Hesitantly Pfenning says yes, he hikes there sometimes. But only on the shorter trails, near the pond and in the bird sanctuary.

"How often do you hike there, Mr. Pfenning?"

"Not often."

"That would be—?"

"Once or twice a month, on a weekend."

"So you're familiar with the area?"

"Not the area. Just the trails around the pond."

"Do you remember when you were hiking there last?"

"Yes. October 30."

"And why do you remember that date so clearly, Mr. Pfenning?"

"Because—Eunice and I were hiking there together, that day. It was the first time—and the last time. I mean, the most recent time."

"Just you and your daughter, and not your wife?"

"Yes. Just me and my daughter. Eunice had never made any special request to hike with me before, so it was flattering . . . She wanted to take pictures for a nature portfolio for one of her classes."

"Was there anything unusual about the occasion?"

"No. But it was special for us."

"In what way?"

Pfenning feels perspiration break out anew on his forehead, beneath his arms.

"As I said—Eunice had never asked me to take her hiking before. She hasn't cared for the outdoors, I'd always had to persuade her. Most children love outings like this but—not Eunice. Her mother can't get her to go out, either."

"Why is this, Mr. Pfenning?"

"Why are you asking me these banal questions, Detective? They can't possibly have anything to do with how Francis Fox died . . ."

"Did your daughter talk about Francis Fox on this hike?"

"No. She did not."

"Did *you* talk about Francis Fox?"

"No! Why would I talk about Francis Fox! I told you, I didn't know the man, I was sick and tired of hearing about the man. I had no idea that he was dead—I mean, I guess he was dead when we were hiking at the pond—and his body would be found out there—but when I heard, I can't say that I was sorry. This freak accident he had, driving over a cliff in the dark, I didn't give it much thought, I don't have time to obsess over local TV news."

"'Driving over a cliff in the dark'—is that what you think Fox did?"

"I don't know—I guess I read that. Isn't that right?"

"Do you know where Fox's car was found?"

"N-no . . . I don't think I know where that would have been. I don't know the area all that well."

"Where exactly were you hiking with your daughter?"

"In the Jorgen Bird Sanctuary. Circling the pond."

"And you didn't hike anywhere else that day, with your daughter or alone?"

"No. I did not."

"Did you hike along the service trail that leads to the ravine? In that hilly area?"

"Where the car was found? No. I did not. I don't really know where that is . . ."

"Are you a serious hiker? D'you hike in the Pine Barrens?"

"I don't really 'hike'—I don't wear hiking boots. I have hiking shoes, that are waterproof. But I don't do strenuous hiking. For one thing I wouldn't hike anywhere dangerous by myself, and I don't have anyone to hike with. Walking around the pond is as much as I did with Eunice, and that isn't really 'hiking.' Just—walking."

"And you stayed on that trail, both of you?"

"Yes. We stayed on that trail."

"You didn't wander off, alone. And you were wearing only hiking shoes."

"Yes."

"Not boots, like the kind you lace up. Just shoes."

"Just shoes, but waterproof."

"You won't mind, then, if we take a look at these shoes?"

"My—hiking shoes?"

"Any shoes or boots you've worn, hiking at Wieland Pond. One of our staff can accompany you after this interview, to pick them up at your home and save you the trouble of bringing them in."

Pfenning feels a wave of sheer exhaustion, as if he has been hiking uphill.

Has he said *Yes* to this outrageous request? Zwender seems satisfied with his response, scribbling in his notebook.

In an affable voice Zwender continues: "You said you'd never had contact with Francis Fox, Mr. Pfenning?"

"That's right. Yes."

"No emails, calls?"

"I said—*no.*"

"Yet—you are a subscriber to a website called *Sleeping Beauties?*"

"'*Sleeping Beauties*'—what is that?"

"A website. 'Adult content.' 'Dark Web.' Aren't you a subscriber?"

A sensation of heat comes over Pfenning's face. For a moment, his heart ceases to beat.

"I—I don't think so. No."

"*Sleeping Beauties 2013.* You are not a subscriber?"

"N-no. I am not."

"Could anyone else be a subscriber to this website, under your email address?"

"Which email address is that?"

"I—I don't know. I will have to check . . ."

Pfenning's heart has begun beating again, a jolting little motor. Now a trickle of sweat runs down his left temple, like a burst artery.

"Are you aware, Mr. Pfenning, that this website contains child pornography which is illegal in New Jersey? Possession of child pornography is in violation of a New Jersey statute and constitutes a felony."

"I—don't know anything about that, Detective. I . . ."

"The law forbids 'possessing, viewing, or having in your control' child pornography, and child pornography includes 'anything that depicts a child involved in a sexual act or in the simulation of such an act.'"

Through a roaring in his ears Pfenning hears these words at a distance. He has the impression that the heavyset young police officer behind him is staring at him with an expression of utter loathing.

Still in his affable voice Zwender adds: "Are you aware, Mr. Pfenning, that until the time of his death on or near October 25 of this year, this website was maintained by Francis Fox?"

"This—what? Which website?"

"*Sleeping Beauties 2013.*"

"I—I don't know what that is . . ."

"Have you let your subscription lapse? Maybe you're not a subscriber right now."

"I—am not . . ."

"You didn't know, had no idea, that Francis Fox was the proprietor of the website called *Sleeping Beauties 2013*?—to which someone with your email address subscribed?"

Francis Fox! Pfenning shakes his head, stunned into silence.

"Sometimes people download pornography onto their computers by mistake, Mr. Pfenning. They click on a link, they have no idea what it is, then they are curious, and maybe then they forget all about it, but it remains in their computer. Is this a possibility?"

"I—I would have to check my computer . . ."

"D'you know, Mr. Pfenning, we can get a warrant to seize your home computer? Not that we intend to, at the present time. Our task force is investigating the death of Francis Fox and not child pornography in New Jersey."

To this, Pfenning makes no reply. Staring at his hands.

Zwender has shut his folder, and has put away his notepad. The interview seems to have concluded.

In a cordial voice Zwender thanks Pfenning for taking time to speak with him. He tells Pfenning that there is a chance he might want to speak with him again, and instructs Officer Odom to escort him out.

The sulky-faced young police officer heaves himself to his feet and leads Pfenning out of a warren of rooms, that pass like a blur before Pfenning's eyes. Almost, Pfenning doesn't know where he is. Phone ringing, voices? Is he under arrest? Weirdly, he sees that Officer Odom's face resembles the fattish-bloated face of Elvis Presley in the final years of Presley's life; his manner is aloof, contemptuous, as if he can't bring himself to look at Pfenning. For a man of his weight and girth he moves quickly.

Pfenning is hoping that Officer Odom has forgotten the fingerprinting even as Odom says curtly: "Prints. Through here."

Pfenning finds himself in another windowless room. Sobbing in rage.

"But I was never in Fox's apartment! Or in his God-damned car! Why are you fingerprinting me! You are harassing me, I'm going to file a complaint!"

Placidly Officer Odom says: "Then there's nothing for you to worry about, is there, Mr. Penny."

"A WRONG KEY"

11 DECEMBER 2013

"That asshole—Pfenning. Couldn't kill anybody if his life depended on it."

Sucking on a bottle of Coke the way a baby sucks on a bottle of formula Daryl Odom makes this observation with a contemptuous chuckle.

"You had him sweating like a hog, man."

At his computer typing up this afternoon's notes H. Zwender seems not to hear the crude compliment from the junior officer though it is rare that the junior officer compliments anyone let alone the senior detective to whom he is obscurely related. An unexpected moment of tender reconciliation between the two which the elder doesn't deign to acknowledge.

"You had him shitting his pants, man! Motherfucker-pedophile."

Odom tosses the emptied Coke bottle noisily into a wastebasket.

"*I* told you the asshole was a waste of time. 'Bristol Myers Squibb.' Frog-faced kid of his, she's no *kitten*. Fox wouldn't look twice at her."

To this outburst of sheer contempt, not altogether typical of the usually lethargic Officer Odom, Zwender responds with a vague assent. Anything related to new tech / pharmaceutical executives like those working for Bristol Myers Squibb evokes local calumny, a kind of choked rage among longtime Atlantic County residents. Still, not typical of Daryl Odom.

In this instance Zwender does not disagree with Odom which is not synonymous with agreeing with Odom. On principle, the two are adversaries: if one makes an overture to agree, or to seem to agree with the other, that other holds back, suspecting entrapment.

"Had to laugh, the look on Pfenning's face when you brought up the kiddie porn. Made my day."

Still, Zwender doesn't glance around. Zwender is preoccupied typing on the keyboard with just two or three fingers, cursing under his breath when he mistypes. Odom, who types rapidly on his cell phone with just his thick thumbs, regards the elder detective's efforts in bemused silence.

"Still, it *was* a waste of time, right? Like you could see, the daughter's not Fox's type, no motive." Odom pauses as if considering whether he should say more. Such pauses in Odom's riffs invariably signal a risky remark, guaranteed to provoke H. Zwender. But he continues:

"At least he didn't try to kill you like that other asshole."

Zwender's heart stops. A pause, and begins beating again, jolting-hard.

Continues with his typing. Not about to allow Odom to know how Odom's remark grates against his nerves like a fork's tines over his brain.

God damn Zwender is *pissed*. Wishes he never had to see/hear Daryl Odom again in his life.

For never will Odom let Zwender forget how he, Odom, saved H. Zwender from being murdered in this very building. *In* police headquarters. At least once a day Odom alludes to the incident in some elliptical, casual way.

So swiftly Blake Healy attacked Zwender, with no warning—even now, a week later, Zwender cannot fully recall what happened. An infuriated man with glaring protuberant eyes shoved the senior detective against a wall at the very end of an interview, an interviewee not under arrest, in fact thanked for his time, released, free to walk out of the police station yet suddenly enraged, crouched over the dazed man as he lay half-conscious half-beneath the table with the apparent intention of smashing his head against the wall—except that in a swift move or two Odom overpowered Healy and knocked him to the floor.

Healy: (estimated) six feet two, two hundred thirty pounds. Odom: (estimated) five feet nine, two hundred thirty pounds.

Most of what Zwender knows of the assault, he's been told by others. Repeatedly the name *Odom* is uttered.

Jesus! D'you know what happened?

Odom saved Zwender's life?

Daryl Odom—Zwender?

No one had seen heavyset sulky-mouthed Officer Daryl Odom, new at the Wieland PD, in any mode that might be called *active, aggressive.* Until this.

A kind of glow about Odom these days. Preening, self-conscious, vain. Even as his Coke habit is accelerating, Zwender has counted at least three bottles tossed noisily into the trash this morning.

H. Zwender is too proud to protest, he was conscious during the attack. He wasn't unconscious for a moment. Taken totally by surprise, otherwise he could have subdued Blake Healy by himself.

In other circumstances, an enraged civilian lunging at him with extreme force, Zwender would have killed *him.* Justified shooting, in close range. If he'd been carrying his weapon, and if he could have gotten to it in time.

But no: maybe not. Killing a local man, however much he may have provoked it, is never a good idea. Killing Blake Healy would be tearing a family apart—Healy is still married, his kids probably love him. The sad runaway daughter probably loves him. Killing anybody local—fucks up the relatives. The community.

Law enforcement is for the protection of the community. Not the individual, the community.

As it is, Healy is being held in the Atlantic County Detention Facility for Men at Red Wing. Aggravated assault against a law enforcement officer, held in lieu of $50,000 bail bond.

With his prison record, Healy will be incarcerated for years. You don't get a slap on the wrist for assaulting a police officer with intent to kill.

Ironically, Healy will probably be incarcerated for longer than he would have been if he'd killed Francis Fox with a plea of manslaughter or self-defense.

Zwender was in the Bridgeton hospital only overnight, his injuries were minor. He was discharged the next morning, head partially/grotesquely shaved, the wound in his scalp secured by black stitches that resemble a half-dozen black spiders spliced together in a row. An MRI revealed he'd had only a mild concussion, nowhere near *killed*.

Dozens of times a day the detective's fingers cannot resist touching, stroking the spider-stitches in his scalp. Like Braille, a secret code he is trying to read, to absorb.

The ideal detective is invisible—no distinctive features, not-memorable presence, even his voice should be low-key, comforting. The intention is to draw out others, allow others to speak, self-incriminate. But now, head half-shaved, row of ugly stitches in his scalp, H. Zwender is too visible.

Sure, he can wear a hat outdoors. But not indoors: he's a gentleman.

Fat-faced Odom, running his mouth again. Condescending to his superior officer. Pitying him—*him*! Not just that Zwender was wrong about Blake Healy, naïvely expecting a confession from the man where the man had no confession to make, he made the elementary mistake rookies are warned against: lowered his guard in the presence of a hostile civilian. He failed to read cues, signals. He (unwittingly) *provoked*.

Allowed himself to be assaulted, overpowered. Authority wrested from him.

Winding up on the *floor*. Bleeding like the proverbial stuck pig.

It is true, Zwender *might* have been killed in police headquarters, a scandal which the small-town Wieland PD would never live down.

Before his eyes the computer screen has darkened. "What did I do wrong?"—Zwender cries.

Daryl Odom comes to stand behind Zwender leaning over his shoulder peering at the screen. With an inspired stroking of keys Odom restores brightness to the screen like sunshine emerging from clouds.

"You touched a wrong key, Horace. I got it."

■

MORE THAN FORTY DAYS since Fox's remains were discovered in the ravine. More than forty days, an investigation moving with glacial slowness, task force headed by H. Zwender, Senior Detective. Sick-sinking sensation of shame, exacerbated by headaches and blurry vision, it is the girl-victims, the *kittens* he must rescue before it is too late.

The detective is deeply unhappy with himself.

Yet: the detective is one who harbors *hope*.

"LITTLE KITTEN"

A t last! After many rebuffs Detective H. Zwender is summoned to the Chambers household to interview twelve-year-old Genevieve Chambers.

Not in a stark-white Wieland police cruiser (which would draw unwanted attention) but in his own ordinary-civilian vehicle Zwender drives to the house at 293 Church Street in one of the older residential neighborhoods in the historic Village of Wieland.

Parking his vehicle in front of the Chambers house. A light snowfall early that morning, melting in midmorning sun. Steeling himself to finally see *her*.

This girl—"Little Kitten."

He has seen in the most intimate of ways.

He has seen tongue-kissed, fondled, sexually abused. Up close.

And Little Kitten has never once seen him. *Knows nothing of* him.

Set back from Church Street, in an elegantly landscaped three-acre lot of tall maples, ashes, and evergreens, the Chambers house is an eighteenth-century white-clapboard Colonial that has been renovated and expanded over many decades; according to county records the price of the property at its most recent sale, in 2002, to Melissa and David Chambers, was nine hundred ninety thousand dollars.

In the driveway is a new-model BMW. Most likely belongs to Genevieve Chambers's mother who retains her married name, Melissa Chambers, though she has been divorced for more than a year from David Chambers, Genevieve's father, living now, remarried, in La Jolla, California.

As the father of an abused girl Chambers would be a plausible suspect in the abuser's murder except he was in La Jolla with his new family, working as a financial consultant for AT&T, in the last week of October when Francis Fox was murdered. Apart from a visit to see his daughter in the hospital in early November Chambers hasn't returned to Wieland for over a year. Zwender has investigated, to his disappointment Chambers has a "perfect alibi."

Evidently Chambers is unaware of the abuse of his daughter by her English teacher. As the girl's mother seems to be unaware.

H. Zwender is well acquainted with victims of crimes, and relatives of crime victims, who rigorously deny that any crime has been committed. Genevieve Chambers has never accused Francis Fox of having abused her and can only explain slashing her wrists by saying she's felt "sad" and "lost" since Fox's death.

These few facts, Zwender has gathered from various sources including Bridgeton hospital authorities. His brief conversations with Melissa Chambers have been frustrating, and not very helpful.

Still, Zwender is resolute: it isn't his role as a law enforcement officer to force the clueless mother, still less the abused daughter, into acknowledging Francis Fox's abuse; it would be cruel on his part, and would serve no practical purpose, since the pedophile-predator Fox is no longer living, and his pornographic website has vanished from the Internet; and Genevieve is reputedly "in therapy."

The point of the Wieland police investigation is to identify whoever is responsible for Fox's death. It is not relevant that Francis Fox may have deserved to be punished; it is relevant to the well-being of the community, that a murderer in its midst be exposed.

Since early November Zwender and his task force team have been interviewing Francis Fox's students—*all* of Fox's students, in order not to appear to be singling out those relatively few girls who might have drawn Fox's attention and were marked with asterisks in Fox's grade book. It would be scandalous if only the most attractive girls were interviewed by Wieland police officers. And so, they have been interviewing boys as well as girls, and girls who would not have qualified as *kittens.*

As serial killers are drawn to a similar type of victim, so the pedophile Fox was obviously drawn to a distinct type of victim: slender, petite, pale-skinned, with delicate doll-like features, inclined to passivity, trust. The dreamy girls in the Balthus paintings—(Zwender has researched the French-Polish painter, the very epitome of European decadence!)—wan, with sleepy eyelids, incapable of pushing away an ardent predator-lover.

Among the forty-eight students in Fox's four classes no more than six were marked in Fox's grade book and of these only Genevieve Chambers has definitely been identified by the detective. (Daryl Odom believes that there are two or three other Langhorne girl-students whose teasingly pixelated *Sleeping Beauty* faces he is determined to identify.)

Fortunately, the Langhorne Academy has cooperated in providing photographs of Fox's students to be compared with the disguised images on the website. Headmistress P. Cady has been true to her word.

Perusing *Sleeping Beauties 2013* has been an arduous and exhausting activity not unlike wading through pungent-smelling muck; frequently, Zwender has felt sick to his stomach. He tells himself that he has as much interest in pedophilia as a carnivore would have in vegetarian foods, definitely *he is not* inclined to find slight-bodied prepubescent girls sexually attractive.

(Of his own sexuality, H. Zwender is not inclined to think. In recent years he has become one of those male persons contemptuously called, in contemporary slang—*incel.*)

Sleeping Beauties 2013 is mistitled, however, since there appear to be lurid photographs and videos on the website that predate Fox's arrival in Wieland. A number of the postings are not set in Fox's office in Haven Hall but in other offices, presumably at other schools. The chronology is jumbled, as if the predator hoped to protect himself in a labyrinthine maze, always a little ahead of his pursuers, eluding their grim efforts to locate him.

Some features recur, no matter the setting: colorful fruit tarts, fed piecemeal to willing *kittens*. A flash of the black onyx ring on the predator's finger, blurred backgrounds of glossy posters on walls, shelves of books.

True to his scavenger nature Fox seems to have appropriated material from kindred child-pornography sites, including sites involving girls who are clearly foreign; these are of a type cruder and more graphic than his own more tenderly observed *kittens*. Alarming videos in which young girls are seen cutting themselves—forearms, breasts, bellies, thighs—with razors or knives; in some cases, male hands are visible, wielding the instruments. Truly alarming, to have seen close-ups of Genevieve Chambers's scarred and wounded body, in selfies taken evidently by the girl herself and sent to Francis Fox.

Disgusting images, that have kept Zwender awake through entire nights.

Awake, *aroused*. Not happy with himself.

Of the two, it is Officer Odom who has been most grimly obsessed with the prurient material, scrolling through *Sleeping Beauties* in a kind of trance, intent upon identifying as many Langhorne girl-students as he can. For only in this way can he and Zwender locate the (male) relative who might have murdered Francis Fox, and investigate him: it will come through the identity of an abused girl.

Zwender has noticed that even after his shift has ended Odom often remains hunched at his computer, eyes fixed to the screen in glassy incredulity. His clammy-pale face is slick with sweat, his lips draw back from his teeth in a grimace of revulsion. He sighs often. He scratches his neck, his armpits, a difficult-to-reach place on his lower back, with a kind of violence; there is always a bottle of Coke within reach. Odom's task is comparing images of onscreen *kittens* to photographs of Langhorne middle-school girls: *kittens* in seductive poses, and stages of undress; middle-school girls smiling hopefully for their school picture, mere children. Odom seems to have branched out beyond the six asterisked girls in Fox's grade book to consider more possibilities.

Zwender wonders if his young assistant is becoming addicted to child pornography as one might come to be addicted to a narcotic ingested without pleasure, without satisfaction, involuntarily, the very molecules of one's being changed irrevocably in the process.

Half-jokingly Odom has remarked to Zwender that his wife (who knows nothing about his police work) is concerned for him: even when he's at home he's in "some other world" where she can't reach him.

Feels like, to him, he's making his way through garbage, filth. Has to wash and wash, scrub his hands, can't get clean.

Some nights, he can feel the Devil tugging at his ankle, to drag him down to Hell.

Zwender is bemused at such speech. Zwender is a bit discomfited.

"D'you believe in Hell, Odom?"

"Do I *believe* in Hell?—doesn't make any difference if I do, or if I don't. Hell is still there."

"It is? Where, exactly?"

"Might be in our souls," Odom says seriously, "—or, might be an actual place."

"Like Heaven?"

"Like Heaven."

Zwender has always been aware, Daryl Odom takes religion seriously. It's the one thing you can't joke about with him.

Between the two is the largely unspoken assumption that Odom, married at nineteen, a father to three young children at twenty-eight, an evangelical Christian from rural Cumberland County, is the *norm;* while H. Zwender, thirty years older, long-divorced, living alone, with adult children of whom he rarely speaks, long lapsed from any kind of Christianity, is *odd, aberrant, abnormal.*

Zwender is amused by this, but also annoyed. There is something smug and condescending about someone who is certain that he is saved and you are not.

That Daryl Odom is *saved,* means he has a *savior.* Which Zwender lacks.

Also, Odom is from a sprawling Cumberland County family of police officers, sheriff's deputies, corrections officers, bailiffs. Zwender was the first in his family to go into law enforcement, unable to afford law school; at the back of his mind is the conviction that he has missed his true calling.

He's sorry, though not entirely sorry, to have to disappoint Odom: turns out, he's going alone to interview the Chambers girl.

(Odom *is* disappointed. A look in his eyes of surprise, hurt. Like a dog realizing you are driving off without him and there's not a damn thing he can do about it.)

Zwender explains: The girl's mother doesn't want more than one cop in her house. She doesn't want Zwender to stay for more than ten or fifteen minutes and he can't make any recording, just take notes.

Anyway, why'd Odom want to meet *Little Kitten* after what he's been seeing of her online? All that garbage, filth? He's a married man, a Christian. Father of young kids. *Lead us not into temptation.*

"With me it's different, I'm going to Hell anyway."

■ ■ ■

PRECISELY FIVE P.M. HE'S expected at 293 Church Street.

Rings the doorbell, briefcase in hand. Likes to think that in his dark gabardine suit, long-sleeved white shirt, innocuous dark-striped necktie and carrying a well-worn leather briefcase with tarnished initials *HPZ* he more resembles a lawyer, accountant, high-school teacher than a plainclothes detective.

(But it's his detective's shrewd eye that has discerned a movement at one of the first-floor windows: a woman's face hovering behind a filmy curtain.)

(Which Zwender doesn't acknowledge. Of course.)

First surprise, a housekeeper answers the stately slate-colored door. Knows who he is, calls him *Detective.*

Second surprise, the housekeeper instructs him *Please remove your shoes.*

Zwender is unprepared for such a greeting. *Remove his shoes?*

"Mrs. Chambers doesn't want wet leaves and dirt tracked into the house . . ."

The housekeeper is apologetic. Embarrassed.

A brown-skinned woman, barely comes to Zwender's shoulder, possibly Filipino, nervous in the presence of a law enforcement officer. Forced by her employer to ask him to remove his shoes and so making a gesture to kneel and remove his shoes for him but Zwender quickly assures her, "It's OK, ma'am. No problem."

He's more embarrassed than angry. Hot-faced stooping to remove his shoes as the diminutive housekeeper looks on with equal unease.

Reminding himself: he's here in this house only because Mrs. Chambers has granted him a visit. He's not here with a warrant. Has to be practical-minded, grateful.

In a foyer with an absurdly high ceiling and a gleaming-white tile floor. To his right is a living room with an ornately patterned rug on the floor, Asian or Middle Eastern, exotically beautiful, no reasonable person would want to track wet leaves and mud onto such a rug.

"Detective Zwender? Hello!"—Mrs. Chambers comes forward quickly to greet him. Staring at the black stitches in his scalp.

Damned if Zwender is going to explain the stitches. In stocking feet he is made to feel diminished, less manly.

Mrs. Chambers is a woman in her early forties, stylishly dressed, with blond-streaked razor-cut hair, overbright eyes. Extending a beringed hand to Zwender—"Hello! Detective Zwender? I'm Melissa Chambers, we spoke on the phone . . ."

Like her housekeeper Melissa Chambers is uneasy in Zwender's presence. He's a tall man, exudes an air of just barely restrained impatience, hard ridge of bone above his eyes, and now the God-damned stitches in his marine-cut hair, all the more need to smile, smile hard, a grave smile to signal to nervous persons like Melissa Chambers that he is *no threat.*

Even as he smiles at Mrs. Chambers perceiving coolly that here is a woman once beautiful; once accustomed to the authority of beauty; retaining still the vanity of beauty even as beauty itself has faded.

A divorced woman, who contested the divorce from her husband initially. From court records Zwender knows that the divorce between Melissa Chambers and David Chambers was particularly acrimonious, dragging on for more than a year.

Formerly a wife and mother, now (merely) a mother. And one of her children, a twelve-year-old girl who has attempted suicide.

Most strategic way to relate to a woman like Melissa Chambers is to allow her to think that he thinks she is attractive, as a woman: sexually desirable. But only in the short run. In the longer run, not a good idea. Not professional. Zwender will remain neutral, asexual.

Chattering nervously Mrs. Chambers leads Zwender through the spacious living room into an adjacent, smaller room with part-drawn blinds where a young girl is lying on a couch beneath a quilt. There is a TV on, fortunately muted; no one seems to be watching its antic screen. The girl's expression is vacant, vacuous; her eyes are heavy-lidded, as if she has just wakened; she looks much younger than twelve and not at all ethereally beautiful as in *Sleeping Beauties*.

This girl—*Little Kitten*?

In stocking feet Zwender stands stunned, staring. It will take him a beat or two to adjust.

In life, the twelve-year-old fetishized as *Little Kitten* online is not exotically pale but sallow-skinned. She is not seductively languorous but listless, enervated. The (luscious) mouth swollen from being kissed hard and long in *Sleeping Beauties* is merely thin-lipped, slack.

Fox has sucked her dry, discarded her. She is nothing now.

"My daughter—Genevieve. She can only talk to you for a few minutes, Detective . . ."

Zwender recovers from his surprise to introduce himself in a kindly-father voice to Genevieve Chambers who barely acknowledges him. Lifting her lusterless eyes only halfway to his face, as if the effort is too much for her.

Zwender has been steeling himself for the girl to stare at the stitches in his scalp so he is spared that, at least. Genevieve Chambers's lethargic manner suggests that she is heavily sedated, no doubt with a battery of prescription drugs.

Her scarred arms are hidden by long loose sleeves. At the base of her neck there is a flesh-colored bandage measuring about two inches by three inches, presumably she slashed herself there as well with a razor or a knife.

Mrs. Chambers cheerfully urges her daughter to *wake up*! She has a *visitor*! A detective from the Wieland police wants to talk to her for just a few minutes . . .

Zwender wonders how Mrs. Chambers has explained him to Genevieve. He told Mrs. Chambers he has several questions to ask Genevieve relating to the investigation into Francis Fox's death, leading Mrs. Chambers to assume that this meant the "accidental" vehicular death in the ravine; but the questions he has prepared to ask Genevieve have little to do with the ravine, or with "accident."

"Genevieve? Can you try to sit up a little? Let me turn off this silly TV . . ."

Genevieve makes no effort to sit up. Beside her on the sofa are several school textbooks and on her lap is a journal with a rose-marbled cover, which looks familiar to Zwender.

Covering Genevieve's legs is a gaily colored children's quilt with the faces of grinning cartoon animals: giraffe, panda, monkey, tiger. Startlingly white bare toes peek out from beneath the quilt in continuous twitchy movement even as Genevieve herself appears listless, indifferent; Zwender is distracted by these toes, which also remind him of something he can't quite recall.

Briefcase in his lap Zwender sits facing Genevieve; Mrs. Chambers hovers nearby too restless to be seated.

"May I serve you some coffee, Detective?"

"Thanks, but no."

"It won't take Irma any time to prepare some . . ."

"Really, ma'am. No thank you."

"I've just discovered this Sumatra dark roast, I have it delivered to the house . . ."

Zwender shakes his head, confounded. *No.*

He has less than fifteen minutes here! He knows, fretful Mrs. Chambers will take up as much of his time as she can.

Zwender begins by asking Genevieve nonthreatening questions about the Langhorne Academy: how long has she been a student at the school, how well does she like it? Genevieve answers in monosyllables even as Mrs. Chambers heartily amends:

"Genevieve *loves* the Langhorne school! She has made so many friends there. She's returning next month for the spring term . . ."

Urged by her mother Genevieve dutifully tells Zwender about her special reading list, how she is keeping up with assignments from her teachers. She is exempt from tests and examinations but she is writing book reports, one a week.

"Because if I take a test, I will fail. And that will make me more *depressed*."

Genevieve giggles. Little white toes peek out from beneath the quilt like mischievous mice.

Mrs. Chambers says, with an air of reproach directed at Genevieve, "It's been so *wonderful,* Genevieve's teachers have all been so *understanding*."

Zwender is accustomed to allowing others to talk. The more they talk, the more they reveal. And when chatter fails them, their eyes will reveal much to the shrewd detective.

In this instance, however, Zwender isn't sure that the strategy will yield much value. What he is searching for is elusive, even to himself. A way into the labyrinth, a route *in*—away from the distracting surfaces of mere contingency.

Only through *Little Kitten* can he reach Francis Fox: and only through Francis Fox, the individual who killed him.

Leaning forward solemnly, keen to hear Genevieve Chambers's small flat toneless voice though little she says is of genuine interest to him.

Mrs. Chambers tells Zwender that Genevieve is *in therapy*. Since the hospital, she has acquired a *wonderful therapist* whom she sees three times a week.

Also, a *physical therapist*. For since the hospital she has had problems with balance, and hand-eye coordination, and is out of breath quickly.

Genevieve smirks, ignoring her mother. She has found something to show to Zwender: a paperback children's book, *A Girl of the Limberlost*—"This is my favorite book now. Mr. Fox gave it to me."

Quietly daringly Genevieve has pronounced the name—*Mr. Fox*. Reverently pronouncing—*Mis-ter Fox*.

Mrs. Chambers is taken by surprise, it seems. For a moment silenced, staring at her daughter who conspicuously ignores her.

Then, Mrs. Chambers smiles happily—giddily. Telling Zwender that *A Girl of the Limberlost* was her favorite novel too, when she was Genevieve's age—"Though the mother in the novel is a terrible hateful person . . ."

Zwender peers at the book cover, which depicts an attractive tomboy-type girl in a long-ago rural-America setting. "Both my daughters loved this, too," says Zwender with a reminiscent smile, "—but I've never read it."

In fact, Zwender has never heard of *A Girl of the Limberlost* by Gene Stratton-Porter. Zwender has no memory of his daughters reading any book when they were young girls, or ever. He has no memory of reading any book himself. He is thinking how ridiculous, anyone who lives in a house like the Chambers house and attends an expensive private school, pretending to identify with a fictitious girl-heroine of a century ago!

But clever of Francis Fox to give "innocent"—"wholesome"—books like this to his girl-students. Impressive to their parents, as to law enforcement officers who might be investigating a pedophile.

Now that *Mis-ter Fox* is out in the open as a festive balloon bouncing in the air between mother and daughter Mrs. Chambers speaks at length about Genevieve's experiences at the Langhorne school—how hard she worked, how challenged she was in her English class—how *encouraging* Mr. Fox was. As well as *wonderful, generous, kind*.

All that Zwender has been hearing about Fox for weeks. Of which he is heartily sick of hearing.

Yet, he takes notes. With seeming concentration, respect. Even as his exasperated pity for the deluded daughter and mother melts outward into pity for all children of all parents, and for all parents of all children.

For what a thankless enterprise it is: not merely procreation but protracted nurturing; caring and loving; dreading, fearing. Almost he has forgotten that he himself has sired children; but now that they are adults, and grown from him, like single-celled organisms breaking off from one another, propelled in counter-directions, he is absolved of having to love and be responsible for them, as they are of him.

But he is sorry, he never noticed any children's book of his daughters. Never read to them in their beds, if that might have been an option.

As Genevieve, or Mrs. Chambers, speaks of how *wonderful* Mr. Fox was, though *also a strict grader,* Zwender finds himself lapsing into an open-eyed dream of suffocating tenderness recalling *Little Kitten* naked from the waist up, on the computer screen just a few inches from his staring eyes. Astonishingly smooth ivory-pale skin, flawless skin, small white breasts of the shape and size of inverted Dixie cups, tiny purple berry-nipples; and how the (faceless) predator gripped the girl tight in the curve of one arm as she slumped forward, clearly drugged, slack-mouthed—a face of exquisite child-beauty just discernible beneath the blurred surface of the video.

And yes, the (luscious) mouth was swollen, the eyelids were bluish, drooping. A seemingly willing girl-victim unresisting as she is tongue-kissed, fondled intimately . . .

"Detective?"—Mrs. Chambers is asking Zwender a question.

Zwender rouses himself from the erotic trance. Tries to recall what Mrs. Chambers has asked him.

Headmistress P. Cady? Yes, Zwender says, he has met the woman. Of course. She has been very cooperative with his task force.

(As if the headmistress has had any choice about it!)

Mrs. Chambers is telling Zwender how Headmistress Cady sent a "gorgeous" bouquet of white flowers to Genevieve in the hospital, and has spoken with her, Melissa, several times on the phone; it is the headmistress who arranged for Genevieve's therapy, which is being paid for by the Langhorne Academy.

Also, Ms. Cady's assistant March, who has taken over Mr. Fox's classes for the semester, comes to the house every other day to bring library books to Genevieve and to pick up Genevieve's homework assignments. March, too, has been *wonderful, so kind.*

Zwender listens to this drivel without comment. If only this foolish woman knew that Headmistress Cady is personally responsible for her daughter nearly dying!—hiring a known, notorious pedophile to teach middle-school children . . .

Mrs. Chambers tells Zwender how Mr. Fox encouraged Genevieve, and allowed her to rewrite assignments; he raised her grade to a high B; he praised her poetry, and asked her to read it to the class. He invited her to join an exclusive book club to which few seventh graders belonged . . .

"Looking-Glass Book Club," Genevieve supplies the name which Mrs. Chambers seems to have forgotten.

Mrs. Chambers speaks of how students at Langhorne are "communally mourning" their teacher who died in a tragic accident, lost on a country road outside Wieland; his "premature death" has been the inspiration for poetry readings, murals, vigils at the school.

"In his death Mr. Fox has brought the school together. Not just his students but all students! The older ones, as well. It's been a kind of miracle. It's a consolation of a kind that Genevieve isn't the only one to have been traumatized . . ."

Zwender is appalled anew, Melissa Chambers has no idea what she's talking about. Praising her daughter's abuser who has most certainly abused other girls at the Langhorne school as elsewhere.

Neither daughter nor mother seems to have the slightest idea what must have happened to Genevieve, to provoke her into attempting suicide. No acknowledgment of how an adult man infected a healthy young girl leaving behind this peevish, sickly-sallow-skinned convalescent.

Zwender knows: He must be cautious, daring to bring up the subject of Genevieve's suicide attempt. He must be indirect, tactful. He has seen how in such families suicide attempts are not addressed but circumnavigated, like a crater in a roadway; even parents who detest each other will bond, in not-acknowledging what everyone else can see.

Zwender asks Mrs. Chambers if her husband came to visit Genevieve in the hospital and she says yes, but he only stayed for two nights, at the Marriott inn.

"He felt guilty. He *is* guilty."

"Had your husband ever met Francis Fox?"

"Francis Fox? Of course not. No."

"You're sure?"

"Of course I'm sure! That man abandoned us long before Mr. Fox came to Wieland."

"So—he knew very little about Francis Fox?"

"Why are you asking about my husband, Detective? *He knew nothing about Mr. Fox.*"

"He didn't spend time with Genevieve discussing her school experiences, any of her teachers?"

"Are you joking? He left us, he 'moved on.'"

"But—over the phone, possibly?"

"Detective, my former husband *did not give a damn about* our daughter any more than he did about me. Ask him."

Zwender has indeed spoken with David Chambers several times on the phone. A harried-sounding man of middle age, guiltily negligent of his left-behind family except that, as he insists, he left Melissa Chambers very well-off, alimony, child support, roughly half his estate plus the house in Wieland. And clueless about his daughter.

Not a man who was involved in his daughter's teacher's death, presumably.

"Is there anyone else in your family who might have met Fox?"

"Why are you asking that? Of course not—no. My family doesn't live in Wieland, they live in Baltimore. They don't come here for visits, we go *there*."

"No brothers in the vicinity, siblings—"

"*No.*"

"And your son is—ten?"

"Yes, ten. Why are you asking?"

"No other relatives in the area?"

"I've told you—*no.*"

Wanting to ask the woman *Is there no one in your family who might have protected your daughter? Is there no one in your family who might be outraged at what has been done to her?*

Obviously the answer is: *no one.*

That sick-sinking sensation he felt in the interview with Blake Healy, the realization that he was (probably) burrowing into a dead-end tunnel, he's feeling now, in the presence of Genevieve Chambers and her defensive mother.

Little Kitten!—Francis Fox would scarcely recognize his favorite now. No place for this sallow-skinned twelve-year-old on the child-porn website.

Of course, *Sleeping Beauties* has been taken down from the Internet. It exists only as Wieland PD evidence. Zwender has to remind himself, he isn't trying to prevent further crimes against children, the pedophile is no longer living.

Genevieve has been paging dreamily through the journal with the rose-marbled cover, not at all interested in the adults' exchange. Zwender's guess is that her allegiance is with *Mis-ter Fox,* other adults are not very real to her.

Recalling now where he saw a journal with a similar old-fashioned, marbled cover: in the hands of the scowling daughter of the youngish executive at Bristol Myers Squibb whom he and Daryl Odom had particularly disliked. Martin Pfenning.

Edith, was it? Eunice? Homely little ferret-faced girl. Her journal had an eye-jarring pond-scum-green cover, not nearly so attractive, so *sweetly girlish* as Genevieve Chambers's journal.

Zwender asks Genevieve why Mr. Fox was *so special* and Genevieve says, with a small sad smile, "He just *was.*"

Adding, "He *is.* Mr. Fox *still is.*"

"D'you think that, possibly, Mr. Fox is still alive? Somewhere?"

"Y-yes. Maybe."

"And who was discovered at Wieland Pond? D'you have any idea?"

"Well, people say—it might've been someone else."

"Someone who resembled Fox near enough to be a twin?"

"I guess."

"Then where would Mr. Fox be? D'you think he disappeared?"

Genevieve shakes her head slowly, no idea.

"*Why* would Mr. Fox fabricate his own death? He was very happy teaching at the Langhorne Academy, wasn't he?"

But this is too harsh: *fabricate, death*. Genevieve stiffens, staring into the journal.

Zwender would like to snatch the damned journal from the girl's fingers and examine it for himself but he has not the (legal) right; and Mrs. Chambers is not an easily intimidated resident of Wieland, whom a cunning detective might inveigle into cooperating with him.

He'd have had no trouble getting hold of Mary Ann Healy's journal if she'd left it behind when she ran away from home, for Mary Ann's mother was desperate to cooperate with Wieland police; but Mary Ann Healy's room was thoroughly searched, and nothing remotely resembling a journal was found. Wherever the girl had fled, and whyever, she'd taken the precious journal with her.

Zwender asks Genevieve more specifically what was special about Mr. Fox, and Genevieve says, "He cares about us. Like, the other teachers don't."

"How does he 'care about' you—that the other teachers don't?"

"He just *does*."

"No other teachers care like this?—like Mr. Fox?"

Zwender smiles encouragingly, as a father might. The hope is that Genevieve might overcome her distrust of him and reply more reasonably. But she does not.

"No. They *don't*." A light flush has come into Genevieve's pallid skin of indignation, impatience.

Zwender asks if Mr. Fox had "private conferences"—"tutorials"—with her in his office, and Genevieve quickly shakes her head *no*.

Shakes her head too quickly, Zwender thinks.

"Not ever? Not once? In his office, I mean."

"No."

"Do you know if your teacher invited other students—girls—to his office?"

"N-no."

"Do you mean you don't know, or—no, he did not?"

"Mr. Fox did not."

Genevieve's voice is low, muffled. She is pressing her chin against her chest, hunching her shoulders oddly. Stiff, steeling herself. Zwender knows, he should be very careful: a twelve-year-old girl is a child, and children can be emotionally explosive if provoked.

"Well, actually—there's a girl we interviewed, she says that she went to Mr. Fox's office quite a few times, and he closed the door . . ."

"He *did not*. He never did. Who is that?"

"There may be other girls, too. Maybe they're in eighth grade, not seventh—you are in seventh grade, yes?"

"They *did not*. They're lying. Who are they? I hate people who lie."

Genevieve is speaking sharply now. Glaring at her mother hovering just behind Zwender.

"Well, some girls are saying 'Mr. Fox closed his door so that no one could see inside.' The window in the office door is 'frosted'—isn't it? So that no one can see in?"

"That is so *not true*. Who is it?"

"Our interviews are confidential. We don't disclose names. If you have something special to tell me, you can be assured that your name will never be revealed."

Genevieve laughs, without mirth. She is beginning to be angry, and anger has enlivened her.

No idea that the detective has fabricated *some girls*. From her manner, Genevieve certainly seems to believe that these girls exist.

Rivals to *Little Kitten*. For the love of (deceased) *Mis-ter Fox*.

"Can you remember any special things that Mr. Fox said to you? Or did? For instance, did he take you to his office? After classes were over for the day? Is that how you knew where his office was?"

Genevieve shakes her head *no*. Can't remember.

"Do you know where his office is?"

No.

"Isn't it in the basement of Haven Hall? Isn't the office number 015?"

Genevieve shrugs. No idea.

Zwender asks if Mr. Fox gave her her journal and Genevieve says, "Yes. He did." Quietly, proudly.

"Where did he give you this journal, Genevieve? Do you remember where you were at the time?"

Genevieve hesitates, shakes her head *no*.

"In his office? When you were alone?"

No.

"After one of your classes with him, Mr. Fox gave you this journal? That's when he gave it to you?"

"Maybe."

"When other students were present? He gave you this special journal?"

Genevieve shakes her head. *Don't know.*

"Why did he give such an unusual journal to you?"

"Because—I was special . . ."

"Mr. Fox gave his favorite students journals like yours—did he?"

"Mr. Fox gave me this. He didn't give anyone else a journal like this."

"Well, we've seen journals like this. Mr. Fox gave them to other students too, didn't he? Girl-students."

"This is the only journal like *this*. Mr. Fox said so."

"Why did he give you a special journal, Genevieve? And no one else?"

"I told you: because—I was special. I am—*special*."

A stricken look comes into Genevieve's face as if she might burst into tears. For clearly, this *Little Kitten* is no longer *special*.

"What sorts of things are in your journal, Genevieve?"

"It could be anything. We could do our homework assignments in our journals. And our own special writing, for Mr. Fox. Like—poetry."

"Did you show your journal to anyone else?"

"No."

"You don't show your journal to your mother? Even now?"

"No."

"Why not?"

"Because—my journal is private. Mr. Fox said not to show it to anyone including him—if there was something private in it, that no one should know."

"What sorts of things, Genevieve? That you don't want your mother to know?"

"Things that are *private,* I said. Things that are *my own.*"

Zwender asks Mrs. Chambers if she has ever been allowed to look into the journal and Mrs. Chambers says *No.*

"I respect Genevieve's right to privacy. I have promised her."

"When she was in the hospital? Didn't you want to see what was in the journal, then?"

Mrs. Chambers hesitates, uncertain how to reply. Zwender can see that yes, she searched for the journal, but didn't find it, probably— Genevieve had hidden it at the time she'd slashed her wrists.

Hidden it somewhere in the house in case she might survive and return to retrieve it.

"I—we—were too upset to think about—anything else . . ."

Mrs. Chambers swipes at her eyes with her fingertips as Genevieve ignores her, embarrassed.

"Genevieve, would you like to read something to us from the journal? That isn't 'private'?"

Genevieve has been turning pages in the journal, slowly. The pages are relatively thick, the journal is comprised of high-quality paper. Zwender can see stanzas of poetry, in purple ink. Red-ink heart surrounding poems. Ornate, old-fashioned calligraphy written with a special pen.

Genevieve seems pleased by Zwender's request. She takes some time selecting a poem which she reads in a hushed, reverent voice:

> *She walks in beauty, like the night*
> *Of cloudless climes and starry skies;*
> *And all that's best of dark and bright*
> *Meet in her aspect and her eyes.*

"That's a very nice poem, Genevieve," Zwender says, "—who wrote it?"

"Who wrote it? Mr. Fox wrote it."

Genevieve looks at Zwender in disbelief that he could be so uninformed. The little white toes at the edge of the quilt wriggle in derision.

Quickly Mrs. Chambers says, "Mr. Fox was a poet, as well as a teacher. A published poet. He won awards . . ."

"Did he give you this poem to copy into your journal, Genevieve?"

"Yes! Of course he did, this poem is for *me.*"

"Do you mean—written for you?"

"Yes! Why are you all so stupid! Mr. Fox wrote this poem for *me.*"

Zwender hesitates. Possibly wisest to retreat before Genevieve becomes even more agitated.

Beside him, behind him, Mrs. Chambers is all but wringing her hands.

It seems clear to Zwender that Mrs. Chambers hasn't a clue what was done to her daughter but possibly Genevieve doesn't understand either. Terms like *pedophilia, sexual abuse of a minor, statutory rape* are not part of a child's vocabulary, still less her consciousness; a kind of merciful amnesia may have numbed Genevieve, like opioids; he has seen, all too graphically, how *Little Kitten* was exploited online, fondled, made to feel sexual sensations by her seducer, involuntarily. Such violations of a child are akin to rape, emotionally; Fox must have sedated the girl to render her helpless, wholly dependent upon him as an infant upon an adult. Not even a question of *consent, trust*—there was scarcely *consciousness.*

Repelled, yet also fascinated, witnessing the young girl gripped tight writhing in an adult man's arms, his hand between her thighs, not aggressively but gently as one might stroke a cat.

Worse kind of sex abuse, forcing the victim to feel intense pleasure. Linking the victim to her abuser in a way more insidious than rape. Fox imprinted his helpless victims in a way too deep to be exorcised for they would remember him always as a lover, not a rapist; their first lover.

So it was throughout *Sleeping Beauties 2013*: the (faceless) male lover is gentle but persistent. Weakly the *kittens* may push at his hands, turn their faces from him, but he always prevails for his power is greater than theirs, he has drugged them, hypnotized them into submission.

Even now Genevieve Chambers is drowsy, drugged. She is a child-convalescent under the control of another adult. Sleepy-eyed, pouting. Stretching her legs beneath the gaily colored quilt, wriggling her bare white toes as she observes Zwender through half-shut eyes, like a cat. Alarming to Zwender, she seems to be emulating the provocative posture of a girl in a Balthus painting.

"Did you ever hear, Genevieve, that your teacher Mr. Fox made any of his students—girl students—feel 'uncomfortable'?"

"'Uncomfortable'—what's that?"

"Embarrassed, awkward . . ."

Genevieve scowls, shaking her head. "That's just *silly*."

"Touching a student inappropriately?"

"'Inappro-pitly'—what's that?"

(Is *Little Kitten* laughing at him? Zwender is feeling unsettled.)

(Unmistakably, the little white bare toes are wriggling, squirming in mockery of him—he knows.)

"Did Mr. Fox ever make you feel uncomfortable, Genevieve?"

Shakes her head *no*. Not looking at Zwender's face.

"Did Mr. Fox ever touch *you*, Genevieve?"

Shakes her head *no*. Not looking at Zwender's face.

"Just by accident, maybe? When he gave you the journal? When he brought you to his office and shut the door? No?"

"No!" That pouting lower lip!

Zwender opens his much-battered leather briefcase with tarnished initials *HPZ*, pulls out a replica of the reproduction of the Balthus painting in Fox's apartment; this, he unfolds to show to Genevieve who stares at it avidly, now sitting up on the sofa.

"Did your teacher Mr. Fox ever show you this picture? Or—pictures resembling it?"

At first glance the girl in the painting appears innocently dreamy, languorous, with closed eyes; she is not a voluptuous female but slender, with a small torso, narrow hips; she might be eleven years old, or twelve. She is sitting with arms stretched above her head and her slender legs are (unconsciously?) lifted, a crotch of white panties revealed.

Mrs. Chambers peers at the reproduction too. "What is this, Detective? Why are you showing my daughter this?"

Zwender ignores her to ask Genevieve again if her teacher ever showed her anything like this.

Genevieve is staring at the reproduction as if mesmerized.

Decisively, Genevieve shakes her head *no*. Never saw it before.

"Was this anywhere in Mr. Fox's office? Or something similar on the wall? A poster?"

Genevieve is certain—*no*.

"Please put that away, Detective," Mrs. Chambers says. "That's—ugly. I don't know why you are showing it to us. What does this have to do with Mr. Fox?"

"We have reason to think that Mr. Fox had a poster of this artist's work in his home."

"But—what does this have to do with my daughter?" Mrs. Chambers is puzzled, disturbed.

With an apologetic murmur Zwender returns the Balthus reproduction to the briefcase and takes out a white pastry bag containing an apricot tart, a cherry tart, and a lemon tart purchased at Wieland's only pastry shop.

"Do these look familiar, Genevieve? Little fruit tarts—for you."

Genevieve stares at the tarts as avidly as she stared at the Balthus reproduction.

"What on earth is this, Detective? What are you doing?"—Mrs. Chambers laughs nervously.

"I think Mr. Fox gave you tarts like these, Genevieve? Do you remember?"

Genevieve continues to stare but makes no move to take one of the tarts Zwender is offering her.

To Mrs. Chambers he says, "We have reason to believe that Fox gave some of his students tarts like these. We've seen photos."

"*Photos?* Where?"

Genevieve says slowly, "Mr. Fox did *not.*"

"Mr. Zwender, I think you should leave soon. You are upsetting my daughter, and you are upsetting me."

"Did Genevieve often stay late at school, Mrs. Chambers?"

"Yes. No. This 'interview' is over . . ."

"Did Genevieve stay late at school, after classes were over, and did you drive to the school to pick her up?"

"I suppose so, yes. It isn't just classes that are important at the Langhorne school, it's *activities.* This special book club that not just anyone could join . . ."

"How often did Genevieve stay late? Once, twice a week? More?"

"It might have been that—once, or twice a week. Activities are so important there. Genevieve would fall asleep in the car going home. She worked so hard . . ."

"Fell asleep in the car when you drove her home?"

Mrs. Chambers doesn't remember, shakes her head *no.* As if she has said something she hasn't meant to say.

"Did it ever occur to you that your daughter might have been drugged, Mrs. Chambers? And that's why she fell asleep in your car?"

"'Drugged'? How?"

"In tarts like these. Which Mr. Fox gave to his 'favorite' students."

"What are you saying! That's ridiculous."

"It never occurred to you? Though your daughter was falling asleep in the car?"

"Genevieve wasn't falling *asleep.* She was just *sleepy.* From all her activities, and a full day of classes. They are all like that, Mr. Zwender! Langhorne students are *special.*"

Genevieve ignores her mother's nervous chatter. Genevieve is glaring at Zwender as if she'd like to spit at him.

"Genevieve? Are these familiar to you—?"

"No! You're just saying this . . ."

"'Saying'—what?"

"You don't *know,* you are just *saying this.* I don't have to listen to you."

"Why are you upset, Genevieve? Is there something about the tarts that is upsetting to you?"

"I told you—*no*. I never saw these before. I—hate sweet things. I hate *you*. All of you. You want to take Mr. Fox from me but you can't. He promised—we would die for each other if that is asked of us . . ."

"'Asked of you'—how? By who?"

"Mr. Fox said—I don't have to care about any of you. Mr. Fox went first, and now he is waiting for me."

"Waiting—where?"

"Just go away! *I hate you all.*"

"Mr. Zwender, you are upsetting my daughter"—Mrs. Chambers tries to intervene but neither Zwender nor Genevieve pays her any heed.

"I love Mr. Fox—there was never a time when I didn't love Mr. Fox. If he is dead there is no reason for me to live, *you can't make me live.*"

Mrs. Chambers reaches to take Genevieve's arm but Genevieve pushes her away. The small sallow face is contorted with hatred for her mother, as for Zwender.

"Genevieve—"

"I said—*I hate you all.*"

Genevieve leaps up from the sofa, several books fall to the floor. She slaps at her mother, and she slaps at the paper bag in Zwender's hand containing the tarts, sending the bag flying, tarts flying, halfway across the room onto the floor.

To Zwender she says furiously: "You look like you have a zipper in your head. Ugly old zipper-head! You're all ugly, I hate you all, *I wish you would die.*"

Genevieve stalks out of the room leaving the adults staring after her astonished.

Zwender's face is burning-hot as if he's been slapped. Hard.

Mrs. Chambers apologizes profusely. Zwender scarcely listens, he has been mortified by the girl's scathing remarks.

Thinking he held all the cards, but the girl has outwitted him—throwing the cards in his face. Naïve male vanity, he imagined that

Genevieve Chambers would respect him, even admire him, as a kindly-father presence, in his way attractive, all along she was staring at the stitches in his scalp, in contempt.

Mrs. Chambers tells Zwender that he should leave now. She should—she needs to be with Genevieve . . .

"It's the medications! The stress . . ."

Zwender professes sympathy. Of course, Genevieve is under much *stress.*

"We think it has something to do with Francis Fox, in fact. There have been complaints about him—maybe you've heard?"

"Heard—what?"

"Complaints about Fox."

"What kind of complaints?"

"That he has behaved inappropriately with some students. Girl-students."

"No. I have not heard this . . ."

"Try to think, Mrs. Chambers. Why did your daughter harm herself?"

"Why did Genevieve *harm herself*? Because she was upset—because . . ."

"Did she give a reason?"

"Because—she said—Mr. Fox passed away, and all of his students are upset . . . That is private, Mr. Zwender."

"Didn't she just tell us, 'I love Mr. Fox'—'there was never a time when I didn't love Mr. Fox' . . . "

"She did *not*! I didn't hear that! Genevieve says many hurtful things, we've been told not to take them personally. Children are always saying *I hate you, I wish I'd never been born*. They are all saying at the school that they 'love' Mr. Fox. It isn't just Genevieve, it's others—many others."

"Your daughter cut herself seriously, might have killed herself, because of this Fox—isn't that possible? Being involved with Fox?"

"Genevieve is just a *child*. Francis Fox is—was—an *adult man*. It's disgusting of you to think such a thing. Nothing like that ever happened."

"And you know that—how?"

"I met Mr. Fox—Francis. More than once. He—he was nothing like that."

"'Like'—what?"

"He would never have harmed Genevieve. He wasn't like that . . . he was a gentleman. I think you should leave now, Mr. Zwender."

"Yes! I will leave in one minute, Mrs. Chambers."

Anticipating such an impasse Zwender has brought a laptop from the office to show Mrs. Chambers the least offensive image of her daughter he could find, downloaded from Fox's website: it's a somewhat blurry picture of a wan, sleepy girl in a swivel chair, arms limp, knees and pleated skirt askew, her face disguised by watery pixels.

The astonished mother stares aghast: "What? What is—?"

"Do you recognize this girl?"

It's obvious, the girl is Genevieve Chambers. But Mrs. Chambers shudders, pushing the laptop away.

"That isn't—who you think it is. That's not my daughter!"

"Could you look more carefully, Mrs. Chambers—"

Mrs. Chambers gives a cry and knocks the laptop from Zwender's hand.

"Go away! Now! *I will sue you.*"

Wisest to retreat. With a murmured apology.

Even as Mrs. Chambers screams after him Zwender is polite, deferential. Yes, yes!—picks the laptop up, slides it back into a black bag, he's on his way out.

The detective has all he needs to know, the interview has not been a failure. Recognizing a *dead end* is not in itself a failure.

Being humbled, insulted is not a failure.

Rapid retreat, in stocking feet. The petite housekeeper has appeared out of nowhere to escort him out. Scarcely coming to his shoulder, she appears stricken with embarrassment. Zwender would like to assure her, he isn't after *her.*

He may be law enforcement but he doesn't give a damn about *illegal immigrants.* If she is, or if she isn't. Fine with him.

Assuring her he's OK. No problem, he can find his own way out, and his shoes too.

Outside on the front stoop, clumsily jamming his feet into his shoes. God *damn*.

Good that Odom hasn't tagged along, been a witness to this. Hasty undignified retreat of H. Zwender, something to laugh about at the Wieland PD where they resent him anyway, head detective, rumored next-in-line to be chief.

■

STILL, THE INTERVIEW HAS been valuable. Every *dead end* is valuable, for fewer possibilities remain and of these, one is likely *the way in*.

That night dreaming not of sickly-skinned brattish Genevieve Chambers but the ravishing *Little Kitten* he first saw on the *Sleeping Beauties* website: pouting lips, dreamy swoon, knees and jumper-skirt askew, bare toes tickling his toes beneath a gaily colored quilt at the foot of the bed.

"SCENE OF THE CRIME"

13 DECEMBER 2013

Ugly old zipper-head.
  Wish you would die.

Forty-third day since Francis Fox's remains were discovered at Wieland Pond, Zwender decides to revisit his office in Haven Hall. Like a bloodhound returning to sniff at a carrion-site that has yielded exciting smells while withholding the origin of the smells.

In this case disinfectant, bleach. Smells annihilating other smells.

"'The scene of the crime.'"

Zwender has no doubt but—how to prove it?

■

GOD *DAMN*.

A shrine for Francis Fox?

First thing that assails Zwender's eye as he approaches Fox's office in the basement corridor of Haven Hall is a makeshift arrangement of flowers, valentine hearts, drawings and watercolors, hand-printed love poems and prayers, newspaper clippings of Francis Fox's dimpled-smiling face on a bench opposite the door of room 015.

IN MEMORIUM MR. FOX—GOD BLESS MR. FOX

WE WILL NEVER FORGET YOU

Predominant are waxy-white calla lilies, crimson-red roses large as a man's fist, sprigs of smaller flowers, sprays of bridal wreath, a scattering of russet-red and gold autumn foliage beginning to dry, crumble. A messy tribute to a beloved teacher—fortunately most of the flowers are artificial, otherwise they'd be wilted and rotting by now.

Wilted, rotting, stinking. The fate of organic matter, to *decompose*.

Affixed to the wall behind the bench are dozens of homemade valentine cards containing verse, prayers, declarations of love for "Mr. Fox" in red ink, signed by student-mourners.

Exasperating to Zwender, how the pedophile is *mourned*. You would think that among Fox's forty-eight students there would be at least one who disliked him, who saw through the pedophile's subterfuge, who frankly loathed the man as H. Zwender has come to loathe him, but if this is so, this student has not (yet) identified himself.

Through much of November, in a room provided by P. Cady for the use of H. Zwender and his team, Fox's students were interviewed. The atmosphere was casual, friendly. There was no hint (of course) that this was part of a homicide investigation. The only (mildly) critical things any of the students said of Fox was that he "graded hard"— "had really high standards"—"made you work."

And: "Mr. Fox would say 'You can always improve. If you follow my instructions, you will improve.'"

If Zwender dared to ask if Fox had ever said "inappropriate things" to them—sent them "inappropriate pictures, emails, text messages"— "touched them inappropriately"—they were likely to stare at him appalled. At *him*.

Girls as well as boys. The most attractive girls, those whose names had been asterisked in Fox's grade book, as well as plain-faced girls.

If Zwender persisted in asking such questions, however obliquely and delicately, the students reacted against him as if he'd said something obscene. He lost their trust, he could not regain it. Clearly they adored their *Mis-ter Fox* who'd become elevated since his death, like a saint. Zwender was slandering their deceased idol, they looked upon him with dislike, disgust.

Others on Zwender's team reported similar responses. The lone woman officer met with less hostility, overall; it seemed to her that one or two (girl) students had been *about to confide in her*—but in the end, had not.

"Not everybody has a dirty mind, sir," a boy named Jeffrey Swanson III with a patrician chin, pale-blond pouf of hair over one eye, told Zwender coldly.

■

THOUGH IN THE RAGING fires of Hell yet the cynical pedophile is passionately defended even by his victims, smirking up at Detective H. Zwender:

You will never catch me, Detective! And since I am dead, deader than dead, hacked to pieces by vultures, you will never arrest me and bring me to justice.

■ ■ ■

TODAY IS FRIDAY THE thirteenth: but H. Zwender isn't superstitious.

Today is the final day of classes at the Langhorne Academy before winter break. In another day or two the school will be vacated until the first week in January. By midafternoon most of the office doors in the basement corridor of Haven Hall are shut, dimmed within.

Though there is an occupant in the office beside 015, one of Francis Fox's (former) teaching colleagues, meeting with students.

Fox's office remains untouched since Wieland police officers and forensic technicians last examined it weeks ago. For the time being it is off-limits to Langhorne staff including custodians, following a directive by Headmistress P. Cady in cooperation with the Wieland PD investigation into Francis Fox's death.

On the doorframe of 015 the neatly handprinted card remains:

FRANCIS H. FOX

OFFICE HOURS 4–5 P.M. AND BY APPOINTMENT

Frosted-glass window in the door, can't peer inside. But you can make out shadowy silhouettes through the opaque glass if the small window high in the rear wall of the office emits light.

Zwender unlocks the door with a key provided by the headmistress's office. Always a mild thrill, entering a *crime scene*. Even one, like this, that has yielded little information.

Weeks after the office was cleaned by an unknown party, still there remain pungent odors. Zwender's eyes water, his nostrils pinch. This too-familiar odor, nauseating.

An odor associated with death, crime scenes. An odor that frequently masks, or fails to mask, a decomposing body hidden from immediate view in another room, in a bed, in a bathtub, in a cellar.

Such smells reminding Zwender of his early years as a police officer. Before he'd lost his youthful capacity to be shocked, saddened by the evil perpetrated upon human beings by their fellows.

Slips on latex gloves, pushes up the small window in the rear wall to let in fresh air.

Fresh air!—relief.

When Wieland police were finally allowed access to Fox's office in November they discovered that the room had been so thoroughly cleaned that no clear fingerprints or DNA remained: not even Fox's. Even the undersides of the desk, chairs, bookshelves had been wiped clean.

The upper drawers of Fox's desk hadn't been disturbed, it seemed: his grade book, class lists, school printouts remained. But other drawers were empty, wiped clean.

Fox would have kept his *kitten* treats in these drawers, Zwender assumed—fruit tarts, chocolates. Possibly, personal items that might have identified the girls. Whoever killed Francis Fox wanted to protect the identities of the girls.

Such thorough cleaning of an office is hardly routine procedure at the Langhorne Academy. Yet, no one to whom police have spoken has acknowledged responsibility.

The scene of the crime. Zwender is certain. You'd only clean a room like this if it required cleaning like this.

Forensic technicians determined that Fox hadn't been killed at the ravine. He hadn't died in any sort of vehicular accident. Nor had he been killed in his apartment. Death was caused by severe blunt-force injury to the back of Fox's skull, with some sort of heavy instrument that also had odd asymmetrical sharp edges; the bone of the skull was cracked, crushed, which would have meant a good deal of blood and blood-splatter, that would have had to be cleaned up, which would not have been easy.

Five–six hours, if it was just one person doing the cleaning. Maybe longer.

One person *who knew what he was doing.*

Who didn't panic, who took his time to be thorough. And had access to cleaning equipment . . .

But the sixty-six-year-old custodian responsible for the maintenance of Haven Hall rigorously denied having cleaned any office in the building in any "special way"—ever.

Not in all his years on the staff had he cleaned an office using disinfectant, bleach, wiping down walls, surfaces—not ever.

Zwender was astonished, the custodian turned out to be Lemuel Healy: the older brother of Blake Healy and the father of Marcus Healy, who'd reported the "accident" at the ravine.

As it turned out Lemuel Healy barely recalled that his son had reported an "accident." And seemed scarcely to know (or care) that his brother Blake had been arrested for aggravated assault against a police officer. Lemuel Healy didn't know who the assaulted police officer was, he wasn't sure if his brother was out on bail; *he* hadn't supplied the bail bond. The two weren't in contact, hadn't spoken in months. Years? Nor did Healy seem aware that a young niece of his had gone missing from home weeks ago.

A brain addled by alcohol! The man's nose was swollen, reddened with broken capillaries. His eyes were watery, veined. His breath smelled of a kind of sour whiskey-mash compounded by decaying teeth. Said to be sixty-six but looked fifteen years older.

All Healy seemed to care about, all that his ravaged brain could focus upon, was his employment at the Langhorne Academy, which

he seemed to think was under threat since the Wieland PD had summoned him to appear at their headquarters on Union Street. As soon
as Lemuel Healy entered the building he was defensive, belligerent.
Insisting to anyone who would listen that in all the years he'd been on
the Langhorne staff, no one had ever complained about him. In fact,
his supervisor praised him. The headmistress of the school herself
praised him. He did a *damn good job.*

In response to Zwender's questions declaring in a loud voice that
he hadn't given any faculty office a "special cleaning" in all his years
at Langhorne. He didn't know a damn thing about it. He'd never
heard of such a damn thing. Sometimes in a boys' lavatory you have
to clean up actual filth from the floor, you can flush it down the toilet
and clean with disinfectant and bleach, and air out the room, but
that's a rare occurrence not anything a custodian did routinely. Small
offices like 015 you clean in five minutes, usually.

When Zwender asked Healy if he'd ever encountered Francis Fox
in Haven Hall Healy cupped his hand to his ear grimacing—*Who?*

It developed that, though Marcus Healy was the one to report the
remains of Francis Fox in the ravine, his father had only a vague idea
that a teacher at the Langhorne school had died in "some kind of accident on a bridge"—he wasn't sure when this was.

He'd never talked with any teachers, that he could remember.
The kind of work he did, he only came to the school after-hours. His
shift ended at eleven P.M. He never met anyone, or hardly ever. He
saw other custodial staff, sometimes he saw his supervisor McGreevy.
Teachers, students—you might see them at a distance. *And if they see
you they look through you.*

Lemuel Healy reminded Zwender of his own father, and other
older (male) relatives: men who didn't read newspapers, paid little
attention to news. Avoided doctors, dentists. Manual laborers who
couldn't afford to retire even as their bodies failed them. Some of
them, like Healy, obsessed with their jobs as if the jobs were lifelines,
all that kept them alive.

Healy's hands were gnarled with arthritis. His fingernails were
broken and edged with dirt. In the creases of his neck, dirt. In his

ears, nostrils coarse black hairs. He carried himself in the cautious way that indicates chronic pain and the anticipation of pain—back, knees, sciatica. His face was ravaged, furrowed. You couldn't tell if he was furious that someone had been telling lies about him or terrified that he was being singled out for questioning for something of which he was, notwithstanding his denials, guilty.

The state of his coveralls, his work-boots, his disheveled hair, the way he'd shaved his jaws oozing pinpricks of blood—sure signs there was no woman at home to look after him.

Zwender guessed: a man who began to go to pieces when his wife died. Heavy drinking, not giving a damn about his health. But the job—*that* mattered.

Reminding Zwender of his father in his final years, crippled with arthritis, hardly able to walk but determined to keep working until finally he'd collapsed, an inoperable tumor in his bowels . . .

Lemuel Healy had fallen silent, then, as if sensing a shift in the detective's mood, he suddenly confessed that he'd (maybe) had help at the school a few times when his arthritis pain had been so bad he couldn't work, and so (maybe) there might've been something he hadn't known about in Haven Hall; a few times, he'd asked his son Demetrius to drive him to school and help with the heavy-duty work, he hadn't told his supervisor because he didn't think it was important because he *always* works, never asks Demetrius to do everything for him, as long as he doesn't have to stand on his feet for long he can scrub and polish, use the vacuum, the floor-polisher, clean erasers and whiteboards, all that matters is that the damned job gets done.

Zwender asked when was this and Healy said evasively that it wasn't any particular time, it was a few times, maybe five or six times, or maybe more, he'd asked Demetrius to help him out, and Demetrius never said no, Demetrius was all you could ask for in a son, never let his old man down, it kind of broke him when his mother died, poor kid never got over it but he was a damned good worker, reliable, more reliable than his brother Marcus, *he'd* moved out of the house to get away from them, but Demetrius stayed with him, he couldn't remember any actual dates when Demetrius drove him to the school, it was a few times, especially when the weather turned cold and wet, he'd never used to mind so much but now he dreaded the cold, the way cold got into his joints; now agitated as if on the brink of sobbing so Zwender said quickly, to spare the older man further humiliation: "I understand, Mr. Healy. You don't want to let anyone down. You're a hard worker and you do a damned good job. We are not going to inform the Langhorne Academy about anything. That isn't our business."

Profusely Healy thanked Zwender. Saying, he hoped they didn't have to question his son, Demetrius didn't know any more than he knew; and Demetrius was a *shy kind of boy, not good at talking to strangers.*

The following day, Demetrius Healy was summoned to the Wieland PD.

In his skittish manner the kid resembled one of those gawky long-legged shorebirds that are in constant motion. Lanky-limbed, bony-wristed, over six feet yet couldn't have weighed more than one hundred fifty pounds. Just turned twenty-one. High-school dropout, expelled for fighting. Working at Kroger, minimum wage.

"So, Demetrius—your father told us you've been helping him out at the Langhorne school? How long has that been going on?"

Nervously Demetrius stammered a reply, he'd been driving his father to work, helping out a little, since the start of the school year . . .

"And no one knew, eh? Your father didn't tell his supervisor? How long did you think you could get away with it?"

Miserably Demetrius shook his head. No idea how to answer.

"Isn't that criminal trespass? Going on school property, into private buildings, pretending to be on the staff . . ."

Hearing these words grimly uttered by Detective H. Zwender Demetrius Healy visibly shuddered. A look in his face of comically raw *guilt.*

Stricken with fear of getting into trouble with the police, or getting his father into trouble. Not a bright kid, not good at expressing himself; inclined to stutter, and hearing himself, stuttering worse. Intimidated by Zwender's harsh confrontational manner as by the

Wieland PD: Uniformed officers, holsters at their hips. Ringing phones. Bright fluorescent lighting.

Zwender had little interest in Demetrius Healy whose connection to the Langhorne school and to Francis Fox had to be incidental: son of Lemuel Healy, brother of Marcus Healy.

He'd just happened to be helping his father at work at the private school. He'd just happened to be helping his father by unloading debris at the landfill, him and his brother Marcus, within walking distance of Wieland Pond.

Typical small-town investigation in which such connections are not uncommon but are time-consuming. H. Zwender has a reputation among fellow detectives for being dogged, exacting.

Zwender asked Demetrius if he'd had anything to do with cleaning Francis Fox's office, 015 Haven Hall, in a way involving disinfectant and bleach, wiping down the walls, all the surfaces of the room, and at this Demetrius looked blank, as a paralytic might look blank, staring at the floor between his feet and slowly shaking his head *no*.

"So, nobody paid you to clean any office at the school, wipe down the walls, with bleach? No?"

Demetrius shook his head *no*. Scarcely daring to raise his eyes to Zwender's face, he was that intimidated.

"Nobody offered to pay you to clean the office?"

Demetrius shook his head *no*.

"D'you have any idea what that room looked like, before it was cleaned?"

N-no.

Zwender mentioned that, under New Jersey law, the Langhorne school could have Demetrius arrested for trespassing. The school could terminate his father for bringing another person onto the worksite who wasn't covered by liablity insurance.

"There are strict state laws about insurance—'workman's compensation.' Not just anyone can substitute for an employee without permission from their supervisor. Work like this, custodial work, you're using machines, chemicals. Some of those chemicals are toxins. Didn't your father know this?"

Demetrius shifted in his seat as if his bones pained him. His shoulders slumped, his head fell forward, poor kid was making himself a smaller target. Stammering he was sorry, he hadn't known, he just wanted to help his father . . .

"They won't f-fire him, will they? I don't know what Pa will do if—if they do . . ."

"Son, I can't speak for the Langhorne Academy. They have their lawyers to instruct them."

Son was to comfort. *Lawyers* was to scare the kid shitless.

Poor sap, all this for your old drunk pa.

Zwender felt a twinge of something like shame, tormenting Demetrius Healy. Really, he should be on the kid's side, *he* should've been a son like this looking after his father instead of letting the old man go his own brazen bluff way.

Zwender knew and cared little about New Jersey workmen's compensation. He knew little about liability insurance. He didn't give a damn about the Langhorne Academy though it reputedly brought in a substantial proportion of Atlantic County's operating budget and he'd come to—personally, privately—respect P. Cady. Most of all he didn't give a damn about how or why Francis Fox had died except he was glad the pedophile was dead and past corrupting innocent children.

He did feel sorry for Demetrius, finally. Rapidly blinking eyes, trying to keep back tears. Big-knuckled hands gripping each other on the table. Twitching nerve above his eye like a flailing worm.

Looking so transparently guilty, so miserable, you'd think the kid had done something actually wrong instead of helping out his half-crippled father and that father a heavy drinker not long for this world.

Demetrius reminded Zwender of young relatives of his, cousins who'd dropped out of school, wound up in dead-end jobs or enlisted in the U.S. military or become involved in drugs, incarcerated or OD'd by the age of twenty-five. As one who'd educated himself, become a law enforcement officer and now a senior detective Zwender looked down upon his fucked-up cousins but in truth, he'd liked them a lot, they'd been his closest friends. He missed them like hell.

In truth he could've been *them*. Who's he kidding?

Saying, in a less hostile voice: "So, Demetrius: There was one day you unlocked the door to 015 Haven Hall, and the office was already cleaned? Smelling of bleach? And you weren't suspicious, and didn't ask about it?"

Demetrius blinked at him as if Zwender were addressing him in a foreign language.

As if, for a moment, he couldn't remember: Had anything like that happened? To him?

"W-who'd I ask about it? I—I don't know anyone there . . ."

"Did you mention it to your father?"

"N-no . . ."

"Why not? Wasn't it strange? You open an office door, you're going to clean the office, you discover it's already clean, in fact sanitized, sterilized. Like an operating room. You don't mention it? Why wouldn't you mention it?"

Demetrius was looking blank, frightened. No idea how to reply to the detective.

"You never met this English teacher, Fox—you said?"

Shook his head slowly—*No*.

"But you know about him, right? What happened to him? You saw his 'remains' at the ravine—you and Marcus?"

Demetrius winced, looking down at the floor. Slow-nodding *yes*.

"Did *you* see, or just Marcus?"

"Maybe it was just—Marcus . . ."

"What led you to the ravine?"

"I guess—Marcus called me. I didn't know where he was, I was looking for him, then I heard him calling me."

"And why'd he climb up the hill?"—Zwender knew the answer, he'd heard it many times before but there was a kind of grim pleasure to hearing it again.

". . . vultures. In trees."

"You didn't actually *see*—you're saying?"

"Marcus t-told me. What he saw. He said there was a head. I— shut my eyes . . ."

"When there's vultures in trees, what d'you expect to see?"

"Dead carcasses, like deer."

"But you wouldn't look? Open your eyes?"

"You can smell it," Demetrius said, with a shudder, "—you don't need to look."

There was a brief pause. Zwender was feeling like a shit, tormenting this kid. It seemed clear to him, Demetrius had nothing to do with Francis Fox, just in the wrong place at the wrong time, bullied by his older brother and bossed around by his father. Still, out of the habitude of a detective, he persisted.

"But you never ran into Fox at the school? At his office? Staying late?"

Demetrius shook his head slowly—*Guess not.*

"D'you ever meet any teachers there? Students? At the school? You must run into students, sometimes."

Demetrius shook his head *no.* Looking miserable, pained.

"Ever talk to any of the girls? Langhorne girl-students, in their fancy school uniforms?"

At this, Demetrius shook his head curtly—*No.*

"Snooty girls, are they? Rich girls?"

Ill-at-ease Demetrius shook his head—*Don't know.*

"Did you ever see any of them, any girls, in a teacher's office? Late? Beginning to be dark? Basement of Haven Hall, no one else around? No?"

No, no. And *no.*

As he'd felt for Lemuel Healy an exasperated sympathy, so he felt for Demetrius Healy an even sharper sympathy, or pity. Sad enough to be the son of alcoholic Lemuel Healy, he had to be one of the Healys out on Stockton Road, their farmland sold off gradually over the decades until they lived in run-down farmhouses on what remained of their property; that was the branch of the family related to the man who'd (allegedly) shot the Nazi dirigible out of the sky back in the 1930s—Romulus Healy.

A recluse who'd lived in the Pine Barrens. He'd kept trespassers at a distance with his rifles and shotgun. Even his own relatives, Romulus warned away. Tales were told when Zwender was growing up of how the Nazi dirigible had burst into flames from a single rifle shot. Hydrogen explosion—sky full of flames. On the dirigible, there'd been the Nazi swastika in black. In these tales, Romulus Healy had aimed for that swastika.

"Demetrius, are you related to Romulus Healy? You know—the man who shot down the *Hindenburg*."

At this, Demetrius hunched forward as if steeling himself against a blow. His face looked like a crucifixion. Guilty, guilty!

"OK, never mind. Not serious, son."

Zwender spoke quickly, seeing how his casual question seemed to distress the young man.

As he recalled, Romulus Healy had never been arrested and charged with any crime. The incident had never been thoroughly investigated. Whether there was anything to the rumor. For maybe it *was* just a rumor. Maybe Romulus Healy hadn't shot down the *Hindenburg,* maybe there was an entirely different explanation for the explosion. Thirty-six people had died on that day but maybe that wasn't Romulus Healy's fault. Maybe people who knew Romulus Healy spun tales of him to hurt him or to elevate him. Maybe it was all spun tales, by the Healys to make them seem important. Reporters, self-styled historians in South Jersey, drumming up "local color."

In the old days—(by which Zwender meant his grandfather's day)—much in South Jersey didn't get investigated including gangland assassinations in Atlantic City. There weren't the financial resources, and there wasn't the manpower. Probably not one first-rate police detective (like H. Zwender) in South Jersey at that time. The official explanation for the *Hindenburg* explosion was a "natural cause"—some kind of electric charge in the air that ignited the hydrogen. At least, that was the explanation given the German government.

"All I knew was, the other kids teased me at school," Demetrius was saying, in a slow halting voice curiously empty of rancor, "—we never talked about it at home."

It was then, as Zwender was about to thank Demetrius for coming to the station, when Daryl Odom, seated at the rear of the interview room, leaned in to say in a matter-of-fact voice, "Y'know, Demetrius, you didn't clean away all the blood in that office. You missed what's called 'blood-splatter'—like, microscopic traces, on the edges of some books."

It wasn't a question, just a statement. Zwender leaned around to stare at Odom in stunned indignation.

For a beat, as stunned as Demetrius Healy.

Odom persisted: "You did a great job, Demetrius. You mopped up all that blood. You threw away things that had blood on them, like a poster. Books. But you missed a few books, just the edges of some pages."

Zwender happened to know there was no blood-splatter on any remaining books. It was all bluff, bullshit. Odom was trying to maintain a pose of calm self-control but his jaw was quivering with the audacity of the stunt.

When Demetrius recovered sufficiently to reply he stammered in a weak faltering voice that he didn't know about any *blood,* he'd never seen any *blood.*

Mostly he emptied wastebaskets, and ran the vacuum . . . He'd never seen *blood* anywhere.

Odom said, "Just 'trace blood-splatter' on the edges of book pages, Demetrius. The naked eye wouldn't pick it up. But a forensic technician would spot it."

Demetrius looked blank. It was evident to Zwender that Demetrius had no idea what Odom was talking about. Zwender slammed the flat of his hand down hard on the table: "What the hell, Odom? You're out of line."

Zwender was furious at this abrupt line of questioning out of nowhere. Nothing Officer Odom had suggested to Zwender. Nothing they'd discussed. Hours of poring over the forensic findings, trying to make sense of the information they had, which was partial and confusing. And now, Odom pulling this bullshit out of the air, he'd been watching forensic documentaries prepared by the New Jersey State

Bureau of Criminal Investigations. All a bluff to intimidate Demetrius Healy and make Zwender look like an inept interviewer.

"It's OK, son. Ignore Officer Odom, he's spinning bullshit theories. Thinks he's Sherlock Holmes. You can leave."

Zwender escorted Demetrius out of the interview room. Tempted to clap his hand on the kid's shoulder to console him. Handed him over to a junior officer, to be led to the front entrance.

In the interview room, Odom stiffly awaited Zwender's return. Trying to maintain an air of composure but clearly apprehensive.

"What the fuck was that about, Odom? You were intimidating my witness."

"He came in for questioning, I was questioning him. He was—"

"You need to confer with me before pulling shit like that! You know better."

"You were letting him go. We need to talk to him longer, Horace."

"Fuck 'Horace'! That's bullshit and you know it. He's a local kid, he works at Kroger's and helps out his old man who's a janitor. He's got as much connection with the Langhorne school as your redneck cousins have—or you. You were showing off, your two cents' worth not worth shit, you can keep that show-off shit to yourself."

So furious, Zwender could hardly speak. Still the younger man insolently held his ground instead of backing off. Might've apologized or at least shrugged to signal he knew he'd overstepped with the questioning, he was (maybe) sorry but stung by *redneck cousins* continued to smirk at Zwender setting Zwender into a rage as if the zipper-stitches in his skull were pulsing electricity, with the flat of his hand Zwender struck Odom's right shoulder sending Odom staggering against a table, instinctively Odom shoved back with both hands forcing Zwender off-balance, reached out then to steady Zwender gripping his arm at the elbow which threw Zwender into a greater rage striking Odom above the right eye with his fist, hard enough to break the skin.

"God damn you, Odom, don't you lay a hand on me. I'll kill you."

Both men were panting. Odom shrank back so the table skidded several inches across the room. Pressing a wad of tissues against his eye, soaking up blood.

Neither was of a mind to apologize. Neither wanted to hear the other apologize.

Odom yielded first, turning away to leave the room. Breathing through his mouth, short asthmatic pants, beginning to cough, choke. Zwender's rage had frightened him, and Zwender's low-muttered threat which no one else would hear, only just Odom.

As Odom exited the room Zwender called after him: "Fuck up another interview of mine and you're out on your ass, Odom. You're on your way to Toms River."

■ ■ ■

LITERALLY, THEY ATE OUT of *Fox's hand: lemon tarts on Fox's opened palm for a kitten to nibble at. Feeding his girls like babies eating from his hand but in the close-up you couldn't know the predator's identity— only just (white) male, adult.*

Girl-children so sleepy, crumbs fell from their mouths. Slow-chewing, too sleepy to swallow. Mouths fell open slack, eyelids drooped shut.

Suffused with disgust Zwender recalls these scenes from Fox's porn website *Sleeping Beauties*. Blurred background for many scenes, had to be 015 Haven Hall. Sometimes you could see the hazy outline of a bookcase, sometimes you could see books, titles of books, book-cover designs blurred as if underwater. High small window in a wall. Posters on walls, the figure of a girl in an old-fashioned pinafore— exactly matching the *Alice in Wonderland* poster on the office wall.

Only a few books remain now on the bookshelves. Most are YA novels. Several copies of *Little Women, A Girl of the Limberlost, The Secret Garden, To Kill a Mockingbird, True Grit*. Selections of poems by Edgar Allan Poe, Emily Dickinson, Robert Frost, Mary Oliver. It was known that Fox kept multiple copies of favorite books to give to students who then praised their English teacher for his "generosity"— "kindness."

These books, you can be sure would pass any decency test if parents took the time to read them.

Always depend upon a pervert to pass himself off as *good, kind, normal, not-a-pervert.*

Zwender leafs through several books in the bookcase, not sure what he's looking for. A love note from a *kitten?*—not likely. No blood-traces on the edges of pages.

Zwender surmises, like Odom, that books that were contaminated were removed from the office along with other bloodstained or -splattered items, which accounts for the relative paucity of books remaining.

Forensic technicians didn't find blood-traces on any remaining books. Overall, no blood-traces in 015.

Yet, Zwender is convinced that this office is the *crime scene.*

Despite the opened window a faint stink of disinfectant and bleach persists.

Faint stink of the predator who, though deceased, body parts cremated, official lifetime ended, yet persists.

There was never a time when I didn't love Mr. Fox.

If he is dead there is no reason for me to live.

Zwender sits at Fox's old desk. Swivel chair, cushioned seat. From this position he can see out into the corridor. (He has left the door open, to help air out the office.) He can see the shrine to MR. FOX messily arranged on the bench, artificial flowers, sprigs of autumn leaves. Valentines on the wall above.

No shrine will mark his life/death, Zwender thinks. If he doesn't hurry and purchase a cemetery plot, he might not have one at all.

On the other side of the aluminum desk is a straight-backed wooden chair, less comfortable than the teacher's chair: for students.

In this swivel chair, and in its near surroundings, much of *Sleeping Beauties 2013* was recorded. In Francis Fox's arms, *kittens* held captive. Fed treats laced with barbiturate. Made to endure tongue-kisses, fondling. Yet, not a trace remains today.

On two walls colorful posters and a third wall empty: too empty. Wiped-down, spotless.

Colleagues of Fox's with offices in the corridor whom investigators interviewed weren't certain what might have been on the wall. They hadn't visited Fox often in his office, Francis was usually "too busy with students."

Some said that Fox "acted like he didn't want anyone hanging around—like he was waiting for a student to come in."

Still, few of Fox's colleagues at the Langhorne school were willing to speak negatively of him. Several, like librarian Imogene Hood who'd claimed to be Fox's *closest friend* in Wieland, spoke of him in the most exaggerated terms, as a dedicated teacher, a person of great integrity . . .

How Fox had fumed against the novel *Lolita*! Proof that *he couldn't possibly be a pedophile himself.*

When Zwender and his team first entered Fox's office several weeks before there were scattered papers on the top of Fox's desk, which were taken away by forensic technicians; now, the top of the desk is clear.

It's an aluminum desk, not large. One large top drawer, three smaller drawers on each side, these smaller drawers wiped clean.

P. Cady, in cooperation with Wieland police, has ordered 015 Haven Hall quarantined as a crime scene; in January, the order may be rescinded, and the office assigned to another faculty member.

Innocent occupant, no idea that its previous occupant has been murdered!

Blunt-force trauma to the back of the head: the medical examiner speculated that Fox was struck repeatedly with something hard, heavy, yet sharp-edged. A weapon brought to the office, or something already in the office? A weapon of opportunity.

No one would choose to kill another person in an office at a school, even after-hours. Had to be an act of opportunity, Zwender thinks.

Premeditated murder would indicate another setting, more private. Myriad other more practical settings including Fox's apartment.

A crime of opportunity is likely to be a crime of desperation, panic. Not-premeditated: not-prepared.

Why Francis Fox's body was removed from the premises, transported miles away presumably in Fox's own vehicle, dumped in a needlessly complicated manner—the murderer must have thought that the body might not be found in the wetlands; or, if found, believed to have died in an accident or as a suicide.

Zwender has thought: Whoever killed Fox didn't want his body to be found in his office because he didn't want suspicion to fall on someone associated with the school; which could mean, the murderer *is* associated with the school. Student, fellow teacher, parent or older relative of a student.

But no young person could orchestrate such a crime. No prepubescent girl.

Whoever it was had to know how to drive a car. Had to be strong enough to carry or drag Fox's body out to the car. Had to know back roads, service roads at Wieland Pond.

Virtually all of Fox's Langhorne colleagues were interviewed, over a period of weeks. A scattering of parents, male relatives of (suspected) *kittens*. Father of Mary Ann Healy.

No one who fit the profile, really. No one *plausible*.

Blake Healy had been Zwender's (brilliant) hypothesis. Yet, mistaken.

Couldn't have been a colleague of Fox's. No man and (especially) no woman in any soft profession like teaching.

All this, Zwender has thought many times. His mind is captive to a loop that keeps repeating. He feels that he is close to grasping the answer, yet it eludes him.

What Zwender doesn't wish to think: that whoever killed Francis Fox doesn't live in Wieland; isn't associated with the school; might be someone who knew Fox in the past, at another school; someone who wanted him dead for no reason that Zwender could ever discover.

Was it possible, one of the sick-pervert subscribers to *Sleeping Beauties* learned Fox's identity, came to see him? Infatuated with *Little Kitten* and wanted to meet her? The sort of deranged thing that happens because of the Internet.

In his maddening way Odom has hinted at this. An "unknown variable."

Even suggesting that maybe, just maybe, Francis Fox wasn't murdered but did actually take his own life.

And you will never know, Detective. You will never "solve" the mystery.

You will die, not knowing a damned thing.

Since Blake Healy assaulted Zwender in the interview room Zwender has had severe headaches. As if the zipper-stitches in his scalp have burrowed into the dermal matter like literal spiders. In the night sleepless, miserable, sweating he can feel tiny pincers sinking deep, deeper into the soft matter of his brain.

Related to this, a sense of disequilibrium. Frequently these days he has to catch his balance, press his hand against a wall. When Odom attacked him shoving him backward he'd damned-near fallen except Odom had the decency to reach out and steady him.

If H. Zwender had had a son, Daryl Odom might've been that son. Smart-aleck, son-of-a-bitch smug insufferable know-it-all worsened by being a self-righteous Christian. But yes, Zwender has to admit, *smart.*

Has to smile recalling the way Odom staggered out of the interview room shaky-kneed and his face drained of blood. Had to be scared shitless.

Disrespecting a senior detective in front of a civilian!

Only vaguely does Zwender recall what he said to Odom. In the heat and confusion of the moment he uttered words he (clearly) didn't mean, should not be used against him.

Soon, Zwender will forget having said anything at all. Though Daryl Odom might not forget.

Zwender does recall striking his junior officer in the face, that hard ridge of bone above the eye that hurt his fist like hell, felt for a few minutes like he'd broken a knuckle or two.

Why a man never fights bare-knuckle if he can avoid it. Have to be very, very stupid or just inexperienced to risk breaking a fist.

God damn Odom for *provoking* his superior officer.

Have to credit him: Daryl didn't slink away to nurse his wounds, or go whining to the police chief. Staggered out to the vending machine for a Coke or two to bolster his courage, then reported back to Zwender having washed his face, composed and contrite and no longer panting like a cornered animal, the bleeding above his eye stanched with Kleenex and turning into a bruise.

"I was out of line, Detective. Sorry."

Zwender was engaged in typing up the interview. Never had learned to type properly so he was striking keys with just two or three fingers, and his right hand hurting. Still indignant, insulted. Did the junior officer expect the senior officer to say with a grin It's OK, kid. Forget it.

It wasn't OK and Zwender wasn't going to forget it.

"It won't happen again, Detective."

Just calling Zwender "Detective" was such bullshit. Daring Zwender to believe that he was sincere.

Or, if Odom *was* sincere who gives a God damn? Zwender's judgment as a detective was challenged, and his dignity. In front of a civilian!

Odom's girth blocked Zwender's view from the single window in his small office. Only a parking lot in front of the Wieland Public Library but Zwender resented Odom just standing there, fuck this fake humility on Odom's part, *turning the other cheek* with typical Christian cunning putting the onus on the other, the insulted, to *forgive.*

Vaguely recalling, he threatened to kill his junior officer. Was that possible?

Not possible. Zwender is the most professional officer in the Wieland PD, the chief of police is always asking his advice.

At last glancing up at Odom as if surprised he was still there. More annoyed than enraged, didn't want Odom to guess how truly upset he was though he was placated (somewhat) by the look on Odom's face of sincere regret, residual fear. Almost visibly trembling like a dog that has been kicked for misbehaving and fears being kicked again.

Above Odom's right eye a yellowish-purple bruise the size of a plum.

Seeing this, the bruise, Zwender felt a twinge of mercy, satisfaction. In the way of a kindly priest absolving a sinner:

"Make yourself useful, Odom: Drive out to Home Depot, Walmart, Sears, hardware stores within a five–six-mile radius of Wieland, see if there were any unusual purchases of cleaning equipment in the last week of October. Check the Bridgeton mall, see what's there."

Relieved, Odom mumbled some kind of grateful assent. Possibly even, without irony, *Thanks, Detective!*

■

"DETECTIVE?"—A KNOCK ON THE frosted-glass window, in the doorway there's a vaguely familiar-looking person baring a mouthful of teeth at Zwender.

"Yes?"—Zwender rouses himself irritably from an open-eyed reverie for a moment scarcely recalling where he is.

With effort summoning up the name of this person: Quinn, Quinlan? Quilty? Former colleague of Fox's he interviewed several weeks ago.

"D'you remember me, Detective? Clarence Quilty."

"Of course. You're on the faculty here, Mr. Quilty. Your office is just next door."

Quilty appears flattered that the Wieland detective remembers him. But Zwender remembers everything associated with an open homicide file until he closes it and moves on.

Or once did, before the concussion perforated his brain.

Here's the killer: no one you suspected, Detective.

Come to gloat over Fox, and over you!

Such thoughts come to the detective like randomly shot arrows. As one long-practiced in the zen of detection Zwender allows all thoughts to sail into his orbit, he repels nothing no matter how preposterous for in Zwender's cosmology *all is possible that is not impossible.*

"Just thought I'd say hello, Detective. Is there anything I can help you with? Any—questions?"

A crafty look has come into Quilty's face. Zwender recognizes this look: the (former) colleague/friend eager to betray the deceased in the interest of "justice."

It is often the case that individuals change their minds over time as their respect, awe, fear of the dead fades. They grasp the elemental truism that the dead are gone and will not return to reciprocate.

For the dead are not permanent in their stature but soon begin to shift, like seismic plates in the living earth. Immediately following death the deceased is bathed in a soft flattering light that eventually fades or turns into garish fluorescence exposing all flaws.

Zwender in a genial mood, indicating that Quilty should step inside the office.

Quilty glances about in nervous excitement, sniffing the air. One of those naïve civilians who imagines that a detective investigating a probable crime will tell him something he doesn't already know.

"Some of us were wondering why this office smells so—like disinfectant . . ."

"Are you one of those, Mr. Quilty?"

Zwender casts Quilty a zinc-eyed smile, in all affability.

"No, but—my office is just next door . . . It's hard not to notice."

"When did you first notice the smell?"

"Oh, weeks ago—it was stronger then. Did something happen in this office, that it had to be, I guess, fumigated? We've asked about it but no one seems to know."

"Who did you ask, Mr. Quilty?"

Quilty shrugs uneasily as if he isn't sure. As Zwender recalls, Clarence Quilty is a middle-school English teacher, like Francis Fox; no doubt, he found himself an involuntary rival of the popular Mr. Fox.

Quilty is a strikingly unattractive man in his mid-forties: no taller than five feet five inches, thick in the torso, almost entirely bald with a fringe of feathery hair. His face suggests a camel's face with a slightly protuberant snout, prominent teeth, the camel's combination of cartoon awkwardness and toothy cunning, menace.

"I guess—Francis's office is going to be reassigned next semester . . ." Quilty pauses as if waiting for Zwender to comment; but Zwender has no comment. "All our offices in this corridor are small like this. About the size of a cell at Attica."

"Actually, no. Cells at Attica are smaller than this," Zwender says. "For two men."

"*Two* men? Jesus!"—Quilty shudders as if he's sharing a joke with Zwender who looks at him imperturbably.

Quilty was evasive in his remarks about Francis Fox several weeks ago. Professing surprise, shock, sorrow at his colleague's death yet thrilled by it, clearly. Now, Zwender guesses that Quilty has become jealous, resentful of the posthumous Mr. Fox—too much student adulation. Right outside his office, a makeshift shrine on a bench he has to see every day.

". . . it's gotten to be a kind of cult. Even my smartest students, who should know better—who hadn't been *his* students. They're still distracted, daydreaming in classes, cutting classes. Girls are fainting in class. There's the most ridiculous talk of Fox 'haunting' his class-room on the second floor. Some students claim to be afraid to enter the room. Others 'seek out Mr. Fox's spirit' in the room. 'Mr. Fox is not really gone but is still with us'—'In bright sunshine you can al-most see Mr. Fox.' Girls in the upper school who'd never so much as glimpsed Fox in person are swooning over him—getting 'Fox' tattoos on their wrists. Last night there was a 'prayer vigil'—before the win-ter break. The school spent a small fortune on a memorial service for Fox in the chapel, I think our headmistress is going a little bonkers over this. Francis was a favorite of hers, for some reason. Did you interview our headmistress, Detective? 'P. Cady'—she calls herself."

When Zwender responds with an enigmatic murmur Quilty laughs nervously saying in a bemused voice that in every issue of the student newspaper there are eulogies for Fox—"Absolutely maudlin drivel. *He* would have laughed at the poems, you know—Fox was like that."

"'Like—'?"

"Well, Francis had a side to him, students didn't know. Kind of a dark side. Francis could be *mean*. He could be *sadistic*. But he was fatuous, too—a *flaneur*-type. Some people thought he was gay and maybe that had something to do with it."

"'With—'?"

"Francis taking his life like he did. Like they are saying. 'Suicide' . . . "

Quilty waits for Zwender to respond but Zwender merely stares at him, impassively.

"It *was* suicide, wasn't it? He drove his car over a cliff, he drowned in a creek?—a pond? People are saying there was a note he'd left behind sent to P. Cady but I guess you would know about that, Detective. If there was one."

Zwender remains impassive. The flat zinc-eyes regard him so coldly, Quilty shivers again.

"There's a small but active LGBTQ community at Langhorne but Fox steered clear of them. They'd have liked to claim him, but—that wasn't Fox's strategy here."

"What was Fox's 'strategy'?"

"Some of us are pretty sure Francis just pretended to like private school teaching. It was a ruse so that he could, y'know, get close to students—girls mostly."

"Girls came often to his office after school?"—Zwender affects a kind of disinterested curiosity.

"Girls come to my office too," Quilty says stiffly. "I mean—students come to confer with us all, it's a Langhorne tradition to hold office hours. Francis *always* had a girl, or girls, waiting to see him; so many, he had to schedule appointments to limit the time a student could spend in his office." Quilty considers, frowning. "This seventh-grade girl who allegedly tried to kill herself—Genevieve Chambers—she was one of them. I'd see her in the hall outside Fox's office looking like she was excited, or scared, or had been crying. She'd sit on the bench doing homework, waiting. Francis scheduled this girl to be the last student he saw. When the rest of us locked up our offices and went home Fox's office would still be occupied—with the door shut."

"Why didn't you knock on the door, Mr. Quilty? If you thought something improper was going on."

"Well, I—I wouldn't have wanted Francis to think that I was spying on him. Or even particularly aware of him. We couldn't always be sure, Detective, that anyone *was* inside. Francis stayed late working every night. He liked to grade papers at school, he said, so he didn't have to take so much work home with him. You know, we give home-work assignments every night at this school, and we have to grade those assignments . . ."

"Were there any other girls who stayed late with Francis Fox, that you recall?"

"Well, yes—lots of girls. The Chambers girl was only one of them but she seemed to be a favorite. She was kind of quiet—somber. There were others who giggled like they were being killed. They'd be hanging out together in the corridor, giggling like idiots. They were all in love with Mr. Fox. There was another one, an eighth grader, who hung around Francis even more frequently, I think she exasperated him. Mary Ann Healy—her family lives in Wieland. A friend of mine on the faculty described how she saw Mary Ann Healy tagging after Francis Fox in the faculty parking lot, seemingly upset, trying to talk to him, and Francis ignored her, got into his car and almost ran her down driving away . . . It seemed clear to my friend that the two of them had been in Fox's office together, that Francis took advantage of her, because at that age—that young—a girl can't give *consent*. And afterward the girl was emotional, and Fox refused to speak to her or even look at her . . ."

"Did your friend intervene? Did she talk to Fox?"

"I—I don't think so. Not that I know."

"Did she talk to the girl?"

"Well—I don't know . . ."

"What's your friend's name?"

"I—I don't think that I should violate my friend's confidence . . ."

"Her name?"

Quilty hesitates, then provides Zwender with a name which Zwender duly notes.

"And the girl's name—'Mary Ann Healy'?"

"Y-yes . . ."

"Eighth grade, you said?"

"She's a scholarship girl. The school gives scholarships to local students, free tuition and costs. But I've been told that she has dropped out of scbool, no one has seen her in weeks."

Mary Ann Healy. Zwender feels rebuked, chagrined. It is looking as if the Healy girl *is* the link to Fox's killer, as he originally thought. Zwender has been distracted by Little Kitten, and nothing has come of that.

Quilty is recounting, bemused, how the Healy girl was always leaving gifts for Fox outside his office—little knitted things—love poems pushed under his door. Once, he and Fox were returning together from lunch and there was a folded note under his office door—"I picked it up and was going to read it aloud but Francis snatched it from me, he was embarrassed and angry, it looked like a love poem and I'm pretty sure the name attached was 'Mary Ann' . . ."

"You saw the name—'Mary Ann.'"

"I saw a handwritten poem in the shape of a heart, in purple ink. I'm almost one hundred percent sure the name at the bottom was 'Mary Ann.'"

"Did you report any of this to the school administration?"

Quilty hesitates, then says yes, he did—"Anonymously."

"Why anonymously?"

"Because I was afraid of recriminations. Our headmistress favored Francis Fox. She never followed through on any complaints about Fox, so it was pointless to make them."

"Yet, you did make the complaint. So you didn't think it was totally pointless."

"What it was, Detective, was *exasperating.* P. Cady makes a show of being 'impartial'—'objective'—but there she was inviting Francis Fox to her house for dinner, and he was just a new hire. I've been teaching here for eighteen years and I've never been invited to dinner with the head of school yet—receptions, yes. But never *dinner.*"

Zwender murmurs something sympathetic, conciliatory.

"The strange thing is," Quilty says, as if he has just thought of it, "—Francis was really something of a prude. He became sincerely upset if anyone spoke of *Lolita*—he thought the novel really was obscene, and shouldn't be sold. He had very particular reasons. He took up very conspicuously with a school librarian—Imogene Hood— (you've probably interviewed her already)—a sweet woman, naïve,

totally taken in by Francis Fox. *She's* the person I feel sorry for—
a kind of collateral victim."

"Is she."

Zwender is thinking that Clarence Quilty with his petty vindic-
tiveness and air of reproach isn't likely his man. No one in a soft
profession like teaching would be capable of such a violent murder.
And the follow-up at the ravine. Quilty would faint at the sight of
blood. A fist in his face would traumatize the man permanently; but
there is no plausible way that that could happen without Zwender
losing his job, so *no*.

Quilty says suddenly, decisively: "I know what's different here—
what's missing. I could see that something was wrong. The bust of
Poe is missing."

"'Poe'—?"

"It was right here, on the corner of Francis's desk. A bronze bust
of Edgar Allan Poe, some sort of poetry prize. Ugly thing. With a
raven on his shoulder."

"'Raven'—?"

"From the poem—'The Raven.' You know, Edgar Allan Poe."

"Some kind of statue?"

"A bust. Y'know—about a foot high."

"Was it heavy?"

"It *looked* heavy. Supposedly it was bronze, and bronze is heavy. It
doesn't seem to be anywhere in the office here, maybe Francis took it
home with him."

"What was it, exactly? Bronze bust of . . ."

"A bronze bust of Edgar Allan Poe, with a raven on his shoulder.
The likeness of Poe was actually quite good—uncanny. Poe had these
sad-puppy recessed eyes. A lock of hair falling over his forehead,
droopy mustache. The bronze head was the size of a man's actual
head and the raven was almost life-sized, with glittery little stones for
eyes. Francis laughed at the thing, he said it was pure *kitsch* but he
was obviously proud of it, too—why otherwise would he display it in
his office? His name was engraved on it—he'd won first prize in a Poe
Society competition. The only time I was actually invited into his of-

fice was when Francis wanted to show me the bust. He said he was going to get married and retire to Italy one day and concentrate on his poetry. That was his goal." Quilty laughs. "He'd say *my poetry.* Like, there was poetry, and there was *Francis Fox's poetry.*"

"How recently did you see this bronze bust?"

"How recently? I don't know—not for a while. We weren't so friendly, really. Francis was always busy, or gave that impression. He didn't seem to want colleagues as friends. Once I rapped on the door of his office, just to discuss something in the curriculum, but he damn near blocked me in the doorway. There was a girl in his office, probably the Chambers girl, he didn't want me to see."

"Was there."

Zwender has been examining the corner of Fox's desk. Nothing to see, no marks or discolorations on the aluminum desktop. If Fox had brought the object with him at the beginning of September, it hadn't been on the desk for very long; wouldn't have left a mark.

The murder weapon. Zwender is excited, exhilarated.

"Thank you for your time, Mr. Quilty. I have to lock up now."

It is always surprising to individuals whom Zwender has been questioning with a flattering sort of intensity, the abruptness with which the detective loses interest in them. As rudely decisive as a grating pulled down over a window.

Ushered out of the office by Zwender, Clarence Quilty looks disappointed, even crestfallen. Zwender is thinking how absurd it was to have ever speculated that Quilty might be capable of killing someone by striking him repeatedly on the head with a heavy object, let alone an adult male like himself; beyond that act, capable of carrying the body out to Fox's own car in the parking lot and driving miles into the wetlands, maneuvering the car up a steep hill and over the edge of a precipice while managing to leap free of the vehicle at the last second and save himself—a feat beyond the capacity of a Clarence Quilty.

IN THE RAVINE

D*etective! Got a surprise for you.*
        Francis Fox, that sick fuck, taunting *him.*

■

TELLING NO ONE, GIVING no hint where he's going. Taking the Wieland police cruiser because the heavy vehicle with four-wheel drive will handle the wetlands terrain better than his own car.

Into the soft-chittering solitude in feathery-light falling snow returning to the ravine near Wieland Pond. Alone, following the rutted service road into the interior.

Alone, so that he can think uninterrupted. For he feels he has been summoned.

Forty-fifth day since Fox's remains were discovered in this very place.

Fox!—no one more detestable. No one more deserving of being *dead.*

Yet: the detective has a premonition. Something unexpected awaits him at the ravine.

Cuts the engine at the foot of the overgrown trail leading steeply uphill where the dead man's Acura was made to topple into the ravine in an improbably silent cinematic sequence which Zwender has imagined so many times, he might (almost) believe that he has seen it, or has executed it himself: for (he thinks) he knows how it was done though he does not (yet) know who did it.

He has surprised himself having begun smoking again after twenty-seven years. Somehow, it has happened. The promise is: just one cigarette at a time.

A way to calm his nerves. Not that Zwender is a creature of *nerves*. He hasn't resumed drinking (yet). Won't give Fox that satisfaction.

What pleasure, to be *alone*. In this place. Lightly falling snow like pollen melting on the cruiser windshield before it can accumulate. He has turned off his cell phone, doesn't want to be interrupted by calls.

How many times Zwender has returned to the Wieland preserve since he first was summoned here six weeks before. At least three times. Since the concussion he has had memory lapses.

About which he has told no one, and will tell no one.

Climbs out of the cruiser, tosses away his cigarette. Makes his way up the hill. Excited to be here, off the grid. But edgy as well. If something is going to happen to a law enforcement officer it is not recommended that it happen when he is alone.

Zwender is discovering, his balance is slightly *off*. The tilted ground is giving him trouble. The hill is badly rutted, crisscrossed with deep tire tracks: tow truck, crane, vans. Trampled grasses, brambles that catch at his trouser legs. At the time of the "accident"—(as it is generally called in Wieland)—the hill was soft from rain, and muddy; more recently the surface of the mud has frozen preserving tracks and prints.

The first time he was at the site Zwender made his way unhesitatingly uphill in knee-high rubber boots. Warned of what he might be seeing, which only first responders and several young uniformed officers had seen so far. *Car wreck, driver killed, body dismembered.*

A collective frisson of excitement, dread. For it hadn't (yet) been determined that the obscene *dismemberment* of the human corpse had been caused by animals. It hadn't been determined that the "accident" had taken place several days before.

Zwender pauses to listen to the soft chittering of birds. These are likely to be swamp sparrows, cardinals, crows, a catbird. Bittersweet sounds of Zwender's lost boyhood.

No turkey vultures (yet) in sight.

Where six weeks before several trees at a safe distance from the hill were festooned with vultures hulked and patient, unblinkingly staring. You could see these creatures in silhouettes so still, it did not seem possible that they were living things.

Six weeks before there had thundered onto the hill such heavy-duty vehicles as a Wieland police van, an Atlantic County mortuary van, a flatbed truck, and a crane to haul the wrecked Acura out of the ravine spilling water as it was lifted and lowered onto the bed of the truck. EMTs in safety uniforms and goggles descended into the ravine to secure the bodily remains of the (yet-unidentified) man in plastic bags to be brought to the county morgue; scraps of clothing, torn and beginning to rot, remnants of a tweed jacket, chino trousers stained with fecal matter, faded blue cotton shirt badly stained with blood, shreds of socks, waterlogged shoes. All carefully bagged and tagged.

All that was definitely known of this luckless person at the time was that he was, or had been, an adult Caucasian male; and that he was alone.

At the time, at the scene, no one had reason to think that the situation was other than an accident. If it was like no accident most of them had seen it was not sufficiently unlike accidents that some of them had seen to warrant anything like immediate suspicion. And so emergency workers and police officers walked at random on the hill with no effort to preserve several sets of older footprints, in this way obscuring/contaminating what Zwender would recognize as a possible crime scene.

Zwender hadn't been summoned to the site initially. He'd been elsewhere, pursuing another investigation. Here, the situation appeared to be self-evident: a freakish vehicular accident resulting in the death of a single individual, presumably the driver. No other body, no other clothing. A young local man had called in a sighting of the wrecked car and a "dead body"—he'd claimed to have been drawn to the site by a large number of vultures circling above it. And so by the time Zwender arrived the battered white sedan was being lifted tremulously out of the ravine, lowered onto the flatbed truck which was atilt on the hillside, facing downhill. For a moment it looked as if the crane would topple over, the battered car would fall sickeningly onto the hill—but this did not happen.

On the flatbed, the Acura spectacularly leaked muddy water. Only one of its doors was open—the driver's door. The trunk was loose, ajar.

Zwender was shown digital photographs of those body parts that had been discovered by this time, bagged and stored in the (refrigerated) mortuary van. Much of the soft flesh on these parts had been devoured, torn by rapacious teeth, pecked by ravenous beaks. Only a portion of the Caucasian male's body would be recovered. The entire right hand, several toes from both feet, ears, tongue, genitals—missing, never recovered.

Zwender steeled himself to examine the close-up photos of the disembodied head. Jesus!—had to be the worst thing he'd ever seen.

Much of the face was missing. Empty eye sockets, missing nose—just a socket where there'd been a nose. The head was nearly scalped, what little (fair, wavy) hair remained was encrusted with mud and dried blood. The back of the skull appeared to be crushed as if struck by a heavy object repeatedly.

At once Zwender was alert, suspicious. There was something stagey about the entire scene. Not likely that the back of the head would be injured in this way, in a thirty-foot fall into a ravine along an embankment of boulders, small trees, and underbrush that would have impeded the fall, lessened the impact at the bottom.

First responders reported not having found a wallet, cell phone, wristwatch, or any personal ID anywhere in the car or in the vicinity of the car.

Had to be deliberate. Whoever was a party to the "accident" had removed these items.

For long minutes the wrecked car on the flatbed truck continued to leak brackish water. The smell of decomposition was acute. While others drew back fearful of vomiting Zwender pressed a handkerchief against his nose and mouth and went about the grim task of examining the interior of the car since he knew from past experience that no one would do so thorough a job as he would, if he delegated this task to a junior officer something crucial might be lost or contaminated that would never be recovered. Even forensic technicians in Newark, he could not entirely trust.

A single shoe, a man's left shoe, was discovered waterlogged on the floor by the driver's seat, and bagged; a matching shoe was found in the ravine. The Acura's glove compartment yawned open filled with muck and leaves. Registration and insurance documents were not to be found anywhere in the car or in its vicinity which would lead Zwender to wonder if the person who'd gone to such lengths to disguise the ownership of the vehicle had no practical knowledge that such ownership can be easily traced by law enforcement.

So much was missing from the scene, had to be deliberately moved but (surely) not premeditated. *Clumsily staged to resemble an accident.*

Leaning into the car that reeked of rot and muck Zwender ran his (gloved) hand beneath the front seats and at last found a small object beneath the passenger seat: what appeared to be a bracelet of feathers, beads, and lace, covered in mud.

A handmade bracelet, something a child might make.

For *him,* he wanted to think. For always the detective wished to believe that fate, or karma, whatever it might be called, left something special for him and for him alone.

And so in this way suffused with meaning for Zwender. Something precious that had been recovered from filth. Lifted in Zwender's hand for others to see.

"Hey, guys: look what I've found."

No way of knowing whether this object had been in the car for days, weeks, months, or whether it had fallen to the floor of the car on the last day of the driver's life and so its identification might reveal what had happened to the driver, and why.

Within a week the little feather bracelet would be identified as having belonged to an eighth-grade Langhorne student named Mary Ann Healy, who lived with her mother on the outskirts of Wieland and who'd made bracelets resembling these for relatives and friends; a girl who was said to have "disappeared" from her home sometime on October 25.

Not long afterward, fingerprints belonging to Mary Ann Healy would be discovered in the bathroom of Francis Fox's apartment on Consent Street.

By this time, the remains of Francis Fox had been identified. It seemed clear that Fox had been involved in some way with his student Mary Ann Healy; if the girl's body had been found it would surely have been her teacher who'd murdered her. But Mary Ann Healy was reported to be alive, in hiding somewhere in Atlantic City, it was asserted by Healy relatives. Mary Ann's parents did not report her as a *runaway,* there was no bulletin for Jersey police to search for her. There was no justification for a high-priority search for her. No arrest warrant, for police to seek her out.

Zwender has tried through contacts in the Atlantic City PD to locate the girl, hoping to speak with her in person or, failing that, on the phone. Her mother, Pauline, has pleaded with police officers not to harass or frighten Mary Ann for that will only cause her to run farther.

A very sensitive girl, Pauline has said. Not such a happy girl, there'd been trouble at school, not her fault but teasing, bullying by boys. Plus, Mary Ann was heartbroken that her father had moved out of the house.

Zwender is (again) convinced: the Healy girl is the link to Fox's death.

Interviewing her father turned out to be a dead end yet still, Zwender is optimistic that this is the right track.

Loathsome to him to consider how Fox must have abused this girl.

By all accounts a shy girl, ill-at-ease at school. For a scholarship student, unusually reticent, inarticulate. Fox took advantage of Mary
Ann Healy's shyness, her lack of friends at the private school. Allegedly, she followed after him in public places, in clear distress. She
was seen crying in the basement corridor of Haven Hall. Quilty
claimed that she and Francis Fox had been seen together on the
school campus, that Mary Ann had followed after Fox pleading with
him, he'd nearly run her down with his car . . .

Even if the relationship is consensual, an adult who has sexual
relations with a child of thirteen is guilty of rape.

Filthy pig, Zwender thinks. His adrenaline surges at the thought
of anything resembling pedophilia.

Yet Odom pointed out, there wasn't evidence that Mary Ann
Healy was one of Fox's abused *kittens.* There were no photos, no videos of the two together. There were no photos, videos of Mary Ann
Healy among Francis Fox's online files at all. In his grim-obsessive
way Odom scrolled through the entirety of *Sleeping Beauties* not once
but twice in pursuit of any female figure resembling Mary Ann Healy
in photographs of the girl with which he'd been provided but he'd
never found one—"Not even close. This Healy girl wasn't Fox's
'type.'"

To this provocative remark Zwender made no reply. His strategy
with smart-ass Odom was to ignore him.

Odom persisted: Maybe the girl was pursuing Fox. Maybe Fox
wasn't the one pursuing *her.*

Sensing how skeptical Zwender was of this notion Odom said that
some thirteen-year-old girls can surprise you, how they behave.

"My own wife, when she was that age. She'd be kind of, you know,
flirting with me at school—I was three years older . . ." Odom
laughed, embarrassed, or pretending to be embarrassed.

Zwender turned away shaking with indignation, disapproval. He
wasn't sure if it was what Odom was saying or the fact of Odom saying it, the insubordination inherent in Odom's continual disagree-
ments with his senior officer, that most infuriated Zwender.

Suffused with dislike of both Daryl Odom and Francis Fox. Determined to (somehow) punish both.

Zwender finds himself short of breath at the top of the hill. Peers into the ravine, feeling a moment's vertigo. All he can see is storm debris, boulders, and rocks, dark water lightly filmed with frost. Organic rot faint as memory lifts to his nostrils.

A vision of the (disembodied) human head. Most of the scalp torn away, eyeless sockets, gaping nose-socket, ears and tongue missing, devoured by scavengers. Zwender recalls that in fact he didn't see the head in the ravine, he saw only photographs, appalling close-ups.

He did not see the ghastly-white torso, the scattered limbs. Bones picked clean that would be identified by the medical examiner. He did not even see the white sedan upended in three feet of water, the driver's door flung open.

Of course the driver's door was open: whoever had driven Fox to this place had had to leap from the car as it was about to topple over into the ravine.

Requiring an individual, certainly male, who is skilled at driving, and fearless, or reckless. For such a desperate maneuver couldn't be rehearsed, it had to be one-time-only.

The killer has to be a local resident. Someone familiar with the service road into the nature preserve, the (near-invisible) trail uphill, the ravine itself.

Zwender believes he knows exactly what this person did: he gunned the motor to get the car to the top of the hill, then put on the safety brake, to secure it; assuming that the body was hunched over in the passenger seat, (probably) covered with a tarpaulin, he had to remove the tarpaulin, and prepare the body in some way to make it seem plausible that this individual had been driving and had driven his car into the ravine. The perpetrator assumed that the wreckage would obscure other details, or he assumed that (possibly) the car would never be found. But he reckoned without turkey vultures, in that he made a fatal mistake.

He had to climb out of the car while the motor was still running; he had to release the safety brake even as with a stick or a board he depressed the gas pedal to urge the car forward and over the edge. He could not have taken time to make his way down into the ravine to see what the staged wreck looked like. To see how the body had fallen—if it looked like the victim had been driving. He wouldn't have wanted to risk this. He must have retreated on foot, unless he had an accomplice in another vehicle. His footsteps would be imprinted in the soft mud of the hill, descending only.

He was wearing gloves, for no helpful fingerprints were lifted from the steering wheel. Even Fox's prints on the wheel were badly degraded.

The wind is picking up, smelling of the Atlantic. Yet it is very quiet here, as if everything is *past tense.*

Zwender's heart is knocking against his ribs. He should not have resumed smoking, that was a mistake: a victory for Fox. He will stop, in another week or two.

The detective is a man of middle age who, if he had a wife, he would try to hide his shortness of breath from her, and the fact that he has resumed smoking; but he has no wife, thus no one to hide anything from.

A younger version of Lemuel Healy, fixated upon his job. And his job wearing him out, eviscerating him.

Another fixation of Zwender's is the *murder weapon.* He is certain that he knows what it was, and he has a strong belief that it was tossed into the ravine at some point, or into Wieland Pond. Very likely, other items (wallet, cell phone, wristwatch, etc.) were tossed into the same place.

Could have been a sinkhole, deep in the Pine Barrens. A quicksand bog.

This object, which Quilty identified as a "bronze bust" of Edgar Allan Poe, is somewhere in the vicinity, Zwender is sure. No idea where.

The Wieland PD doesn't have resources for searching a body of water as large and as deep as Wieland Pond, let alone the countless sinkholes and bogs of the wetlands. Doesn't have the manpower, can't afford overtime. Can't hire someone from another PD, all small New Jersey PDs are understaffed.

Zwender is at the point of obsession at which he'd work for no salary if necessary. He has the distinct feeling that the police chief is going to dismantle his team early in 2014. If he doesn't solve this case by then he will have to give it up, or continue it on his own as a kind of rogue detective.

Then again, he tries to consider a Buddhist objectivity: none of this matters, it is all passing, past.

Making his way along the ridge of the hill. Casting his eye about for something—anything . . . He'd had luck finding the little feather bracelet belonging to Mary Ann Healy, and he'd had luck encountering Clarence Quilty the previous day. Otherwise, a rivulet of bad luck like dirty water.

Since police officers and emergency workers wore standard-issue boots with distinctive soles, forensic technicians were able to eliminate most of the tangle of their footprints from the footprints photographed on the hill; what remained were somewhat degraded footprints belonging to the Healy brothers Marcus and Demetrius, which could be traced ascending the hill, and descending the hill, in exactly the area one would expect their footprints to be found. But there was a set of other, older and more degraded footprints, descending the hill a short distance away; no way to determine when these footprints were made for they were not clear enough. Could have been weeks before, possibly. Or just days. Or hours.

An expert in forensic footprints could provide more precise findings but no one at the New Jersey State Bureau of Criminal Investigations is willing to spend more time on the Wieland case which is no high priority, as nothing in Wieland, New Jersey, is considered a high priority.

"Fuck it."

Almost, Zwender can see the face jeering at him. The face of Fox's killer yet also Fox's face, the two have conflated as in a funhouse mirror.

∎

ZWENDER GIVES UP THE search, for today.

In the near distance is Wieland Pond, dully gleaming in the light-less light. And somewhere near, the cry of an owl: a screech owl. A cry of melancholy yearning, resignation. A sound Zwender remembers from boyhood, that never fails to move him emotionally.

Thicker tufts of snow are falling, and not melting. Zwender descends the hill a little faster than he intends, skidding on his heels. Seeing then, at the foot of the hill, in a patch of brambles, what appears to be the scat of an owl, a cluster of tiny bones, and among these a larger object resembling a human toe bone, a man's big toe, with what looks like a dark-gnarled nail.

Jesus!—did an owl devour one of Francis Fox's toes, digest the flesh, and excrete the bone? To be discovered in this place, at just this hour, by Detective Zwender? He laughs aloud, this is fucking weird. What's meant by *grace.*

For the first time feeling, for Francis Fox, something like pity. The sympathy of one mortal being for another.

With his (gloved) hand picking up the little toe-bone. Detaching it from the owl scat surrounding it. No need to turn this in, Fox's big-toe-bone with the dark-gnarled nail has become *his.*

GOOD-LUCK PIECE

A *good-luck piece. You deserve it, Detective.*
Stopping by the house in which Pauline Healy is living without a husband—as a "single mother"—on his way back to the Wieland PD.

Feeling the need to try one more time looking through the missing girl's room.

With Odom and others he'd done a search at the residence but they found nothing to connect Mary Ann Healy with Francis Fox— nothing to suggest where the missing girl might be—but Zwender is thinking he will try again for possibly his luck *has* changed.

Five miles south of Wieland on Stockton Road. Much of the farmland here is no longer under cultivation, pastures have become overgrown. There are mobile homes amid weedy fields, small "ranch houses" alternating with farmhouses originally built in the late 1800s. North of Wieland are new upscale housing developments with names like Pheasant Meadows, Greenway Hills, Juniper Acres; south of Wieland is farmland reverted to the wild, unnamed.

Zwender stares at names on mailboxes. *Healy, B.*—faded letters almost unreadable amid a cluster of tall grasses.

At the end of the lengthy eroded driveway is the luminous pale-yellow farmhouse he remembers from the previous visit but had forgotten until now.

Pale-yellow-jonquil! Unexpected color amid the faded-sere colors of December, the detective feels a stirring of something like—hope?

Rusted cattle guard at the foot of the driveway. Dull galvanized roofs of farm buildings. Hay barn, cow barn, silo weatherworn and on the verge of collapse. Scattered hulks of abandoned cars, a pickup truck, John Deere tractor. Rusted drums, metal piping, rotted tarpaulin in piles. The barnyard is overgrown, fence posts have fallen. Most of the farm's acreage has been sold. Decades since anyone living on this property has raised cattle.

So thinly has the sprawling old farmhouse been painted jonquil-yellow, patches of bare clapboard have begun to push through. Typical of Blake Healy, painting the house himself, with local help, using the cheapest paint and only giving it a single layer.

The shingled roof of the house is sagging, miniature saplings sprout out of rain gutters. On the veranda are a soiled bamboo mat, outdoor vinyl furniture, empty clay pots. Against a veranda railing, a rusted bicycle with flat tires.

Zwender feels a twinge of guilt: it's because of him that Blake Healy, Pauline's husband, has been jailed in the county detention at Red Wing on a charge of aggravated assault against a law enforcement officer; because of Zwender unwittingly provoking the man, or perhaps not so unwittingly, the Healy family has been further sabotaged.

Not that Blake Healy was living here at the time of the assault. He'd moved out of the house at least a year before, Pauline was living alone with Mary Ann. There are two older brothers in this branch of the Healy family, one of them in the navy, the other living and working in Edison, New Jersey.

Both brothers, as well as the father, have been interviewed, as possible persons of interest who might have had reason to inflict harm upon Francis Fox, but nothing has come of the interviews.

The detective is obliged to follow a protocol of *elimination*.

If/when all other suspects are *eliminated,* the suspect remaining is (likely) to be the guilty party.

Unless (the detective must acknowledge) a fatal blunder has been made, and the protocol has failed to include the guilty party: in which case there will be no closure.

Blake Healy will plead guilty to the charge, with his record he will spend at least five years in prison, probably maxing out, no parole. If he'd killed Francis Fox, and pleaded guilty to manslaughter, he might've drawn a shorter sentence, with a possibility of parole. The left-behind wife, Pauline, will lose even the reduced income Blake Healy was providing her, his daughter will lose what minimal child support he might have been providing. The service station he co-owns, heavily mortgaged, will probably shut down.

Pauline Healy should divorce her husband but probably will not. In rural Jersey broken marriages like theirs persist for years out of inertia until something catastrophic happens—the husband falls ill, the wife takes him in and cares for him until he dies. Or, the wife dies of some kind of cancer, the husband is heartbroken, remarries within months.

At a point in life, a man wants someone to care for him; but has become leery of caring for others, with a likelihood of ending up alone (again).

In Zwender's case, his ex-wife isn't likely to take him in; she has remarried, moved out of state.

Too young yet, to wonder who will take care of *him.*

But since the concussion, maybe not.

Zwender parks the cruiser in front of the house beside Pauline's compact Nissan. The dull-opalescent sky feels too large overhead, his eyes ache. He's conscious of the ugly wound in his scalp. As he approaches the veranda the front door is opened abruptly—"Yes? What do you want?" Pauline Healy stands in the doorway, in her face a look of anxiety, dread.

Expecting to hear that her daughter is dead.

Quickly Zwender assures Pauline, he isn't a bearer of bad news.

"Jesus. You scared me half to death . . ."

Pauline tries to laugh, pressing the flat of her hand against her chest. Her eyebrows have been plucked thin, her eyelids seem to be lashless. She regards Zwender warily, distrustfully. He has no need to identify himself, Pauline knows who he is.

Zwender asks if he can come inside—"Just for a few minutes."

Never invite law enforcement into your house! Zwender knows exactly what Pauline Healy is thinking. Wordlessly Pauline opens the door wider, invites Zwender inside. She'd like to close the door in his face but fears antagonizing him.

Pauline Healy is a cashier at the 7-Eleven where Zwender stops for coffee, in recent weeks Pauline hasn't been so friendly toward him.

First thing Zwender notices about Pauline, she isn't wearing makeup, as she usually does at the 7-Eleven. Her lipstick has worn off, hasn't been freshened. Her shoulder-length hair which is some kind of streaked dirty-blond hasn't been combed. She's wearing a loose-fitting beige sweater, faded jeans tight across the buttocks. On her feet, water-stained sneakers with twin worn spots, oddly, at each of her smallest toes. And on her left wrist, a little homemade bracelet of feathers, beads, glitter, yarn.

Zwender has never seen Pauline wear this bracelet at the 7-Eleven. Maybe just at home, in private.

It's clear that Pauline is alone in the house, wasn't expecting a visitor. There's a special aura a woman exudes in such circumstances like (for instance) being wakened, roused out of bed unexpectedly.

As Zwender passes close by Pauline Healy a sensation of unease, excitement leaps between them like an electric current.

He sees Pauline glance at his head, the shaved swath of scalp, zigzag stitches. A quick, intimate glance. That Pauline doesn't react as most people do, doesn't ask Zwender what the wound is, allows Zwender to know that she knows what it is, and who caused it.

The woman is self-conscious, wary. It's her bright-bantering way in the 7-Eleven, to keep men at a distance: "Seeing the police car out there, Detective—seeing you coming up the driveway—like army officers coming to somebody's house to inform them that their son has died 'in action.' The officers are in dress uniform, they wear white gloves, they're all spiffy and shiny and you have no choice but to let the bastards in."

Pauline laughs a little too loudly. Wanting to assure Zwender that she isn't being sarcastic or reproachful, she is just trying to be funny.

"If there was news of Mary Ann you'd be contacted by phone, Pauline. I'd contact you myself. I promise."

Something tender about *promise*. Pauline seems mollified.

It is believed that Mary Ann Healy has sought sanctuary with relatives, or friends of relatives, in Atlantic City. They are hiding her, harboring her. Exactly why isn't clear but (Zwender supposes) it must have something to do with Francis Fox, or it might have something to do with family squabbling. Mother, daughter. Estranged father.

Adolescent girls trying to take their own lives in the past twenty years or so, it's something like an epidemic. Mostly they don't succeed, it's male adolescents who more often succeed.

Pauline leads Zwender into the living room where she switches on a lamp. A cluttered cozy interior, reminds Zwender of the living rooms of his childhood, aunts, grandparents; probably some of the furnishings in this room date from earlier generations. There's a smell of cigarette smoke here, on a side table is a half-filled glass of red wine.

Not good to drink alone, Pauline should have company.

Colorful pillows are scattered on the sofa, a knitted afghan. What looks like dog hairs on the cushions. The TV is medium-sized, not new. Flickering images shimmer on the screen in the forlorn foolish way of TV not being watched.

Nervously Pauline turns the feather bracelet around her wrist. Unlike the mud-stained bracelet in the evidence bag at the Wieland PD this bracelet is brightly colored, russet-red, jaybird-blue feathers, shiny little glass beads.

"Nice bracelet. Something your daughter made?"

"Y-yes. It is."

"Did Mary Ann make many bracelets like that?"

Pauline looks at the bracelet as if she hasn't been aware of it. As if she resents Zwender noticing it.

"No, just something she did one summer. Each bracelet is different . . ."

"How many d'you think she made?"

"How *many*? Christ! Who'd know? Who's keeping track?"

"Were they for sale, or just for special people?"

"Just for special people."

Each bracelet, for someone she loved.

"That looks like something you could sell, in a gift store . . ."

Pauline ignores this remark. Since they passed close together in the hall she has been keeping a little distance between them.

Nonetheless, Pauline asks Zwender if he'd like a drink?—Zwender guesses that she wants to finish that glass of wine herself, he tells her thanks, no.

"Because you're on duty, Detective?"

On duty is intended as some sort of rebuke, sounds so prim, pious.

"That's right."

"And you never drink 'on duty,' Detective—is that possible?"

"It's possible."

"Well, then—coffee?"

"Maybe later."

"How much later?"

Pauline laughs seeing that Zwender is looking pained.

Adding, in a less abrasive tone, that it must be hard, hard on the nerves, delivering bad news to people. Seeing that, when people see you, they want to run away.

Zwender says it *is* hard. Especially in a small town like Wieland where you're likely to know almost everyone.

This comes out sounding more serious than he intended. Pauline regards Zwender with a quizzical look.

Does she blame him for Blake, he is wondering. No? Yes.

Pauline is telling him that today is an early day for her at the store. Early shift, home by three P.M. She liked to be home when Mary Ann came home from school but that wasn't always possible and she regrets it now.

Being a parent, having a kid, having kids with another person, the two of you *parents*. Nobody tells you how weird that is.

Needing to unwind, today.

Why today?—Zwender asks.

It's stressful at the 7-Eleven, nowhere to hide if you're a cashier. People asking about Mary Ann, what's the latest news, rumors she doesn't want to hear, they make her crazy. And now Blake in jail, Jesus!—like it's anybody's business but her own. Like she wants to put a paper bag over her head so no one knows who she is. People mean well—mostly. The worst are the ones you went to high school with, or Blake went to high school with. Or Healy relatives. Or *her* relatives. But going home is worse because the house is *empty*. Not just that Mary Ann is missing but the boys, and Blake, though they haven't been living in this house for a while still she misses them, heavy footsteps on the stairs, voices not TV voices, making supper for someone not just herself. *That* is the worst.

She'd never be living alone in this remote damned place if she had any choice.

Don't tell her, the countryside is *beautiful*. Not to her, it isn't.

Zwender tells Pauline that she shouldn't assume Mary Ann won't be back. If they're in contact, that's the important thing. It's a statistical fact that missing teenagers usually return home in a month or two.

"Do they! If they are alive, you mean."

"But Mary Ann has called you? When was the last call?"

"Last Friday. We talked only for about five minutes . . ."

Pauline's voice trails off, she doesn't want to tell Zwender anything more.

Police can't track Mary Ann Healy's cell phone since she keeps it turned off most of the time. Zwender has wondered if the thirteen-year-old is canny enough to know about tracking via cell phone or whether the girl is in the company of someone older who has taken charge of her.

"You haven't seen her, since she left home?"

"No! Mary Ann doesn't want to see anyone from Wieland—including her mother."

"And you don't know where she is?"

"I—I don't know where she is. I've told you."

Pauline speaks haltingly, not looking Zwender in the face. Very likely she isn't telling the entire truth which isn't the same as lying.

In an interrogation, that would be the "tell": not looking the detective in the face.

Pauline sits on the sofa, lights a cigarette. Saying in a rush of words: "I hate this! I hate this waiting and not-knowing. First, people were saying that Mary Ann ran away with her English teacher, then they were saying that Blake 'abducted' his own daughter—they were hiding in Atlantic City! Now Blake is in jail, and Fox is dead, so I don't know what they're saying but *it isn't true*. Jesus knows what I did wrong, my life is shit now. There's a pounding in my ears, someone told me that's high blood pressure. You can have a stroke. I tried to be a good mother—I think I *was*. But what could I do, if kids picked on Mary Ann? If guys stare at her, and follow her, and try to get her into their cars? I had her wear loose clothes, clothes too big for her, she never wears makeup like other girls her age, she wouldn't *dare*. I used to have low blood pressure! I used to weigh twenty pounds less than I do now. I'm always feeling that I should be here, at home, in case Mary Ann comes back, in case she needs me, but when I'm here in the country the quiet drives me crazy, I keep the TV on. At work I feel that I should be home, and at home I want to be somewhere else. When I drive back and forth I'm in this weird state, like panic. Today at the 7-Eleven I had a premonition that someone would be waiting for me here, or was already here, and I couldn't remember if I'd locked the door—lots of times I forget, and I get back home after dark, and the damned door is unlocked, and I'm scared to step inside. There's guys who talk to me at the 7-Eleven, that I can't avoid, I don't mean that they are harassing me, or hitting on me exactly, but they say things to me, they ask about Blake, and if I'm living alone, and I don't know what to do about it. Because I need my job. Because I can't just quit. Because I'd be alone out here full-time.

With Mary Ann here, I never worried about living out here. With just one other person, you don't worry."

Zwender is moved that Pauline has confided in him. He's wondering if she has forgiven him, for Blake.

"Has anyone showed up here at the house, uninvited?"

"N-no . . . I don't know."

"What d'you mean, you don't know?"

"I don't *know*. I'm on the sofa here watching TV late at night, sometimes I think I see headlights out on the road, I'm scared as hell. Blake had guns, when he was living here—he took them . . . Not that I'd know how to use a gun. For all I know it could be Blake himself out there, or might've been, before he was arrested. Sometimes I turn off the lights so if someone is out there he can't see inside. I run upstairs, lock myself in the bedroom . . . There's a lock on the bedroom door."

"If anyone bothers you, Pauline, let me know? I'll talk to him."

"Oh no—really . . . There's no one, really. I don't want to cause any trouble, like with my job—that's the last thing I want. Nobody wants to hire a woman if she's going to cause trouble. You have to keep it low-key. It's being 'single'—a 'single woman'—you can attract the wrong kind of man without realizing. Some men, they assume that a woman who's alone will be interested in them, they have no idea what a relief it is, just to be alone—that is, a 'single mother.' But I'm not ready to be actually *alone*. I guess that's what I'm saying."

Pauline is speaking disjointedly, her words are slightly slurred.

A random thought comes to Zwender: This woman needs protection, *he* might protect her. Might marry Pauline Healy if she divorces Blake Healy. If Pauline could be interested in him, H. Zwender, a divorced man fifteen years older than she is, with a permanent zigzag scar in his scalp.

Thoughts like arrows flying at him, that pass him by. What Zwender has read of zen, this is zen. He has learned not to be surprised by his most outlandish thoughts but to let them pass, vanish. Zwender asks if he can see Mary Ann's room one more time.

"Oh Christ! That's what I was afraid of. I haven't even gone in that room, Horace. Nothing has changed."

Zwender promises, he won't disturb things. Not like the previous time. He isn't sure what he's looking for but he has a feeling, he might find it.

"I told you—I've had the door closed. I don't go inside. No one has gone inside. I'm just waiting for Mary Ann to come home and things can be the way they were."

Zwender considers this. Pauline Healy is as deluded as Melissa Chambers. As if *things can be the way they were.*

As if Francis Fox hasn't brought destruction to both girls' lives. How many girls' lives. The most insidious destruction, that is invisible, immeasurable.

In early November Zwender led a team that searched not only Mary Ann Healy's room but the entire Healy house (including cobweb-ridden attic, mildewed cellar); the long-abandoned outbuildings, and the fermented-smelling silo; the grassless front yard, the overgrown backyard, acres of adjoining fields. All this, with Pauline's permission. It was a thorough search requiring days since at the time it hadn't been known that Mary Ann had (allegedly) made her way to Atlantic City after disappearing from home on a weekday morning and failing to appear at school; there was the possibility that the thirteen-year-old had been abducted, sexually abused, and murdered and her body buried close by her home.

Dozens of volunteers helped search for Mary Ann Healy in the fields and wooded areas near her home and along Stockton Road. Since Mary Ann's English teacher Francis Fox seemed to have disappeared at about the same time Mary Ann disappeared it was naturally suspected that Fox had had something to do with the girl's disappearance.

In actual fact, as Zwender determined, Francis Fox taught classes at the Langhorne Academy *after* Mary Ann Healy was believed to be missing. Which still didn't remove the possibility that Fox had abducted the girl, and knew where she was.

(At the same time, law enforcement officers had to consider that the girl might have been abducted by someone in her family, namely her father; which was why the house, outbuildings, and adjoining fields were so carefully searched. Nothing came of this suspicion of course: never mentioned to any civilian.)

(Whenever a child is murdered, or missing, the first suspects are likely to be the parents, outrageous as that might sound to civilian ears.)

Reluctantly Pauline leads Zwender to Mary Ann's room at the rear of the sprawling farmhouse. The detective feels a quickening of excitement as if (he knows) something awaits him there, which would otherwise be lost.

As he seemed to know, though he could not possibly have known, that something would be awaiting him at the ravine—no idea it could be something so small, so negligible, so easily overlooked, as a toe-bone in the scat of an owl.

Excitedly fingering the *good-luck piece* in his jacket pocket.

As Zwender recalls the girl's room is small: low ceiling, single narrow window, bare floorboards on which a shag rug has been laid. Typical room in an old farmhouse, in a family of limited resources, the kind called, cruelly, *poor whites*—Zwender stiffens at the thought for he, H. Zwender, is of that background, in South Jersey; old families that have failed to thrive in the twenty-first century, left behind by the computerized, high-tech economy.

Mary Ann's room is just large enough to contain a (narrow) bed, a maple bureau of drawers, a single rattan chair, and a makeshift bookcase (bricks, boards). The walls are covered in faded-rose floral wallpaper. No curtain or blind on the window, that overlooks a bleak wintry scene of broken sunflower stalks as in an ancient Chinese scroll.

On the walls are glossy-lurid posters of rock music performers (none of whom Zwender recognizes, or would expect to recognize: glamorous-garish heavily tattooed figures posed in sexually provocative poses, bare midriffs, skintight silk) as well as a calendar for October 2013 with a grinning Hallowe'en pumpkin. In cheaply shiny frames on the bureau top are photos of Mary Ann Healy with family, relatives, friends; Zwender recognizes Mary Ann from photos he has seen of her, though the girl is younger and less physically "mature" in these photos of years ago; he recognizes Pauline Healy, a young mother, smiling at the camera, in T-shirt and shorts, years younger than the unsmiling woman regarding him now with shadowed eyes.

"Is this you, Pauline?"

"Yes. And that's Blake . . ."

Beside Pauline in the photo, smiling with half his mouth, squinting at the camera, is a lean young man only vaguely recognizable as thickset Blake Healy.

". . . before he went all to hell."

Zwender opens the bureau drawers, can't not. But finds nothing out of the ordinary, no secret note or card from Francis Fox hidden beneath socks, underwear.

The narrow bed has been neatly made up. Here is a colorful quilt made by Mary Ann's grandmother, who is no longer living; atop the bed, a half-dozen stuffed animals.

This, Zwender recalls from the first search. Stuffed animals, teddy bear, panda, giraffe, too childish for an eighth-grade girl.

At the time of the first search the bed had to be opened, sheets, pillowcase, and mattress cover examined, and between the mattress (which was faintly stained) and the box spring; and Pauline, mother of the missing girl, said angrily to Zwender and his team, "I made up this bed! These are all clean sheets! What are you looking for? You can go fuck yourselves."

Today Pauline is silent, subdued. Zwender too is silent, lifting just the quilt, not the rest of the bedclothes, conscious of Pauline watching him resentfully, seething with dislike. How intrusive, a stranger has entered her house, the privacy of her house, and is examining intimate sights: her daughter's bed, a bureau of drawers, a closet.

The detective has seen things that no one has wanted him to see, in other bedrooms, in other houses; he has seen some very ugly things; what is freely available for the detective to see, the detective usually doesn't value. It is only the hidden, the secret, the shocking, the obscene that has value to the detective.

What pains another, what causes another to wince, to flinch, to bite her lower lip in distress—only that is of interest to the detective.

Zwender stoops to peer beneath the bed. With his (gloved) hand swiping beneath the bed, finding nothing.

Inside the closet, a girl's clothes on hangers, the Langhorne uniform—maroon jumper, pleated skirt.

The school uniform, left behind when the girl fled.

Pauline says, reminiscing: "Mary Ann loved the uniform, at first. So much better an idea, than letting kids dress the way they want to dress, especially at the school here. The boys dress like thugs, the girls—some of the girls—like hookers . . . As young as seventh grade."

"She liked—loved?—the school? The private school?"

"At first, she did. She loved the idea of the school. But then, there were boys who tormented her. She didn't tell me much about them but I'd hear her crying in here at night."

"Did she tell you much about her teachers?"

"Not too much. I didn't really have time to talk to her, listen to her . . . It was complicated, I'm sorry now."

"If she wasn't wearing this school uniform when she left home what would she have been wearing?"

"Just—her usual clothes, I guess. I don't think I even saw her that morning, I had to be at the 7-Eleven by seven A.M."

Zwender brings up the subject of the journal with the fancy "marbled" cover, that Francis Fox gave Mary Ann. He has asked Pauline about this journal in the past, but Pauline hasn't remembered much about it; she thinks she remembers a journal with a purple cover, but she never saw what Mary Ann had written in it.

"She'd written poems, that Mr. Fox seemed to like. He praised her, he gave her high grades—B's and B+'s. She was almost crying, it meant so much to her. Or maybe she *was* crying. She said, 'I'm so happy *I could die.*'"

"Is that how Mary Ann talked sometimes—*I could die*?"

"Oh, it was just—talk. Girls that age say things like that. She didn't really mean, you know—*die.*"

Zwender asks if Mary Ann ever tried to hurt herself and Pauline says *No.*

Zwender asks if Mary Ann ever threatened to hurt herself and Pauline says *No*.

"I see now, I should have paid more attention to her. I'm so sorry! She'd hide in her room after school doing homework, or writing poems, book reviews in her notebook to hand in to Mr. Fox, I was mainly relieved, she wasn't going to that awful Wieland school. If I knocked on her door she'd tell me to go away, she was too busy. She'd help me with supper and cleanup and that was it. They all have secret lives—I guess. Maybe she had a crush on this Mr. Fox which is how girls are at that age but I didn't think it was anything serious . . ."

"She never let you read her journal?"

"No. But—I never asked . . ."

"What about her father?"

"Are you joking? Blake? *No*."

Through the bureau mirror Zwender sees Pauline in the doorway, eyes shining with tears. He would comfort her except he knows that if he were to approach Pauline she would shrink from him. She might push him away with the palms of her hands against his chest—*Get away! Get away, I hate you*.

No sign of Fox in this room. No journal with a marbled-purple cover.

The books in the makeshift bookcase date back to elementary school, nothing relates to Francis Fox. (Evidently) Fox didn't give Mary Ann Healy books from his office as he gave other students. Zwender recalls how proud Genevieve Chambers and her mother were, that Fox had given Genevieve a paperback copy of *A Girl of the Limberlost*.

What did Odom say?—just maybe, Mary Ann Healy wasn't Fox's *type*.

"Mary Ann was moved to tears when Mr. Fox gave her a high grade. Did she cry over Mr. Fox at other times?"

"No! I don't think so! Can we change the subject?"

"But—the subject *is* Fox . . ."

"No. The subject *is not* Fox. My daughter had more than one favorite teacher, Fox was just one of them. He was her first male teacher, I think all the girls had crushes on him. That's what I gather. She also had a kind of crush on a librarian at the Langhorne school, a woman, who gave her books to read . . . All Mary Ann really liked, was reading—here on her bed, she'd cuddle with one of the stuffed animals, that was her favorite time. She said, a book is like a little door, I can open the door and climb through, and nobody can follow me."

"But Mary Ann spent time in Fox's office, didn't she? When she stayed late after school."

"Why do you keep asking about Fox, Horace? I'm sick of being asked about Fox!"

"Because Mary Ann's bracelet, like the one you're wearing, was found in Fox's wrecked car. You know that, yes? And Mary Ann's fingerprints, in his apartment."

"I don't know if I believe that. Why should I believe that."

"You saw the bracelet yourself, Pauline. You ID'd it at the police station."

"But I don't know where you found it, do I? Or when? You say it was in Fox's car, but can I believe you?"

"Why would we be lying about the bracelet? Or fingerprints?"

"Cops lie all the time, don't you? You plant false evidence, you lie on the witness stand. Look what happened to Blake, he went to the police station for what they called an 'interview,' and wound up at Red Wing."

To this, Zwender has no reply. He is stricken, silent. Pauline swipes angrily at her eyes.

"I know—Blake showed up at the station drunk. He brought the trouble on himself. He should have known better. God damn him!"

Still, Zwender doesn't speak. Recalling how he showed the little feather bracelet to Blake Healy, with the deliberate intention of provoking him.

And how close Healy came, to killing *him*.

An ironic death, Zwender's skull bashed in. Very like the way Francis Fox died.

"I have to blame Blake for this—the trouble with Mary Ann. If he'd had a different attitude she might be all right. He started acting funny around her when she was three, four years old and starting to 'mature.' He'd been crazy for his little daughter but then suddenly he was afraid to look at her. He kept his distance. He didn't touch her. He avoided the bathroom if it was her bath time. He stopped coming into her bedroom to say goodnight. Her brothers started behaving strangely to her too. They'd loved their baby sister until one day they didn't. Kyle was the first, then Pete. Mary Ann was getting chubby, they called her Little Piggy. Pete pinched her breasts to make her cry—she was just five or six. He was ten. Blake walloped him, knocked him down. He'd have beaten the hell out of Pete if I hadn't stopped him and that made her brothers resent Mary Ann all the more. Oh, I wish I'd looked out for Mary Ann! I guess I was embarrassed too—the changes that came over her. It was just so—kind of *freakish*. I took her to the doctor. He said it was some kind of 'condition'—it had to do with processed foods, hormones, additives in food, like chicken . . . But not every girl looks like Mary Ann at the age of five or six or nine, so why *her*? It wasn't fair, she had to grow up so soon!—she started her period when she was not even nine. Imagine—nine! A child that young could have a baby—it's just not right. People look at Mary Ann, they see her body and not *her*. Then they get disgusted with her, or angry at her, they say cruel stupid things. Not just nasty-minded boys but adults too. Her own relatives. Her own grandmother—Blake's mother! I know exactly how Mary Ann felt. You want to *scream*. You want to *run away*."

"Do you know where Mary Ann ran, Pauline?"

"I—I don't know . . ."

"You can tell me, Pauline. I'm your friend."

"I said *I don't know*. I promised Mary Ann I wouldn't tell anyone."

"But she's safe?"

"She's safe! She says."

"Have you seen her, Pauline?"

"We do FaceTime. When she calls me. She has lost a little weight but—I guess—she's all right."

"She isn't in Atlantic City? With relatives?"

"N-no. We were saying that so that Blake couldn't find her. He's driven to Atlantic City twice, he's been harassing my cousins. He's one of those who seems to blame *her*, for whatever happens to her."

"If not Atlantic City, where?"

"I can't tell you, Horace! Can't we let it go at that, it *isn't* Atlantic City?"

"Does anyone know where she is, apart from you?"

"I don't think so. No."

"There's no one else in the family she's close to? A cousin? Another girl?"

"She used to be close with one of her girl-cousins, but not so much any longer. They're all jealous of her, for looking the way she does, and for the special scholarship to the private school. The Healys will never forgive her." Pauline pauses, considering. "I guess—her boy-cousin Demetrius, *he's* kind of close to her."

"Demetrius?"

"Lemuel's son. One of Lemuel's sons. 'Demmie.' He's out of school now, he works at Kroger's. We've kind of drifted apart, the families, since Ida Healy died about two years ago . . . Ida was a lovely woman, Lemuel fell apart after she died. He's a wreck now, people say. Demetrius was her caretaker for maybe a year."

"Mary Ann was close with Demetrius Healy? He's her cousin?"

"Yes! Her closest friend among the cousins."

"Did they see each other often?"

"Well, yes—for a while—when the kids were younger. Demetrius was the only boy who was quiet, kind of thoughtful, he'd treat girls with respect. He was polite to women. He was like some kind of *saint* you hear about, who is kind to everyone, even animals. He didn't get along so well with other guys, I think—they're so *loud,* and *rough;* and Demetrius is the opposite. He and Mary Ann were always friendly, she wasn't afraid of him. He'd sort of protect her if boys were teasing her."

"'Protect her'—how?"

"Just—protect her. The way a boy might do, if a girl was being harassed."

"Did he protect her from her own brothers?"

"Y-yes. Sometimes."

"Did he get into fights?"

"No, I don't think so . . . Demetrius didn't *fight,* that I remember. Unless he was really provoked."

"Did he ever hurt anyone? Injure anyone?"

"Of course not! No."

Adding: "I just now remembered—Demetrius was over here, just before Mary Ann left home. He's been helping his father at the private school, his father's a custodian there, and now Mary Ann is a student there, or was, so they'd see each other at school. Demetrius came over one night after supper, it was kind of late, he had something to ask Mary Ann, or to tell her, he said it was important. He didn't say what it was, only that he wanted to see Mary Ann. He seemed kind of excited, which was strange. Coming over here at night was strange. Demetrius went into Mary Ann's room, she'd been doing homework, whatever they talked about their voices got loud—Mary Ann said afterward that he'd snatched the notebook from her and was reading it, and tore out a page—by the time I went to check Demetrius had run out the back door and Mary Ann was crying, furious . . ."

"'Tore out a page'—why'd he do that?"

"Horace, I don't know! How would I know?"

"Did you see the page he tore out? What was on it, did Mary Ann tell you?"

"No, no! No! I don't remember anything, just that they were shouting at each other which I don't think they'd ever done, I'd never heard Demetrius raise his voice at anyone, I swear. Mary Ann was crying, she was so angry and upset. She refused to tell me what the quarrel was about but she said that she never wanted to see Demetrius again."

"So you never saw the page? You don't know what was on it?"

"No! I said *no.*"

"Did Demetrius touch her, d'you think? Threaten her, hurt her?"

"Oh, no. It wasn't anything like that. Since she went missing he's been calling me, he's worried. I think he might actually have driven to Atlantic City though I told him not to—to leave Mary Ann alone right now. I guess, Demetrius *was* pretty upset, that Mary Ann had been angry with him. He kind of blamed the Langhorne school for making Mary Ann unhappy. People out here resent the private school—not that they know anything about it."

"Mary Ann was sad because—? Something about the school?"

"All I know is, she was worried about her grades. She spent hours on homework each night. And not fitting in, being teased. She didn't want to tell me, but I knew. It's always been like that with Mary Ann, she loves school but something happens to poison it. Just a few boys harassing her . . ."

"Would Demetrius protect Mary Ann, if he knew that someone was hurting her? Threatening her? Abusing her?"

"God, yes! I hope so. Demetrius loves Mary Ann."

■

AS ZWENDER IS ABOUT to leave Pauline asks him another time if he'd like a drink?—and again Zwender thanks her, *no.*

His heart is beating quickly, foolishly. He lingers in the front doorway, Pauline follows him outside onto the veranda, shivering. She seems friendlier now that Zwender is leaving. In a way, reluctant for him to leave.

The glowering sky has dimmed, still the cloud cover remains opaque. Not a hint of sun at the horizon.

Zwender says, as if he has just now thought of it: "I could come back later for a drink, Pauline."

"How much later?"

"After eight."

As he's getting into the cruiser Pauline calls after him, "Maybe I'll make supper too. Would you like that?"

Zwender tells her yes, he'd like that.

Good-luck piece in his pocket, Zwender has been gently fingering.

THE CONFESSION

J*ust a feeling like something wasn't right.*

Saw the tire tracks in the mud, going up the hill . . . Turkey vultures in the trees.

Jesus! Wish I hadn't gone there.

■

"DEMETRIUS!"—HIS NAME IS CALLED. "Tell us what you see here."

Glossy photographs spread out on the table before him. All color has been bleached from these photographs. Wipes his eyes, stares numbly for what have these photographs to do with *him*?

It is a summons. It is *the summons* which he has been awaiting.

He has been led into a room. A chair has been jerked away from a table, weak-kneed and shivering he is made to sit.

Fluorescent lights overhead, glaring. Blinding.

Blinking, staring. Eyes fill with moisture like ammonia fumes.

"Demetrius? See here. Tell us what you see. Here."

A finger tapping the glossy surface of the photograph. A man's forefinger, dark hairs on the back of his hand. Beneath glaring fluo-

rescent lights the surface of the photograph is shiny, almost you can't
see what the photograph is.

Rubs at his eyes, his knuckles might gouge out his eyes. (He
could do that—could he? Gouge out his eyes before they can stop
him.)

"Here. This one."

Belches beer, a taste of beer-bile at the back of his mouth.

Mingling with the sickish-dry taste of sleep in his mouth. When
you sleep for only two hours that sleep is intense, hurtful. The brain
hurts like a strained muscle.

On his knees praying that morning. *Jesus help me.*

Jesus help me do Your bidding.

His heart is empty, Jesus has abandoned him.

That morning, Marcus gaping at him astonished. Unshaven,
stubble-jawed, in just a grimy T-shirt, the shorts he sleeps in, haven't
been laundered in weeks. Broken capillaries in his eyes. Barefoot in
the kitchen guzzling beer from a Coors can.

Not showing up at Kroger's? Did he call, let the manager know he
wasn't coming in?

It's rare for Marcus to be concerned about his brother. Actually
looking at Demetrius, for once. Says he'd better drive him to the
Wieland PD, the shape he's in.

Jesus—what the hell? What'd you do to yourself?

Insisting to Marcus he can drive himself. Shivering so, you can
hear his teeth chattering.

Shaking so badly, has to grip his hands together to steady them.

Popping a second can of Coors, after he's got some clothes on.
Taking it with him in the pickup.

Marcus has come to the house concerned for how weirdly Demetrius has been behaving. He had a call from their father, also a call
from their aunt Pauline.

Around the time Mary Ann left home without telling anyone.
Marcus is sure that's it: their girl-cousin Mary Ann "disappearing."

Later, they learned she was staying with relatives in Atlantic City.

Demetrius took time off from work, drove there, made inquiries but never found her.

Why's Demetrius care so much about Mary Ann?—that's just how he is. Might be he's hurt that she left without telling him, and hasn't called him since she's been gone; if he calls her cell phone the call goes to voice-mail that's never returned. If he calls Mary Ann's mother Pauline, Pauline will say she can't help him, can't talk with him right now, she's too busy.

Not friendly-sounding. Not encouraging Demetrius to call back.

Marcus is incensed that Demetrius has been summoned back to the Wieland PD.

Why the *hell*. Why're they asking *him* to come back a second time?

Marcus Healy is the one who found the body parts in the ravine. Everybody knows. It was in the Wieland newspaper.

Or, no: not Marcus. Marcus was the one who *said* he'd found the body parts but really it was Demetrius. (Marcus has to admit.)

Lying to a law enforcement officer is a crime. Marcus was threatened but nothing came of it. Fuck the motherfuckers.

Both Marcus and Demetrius brought their work-boots to the police station, as requested. Both Marcus and Demetrius were fingerprinted.

Assured it's just *routine*. *Process of elimination*.

You'd think that would be the end of it but you'd be wrong.

Over the phone cops don't explain shit. Come in the morning, just an interview, won't take long. When Demetrius hesitates the voice asks if he'd like officers to pick him up at his house and bring him in or would he prefer to come to the station voluntarily, he says no, he says he means yes, he will come voluntarily.

Their father would have a heart attack, a Wieland police cruiser pulling into his driveway. Uniformed officers coming to the door taking Demetrius away. His only son who lives with him now.

His only son who gives a damn for him.

Word is spreading among the relatives and neighbors on Stockton Road, there's an arrest warrant for one of Lemuel Healy's sons. Could be a warrant for—what?

Their girl-cousin, the one who's gone missing?—maybe the Healy boys did something to her . . .

Marcus protests: It's not an arrest. There's no warrant. Marcus explains to whoever asks him and eventually whoever will listen.

Not an interrogation. What they call an *interview.*

Marcus explains, Marcus is becoming seriously pissed, the asshole questions people are asking him about his brother.

Marcus guesses it's about their cousin Mary Ann, why they're calling in Demetrius to ask him questions. Maybe something has happened to Mary Ann in Atlantic City, that's being kept secret. Jesus!

But the photographs spread on the table in front of Demetrius have nothing to do with Mary Ann Healy.

For weeks Demetrius has been bargaining with Jesus: he will accept the worst for himself as long as Mary Ann is OK and not hurt. Dreading whatever it is they are going to tell him and show him which he does not want to see. Wiping moisture from his eyes roughly as the photograph positioned in front of him comes into sharp focus.

"D'you recognize this, Demetrius?"

"Recognize who this is?"

"Here. Look here, son. Look *here.*"

His stunned eyes are seeing: a ruin of a human head, a human head detached from a body like random debris in mud. Like something kicked across a field.

Skin missing from the face, or what had been the face. Eyes missing, just empty sockets. Ears missing. Hole where there'd once been a nose.

A man's head, what remains of it. Scalp partly torn off, hair matted with blood, what looks like teeth marks on the forehead.

Mouth agape, jaw fallen. Soft flesh at the lips is gone, devoured. Gums have been devoured, pecked by birds. Yet, rows of ghastly teeth remain.

Other photographs are pushed toward him. He is helpless not to see: a male torso, remains of a rib cage, stark white bones exposed.

Eviscerated belly, groin. Genitals torn by ravenous teeth.

"Demetrius! Open your eyes."

"Look here, son. Where I'm pointing—*here*."

"You know who this is, yes?"

Staring at a close-up of the ravaged head, the head without a body, now positioned on a metallic surface as in a morgue. Here, details are larger, sharper than in the photographs taken at the ravine.

Transfixed in a paralysis of horror as the empty eye sockets stare back at Demetrius in derision. Ghastly fixed grin, gaping jaw, faint mocking voice—*Hey: you seem kind of young to be a janitor.*

A vise tightens around Demetrius's chest. In his ears a roar like a cataract. The table shifts beneath his elbows, he has been leaning hard on his elbows.

Taste of beer-bile sharp as acid at the back of his throat. He begins to gag, choke.

YOU, you seem kind of young . . . Hey?

A rush of hot liquid into his mouth. He begins choking, coughing. The older police officer lurches back from him, cursing.

"God damn! Get him out of here."

Too late: Demetrius is gagging, heaving. Puking. Mostly beer, liquid acid onto the table, onto the glossy photographs, spilling onto the tile floor. Hot shame of being sick to his stomach in front of (male) others staring at him in contempt. Like pissing his pants. Losing control of his bowels. Worst nightmare at school, as a kid. Flu, sudden stomach cramps, diarrhea.

Slip-sliding in his own vomit he's led away to a lavatory hearing behind him the elder of the two interrogators cursing in disgust.

■

JESUS HELP ME TO do what has to be done.

On shaky legs Demetrius is led back to the interrogation room. He has washed his face in cold water, he has rinsed his fetid mouth. His brain is filled with static, he has been unable to think coherently since stepping inside the police station.

The photographs have been wiped clean. The top of the table has been wetted, wiped.

A smell of vomit in the air, still. Though the single window in the room has been opened several inches.

He is seated in the same chair. He is unable to lift his eyes to the detective's face.

Nonetheless hoping the detective will call him *son* again.

Addressing Demetrius in a matter-of-fact voice neither kindly nor cruel with the equanimity of a great wheel rolling over him crushing him.

Asking why he returned to the ravine. Why he climbed the hill. Why he called his brother Marcus to join him.

Why he and his brother lied about which of them saw the wreck first?

Demetrius is unable to answer these questions. He is not sure that he has heard them correctly, the static in his brain is so loud.

A new set of photographs is spread on the table. These have been marked in red ink.

A steep hillside, trampled grass and mud. Deep-rutted tracks of vehicles, gouges in the earth. Trails of dozens of boot-prints criss-crossing one another.

Detective Zwender speaks in his matter-of-fact voice instructing Demetrius to observe these boot-prints which have been highlighted in red: his brother Marcus's prints, and his prints.

Going up the hill, coming down the hill. See?

But to the left, there is another set of Demetrius's boot-prints which appear to be older, and not so clear, but recognizable as his prints, *which only descend the hill.*

"How's that possible, Demetrius?"

"How'd you climb down the hill that day without walking up the hill first?"

"Because you'd driven Fox's car up the hill? Was that you?"

"If these footprints are yours, Demetrius, it's you."

Demetrius stares at the photographs. A leaden sensation suffuses his limbs.

If required to swim for his life in a fast-running stream, he could not.

As when his mother was dying. In his arms her frail ardent body. In his arms his mother breathed, breathed, breathed through hours with no diminution of the determination of her lungs to live. And so entranced he did not truly think that his mother could die for to die would be to cease this ardent breathing and would be to abandon him; yet finally the breathing accelerated, grew more labored and intense and suddenly came the deepest breath of his mother's life which was to be her final breath leaving him abruptly alone in silence as he is alone now in his life still disbelieving, stunned in a suspension of being that continues to this hour like a subterranean stream.

"I guess . . . I didn't want him to be alone."

Now Demetrius has spoken, in naïve simplicity uttered these words that cannot be retracted, there is a quickening of the air in the interrogation room like an electrical charge before a storm.

"What's that, son? What did you say?"

". . . that he should be buried. Not left by himself. And if he had family, that they would know what had happened to him."

"And you knew—how?"

"Because I—I was the one, I drove him there . . . I left him there but then I had to go back, he had to be buried."

"And he was dead, when you drove him?—Mr. Fox? When you left him?"

"Yes. He was dead."

"And—who killed him? Did you kill him?"

"I—I did."

Hearing his own words Demetrius is stricken silent even as Officer Odom rises to his feet with that remarkable alacrity in one so heavyset and seemingly lethargic and comes to Demetrius laying his hand on Demetrius's shoulder asking is Demetrius a Christian?— and Demetrius nods *yes* and Odom says quietly, "Would you like to pray with me, Demetrius? Ask Jesus the best way forward?"

Tears spill from Demetrius's eyes. *Yes, yes!*

It will be one of the astonishments of H. Zwender's career as a police officer how his junior officer and lanky-limbed Demetrius Healy lower themselves to their knees on the tile floor of the interrogation room, without hesitation; Odom with some effort and a creaking of his leather belt, breathing audibly, and Demetrius with a soft sigh like a child who has sobbed himself to sleep.

Of all sights beneath these fluorescent lights, ridiculous! Religious fanatics! Zwender is disbelieving, incredulous. A glance upward at the video recorder in a corner of the room, a startled smirk to register the absurdity and detach himself from it.

Feeling himself superior to such folly. Even as he is excluded.

Daryl Odom with gravest sincerity, shut eyes and clasped hands leading the prayer, the Healy boy so frightened his teeth chatter audibly with cold, tears streaking his stubbled cheeks murmuring with Odom *Our Father who art in heaven hallowed be thy name* . . .

Forgive us our sins . . .

■ ■ ■

ALL HE CAN REMEMBER (he says) is the blood.

Sudden stench of blood, overwhelming. And the stench of released bowels, panic and molten excrement staining the man's sharp-creased chino trousers where he lay fallen and unmoving on the blood-puddled floor.

Surprise of the skull breaking as easily as a melon with a tough rind.

Blood wetting the fair-brown wavy hair. Blood glistening on the floor, on the desktop, on papers strewn across the desktop, fine-spray-splatter on the glossy wall poster, and on the wall surrounding the poster. Blood blood blood on the latex gloves, on his custodial coveralls, and on the cloth cap on his head.

Slipping from his blood-slick latex fingers to fall heavily to the floor the dense weight of the unwieldy bronze object covered in blood and hairs that was the sculpted head of a man with mournful sunken eyes and on the man's shoulder the figure of a bird resembling a crow, no memory of picking up this weight in his hands but seemed to know or to recall that it had been positioned on a corner of the teacher's desk with the mournful eyes gazing outward and the fine-chiseled lips so tight-pursed that all screams of terror and of agony were muted within that dense obdurate bronze.

It came to me then that I had a choice: I could run shouting for help for the man already dead and beyond help or quietly I could switch off the office light and shut and lock the office door and continue on my rounds and meet up with my father and drive my father home as on an ordinary night and later I would return to clean the office and remove the body and no one would know that anything had happened there nor would they guess to blame me.

Already he was wearing the tough-fibrous latex gloves provided for the custodial staff at the Langhorne school, which his father had given him. Already his hands were protected from the blood dripping down the side of the aluminum desk and would be protected from the virulent cleaning fluids required to clean the befouled office through the long hours of the night.

Already in his possession the cloth mask over his mouth and nose to protect his lungs from powerful fumes.

Already staggering to a high window at the rear of the small rectangular office to force it up an inch, two inches to air out the worst of the stench.

Why this has happened he isn't sure. Why *him*, he isn't sure.

For (possibly) it was something meant to happen; and he, blundering upon the scene, has been the agent of its happening through no volition of his own.

For (possibly) it was needed?—because there was no one else to raise a hand against the predator Fox.

For a twelve-year-old girl had cut her beautiful smooth arms because of him—"Mr. Fox"?

For "Mr. Fox" took pride and vanity in such, you could see in his bearing what pride and vanity he took in his power to hurt the innocent.

For even those children Fox had not (yet) hurt, his shadow fell upon them like the shadow of a predator bird, to poison them.

For Demetrius had not meant to observe and yet had been helpless not to observe how the predator Fox shut his door and dimmed the light when certain girls came into his office in the late afternoon. How Demetrius had seen girls crying, and he'd heard the high shrill laughter of girls, screams of laughter, he was made to feel fury, help-lessness.

Yes, and one of these girls his own cousin. To his shame.

Crying as if her heart would break, that Fox had harmed her. He, Demetrius, had not wanted to be a witness, yet he had been a witness. You cannot erase what your eyes have seen and your ears have heard and the shame and disgust you have felt. That his cousin was in love with Fox and Fox did not love her nor care for her in the slightest except to take advantage of her. How in the parking lot Fox had struck her with the fender of his car and knocked her to the ground and driven away without a backward glance and yet she denied what Demetrius had seen with his own eyes. *Love Mr. Fox more than anybody in the world . . . don't care who knows it.*

Girls crying, hiding their faces in shame. And one of the youngest, who tried to kill herself.

One of the girls he'd seen weeping in the corridor outside Fox's office when another girl was in Fox's office and the door was shut and the light dimmed quietly Demetrius approached to ask if she was all right but the girl ran away from him not wanting him to see. But he'd seen.

Except for his cousin he did not know names, he did not know faces. He had no wish to know and prayed upon it many nights, what to do.

Think not that I am come to send peace on earth: I came not to send peace, but a sword.

As Jesus sacrificed Himself on the cross for the salvation of humankind so Demetrius would sacrifice himself as an executioner to spare Fox's girl-victims now and in the future and to sow the seeds of justice which others more responsible than he had shirked.

■

AND YOU DID ALL *this alone, Demetrius?*

Alone! Alone in the night through the entire night not-hurried but calm, methodical with a slow-beating pulse that had the effect of stretching out time, never did he doubt that he would have enough time.

So strangely, he did not worry that he had no plans. He *had not planned* that this would occur and yet, as it had occurred, and he was at the center of its occurring, he did not doubt that a plan existed, and had existed from a time deep in the past, that this plan would be revealed to him as he required knowing, and not before.

As if a great cobweb enveloped him rendering him helpless to break free and yet was a comfort to him, that he was secured, he was not in free flight, he was not falling helplessly.

Telling the detective that yes he was alone except for Jesus in his heart of which he was not (always) certain. For the way of Jesus (he believes) is not to lead but to allow you to *feel what must be done.*

As the skull of the predator Fox was broken easily and the danger he had wielded to the innocent so abruptly ceased so too Demetrius would come to understand that something brittle and unyielding had broken in his brain, he would not ever be the same again.

Rendering unto Caesar that which is Caesar's and unto God that which is God's. So a great peace came over him, if he was punished for what he had done he would accept the punishment; if not, he would not give it a second thought.

And so, through the long night he was not hurried. He did not act in haste. Unlike his brother Marcus, he was not impatient, he had learned from his carpenter-father (whom he had assisted from boyhood) to be methodical, precise.

Even as Demetrius's thoughts came more slowly than thoughts came to others, and the words he uttered seemed to be shaped with effort like those tortuous-shaped clouds passing overhead as if with difficulty though mere wedges of vapor.

On this occasion, his heart too was beating with unnatural slowness. Calm, precise as a clock that ticks slower and slower yet continues, will not stop.

He would rinse the still-wet blood from his hands in the latex gloves; he would dab with a wetted soapy sponge the bloodstains on his coveralls and on the cloth cap, that registered, to the eye, as merely dark stains, like oil. In case he was observed in the corridors of Haven Hall: which he was not.

Only vaguely was the custodian's son Demetrius aware that fall break at the Langhorne Academy began at the end of this day and that classes would not resume until November; like water disappearing down a drain, students and faculty had been retreating through the afternoon, now the residence halls were virtually deserted, and teachers had been steadily departing the campus.

With robotic calm and precision continuing the custodial tasks he was performing in Haven Hall for his father's sake and afterward meeting his father in the usual place on the first floor at the usual time to drive him home listening to his father's ruminative voice variously aggrieved, jocular, resigned, and again aggrieved, without comment or judgment smelling alcohol on his father's wheezing breath and replying to his father as required, if tersely. In a trance of certainty he accomplished this, bringing with him a flashlight from his home and returning then to the darkened school campus where few vehicles remained in the faculty parking lot and one of them the white Acura sedan belonging to "Mr. Fox" that had knocked his girl-cousin so ignominiously to the ground.

None of this planned. All opened before him like a scroll. It was imperative to clean Fox's office in its entirety, not just the circumscribed area between the desk and the bookcase which was most befouled with blood, as it was imperative to clean out Fox's desk drawers removing handwritten notes, cards, valentines, and other items that might identify any of Fox's girl-students. He did not take time to peruse these, he did not want to encounter ardent poems in purple ink written for "Mr. Fox" by his cousin Mary Ann or from any other girl-victim. He did not want an innocent child identified, humiliated.

The (digital, expensive-looking) wristwatch removed from the wrist of the dead man, the wallet removed from the trouser pocket with cash, credit cards, laminated Langhorne Academy ID intact—shoved into a large trash bag. Fox's cell phone that glimmered and gleamed with a semblance of life when Demetrius's fingers brushed against its screen like a living thing that lapses into darkness when neglected. In several trash bags scissored lengthwise he would wrap the body in as many as six layers to disguise it and to prevent blood smearing onto the corridor floor along which he would drag the body to the elevator. The key to the Acura he would remove from a pocket of the stained chino trousers to secure in his own coverall pocket for use in transporting the body and the car to a remote place, a ravine he had in mind, a mile or so beyond Wieland Pond.

The heavy sculpted bust covered in blood, blood-sticky hairs on its sharp edges, bronze bust of a man's head and shoulders with a malevolent bird of the size of a crow digging its talons in the left shoulder—this freakish object identified on its bronze base as *Edgar Allan Poe 1809–1849* he would shove into the trash bag along with Fox's personal items and a sizable quantity of bloodied paper towels and other detritus to be dumped from a bridge into the Millbrook River en route to the Wieland nature preserve.

All this, you did by yourself, Demetrius? You expect us to believe that?

By himself! Alone! For no one else could know.

Hours were required for the task but not more hours than Jesus had endured on the cross at the bidding of His Father.

As he hopes to be forgiven by Jesus, for this task placed upon him by God.

As he has acquiesced, for it is rendering unto Caesar. He is willing to be punished by the state if that is the decree—his soul is untouched, and will prevail.

And so—acting alone—he cleaned 015 Haven Hall thoroughly. Mopping, scrubbing, wiping with powerful cleaning fluids, any and all surfaces and interiors and the undersides of things, a task not very different from the myriad robotic tasks of his life he'd learned to execute in the service of others for as long as he could remember.

Having access to cleaning materials in this very building in the custodian's storage room. And through the night there was no one in Haven Hall.

Quiet of the tomb. Jesus in His sepulchre not yet risen from the dead.

Once the body was secured, he did not fear the body. He had ceased thinking of the body as *him*. Practically speaking, the body was *it*. As a custodian you are required to clean, to scrub, to wipe. To fumigate if needed.

The stench of the office you would think would make him ill but it did not for the harshest of smells, soon you cease to notice.

At the landfill, even smoldering rubber tires, fertilizer, and chemicals spilling out of drums, soon you ceased to smell.

And a strange peace in the very inertness of the predator's body on the floor unbreathing, unthreatening, now an object, a weight wrapped in black plastic trash bags secured with twine neatly knotted. *In such ways it is the sword that brings peace as evil is vanquished.*

After the initial cleaning he took time to reexamine the room. A careful scrutiny of the bookcase revealed feathery-fine blood-traces on the edges of pages in several books and these books he would shove into the trash bag to be disposed of at Wieland Pond.

The remaining books, he examined yet again. Untouched, no blood, he would leave them behind. So alien to him was the world of *books, printed pages, reading* since he'd left school that his eyes glided over the titles of these books and the names of their authors without translating them into words.

In a lower drawer of the teacher's desk there was a pastry bag, very like the one he'd discovered weeks before. Seeing the white paper bag, smelling the pastries, he was seized with a sudden hunger for he had not eaten in a very long time since midafternoon of the previous day on his ten-minute break at Kroger's.

A lemon tart, an apple tart. Chocolate-covered strawberries, broken oatmeal cookies with raisins. He chewed, swallowed. A rush of sugar in his mouth like stinging red ants.

These pastries, Fox had fed to his girl-students. To those special girl-students he'd invited into his office and shut the door feeding them (Demetrius envisioned: he had not ever actually seen) out of his hand as you might feed a tamed animal for which you felt an affectionate contempt for its very tameness.

Afterward, all crumbs removed. All evidence. Desk drawers wiped clean inside and out.

Desk drawers emptied, except for the top drawer containing nothing of interest only school printouts, Fox's grade books, several ballpoint pens, paper clips.

During this long night he was several times overcome with lightheadedness, fatigue. Weak-kneed standing on his toes at the window high in the rear wall breathing in fresh air to restore his strength. Sometimes despite his resolve stricken with nausea. His eyelids drooped. So leaden-limbed he had to sit in the swivel chair, lay his head on the desktop smelling of disinfectant and sleep for dazed minutes at a time. A black mist obscured his brain. He saw his mother's pale face, he grieved that her frail beauty had faded. Her skin, once smooth, now crisscrossed with fine lines like glazed cracks in crockery. She reached out to touch him: to bless him. Fleetingly, he saw the face of Jesus even as he was given sternly to know—*This is not my face. No one has seen my face.* But he did not dream. He had no sense of time. It might have been shortly past midnight, it might have been the middle of the night. Though he had not the strength to force his eyelids open yet in time they would open of their own volition startled and alert as if from somewhere far away he'd been summoned to return.

With his slow heartbeat he was empowered with an unusual strength.

Relating all this to Detective Zwender and Officer Odom like a man in a spell, speaking in a raw young-male voice both halting and assured as if recollecting events that had happened long ago to another person.

You carried an adult man's body out to the car, Demetrius? By yourself?

No! Not like that.

He'd driven Fox's car to the rear of Haven Hall. He had only to drag the body wrapped in trash bags along the basement corridor to the elevator which he would take to the first floor; the rear exit was close by the elevator.

Outside the exit door, he had only to drag the body a few feet farther and lift it into the passenger seat of the Acura.

The body *was* heavy, he did struggle lifting it, shoving it into the front seat. Dazed with exertion, sweating. The muscles in his upper arms not large but ropy-hard, tight.

The kind of soft-eyed boy you might misjudge: hard-rippling muscles in shoulders, upper arms, back, thighs.

So Detective H. Zwender thinks soberly observing Demetrius Healy across from him on the opposite side of the table in the Wieland PD interrogation room.

■

HORACE, SHOULDN'T WE ARREST *him now?*

No. Not yet.

But—

I said no.

■

IN THE WHITE ACURA driving south of Wieland into the countryside.

At the bridge over the Millbrook River pausing to dump the trash bag weighted with the bronze bust into the water.

As the vehicle gathered speed beginning to breathe more easily. For he was entering now the region of his childhood.

Knowing that behind him *no trace* remained of what had happened in the teacher's office in Haven Hall. *No trace* even of memory. Nothing in that place to link Demetrius Healy to it.

Overhead, a night sky of splotched moonlight, froth-thin clouds driven by invisible winds. Below, the blacktop highway with its myriad cracks and potholes rushing into the beams of the Acura's headlights.

Past the turnoff for the Wieland Township landfill, that looked to be, from the highway, nothing more than a dense wooded area; from this, a narrower road, and another, roads he'd known so well as a boy bicycling he'd long forgotten their names if he'd ever known them. As if by instinct or memory turning onto an unpaved service road into the interior of the preserve, and from this to a lane leading up the steep grassy hill he was certain he recalled, knowing there was a (hidden) ravine accessible from the top of the hill though not sure of its depth, and whether a vehicle the size of the Acura sedan could plunge over the side and into it unimpeded by small trees and underbrush.

A risk he'd have to take for otherwise he'd have to drive seven miles farther south for another service road into the Pine Barrens, less familiar to him.

The landfill he knew, had known since boyhood. The more densely wooded area beyond Wieland Pond where nature trails faded into oblivion, old ruins of kilns and forges emerged out of tangles of vines he knew, or had known.

Mild panic came to him, did this lightweight suburban vehicle have four-wheel drive?

Every vehicle he'd ever driven was equipped with four-wheel drive. All of them heavier than the schoolteacher's fancy white Acura, manufactured for rough terrain, roads clogged with snow, stretches of mud; many vehicles he'd driven had stick shifts. Contempt he felt for Fox he was feeling for Fox's car, it would give him pleasure to wreck it.

Where the hill began its steep ascent he maneuvered the Acura slowly and joltingly along a trail overgrown with knee-high grasses and underbrush illuminated by the car's headlights with oneiric overclarity; several times, he had to put on the emergency brake and climb out of the car, to clear away brush; cursing himself, that he'd neglected to bring even a hoe. Fortunately the trail ascended not straight up the hill but at an angle, there was less risk of overturning. Many times he'd operated tow trucks, bulldozers, backhoes with no difficulty if he took care.

As the vehicle labored upward, headlights tilting drunkenly, tires grinding into the soft earth, he saw that the body swaddled in trash bags in the seat beside him had slumped against the passenger door, as if scheming to escape from the car. Even in death, the predator Fox could not be trusted.

Not good, he was smelling exhaust. More exhaust than he should have been smelling. Opening a window, breathing in air borne by the wind from the Atlantic fifty miles away, smelling of something metallic, wet.

Healy relatives assured him Mary Ann was fine, but Demetrius knew that they were lying, and that they were lying because Mary Ann had told them to lie—to *him*.

His heart was sore, remembering. That Mary Ann had told them to lie to *him*.

Renewed rage, for the predator Fox. *He* would pay.

As if this demolishment of Fox's car, with Fox inside it, was the final step in Fox's execution: his erasure, extinction.

At last, as the front wheels of the Acura approached the precipice, Demetrius knew by a wild tingling in his scalp that he was very near the edge, and stopped; put on the emergency brake; got out to examine the situation, yes he had only a few more inches before the car plunged over the edge unless it was impeded by underbrush.

It was Demetrius's calculation that the weight of the Acura would be sufficient to break it free of underbrush and plunge it all the way down into the ravine, but it was a gamble, a *one-time-only* gamble never to be repeated. He'd become bathed in sweat. His slow-beating heart was gradually quickening.

Returning then to the car, to remove the trash bags from the body and to position it behind the steering wheel. For it must seem likely, if the wreck were ever discovered, that Fox had driven himself here, and precipitated his own death.

Better to have submerged the car in water, in the Millbrook River, or in Wieland Pond—except he could not figure how to execute these maneuvers, in the small amount of time granted him; especially, Wieland Pond would have been impossible since it was deepest at its center, and shallow at its shore, and no bridge led over it.

In a gesture of humility, or rue, the battered head fell forward against the steering wheel, like the head of a penitent at prayer; the eyes were partially open, as if alert and aware, in mockery. The commingled smells lifting from the corpse were suffocating now, Demetrius crawled out of the car as his lungs were about to burst.

He would take with him the soiled trash bags and out of the car's glove compartment documents regarding the car's ownership.

With the flashlight he managed to find a broken tree limb neither too short nor too soft-rotted to be of use. He returned to the car with it and leaned in to release the emergency brake; very cautiously he moved, not daring to breathe; and now with the limb he pressed down on the gas pedal to ease the vehicle forward, as a bull might be urged forward with the lightest tap on the nose or the rump; until the vehicle seemed to rouse itself to inch, then lurch, forward until momentum seized the car sending it over the precipice and down as if drawn by the glare of its headlights careening headlong bringing with it a small avalanche of mud, stones, and underbrush into several feet of dark water thirty feet below.

At once the Acura's headlights were extinguished. The taillights remained red, unblinking. Exhaust lifted in a steady ill-smelling stream from the tailpipe.

The motor wouldn't run long, he thought. Submerged in several feet of water.

Somberly now making his way back down the hill. Slipsliding, skidding on his heels. Grabbing at underbrush to keep from falling.

At the foot of the hill he aimed the beam of the flashlight about. All was still, where the car's tires hadn't spun in the soft earth there remained waist-high grasses, spindly trees casting stark shadows.

Still, the motor persisted. In the ravine, not visible to him.

And the lingering stink of the exhaust, making his nostrils pinch.

Above, a sky like darkened glass. Filmy clouds parted, there was a smudged-looking moon emitting just enough light that Demetrius could turn off his flashlight.

"Thank you, Jesus."

He had now to return to the Langhorne school where in the deserted staff parking lot his father's pickup truck waited. Though he should have been exhausted after hours of intense concentration and effort yet (in fact) he would discover in his legs and in his lungs a renewed strength, exhilaration.

For he was convinced, *no trace* of Demetrius Healy remained in the wrecked vehicle in the ravine as in room 015 of Haven Hall. *No trace* in anyone's memory including his own.

By 5:20 A.M. arriving at the rear of the darkened school. Near two hours before dawn.

Driving the pickup to his darkened house in the country, parking it in the driveway exactly as he'd parked it the night before.

(His father was sleeping, he would not awaken until after dawn. His father would have no idea that Demetrius had been away for most of the night.)

Collapsing onto his bed and sinking at once into a deep dreamless sleep with no thought to remove even his work-boots or coverall he would sleep for however long his eyes remained shut.

Following which, days followed days. As if a great wheel had been halted but had then begun again, resuming its usual pace.

At Kroger's they believed sympathetically that he'd been sick with flu and so missed a day's work. They commiserated with "Demmie" whose face did indeed appear sickly-pale, fatigued.

Now it was a routine, driving his father to the school in the late afternoon. Where at first in the late summer it had seemed that Lemuel Healy would require his son's help on his shift only occasionally as his arthritic pains waxed and waned now it was taken for granted that Demetrius would accompany his father on each shift, each day of the week.

It was an interregnum at the school: fall break. No one would miss Fox until classes resumed in November and Fox did not return.

This season when daylight rapidly wanes, dusk comes earlier and earlier.

He checked Fox's office. He could not keep away from Fox's office. In that narrow space, nothing had changed. No one had (evidently) entered the room. Paperback books in the bookcase, exactly as they'd been after Demetrius had removed the blood-splattered books, shoved them into the trash bag.

The smell of bleach remained strong despite the window Demetrius had opened in the rear wall.

It should have been, Demetrius knew, that he'd find the excessively clean faculty office a surprise and so would have reported to his father who might have looked into the office himself and wondered at the novelty and (possibly) notified his supervisor. But Demetrius could not bring himself to mention the condition of the office to his father for almost it was coming to seem to him that since nothing had apparently happened in that place, nothing had happened.

Jesus consoles—*One day at a time, Demetrius. This will be your life.*

"THE OTHER SIDE"

17 DECEMBER 2013

"**G**od help us."

Fumbling to light a cigarette. His hands shake, he is dismayed with himself.

Like a man operating a bulldozer who steeled himself for a difficult task but finds to his surprise that he has completed the task with little effort.

Jesus! How many hours listening transfixed to the Healy boy's confession. As if Demetrius had read H. Zwender's mind, describing almost literally what Zwender had imagined had happened in Fox's office and at the Wieland ravine.

Never has Zwender felt so vindicated, so thrilled with the outcome of a case that has plagued him for weeks; yet, so stunned, disbelieving.

"Is it possible? *Him?*"

He'd declared the interview concluded for the present time for Demetrius was slumping in his chair, unable to keep his eyes open; laying his head on his arms, on the tabletop, like a kid who has fallen asleep at his desk. Excusing himself to hurry to the lavatory needing badly to empty his bladder.

No wish to examine the hue of the hot liquid that rushed from him, a new fear in the detective's life is kidney trouble. That son of a bitch Blake Healy struck him hard in the lower back, sometimes the pain is paralyzing.

Washes his hands with care. H. Zwender is particular about his hands, keeps his fingernails clean; notes with disdain dirt beneath the nails of certain of his colleagues, including Daryl Odom. Somberly he peers at his reflection in the mirror above the sink. Apart from the zigzag scar on the right side of his head he is not a bad-looking man for his age, and indeed might be mistaken for someone much younger; even the two-day stubble, glinting with silver, exudes an air of noir glamour that might appeal to women themselves no longer young, like Pauline Healy.

Not always easy for H. Zwender to confront his own face, his own zinc-flat eyes gazing at him bemused—*This is what you wanted, right?—a solution to the Fox case. And so, this is what you got.*

Pushes out the rear exit into the parking lot. Wanting to avoid his junior officer, Zwender needs time to think for himself.

He *is* astonished at what Demetrius has been telling them but hell, Detective Zwender shouldn't be surprised.

Not surprised that someone has confessed to killing Francis Fox in the way that Demetrius has described for he knew that such a person had to exist; but yes, he's surprised that it's Demetrius. How certain Zwender has been, the person who killed Francis Fox had to be an older male, (surely) the father of one of Fox's *kittens.*

Feeling dazed. Smoking too many cigarettes lately. The zipper-scar in his scalp is tingling like a raw nerve.

Like jigsaw-puzzle pieces fitting together. The final hours of a problematic case. At first you have a jumble of crazily disparate pieces but eventually a pattern emerges, a *fit.*

The word *love* was the final puzzle piece. Pauline confiding in him—*God, yes! I hope so. Demetrius loves Mary Ann.*

Ironic, the Healy kid (allegedly) committed a homicide out of love for his girl-cousin, as if trading his life for Fox's. Otherwise, what motive? None.

Like a saint—Pauline said of her nephew. *Kind, protective. Not like other boys.*

Zwender feels a pang of guilt, he took advantage of Pauline Healy. Asking questions of her that might incriminate her nephew, she was trusting of Zwender, scarcely aware that he was interrogating her, Christ!—*betraying her.*

As he is falling in love with her. What a blunder!

And what a shit he is, Detective Zwender who provoked Pauline's husband into assaulting him, assuring the man years of incarceration; in effect, removing him from Pauline's life. If Pauline forgives him for Blake Healy, she isn't going to forgive him for Demetrius.

Everyone he's ever known intimately, he has betrayed, H. Zwender has to concede.

Why this is, he has no idea. Because he became a police officer, giving over his allegiance to the community, and not to a marriage, or a family? Or maybe Zwender's personality is such that he cannot resist using others, manipulating others to the revelation of elusive and devastating truths that would remain hidden except for his effort: therefore, he became a police officer, an enforcer of (impersonal) law, eventually a detective.

Crazy-obsessive as one of those hunting dogs—bloodhound, terrier, retriever—that exist to track the faintest scent of their designated prey; unable to rest until they track the prey to its lair or perch. So Zwender prowled the area at Wieland Pond the other day peering into the ravine, into underbrush, into the very scat of an owl in search of just one more puzzle-part of Francis Fox he'd known would be there, overlooked by other searchers.

Zwender's *toe-bone good-luck piece*, he has in his right-hand trouser pocket with his key-ring and wadded tissues.

About which he isn't likely to tell anyone and especially Pauline Healy.

But this obsessiveness, like his penchant for betrayal, is the essence of Detective Zwender's being. His task, his role. His function in the community, to protect the community even without the community's awareness.

His allegiance isn't to individuals but to the commonweal. Zwender admires the word, so rarely heard in the United States: *commonweal*.

Recalling Buddhist teachings he discovered years ago as a young man. As a young police officer who'd had no choice (this was the official ruling, he'd never quite convinced himself) except to use his service revolver in a fatal exchange.

This religion, if it was a religion, so very different from the Protestant Christianity into which he'd been born: the assurance that there is no Heaven and no Hell and no likelihood of reuniting with loved ones after death, still less is there a savior. Nothing is permanent, all is continually passing away, leaves drying and falling from a deciduous tree, pointless to lament their loss, futile to try to prevent it. The *self/soul* seemingly so important is of no more significance than a fallen leaf, and desire feeds upon itself, insatiable.

This seems to Zwender the most evident interpretation of human life amid so much that is inhuman, as it is the most stoic, resigned; though he is surrounded by persons who believe very differently, like his own relatives, and like Demetrius Healy.

Yet, Zwender has become less confident in recent months. He has made notable errors of judgment, followed dead ends, feels as if Francis Fox has occupied his waking life for years and not (merely) forty-seven days. Possibly, the interrogation and "confession" of Demetrius Healy will prove to be another blunder.

He'd asked Demetrius at intervals if he wanted to stop for a while, to rest; or whether he wanted to continue. Each time Demetrius indicated *yes*, he wanted to continue.

Like a swimmer who is becoming exhausted, at risk of drowning but dares not stop swimming, dares not rest for he will sink immediately beneath the waves and never again emerge.

Zwender understood: Demetrius had become the Acura toiling up the hill an inch at a time. You needed to go all the way. You needed to push to the end. You needed to risk collapse. You could not stop speaking until you'd said all that you had to say, then you could be silent, you could slump forward in sleep, blameless as a child.

Through the hours in the bright-lit interrogation room there was Daryl Odom seated to Zwender's left. From time to time he shifted in his seat, exhaled his breath sharply as if in surprise or disbelief, but said nothing; mostly he listened in silence, mouth agape.

Zwender has to laugh, Odom's stunned-oyster look. The smart-ass speechless for once.

Still it was lucky, that Odom invited Demetrius to pray with him. Zwender had never witnessed such a spectacle in the interrogation room, he'd seen a number of people breaking down in tears, and praying, even praying on their knees, but he'd never seen a fellow officer praying with one of these.

It would become something of a local legend, maybe. How Daryl Odom precipitated a confession of homicide by praying with the perpetrator at the Wieland PD.

A local legend, if anyone outside the interrogation room is told of it.

Zwender has been pacing in the parking lot, smoking. Coughing as he inhales. He is reluctant to admit it, his balance is just perceptibly *off.*

With a part of his brain he is disbelieving, incredulous. All that Demetrius Healy has said, could it be invented? Imagined? What's the fancy word—*confabulated*?

At the most—if he'd paused to examine his assessment of the situation—Zwender might've guessed that Demetrius was involved in some peripheral way with whatever happened to Fox. The kid has the look of a bystander, an (innocent) accomplice after the fact; the younger brother cajoled by an older brother into participating in a robbery, remaining loyal to the brother while the brother pleads guilty to a lesser charge, leaving the kid to fend for himself.

But Demetrius has confessed, at length. He has revealed a number of facts not released to the public. He knew that the bronze bust was the blunt-force instrument used to bash in Fox's head, his description of cleaning Fox's office and driving Fox's car up the hill fit with the facts. He has told them that he dumped incriminating evidence into the Millbrook River.

Except: Zwender hadn't figured this soft-spoken kid had enough rage in him to bash in a man's head, for any motive.

Except: Demetrius *is* obviously strong, wiry. He may appear to be slight-bodied but his shoulders and upper arms are tight with muscle. When Zwender laid a hand on the boy's shoulder at their first interview he felt the hard muscle. The kind of lean quiet kid who keeps things to himself and can surprise you. One of those venomous snakes that gives no warning, just leaps and sinks its fangs into you.

Fact is, H. Zwender has arrested kids in rural South Jersey not so different from Demetrius. Maybe more steely-eyed. If there's been a homicide it's usually dropped to manslaughter, voluntary.

The Atlantic County medical examiner Orin Matthews (for whom Zwender feels infinite contempt) has been vacillating for weeks on the probable cause of Fox's death. He has failed to totally agree with Zwender, and the forensic investigator in Newark, that the injuries to Fox's skull could (probably) not have been caused by the car plunging into the ravine; there were boulders at the base of the ravine, and Fox might well have been thrown from the car, and his head struck on these. (Examining the boulders for Fox's blood or DNA proved "inconclusive.") In Matthews's opinion it is *likely* that the injuries were caused by blows to the head by a blunt object, yet it is *not definite*; if there were a jury trial, and if the defendant could afford to hire a medical forensic expert to argue for "accident," there could be a strong case for acquittal.

Matthews is an elderly physician who has held the office of county medical examiner since his retirement from private practice in 1987. His rulings are invariably cautious, conservative. His favored cause of death is "inconclusive."

Twelve years ago Matthews garnered criticism and ridicule in the press by ruling "accidental" the death of a middle-aged woman found drowned in her bathtub in suspicious circumstances; months after the case was closed the woman's husband abruptly confessed to having murdered her, by holding her head beneath the water.

There have been other questionable decisions on the medical examiner's part but Matthews hasn't been relieved of his position for political reasons.

Zwender has asked the medical examiner sarcastically what the hell caused Fox's death if it wasn't a homicide and all Matthews can come up with is "accident"—or "suicide." In the meantime, pending the investigation, the ruling remains "inconclusive."

No need to discuss the issue with Police Chief Paradino, another older officer approaching retirement who is uncomfortable with controversy. *Accident, suicide:* either ruling will close the case, which will be a relief.

There's growing sentiment in the Wieland PD that Zwender is squandering time, money, manpower on the Fox case, it's only because he's the senior detective that he's being humored by Paradino.

"Fuck them all."

■

ZWENDER RETURNS INSIDE, THERE'S sweaty-faced Daryl Odom awaiting him in the corridor looking exhausted, anxious.

Pleading with Zwender, what're they going to do with the Healy kid? Why didn't Zwender want to arrest him? Read him his rights? The damned confession is "inadmissible"—they failed to follow protocol.

Zwender is amused, unless Zwender is annoyed, that Odom has been skulking in the corridor here just inside the back door, peering out at Zwender pacing in the parking lot, smoking, arguing with himself, hesitant to go outside and speak with Zwender as he is dying to do.

"What the fuck are you saying, Odom? 'Arrest'—who? There's no evidence that anything the kid said is true. There're no fingerprints. There're no witnesses. The boot-prints on the hill—they're too 'degraded' to identify. Forensics told us that. We made it up, that they're his prints. We didn't arrest the kid because we were accumulating evidence and we didn't get enough. We didn't read Demetrius Healy his rights, you are right. The confession *is* inadmissible. And I erased the video."

"You—what?"

"It's all bullshit. The kid is a religious fanatic, he's confessing to something he never did. Psychologists call it 'confabulating.' I'm not going to let a local kid ruin his life because we ambushed him and he thinks he's Jesus Christ."

Odom stares at Zwender stunned. Feebly he protests they can search the river beneath the bridge. The bronze bust Healy used to kill Fox, other incriminating evidence, a trash bag with bloody rags . . .

Now Zwender is getting angry. *No.*

"That's bullshit too. 'We' are not going to search the fucking Millbrook River. It's thirty feet deep down there. The department doesn't have resources for that, we're running over budget. Even if we found something, who could prove whose it was? Maybe he disposed of it for someone else? This Healy kid, he's in another world. The public defender on the case, he'll file to dismiss the charges, there wasn't proper protocol, the confession was coerced. Paradino will never pass on this."

Odom stumbles back, weak-kneed. Leaning against a wall.

Staring at H. Zwender, baffled. Wounded, as a (favored) son might be wounded. But wary too. A rivulet of perspiration runs down the side of his face like a tear.

In the past twelve hours or so Odom has consumed several bottles of Coke. It seems he's emptied the vending machine of regular Coke, he's reduced to Diet Coke.

"I've been consulting with the medical examiner," Zwender says, "—he's still leaning toward 'inconclusive.' He thinks there's too much margin for error. It's possible that, weighing the evidence we have, Fox's death *was* accidental. There wasn't any crime—possibly. No connection with the pedophile site, that was a dead end. No connection with anyone in Wieland. Just, Fox made a wrong turn. He got lost in the preserve. Maybe he was looking for some little girl he'd hooked up with online, and got lost. Probably he was drunk. We know he drank, we saw the bottles. He was a known predator, a sick fuck of a fuck, he got himself smote by the hand of the righteous God you believe in, Odom. How's that? That make sense to you? The chief will be relieved. If there wasn't any crime we don't have to make any arrests. We can let the kid go, and go home ourselves. Nobody's going to be a fucking martyr."

Grave-faced Daryl Odom listens, in silence. His eyes are veined with broken capillaries from so long without sleep, he's not about to challenge his superior officer. Wipes his mouth with a tissue, his damp forehead. Zwender is thinking, Odom *is* a kind of good-looking guy despite his fattish face sickly-pale as an oyster bereft of its shell, and his smart-aleck personality. Shrewdest move you can make at times is be humble, Odom is beginning to see.

Zwender says, in a friendlier tone, he's been reading Buddhist stories. He thinks Odom would find them interesting.

"One day a young Buddhist on his journey in quest of enlightenment comes to the banks of a wide river. No way to get across!—no bridge, or boat; no magical eagle to carry him over. He can't swim well enough to risk drowning in such a river and so for a day and a night and another day he walks up and down the bank pondering what to do and just as he is about to give up he sees a great Buddhist teacher on the other side of the river. The young Buddhist calls to the teacher eagerly: 'Oh Wise One, can you tell me how to get to the other side of this river?'

"The teacher ponders for a moment, looks up and down the river, smiles, and says: 'My son, you are on the other side.'"

A WALK IN HELL

Come walk with me in Hell!—a figure appears before Demetrius shadowy and beneficent laying his hand on Demetrius's shoulder.

In his deep black-muck pit of oblivion the sleeper shudders, shrinks away. Terrified yet unable to resist. Unable to throw off the warm weight of the hand.

"Hey: wake up. C'mon."

Beneath blinding lights he has fallen into the deepest black-muck sleep. The most pleasurable sleep. Burrowed deep, heartbeat slowing to less than fifty beats a minute, almost he has gone into hibernation.

"Son, you're free to go home. Y'hear me? But you don't look like you should be driving yourself."

Lifts his head from his arms. His neck aches. One of his legs has gone numb.

Shaking his head as a dog shakes its head, to wake itself up.

"We're not holding you, Demetrius. We just wanted some background information. We've been calling people in to help us wrap up the investigation. It's a matter of insurance. It's a matter of liability. The county might be liable, there's no warning about roads coming to an end in the Wieland preserve. You could mistake a trail for a road. If you were from out-of-state, and got lost."

Demetrius rouses himself to his feet, swaying. No idea in hell what the elder detective is talking about in a matter-of-fact manner verging upon the jocular.

Like there is some joke in the air Demetrius isn't getting but it's here to be got, if he can just wake up.

"About that ring, Demetrius? How'd you know there *was* a ring? Somebody told you?"

Ring? Demetrius tries to think.

H. Zwender smiles his enigmatic smile. His eyes are cold, flat yet kindly. But Demetrius stands mute.

"You want to wash your face, Demetrius? Call somebody at home?"

Demetrius manages a reply, he isn't sure. Just barely audibly he mumbles the word *sir.*

Zwender is touched, he's being called *sir.* He'd glance over at Odom to exchange an amused look but Odom isn't in sight.

It is then that in a lowered voice H. Zwender tells Demetrius a number of things following in quick succession which Demetrius will try to retain as one might try to recall a particularly powerful dream that begins to fade upon waking.

"It's our thought, Demetrius, that you have imagined what you've told us. Some of this might have happened, but not all of it. And maybe not to you. You know, the medical examiner thinks that Fox killed himself. But the public needs to be told it was an accident. That's for morale—y'know what morale is? A schoolteacher kills himself, it's not a good look. For young people. Also you know, the things you told us are not 'admissible.' You were never arrested. You were 'interviewed.' You were not 'interrogated'—tell your friends. In fact, none of this happened. There's no videotape or recording. Think of your mother's memory, Demetrius. I knew your mother, just a little— Ida. Your mother is in Heaven, Demetrius, looking after you. She doesn't want you to sacrifice your life needlessly. You have to wash up, go home, and see what the rest of your life will be. You believe in Jesus, yes? Well, Jesus is watching over you, too. Jesus knows what's

in your heart. Jesus forgives, that's His special gift. I don't believe in
Jesus personally—I admit it: I'm not proud—but I believe that there
is a God who made the world and it got away from Him and He can't
unmake it. He made man and woman in His image, now He can't
control them.

"But I know this, Demetrius: God does not want you to spend
years of your young life in prison. That is not God's plan. His plan is
for you to lead a normal life. You will marry in a few years, you will
become a father. That's what we do. You will be beloved. Your mother
expects that. Your father, too. That's God's plan for you."

Zwender ushers Demetrius out into the corridor, as one might
lead a convalescent. Beside the vending machine, there's Daryl Odom
seated in a chair glassy-eyed, an empty Diet Coke bottle in his hands.

"Hey: Odom. You can drive Demetrius home, he's not in good
shape for driving. Also, take him out to breakfast en route. He's starving, hasn't eaten in twelve hours."

Odom rises to his feet, with some effort. His expression is resolutely neutral, he isn't going to risk H. Zwender's temper.

"Where'd I go, that's open now?"

"One of those truck stops on the highway. Wendy's? McDonald's?
How should I know?"

"Is this on the department? Both of us?"

"Here—you can charge it on my card."

THE COVENANT

19 DECEMBER 2013

How the detective came into my life. And altered my life.
Speaking to me as no one has spoken to me. Peering into my
soul that was bloated and blemished with pride. Humbling me, but not
humiliating me. Having mercy on me.

A final time H. Zwender has come to speak with P. Cady.

This time also walking together on the Langhorne school grounds beyond the playing fields deserted at this time of the school year.

A light-falling snow, fallen leaves underfoot. Poplar leaves like the palms of open hands and like human hands lined, veined. Smaller red-maple leaves, dried and broken on the pathway.

Bringing me the solace that I have been spared whether I deserved
such mercy or not.

Taller than P. Cady by no more than an inch or two H. Zwender walks beside the Langhorne headmistress in her charcoal-gray military-looking cashmere coat that falls to midcalf. Black leather boots, soft Italian leather of such high quality they appear to be almost plain, self-effacing. On her head a smart beret-like cap of dark maroon cashmere.

And that the school has been spared, that is as close to me as my life.

Zwender is bemused by P. Cady, once so haughty in his presence and now so eager to believe what he tells her. Like a starving creature, lifting its head, opening its mouth, or beak, so grateful to be fed whatever she is being fed there is no motive to question it.

". . . just so you know, Ms. Cady, the investigation has ended. We have reason to believe—the medical examiner has reason to believe—that, as you anticipated, Fox may have taken his own life."

"Oh! Poor Francis! He must have been so, so depressed . . ."

"Since it can't be definitively proven, the medical examiner is ruling it an accidental death."

"Yes—thank God! 'Accidental.'" P. Cady pauses, wiping at her eyes. "That's what our students believe."

"But you say, Ms. Cady, no suicide note ever turned up?"

"No note. No."

P. Cady's voice is hoarse, hushed.

"I mean, not that I know of. Francis might have sent a note to—to someone . . . He has—had—a stepsister in Florida but they don't seem to have been very close."

"There's a woman on your staff, a librarian, who claimed to be Fox's closest friend in Wieland."

P. Cady stiffens. Is this Imogene Hood?—the headmistress hesitates to say anything critical about any of her staff.

"But possibly," says Zwender, "this woman was mistaken."

"She *was* mistaken," P. Cady says. "She's decided to leave Wieland at the end of the term. I tried to dissuade her but she said it was impossible to stay here any longer."

"And why was that?"

"Because—I think—too much here would remind her of him. Of Francis."

Zwender considers this. Recalling that Imogene Hood was tremulous with emotion, he felt pity for her, and impatience; he never questioned her a second time seeing that the information she could provide him about Francis Fox was worthless.

"You'd thought, Ms. Cady, Fox took his own life because he was stricken with remorse."

"I—I think so . . . Did I say that, Detective?"

"I think you did, yes. 'Remorse'—'conscience.' Because of things he did to underage girls, that would have sent him to Rahway for a long time."

"Rahway?"

"Sex crimes. Child molesters."

P. Cady is looking distressed, as if she doesn't understand.

"And because you knew him so well."

"I—I did know Francis . . . Probably better than anyone in Wieland."

P. Cady's voice trails off uncertainly. As if in acknowledgment that this is a preposterous thing to say, though Zwender listens politely.

The more intelligent the woman, the more likely to be mired in delusion. P. Cady, Imogene Hood. Precisely because the woman cannot imagine that she is mired in delusion.

". . . still so very hard to believe. But . . ."

"What is hard to believe, Ms. Cady?"

"What you told me. The things Francis did—allegedly. And the website. It just didn't seem like Francis . . ."

"Not the Francis you knew, Ms. Cady."

"It's such a tragedy, he never had the opportunity to defend himself. If there'd been a trial . . ."

"But you wouldn't have wanted a trial, Ms. Cady. I don't think so."

"Oh no—of course not. I didn't mean that. I meant that Francis never had a chance to—explain . . ."

"To explain pedophilia? Posting pornography for subscribers, making a little untaxed money on the side?"

"There were—subscribers?"

"Almost eight thousand."

"Eight thousand!" P. Cady is shocked, dismayed. "Who—who are these people?"

"People like Francis Fox."

Zwender speaks gravely. For P. Cady is genuinely shocked, though none of this should be new to her; it's as if a kind of amnesia seeps inexorably into the woman's brain, so strong is her opposition to knowing the truth about Francis Fox.

"It's just so—so difficult to believe . . ."

"Is it?"

Anticipating such a moment Zwender has brought with him his laptop, in an unobtrusive black bag; this, he now activates, to show P. Cady the image he showed Mrs. Chambers: a young girl, face crudely pixelated, in a maroon jumper immediately recognizable as a Langhorne uniform, seemingly asleep, her pleated skirt uplifted, bare white thighs visible as a man grips her between the legs. On one of the man's fingers a ring with an octagonal black stone.

P. Cady stands staring. That ring! That school uniform!

Weakly P. Cady pushes the laptop away. No! No more.

"There's worse. Self-harm, cutting—girls cutting their arms, bleeding in videos. Cutting the insides of their thighs with razors."

P. Cady stumbles, feeling faint. Zwender reaches out to steady her.

The touch of the man's hands! P. Cady shuts her eyes, dazed. She feels as if her brain has been obliterated, she has been utterly humiliated, humbled.

"But the website is down, Ms. Cady. I took it down. Weeks ago. *Sleeping Beauties 2013* he called it. No one can access it. No need to be upset."

"But—you have it on your laptop. You have it, in your police files?"

"Of course, Ms. Cady. We don't erase our files. But the public will never know, so don't worry."

P. Cady looks worried. But Zwender isn't going to placate her further.

"I—I can't tell you how grateful I am, Detective. You have done so much for our school, for the poor girls, and for me . . . If it were not for you, what would have happened to us!"

"What would have happened? Eventually, Fox would have been caught. One of the abused girls would tell her parents. It would all come out, and you'd have been blamed for hiring him, and the Langhorne Academy might have gone bankrupt. But that didn't happen because Fox's 'conscience' won out, he rid the world of his depraved self. So all has ended well for everyone."

"'Ended well . . .'" P. Cady laughs sadly.

Zwender has come to feel more positive about the Fox investigation ending abruptly as it did. Police Chief Paradino has expressed satisfaction and relief that it's closed with a ruling of accidental death. No more homicide investigation, no drawn-out negotiations with Atlantic County prosecutors, no scandal involving a young local man.

Indeed, Leo Paradino has told H. Zwender privately, what will be officially announced in January, that he is stepping down, and H. Zwender will be promoted to chief.

Is this good news? Zwender isn't sure. It means more money, slightly more local prestige: Pauline will be impressed, and happy for him. But most of a police chief's work is administrative, which will be dull, boring.

Also, at Zwender's urging, Officer Daryl Odom will receive a boost of one-quarter of his first-year salary, for his "exemplary" work in assisting Zwender in the investigation; when Zwender is chief, after a year or two he'll promote Odom to sergeant.

His man on the force, in thrall to H. Zwender. For it seems to Zwender, he and Odom make a useful team.

P. Cady tells Zwender of plans the school has to establish annual poetry prizes in honor of Francis Fox. Her art historian niece Katy Cady will be joining the Langhorne faculty, and will live with P. Cady— "My house is too large for just one person! I've been lonely." The niece has ambitious plans to preserve the memory of Francis Harlan Fox by building an endowment . . .

Zwender is amused, P. Cady doesn't seem to see the irony here. She speaks with girlish enthusiasm about prizes, scholarships, endowments in the name of Francis H. Fox. It is hard not to fall in with such enthusiasm in planning for a future that will benefit students.

Headmistress Cady is fascinating to Zwender: a woman in her fifties with a curiously unlined face, never wears makeup, no (evident) female vanity, perfect posture, poise. Most women he knows in Wieland wear makeup, lipstick, alert and aware of a man's attention as P. Cady is not.

Pauline, with smudged lipstick. Smudged mascara. Inky rivulets beneath her eyes if she has been crying.

"Ms. Cady, there's someone you should know about, that you're indebted to."

Indebted! P. Cady listens intently, for she doesn't doubt that the detective is telling her something important.

Zwender tells P. Cady that, for reasons he can't divulge, she owes a favor to a young local man who is the son of one of her employees, a custodian.

"It has to do with the school's reputation. Getting rid of pornographic material belonging to Fox, he'd found in Fox's office at the school before the office was searched."

"I—I see . . ."

"This young man has been helping his father—the custodian. I can't go into details because it's confidential but believe me, he spared you all considerable humiliation. There are some things that have to be suppressed. Between making the truth public and protecting the innocent, like the innocent victims of Francis Fox, I believe in protecting the innocent."

P. Cady listens, not sure what she is hearing. *Humiliation, protecting the innocent . . .* She is deeply moved, even dazzled by Zwender's impassioned words.

"What I suggest, Ms. Cady, is that you extend financial help to Demetrius Healy and his father, Lemuel. The father is becoming incapacitated—he should be retired with a generous pension. Demetrius should be hired for something suitable, that pays well: not as a custodian, maybe a personal driver? A headmistress is in need of a driver, yes?"

"A—driver?"

"A personal driver. An assistant. Not an academic. A local hire, who can do things with his hands."

P. Cady is not in need of a personal driver, she drives herself everywhere in her own vehicle. She is an administrator who believes in self-maintenance, no expense account. She has always prided herself on her self-sufficiency!

But hearing the urgency in Detective Zwender's voice, seeing in the man's face the strong imperative that she say *yes*, P. Cady says *Yes*.

She will hire this person—"Demetrius Healy"—whom she has never met. She will pay him a generous salary out of her own private income, more than his custodian-father has been making. (Headmistress Cady knows the salaries of all of her staff as well as her faculty, she has an uncanny memory for such details.) It will be a relationship of meaning to them both though the connection between them, through H. Zwender, will remain obscure.

Seeing that she has pleased the detective P. Cady feels elated, relieved. She has no curiosity about what exactly Demetrius Healy did to protect the Langhorne school.

She is charmed by the name "Demetrius." A son of working-class people in rural Atlantic County. And his father a custodian at the school—possibly, she has spoken with Mr. Healy, and would remember his face; as an administrator, P. Cady is admired for taking time to meet all of her staff.

P. Cady has always intended to become better acquainted with her neighbors in Atlantic County. If Demetrius is interested, she might pay his tuition at the community college. The sick-sinking sensation evoked by the memory of *Sleeping Beauties 2013* has vanished.

Suffused with joy, a sense of purpose. As if Francis Fox is the benefactor, making reparations for his sins after his death.

Impulsively P. Cady reaches for Zwender's hand, to shake it in farewell, or to grasp it tight. For a moment is seems as if P. Cady might lift Zwender's hand to her face, pressing it against her cheek in a gesture of ecstatic self-abnegation.

You have changed my life, Detective. You have saved my life. I love you.

Quickly recovering, and merely shaking the man's hand. "I owe you everything, Detective. I am so, so grateful."

Zwender listens to this declaration with something like amazement. It crosses his mind—(one of those random arrows that flies through his brain at unpredictable moments)—that he and this woman might have a more defined relationship with each other. "Paige" seems to admire him, she is certainly intimidated by him; he guesses that in her life there have been few men who've intimidated her as there are few men as tall as she, with as assured a bearing.

And a wealthy woman, to boot.

Among all of the Zwenders, no one like Headmistress Cady.

Not a bad-looking woman, either.

Make a fool of yourself, overstep a boundary.

Be an asshole, take a chance.

(The look on Odom's face!—that alone would be worth it.)

But no? Not a chance?

Can't risk embarrassment? Humiliation?

No, and no.

No.

EPILOGUE

MAY 2022

MYSTERY-JOURNAL

BY E__ P__

A senior thesis submitted to the Program in Creative Writing at
Princeton University in a partial fulfillment of the requirements
for the Degree of Bachelor of Arts

ADVISOR: JOYCE CAROL OATES

May 2022

Princeton University

Princeton, New Jersey

1.

There was never a time when I was not in love with Mr. Fox.

There was never a time when Mr. Fox was not my life.

Because before Mr. Fox came into my life our souls knew each other *in* the time before *where there is no time.*

Because *we are born of such knowing. Of* the time before *as when waking in the morning we carry the memory of the beautiful dreams we have lost in waking.*

In the time before *there is no time as we understand it on Earth, it is a great void like the ocean in which droplets of rain fall & vanish.*

In the time before *we are children together, there is no "age" that* separates.

This, Mr. Fox explained.

Saying, *My darling there will never be a time when our souls are not* joined.

Saying, Our (secret) pledge will be, we will die for each other if that is asked of us.

We will never reveal our secret, we will die together & our secret will die with us.

For there is no Death in the time before. *Souls are joined in love in* the time before.

This, Mr. Fox explained.

To me only, Mr. Fox explained.

2.

"This is for you. Because you are *you*."

In his hand a journal with a marbled cover like the lush green of new-budded leaves.

I could not breathe. Tears hot as acid welled in my eyes. I had never seen anything so beautiful.

"Don't cry, my dear! Please."

His fingertips brushing tears from my cheeks.

Kissing me then. That first time. So gently his tongue entering my mouth, I felt that I would faint.

Swooning it is called. *Swooning* is not a joke but a real thing.

■

THERE WERE OTHERS BEFORE me, I knew. But Mr. Fox made it clear, he adored ME most of all.

My name in his mouth became beautiful as music. Where always before in the mouths of others my name was ugly.

Eu-nice. You-nice!

So many little jokes between us. Whisperings, cuddles and tickles.

Sharing a lemon tart with Mr. Fox. Chocolate-covered strawberries. My mouth filled with saliva like pain. I was ravenous with hunger, I never ate like that at home.

Mr. Fox laughed at me kissing me, you are special because you are
You-nice.

The tarts were so sweet, my eyelids grew heavy. On Mr. Fox's office wall was a glossy poster of Alice in Wonderland with Alice's neck
eerily elongated, her hands lifted indecisively. Her flat-chested torso
was eerily elongated as well, and her feet in prim black strap-shoes
freakishly small, smaller even than her hands . . . In appalled fascina-
tion Alice observed me in Mr. Fox's embrace as I fell asleep and when
I awakened my (white, cotton) panties were down around my ankles,
a strange warm sensation thrummed at the fork of my legs.

Mr. Fox's face was flushed, his eyes shone with love.
Eu-nice! My special love.

■

THERE WAS NEVER A TIME

              when I was not in love with Mr. Fox
      but there are times when the love comes so strong
            my heart is near-bursting and I know that
                I will be joining Mr. Fox soon

because

           the hunger is more than I can bear
             now there is no one to feed me

     the food
     I require

■

ALL THIS WAS NINE years ago. I was just a child: thirteen.

Though (in fact) I was an unusually mature thirteen, intellectually.

Nine years ago Mr. Fox was taken from me.

But nine years ago is *now.* For Mr. Fox is with me *here.*

Always the first time entering Mr. Fox's office in the basement of Haven Hall scarcely daring to breathe for I feared my stern English teacher staring and glaring at me in contempt as I had never feared any teacher or indeed any adult before; and then so unexpectedly there swept upon me Mr. Fox's (blue, pale) eyes startled as if, for the first time, close-up, Mr. Fox was seeing *me*.

"Come in, Eunice! I've been waiting for you."

(Waiting for *me*? I was stunned by this remark, I could not think of a reply.)

(For I was not one of those slutty girls who knew by instinct how to *flirt* with handsome Mr. Fox.)

Instead, there was a roaring in my ears like a chorus of frogs. As I stumbled to sit down my bookbag slipped from my shoulder, fell to the floor.

Mr. Fox gazed upon me with affectionate amusement which in my anxiety and self-consciousness I mistook as scorn.

And, on the corner of Mr. Fox's desk, at eye level the stony blind eyes of a sculpted male head gazed at me as well.

It was a life-sized head, or even larger. Head, chest, shoulders and on one of the shoulders a large bird with a sharp beak perched with malevolent intent.

The carved face was wanly handsome, and exuded an air of melancholy. There was something accusatory in the mournful eyes. Something soft, wounded in the mouth.

The style of the hair, the drooping mustache suggested an era long past when *hauntedness* was pervasive.

Mr. Fox would explain, this was a bust of the great nineteenth-century poet Edgar Allan Poe. And on his shoulder—did I know what the bird was?

"A raven?"—shyly I guessed.

"*The* raven: correct! The raven who quoteth—*Nevermore.* I see that you've read ahead in our anthology."

"Oh no—I read 'The Raven' last year. And 'The Tell-Tale Heart' and 'The Black Cat' . . . "

"In your English class?"

"Oh no—just—just by myself."

Mr. Fox's blue eyes moving upon me, approvingly.

The choking-tight constriction in my chest began to relax. I began to breathe more freely. Knowing that I had passed a test that few others in this chair had passed.

And from this time Mr. Fox began to favor me. It was as if Mr. Fox had *recognized me,* as I had *recognized him.*

Later this would be explained to me. But on this occasion, I felt it keenly.

In our classroom amid the distractions of those others vying for his attention Mr. Fox had scarcely seemed to notice me though I was seated, not entirely by chance, in the very center of the room. For Mr. Fox's fullest attention was lavished elsewhere. (Yes, I could see where! Faces of vacuous prettiness, I held in such contempt I rarely so much as glanced at them.) Seeing now that *Eunice Pfenning* who'd been but a name on the class list was superior to those others, boys as well as girls, who'd drawn Mr. Fox's initial attention. Now across the width of his desk Mr. Fox was looking seriously at *me.*

Mr. Fox explained the sculpture on his desk: a bronze bust commemorating first prize in the annual Nevermore Poetry Competition sponsored by the Poe Society of America which had been awarded to—*Francis Harlan Fox.*

Mr. Fox spoke with quiet pride. I would recall how Mr. Fox was not one of those mealymouthed hypocrite adults who pretended to false modesty.

How impressive this information was to me: *First prize! Poe Society!*

It was a revelation: Mr. Fox was a *poet.*

Eagerly I asked if I could read the prizewinning poem but Mr. Fox said that could wait for another time for today our subject was *me.*

(Though Mr. Fox was clearly pleased, that I had made the request. Few eighth graders would have expressed an interest in a poem, *his poem.*)

"We need to reexamine your Sandburg critique, Eunice."

A hot flush came into my face. I was deeply ashamed, mortified by my grade on the assignment; I'd been thinking of nothing else since Mr. Fox handed it back the previous day marked, in glaring red ink, C–.

One of the lowest grades in the class, I was sure. I *was* sure, for I'd overheard others boasting about their grades including the most insipid girls.

That night I'd barely slept and in my sleep the C– shimmering in red as in blood danced inside my tight-shut eyes.

And now, that Mr. Fox would bestow mercy on me, that he would take the time to reread the paper with such patience, inviting me to "correct" sentences he'd marked in red ink—this was astonishing to me.

In this way, with Mr. Fox's assistance, *improving my ability to critique a work of literature and also to express myself in good clear English prose.*

In this way, saving my life. For a grade of C– was so humiliating, I had considered killing myself. I had crept into the kitchen in the night to examine knives and cutlery. Several razor-sharp knives attached to a magnetic board above the butcher-block island drew my close attention.

My critique of Sandburg poems was easily twice as long as the other students' critiques, what had I done wrong? Killing myself would be a way of punishing Daddy too.

(I tried not to think of Daddy when I was at the Langhorne Academy. It was bad enough that, at home, when Daddy was no longer *at home,* I had to think about him.)

Yet, Mr. Fox rescued me from such thoughts by showing how *improving/raising a grade* could be accomplished by a careful reexamination of language.

Each of the offensive sentences, which Mr. Fox read aloud, I was allowed to "correct." First, orally; then, in my own handwriting on the critique.

When the corrections were completed Mr. Fox smiled at me and asked which of the Sandburg poems was my favorite?

I could not discern if this was a friendly question or a trick. For Mr. Fox *was* tricky!

Hesitating to reply dreading to give a foolish answer and losing what meager approval I had won with Mr. Fox so far.

Seeing that I was tongue-tied and blushing Mr. Fox volunteered that *his* favorite Sandburg poem was "Fog."

This was, Mr. Fox said, a perfect little poem for middle-school readers containing a single catchy metaphor: "Little cat feet."

Mr. Fox asked me what the "poetic effect" would have been if Sandburg had said "little kitten feet" instead?

This was a novel idea to me, that anything in a poem could be other than the way it is in print.

That anything in the adult world could be other than it is because they want us to think *this is how it is, there is no other way.*

I told Mr. Fox that "little kitten feet" would be silly!

"Why would 'little kitten feet' be silly, Eunice?"

"You wouldn't say 'little kitten'—a kitten is already *little*."

"And so, 'little kitten' is redundant?"

"'Redundant'—y-yes . . ."

"And what is the figure of speech of 'little cat feet'—?"

"A metaphor."

"And what *is* a metaphor, Eunice?"

This rapid-fire exchange was dizzying to me. Yet exhilarating.

"'A metaphor is a figure of speech in which a word or phrase is applied to an object or action to which it is not literally applicable'"— this was the definition Mr. Fox had written on the whiteboard for us, which I had memorized.

"Very good, Eunice!" Mr. Fox said. "And what is another example of a metaphor? Give me one of your own."

I tried to think. If this were a homework assignment I would have composed any number of metaphors without difficulty but in the exigency of the moment with Mr. Fox looking at me, and the stony eyes of Edgar Allan Poe looking at me, my brain went blank.

"'The fog comes trudging in on ponderous elephant feet.' Is that a metaphor, Eunice?"

I had to laugh, Mr. Fox was so funny.

"'The miasma comes staggering in on drunken camel feet.'"

I giggled harder. *Miasma* was a funny sound and so was *drunken camel feet.*

Could not stop giggling, it was like Mr. Fox was tickling me.

Like the sun rising on a mudflat. A nasty mudflat stinking of rotted things. But the sun *rising and shining on the mudflat.*

That was the surprise of Mr. Fox smiling at me, laughing with *me.*

In just these few minutes, Mr. Fox said, I'd raised my paper to an A—except, unfortunately Mr. Fox couldn't record that grade because it would be unfair to other students who hadn't had the opportunity of improving their grades, did I understand?

It was sad but yes, I understood.

"D'you know why I've taken so much time with you, Eunice?"

Shook my head shyly *no.*

"Because you are unique, Eunice. Even in your first paper on *The Call of the Wild* I recognized this. Though the paper was not perfect, yet the potential was evident. And your subsequent work confirms it."

Confirms—what? I sat there, dazzled.

"That you are exceptional. In essence. I wonder if your parents quite realize who you are—*their daughter*? No! Not at all."

Disbelieving I sat staring at Mr. Fox. His moving mouth, that was so beautiful in my eyes.

"You dwell among us as a stranger, Eunice. In your innermost heart you must know this."

I could not speak, I was so moved.

I could have cried. *Mr. Fox has peered into my soul.*

For yes, I did know this—I had always thought this. My other teachers had praised me, and given me A's. I knew—of course. *I was special.*

But no one except Mr. Fox had ever spoken such words aloud to me.

Returning the paper to me, now marked C+.

C+! Where C– had made me want to kill myself, now C+ filled my heart with hope.

For it was a C+ *from Mr. Fox's own hand, in red ink.*

For a C+ is close to a B–.

I would strive for a B, and I would strive for an A. And one day—A+.

That seemed to be the promise. I was sure, that was the promise.

I would show this critique to my mother with the grade raised to C+. And (possibly) to my father.

(Though I was angry at Daddy. I did not trust Daddy. He had moved away from us saying it was not *his choice*. But I did not believe Daddy for it was Mommy who hid away crying in her bedroom, not Daddy.)

"Thank you, Mr. Fox. I will try to do better."

"Eunice, you *will* do better."

As I gathered up my bookbag to leave the office Mr. Fox bade me *Wait.*

Lifting, out of a desk drawer, a journal with a beautiful marbled-green cover, to give to me.

"A special gift for you, Eunice. For your class portfolio, due at the end of the term."

This was so unexpected, I could only stare speechlessly.

"It's a magic journal, Eunice. You must tell the truth when you write in it, otherwise there will be a curse on you."

Mr. Fox spoke so gravely, I could not be sure if he was joking.

"What kind of curse?"

"Ah! It's forbidden to say."

A fit of wild giggling overcame me. I would come to love how Mr. Fox *joked.*

Warning me: "Mr. Fox never jokes! Haven't I told our class—*There are no jokes.*"

Warning me: "You must keep the contents of your journal secret from everyone—parents, relatives, friends."

(Friends! As if I had friends, or even relatives close to me. It was flattering to me, that Mr. Fox assumed this.)

These words would reverberate in my memory every day of my life.

Until this very time—*now.* For always, I must record the truth in my Mystery-Journal (as I would come to call it.)

It was wonderful to me, to lift the journal in my hands, to leaf through the (slightly yellowed) pages, that were unnervingly blank. It was an old-fashioned journal, to be written in by hand.

I scarcely dared whisper, "Thank you, Mr. Fox."

Mr. Fox instructed me: I would be expected to hand in the journal to him every Friday. Soon, if all went well, I would be of the élite to qualify for the Looking-Glass Book Club.

In the journal I could write about anything—everything. Homework assignments, formal critiques, creative responses to work from our anthology. Things that I would never say aloud, I could write in my journal. Things that would shock my parents and make them unhappy with me and say of me *This is not you, Eunice!*

"But of course, Eunice: *it is you.*"

Telling me that I should explore the outside world: trees, waterways, birds.

Must get outdoors. Out of your hard little skull.

"Push yourself out of your comfort zone, Eunice. Experiment with writing with your nondominant hand. Illustrate your journal with colored pencils, crayons. Take photos. Wander in the woods and get lost.

"Have you ever been *lost,* Eunice?"

So gravely Mr. Fox gazed at me, I could only stammer *No.*

One cannot be found who has not been lost.

"You see, dear Eunice, you are an exceptional student who has been untested until now. Being superior to your classmates is a very low bar; it doesn't mean you've achieved your potential—far from it: being superior to others will limit your potential when *those others* are mediocre.

"But I have come to the Langhorne Academy to challenge you: for your destiny is sheerly potential, it is far from realized."

It was Mr. Fox's way to speak like this. You felt you might burst into wild laughter, or wild tears.

Almost you would think—*But he is joking, he can't be serious—is he?*

Seeing that my eyes brimmed with tears of gratitude and wonder Mr. Fox leaned forward suddenly as if he could not help himself, and gently framed my face in his hands.

Kissing my eyelids, to kiss away the tears.

Tenderly kissing my mouth, that no one had ever kissed before.

"*My* unique Eu-nice."

3.

Love love love you *Eu-nice*.
 Eu-nice is SO UNIQUE AND SO NICE!

Love you more than anyone else has been loved—ever!

Each time when I entered his office now Mr. Fox closed the door quickly.

Closed and locked the door safely, to keep others out.

I came then to understand that I had always been in love with Mr. Fox—even before I knew him.

Even before I knew him in the time before time, we had loved each other.

As soon as our eyes met, we recognized each other. For our knowledge of each other is in our *souls,* not our outward beings.

And there will never be a time when our souls are not joined.

In careful words like a poet Mr. Fox explained. It was clear to me when Mr. Fox explained but not so clear afterward when I lay in bed trying to remember his wonderful words.

He spoke of the "plasticity of time." How time loops back upon itself like a Möbius strip.

Like a Möbius strip, that is a continuous strip of one side only, the soul is immortal.

At the crossing of the (immortal) soul of the lover with the (immortal) soul of the beloved there is a union.

This union defies all clock-time, calendar-time, and cannot be measured.

We knew each other, Mr. Fox said, in the time before we were known to the world by the names assigned us at birth. For these are names imposed upon us, not freely chosen.

Names imposed on us by strangers—our "parents." Not souls that would bind together in exclusion of all else.

He would teach me to be wild, reckless. He would teach me to be *me*.

In my journal in which I would bare my heart, and in Mr. Fox's office with the door safely shut and locked and the overhead lights switched off.

With that special look summoning me in our class. Lifting my eyes to his Mr. Fox would nod at me for just a second, the smallest glimmer of a smile no one else saw.

Sharing lemon tarts, chocolate-covered strawberries fed to me by Mr. Fox's hand, so delicious!—I never devoured anything so ravenously at home, Mr. Fox laughed at me affectionately saying that I was a little girl with a big appetite, that would have to be satisfied.

Sugary-sweet tarts, that made saliva rush into my mouth. And Mr. Tongue poking, prodding as Mr. Tongue did for you could not keep Mr. Tongue away, Mr. Tongue could be *naughty.* Strange how sleepy I became, my eyes could not stay open. Cuddling in Mr. Fox's arms and when I was sleepiest there came Mr. Teddy Bear to slip his warm firm bear-paw between my legs.

Sometimes I cried in Mr. Fox's office (because I was so happy) and sometimes I cried myself to sleep in my bed (because I was so lonely).

. . . *never a time when you were not in love with Mr. Fox and Mr. Fox was not in love with you. Never.*

■

THERE WERE GIRLS IN our eighth-grade class who were in love with Mr. Fox—I knew.

These were slutty girls who hung about Mr. Fox's desk after class with silly questions to ask him. Like chittering birds following him in the hall. Waiting outside his office to see him without having an appointment.

But I was the only one Mr. Fox ADORED.

And there were other girls, in other classes. I could recognize them: they had journals like mine with marbled covers.

Mooning after Mr. Fox in the corridors, on the stairs. Following him outside on the walkway.

Mr. Fox? I have a question . . .

Mr. Fox? What do you think of . . .

Giggling together, ridiculous.

Most ridiculous, and most disgusting was an eighth-grade girl who if you didn't see her silly insipid face you'd mistake for years older than she was—a senior in high school at least. Sickening how boys stared at her and followed her and some of them laughing and jeering calling after her *Baby Tits! Baby Tits!*

Especially it was sickening to me, to see how Mr. Fox looked at this girl as if helpless to look away.

There were even girls from the upper division who hung out sometimes at Mr. Fox's office. Pretending to be interviewing him for the school paper or the yearbook. *As a new faculty member what do you think of the Langhorne Academy? How does it compare with your previous schools?*

Asking if they could take selfies with him but Mr. Fox laughed saying curtly *No!*

All these girls, I came to hate. I will confess this, I am not ashamed. For they were hateful, all of them.

In my journal I listed their names. Lay in bed thinking how I could kill them one by one.

I *could* have killed them if I'd had a gun or a hammer to pound at their heads like melons until they cracked or possibly a knife, instead of turning a razor-sharp knife on myself why not on one of them? A plan came to me in a dream: on Hallowe'en there was a stupid dance at school to which I was not going (of course) but if I did go to this dance (in costume and mask) there would be opportunities for me to slash their throats in the girls' restroom in toilet stalls and no one would know until the end of the dance but (of course) I DID NOT REALLY MEAN THIS, it was just that my heart was raw with hurt when Mr. Fox did not summon me for several days at a time and if I crept to his office, the door was closed and locked.

Why this began to happen, I did not know.

In our class Mr. Fox smiled outward at us all but I did not see him smiling and winking at *me*.

It was hard to pay attention in class. In Mr. Fox's class or in any class.

Too much pride to creep to Mr. Fox's office to see if the door was closed. To see if anyone was inside. To knock on Mr. Fox's door shyly and hope that he would have time for me.

Too much pride to press my ear against the frosted-glass window, to hear what was being said inside.

For I *was not* jealous.

For I *was not* jealous of the stupid girls mooning and giggling in the hall outside Mr. Fox's office. Stayed away from Mr. Fox's office for one, two, three days and on the third day I was coughing so hard my mother would not drive me to school but to urgent care where the doctor diagnosed me with bronchitis.

I was never jealous of Mr. Fox, it was Daddy who was jealous of Mr. Fox. I had begun to tell Daddy about Mr. Fox because I did not need Daddy any longer, I did not care if Daddy stayed away. I did not care if Daddy died.

I would not (ever) forgive Daddy for going away and leaving me. He said it wasn't his choice, it was Mommy who had asked him to go away but he was the one to *go away*.

Mommy said it was *an interim time—in-between time*. Until things were *worked out*.

I felt sorry for Mommy who was left behind—(like me). I did not love Mommy and so I did not hate Mommy, much.

Like drops from a faucet the hate came slow, then faster. Disappearing down a drain.

I turned off the shower knobs so hard, something broke inside one of them. I didn't mean to do this but somehow it happened.

So now, there was a drip from the showerhead. I could hear this drip in my room. With the door closed, and the door to the bathroom closed, and the door to the shower stall closed I could hear this drip.

Mommy called a plumber, while I was at school the drip was fixed one day. Yet sometimes I could hear it through the closed doors.

I did not love Daddy, it made me sick to love Daddy. I began to hate Daddy. Daddy came for me each weekend. I hated the name—*Dad-dy*. What a silly insipid name! Daddy asked me where I wanted to go for dinner and I shrugged and said *Anywhere. Doesn't matter.* Daddy asked if I would like to spend the day at the Jersey coast and I made a face crinkling my nose—*No.*

Nothing that Daddy could give me was of interest to me now. Now that Mr. Fox loved me.

Wanting to curl up like a little kitten in Mr. Fox's arms.

Wanting to suck Mr. Tongue into my mouth deep, and deeper until I choked.

And Mr. Teddy Bear, I wanted him to touch me between my legs in Mr. Teddy Bear's special way until I died.

■

THIS POEM, MR. FOX whispered in my ear.

The most perfect poem, Mr. Fox described it.

> *She walks in beauty, like the night*
> *Of cloudless climes and starry skies;*
> *And all that's best of dark and bright*
> *Meet in her aspect and her eyes.*

I knew that Mr. Fox had not written this poem; I knew from a computer search that it was a poem by Lord Byron written in 1814 in iambic tetrameter. Yet still, it was a poem *for me*, and it was a poem *from Mr. Fox* which I would cherish always.

4.

In an instant, a life is altered.

Mr. Fox's affable face, eyes of the chemical blue of Windex.

"Eunice: what happened this week?"

Handing back critiques in our English class, casually addressing you in mild surprise but only in passing, not lingering with you, not absorbing the look of utter shock in your face, trading jokes with other students *as if a blade had not pierced your heart*.

Fortunately it is at the end of class. Quickly you can shove the paper into your bookbag, flee the room with a bowed head, blinking tears from your eyes.

You know, they are laughing at you.

You know, Mr. Fox is surprised (and sad) for you.

Another time, a C– in glaring red ink. After a steady succession of B's and B+'s at a time when you might certainly expect your next grade to be A– or even A for you have *worked so very hard* on this critique of a lengthy excerpt from *Huckleberry Finn*.

You are so upset, you crumple the paper in your hand. Can you—should you—ask Mr. Fox if you can rewrite it and resubmit it?—you are fearful of annoying him, he has not been smiling so freely in your direction lately.

Know that you have disappointed *him,* failed *him.*

Run away, hide in a toilet stall. Bitter tears, no one needs to see how Eunice Pfenning's frog-homely face becomes homelier still when she is crying.

■

NOT JEALOUS. BUT: IN the stairwell observing.

How *she* has come to Mr. Fox's office (obviously by appointment) at the very end of Mr. Fox's office hours, five P.M.

And (as you stare, blood rushing into your face) the door is opened to her soft knock and she slips inside wraithlike and welcome and the door is *closed, locked behind her.*

Not jealous but: press your ear against the frosted-glass window. Hearing the beat of your blood which is shameful and ignoble but *it is yours.*

Hearing them inside—whispering, giggling.

You can envision: Mr. Fox holding a lemon tart to her mouth. Breaking the tart in two, sharing it with *her.*

Love love love you, Little Kitten. No one but you.

Mr. Tongue darting, licking. Tasting of sugary-sweet lemon.

Stricken to the heart. Homely Eunice!—run, run away.

Wait outside in light-falling rain for your mother to pick you up, shivering in your cotton-and-polyester raincoat that is new, and pretty, pale rosy-red with a sash.

■

Wanting to die you, I
If not you die, I
Die wanting you
Not I

Scribbling poems in your journal which you tear out in disgust. Or, tear out to push beneath Mr. Fox's door the next day.

In the hope that Mr. Fox will read them and be deeply moved. And sorry for his behavior. And sad on your behalf. And forgiving.

Hoping that he will summon you with his eyes in class signaling *Yes, Eu-nice! This afternoon.*

As he has not for five days.

■

GROWING DESPERATION, IT WILL soon be fall break.

Nine days without Mr. Fox will be unbearable.

Your brain clattering with useless rhymes: *nine, die.*

If nine you (will) die
(You) die if nine

In fact you are proud of this (ingenious) rhyme but it is useless, you fail to compose a poem to contain it.

■

"YES, EUNICE? WHAT DO you want?"—flush-faced Mr. Fox opens the door abruptly, glaring and unsmiling.

Pretend there is nothing wrong, you have just dropped by. Though it is late Friday before fall break, not a good time.

But he is alone now, as you know. *She* has fled.

Telling you in a choked voice, a voice determined not to betray exasperation, disappointment that his office hours are over, he's just about to leave . . .

You don't quite hear. You are eager with hope. So yearning, and your face so luminous with expectation, how can Mr. Fox disappoint you?

You will only be a few minutes, you tell Mr. Fox. Please!

With a sigh, a most audible sigh Mr. Fox relents. For Mr. Fox is fond of you, you tell yourself. Alone amid the others you are *special.*

Sitting heavily in his swivel chair, as you sit in the hard-backed chair with the flattened cushion. Handsome Mr. Fox in tweed jacket, pale-blue button-down shirt, chino trousers. *That preppy look.*

It is *so good* to be sitting here. Such a relief! You've been in terror that you were banished forever without knowing *why.*

Though there is Mr. Poe staring at you with disdainful eyes.

And the raven perched on Mr. Poe's shoulder, long sharp beak pointed at *you*.

In a soft not-accusing voice you inquire if Mr. Fox has had time to look at your new poems and for a moment Mr. Fox looks blank as a man just waking from sleep in an unfamiliar place.

(Is Mr. Fox hoping that *she* will return?)

(Your rude knock sent Little Kitten scuttling away like a cockroach. Not likely she will be back.)

No matter if Mr. Fox seems to have forgotten your new poems, you have new copies to give him. Including the fragments with the ingenious rhymes, you are sure Mr. Fox will appreciate.

Jerkily his eyes move along the short stanzas, face empty of expression.

Just perceptible sulky downturned mouth. If this mouth has been kissing/nibbling/sucking at Little Kitten it is a disappointed mouth now that Eunice Pfenning has arrived.

You feel your mouth watering, a smell of lemon tarts in the air. Chocolate-covered strawberries beginning to go soft.

When you entered Mr. Fox's office you pushed the door over, not quite closing it. And now Mr. Fox glances past your head unable to see into the hall which is vexing to him but (you surmise) he doesn't think it's worth it to go to the door and open it fully to the hall since this conference with you isn't going to last long.

It *is* the end of the day, and the end of a week; Friday heralding the start of fall break.

None of which seems to matter to you, Eunice Pfenning. Of serious, devoted, obsessive eighth graders, you are exceptional.

Exceptional, unique. Sheer potential.

Mr. Fox says of your new poems that they are *very good, for first drafts.*

You wait for something more—anything. But there is (evidently) nothing more.

You tell Mr. Fox that you've been experimenting with iambic pentameter, iambic tetrameter, and "free verse" in the style of e. e. cummings. In a girlish voice you recite:

Wanting to die you, I
If not you die, I
Die wanting you
Not I

Mr. Fox seems to be stifling a yawn. But Mr. Fox is too gentle-manly to *yawn*.

Saying, as if reluctantly, though perhaps with an undercurrent of satisfaction, "Sometimes magic just vanishes, Eunice. It's the nature of magic that it comes out of nowhere, and can disappear into no-where. That's what magic is."

You are smiling inanely. But Mr. Fox fails to smile back.

Now you utter those words you have memorized. Lying awake in your miserable bed moving your lips. How thrilling it is, how fright-ening to be saying these words to another person, to the very person to whom they are addressed.

". . . lately thinking I don't know if I, if I really want to . . . live. Thinking I might die. Like Annabel Lee. *She* was missed."

Mr. Fox nods vaguely. Mr. Fox is perhaps not altogether alert, aware of what you are saying.

". . . suicide."

Hastily correcting: ". . . take my own life."

Take my own life is so much more eloquent than *suicide*.

There is a blunt clinical sound to *suicide*.

". . . lonely, and what's the point. Each day getting up, going to bed, now it's getting darker earlier, you have to get up in the dark, what's the point . . . Is there a point, Mr. Fox?"

"*Is* there?"—Mr. Fox seems to be considering this. "Hamlet pon-ders, 'To be or not to be'—*to be* is the riddle. As John Berryman says, 'Life, friends, is boring. We must not say so.'"

Mr. Fox is speaking now with more animation, interest. It is con-fusing to you that Mr. Fox does not dissuade you from your dark thoughts as, it's expected, adults will naturally do: teachers, parents.

"Many have agreed, Eunice. Marcus Aurelius considered suicide every day of his life and eventually killed himself, probably none too soon. Suicides are bores if they're serious and worse bores if they are not. Virginia Woolf, Berryman, Sexton, Plath—all. Hemingway— with a shotgun, what could be more macho? But very messy, probably as he'd intended since he was peeved at his wife."

You are staring at Mr. Fox in dismay. Your wizened little prune of a heart is beating sadly. Can it be, Mr. Fox cares so little for you? This must be a mistake, a Fox-trick.

Seeing the expression in your face Mr. Fox relents: "Well, Eunice! It's a solution to a problem that simply eradicates the problem. Life *is* pointless but no one should 'take their own life' unless . . ."

"'Unless'?"

"Unless you have peered into your shallow soul, black muck and algae, and decided *yes, this is it, I've had enough.*"

Still you are not sure that Mr. Fox is saying what he is saying. You wait for the warm smile, the blue glimmer of a wink.

"D'you know the poetry of Sylvia Plath, Eunice?"

"N-no . . ."

You know the name, of course. Plath: a heroine of poetry who took her own life at a young age out of spite, to hurt her estranged hus- band.

Or, a heroine of poetry who'd decided *yes, this is it, she'd had enough.*

"A brilliant poet, a sort of anti-feminist. Gutsy."

Gutsy! This word in Mr. Fox's mouth is so alluring, you wonder what you would have to do, what enormities, to earn it for yourself.

"Plath wrote the great poem on the subject of female suicide— 'Lady Lazarus.' Purely performative, exhibitionist, a kind of prancing- on-a-tightrope poem:

"*Dying*
Is an art, like everything else.
I do it exceptionally well.

"But let me look it up, I don't want to misquote. Poetry is a precise language, as in Emily Dickinson."

Affably smiling Mr. Fox turns to reach for a book on a lower shelf of his bookcase and in that instant a red mist obliterates your brain, gripped in your hands is the heavy bust of Edgar Allan Poe uplifted, you are leaning over the edge of the desk and your hands are bringing the bust down hard on the back of Mr. Fox's head, so swiftly it happens, has happened as Mr. Fox falls forward from the swivel chair with a soft bleat of utter astonishment. Frantic then to escape the second blow which animal instinct tells him is coming he tries pitifully to crawl away drawing breath to cry out but unable to cry out even as your hands lift the weight again and bring it down hard on the back of his head, hard and harder, beyond the capacity (you would think) of a scrawny-wiry thirteen-year-old.

A high-pitched sound like a bat's cry *I hate you! hate you!*—which you have never heard before in your life and will never hear again.

The bronze bust slippery with blood, slip-sliding from your hands to a soft landing on Mr. Fox's back, and onto the floor.

Mr. Fox is fallen, and quivering. His breath comes in sharp pants. His head is turned from you, his face is hidden. Only the soft-wet wound in the wavy hair, roiling with blood.

On your knees disbelieving. Staring, blinking. So swiftly—it has happened . . .

On the wall long-necked Alice in her blue schoolgirl dress and pinafore stares in appalled astonishment as well.

There is something *so wrong* about an adult who has fallen. A *teacher, an adult* fallen lying with sprawled arms and legs on the floor, terrifying to see. You want to touch Mr. Fox's shoulder to say that you are sorry but you dare not touch him, there is a taboo against touching adults even your parents unless in their eyes is the signal that you are known to them, you are wanted.

Even more *wrongness,* the size of a fallen man. Mr. Fox is *large.* Yet he is not looming above you, you are looming above him.

Mr. Fox was quivering, but he is not quivering now. Mr. Fox was breathing, but he is not breathing now. His body is hot, a foul smell makes your nostrils pinch, as if bowels have been released. And this too, a terrible *wrongness.*

You are thinking—*Now, my life is ended. We will die together.*

Even now, it does not seem that what has happened, has happened. It is something impersonal as an earthquake that has thrown both you and Mr. Fox onto the ground, you could swear that the floor sharply tilted.

You reached for something to stop you from falling—something sizable, substantial. The bust of Edgar Allan Poe, on the corner of Mr. Fox's desk. Somehow it was in your hands, and as the floor tilted it fell from your hands and onto Mr. Fox's head, stunning him—is that what happened?

In this sharp tilting of the floor Mr. Fox's ring must have slipped from his finger. A heavy ring, a man's ring, a black octagonal stone in a silver setting, many times you have stared at this ring on Mr. Fox's finger and now you snatch it up to keep it from being contaminated by the widening pool of dark blood beneath the fallen man.

You will keep the ring safe, to return to Mr. Fox. Monday morning.

But no: next week is fall break. Monday morning will not be until November.

A panicked breathing in the room, loud in your ears. You are in danger of fainting, hyperventilating. Barely can you speak—"Mr. Fox? Mr. Fox—"

Weakly your legs move, like an insect's broken legs skittering to the office door. In the hall you have been hearing a thrumming: vacuum cleaner, floor-polisher.

In the near distance, this sound of adult activity. By instinct drawn in this direction sensing that there will be help here, there will be protection here, there will be solace here and not in panicked flight.

Already the custodian has sighted you, he has turned off the floor-polisher.

Hurrying to you as you stand crouched, panting and unsteady on your feet in the corridor. Asking you what has happened? Are you hurt?

Staring at you in astonishment: the splattering of blood on your raincoat, on your face and hands. Your face is ghastly-pale stunned in a kind of blank bafflement as in the aftermath of a great explosion.

The custodian is a *worker, employee*. He wears coveralls, gloves, work-boots. On his head a cloth cap. Surprisingly, he is a young man of about twenty not an older adult as you'd have anticipated. He is nearer in age to you than to your parents, you feel that you can trust in him.

Did someone hurt you?—the young custodian asks.

Did *he* hurt you?—indicating Mr. Fox's office.

In his face an expression of indignation, vehemence. Revulsion.

As in that instant you understand even in your stunned state that this young custodian in coveralls is *on your side.*

Though your jaws feel locked and your tongue numb as if with novocaine you manage to stammer *He hurt me, he was hurting me— he did bad things to me . . .*

Warily the young custodian pushes open the office door, steps inside—"Jesus!"

■

HE WILL TAKE CARE of it, he says. He promises.

You did nothing wrong, it was self-defense.

He too is trembling. With excitement, with a kind of exhilaration. Though he is very pale, the blood has drained from his face. Still he is primed for action, he is one who *acts.*

Adamant repeating you did nothing wrong, it was self-defense.

He hurt you. That son-of-a-bitch. You are not the only one that son-of-a-bitch has hurt.

The young custodian knows who Mr. Fox is! You don't doubt this, you will doubt nothing.

In a state of shock you are not hearing clearly. It is enough, the young man in the coveralls will take care of you.

With a part of your mind you might have registered this. Hearing the thrumming of a machine, the presence of someone responsible.

It is true, Mr. Fox *did* hurt you. This fact you will clutch as you clutch Mr. Fox's onyx ring in your hand and never lose it.

Brushing at your pretty raincoat to wipe away the stains as a child might.

Dimly you hear the young custodian speaking to you. Through a rustling-roaring in your ears like fire. You understand: a person in work-clothes will deal with this. No doubt, the young custodian is accustomed to cleaning up messes made by Langhorne students.

He will take care of the office, he says. What's inside the office.

You need to go to the nearest restroom and wash your face, hands. He will take away the soiled coat, bookbag. He will dispose of them.

In a lowered voice asking if you live on campus in a residence and you are alert enough to tell him *No*. Do you live in Wieland, is your mother coming to pick you up?—you tell him *Yes*. Six P.M.

He tells you to text your mother on your cell phone, tell her that someone else is driving you home. Do this quickly, now.

So that he can take you home. Away from this.

The building is near-deserted but it is not completely deserted. Voices in a stairwell, footsteps.

Too weak to stand. You are sitting on the bench outside Mr. Fox's office. Your heartbeat is erratic, it is difficult to breathe. Try to remember what the young custodian has told you so urgently but his words are like dreams rapidly fading.

Your eyelids droop, you are so very tired.

Mr. Fox, I am so sorry! But I have your ring, I will save it for you.

Wake up!—the young custodian is standing over you, alarmed. He has finished in Mr. Fox's office for now, he has partly filled a plastic trash bag. He asks you if you have texted your mother and you tell him you have not. Fumble for your cell phone in your bookbag as he looks on in exasperation. Your fingers are stiff with cold, it is hard for your thumbs to type but finally you manage to type *I will getting a ride hom with someone else, no need to pick me up* which the young custodian tells you has something wrong with it, you reread, you correct *I will be getting a ride home with someone else, no need to pick me up* and this is OK to send.

Next you must remove your raincoat which is splattered and smeared with blood. Your fingers are icy. Fumble with buttons too large for their buttonholes until the young custodian removes his latex gloves to unbutton the coat, helps you out of the coat, a stylish polyester raincoat for teen girls, the single article of clothing you have liked in years, the pale-rose color is flattering to you, or so you imagine. You selected this coat online, your mother ordered it, your father has not (yet) seen you wearing it.

Your eyes fill with tears, you are losing your pretty new raincoat which the young custodian folds over carefully, lining on the outside, (stained) front hidden, shoving the coat into a plastic trash bag.

Tell your mother your coat was stolen, the young custodian says.

Your bookbag too, in Langhorne school maroon, is too soiled for you to keep, briskly the young custodian turns it upside-down and out spill your wallet, tissues, cough drops, textbooks, the journal with the marbled-green cover.

What's this?—the young custodian asks with a sneer.

No idea why he is hostile suddenly. No idea how to reply.

You are anxious, all these items you will have to carry home in your arms. Especially the journal, you are anxious not to lose.

The young custodian finds a smaller trash bag for you, you are absurdly grateful.

Next, the young custodian stiff-walks you to a lavatory for the handicapped, a single room. Shuts and locks the door behind you. Hurriedly washes your face, hands. Swipes at your disheveled hair with wetted paper towels. The smell of the hand sanitizer makes your nostrils pinch.

Faint blood-streaks in the wetted towels. A considerable quantity of paper towels, the young custodian will shove into a trash bag.

Still you are trembling convulsively, your teeth are chattering. Hallowe'en skeleton, castanets.

A wild fit comes over you, you begin to laugh. The young custodian says sharply—*Stop.*

When it's determined that no one is in the basement hall the young custodian leads you out of Haven Hall by a rear door, with stone steps to the pavement. This is an exit no one uses, you have never seen it before.

By this time it is dark, no one is near.

The young custodian walks you to the parking lot stiff-legged, briskly. You would stumble and fall, your knees are weak but he holds you aloft, moves you along. He is giving you instructions. You force yourself to listen, memorize.

Don't tell anyone. Ever.

Don't tell your mother—anything.

Just that your coat and bookbag were stolen. Just that you are feeling sick, you have the flu, everybody at school has the flu, you want to go to bed.

Don't let her look at you. Keep moving.

You are sick, you need to be alone. In the bathroom, alone.

You are not to blame, *he* is to blame.

It was self-defense. But don't tell anyone.

I will take care of it. He was an evil man. It was self-defense, he'd hurt you.

Other girls he has hurt, and he has hurt *you*.

Get past your mother when you come inside the house, don't let her look at you.

Is there some door you can use, not the front door probably a back door? Kitchen door?

Get into the bathroom, run hot water into a tub.

Tell her you're sick to your stomach, you need to sleep. Never tell her anything. Never tell anyone anything.

Run hot water in a tub, make sure that you are scrubbed clean. Make sure that the tub is scrubbed clean.

Go to bed, don't talk to anyone.

Don't feel bad about this. It was self-defense.

It was something that needed to happen, now it has happened.

By the morning, what's inside the office will be gone.

By the morning, there will be nothing to worry about.

Are you listening? Are you OK?

Mutely you nod *yes. OK.*

■

NEVER BEFORE HAVE YOU given directions to anyone, to your house across town. In a panic now that you have forgotten the way but the young custodian is patient with you.

It's a vehicle you think must be a pickup truck. A high cab, hard for you to climb into with your short legs and your weak knees.

Smell of something acrid like beer, cigarette smoke. Male sweat.

This ride across town you will remember for the remainder of your life: a close-up intimacy as in a movie scene decontextualized and detached from anything preceding or following. The driver of the pickup, you see in profile. A long lean mournful-boy's face, you never see clearly.

Never learn his name, nor make inquiries.

Driving you in the dark past houses ablaze with Hallowe'en decorations: plastic pumpkins, ghost-mannequins hanging from trees, dazzling-white skeletons. Only vaguely in your distraught state are you aware of seeing these, you will recall them later in fleeting spasmodic flashes.

Smiling to think that your silly Daddy has suggested that the two of you go out on Hallowe'en trick-or-treating, just you two, you can wear a Gypsy costume, something of your mother's. Embarrassed for Daddy knowing you so little, imagining that you're still a young child and not the person you've become.

At your house the young custodian cuts the pickup lights. Cradling the trash bag in your arms you jump down, begin to run even as you call back in your girl's thin voice *Thank you* without glancing back over your shoulder at the young custodian already driving away from the curb and out of your life forever.

Entering the house by the back door. Already halfway upstairs when your mother calls after you surprised—*Eunice? Eunice*—call to her in a pleading voice you are feeling sick to your stomach, there is flu at school, hurry to the bathroom before she can see you.

Faucets so loud gushing hot water into the tub, you can't be expected to hear your mother through the door.

Peeling off your clothes, tossing them onto the floor. Abashed to see that you have wetted your panties, only just a colorless odorless stain. You will throw away the panties, you will throw away your white light-woolen socks splattered with blood, wrapped in the plastic trash bag, buried deep in the trash container in your garage.

In the medicine cabinet, there is a container of pain pills. From when your father had dental surgery. Large chunky white pills, oxycodone, take one to four tablets every six hours for pain, you may become dizzy, do not operate heavy machinery.

Swallow just one of the pills. Near-choking it's so big.

The rest of the pills, in the container, you balance on the rim of the bathtub. In case you want more.

Lower yourself into the water that is steamy-hot, too hot.

Smell of Mr. Fox's blood, smell of Mr. Fox's bowels you must cleanse yourself of.

Dying is an art like everything else

5.

But you don't die.

You don't die because your secret is: you are already dead.

With Mr. Fox in your arms, you died; on the blood-smutty floor of Mr. Fox's office, both your lives ended.

Through the remainder of your leftover "life" this secret knowledge to be shared with no one except (elliptically) in this Mystery-Journal.

Into late adolescence, into early adulthood: now twenty-two, a year or two older than others in your class at Princeton.

Perceived by these other more "normal"—(i.e., ordinary, average)—contemporaries as *aloof, standoffish, condescending.*

Still, you have acquired a few undergraduate friends. Very special individuals, of whom two are, like you, writing novels, or memoirs, or (teasingly!) *memoirist novels* as senior theses.

These friends will claim they'd known that there was *something very strange* about you, in months and years to come. You will not contradict them, you will not be in contact with them at all.

Break with the past, a matter of survival that has acquired the apt term *ghosting.*

To *ghost* another is to make of yourself an absence in the life of the other, very possibly a tear in the fabric of their lives that can never be mended.

For this, you feel not the slightest repentance. Francis Fox has taught you: you owe nothing to those who love you, if you feel no love for them. *They* are the ghosts.

Your break with your *merely personal past*—your "parents"—you have made complete: moving out of your mother's house without a backward glance, ignoring her frantic calls, emails; your father, that figure of pathos, divorced by your mother as a passenger in a lifeboat near-capsized by gigantic waves pushes overboard another who threatens to sink the lifeboat, years ago exiled to whatever *executive position* he occupies in whatever dreary upstate New York city whose very name you have erased from your memory.

You *are* unique, your friends have guessed. You are legendary, or will be.

For your salvation has been Mr. Fox's admonition—*Push yourself out of your comfort zone, Eunice.*

Experiment with your nondominant hand.

■

CLOSE YOUR EYES: THE apparition beckons.

It is always here. *He* is always there.

Mr. Fox's (kindly, handsome) face in which Mr. Fox's (blue, adoring) eyes are fixed upon *you.*

Or is it Mr. Fox's (cruel, monstrous) face in which Mr. Fox's (icy-blue, killer) eyes are fixed upon you?

You see, my darling—I am not dead! I am exactly as you remember me.

Make your way gliding enchanted along the basement corridor of Haven Hall blurred as in shimmering water at last at 015 Haven Hall Mr. Fox's office door with the frosted-glass window and the small white card listing Mr. Fox's office hours—(so banal! trite! the beauty is in the very banality and triteness of *office hours*); and inside the office the single window set high in the wall emitting an autumnal late-afternoon light, desktop covered in miscellaneous papers and a swivel chair, teacher's chair, behind the desk facing a smaller, abashed-looking chair with a flat cushioned seat.

On a corner of the desk, to your left as you enter, the bronze bust *Edgar Allan Poe 1809–1849.*

Bookcase, shelves half-filled with "suitable for middle-school" books. Mr. Fox is still new at the Academy, he has not quite moved in.

Not quite ever, Mr. Fox will move in.

Immediately your attention is drawn to Alice (in Wonderland) with her snaky long neck, waxy-white girl's face, and affrighted hair, gazing out of the glossy poster across decades.

You, I. Wonderland!

Of an era more than a century ago when *girls of good family* wore proper dresses for everyday, certainly for school, pinafores like little aprons over them, white cotton stockings, and prim little black shoes on impossibly small feet.

Posters of dreamy flowers, African big cats. Flowers aching to be penetrated, big cats salivating to tear you into bloody pieces.

But it is the bust of Edgar Allan Poe with the raven hunched on its shoulder that commands attention.

From the first, the blind eyes snatched at your eyes. Long before you knew what use the bronze head would make of you, you knew.

At its base engraved in script so small you have to squint to read:

Francis H. Fox first-prize winner Nevermore Competition,
Poe Society of America 2011

Mr. Fox laughs, your childish awe is delightful to him. He will close the door behind you, he is beckoning to *you.*

For this is the time before time when already without awareness you were in love with Mr. Fox.

Never a time when you were not in love with Mr. Fox.

Never a time when Mr. Fox was not your life.

Never a time when your souls were not joined.

Because we are born of such knowing: of the time before as when waking in the morning we carry with us the memory of the beautiful dreams we have lost in waking.

In the time before there is no time as we understand it on Earth, it is a great void like the ocean in which droplets of rain fall & vanish.

These droplets are many, but also one.

As in the time before we are children together, there is no "age" that separates.

This, Mr. Fox explained.

Saying, My darling there will never be a time when our souls are not joined.

Saying, Our (secret) pledge will be, we will die for each other if that is asked of us.

We will never reveal our secret, we will die together & our secret will die with us.

For there was never a time when you were not in love with Mr. Fox and there was never a time when Mr. Fox was not in love with you.

JOYCE CAROL OATES is a recipient of a National Humanities Medal awarded by President Barack Obama, the National Book Critics Circle's Ivan Sandrof Lifetime Achievement Award, the National Book Award in Fiction, the Jerusalem Prize, the Prix Femina, and the Cino Del Duca World Prize, and is a five-time finalist for the Pulitzer Prize. She has written some of the most enduring fiction of our time, including the bestsellers *Blonde* and *We Were the Mulvaneys*. She is the Roger S. Berlind '52 Distinguished Professor of the Humanities Emerita at Princeton University and a member of the American Academy of Arts and Letters.

X: @joycecaroloates

ABOUT THE TYPE

This book was set in Fairfield, the first typeface from the hand of the distinguished American artist and engraver Rudolph Ruzicka (1883–1978). Ruzicka was born in Bohemia (in the present-day Czech Republic) and came to America in 1894. He set up his own shop, devoted to wood engraving and printing, in New York in 1913 after a varied career working as a wood engraver, in photoengraving and banknote printing plants, and as an art director and freelance artist. He designed and illustrated many books, and was the creator of a considerable list of individual prints—wood engravings, line engravings on copper, and aquatints.